PROLOGUE

BREMERHAVEN - OCTOBER 3. 1944

Kommandant Kaufmann was standing on the pier inside the harbour, watching the seagulls gliding overhead in what was now building up to become gale-force winds. It was late in the afternoon, and as the low grey clouds raced across the sky, it was quickly becoming dark. The rain had not stopped falling for several days now, and the Kommandant was becoming annoyed. He was supposed to sail on the water, not have it fall on his head. Dense curtains of rain were sweeping across the harbour, and through the haze of water droplets, he could now only vaguely make out its outer perimeter.

The temperature was close to freezing, and occasionally snowflakes would mix with the raindrops. The only positive aspect of the storm was the fact that the heavy clouds completely obscured the harbour from the view of enemy war planes as they made their way overhead to bomb Berlin and other German cities. The war in Europe was now inexorably turning against The Reich, with enemy forces pushing in from both the East and the West. It would not be long before it was all over.

Kaufmann was wearing his long black leather coat, which glistened as it reflected the bright floodlights on the pier, and in his mouth was a pipe from which the occasional puff of smoke rose, only to be swept away instantly and then vanish.

It had been one year and four months since he had taken command of U-303, and since then he had distinguished himself by sinking a total tonnage of 64,500 of enemy shipping. Most of this had happened in the Atlantic Ocean, and almost all the ships sunk had been part of convoys crossing over from the United States to Britain. The aim of the convoys was to relieve the shortages of military equipment that Allied forces were experiencing, so along with a large number of other U-boats, Kommandant Kaufmann had been tasked with hunting these convoys down and sinking as many ships as possible.

U-303 was a fairly new Type VIIC from the *Kriegsmarinewerft* in Wilhelmshafen. At 67 meters and just over one thousand tons, it was one of the largest U-boats in the fleet. It was powered by two BMW diesel engines producing a combined three thousand six hundred horsepower, which enabled it to travel at a respectable speed of eighteen knots when surfaced and a little over seven knots when submerged. It was armed with fourteen torpedoes, and able to fire from four torpedo tubes in the bow and one in the stern. Its hull was designed to withstand the pressure of a depth of two hundred and fifty meters, and its maximum range was nine thousand miles, giving it ample range for stalking allied shipping over extended periods of time. On its deck was mounted an 88mm gun, now readied with 220 rounds of armour-piercing shells. It would be capable of delivering a powerful punch to most surface ships, but it was only to be used as a last resort. Staying hidden was the most important objective for any submarine commander.

The fact that Kaufmann and his crew of 49 sailors were still alive at this point in the war was no small feat in itself, particularly now that luck had turned against The Third Reich. Hitler himself had taken a special interest in the efforts of the U-boat fleet, believing that if Germany could choke off the American aid, Britain would not be able to mount a serious threat to continental Europe, thus allowing Germany to concentrate fully on stopping the Russian advance. Now that Germany was fighting a losing battle on two fronts, it had become clear to even the most optimistic German generals, that it had been a mistake to engage both Britain and Russia at the same time.

Kommandant Kaufmann was not a politician, nor was he a general, and even though he was unhappy with the way the war was conducted, he remained fiercely loyal to his Fuhrer and to his Fatherland. He had started his career in October 1929, when at eighteen years of age he had joined the Reichsmarine as a simple seaman. He spent the next few years on a torpedo boat.

In September 1935 he transferred to the new U-boat force, and after some six months of training, again transferred to the U-boat force proper in June 1936. In March 1937 he entered the Navy school where he received several months of officer training, and during the following two years, he served on the cruiser Admiral Graf Spee. When war broke out in the autumn of 1939, he took the helm of the Type IID U-boat U-141, with which he completed five patrols, mostly in the Atlantic, receiving an Iron Cross, Second Class.

Standing on the pier, his thoughts were on the mission ahead. To his right his men were working alongside the dockworkers, hastily loading supplies onto the submarine. Most of it was food since the journey upon which they were about to embark was expected to be long. As the men were hoisting a big net filled with all manner of food and other supplies, an army truck cleared the security check point at the harbour entrance and made its way to the loading area, its headlights fanning out into the rain and snow.

The truck pulled up next to the crane, and immediately, four soldiers in black uniforms jumped out of its back and started lifting a large wooden crate out of the truck and down onto the ground. The crate was unmarked except for one arrow on each side indicating which way was supposed to be up, and a seal with the German eagle printed on its top. The corners were reinforced with steel caps, and the lid seemed to be bolted shut with no apparent lock. The soldiers then brought out a large polished steel cylinder, that appeared to be very heavy.

When the two items had been placed on the ground, an SS officer climbed out from the truck's passenger seat and walked to the crate where the four soldiers had now fanned out, weapons at the ready. He waived at the man operating the crane, and a few minutes later the crate was lifted aboard U-303 where it was placed in the cargo hold in a separate compartment. The steel cylinder was brought forward to the torpedo room.

'This is it?' Kommandant Kaufmann asked.

The SS officer spun around not having heard the Kommandant approach. His black uniform signalled authority, and the Iron Cross on his collar made it clear that he too was a battle-hardened war veteran. Apparently unaffected by the strong wind and the cold rain and sleet, he looked at Kaufmann for a few seconds, before tilting his head slightly to one side and asking, in an almost accusatory tone of voice. 'My name is Colonel Springer, and you Kommandant Kaufmann, do not seem very impressed?'

Arrogant arse, thought Kaufmann and returned the SS-officers suspicious glare. He was about to join in the building confrontation, but then thought better of it, and ended up smiling disarmingly. 'I'm sure that whatever is in the crate is very important. But I would appreciate it if you would tell me where we are going.'

The SS officer nodded, unbuttoned his coat, pulled out an envelope and handed it to Kaufmann.

'These are your mission orders. You will leave this harbour tonight and then head out to sea before opening this envelope. We cannot risk any of your men leaking anything to anyone. This is of the utmost importance to the security of our Fatherland.'

Kaufmann took the envelope, held it for a few seconds as if to try to guess its content, and then tucked it under his coat. 'We are ready, Colonel.'

'And Kommandant,' the SS officer added. 'You may need this, although I hope you will not. When you have read your orders, you will understand.'

He handed Kaufmann a small radio transmitter with a set of dials acting as a combination lock. The correct combination would allow the transmitter to send out its signal. Next to the dials was a small black button.

'Very well, Kommandant Kaufmann. I wish you the best of luck, and may your journey be safe.'

★ ★ ★

Four hours later, U-303 was heading out to sea. The ocean was almost black with streaks of white foam showing as the waves broke. Even close to shore the waves were severe, and the sea seemed more than anything like a raging monster showing its teeth, ready to devour any prey foolish enough to venture out of the harbour.

'Make your depth 40 meters as soon as you can,' the Kommandant ordered.

'Ay-ay, Kommandant,' replied the helmsman. 'Making depth 40 meters.'

Even though he had been a sailor for most of his adult life, Kaufmann did not exactly enjoy the violent rolls his vessel was experiencing, and so he wanted to dive as soon as possible to lessen the effects of the great swells rolling overhead. After just a few minutes the U-boat was gliding along at 6 knots, virtually unaffected by the storm raging on the surface. The Kommandant instructed his second in command, Obersteurmann Jürgen Schwartz to clear the British channel into the Atlantic Ocean, and then he went to his cabin. He had been up since early that morning and was in need of some sleep. He looked at the clock mounted on the wall over his desk and yawned. It was half past ten in the evening. He might as well try to get some sleep now. The trip out into the Atlantic was far from safe, but he could do nothing better than try to relax and let his capable crew handle things like so many times before. Every crewmember was experienced and knew how to handle himself. Kommandant Kaufmann sat down on his bed, swung his legs up and eased himself down onto the bunk. A few minutes later he was fast asleep.

★ ★ ★

There was a knock on the door. 'Kommandant,' said a voice from outside. It was Schwartz. 'Kommandant, we have cleared the English Channel.'

Kaufmann opened his eyes and glanced at the clock. Ten minutes to seven in the morning. 'Thank you, Jürgen. I'll be right out'. He rubbed his eyes as he staggered out of his bed, still a bit tired but feeling much better than the night before. After washing his face and putting on a clean uniform, he sat down at his desk and took out the envelope given to him by the SS Colonel Springer. He fetched his silver letter opener and pulled out the single sheet of paper that lay inside. It was dated October 1. 1944 and across the top were written the words 'Top Secret'. The letter was typed but had two signatures at the bottom. They were written in dark blue ink, and it took Kaufmann a few seconds to realise that the first was that of the head of the SS, Heinrich Himmler, and the second that of none other than his supreme commander and *Fuhrer*, Adolf Hitler.

Kaufmann put down the letter opener and started reading. As he did so, he felt a chill run down his spine, and all of a sudden, his fingers became cold and sweaty. The wording of the letter was clear and unequivocal, and its orders correspondingly unambiguous. He knew instantly that this would without a doubt be his most important mission ever. Having read every word carefully, he stared for a few seconds at the last sentence. *Crew expendable.*

He read the letter once more, and then slowly put it back in the envelope. As if in slow motion, he placed the letter in his personal airtight safe, to which only he knew the combination. As he sat back in his chair, he took a deep breath and closed his eyes. He was still the Kommandant of this U-boat, but he somehow felt as if his life and those of his crew were now in the hands of fate. He could only pray that their journey would be without incident, and that they would make it safely to their destination without being detected either by allied war ships or anti-submarine aircraft. He had sworn an oath to his *Fuhrer* and his country, and he would not let them down, even if it were to cost him his life.

Opening the cabin door, he was met by the familiar and welcome smell of fried eggs being prepared in the galley. He knew that the best way to maintain his men's motivation and morale was to serve proper food for them. It could make all the difference in the world during the never-changing routines in the life of a submariner. Being in a confined space for weeks could drive a man crazy, so anything that reminded the crew of home was welcome, and what better way than to serve good healthy food. The Kommandant put on his jovial face and made his way forward to the bridge.

'How are we doing, Jürgen?' he asked as he entered the bridge.

'I have taken the ship out along our previous route as you ordered,' replied Jürgen Schwartz. 'We have cleared the channel and are now 50 miles from the coast of France. How shall we proceed?'

Kaufmann looked at Schwartz and smiled. 'My friend, we are not here to hunt convoys.' He then reached for the microphone and flipped a switch that allowed him to address the entire crew.

'This is your Kommandant speaking,' he started in his usual calm but stern voice. 'I have an announcement. Our Fatherland has given us a mission of extreme importance, and I expect us to carry it out in accordance with the direct orders delivered to me yesterday and signed by our *Fuhrer* the day before that. We have been tasked with transporting an exceedingly important cargo to a destination that can be known only to me, at least for some time to come. I am not in a position to reveal to you the nature of this cargo, except to say that if delivered safely to its destination, it may very well win the war against England and America.'

He paused for a short moment to let the significance of his message sink in among the crew, who stood still all through the U-boat to listen to their Kommandant's words.

'It is vital that we reach our destination safely and that this cargo does not fall into the hands of the enemy,' he continued. 'I expect you to show the utmost diligence on this journey, and I have been instructed to say that we will all be richly rewarded upon our return to Berlin. That is all.'

Kaufmann put down the microphone and looked again at his trusted friend. 'Jürgen, I cannot adequately stress the importance of this.' He said in a low voice. 'This cargo must reach its destination, and never fall into the wrong hands. We are to plot a course for Argentina, where the cargo is to be handed over to a task force already in place. This mission must be accomplished at all cost.'

Kaufmann held his gaze at Schwartz for a few seconds to make sure he understood the implications of his words. Schwartz was clearly unsure of how to react. He had never seen such determination in the eyes of his Kommandant, and he couldn't help but feel slightly uneasy about what he had said. But instead of asking questions, he resolutely walked over to the map table and spread out a large map of the Atlantic Ocean.

★ ★ ★

Two days later, U-303 was closing in on the Azores Islands in the middle of the Atlantic Ocean. Kommandant Kaufmann, along with Jürgen Schwartz had plotted a course that would take them between the main island of Sao Miguel and the island of Terceira. They knew very well that the United States Airforce had an airbase on Terceira, which was also used by British anti-submarine dive-bombers, but as long as they stayed submerged, they would be safe. The water is deep between these islands and it would be relatively easy for a submarine to stay hidden beneath the waves. Dive-bombers regularly flew missions from Terceira to provide cover for convoys crossing the Atlantic, but since there was no significant allied shipping in this area, it was thought unlikely by the allies that German U-boats would be prowling these waters. And for that reason, none of the dive-bombers operating from here were ever looking for enemy vessels this close to their own airbase.

U-303's journey had gone without incident until one of its batteries in the engine room suddenly started leaking acid onto the floor of the U-boat. The batteries were several years old, and one of them had eventually given in. As the acid hit the floor, it started eating away at the metal, and in the process developed toxic fumes that would eventually become harmful to the crew. The leak occurred at night when most of the crew was asleep, so it was several hours before it was discovered. There was, however, no need to panic. This had happened to many a submarine in the past, and having stopped the leak, the problem was basically solved. However, the acid had by then caused a low cloud of toxic fumes to creep along the corridors of the U-boat. The air inside thus needed to be vented, and so Kommandant Kaufmann ordered the submarine to rise to a depth of 10 meters after which he ordered the periscope up. It was early in the morning as the periscope broke the surface and started to sweep the horizon to check for surface ships nearby. Having convinced himself that it was safe, Kaufmann ordered the U-boat to surface briefly to vent the air and to top off the air tanks that were needed for extended dives.

★ ★ ★

Heading home from an uneventful mission, the pilot of a Blackburn Skua dive-bomber spotted what he initially thought to be a whale. The island of Pico had served as a large whaling station since as far back as the end of the 18th century, and it was not unusual to see whales breaking through the waves and shooting a jet of steam into the cold air. Coming in to land at Terceira Airbase, the pilot of the dive-bomber was just about to look away and concentrate on the approach, when the shape of the whale struck him as unusual. He banked the single-engine aeroplane slightly to the left, peering down through the clouds when it finally dawned on him that this was no whale. What he had spotted was a submarine.

His mission was to locate and attempt to destroy German U-boats, but because the submarine was so close to The Azores, he initially thought that it had to be a British hunter-killer submarine. But what would that be doing all the way out here? There were no naval bases to support submarines here, and the German wolf packs usually hunted much further north. He banked his plane to the left, and dove towards the unsuspecting U-303. As he did so, it became clear to him that this was indeed a genuine German U-boat. He had no clue what it might be doing here, but at this point that was irrelevant. A kill was a kill.

He flicked the safety switch from the bomb release button and aimed his aeroplane carefully. With a range of 760 miles, the Skua carried a lot of fuel for these patrol missions, but it was a lot lighter now than at take-off because of the reduced fuel load. The bomber consequently responded well as the pilot attempted to aim it at the submarine below. The Skua's maximum airspeed in level flight was 225 miles per hour but it quickly exceeded that as it dove through the low clouds towards its unsuspecting prey.

On U-303, Jürgen Schwartz had just opened the hatch to speed up the ventilation process, when he heard what he feared the most. It took a few seconds before he could get a fix on where the sound was coming from, but it was instantly clear to him that what he could hear was an aeroplane. Out here, that could only mean trouble. He spotted the dive-bomber just as it banked to the left and started its run towards the submarine. In an instant, Schwartz slammed the hatch shut and slid down the ladder into the U-boat yelling at the helmsman to dive.

Kommandant Kaufmann ordered the forward planes on the U-boat to be set to a maximum of 45 degrees down, engines were set to all ahead, and ballast tanks were filled as fast as possible. The U-boat quickly began to submerge as it shot ahead through the waves of the Atlantic Ocean. In a few seconds, the U-boat would no longer be visible to the enemy pilot.

But it was too late. The dive-bomber pilot released both of his bombs and pulled back on the stick to level off and evade the shockwaves from the explosions. One of the bombs missed, but the other struck four meters from the stern. It slammed into the hull at a slight angle and so failed to penetrate before it exploded. But the blast was enough to open a gap in the hull not far from the cargo hold, and immediately water started pouring in. All hatches aboard the U-boat had been shut, so the damage could have been containable. But the vessel was doomed. The engine room was flooding fast, and it would be a matter of minutes before the diesel engines would die, leaving U-303 a sitting duck and vulnerable to further attacks.

'Kommandant,' Jürgen Schwartz yelled through the noise. 'We must abandon ship now. She's going to go down sooner or later. Engine room reports the engines flooding. The hydraulics are failing and the dive planes are still stuck at negative 45 degrees, so even if the engines can hang on for a bit longer, we can't get out of here. We have to stop the engines, blow the ballast tanks and attempt to surface immediately!'

Kaufmann faced Schwartz with an angry look on his face and yelled. 'We will not surface. We will stay the course until we are out of danger. Those dive bombers have only two bombs so there is nothing he can do to us now.'

'Kommandant that will not matter if we are at the bottom of the sea! I told you, the hull is severely damaged. We do not have structural integrity to dive now. We must re-surface!'

Schwartz was now becoming very agitated, and the rest of the crew looked on anxiously while the hull was making uncomfortable groaning noises. They knew as well as anyone the grave danger they were in, and none of them had any intention of staying on board a sinking ship for longer than they had to. The U-boat was now 25 meters below the surface and rapidly heading deeper.

'Jürgen Schwartz!' shouted Kaufmann. 'We cannot risk it. If we surface now, our cargo will be captured. I cannot let that happen.'

'But we will all die,' pleaded Schwartz in a nervous voice, beads of sweat running down his face.

Kaufmann said nothing but simply looked around the bridge at his men, as if trying to gauge what they might do.

'Kommandant!' Schwartz yelled. He was now becoming desperate. The hull made another loud grinding noise, making it clear that it had suffered serious structural damage. Kaufmann returned his gaze to his second in command and stared sternly at him.

Suddenly Schwartz turned to the helmsman and screamed. 'Blow the ballast tanks! Prepare to surface!'

'Ignore that order, helmsman!' Kaufmann countered angrily, pinning the helmsman down with his stare.

'Do it now or you are a dead man!' Schwartz shouted to the young man. His voice revealed his growing panic.

The teenager hesitated for a few moments but then pulled back hard on the lever controlling the forward ballast tanks. Without hesitation, Kaufmann pulled out his pistol, pointed it at the helmsman and fired twice. The bullets struck the helmsman in the temple and blood and brains were splattered all over the controls in front of him as his body slumped down onto the controls, his arms dangling at his sides.

Kaufmann then pointed the gun at Jürgen Schwartz. 'There are things more important than friendship. Take the controls and hold this depth.'

Schwartz did not move a muscle. At that moment the engines died along with the alarm, and the U-boat was now drifting slowly and silently towards the surface. A bead of salty sweat started to make its way from Kaufmann's forehead and into his left eye. He was forced to blink quickly twice, which made him appear even more unstable as his gun started to tremble.

'DAMN YOU,' yelled Kaufmann, waving the gun wildly at Schwartz who stood still as a statue staring at his Kommandant. 'You have been by my side for all these years, and you will not fail me now. Take the helm and hold this depth!'

Schwartz remained motionless, simply lowering his head and closing his eyes. He was not going to be the architect of his own death. The U-boat was surfacing and there was nothing Kaufmann could do about it.

Kaufmann pointed the gun at his friend's head and pulled the trigger. Jürgen Schwartz's head jerked back as the bullet struck. His body then collapsed and hit the steel floor with a thump. The rest of the crew was too shocked to react as Kaufmann ran past his dead friend towards the front of the U-boat. He held his gun in front of him, and nobody dared to stand in his way. When he reached the torpedo room, he sprinted to the second torpedo tube and flung it open. Inside was the steel container with 20 kilos of high explosives. He then pulled out the small radio transmitter he had been given by SS officer Springer, rolled the dials to the correct combination and put his finger on the little black button.

'May God have mercy on me,' he whispered, and then he pressed the button.

★ ★ ★

From above, it looked like a giant blue whale blowing out air in a huge geyser. The pilot of the dive-bomber had initially cursed what he thought was the submarine's escape, thinking he had done too little damage to cause her end. As he saw the explosion and the column of water and steam, he concluded that his bombs must have started a chain reaction, leading to a secondary explosion inside the submarine. He stayed over the site for a few more minutes to look for survivors, but there were none. With a grim face, he finally banked the aircraft over and headed for the airfield on Terceira.

Hunting submarines was his job, but coming to terms with taking human lives was something else entirely.

'Better them than me,' he muttered to himself, and then he called in for his approach to the runway.

ONE

BERLIN – MARCH 14. 2002

The man in the guardhouse by the entrance to the National Archives had his eyes fixed on a small television set, that was placed on a stool by his desk. Hardly anyone was out now that the German national football team was playing the Spanish team. The streets were almost empty, except for a few buses and taxis, and only when cars stopped in front of the guardhouse, did he take his feet off the desk and get up to check IDs. Of the few people who needed to pass through the entrance to the 18th-century building, more were leaving than were going in, and the ones leaving he would just let pass without showing an interest. There were two cars left in the parking lot now, and one of them was his own. He had often wondered exactly what it was he was guarding. There was nothing in the archives of any significance as far as he could tell. Only the Stasi records might be of some value to certain people who refused to leave the past behind, but those documents had been examined a thousand times since they were opened more than ten years ago.

It was late in the afternoon and darkness was closing in, but with the ground covered in snow and the street lights on, it never got completely dark. There was a small courtyard beyond the tall gate to the National Archive, and it and the guardhouse were lit up by bright floodlights. But along the sides of the building, there were no lights, and it was here that a single black-clad figure crept over the grounds towards the main building. After reaching a window, the man stood up, and within a minute he had cut out a piece of glass, stuck his arm through the hole and opened the windows just enough to let him slip inside.

Moving along the walls, the man-made his way purposefully towards a room at the back of the ground floor. He had been told that no motion sensors had been installed, so he proceeded briskly but quietly to a door and opened it. Information on alarm systems installed in the doors was poor, so he had to take the chance. To his surprise, nothing happened as he pulled the handle, and he continued to the far wall of the windowless room. Here he opened a cabinet, and then pulled out a small flashlight that gave him just enough light so that he could read the names on the files stored in it. Putting some of the thick files aside, he placed several others in a bag that he had slung over his shoulder. He zipped the bag shut and closed the cabinet. Then he made his way back to where he entered the building and climbed out onto the lawn.

After a few minutes of crawling, he was back at the fence which he had cut open half an hour earlier. He slipped through silently, and once on the other side he stood and took off his hood. After making his way down the quiet street next to the fence, he started walking casually to a parked car about a hundred meters away. He got in and drove off without arousing any suspicion in the quiet neighbourhood. Handsome rewards would await him upon delivery.

★ ★ ★

LONDON – SEPTEMBER 2. 2003

Being stuck in traffic in the middle of London was not Andrew Sterling's idea of a good time. But he was in no hurry, and The Firm paid his bills, so he took the opportunity to sit back and relax, while he looked out at the busy streets. Not that he had any problems paying for cab rides. Sterling was from a wealthy family, his grandfather having made a small fortune on sugar plantations in South Africa. Following his death, Andrew's own father Charles - then 28 years old and an only child – had left for London with the money from the sale of his father's plantations. A few years later he had met the girl who was to become Andrew's mother, a nurse at Chelsea Royal Hospital. Andrew's childhood had been similar to that of most other children, except that his family was rich. Having money was nice, but it didn't necessarily make life that much easier for a youngster.

Childhood and adolescence had presented exactly the same problems and issues that every other person experienced. At eighteen his world had suddenly come crumbling down when his parents were both killed in a car accident on the M1. They had been on their way home late at night after visiting friends, when the driver of a lorry travelling in the opposite direction had fallen asleep at the wheel. The lorry had smashed across the fence separating the two lanes of cars racing in opposite directions and had struck his father's car head-on. The doctors told him that they probably wouldn't have had time to feel any pain and that perhaps it had been all over before they'd had time to realise what was happening.

Being an only child like his father, Andrew had been the sole heir to his parents' wealth, and inherited among other things, the mansion his father had bought after coming home from South Africa. A large three-story estate in Hampstead, it was built in a late Victorian style with a large garden including two small ponds in the centre. Having grown up there he initially had trouble living in the house alone following the accident, as the house constantly reminded him of his parents. But as he grew older, he had come to terms with what had happened, and he now thoroughly enjoyed coming home to his quiet residence, feeling a sense of comfort knowing the house was a part of who his parents had been.

Initially, though, he had spent little time there as he had joined the army just a few months after his parents passed away. Becoming a professional soldier had never crossed his mind before the accident, but it represented a means of escape during those first difficult months when he had trouble finding his feet in a world where he was now alone.

He soon realised that the army was beginning to take on the role of a family for him. They were a close-knit bunch, and with every new experience they shared, they became more like brothers or cousins. As the years passed, Andrew acknowledged that the army had provided for him the stability and sense of belonging that had been taken away from him at a young age. Even though he couldn't credit any one person with that, it still meant that he felt a deep sense of loyalty towards the military.

Andrew was passing through The City, London's financial district, and although men dressed in suits were a common sight in the capital as a whole, hardly anyone wore jeans in this part of London. They were mostly young people walking briskly along the pavement making every effort to look the part of important businessmen. Sterling looked very much like a banker himself as he sat there in the back of the cab wearing a three-piece pin-striped suit, although he couldn't bring himself to add the gold watch chain in the vest pocket. He liked wearing suits and sometimes thought that he would have made a great banker – except he'd probably die from boredom.

The weather was getting quite cold now after an extremely hot summer. The leaves on the trees and bushes in the parks and on the boulevards were turning shades of yellow, red and brown, and every day they littered the streets leaving no one in doubt that autumn was here and winter was fast approaching. The city had commandeered dozens of workers out to clean the streets, but this week it seemed that they were fighting a losing battle.

Andrew had been called into the office for a meeting with his senior officer. That didn't happen very often, so he assumed it was important. Come to think of it, he hadn't been called anywhere urgently for a long while now. Not since he left active duty with the SAS one and a half years earlier. At thirty-five he could easily have stayed on for several more years but was asked to accept a job as the head of a new team in the anti-terrorism division of the special operations unit. The team was to engage in identifying and fighting chemical and biological terrorism, preferably before it occurred. And that was the problem with terrorist acts, wasn't it? You hardly ever knew beforehand that such things were going to happen. Mostly you were left to pick up the pieces, and if you were lucky, you'd be able to go after the bastards that did it. But actually, preventing it from happening in the first place, that was the really tricky bit.

For many years the scenario of a suitcase-sized nuclear device falling into the hands of terrorists had scared people witless, but in reality, it was more likely that chemical or biological weapons would be used in terrorist attacks. The availability of such weapons was much greater, and the technological sophistication required to handle, transport and detonate a nuclear device was quite significant, thus making a nuclear attack unlikely.

The fact that he was responsible for chemical and biological anti-terrorism efforts didn't exactly make it easier though, since most people could go online or walk into a library and pick up a book on how to make a deadly mix of chemicals. Biological weapons were more difficult to manage for would-be terrorists but they were also potentially much more dangerous. A virus or bacterium on the loose in a major city would likely infect thousands of people before anyone ever realised what was happening. In addition, it was likely to create a panic that could cripple a city or a whole nation.

Andrew often felt that, more than anything else, his current job was that of an investigator. It was definitely far removed from his days of being inserted behind enemy lines, with a few other men from the SAS and nothing but an MP5 submachine gun, a couple of days' worth of food rations and a laser designator for marking targets for incoming bombers. He missed the comradery but not the danger that the job entailed. Several soldiers from the SAS regiment at Hereford had lost their lives in covert operations during Desert Storm in 1991. But he certainly did miss the rush of adrenaline that came with low-level parachute jumps out of helicopters at night, not knowing exactly where they were going to land and who they were going to run into.

During Operation Desert Storm, his involvement had been limited to two missions, of which only one had been a success. At that time, he was still a relatively young, although capable sergeant, and he learned a great deal from those two missions. Above all, he had learned how crucial it was to stay hidden. His SAS squad leader had blundered right into a small enemy camp atop a sand dune. The squad had quickly neutralised the poorly trained Iraqi soldiers, but not before the squad leader had taken two bullets to his chest. He died two hours later. They had to bury him right there and then in the desert without much ceremony, since they were unsure whether more soldiers were on their way. The second in command had taken over leadership of the squad and they had eventually completed their mission by destroying a SCUD missile launcher, after which they were extracted from the area by helicopter the following night. His next mission had been a washout since they had been dropped near what turned out to be a long-abandoned SAM-site, which by then contained about £5 worth of scrap metal. For all the satellite imagery that was available, things didn't always go according to plan, and that was an important lesson in itself.

Operations in Afghanistan in the autumn of 2001 had been different. By that time, he had risen to the rank of Captain, and units of the SAS along with units from the 10th Mountain Division of the United States Army, had been inserted in the mountains of that barren central Asian country. It had happened just weeks after the destruction of the World Trade Centre in New York and the attack on the Pentagon in September of 2001. It hadn't taken long for the intelligence services in the US and the UK to determine who was behind those acts of mass murder. In Andrew's mind, the people who had killed almost three thousand civilians were beyond simply being terrorists. They had declared war on western civilisation in general and the United States in particular. Governments had apparently seen it more or less the same way, and within twelve hours of the events, all available members of the SAS had been ordered back to Hereford, where the usual training had taken on a new sense of urgency. No one knew exactly what was going to happen, but everyone knew that it would only be a question of time before they were going to get thrown into the thick of things.

Back then, Andrew was already familiar with the Al Qaeda terrorist network, and he knew as well as anyone that these people did not represent an organisation that one could easily track down and go after. Little was known about the people involved, except that they were fanatics willing to die for their cause and that the network had a very loose structure, with little to no central command. They were almost like task forces with specific missions, that would quietly dissolve once their mission was completed. As a rule, the group members rarely knew the identities of each other, and chances were, they would never see each other again after a mission. That made the activities of Al Qaeda extremely difficult to investigate and deal with. At the time though, it was clear that there had been Al Qaeda terrorist training camps dotted around the mountain ranges of Afghanistan for years. Inexplicably these had been tolerated by the rest of the world until that day in September 2001 when the terrorists had struck in a way that could not have been anticipated.

Only days later, Andrew and eighty other members of the SAS had been flown to an airbase in Uzbekistan from where they would operate along with special forces units from other countries. At the start of the conflict, they had usually been suited up for their missions just after midnight, boarded their Blackhawk helicopters and, after a couple of hours of low-level flying had been dropped in enemy territory, with dawn only a few hours away. Just enough time for them to find a suitable place to hide, get dug in and camouflaged, and then begin the initial reconnaissance.

The special operations teams were usually dropped some distance from known enemy positions, but on his first mission, his squad had found itself just six hundred metres from a training camp. They had been given orders to avoid engaging the enemy. It was still very early days in the military campaign against the Taliban and the Al Qaeda forces, and it was wiser for Andrew and his men to report the exact nature and position of any targets found. If possible, they would then aid the incoming strike aircraft by pointing a laser designator at those targets. Taking on an entire camp of more than a hundred soldiers was decidedly unwise for a squad of five men, even if they were far better trained and had superior equipment. The soldiers in the camp all had AK47s and hand grenades, and they would be able to annihilate the squad if they had been willing to take casualties.

During the first days of the campaign, the allied forces had flown only night bombing missions and so his squad had had all day to get in position for the strike. Staking out the camp was not entirely without risk, and they experienced their first tricky moment when a two-man patrol had walked along a path only meters from their position. Remaining stealthy was one of the things that members of the SAS did best, but as the soldiers passed their hideout, all members of the squad released the safety switch on their suppressed MP5s, ready to take the men down if they were discovered. Luckily the soldiers passed without noticing the hidden danger.

As night came, Andrew and Lieutenant Colin McGregor had advanced towards the camp in a slow silent crawl until they were about three hundred meters away, where they found a suitable indentation in the rock that provided good cover as well as an excellent view of the camp. Andrew had fought with McGregor in Operation Desert Storm as well, and they complemented each other extremely well, together making a deadly team. They had established encrypted radio contact with the pilot of the low flying Tornado bomber operating out of Uzbekistan, and as he called his approach to the target, Andrew had switched on the laser designator and pointed it at the main building in the compound. The men on the ground could hear the distant roar of the jet engines, and Andrew noticed that some of the soldiers in the camp turned their eyes skyward in an attempt to see the aircraft. The bomber was much too low to be spotted by the insurgents in the middle of the night. Suddenly the jet was on top of their position, and as it screamed over the heads of the two SAS men, the pilot called out bomb release. Andrew and Colin instinctively pressed their bodies into the dusty ground and waited. Less than ten seconds later there was a bright flash lighting up the sky, and half a second later the sound of the explosion hit them along with the shock wave. They both looked up cautiously towards the camp, where smoke and an oily fire was now billowing out of where the main building had been just seconds earlier. Most other structures in the vicinity had been completely flattened, including what seemed to have been the barracks building. The two men remained flat on their stomachs for a few minutes, in order to ascertain the extent of the damage to the camp. They then moved out to return to the rest of the squad. As they lifted themselves from the ground to crawl away, they heard the sound of feet running towards them.

Seconds later two men dressed in shabby clothes, each with a rifle in their hands, jumped over a couple of rocks and landed right on their position. The two insurgents were stunned to find anybody this close to the camp and frantically tried to scramble to their feet, clawing at their weapons. Resting on one knee, Colin had gripped one of them by his belt and in an instant, he tore his knife from its sheath strapped to his leg and slammed it into the chest of the stunned soldier who promptly dropped his rifle, which fell clattering onto the rocks. A split-second later, Andrew was on his feet aiming his MP5 at the other man's head just as he was bringing up his rifle to fire at Colin. Andrew fired a quick double-tap into the soldier's forehead causing his head to jerk backwards. The suppresser muffled the shots to an almost inaudible 'pop-pop'. Colin quickly pulled out the knife and both of the two insurgents fell heavily to the ground almost simultaneously. Andrew and Colin knelt down without a word, listening for more soldiers who might be on their way. They could hear nothing except for the crackling of the fire in the camp. They then slipped away towards their hiding place where the rest of the team had already started packing up for the extraction that night. Six hours later they were resting at the airbase in Uzbekistan.

Andrew's new job in the anti-terrorist division was certainly a lot safer but also a lot less exciting. If he'd had a girlfriend, she would have appreciated that. *Christ*, he thought. His love life had been in hibernation for longer than he cared to remember. He was considered relatively good looking with his blue eyes, black hair, chiselled jaw and muscular body. And there had been quite a few women in and out of his life over the years. Some had been short flings. Others, he had to admit, had been attempts at serious relationships. But they had all ended unhappily. *Of course, they had all ended unhappily*, he thought. *Otherwise, they wouldn't have ended, would they?*

It was not that he wasn't interested in eventually settling down and even having a kid or two. Things had just never worked out that way. It was easy to blame it on his work and the fact that he had been away from home a lot, so that was mostly what he did. But deep down, he knew that that was not entirely correct. Most men are boys at heart, and boys seldom like to commit to anything. Partly because they don't like to get tied down, and partly because they are always wondering what might be just around the next corner. A childish way of looking at it, but nonetheless true for quite a few blokes he had known, including himself.

The cab passed Buckingham Palace, where, true to form, a gazillion tourists had lined up to watch the changing of the guards. He found it amusing how the royal family had been reduced to a tourist attraction. Having once been the most powerful family on the planet, during the heydays of the British Empire, it struggled to keep the respect of its own people through largely ceremonial activities.

As the cab made its way along Constitution Hill towards the West End, Andrew thought back to the 'good old days' when terrorists were mostly young men and women with guns, ski masks and a slightly rosy view on communism. Sure, they represented a danger to the public and they did present serious challenges to the anti-terrorist community. But at least they only carried guns and the occasional pack of explosives, and only very rarely did they view the prospect of dying for their cause as an attractive proposition. And in addition, it was possible to get inside their heads and to understand what their intentions were and even why they did what they did. That made it all so much easier to work with.

Now the terrorists were completely unpredictable, and at the best of times, their motives were difficult to determine, let alone understand. That made it correspondingly difficult to predict and prevent new attacks. What was clear to people such as Sterling, and even to the general public, was that the motives of this new breed of terrorists were more akin to those of fanatic warriors of old. They did not fear death, and they did not really care whether their victims took notice of them or not. They were simply zealots, bent on the destruction of their perceived enemies, even at the cost of their own lives. Chemical and biological weapons in the hands of such people was truly a terrifying thought.

The cab turned onto Sheldrake Place close to Holland Garden in the West End and pulled up to the curb in front of a large non-descript steel and glass building with no name plaques on the outside. The operational headquarters of the SAS in London was not keen on advertising its presence, let alone its activities to anyone.

The cab driver turned his head slightly to the left and looked at Andrew in the rear-view mirror. 'That'll be eighteen fifty, Gov.'

Andrew got out of the cab and handed the driver thirty pounds. 'Could you do me a receipt for twenty-five, please?' he asked the cabby. 'Just keep the change.'

'Thanks, Gov,' the taxi driver said and handed him the receipt. Then he drove off.

Andrew walked through the revolving door into the large reception area where two men in suits without badges or name tags were standing guard.

'Good morning, Helen,' smiled Andrew as he received his access badge and signed his name. 'How are you today?'

'Very well, thank you Mr. Sterling,' smiled the girl at the reception and handed him his badge. 'Have a good day.'

Andrew ignored the elevator and took the stairs to the fourth floor. He liked to stay fit even though it had proved more difficult than he imagined with no exercise on the job anymore. He had purchased some home exercise equipment but had never really come to like using it. Granted, it did save him some time now that he didn't need to go to the gym anymore, but there was just no substitute for the good old-fashioned drills on the SAS training grounds at Hereford.

As he entered the office of his boss Colonel Strickland, his superior got up from his desk and walked towards him with a broad smile.

'Andy,' he said and stretched out his hand. 'Good to see you again. Sorry to have to drag you in here on such short notice, but something rather important has come up. Close the door, would you?'

'Certainly, Sir,' said Andrew and closed the heavy wooden doors. He sat down in a big soft armchair across from Colonel Strickland's desk.

'Tea? Or perhaps a Brandy?' The Colonel smiled teasingly.

'Thank you, Gordon. I'll just have tea for now,' grinned Andrew while he looked around the office. It was actually a rather nice place to work if you had to drive a desk for a living. The room featured large windows with a view to a park, beautiful wood-panelled walls with several full bookcases reaching the ceiling. On the floor was a thick Turkish carpet that seemed to want to swallow up anyone daring to stand on it. Colonel Strickland's desk was made of dark rosewood.

Very old and very expensive, Andrew thought.

The Colonel poured two cups of freshly made tea and sat down, pushing one cup across the desk to where Andrew was sitting.

'Andy, I'll come straight to the point,' he said. 'Eight months ago, there was a fire at the Office of Historical Records at the Admiralty of Her Majesty's Navy. Do you remember?'

'Vaguely,' Andrew responded sipping his tea.

'Well, at the time it was treated as arson committed by some deranged person. It now turns out that it *was* indeed arson but that the fire was started to cover up a burglary. They've had one burglary before this one, but the first time it happened it was only computers that were stolen, and of course, no fires were started. The computers were probably to be sold on to people who were not very happy about paying the full price for a new one. Their content is backed up every night on a central storage network, so no data was lost. In other words, it appeared to be a simple case of theft.'

Strickland took a sip of his tea and then leaned forward in his chair, placing his elbows on the table. 'But here's what was peculiar about the second break-in. In addition to starting a fire, several original documents containing historical records of military activity during the Second World War were taken. Apparently, only records pertaining to the British and American anti-submarine activities in the Atlantic Ocean have been removed. These are not publicly available, so someone decided to go in there and take them out for themselves. Why? We don't know yet. The truth is that these records have never been used for much, except by scholars tallying up the number of German U-boats sunk and the effectiveness of allied war efforts. But that sort of analysis had been completed many years ago, and all the research is publicly available. There isn't anything secret about the documents as such, but they were clearly sufficiently important to risk going to prison over. Breaking into a facility of the Royal Navy is not to be taken lightly. Combined with one count of arson, the culprit could face several years in prison if they are caught.'

'I must say that I still fail to see what this has to do with us,' said Sterling. He hadn't had much sleep lately and it was difficult for him to get excited about someone stealing what appeared to be useless old documents.

'Bear with me for a second, Andy,' said the colonel and raised his hand. 'There's more. This is not the only burglary that has occurred in locations such as this over the past couple of years. We would probably have accepted this as the work of an arsonist, had it not been for the fact that similar documents had been stolen in Paris, Berlin and Munich.'

'So, someone steals historical documents and sells them to the highest bidder,' Andrew interjected. 'That's happened many times before, hasn't it? I bet there's a lucrative black market for those things.'

'Indeed it has, and there certainly is. But in this case we are dealing with a very large number of documents, that quite frankly should be of no interest to anyone except a few history buffs. But apparently, none of the documents have appeared on any black market that the police here or indeed in France or Germany have any knowledge of. That in itself is unusual.'

Becoming a bit impatient, Andrew shifted in his chair. He didn't think of himself as a man particularly interested in solving mysteries, and this was beginning to test his mental endurance.

'Gordon,' he said. 'I don't mean to be rude, but what on earth is this all about. And what does it have to do with us?'

'I will grant you that it does appear rather far from our area of expertise and I can understand your scepticism. In fact, I myself failed to see the relevance until our German colleagues insisted on seeing us last week for an unofficial meeting. They claim that the break-ins in Germany, and quite possibly over here as well, were carried out by the same group of people.'

Andrew sat up in his armchair and put his teacup down on the desk. 'The same people? And what people might that be? And what on earth for?' he frowned.

'Well, Andy. This is the worrying bit. Apparently, our intel chaps say it points to a fundamentalist Islamic group calling itself 'New Dawn'.'

Finally, Andrew's mind snapped to attention. 'You sure about this? It sounds a bit far-fetched.'

'Indeed it does. No one has ever heard of them before, and the only reason the German police know anything about this and were able to tie the burglaries together is due to an arrest they made a few months ago. It seems that the man they arrested in connection with a drug-smuggling ring belonged to the shady organisation that appears to be behind these burglaries.'

'How did they determine that?'

'Well, it was quite simple, really. The chap they arrested was involved with bringing drugs into the European Union via Albania and Italy. Upon searching his apartment in Dortmund, the German police found a package about to be sent to Syria. In the package, they found some of the stolen documents. Most of them are from the National Archive in Berlin which was broken into early last year. But one was from the Office of Historical Records right here in London.'

Andrew looked at Colonel Strickland for a few seconds then shook his head. *Drugs and documents. What's the connection here?* he thought.

'So, what does this mean, precisely?' he asked. 'Islamic fundamentalists who specialise in burglaries. Why is that important to us? I mean – is there any indication that these people are planning violence? Do we even know what the purpose of their organisation is? New Dawn, you say?'

Strickland pressed his lips together and shook his head. 'No. There were no acts of violence in any of the break-ins, except for the arson, but no one was hurt as a result of the fire. However, the German police recovered two names of other members of this 'New Dawn' organisation from the apartment of the man they arrested in Dortmund. They are both Palestinians and both previously lived in Germany but have since moved to Saudi Arabia according to what the arrested man says. At least one of them is known to be affiliated with the terrorist groups Hezbollah and the PFLP. Both groups have tried for years to get their hands on various chemical agents, particularly from the former Soviet Union.'

Andrew leaned forward in his chair and placed his elbows on his knees. 'So, what this all adds up to,' he said as he rubbed his temples with his fingers, 'is that these gentlemen were not just pursuing an interest in history. They were looking for something that might be applied for a more sinister purpose?'

Strickland sighed as wrinkles formed on his forehead. 'Something along those lines. Well, to be perfectly honest, at this moment we don't have the first clue as to exactly what they were looking for, which is why I would like you to pursue this matter. I've already set up meetings for you with several experts on the stolen records, and I'd appreciate it if you could get cracking, right away.'

Andrew nodded and ran his fingers through his hair. *Time for a haircut*, he thought. 'Alright. Who would you like me to see?'

'Well, the first person I'd like you to speak to is the curator of the Office of Historical Records, Professor Maltby. He is probably the one person here in London who knows most about the content of the stolen documents. He's worked on cataloguing them for some years, and he has written extensively about allied war efforts in the Second World War.'

'Alright. Anyone else?'

'Yes, I've arranged for a video conference at five this afternoon with the head of the German investigative team, Dietrich

Obermann. It's in Meeting Room B on the seventh floor. He can probably provide some details about what was taken from the archives in Berlin, as well as any progress they may have made in the investigation of the New Dawn organisation. As it stands, they probably know more about it than we do.'

Andrew rose and adjusted his tie. 'Very well. I'll get right on it. If I go and talk to Professor Maltby right now, I'll make it back here by five.'

'Thank you, old chum. I'll advise him that you are on your way. Best of luck.'

'Thanks, Gordon.'

'Oh, and Andrew,' said the Colonel as Sterling opened the door to leave the office. 'There's no need to tell either of them too much of what I just told you. We keep our own investigation quiet for the moment. It's all on a 'need to know' basis for now.'

'Don't worry,' replied Andrew. 'I'll just ask them a couple of questions, and see what they've come up with.'

'Good man. Report back as soon as you have something.'

'Will do.'

TWO

Andrew Sterling left the office at Sheldrake Place and walked down the corridor to the stairs leading to the reception. A moment later he handed over his security badge at the front desk and signed his name once more. Twenty minutes after that, he entered the Office of Historical Records on Cromwell Road a short walk from the SAS's London headquarters. The building was a massive grey Victorian construct with a huge wooden door painted dark blue. As he entered, Andrew had the distinct sensation of stepping back in time to a bygone age. There was no reception in the hall so Andrew walked casually across to the doorway leading further into the building. Everywhere he looked, there were paintings of people he had never heard of, but judging from their appearance they had to have been prominent naval officers of years past. The floor was set in dark marble and the walls were made of light grey granite giving the impression more of a castle than what was effectively a storage house.

He entered a large room filled with row upon row of bookshelves and file cabinets, containing what seemed to Andrew to be several centuries worth of records and publications. From one of the aisles appeared an older man with spectacles and a white beard. He was impeccably dressed in a striped suit and shiny black shoes. He appeared to be in his mid-sixties, with keen blue eyes, hinting at a sharp mind. Upon spotting Andrew, he immediately stretched out his hand to greet the visitor with a broad smile.

'Mr. Sterling?'

'Yes, I am Andrew Sterling. How do you do, Sir?' asked Andrew not sure if the curator might have military rank, possibly one superior to his own. One never knew about these things. He wasn't exactly what Andrew had expected in a curator. He had expected to meet a dull scholar buried in his books and files, but this man was very different.

'Not too bad,' said the man. 'Not too bad. I'm Professor James Maltby.'

The two men shook hands, and Andrew couldn't help noticing what a firm handshake he was greeted by.

Might be a former sailor, thought Andrew. He wondered how a man of such apparent vitality and spirit could be content with a job such as this.

'Good to see you, Professor Maltby. I expect Colonel Strickland has informed you of the purpose of my visit?'

'He has indeed. But may I inquire as to your title. I didn't quite catch that.'

'Certainly. I'm with the chemical and biological anti-terrorism unit at the SAS.'

'Really? You are a scientist then?'

'No,' laughed Andrew. 'Far from it. I've spent most of my career in the army and the SAS, but during that time I acquired a Master's degree in biochemistry. The SAS likes its people to know about other things than just weapons and explosives.'

'Quite,' said the professor. 'Does what happened here at 'Records' have any bearing on that sort of work?'

'Well, it might. The police are investigating, as are we, and there may be a link to some of the work we are engaged in back at the office. But I have to tell you that I've been instructed not to speak to anyone about the finer points of the investigation.'

Andrew was slightly annoyed with himself. He had already revealed more than was necessary.

'Top secret, eh?' the professor smiled cunningly, clearly enjoying the cloak-and-dagger element of their exchange.

'Something like that, yes,' said Andrew, feeling a bit uneasy about Maltby's enthusiasm. 'Professor, do you have an office where we can talk privately?'

There was no other person in sight, but Andrew thought it safer to discuss things in the relative privacy of an office.

'Certainly, young man. Please follow me.'

The professor's office was small but comfortable and pleasant looking. It was very orderly indeed, with hundreds of books and publications arranged neatly on the shelf-covered walls. The furniture was all made of dark wood, and from the ceiling hung a beautiful chandelier that filled the room with a soft yellowish light.

'Please sit down Mr. Sterling.' said the professor and gestured to the chair across from the professor's desk.

'Thank you, professor.'

Andrew unbuttoned his jacket to make himself more comfortable and then looked at Maltby. 'First off. Could you tell me a bit about the burglary?'

'Oh, yes. That!' exclaimed the professor as though he had forgotten the purpose of Sterling's visit. 'I must say that I was most astonished that somebody would break in here and set fire to the whole thing. I don't know what the world is coming to. But with regards to the stolen documents, I can tell you that they were all from the section of naval records made during the Second World War. Typically, these include original briefings and de-briefings from naval operations of various kinds, but the ones that were taken all concerned the Royal Air Force's efforts to protect naval and commercial convoys crossing the Atlantic Ocean with supplies from America. Trucks, food, oil, weapons, ammunition. That sort of thing.'

'Approximately how much was stolen and how much was destroyed in the flames?'

'Well, judging from what was left behind, I'd say that what was stolen must have been quite heavy for one man to carry out of here by himself.'

'So, you think there were more than just one thief?'

'Not for me to speculate about such things, but I'd say that that is conceivable.'

'Can you be more precise as to the content of the files taken from the cabinets?'

'Well, as I say it is rather difficult to be precise about this since the files are no longer here. But if my memory serves me correctly, those particular files contained exact records of German U-boats sunk during the latter half of the war. Every time a pilot came back from a mission, he had to fill out papers accounting for his flight, including the time taken, his approximate route and of course targets attacked, if any.'

'How precise was this information typically?'

'As I recall, that tended to vary quite a bit. Most pilots doubtless failed to see why such debriefings were important. After all, they had made it back in one piece, and I would imagine that more often than not, they had their minds set on either the next mission or the night ahead. Of course, they had no precise navigational aids like GPS at the time, but approximate positions were always logged.'

Andrew had taken out a small notebook and was scribbling away. He began to feel rather a lot like a crime scene investigator. *I could get the hang of this,* he thought.

The professor was easy to interview. He thought carefully about what he wanted to say and relayed it in a clear and precise manner.

'Ok,' said Andrew. 'So, the written debriefings weren't necessarily very accurate, but presumably they would always mention any U-boat engagements?'

'Oh, yes most definitely. After all, that was what the pilots were there for. And if possible, the pilots would use coastal landmarks to indicate the position of a sunken U-boat or surface vessel. But since most of these events occurred hundreds of miles out to sea, such landmarks were naturally few and far between.'

'And this would be the only type of information contained in the stolen files? Nothing about other aspects of the war or the convoys? Just submarines?'

'Correct. Just submarines.'

'Alright. Getting back to the burglary. Did the files seem to be taken out in random order, or did the thief appear to know what he was looking for?'

'Very difficult to say. The fire brigade was here in a flash, but I'm afraid the fire still had time to destroy many other documents. But I did note that some files were laid aside as if they weren't what the culprit was looking for,' said the professor pensively. 'So, I suppose you could say that there were indications of some form of purpose to his actions.'

'Might you have any idea why anyone would be interested in these files?' asked Andrew.

The professor shook his head and held up his hands with his palms facing the ceiling while smiling in resignation. 'I've wondered about that myself ever since it happened, but I suppose it's fair to say that someone must have thought them very important indeed to go through all this trouble just to get their hands on them.'

'Yes, indeed,' said Andrew. 'Professor you've been most helpful. Could I have your card just in case I have more questions?'

'Certainly, Mr. Sterling,' he said and dug a hand into his top drawer, fetching a business card which he handed to Andrew.

'Thank you, Professor Maltby. I might make use of that. Here's my card. If you think of anything please don't hesitate to call me.'

'I shall ring you straight away if I remember anything else,' he said as he escorted Andrew to the hall.

The two men shook hands once more and Andrew exited the building feeling enlightened but confused.

Burglaries, documents and submarines, he thought. *What's the connection? I wonder if we are chasing something that isn't there. Wouldn't be the first time.*

In the past two years, many people around the world had spent a great deal of resources in the form of people and money, chasing after threats that turned out not to be there. It was all a result of the heightened awareness and indeed increased fear that resulted from the destruction of the World Trade Center a couple of years earlier. In that respect, it seemed the terrorists had achieved their goal - to spread terror.

★ ★ ★

The winds were buffeting the small twin-engine turbo prop passenger plane as it made its final approach to the small airport. There were hardly any clouds and as Mohammed Yusef looked out through the small window by his seat, he could clearly see the tall volcanic peak on the island of Pico. Forty-two kilometres long and with a maximum width of fifteen kilometres, the tear-shaped island was the most spectacular among the nine Azores islands. All the islands were volcanic in origin, but none of the others had a profile as impressive as that of Pico. With its cone-shaped volcano a little over ten kilometres wide at the base, 300 meters wide at the top and at 2553 meters tall, it was almost perfectly symmetrical. At first glance it looked very much like Mount Fuji in Japan, but smaller and without the snow on the peak. From the air, Mohammed could just make out the small 100-metre high cone on the edge of the crater at the summit, indicating the location of the most recent eruption.

Yusef had flown out from Lisbon the day before, and much to his regret, he'd had to spend a night in the town of Ponta Delgado on the main island of Sao Miguel. He had not ventured outside his hotel room once, and the next day he had driven back to the airport for the flight to Pico at half-past three in the afternoon. It was approximately a hundred kilometres to Pico from Sao Miguel, which meant that all the locals travelled by plane and never by boat between the islands. As the plane approached the landing strip, he checked his seatbelt again. He had never been very happy about flying, and the small plane did not deal well with turbulence.

As the wheels hit the runway with a screech the pilot reversed the propeller blades on the engines and increased the throttle to reduce speed. Then he engaged the brakes and the plane rolled off the runway and towards the small building that served as both arrival and departure lounge.

It was mostly locals flying out here at this time of year, but during the summer months, the planes were packed with tourists. Most of them were Portuguese, the relatively cool islands in the middle of the Atlantic Ocean serving as a welcome break from the searing heat of the Portuguese mainland.

Yusef unbuckled his seatbelt and rose to collect his luggage from the overhead compartment. Along with the other passengers, he moved slowly along the aisle towards the front of the plane where he was met by the fresh cool air from outside the plane. The engines were being spun down as they exited down the stairs to the black tarmac. Clean-shaven and wearing light beige trousers, a white short-sleeved shirt and sunglasses, he looked every bit the rich tourist he wanted to appear to be. Indeed, he was rich, in a manner of speaking. He had plenty of funds, but the money wasn't his own. Truth be told, he didn't know exactly from whom it came, and he wanted to keep it that way. He had no need to know the names of his benefactors, as long as they provided him and his brothers with the means to do what had to be done. Not knowing, was in many respects an advantage.

With a smile, a member of the plane's cabin crew waived the passengers towards the small building, where most of them started to line up along the conveyor belt, anxious to receive their luggage and head off for their pre-booked hotels and resorts. Yusef made his way through the crowd and exited a few seconds later on the other side of the building. He quickly spotted the rental car that had been arranged for him. A small Seat, it was a suitable vehicle for the narrow roads on the island.

He opened the door and slung his bag over onto the passenger seat and got in. The key was in the ignition and as he turned it, the engine sprang to life. He drove away from the airport along the newly laid asphalt road while listening to the radio that played endless hours of Portuguese pop music. After a few minutes, he had reached the main road that ran the length of the island from the town of Piedade in the east to the small port city of Madalena in the west. As he had been instructed, he turned right towards Madalena and drove calmly along the road, and ten minutes later he reached the town. Glancing up and to his left he could see the volcano now towering over him as he drove towards Madalena. It looked barren and inhospitable as the clouds slowly began forming in the rapidly cooling air that swept around its top late in the afternoon.

It made him think of his mountainous homeland far away. Mountains and the desert had always made him feel at home even though he had spent most of his life in cities. There was a quality to mountains that made him feel small. Made him realise that he was but a tiny speck on the surface of the planet and that there were things - places as well as ideas, thoughts and dreams - much greater than he was. And he was now part of such a great dream. He knew that now. Having been chosen to take his place in the plan as laid out to him only a few months earlier, had been the greatest privilege of his life so far. He only prayed to God that he would be able to fulfil his duty in helping to achieve the objective.

Whatever happened, he felt confident that God would look favourably upon his efforts and reward him.

Driving across the central square with its post office, bank, grocery shops and a church, his rental car rolled slowly onto the harbour area where a few small fishing boats were moored. Over to the right was a long wharf that extended a couple of hundred meters into the inner harbour area. At its tip lay a large ship fitted with a tall crane at the centre. With its 31 meters in length, a gross tonnage of 235 and its 660 horse-power diesel engine, the salvage ship could make 12 knots in calm seas. Its hull was painted dark blue and its bridge and superstructure were white with a red band at the very top. The crane could lift close to 2.5 tons from as deep as 350 meters, but operating at those depths happened very rarely. Most ships that were deemed worth salvaging were coasters or other commercial transport ships usually sailing close to the shore where waters were much shallower.

With seagulls squawking away above him, he parked the car next to the ticket office selling fares for the short trip to the small island of Faial that lay directly opposite from Madalena. He got out and headed along the pier towards the blue and white ship that lay waiting with its engines running and a couple of people loading supplies. Seeing Yusef approach, one of them, a big brawny man with dark curly hair and a short black beard set down the crate he was carrying and began walking slowly towards him. As he approached, his smile widened and he stuck out a big strong hand to greet his comrade.

'Mohammed, my friend,' he said as he grabbed Yusef's hand a shook it forcefully. 'You are here at last. We've been expecting you all day. Do you have what we need? The co-ordinates?'

'I have them, Hamza' replied Yusef affirmatively as he embraced Hamza Masood. 'It's good to see you again, Hamza. Is the boat ready?'

'The boat is ready and we have loaded supplies for a week. That should be enough.'

'You appear confident, my friend,' smiled Yusef as the two men started walking towards the ship. 'But you may be correct. The coordinates that were given to me by Arrowhead appear to be very precise, so we will be able to start our search early tomorrow.'

'Good. I have waited for this since the day I was first granted knowledge of the project. I am confident we will secure our prize.'

'Hamza, you are a man of great optimism,' smiled Yusef as he stepped onto the deck of the ship. 'As you know, I personally requested that you be assigned to this task. I know you well and I have faith in your abilities. I can reveal to you that we have both been promised great rewards upon the successful completion of this most delicate and difficult mission.'

Hamza Masood's eyes lit up. An expert in salvage operations, this was what he lived for.

'What of the harbourmaster? You have spoken to him?' asked Yusef leaning back his head to look at the top of the large crane that was mounted at the front of the ship.

'Yes. He believes that we are going to search for a small private aeroplane, which crashed into the sea a few miles from the runway a couple of years ago. I told him that the pilot who died was my brother. He has asked no further questions after that.'

Hamza smiled, pleased with his own ingenuity. 'By the way, I was requested to ask you to report to Arrowhead as soon as you arrived here. You have a phone?'

'Yes,' said Yusef and pulled out an Iridium satellite phone from a pocket in his jacket. 'I'll do it now.'

'I'll be in the galley,' said Hamza. 'The cook is almost done with the meal. He's good,' he smiled and ambled off to get himself some food.

Yusef dialled a number and the signal was beamed to a network of orbiting communications satellites where it was relayed down to a point far beyond the horizon to a place in the desert where it was already dark. A phone there chirped a few times before a voice answered hesitantly.

'Arrowhead.'

'This is Quest.'

'Quest! It is good to hear from you. You have arrived?'

'Yes. The vessel is ready. We will leave early tomorrow morning. Hamza is in charge of the team,' said Yusef and looked over his shoulder towards the crewmen hoisting the last supplies aboard.

'What about the crew. I trust they know nothing?', asked the voice in the desert.

'That is correct. They are all professional divers from Lisbon and they have been paid handsomely not to ask any questions. I'm confident that they will cause us no problems as long as they get their money. All you have to do is flash dollar bills in front of their eyes, and these people will do anything,' he scoffed.

'You will report back tomorrow?' asked the voice.

'I will. We begin with a broad sweep of the area. It shouldn't take too long to locate it. It is big, so we should get a sonar ping quite quickly.'

'Excellent,' said the voice. 'We await your report tomorrow evening then. Good luck and may God be with you.'

'Thank you.'

Yusef put down the phone and switched it off. Tomorrow would be interesting indeed. He headed for the galley to join the rest of the crew. He might as well get acquainted with them, as they would be working closely together, at least for the next few days.

A few hours later the ship cast off its moorings. It then slowly exited the harbour area and made its way Southeast on the calm seas along the coast of Pico. Most of the crew was either working on the bridge or gazing at the peak of the volcano, where a flimsy layer of cloud was forming as the wind pushed warm air from below, up along the side of the mountain, cooling it as it did so. It made for a spectacular sight. Yusef and Hamza were in the mess hall going over the next few days' work plan with the head of the dive team, Augustino Pieza. They were to start by using sonar to pinpoint the exact spot. Then they would send down the team of divers they had employed in Lisbon. From then on, they would have to improvise. It was dangerous work in more ways than one, so they had to be careful and take their time. Yusef felt the excitement grow inside him with each passing minute, knowing that he was moving ever closer to the prize.

★ ★ ★

Sterling made it back to the anonymous-looking building on Sheldrake Place at ten minutes to five in the afternoon. After signing in, he proceeded to Meeting Room B, where a technician was already setting up the teleconferencing equipment. A desk and two chairs were positioned in the middle of the room, and opposite them was a 64-inch Toshiba display. On top of the screen was a small camera pointed at where Andrew was sitting.

Andrew sat down at the desk and looked self-consciously at the camera. There was no image feed from Germany yet, but his own image might very well be blown up on a big screen in Dortmund right now. To be seen, but without being able to see anything himself, went against everything Andrew had been trained for, and it felt decidedly unsettling.

'That's got it,' said the technician and instantly an image from an office in Dortmund was displayed on the big screen. 'We're live.'

Andrew shifted in his seat and sat up straight as the technician left the room. On his screen, an amiable looking man in his fifties sat down at his own desk and looked at Andrew. Amusingly, he seemed to be looking straight at Andrews's hair since the camera he was looking at was mounted below his own screen.

Right. Let's get on with it.

'Good afternoon, Inspector Obermann.' said Andrew and smiled at the screen.

'Good day, Mr. Sterling. Very happy to meet you.' The Inspector spoke surprisingly good English and seemed very open to this exchange of information.

'You too,' said Andrew. 'Let me start by introducing myself. I'm attached to the chemical and biological anti-terrorism unit of the SAS, as you probably know. We are part of the SAS, but it's really more of an investigative division. We're currently looking at a potential threat developing over here, and would appreciate it if you could assist us in this matter.'

'Certainly,' nodded the inspector, furrowing his brow, and shifting slightly in his seat.

'Excellent. As you know, we've both encountered break-ins at facilities that store historical documents. And similar break-ins have happened in France, as I understand.'

'Correct,' said the inspector.

'I wonder if it would be alright with you if I went straight to some questions?'

'Please do,' said Obermann and sipped some coffee from a Styrofoam cup.

'Ok. First of all – I understand that you have arrested a man in connection with a drug-smuggling operation. Is that correct?'

'Yes, it is,' replied Obermann and cleared his throat. 'He had been receiving large quantities of heroin from a source in Pakistan. This was to be distributed to several European countries and the money channelled back to Pakistan. At least, that is what we could gather from what we found in his apartment. He was very sloppy with leaving evidence there for us to find.'

Andrew was already taking notes, even though the conversation was being recorded. Not that he doubted the recording system, but taking his own notes helped him remember the details.

'And you also found some documents there, is that correct?' he asked.

'Yes. By the way. Finding drugs is not very unusual,' continued the inspector. 'We have a big problem with drug smuggling and drug addicts, as I believe you have as well. What was unusual was that we found some of the stolen documents from the National Archive in Berlin when we searched his apartment. Almost all of them were there. And along with that, we also found evidence linking him to a person who we know is affiliated with at least one terrorist organisation.'

'Have you been able to establish any link between the two sets of documents?' Andrew asked and looked up at the screen.

'No. No links. We cannot see why the documents were of any interest to these people. At first, we thought that it was a mistake and that perhaps they had taken the wrong documents or something, but it appeared that they had actually been analysed methodically by the man who is now in our custody. He had made several pages of notes on the content of the files, and it did seem very purposeful. But his notes make no sense to us, I'm afraid. They are in Arabic, but the translation didn't help us determine what the purpose of the break-in was. Obviously, the man in our custody isn't talking.'

'What exactly did the documents from Berlin contain?'

'Well, they have a very orderly filing system over there, and since they had catalogued all of their records thoroughly, they can actually tell us exactly what is missing. It seems the documents are all from the last two years of the Second World War. It is quite extensive, and scholars have written several papers on their content. It seems they all had to do with the many expeditions that the National Socialist Party financed in those days.'

'Expeditions? I don't believe I've ever heard of those,' said Andrew. *Nazi expeditions? Interesting.*

'Well,' said the inspector, clearly uneasy and perhaps even a bit embarrassed at what he was about to say. 'There were some expeditions that were supposedly looking for a way to prove the racial superiority of the German people. They went all over the world, looking for clues.'

Andrew cleared his throat and went on calmly. 'So presumably the documents were records of these expeditions?'

'Among other things. Yes.'

'Do you have details on their content?'

'Well, I could find out for you, but I can actually do better than that. As the files were catalogued at the National Archive, every document that was stored there was also recorded on microfilm.

The archive has begun digital scanning of all documents as well, but have not yet got round to these particular ones. Anyway, the microfilm is available, if you would like to see them. I could have a copy made and sent to your office within a few days. Would you be interested in that?'

'I'd be very grateful if you could arrange that,' said Andrew, pleased that the inspector was so willing to assist him. 'We would definitely appreciate seeing what was taken and if there is any relation to what was stolen over here in London. And I'll see to it that our Office of Historical Records extends you the same courtesy if possible.'

'Thank you,' said the inspector and smiled. 'Is there anything else I can do for you?'

'No, thank you. You've already been most helpful. I don't think any of us over here are sure exactly what is going on, but we are nonetheless very appreciative of your help. Thanks again.'

'My pleasure. Have a nice day,' the inspector smiled and looked off to the side.

'You too, Sir.'

Then the screen went black and Andrew leaned back in his chair rubbing the back of his head. It was difficult to make sense of it all, particularly this late in the day. He could feel his brain yearning for some peace and quiet and decided to leave for home as soon as possible. Before he went home for the weekend, he stopped by Colonel Strickland's office to brief him on the progress, if one could call it that. It seemed that every question asked, resulted in several new ones raised, and without any answers necessarily coming out of it.

At a quarter to seven in the evening, he went outside and looked up at the sky. The clouds were receding rapidly towards the east and clearer skies began to emerge as the sun crept slowly towards the horizon, taking on an ever-darker orange glow as it did so. It was going to be a cold clear night in London. The leaves clattered along on the pavement. Even mild winds could cause strong gusts in the middle of a city, and every few minutes a heap of leaves would get swept up into the air, temporarily finding a new resting place, only to be swept further along the street a few seconds later.

I wonder where it all ends up, thought Andrew, as he headed into Hyde Park for his walk home.

He crossed over to The Serpentine to sit on a bench for a few minutes watching the ducks paddle themselves along the long shallow pond. There were always some old ladies feeding them, it seemed. The ducks would probably die if it weren't for those women. Maybe the opposite was true as well.

He rose and walked the rest of the way home. It took him around an hour of brisk walking to reach his house, but the fresh air cleared his head. He spent the evening in front of the TV watching BBC World, and at ten he shuffled off to bed.

★ ★ ★

Early the next morning just south of the eastern tip of Pico, the salvage ship had begun its slow arduous sweep of the ocean floor, its advanced active sonar hammering away at the sea bed in an effort to find what the crew was searching for. Hamza was engaged in checking and re-checking all the equipment on the ship, including the semi-autonomous submersible Manny.

The remotely operated vehicle or ROV was a so-called 'Hyball'. It was named so, because it looked more like a ball than anything else. It was made of yellow hardened plastic and had two powerful lights pointed forward. Two thrusters pointing up and to the right and to the left respectively, and a similar pair pointing down, ensured that it could hover underwater in the same spot, even with powerful currents trying to push it around. Two additional thrusters that were pointing backwards were built into the body of the submersible, thus providing a means of forward and backward propulsion. Two circular aluminium bars made their way in an arc around the body of the ROV, functioning as a fender if the Submersible should bump into something. This gave it its ball-like shape. Inside the yellow ball was mounted a camera and a range of sensors that were visible through the Plexiglas at its front. It had been bought a few months earlier from a salvage and rescue company in The Netherlands, which was experiencing economic woes and thus had to trim their costs and sell off some hardware.

For Yusef and his team, it was more than adequate for what they needed to do. The ROV was a sturdy little machine, and they were not going to get even close to its maximum service depths of 350 meters. It was operated by Antonio Pieza's right-hand man, Ramon Salinas. A young thin man with large spectacles and messy brown hair, he was the archetypal nerd. A very bright engineer, Ramon was more interested in the technical details of operating Manny, than in the actual search itself. That made for a perfect working relationship with Antonio, who was thoroughly unimpressed with the capabilities of the small sub. After all, it wasn't able to do anything that a diver couldn't do just as well.

Antonio was, however, very enthusiastic about the task at hand. It had been a long time since he and his team had been tasked with participating in a mission to retrieve items of historical value, and he felt sure that they would find many interesting and historically important items in the days to come.

THREE

Disappointingly for them all, the first day's search was without result. They had produced a beautifully detailed map of the seafloor in a one square kilometre area, but there had been no sign of their objective. On several occasions, large objects had seemed to present themselves near the bottom, but every time it had turned out to be large schools of fish moving slowly through the water near the sea bed. Late in the afternoon on the second day, Yusef was standing in the bow of the ship, watching the waves glide underneath. He was becoming increasingly impatient and had had to report the lack of progress back to Arrowhead the previous night. An unpleasant experience that he didn't much want to have to repeat again that evening. He wouldn't let himself fail this test. He knew that the information on the exact position was uncertain and that they would need a bit of luck, but he had no intention of keeping his superiors waiting for longer than absolutely necessary.

He was on his way back to his cabin for some sleep when Hamza stuck his head out from the bridge and called to him. 'Yusef! Come,' he shouted, waving his hand.

Mohammed Yusef walked quickly to the bridge and joined the others by the sonar screen.

'Look here,' said Hamza and pointed to a large green area on the screen. 'This could be it. It has the right size and shape, and we are well within the area of the seafloor that was designated as the most likely location.'

'Can we take another look?' he said and looked at the helmsman, as the long green area on the sonar screen disappeared on the bottom of the screen.

He nodded and started to turn the ship around for another pass. A couple of minutes later they were approaching the position that had presented the image they'd hoped for, and right on cue, it reappeared at the top of the screen.

'Shut down the engines,' Yusef ordered. 'We stay in this spot.'

The engine noise dwindled, and as the ship coasted forward, slowly losing speed, the image on the screen moved ever more slowly down towards the centre. When the ship was directly above the sonar contact, the loud clattering of chains signalled the deployment of her two anchors.

'Ninety-two meters,' said Hamza and looked at Antonio who was standing next to him by the sonar screen. 'We are fine with that, are we not?'

Antonio nodded confidently. 'No problem, Señor. I recommend we commence the initial stage tomorrow morning at first light.'

'Tomorrow?' asked Yusef disappointedly. 'Why not now?'

'There is no need to take risks,' said Antonio Pieza in a stern voice. 'We have determined the position, and my men are used to working in daylight. The deal was for us to do it our way, right?'

Yusef hesitated but then thought it best to comply with the suggestion of the dive team leader. Despite his growing impatience, he didn't want to start an argument.

'Alright then,' he said. 'Tomorrow at daybreak. Good work, men.'

He then walked outside and fetched his satellite phone to call back to the base and deliver the good news.

★ ★ ★

Sterling had spent the weekend reading up on the intricate web of terrorist networks in the Middle East. Nowhere did he find a reference or even a small hint of an organisation by the name of New Dawn or anything similar to that. He even spent several hours browsing hundreds of news sites on the internet, but without result. Early Monday morning he went to SAS headquarters, and on his desk he found a note from Colonel Strickland, asking him to ring as soon as he got in.

'Colonel Strickland. Andrew here. You asked me to call?'

'Ah, yes Andy. Following on from our talk on Friday, I made a few inquiries here and there, and I'd suggest you call a lady named Fiona Keane. She's a historian and archaeologist currently working with the British Museum, and it has been recommended to me that we contact her in this matter. It appears that she is the one to talk to for information on the more clandestine archaeological activities of the Nazi regime before and during the war. As it turns out, she's actually one of just two people here in Britain that has so far been allowed to access the German files. I think she might be of use to you. Give her a ring and arrange for a meeting.'

'Will do,' said Andrew. 'By the way, I've tried to find some information about this New Dawn organisation, but there is nothing to be found anywhere. It seems that it is quite new. Either that, or it has stayed well hidden up until now.'

'I've asked around concerning that too. Apparently, the German police are the first to have uncovered anything about the group. The French police have made no progress in their investigation of the break-in that occurred in Paris. For some reason, they seem reluctant to treat it as anything but simple theft, so no help from them I'm afraid.'

'Alright. I'll try to reach this Keane lady today. Anything else from your side?'

'I'm afraid not. It is rather slow going, isn't it?'

'A bit. I just wish we had a better sense of the big picture here. It feels like there's definitely something odd about this whole thing, but I can't put my finger on it.'

'I know what you mean, Andy. Speak to Miss Keane, and we'll see where that leaves us.'

'Right. I'll talk to you later.'

Andrew put down the phone and pressed the button for his secretary Catherine Swanson, who was sitting just outside his door in the front office. She was a woman in her forties with a heart of gold and a broken marriage, and she worked a lot more than her salary could justify. With two adult children, she never missed an opportunity to advertise their exploits. She was actually quite pretty, and Andrew sometimes wondered how she avoided being swarmed by suitors, but perhaps she had decided that she was happier alone.

She and Andrew enjoyed a warm but professional working relationship with one another. She took immense pride in her work, and she was the envy of all the other officers in the building. She would see to it that there would never be an appointment or a meeting that Andrew missed, and she was always sensitive to when he needed to be left alone.

'Cathy. Will you try to reach a Miss Fiona Keane at the British Museum for me?'

'Certainly Mr. Sterling.'

He always called her Cathy, which he suspected she appreciated, but she never refrained from referring to him as 'Mr. Sterling'. That was the proper thing to do, and she wasn't about to change that. A few minutes later the phone rang, and Catherine's soft voice reached his ear.

'Mr. Sterling. I have Miss Keane from the British Museum on the line for you.'

'Thanks, Cathy.'

There was a short pause, and then the voice of what seemed to be a young woman came on.

'This is Fiona Keane speaking,' she said, her Irish accent immediately apparent to Andrew.

'Miss Keane. This is Andrew Sterling. I'm with the SAS.'

'The what?' she asked.

'The SAS. Special Air Service?' He shifted slightly in his seat.

'Is that an air freight service?' she asked.

'Uhm, no,' said Andrew slightly off balance.

'I know who you are,' she exclaimed. 'You are the lads who run about blowing up bridges and railways and such. Is that correct?' He could hear her smiling as she asked the question.

'Well, among other things. Yes,' he responded, a bit thrown off by the remark. 'But that is not why I'm calling you. I'd like to request a meeting with you as soon as you are available. It's rather important. Is that alright with you?'

'Well, I can't see why not,' she said in a more serious tone of voice. 'I'm actually free this evening, so I'll let you buy me dinner. How does that sound?'

Pleased with her answer, Andrew smiled and agreed. He had no plans anyway. 'That sounds fine. Where do you live? I'll come by and pick you up if you like.'

'Just come by the British Museum at seven. I'll be working late.'

'Alright, then. I'm driving a dark green Jaguar.'

She laughed, although he wasn't sure why. 'I think I'll be able to spot that,' she said 'And I'll be wearing a red leather jacket.'

'Red leather jacket,' Andrew repeated. 'Got it. I'll see you then.'

'Ok. Bye-bye.'

★ ★ ★

Meanwhile, in the city of Karachi in Pakistan, a group of dedicated men were getting ready to carry out their raid. They had planned this for a long time, and they had needed to wait for the right moment. Tonight, that moment had come. Most of them were former Mujahedin fighters who had fought many wars in Afghanistan in an effort to keep the country free of western influence. They were trained in weapons and explosives, and there was not one among them who had not taken the life of another man. And what they had been told at the training camps when they were young, had turned out to be true for all of them. Once you had taken one life, doing it again would be easy.

Night had already fallen over the Pakistani city of some 10 million people, many of them living close to the poverty line. Pakistan was rich measured in people, some 140 million of them in an area the size of France and Spain put together, but poor in monetary terms. And yet the country had pressed on with a multibillion-dollar nuclear programme, that involved energy for civilian purposes as well as weapons manufacturing.

Cynics argued that the energy programme wasn't established out of care for the ordinary Pakistani, but rather because it enabled the country's leaders to obtain the depleted uranium necessary for a nuclear weapons programme. For all its many millions of people, mainly Muslims, Pakistan was small compared to its giant neighbour to the Southeast. India, with a predominantly Hindu population of over a billion people, dwarfed Pakistan. And now, with a nuclear arsenal to match that of its neighbour, the conflict between the two countries over the region of Kashmir was becoming increasingly worrying to the previously dominant superpowers of yesteryear.

Inside the state prison near the river on the outskirts of the city, the prison guards were making their last rounds, checking that all of the cells were securely locked after the walk in the courtyard that afternoon. All was relatively quiet, except for the occasional shouting from one of the prisoners. None of them were violent criminals, but rather they were in prison because of their opposition to the military government.

Officially, political opposition was allowed, but in practice, it was very different, at least if the opposition became too vocal or too popular with the masses. The government was constantly fighting radical Muslim elements within what was otherwise a peaceful religion. Some of the radical groups had wanted to overthrow the government for many years, in order to replace it with non-democratic religious rule. Their aim was a country governed by an Islamic council of elders, religious leaders and scholars. Once established, such a government could never be replaced by the people, because its stated aim was to reject democracy on the basis that the individual is unable to make responsible decisions for itself as well as for the society as a whole. The only solution was thus a society constructed around the legal interpretation of the Koran, the Sharia. The only problem with this idea was that the interpretation of the Koran was just that, an interpretation, and there were about as many of those around the world as there were Muslim communities. Even within Pakistan, there were a plethora of Muslim factions, and if one added to that the diverse ethnic composition of the whole society, it was clear that the government had a difficult task in just keeping the nation from falling apart. Knowing this, the government would frequently imprison large groups of people suspected of organising subversive political activity, or of plotting to overthrow the government.

These were the men sitting in the cells in the prison, as darkness fell over a seemingly peaceful city. Most of them had been rounded up by the security forces and were now awaiting hearings or trials. Many of them were innocent but had been unfortunate enough to know someone who was actively opposing the government. Others had simply found themselves at the wrong place at the wrong time.

Prisoner #4264 was an outsider in the compound. He had committed no violent acts, had never been affiliated with an opposition group, and didn't subscribe to any of the extremist religious views that were prevalent in this society. In fact, he had never been known to hold any political views at all. He had, however, been convicted of spying for Russia. He was a Pakistani national but had worked for years for Russian intelligence agencies, gathering and passing on information about the work he did for the Pakistani military. His reasons for doing so had simply been money. He was sure that Russia knew as much about these types of weapons as Pakistan did, but Russia wanted to keep an eye on the progress of that work within Pakistan. As far as he was concerned, him passing on that information would make no difference to anyone, since the Russians already knew what was going on, and they even knew what his research would lead to in the end. So, taking a huge amount of money for delivering a little information that would probably be public knowledge five years later, was no crime in his eyes. The only thing that saddened him a bit, now that he had spent six months in prison and had no hope of ever getting out, was that he had truly enjoyed his work in spite of its sinister purpose. He had been an extremely gifted scientist, and so he had quickly been awarded the overall responsibility for the whole programme. Allowing his great talents to be squandered in a poorly paid job for the Pakistani military just seemed such an awful waste. And the Russian money had been nice. Very nice indeed. Enough to pay off tonight's guard. In a country as poor as this, money could truly do wonders.

At that moment, he heard the expected footsteps on the cement outside in the corridor. They became louder and then stopped right outside his cell's solid steel door. A few seconds went by without a sound, but then a key was inserted in the lock, and then slowly it was turned to unlock the door. The guard obviously made an effort to produce as little noise as possible. The door slowly swung open without making a sound. No one stood in the doorway, so prisoner #4264 stood up and moved apprehensively out into the dimly lit corridor. The guard was standing still like a statue a few feet away. He raised his hand and beckoned the prisoner to follow him. The two men walked silently down the corridor, both of them certain that their lives were about to change for the better.

Having made their way from the road outside the compound to the prison grounds, the man who was in charge of the small band of fighters, took out a piece of paper with a picture on it. It was an official Interior Ministry document, detailing the exact location of prisoner #4264. This information was highly sensitive and was supposed to be classified, but the group of men had friends and sympathisers everywhere, including several within the government apparatus. It was shown to the others in silence so that they would be able to recognise him.

The back doors of the van swung open, and the men jumped out and started sprinting towards the prison wall. Halfway there, all but two men lay down on the ground. Within thirty seconds the two men were right next to the end wall of one of the prison blocks, outside the mess hall. No fence had been built here, and it was the only part of the prison where there was just a single, although heavily reinforced wall, separating the prisoners from the outside world.

The two men knelt down next to the wall and placed a heavy bag next to it. Then they ran back to the others. Having thrown themselves on the ground, one of them pulled out a small box, flipped a switch and pressed a button. For an instant, the whole sky was lit up in a bright white flash above them. The noise of the explosion was deafening, and pulverised pieces of brick and cement burst out from what was now a gaping hole in the thick prison wall. They had certainly brought enough explosives, but better too much than too little.

Slowly lifting their heads to look at the carnage, several of the men brought forth their weapons and aimed them at the hole where the dust was slowly drifting away in the light breeze. Suddenly a man bolted from the opening and started running straight for them. The leader of the group raised his arm and two of the men stood up to make their way towards him. Prisoner #4264 was easily recognisable with his glasses, his clean-shaven face and his smooth black hair. The others began to retreat back to the van. It had been about a minute since the explosion, and only now did a siren go off, and the prison floodlights were turned on. But there were still no guards in sight. They were probably still confused by what had happened, and they most likely had no idea exactly where the explosion had come from.

At that moment a second figure emerged from the rubble and started making his way quickly towards the small group of men. Upon seeing this, the leader took out his pistol and pointed it at the advancing man. It was the prison guard, and as he spotted the gun pointing at him, he froze with a confused look on his face. He had been promised a lot of money for this.

Looking briefly at this pathetic government lackey, the leader pulled the trigger three times in quick succession, and three shots rang out in the night. The guard's body spun around as the bullets smacked into the right side of the chest. Small spats of blood shot out from the wounds, and he fell backwards onto the ground where his open eyes stared blankly at the black sky. A few seconds later he was dead. The shooter quickly turned, holstered his weapon as he made his way back to the van. He was the last to get in, and as soon as the doors slammed shut, the van drove off into the night.

★ ★ ★

At ten to seven that evening Andrew parked his car on Bedford Square just opposite the British Museum on Bloomsbury Street. He got out and stood next to the car, waiting. He was good at that. Patience is a virtue for any soldier, but particularly for the members of the SAS, who often spend more time avoiding the enemy than pursuing it. He had spent more hours and days sitting in one place not doing anything than he would care to remember. This particular wait, however, was short. At exactly seven o'clock, an attractive young woman with shoulder-length dark hair and wearing a short red leather jacket exited the building and made her way down the stairs to the pavement in front of the building. A small bag slung over her shoulder and wearing a light grey turtleneck sweatshirt, she looked like someone that cared about her appearance. She also struck him as the sort of person who was usually busy, and who probably enjoyed it.

Punctual, he thought approvingly as he moved a few steps towards her, waiting for her to spot him.

As she did so, she waived and quickly darted across the road. 'Mr. Sterling?' she said with a smile.

Andrew extended his hand and smiled back at her. 'Call me Andy. Nice to meet you. Is it *Miss* Keane?'

'Yes, it is. Please call me Fiona. Have you booked a table for us?' she asked.

'I've taken the liberty of making reservations at a Chinese restaurant. I hope that's fine by you?'

'Excellent. I love Chinese. This is your car?' she asked and pointed to the Jaguar.

'Yep. You like it?' asked Andrew as he unlocked the car with the RF unit in his key ring. Things suddenly began to feel a bit corny.

'I guess it's alright if you like that sort of thing,' she said as she opened the door on the passenger's side.

Andrew got in behind the wheel and they drove off. The drive to the Chinese restaurant in Mayfair took about five minutes, and as he drove, Andrew outlined for Fiona the events surrounding the burglaries in London and Berlin. They got out of the car and went inside, where they were shown to their table in a quiet corner. It was where Andrew usually sat, and the waiters made an effort to make him feel at home and welcome.

Having ordered, Fiona leaned forward in her chair and looked Andrew in the eyes. She really was quite beautiful.

'You know, you don't look like a soldier at all,' she exclaimed studying him inquisitively. 'Do all you chaps get sent off to boarding school after they have trained you?'

Once again, Andrew was caught off guard by the young woman. 'What do you mean?' he asked, trying to keep a straight face.

'Well. You just seem too… educated. And your manners are far too good for a soldier,' she said picking up her glass of wine while still waiting for his reaction. He couldn't figure out if she was deliberately trying to rattle him to see what he was like beneath the suit, or if she was just being Fiona Keane.

She smiled at him and said, 'I wasn't joking about the boarding school, you know.'

Andrew shook his head and chuckled. 'No, I didn't go to boarding school. But I'll admit that I grew up with a butler and a nanny. Perhaps you can picture it'

'Oh?' she said with a smile, raising her eyebrows pretending to be impressed.

He saw that she was just teasing him, and he actually rather liked that in a woman.

'Rich parents, eh?' she said and winked at him.

'Something like that,' he said. 'My parents died when I was young and left me some money.'

She looked straight at him for a few seconds. 'Oh, shit. I'm sorry Mr. Sterling,' she said embarrassed. 'I can be very clumsy.'

Andrew shrugged and smiled. 'Don't worry. You are not the first person to feel awkward about this. But there's really no need. I'm perfectly alright with it. It was a long time ago,' he said and picked up the wine bottle. 'Would like some more?'

'Yes please,' she smiled, her eyes conveying her apology.

Andrew filled her glass and then his own with the Margaux '86. As he placed the bottle on the table again, he cleared his throat and looked at her. *Time to get down to business.*

'Miss Keane. Fiona,' he smiled. 'The reason I've asked to see you is because I've been told that you are quite an authority on certain expeditions that were undertaken by the Nazis during the Second World War.'

'Well, that isn't too far off the mark,' she replied. 'I wouldn't call myself an expert, but I've spent quite some time researching the Nazi expeditions during the last three or four years. I was actually granted access to some of the original files stored in Berlin.'

'Yes, I know. The National Archives, right?'

She looked at him in surprise. 'You've certainly done your homework, haven't you?'

'That's what I get paid for. I'm probably not what most people think of as a member of the SAS. I've taken on more of an investigative role for now.'

'I see,' she said. 'Well, anyway. Most of these expeditions were actually carried out long before the war, in the late thirties. The National Socialist Party, as it was actually called, was establishing its power throughout the entirety of German society, and one of their projects was to, shall we say, revise history where possible.'

At that moment the waiter returned, placing a large dish of food that was oozing exotic fragrances in front of each of them. Fiona continued talking as she picked up her knife and fork, leaving the chopsticks on the table.

'The expeditions weren't very well publicised at the time,' she continued. 'But the official purpose was to locate the origin of the Aryan race.'

Andrew frowned, looking incredulous, and Fiona chuckled as she saw his face. 'Most people react that way when they first hear about this. And I'll admit that it does sound a bit daft, but the fact remains that the German government at the time poured huge resources into these efforts. There were four or five major expeditions in total, not counting the many undertakings on

German soil. There was definitely one to Thule in Greenland, and one to Tibet. I have found no details on the third and fourth expeditions yet, except that they definitely happened. There may have been a fifth expedition, but so far, I have only been able to find hints of this. Some scholars reject a fifth expedition altogether, but I'm not convinced.'

'How many resources were allocated to this effort?'

'I'm not sure exactly, but I estimate that several thousand people were working on this for more than five years, so you can understand that this had a high priority back then.'

'I dare say,' mumbled Andrew and took a sip of his wine.

'In fact,' continued Fiona. 'This is what leads me to believe that there was much more to these expeditions than mere anthropology and archaeology, however twisted it might appear.'

'What do you mean?'

'Well. It is well known that Hitler and many of his followers were fascinated – some would even say obsessed – with the occult.'

'Really?' said Andrew.

So far, this young lady is at least right about one thing. It does sound a bit weird.

'Yes. Ever heard of the Thule Society?' she asked.

'No, but right now I'm guessing it has something to do with the Nazi expeditions to Thule, right?'

'Yes and no,' she responded, really getting into the swing of things. It was obvious that she had a genuine interest in the subject, and Andrew couldn't help being swept along by her engaging and energetic personality, as her mind raced across this most peculiar topic.

'The Thule Society was an occult society founded in Germany around 1915,' she continued. 'Its driving force was a man called Rudolf Von Serbottendorf, who had been schooled in occultism, Islamic mysticism, alchemy, Rosicrucianism among other things.'

'Sounds like a very open-minded chap,' smiled Andrew.

'He was indeed. The Thule Society was an occultist spiritual and political entity that thrived on the turmoil that followed from the First World War. One of the many associations that it founded was the German Workers Party, which in 1920 changed its name to the National Socialist German Worker Party. And as you can guess, that was when the Nazi party was born.'

'So besides being a bunch of occult enthusiasts meddling in politics, what did this Thule Society do? What was their aim?'

'The belief system of the Thule Society was founded in the conviction that Thule was a legendary island in the far north, basically like an Atlantis. It was supposedly the centre of a lost, high-level civilisation that mysteriously vanished thousands of years ago, possibly in some sort of natural disaster. The Thule Society held that not all secrets of that civilisation had been lost completely. Those that remained were being guarded by ancient, highly intelligent beings, and the truly initiated could establish contact with these beings by means of occult mystical rituals. Upon completion of these rituals, the initiated would allegedly be endowed with supernatural powers and energies. It was believed by some of the Nazis, that these would enable the faithful to create a race of superior beings of Aryan stock, who would then exterminate all inferior races and conquer the world.'

Andrew stopped chewing and looked at Fiona, who actually looked as if she herself might give some credence to these tales.

'You're not buying any of this nonsense, are you?' he asked.

'Well, obviously I don't believe in supernatural beings that one can phone up with a few rituals,' she said as if having been insulted. 'But I don't see why it shouldn't be possible that an ancient civilisation long before ours once existed, and that it might then have been wiped out by a natural disaster.'

'So how long ago is this civilisation supposed to have existed?'

'About 10,000 years ago. Maybe a bit more. It is thought that it was the first true civilisation on earth, long before the Egyptians, the Mayans, the Incas, or the ancient Chinese Dynasties. And the Nazis quickly latched on to this idea, since it presented them with an opportunity to scientifically explain and justify the origin and superiority of the Aryan race. In other words, this was supposedly proof that they were the true descendants of a highly developed race that pre-dated anything else in recorded history.'

Andrew raised his eyebrows. 'A highly developed ancient civilisation that left no trace? That doesn't strike you as odd?'

'Well, that's the thing. The Nazis clearly believed that traces could be found, and this is exactly why they financed all these expeditions all around the world.'

'And do you believe that such traces remain?'

'Yes, I do,' said Fiona and lifted her head with a defiant look. 'I actually happen to believe that this civilisation must have left traces all over the world, and I wouldn't rule out that the Nazi expeditions actually found some of them.'

'Really?' he said sceptically.

'Yes. Really!'

Fiona could tell from his reaction that he was far from convinced. 'Look. This isn't fantasy and it isn't just an old wives' tale. The Nazis did send out hundreds of scientists all over the world. These are all well-established historical facts.'

Andrew had never been religious, and frankly hadn't ever given much thought to the occult or supernatural. Such things were of course hard to disprove, and for all he cared, people could believe whatever they liked, but this was getting ridiculous.

'Alright,' he said and lifted his hands as if to concede. 'Let's assume for a minute that such an ancient civilisation did exist, and that the Nazis sent out expeditions to search for its remains. What exactly do you think they were hoping to find?'

'Well, I don't think that the expeditions were financed just for anthropological reasons, such as proving the legitimacy of the Aryan race as the rulers of the Earth. Even though that does sound like quite a task in itself. But given the scale of the whole operation, I think there was much more to it than that.'

'Like what?' Andrew sat back, holding his glass of wine.

'My guess would be that they were hoping, not only to find but to bring back to Germany, artefacts that could be used to acquire the supernatural powers that they believed the ancients mastered. Making a long story short, I think they were looking for the source of that power, hoping to be able to control it and intending to subsequently use it as some form of weapon.'

'A doomsday device?' said Andrew.

'Not necessarily,' said Fiona and shrugged. 'But I believe they thought it could help them win the war.'

'And you believe that such a power or energy might exist?'

'Why not?' she said and lifted her eyebrows.

'Ok. So far so good.' Andrew sighed.

He had stopped taking notes. It was all a bit confusing. He wasn't used to occupying his mind with such metaphysical topics, and it was rapidly draining his brain of energy.

'Let's go back to the topic of Thule. What you are saying is that Thule was what the Nazis believed this lost continent or civilisation was called. So, they actually went to Thule in Greenland?'

'Yes, they did. I haven't found any information about those expeditions other than the fact that they happened. My guess is that they came back empty-handed.'

Andrew sat for a few moments whirling his wine around in his glass and pondering the significance of what he had been told. Again, he wondered what the possible connections to the break-ins, the drug smuggling and the New Dawn organisation might be.

'What about expeditions to Central America? Why would they go there?' he asked. 'Wouldn't it seem more obvious to look for an original Aryan race somewhere that is land-locked with Europe?'

'I would agree, but if we assume that the ancient civilisation was actually based on a great island in the middle of the Atlantic as some have suggested, then it would make sense to look for remnants of its people on other continents. After all, if they were so advanced, they would almost certainly have colonised or at least visited much of the world.'

'Good point, I suppose. So, I guess the theory is that this original civilisation spread its influence around the world?'

'Exactly. Some people say that the pyramids are clear evidence of this. They can be found on every continent, and they are all aligned with the stars in some way, demonstrating precise astronomical knowledge and insight. Extrapolating from that, some researchers claim that such knowledge would have enabled them to navigate the Earth and that this is exactly what they did.'

'By sailboats presumably?'

'Yes. Although there have been claims that they were able to fly as well.'

'Right,' he said and smiled overbearingly. 'Uhm. Getting back to what I told you on the way over here. As far as you can see, might there be a connection to the burglaries?' asked Andrew, wondering if Colonel Strickland might not get a bit twitchy about him discussing these details with what was effectively still a civilian, even if she was a very clever and pretty one. 'I realise of course that you are not a criminal investigator, but I'd still like to hear your opinion.'

Fiona nodded and sat back in her chair, thinking for a few moments before she spoke. 'Well, if I were a member of a terrorist group, I'd obviously try to get my hands on some weapons, right?'

Andrew nodded. 'Obviously.'

'And if the expeditions actually did find something that could be used offensively in some way, that might be plenty of reason for whoever broke into the National Archives and the Office of Historical Records to go looking for information that might lead them to such a weapon.'

She paused for a few seconds and stared at the ceiling. 'But that doesn't explain how they made a connection between the two in the first place. With sufficient time on their hands, I guess they could have figured out that the two sets of files were stored in those two locations, but how did they know what they contained and that they might be connected?'

Andrew nodded again. 'Another good point.'

She's actually quite good at this, he thought as he signalled the waiter.

'Yes. There has to be something more here, that we just don't know about. And how allied war records regarding anti-submarine efforts fit into all this, I have no idea.'

'Well,' she said. 'Perhaps if I could have a look at those microfilms you mentioned, I might be able to come up with something more. It might jog my memory.'

'That sounds like an excellent idea,' replied Andrew. 'Let me arrange for that, and perhaps you could come by my office? How about tomorrow afternoon. Say around three-thirty?'

'That sounds good. I'll have to speak to my boss, but I don't think it'll be a problem.'

'Excellent,' Andrew smiled.

The waiter swung past their table and discreetely placed the bill on the table in front of Andrew. He took out his credit card and laid it on top of the bill. On his way back, the waiter moved smoothly past the table picking them up and then vanished behind a red curtain at the back of the restaurant. In less than a minute he was back with the card and a receipt, and then Andrew and Fiona left the restaurant.

Standing outside in the light rain, he turned to her. 'Thank you very much, Miss Keane,' he said taking her hand. 'It has certainly been one of the most interesting dinner conversations I've had in a while, although I must say that I'm having trouble following you on the finer points of the occult.'

She beamed back at him. 'It was nice to have such an attentive listener,' she said bowing her head slightly in gratitude.

It was clear that she had enjoyed his company as well. When she looked up at him again and their eyes met, he was tempted for a split second to ask her to join him for a drink somewhere, but he decided against it, and let go of her hand. *Better keep this strictly professional.*

'Goodnight, Andrew. And thank you for a lovely dinner.'

'My pleasure. By the way, can I drop you off somewhere?'

'No thanks. I'm fine,' she said as she pulled out a telescopic umbrella from her bag. 'I'll just walk home. It isn't far.'

'Are you sure?'

'Yes,' she laughed. 'I'm a big girl, Mr Sterling.'

'Alright, then. Have a good night.'

'You too. See you tomorrow.'

As the Jaguar sped north along Park Lane, the car that had followed them from the British Museum to the Chinese restaurant and now to this spot, turned right and parked at a distance from where the young woman was now unfolding her umbrella. No sooner had the car come to a halt, before a man stepped out of the passenger side and hurried across the street. Here he walked to the corner and peeked around it. The woman in the red leather jacket had started walking briskly along the pavement on Park Lane, and the man began to follow. An athletic man in his thirties, he had short dark hair under a hat, and he was wearing a black leather coat and a pair of black gloves.

Just as he began walking after her, she turned down a side street, and he moved into a slow jog to catch up with her. Shortly before reaching the corner where he had lost sight of her, he slowed to a walk again and proceeded casually out from the corner, while looking down the side street. He immediately spotted her again, as she walked along the wet pavement hurrying to get home, and then he continued to follow her at a distance. After a few minutes, she stopped by a small shop to purchase some fruit and a magazine. Waiting outside the shop in the rain, he began to get nervous when she hadn't come back out after almost five minutes. But then she reappeared and jogged across the street, where she resumed her walk towards her flat.

After another ten minutes of following her, the man was gratified to see her walk up to a house and take out the key for the front door. She hurried inside and the man walked past the house noting the address.

FOUR

Yusef was watching as the sun came up and turned the calm sea into a fiery undulating yellow carpet that stretched all the way to the horizon. Growing up in Riyadh in the middle of Saudi Arabia, hundreds of miles from the sea, he had surprised himself by not becoming seasick during the night. He hadn't slept much but had spent most of the night awake in his bed thinking about the day ahead. Now he was up and eager to get started.

'That's good right there,' shouted Antonio Pieza, waving at Ramon Salinas who was operating the ship's crane from the bridge. 'Start lowering it.'

Dangling at the end of a steel wire, the small unmanned submersible Manny was being lowered towards the water. Next to the hook where the wire was secured, was attached a yellow communications cable about the thickness of a garden hose. It would ensure Ramon's ability to control the vehicle as well as send live images to the control room aboard the salvage ship. In an emergency, it could also serve as a crude means of recovering the submersible, in the unlikely event that it should experience some mechanical or electrical failure.

In theory, the craft could operate completely autonomously if need be, but Ramon liked to have control of its every move. After all, he regarded himself as being the brains on the team.

The calm seas made it easy to launch the submersible, and as soon as it reached the water, the steel wire was released. Manny instantly dropped beneath the water but then quickly resurfaced next to the salvage ship. There were no currents to speak of, and as it bobbed calmly on the surface, Ramon tested the thrusters one by one, and simultaneously the onboard navigation computer performed a comprehensive self-test cycle. Within a few seconds, it displayed a message on the computer screen to the effect that the submersible was functioning flawlessly.

'He's fine,' yelled Ramon from the bridge where a temporary control centre had been established. 'Electrical systems and navigation are online. Thrusters are functioning nominally. We are ready to roll.'

'Excellent,' Yusef shouted back at him. Finally, they could get underway. He had been anxiously watching Ramon and the other men from the diving team preparing the submersible for the last hour. He had to admit that they were very professional about what they were doing, and although he had wanted to step in to assist in an effort to speed things up, he had decided to keep quiet and let the men do their work. Hamza had spent the morning going over maps as well as the result of the sonar sweep from the day before, trying to determine if there might be unseen crevasses on the seafloor. If there were, they might present a problem depending on the extent of material that needed to be brought to the surface. Hopefully, they would be able to complete their task, without having to bring up more than a few kilos.

'How long before he reaches the bottom,' asked Yusef, and looked at Antonio as the two men were leaning on the railing watching Manny silently awaiting its commands.

'About fifteen minutes. We'll have to go more slowly as we approach the seabed. We will begin by searching the perimeter at first, and I expect that within about an hour we should be able to move in for a closer look.'

Yusef nodded approvingly. 'Excellent.'

He was satisfied with the way Antonio handled the job. What was needed for this task was a steady hand and a sharp mind, and Antonio seemed to have both.

Antonio turned to look at Ramon who was standing on the bridge and gave a wave with his hand to start the descent. Ramon engaged the submersible and after it whirled up the water around it for a few seconds, it started pulling itself forward and down into the ocean. It would be very dark near the bottom, particularly this early in the morning, but fearlessly the small vehicle made its way deeper and deeper as the darkness closed in around it. During its descent it would be running autonomously, not needing any points of reference as it made its way to the seabed. Accurate pressure sensors told it exactly how deep it was, and the gyroscopic system kept track of its exact position relative to the salvage ship as well as its heading. Upon reaching eighty meters, its thrusters reversed for a brief moment and then it held its position in the water. It was now hovering in almost complete darkness approximately ten meters above the ocean floor.

Above it, the yellow control and communications cable extended as an umbilical cord swaying ever so slightly in the weak currents.

On the bridge, Ramon shouted to the rest of the team. 'He's at eighty meters. I'm going to switch on the lights.'

The crew gathered around the fourteen-inch colour screen on the control station. Yusef made his way to the bridge and sat down next to Ramon. The engineer flipped a switch, and the seabed became flooded with white light. The water was murky, but they could clearly see the silt-covered ocean floor. As Ramon disengaged the autonomous navigation system, the submersible jerked slightly and then began drifting very slowly to the left.

'Weak easterly currents. 1½ knots,' said Ramon and then entered a command that would compensate for any drift. He then gripped the control stick firmly with his right hand and the thruster control with his left. In addition to having worked the controls on numerous occasions before this one, he regularly practised on a PC-based simulation system that came with the submersible.

'Let's see what we can see,' he said and pushed the control stick gently forward.

The submersible came to life, its thrusters pushing it forward, and ever so slowly it started gliding towards its objective.

★ ★ ★

Fiona had difficulty concentrating on her usual chores at the British Museum. Her dinner with Andrew the previous night had really made her think in a way that she had not done in a long time. She could feel the puzzle of the stolen documents gnawing away at her brain. Whenever she had tried to focus on other things, question after question would suddenly pop up in her mind. Was there a connection between the break-ins and those expeditions? Might this all be a cover-up for some larger crime, the results of which had not yet seen the light of day? What would the microfilm reveal? And who was this man, Andrew Sterling?

She left work just before lunch and headed for Covent Garden as a mental diversion manoeuvre. There were always things going on there that could take her mind off almost anything. She picked up a slice of pizza and a bottle of mineral water, and as she was walking along next to the shops, it suddenly occurred to her that she might know somebody who might be able to help. She would have to mention it to Andrew later in the day.

She walked all the way to Sheldrake Place where she entered the anonymous building described by Andrew. At the reception, she was equipped with a visitor's pass and was then escorted to Andrew's office on the second floor. As she was led to the front office, Catherine got up from her desk with the warmest smile imaginable.

'Hello Miss Keane,' she said and offered to take Fiona's coat. 'I'm Miss Swanson, Andrew's personal assistant. Let me show you to his office,' she said and beckoned Fiona to follow her.

Catherine tapped softly on the door and then waited a few seconds before opening it. 'Miss Keane here to see you, Mr. Sterling.'

'Thank you very much, Cathy,' Andrew smiled and got up to greet Fiona. 'No trouble finding your way here?'

'No,' said Fiona. 'Although you people don't exactly advertise your own presence. Is this whole building yours?'

'Yes, it is. We're not hiding exactly, but we do like to keep a low profile, as I'm sure you can understand.'

'I would expect so,' nodded Fiona.

'Please sit down, Miss Keane,' said Andrew and motioned to the armchair in front of his desk.'

'Thank you. Before we start, I should tell you that I've just remembered someone who might be able to provide more detail about those Nazi expeditions.'

'Really? And who's that?' said Andrew and sat down.

'His name is Doctor Phillip Eckleston. Rather eccentric chap. He used to work for the British government years ago - in the 70's I think, in a special branch of the MI5 that researched supernatural occurrences. The programme which included everything from remote viewing to various forms of telepathic mind control was similar to those carried out by the CIA during the same period. So, I guess he is quite old by now.'

'Remote viewing? That's similar to clairvoyance, correct?' asked Andrew apprehensively.

'Right.'

'So, what happened to the programme?'

'Well, he was highly regarded among his peers, but funding was eventually taken away in the early 1980s. I guess it all became a bit too exotic for whoever had to decide on funding. Partly because Eckleston eventually began spending a lot of time on some rather amazing theories that included ancient civilisations and weapons. I won't bore you with the details right now, but eventually, the politicians failed to see why they should finance the efforts of this man. Pity really, when you consider the fact that the chap was actually paid to investigate things that fell outside what would be called conventional science.'

'So, they more or less decided that he had lost his mind then? Is that what you're saying?' asked Andrew.

'Yes, that's probably what happened,' said Fiona.

'How do you know him?'

'Well, I've read one of his books, and I even went to see him once when I was looking into the activities of the Thule Society.'

'That esoteric Nazi cult you mentioned?'

'Yes.'

'How do you think he can be of any help to us?'

'Not sure frankly, but I think it's worth a try. Regardless of what people think of him, he is definitely an authority on theories about ancient civilisations. Talking to him could help us better understand and put into context any information about the Nazi expeditions we may obtain from the German microfilms.'

Andrew shrugged. 'Yes, I don't see why not. Can you set up a meeting?'

'I'll try this evening.'

'Great. Ok, then. Let's go and have a look at those films. They are in a room just down the corridor. If you'll follow me.'

They rose and went to the end of the corridor, where they entered a windowless room that had equipment for handling microfilm and projecting it onto a big screen covering an entire wall. At the centre of the room facing the wall were two desks and a couple of chairs.

'I've had this set up especially for you,' said Andrew and pointed to the projector. You'll have it as long as you need.'

Impressed, Fiona walked to the table where copies of microfilms of all the documents stolen from the National Archive in Berlin were placed.

'This should be interesting,' she said, taking off her jacket and placing it on a chair.

'You go ahead,' said Andrew. 'I'll just go and arrange for something to drink. What would you like?' he asked halfway through the door.

'Oh. Just coffee, please. Helps me think.'

'Got it. Won't be a second,' he said and closed the door behind him.

As he passed his own office, he asked Cathy to fetch some coffee, and then he proceeded to Colonel Strickland's office. He wanted to brief the Colonel on his meeting with Fiona, and also obtain proper authorisation to bring a former MI5 employee into the investigation. Having been told of Doctor Eckleston, Strickland could see no problem with it, but once again asked that Andrew didn't go around town talking to everyone about the whole thing. He also handed Andrew a file on Fiona Keane.

'I've had this prepared for you,' said the colonel. 'We have to be careful with these things, as you well know, Andy. I have complete faith in your judgement, but I would still like for you to read through this. No indication of anything unusual that I can find, but just so you know a bit more about her.'

'Thank you, Sir. I will do that right away,' said Andrew. 'She's in the projector-room down the corridor right now, analysing the microfilms.'

'Good,' said Strickland and looked at Andrew as if troubled by something. 'Let me just ask you one final thing.'

'Certainly, Sir.'

'Are you sure we need to engage in this type of investigation?'

'Look, I know it all seems a bit bizarre,' replied Andrew. 'But if the New Dawn organisation really is a terrorist organisation as the Germans suspect, and if there is a connection between them and the break-ins, we need to investigate this and find out what they might have been looking for. At the moment it's really all we have.'

'Fair enough,' nodded Strickland. 'Carry on.'

Andrew left for his own office, where he promptly sat down at his desk and began reading through the intelligence report on Fiona Keane. It wasn't very long, which was usually a good thing in this business.

Fiona Keane, 31 years old. Unmarried and living alone in a flat in Chelsea. Born in Dublin. Moved with her parents to Manchester at the age of fifteen when her father got a job as an accountant with a local solicitor. Moved to London at eighteen to study at Kings College where she received a Master's degree in history and archaeology, and subsequently stayed on after being offered a PhD. Worked at the British Museum during most of her studies, and here she eventually accepted a full-time research position. Apparently, no affiliations with any political organisations.

Bright girl, thought Andrew. *I wonder if she might not be useful to have about on this task on a more permanent basis. I might suggest that to Strickland as well.*

He then picked up the phone and dialled the number for Professor Maltby at the Royal Navy's Office of Historical Records, hoping that he hadn't gone home for the day. It rang several times before being answered.

'Professor James Maltby speaking.'

'Professor. This is Andrew Sterling again.'

'Ah, Mr. Sterling. What can I do for you?'

'Well, I was wondering if the stolen documents might have been photographed and stored on microfilm or some other medium prior to the burglary?'

'Microfilm, eh? What a marvellous idea. No, I'm afraid we never got around to that here. Sorry.'

'Oh,' Andrew said disappointed. 'What a shame.'

'Are you making any progress?' asked Maltby.

'No. Not yet. But it's still early days. Look, Sir. I really must be going. I'm quite busy this evening. But thanks again for your help.'

'Not at all, Sir. Goodbye.'

When Andrew got back to the projector room, Fiona turned to look as he entered. 'What kept you?' she smiled.

'Just some admin. Any luck?'

'Not much. I'm just scanning all the documents and sorting them by topic. There are several hundred here. Did you know that?'

'No. I didn't. Need some help?'

'No, I'm alright. But I think I'll need some more coffee,' she said and tapped the lid on the coffee can. 'This stuff usually works wonders for me, and I have a feeling I'll be sitting here all night. Care to join me?'

'Absolutely! What can I do?' he said as he sat down next to her.

Oblivious to the darkness closing in on the city outside the building on Sheldrake Place, the two of them worked through the night sorting and examining the endless rolls of microfilm, placing each one in the projector and then methodically analysing and discussing the content of those that appeared relevant. They quickly found references to several pre-war Nazi expeditions, but details on their actual purpose were elusive.

When Andrew went out for more coffee and a couple of sandwiches from the vending machine in the cafeteria, he was astounded to find that there was no one left on that whole floor of the building. Only then did he look at his watch, surprised that it was already five to nine in the evening. Having picked up a pair of chicken sandwiches and two cans of orange juice, he returned to the projector room and walked in.

'Fiona. Do you think that...'

She held up her hand to stop him from talking and then pointed it at the screen without saying a word. When he turned to look at the wall opposite her, an elderly man with sharp facial features, short thinning hair at the temples and a pair of round spectacles was staring back at him. Wearing a brown shirt and a black tie with a small white swastika embroidered at its centre, he didn't exactly look like the typical Nazi goon. He had the appearance of a scientist.

'I'm pretty sure that I wouldn't like this chap,' said Andrew and closed the door, not taking his eyes off the man on the wall.

'Don't worry,' smiled Fiona. 'He's dead. At least I think he is. This picture was taken in the summer of 1942. He was thirty-eight at the time. That would make him over a hundred years old today.'

'It has happened before you know,' grinned Andrew and walked closer to the screen. 'Who is he?'

'This is our friend Rudolf Von Serbottendorf, member of the SS and founder of the Thule Society. He was also coordinator of the expeditions with the aim of uncovering the origins of the Aryan race.'

'Charming,' said Andrew and sat down next to her.

'And look at this,' she continued and flipped through a few more slides. 'It seems that he actually took part in at least one of them himself. Strangely I can't find anything to indicate which one, what he might have found, or even if he and his team ever made it back to Germany.'

'What of the other expeditions? Have you found any more details on them?'

'A little bit. As we have already established, there were at least four major expeditions. Destinations were the Yucatan Peninsula in Mexico, southern India, Peru and Tibet. I believe they were carried out in that order. From the looks of these documents, all expeditions returned with artefacts, but there are no details of what they were. And if they attempted to harness some sort of supernatural energy from any of them, there's nothing here to suggest what the results might have been if any.'

'About this Von Serbottendorf. He could have headed your fifth expedition, you know,' suggested Andrew.

'Exactly what I was thinking. It's just strange that there is no trace of him returning. But he definitely did leave Berlin early in 1943. See this? It's a materiel request form submitted by Von Serbottendorf. It's basically a sort of shopping list for all the equipment he asked for, prior to leaving.'

Andrew sat down in his chair and looked at the photograph of the form. It had turned yellow with age and the items were typed. In the top left corner was a swastika and a small German eagle.

'Look at this. An ocean-going ship to embark from Naples in Italy. Tons of food. Large snow sleighs and lots of dogs. Weapons. I'm guessing that there were at least fifteen men along with him.'

'Another expedition to Thule, perhaps?'

'Possibly. But as I said, there's no trace of any of them returning.'

Andrew leaned back in his chair looking at the ceiling for a few seconds before he spoke. 'Why don't we let this Phillip Eckleston of yours have a look at the files we think are most interesting? I'll have them printed out, so he can go through them at his own pace.'

'Hey, that's a good idea,' said Fiona. 'He's bound to come up with something we haven't thought of ourselves.'

'Let's do that tomorrow.'

'Ok. Look, there is one final thing that I thought might be useful to us. Look at this,' she said and quickly flicked forward a few slides. 'Apparently, all the artefacts that were brought back from these expeditions ended up in a storage facility outside Berlin, where they were probably studied and tested. There is no mention anywhere of the exact location of this place, but one name keeps coming up whenever that facility is mentioned. A Doctor Friedrich Henke, who seems to have headed the whole affair. If he is still alive, we might be able to extract some information from him. He is the only name that we have, apart from Rudolf Von Serbottendorf.'

'Alright. Why don't you go out to see Doctor Eckleston tomorrow? I'll ask Dietrich Obermann to help me locate this warehouse administrator Doctor Friedrich Henke, if he is still alive.'

'Sounds good. But now I'm completely spent. I need to home and get some sleep.'

'Fair enough. I'm starting to get a bit tired myself. Let's just call it a day and go home.'

They left the office, and on the way back to his house Andrew dropped off Fiona on Park Lane, so that she could easily walk home. She insisted that he just drop her off and not take her all the way home. Maybe she didn't want him to get too close. Maybe she fancied him. Whatever it was, Andrew realised that he wouldn't be thinking about her that way unless he himself was attracted to her. 'Shit,' he muttered as he drove through the gates towards the mansion. He wasn't entirely sure whether to be happy or annoyed about it. Women were the best and the worst that could happen to a man. And strangely, sometimes they were both of those at once.

★ ★ ★

As the small submersible made its way slowly through the murky water, the crew of the salvage ship stood quietly around the control station, watching the screen. Manny was about eight meters above the ocean floor and moving towards the spot where the large sonar contact had been. Its floodlights were powerful, but as long as there was nothing but silt floating in the dark waters ahead of its camera, it was very hard to see anything on the screen, let alone make out any familiar shapes.

In a small window at the bottom left-hand side of the screen was a virtual top-down view of the ocean floor, with a large blue dot where the sonar contact had been, and a small red blinking arrow indicating the position and heading of the submersible.

'About 15 meters now,' said Ramon without stirring. He was concentrating hard, with his eyes fixed on the screen and his hands constantly making tiny adjustments to the submersible's course.

'So dark it is down there,' whispered Hamza. 'Will you be able to see what you are doing?'

He didn't have to wait for an answer, because at that moment a large shadow emerged directly in front of the submersible. At first, it was impossible to see exactly what it was, but as Ramon guided Manny closer, it became clear that it was the forward diving planes on the U-boat. Or rather, what was left of them. The entire bow of the U-boat was ripped open like a sardine can.

'What the hell happened here?' said Ramon staring at the wreck.

'Torpedo malfunction?' asked Antonio.

'Maybe. It looks like it exploded from the inside. What a mess. We won't be able to enter from this end.'

'Let's move towards the back of the boat,' said Yusef.

He was anxious to start the real search.

Manny glided along the hull, and it was clear that U-303 had come to rest on the seafloor in a near upright position, despite the severe damage to the front of the U-boat. The submersible was now approaching the tower of the submarine, protruding up about six meters from the hull at a slight angle. They could see the badly corroded railing at the top of the tower, where the captain would have stood many times, either going out to sea or coming home.

'Look at this,' said Ramon triumphantly as he rotated Manny slightly to get a better image.

Across the tower was written in large letters; *U-303*. The paint had almost worn off, but it was now clear to Yusef that they had found what they were looking for. He placed his hand on Hamza's shoulder. 'We are here.'

As Ramon guided Manny further towards the back of the U-boat, they saw the large indentation that had started the chain of events that had brought her to the ocean floor.

'What's this?' Yusef asked Antonio.

'Looks like a bomb or a depth charge detonated on the side of the hull. But I think that it would have been enough to sink her. Look at this,' he said and pointed to the screen. 'Severe structural damage. I'm pretty sure that she would have been doomed regardless of the explosion in the bow.'

At that point, Hamza pointed to the right side of the screen. 'We need to move down this way. The cargo hold is just aft of the engine room. Move the submersible towards this spot,' he said, placing a finger on the screen.

Manny glided across the body of the U-boat and down along its side towards the seabed.

'There. That's where we will go in. There is a corridor here that runs all the way down to the cargo hold. If we can access that corridor, we should be able to move to the cargo hold itself. Will that present a problem for you Mr. Pieza,' he said and looked at Antonio.

'No,' said the diver. 'We'll just cut right through the double hull. It is going to take a couple of hours, but we can do it.'

'Good. Get your men suited up.'

With that, Antonio stood. 'Ramon, bring Manny to the surface. I'll go and prepare the divers.'

Half an hour later the submersible surfaced, and a diver jumped in to secure the hook to the steel wire. The crane pulled it from the water, and a few minutes later it was sitting on the deck, being detached from the wire and its control cable. At the same time, three divers were putting on their dry suits, getting ready to dive to the wreck. Yusef was pacing the deck while watching the activity and wanting to join in himself, but knowing full well that he'd probably get himself killed in the process.

★ ★ ★

Early the next day Dietrich Obermann called Sterling with the address of Friedrich Henke the warehouse administrator. At ninety-seven years of age, the former warehouse director now lived in Munich, but he was very much alive. Andrew managed to book an early afternoon flight to Munich that same day. Things were moving swiftly now, and Andrew liked that. Obermann had been kind enough to call Henke in advance, to warn him that 'the British were coming'. He had initially been a bit apprehensive about meeting Sterling, but had eventually yielded to the inspector's request.

Sterling hailed a taxi outside Munich's International Airport and showed the address to the driver. A few minutes later he was on his way, speeding along the wide *autobahn* towards Henke's apartment on the outskirts of town. As he sat there in the taxi, he thought about how quickly he had been yanked away from his usual style of thinking to now having to concentrate on things that he would normally have paid no attention to. But they were actually making progress in the investigation, and he had to admit that most of it was due to Fiona. Not just her dogged efforts to find the truth, which was in itself an admirable quality in any scientist, but he also benefited from her open-mindedness. Had it all been up to him, he might have dismissed the stories about occult Nazi expeditions simply as nonsense, made up by people with too much time on their hands.

FIVE

The taxi pulled up to a row of dull apartment blocks in a quiet neighbourhood by a small stream. The driver pointed to one of them. 'Hier,' he said, and then tapped his finger on the meter.

A man of few words, thought Andrew. He paid the man, got out of the taxi and started walking towards the front door of the building. The stone path was covered with leaves that had fallen off the tall oak trees scattered along the grounds in front of the buildings. By the door, he looked at the array of buttons. Few names seemed familiar to him, but as expected there was an F. Henke on the third floor.

He pressed the button and waited. A few moments passed without an answer, and as Andrew turned to look over his shoulder to the street, he felt strangely out of place. At that moment, there was a loud buzz from the door, and he pushed it open. When he reached the third floor, there was an old but tall and vigorous looking man standing in the doorway.

'Friedrich Henke?' asked Andrew and stretched out his hand to greet the man.

'Yes. I am Henke,' said the man apprehensively. He spoke excellent English.

'How are you? I am Andrew Sterling of the British SAS. Are you familiar with us?'

'Yes, I know of you,' he said, as he beckoned for Andrew to enter.

'It's very good of you to see me on such short notice. I expect Inspector Obermann has told you a bit about why I'm here?'

'He has told me a few things. Yes. Would you like to sit down?' he asked and pointed to a sofa in the living room.

It was a small but cosy apartment with a view to a large park. On the walls were rows of pictures of what appeared to be family members. Most were black and white. The old man sat down in front of Andrew and began pouring coffee for the two of them.

'Ah, thank you,' smiled Andrew. 'Just what I need.'

'My pleasure,' Henke smiled.

The old man seemed a bit more comfortable now that they had sat down. He probably didn't get too many visitors, but then not many nonagenarians do. Except for their family, it was an increasingly lonely life with fewer and fewer friends still among the living. But Henke looked cheerful and in good physical shape for a man of his age.

'What can I help you with?' he said and leaned back in his large soft armchair, holding his cup of coffee.

'Well, as I think you know, we are investigating the burglary of some records in London as well as in Berlin. And of course, we are working with the German police in this matter.'

Henke nodded approvingly. 'Yes. Hr. Obermann has explained that to me.'

'Ok. We have examined copies of these records, and you are mentioned in several places as having been employed at a storage facility outside Berlin during the Second World War.'

Andrew did his best to look casual, but he could feel himself tensing ever so slightly as he mentioned the war. Henke apparently didn't seem to mind discussing that, but simply nodded, still looking at Andrew.

'That is correct. I was the head of a facility there for quite a few years.'

'Right. What I would like to ask you about, is the content of this storage facility. I have learned that Germany sent out a number of expeditions to places around the world, and that the storage facility you managed contained what was brought back. So, if you don't mind me being blunt: What was actually stored there?'

Henke shifted slightly in his armchair before answering with a smile. 'Well. You are right. There were many things brought back from all over the world, but it is many years ago now. And to be honest, it was probably worthless old rubbish if you ask me. The SS was very keen on discovering things that could support the idea of the Aryan race, so they went all over the world to look for such things. I don't think they ever found anything important. If they did, why has it never been revealed? Anyway – I wasn't even allowed to see what came back. It was all locked in containers and crates.'

'Yes. I see what you mean,' said Andrew pressing on.

'So, you never actually saw any of the items yourself?'

'No. I never saw any of them. It was all top secret, you know? As far as I was concerned, I could have been the chief of the cargo storage of the public railway system. I was just the administrator, and I was never allowed to see what I was actually in charge of. Next to the storage halls were laboratories or something, where they would take each item, one by one. What they did in there, I don't know.'

'Do you remember the names of anyone working there?'

'No. I didn't even know who they were back then. But I do remember a couple of very strange things that would probably not have happened anywhere else. The only reason that I still remember them, is because they seemed so peculiar to me.'

Henke was looking at the wall above Andrew's head as if trying to recover files from his memory that had been tucked away long ago.

'Like what?', asked Andrew.

'Well, there was always very tight security around the shipments of items to the facility, and usually there would be a couple of soldiers riding along with the trucks. But one day there was this troop transport offloading soldiers outside. They ran to the gate of one of the largest storage buildings, which had a huge refrigerator inside. They opened the gate so a truck could back up to the loading area which was elevated about one meter from the ground.

Seeing this, I went down to the storage building to see what was happening, because nobody had told me anything about this. But I was stopped by an SS Colonel, who said that I had to stay out of the way and let the soldiers do their job. So, I stood by and watched them unload two huge metal containers, and as I did so I overheard what appeared to be a scientist say something to the Major about a dangerous substance, but I couldn't quite hear what was being said. But what struck me as really odd was that water was dripping off both of the containers.'

Andrew was busily taking notes, but the old man didn't even seem to notice. He was travelling back in time and seeing now what he saw back then.

'It seemed like they were in a hurry, because the containers were quickly put down on large wheeled pallets, and rolled into the refrigerator in a rush.'

'Could you see what it might have been?'

'No. I was instructed to keep away from that particular storage building. But that same night when the soldiers had left, my curiosity got the better of me, and I entered the building. It was completely empty except for the big refrigerator room. Strangely it wasn't locked so I went inside and quickly found that the temperature was well below freezing. I hurried over to one of the containers which was about two or three meters in length, a meter wide and a meter deep.'

As he recounted his experience, the old man gesticulated vigorously with his arms and hands.

'I then climbed up onto the carriage and lifted the lid. It was very heavy. I had to use all of my strength to do it, and back then I was no weakling, I can tell you. When I looked down, I was stunned to discover that inside that container was a man frozen in a solid block of ice.'

Andrew looked in amazement at Henke, who in turn was lost in the images now sweeping past his mind's eye.

'The ice was clear as crystal, as if the man had been carefully and deliberately frozen inside the ice block. I could see his face as clearly as I can see yours now. I'll never forget him. He was in his late thirties, with a thin face and he was still wearing a pair of round spectacles. That is why I remember him still. The spectacles were just sitting there on his nose.'

Andrew looked at the old man and tried to recall the image of Rudolf Von Serbottendorf that Fiona had shown him the day before. Could this be him? Maybe he did make it back from his expedition after all.

'Did you look in the second container as well?'

'Yes. There was another man there. They were both dressed in strange clothes. The sort you would wear in extreme cold. Big brown leather jackets with wool on the inside, thick trousers and big heavy boots. Their faces looked as though they had been burned by something. It was quite unpleasant to look at.'

The old man shook his head slowly, lost in his reverie.

'That sounds incredible,' said Andrew after a few seconds.

'Yes, but it is true. Every word,' said Henke forcefully, and looked Andrew straight in the eye.

'I believe you,' said Andrew disarmingly. 'What did you do then?'

'I hurried out of the refrigerator and left the storage building. From the next day onwards, there were always soldiers outside, day and night. And scientists in white clothes went in and out of there for the next few weeks. Then one morning they were all gone. Even the refrigerator room had been removed. It was as if it had never happened, and when I asked my superiors about it, they refused to accept that there had ever been anyone there.'

'So, you didn't go any further with it?'

'How could I?' he said and held up his hands. Officially there was nothing to go anywhere with.'

'Do you remember any other events that were unusual?'

'Well, there was one more episode that was a bit strange, but perhaps not as interesting.'

'What was that?'

'Well, I distinctly remember once signing for a crate to be delivered to Bremerhaven, because it was the only item ever to leave the storage warehouse, except for the containers in the refrigerator room. It was picked up by four or five soldiers commanded by the same SS Colonel that had been in charge of transporting the containers with the ice blocks. I was told that it was going to Bremerhaven that night, but I managed to get a glimpse of the transport papers. They said that it was going to be loaded aboard a U-boat, and shipped to Argentina.'

'Argentina?'

'Yes. But that was all I could see. I don't know why?'

'And you didn't know what was in the crate, either?'

'No. The papers in our files indicated that it had been brought to the storage warehouse about a year earlier, and that extensive experiments had been carried out on its content. But there was never anything in the files about the content of any crates. But that wouldn't have mattered anyway, because as soon as the crate had left the warehouse, the files were burned.'

'Burned?'

'Yes. Nothing was left.'

'Sounds very secretive,' said Andrew.

'Yes. It was. As the war was coming to an end, I left the city with my wife. We went to live with family in the countryside because the bombing of Berlin was getting very heavy. I don't know what happened to all the other artefacts after the war, but when I walked past the warehouse a couple of months after the capitulation, it was all gone. Nothing was left.'

'And you never heard anything about it ever again?'

'No. I took a job as a logistics supervisor at Siemens, and worked there until my retirement some years ago.'

'Have you written or spoken to anyone about this since then?'

'No. Except for my wife of course, who passed away six years ago. We all needed to move on after the war if you understand. No one was very keen on discussing their previous employment during those years.'

'I understand,' nodded Andrew. 'Mr. Henke, you have been very helpful. I'm very grateful for the information that you have given me.'

'It's been a while since I've managed to remember this much about it. I haven't really thought about it for years now,' he said escorting Andrew to the front door.

'Well, I'm sure we'll be able to benefit from it as we investigate these matters further. Thank you again, Sir.'

Andrew went down the stairs and outside, and looked at his watch. Plenty of time to catch the flight back home. He started walking down the street, and a few minutes later he was able to hail a taxi. He was still a bit stunned by what he had been told, and on the way back to the airport, he wondered how it was all connected. What seemed clear was that the burglaries were carried out by people who knew exactly what they were looking for. And more specifically, they knew at least some of what Friedrich Henke knew, but not from him if he was telling the truth, and Andrew didn't think that the old man had lied.

At 7.30 pm, Andrew was sitting in the departure lounge at Munich's International Airport, waiting for his flight back to London when his mobile phone started chirping away in his coat pocket.

'Andrew Sterling.'

'Andy, this is Fiona.'

'Oh, Hello. You alright?'

'Yep. I'm fine. I got your message. How's Munich?'

'Good so far. I've met with Friedrich Henke. He's old but he remembers things remarkably well. Or else he has been pulling my leg the whole time, but I don't think so. Let me tell you about that when I get back. It's all a bit confusing right now. I am still trying to put the pieces together.'

'Alright. I've just had a very interesting meeting myself with Doctor Phillip Eckleston.'

'Oh? Start talking. I have plenty of time. It's at least twenty-minute until we board the plane. What did you find out?'

'Well, let me start by warning you that he is a bit eccentric, to say the least, and you'll probably laugh at some of the things he said. They sound a bit fantastic even to me,' she chuckled.

'I'm beginning to get used to that by now. Try me.'

'Alright. He lives in a small house on the outskirts of London, basically just minding his garden and his own business. But as it happens, Doctor Eckleston knows quite a bit about the German expeditions and the Thule Society. In fact, he knows a lot more than I do, and he was even able to add some information that definitely wasn't in the stolen files.'

'Such as?'

'Such as information about some of the artefacts that were brought back. It's not what you would consider hard facts, but he believes that in several of the locations to which the Nazis sent out expeditions, they found what Eckleston called 'parts of a medallion'. Apparently, legend has it that there was once a medallion made up of four irregular and uniquely shaped triangles, that would fit together to form a square, about the size of a human hand, with a pentagonal hole in the centre. In that hole would fit a ruby, and correctly assembled, this medallion was supposed to indicate the way to the gates of an ancient and now lost civilisation.'

'Just… wait a minute,' sighed Andrew. 'Isn't this what one could call utter rubbish, without offending more than a handful of hermits living in trees in the Welsh forests?'

'Andrew, I will concede that this all sounds a bit absurd. But isn't the point of this whole thing to investigate this matter as best we can?'

'Yes?'

'So, whether you and I believe these stories or not is really not relevant. What is important, is that we may be able to track the people who stole the documents and uncover what they intend to do with them. And if they believe this stuff, we need to understand what that might mean. Let's say that it was some Neo-Nazi group that is trying to resuscitate the idea of an Aryan master race. Shouldn't we then try to get inside their heads?'

Grudgingly Andrew had to agree. 'Yes, when you put it that way. But I have to tell you that I'm having a very difficult time taking this seriously.'

'I know that, Andy.'

'Ok,' said Andrew and bowed his head. She knew how he felt, and that was good enough for now. 'Anything else?'

'Well, Eckleston said that he was sure that there really was a fifth expedition.'

'Really? Where to?'

'Antarctica of all places.'

Andrew hesitated. 'Antarctica? But there's nothing but snow and ice down there.'

'I know that and Phillip knows that, but what he's saying is that it wasn't always like that.'

'How do you mean?'

'Well, it's all a rather lengthy tale I'm afraid, but Eckleston has become a great fan of a certain Charles H. Hapgood of Keene College. In the 1950s, Professor Hapgood proposed a radical geological theory regarding something he called Earth Crust Displacement.'

'Earth what?'

'Earth Crust Displacement.'

'You'll have to enlighten me on that. I don't believe it was in my curriculum back when I was in school.'

'Well, no. I am not surprised. It is not exactly mainstream science. Anyway, you know that the Earth is really a giant ball of hot liquid rock, with a cool and very thin crust of rock?'

'Yes?' replied Andrew hesitantly.

'That ball of lava is essentially suspended in the vacuum of space, and because of its own mass and gravity, it takes on the shape of a sphere. Much like when you see astronauts playing with spherical water droplets inside the International Space Station. Except the Earth is slightly flattened because of its rotation. Still with me?'

'Still here,' Andrew said as he glanced out of the window of the taxi at the passing German landscape.

'Alright. The Earth constantly generates heat internally from its magnetic forces and the movement of the liquid interior. But floating along in empty space, which is around 263 degrees Celsius below zero, it also loses heat mainly through radiation. In other words, the only reason life has evolved on this planet is because the surface is relatively cool, at least compared with the thousands of degrees of heat at the Earth's core.'

'And the theory of this Hapgood fellow?'

'Just wait. I'm getting to that. Professor Hapgood's theory had its inception in the realisation that only a tiny proportion of the

Earth's matter is solid, namely the crust. From the Earth's surface to its centre is a distance of about six thousand kilometres, but only the first few of those are the solid crust. If you imagine a cross-section of the Earth, you would see that the crust is just a thin membrane of solid matter, floating around on the liquid interior. This is essentially what plate tectonics is all about. But Professor Hapgood took this one step further. He argued that it was possible for the entire crust of the Earth to shift or rotate all at once.'

'How so?'

'Well, the idea is that as massive amounts of ice builds up on the poles over tens or hundreds of thousands of years, the Earth's rotation becomes unstable. In other words, the centrifugal force of the Earth's rotation would cause the heaviest part of the Earth's crust to shift towards the equator. This would occur specifically if the build-up of polar ice happened in an asymmetrical fashion, causing the Earth to wobble violently in its rotation.'

'Fiona. Come on,' said Andrew overbearingly.

'I know. I know,' she laughed disarmingly. 'It all sounds pretty extravagant, but let's try to keep an open mind about this, shall we?'

'Ok. Go on.'

'Right. Think of a basketball that you rotate on your finger. The only reason it is possible to do so is because the ball is perfectly round and symmetrical. If you were to suddenly fix a heavy object to the ball somewhere close to the top, the weight of the ball would no longer be symmetrically distributed, and it would rotate wildly out of control. It is basically the same thing that Hapgood proposed for the Earth, except his idea actually seems more plausible when you think about it, since in the case of the Earth, it is not the entire ball that suddenly shifts, but just the surface of the ball that shifts on top of a liquid interior.'

'Hmm. Let me guess. This theory wasn't very well received in the scientific community?' probed Andrew.

'You are absolutely correct. Scientists are difficult to convince, as they should be, and Hapgood's ideas certainly challenged conventional scientific dogma. But I should add that one of the greatest scientific minds in history, Professor Albert Einstein was an enthusiastic supporter of Hapgood's theory. It is quite evident from the lengthy correspondence between the two during 1952 and 1953. In fact, Einstein urged Hapgood to press on with certain aspects of the theory involving centrifugal momentum, and on the whole, it is clear that he found Hapgood's ideas very plausible. Listen to this excerpt from a foreword to Hapgood's paper, written by Einstein.'

'I frequently receive communications from people who wish to consult with me concerning their unpublished ideas. It goes without saying that these ideas are very seldom possessed of scientific validity. The very first communication, however, that I received from Mr. Hapgood electrified me.'

Andrew was now beginning to listen more carefully. It was a thoroughly intriguing idea and it actually made good logical sense when he thought about it, but he still had a hard time getting his head around the implications of such a theory. 'Look, Fiona. I guess it does sound plausible, but there are a couple of things that do not make sense to me.'

'Yes?'

'For example. How could this ice on the poles suddenly build up? Doesn't something like that take tens of thousands of years?'

'Yes, it does. But in geological terms, ten thousand years is a blink of an eye. It really is a very short time, considering that the Earth is at least five billion years old. Hang on. Let me get my calculator out?' she said and started rummaging about in her handbag.

'You carry a calculator with you?'

'Yes, I do actually. So?'

'Nothing. Nothing at all,' Andrew exclaimed disarmingly.

After a few seconds, she was back.

'Ok. If you think of a 24-hour period as the approximate age of the Earth, then the passage of ten thousand years would take about one-fifth of a second. And that could be how long it would take for a sufficient amount of ice to build up, in order to cause the Earth to become unstable in its rotation.'

'Right. If you put it that way, I guess it is a short time,' said Andrew as he scratched his head. 'And I guess it goes without saying, that if such a displacement of the Earth's crust happened, any civilisation that existed at the time would have suffered severely.'

'Very much so. That is actually what Eckleston is convinced of.'

'But if it really did happen, there is no reason to believe that it hasn't happened several times before.'

'And there is no reason to think that it might not happen again,' said Fiona thoughtfully.

'When was the last time this was supposed to have occurred?'

'Supposedly some 12,000 years ago, judging from the evidence.'

'Over how much time would such an event stretch?'

'Well, obviously that is really difficult to say, but estimates range from many years to just a few months.'

'Months?' said Andrew. 'Christ. No civilisation would survive that, would it?'

'No. I don't think so. It would truly have been a cataclysmic event. Eckleston is convinced that there once existed such an ancient civilisation and that it really was wiped out by a rapid crust displacement. He thinks this is where all the legends of Atlantis originated.'

'Atlantis, eh?' said Andrew. He had always thought of Atlantis as an old wives' tale. But if this theory was correct, and if such violent shifts in the Earth's crust had actually taken place, an ancient civilisation would almost certainly have perished. And regardless of whether they chose to call it Atlantis or Thule or some other name, he couldn't completely rule out that it might have existed. Which of course meant that the Nazis might actually have been on to something. This in turn meant that whoever stole those records, thought the expeditions actually found remnants of this civilisation. But what remnants, exactly? And precisely what were they hoping to do with them? And how did they even know what to look for and where?

'Well,' said Fiona. 'I'm not really too interested in whether people call it Atlantis or Thule or something else. The important thing is that there may have been an ancient civilisation long before ours came along. And if there really was one, then I'm quite sure that the Nazis would have tried to find it. What do you think?'

'Fiona, I think my brain is completely fried. I can't even remember my own last name anymore. I need to get some sleep.'

'Alright. Fair enough. Let's talk about it tomorrow, Ok?'

'Yup. Let's do that. My office at ten o'clock'?

'Sound good. I'll see you then. Good night.'

'Good night, Fiona'

★ ★ ★

Fiona put the phone down and rose from her desk at the British Museum. She had just come by to read and answer her e-mails and chat to the other people in her office.

'Eckleston, eh?' said a female voice from behind her.

In the doorway stood a colleague from the museum library. A thin bespectacled redhead, with a green skirt and a white shirt, she poked her head inside the office and looked curiously at Fiona. Edwards, was her name, as far as Fiona could remember. Pauline Edwards.

'Uhm. Yes?' asked Fiona suspiciously. 'Do you know him?'

Pauline entered the office. 'Yes. A little bit. I have read a few of his books. They are quite interesting. We have several of them ourselves. Would you like to borrow any?'

'No thanks,' smiled Fiona. 'I'm going to see him tomorrow.'

'Really?' said Pauline puzzled. 'What for, if I may ask?'

'Oh, nothing. I just have some questions about an old theory he is excited about.'

Pauline nodded, and Fiona couldn't help but feel that her colleague was a bit more than just nosy. They had only spoken a few times before, and on each occasion, Fiona had felt slightly uneasy. It was as if Pauline had trouble interacting with other people in a relaxed fashion. Whenever they would talk, things always felt stilted and awkward, and it never took them more than a few seconds to discover that yet again, they had nothing to talk about, except for work.

'Well, good luck. I must be going. I'm a little bit busy today,' said Pauline and then she turned and walked out of Fiona's office.

Fiona looked perplexed at the empty doorway where Pauline had been standing. 'Thanks,' she muttered.

★ ★ ★

The flight back to London felt much shorter than the flight to Munich, partly because Andrew nodded off a few times, only to be disturbed by a stewardess. He tried several times to force himself to start making sense of the information he had obtained during the day, always keeping in mind that his aim was to look for connections to possible terrorist activity, but there was simply no energy left in him. He boarded the shuttle at Heathrow Airport, and twenty minutes later he was in a cab, leaving Paddington Station for home.

It was almost ten in the evening. In twelve hours, he would be meeting with Fiona again. Gradually he had begun thinking of her as his colleague, although she was really just a historian and archaeologist. Andrew decided that he needed to have a talk with Strickland the next day. Perhaps they could reach an agreement with the British Museum about temporarily 'borrowing' her for a while. For national security reasons, and all that. Shouldn't be a problem.

It's definitely worth a try, he thought as he walked to the front door of his house.

Six

The seawater regularly came in over the bow, as the salvage ship cut through the waves. It was heading almost due east and had been underway for approximately eighteen hours. Yusef was sitting in his cabin, trying to stop himself from throwing up. He hated being at sea in weather like this, but he had to stay on the boat now that they had recovered their prize. Calling back to Arrowhead the previous evening had been a great triumph for him.

Tomorrow afternoon they would be entering the Mediterranean Sea, which they then had to traverse. It was a slow mode of transport, but it was safe and that was essential. Speed would not be a goal in itself. They had all the time in the world now. There was just one little detail that they needed to take care of first. A small disappearing act had to be prepared. But that would be easy.

★ ★ ★

The next day, Fiona entered Andrew's office a five past ten. He had only just got into the office himself, having been badly in need of sleep the night before.

'Good morning, Andrew,' she smiled.

'Hello. Did you get a good night's sleep?'

'Yes. Except that I kept thinking about what Eckleston told me. I've always been fascinated by the idea that maybe there were other people before us, you know? Maybe this civilisation is not the first one to build great cities, travel the world by boat or by planes, even.'

'Planes?' said Andrew and looked at Fiona.

'I'll tell you about that some other time. Are you alright?'

'Yes. I slept like a log,' said Andrew and stretched, still sitting in his chair. 'I was pretty tired after yesterday's trip, although it is quite amazing that one can go to another country and come back in just one day.'

'So, what did Doctor Henke have to say?' she said and sat down in an armchair.

'He was actually very forthcoming,' said Andrew and started telling Fiona about the old man and his stories. Afterwards, they both sat back silently, contemplating the whole thing, each waiting for the other to make an observation. Fiona was the first to do so.

'Well, it's obvious that the Nazis located several sites on those expeditions, and that they did find several relics that they thought were sufficiently important to haul all the way back to Germany.'

'Even if they turned out to be old pieces of junk, as Henke thought they were,' Andrew observed.

'Right. But then they couldn't know that until they had been examined properly. Speaking from experience, having participated in archaeological expeditions to a few far-off places, it is extremely difficult to accept not finding anything that is worth bringing back. After all, these expeditions usually cost a ton of money, and judging from what Eckleston told me, the Nazis poured huge amounts of money into this venture. Add to that the political significance of making progress in the quest for the origins of the Aryan race, and it becomes quite apparent, that one wouldn't want to be the leader of an expedition coming back to Germany and the *Fuhrer* emptyhanded.'

'Good point,' mumbled Andrew. 'So that would argue for what Henke said to me, namely that most of the items that were stored in the warehouse outside Berlin was essentially just junk.'

'Yes, it would. If Henke's account is to be given any credence, some of the items actually did get significant attention from the powers that be. Enough to have them seal off the whole thing, even from the facility's administrator, and enough for them to remove all documentation of the presence of these items.'

'Right. But the most peculiar part of Henke's story was the two men encased in ice. What do you suppose that was all about? If it really is true,' she said.

'Your guess is as good as mine, but from what he told me, it seemed that they were wearing clothes suitable for arctic conditions. And that they had been deliberately placed in water tanks, which were then filled with water, and then frozen. Why would anybody do that?'

'I guess they'd only do it if they were already dead, right?'

'I guess so. Particularly if Henke's description is accurate, and one of the men really was Rudolf Von Serbottendorf, head of the Thule Society. You wouldn't put your boss in a deep freeze unless he had already gone on to meet his maker, would you?' asked Andrew with an insidious smile.

'Well. The thought has actually crossed my mind once or twice,' she chuckled. 'But I guess you're right,' she said, now with a more serious tone. 'They must both have been dead before they were frozen. In fact, it might have been quite natural to freeze them, if their deaths occurred far from home in a cold environment. Let's just for argument's sake say that Von Serbottendorf and his team had gone back to Thule again, and that he had died in an accident along with another member of the expedition. It would have taken them a long time to get back home, so they would have needed to prevent the bodies from decaying, wouldn't they?'

Andrew hesitated. 'You are right. But what about the burns to their faces?'

'Well, if there was an accident, that could have caused it. An explosion or fire of some sort.'

'Yes. That's what I thought as well. Except of course, if you wish to go for the more exciting option,' Andrew smiled.

'And what might that be?'

'Imagine for a second that the expedition actually did uncover some form of energy or power, linked to an ancient civilisation.'

Now Fiona was the one looking very sceptic. 'Yes?'

'Then they would probably have experimented with it, and that may have gone wrong, causing Von Serbottendorf and his mate to suffer burns and die,' said Andrew offering her his most cunning face.

'Andrew, I appreciate your attempt at allowing for an alternative view, but how do you suppose their faces got burned, without their clothes going up in flames or even being scorched? He didn't mention anything about that did he?'

'No, he didn't,' Andrew conceded.

'What about the crate that was removed from the warehouse by the SS Colonel?'

'What about it?'

'Well. Any idea what it was?'

'None, but it must have been damn important for them to try to get it out of the country. And why Argentina?'

'Well. The Argentineans had sort of a friendly or at least non-hostile relationship with Nazi Germany during the war. It might very well have been one of the only relatively safe havens for the Nazis.'

'Still doesn't give us a clue as to what it was, though,' said Andrew and sighed.

'Hey, wait a minute,' said Fiona suddenly and sat up in her chair. 'Didn't Professor Maltby tell you, that the documents stolen from there had contained information about the allied hunt for U-boats in the Atlantic?'

'Yes. So?'

'Well, if you are going to sail from Bremerhaven to Argentina, you obviously had to cross the Atlantic.'

Andrew still didn't see her point. 'So what?'

'Andy, let's say that whoever broke into the National Archives in Berlin are the same people who stole files from the Office of Historical Records. If they knew that U-303 had sailed from Bremerhaven, and if they knew where it was going and when it had left, they might also be able to find out what happened to it.'

'How do you mean?'

'Well, the stolen documents from London would indicate that they think or even know for a fact that it was sunk. Why else would they steal documents on anti-submarine effort?'

'Right.'

'And if they had all the records of sunken U-boats, it would be pretty easy to determine which allied sortie had sunk it, and from there work out approximately where that might have had happened. It's the only thing linking the two burglaries.'

Andrew looked at her, impressed with her deductions.

'But they would also have to know what it was carrying, wouldn't they? Why else would they go through so much trouble?'

'Yes, I think you are right. That means that there is at least one more source of information that we are not aware of.'

'But in any event, doesn't it seem quite clear to you, that those people have the intention of actually finding the U-boat themselves?'

'Yes. I guess that would be logical. If it was indeed carrying that crate, and if the crate contained something important or valuable, they must have had a plan to retrieve it.'

'That means that they may already have found the U-boat. It could have been sunk anywhere in the area that dive-bombers and patrol ships covered at that time. That would have been a huge area. Finding it would be like looking for a needle in a haystack.'

'Unless you had detailed information on every sunk U-boat.'

'Which the thieves now have,' sighed Andrew.

'So, we're stuck again, aren't we?'

'I'm afraid so. If only there was some other source we could use.'

Andrew looked at Fiona, suddenly remembering. 'Oh, by the way. I've talked to my superior, Colonel Strickland, and he has arranged for you to work with us for now,' said Andrew a bit hesitantly. It just occurred to him that he hadn't actually asked Fiona first.

'Oh, really?' she said in surprise. 'You've talked to the British Museum about this, have you?'

'Yes, we have. Sorry, I didn't mention this to you before, but it didn't occur to me to do so. Hope it's alright. This really is very important to us. Both Strickland and I feel strongly that we have to try to get to the bottom of this as fast as possible.'

'Well, I'm not used to having decisions made for me, but in this case, I'll be honest and say that it's alright. I agree that this may be quite serious, and I want to keep digging.'

Andrew smiled. 'Excellent.'

At that moment Strickland entered Andrew's office. Upon seeing Fiona, he stopped. 'Oh, I'm sorry. Am I interrupting?'

'No, not at all,' said Andrew and rose from his desk. 'We are a bit stuck at the moment. Colonel, this is Miss Keane. Fiona this is Colonel Strickland, my superior officer.'

The two shook hands.

'I just thought I would stop by your office, because I have some information that you might want to have a look at,' said Strickland and handed Andrew a stack of paper.

'Our boys at MI5 have run a background check via Interpol on this chap who was picked up in Germany. They've unravelled quite an interesting money trail connected to him. It seems that he was instrumental in directing funds from an account in Switzerland to a company in The Netherlands.'

'I wonder who is financing all this,' said Andrew.

'We don't know yet. There are usually quite a few dead ends in such a money trail, not least because some banks do not under any circumstance hand over information about their clients' money transfers. So, we can't see where the money originally came from. But we were able to learn that the Dutch company used the money to buy a salvage ship registered in Rotterdam.'

'Really?'

'Yes. And that seemed sufficiently unusual to them that they ran a check of where it might have gone after being bought, and it turns out that the ship left Rotterdam a few days later, and entered the port of Lisbon two days after that.'

'How do you know all this?' asked Fiona.

'There are records of these things in every harbour. Every time a ship enters or leaves a harbour, it requires permission from the harbour master. Much like at an airport. Every ship gets logged upon both entry to and exit from a harbour.'

'Ok. So, it went to Lisbon. Then what?'

'Well, there it took on a diving crew, and immediately sailed for the Azores. Knowing this, all the boys at MI5 had to do was request information from all the harbours on the Azores, to see exactly where it went. And sure enough, it turns out that the salvage ship had been moored in the harbour of Madalena on the island of Pico until last week. Then it supposedly left port to investigate the site of an aircraft crash that happened in the sea close to the island of Pico. It never returned to a port on any of the islands, but it definitely was there in Madalena harbour.'

Strickland smiled at the two. 'As the chaps at MI5 told me: It's all very simple if you know where to look.'

Andrew's face lit up. 'This definitely sounds like the people we are looking for. The salvage ship hasn't put in at any other harbour anywhere?'

'No. At least, not any that we know of.'

'What was the name of that island again?'

'Pico. I had never heard of it myself either, but I guess you learn something new every day. Anyway, it's all there in the report,' said Strickland. 'Now, if you don't mind, I'll get going. I have a meeting in a couple of minutes. I hope this helps you turn up something for us.'

'It just might,' said Andrew and looked at Fiona as Strickland left the room. 'The Azores, eh?'

'Well. As I told you, you can't sail to Argentina without crossing the Atlantic, and the Azores are sort of in the way.'

'So, if a submarine was actually sunk that far south and that close to an allied airbase where anti-submarine bombers were stationed, it could easily have been U-303. No German U-boat captain in his right mind would get that close to the Azores unless he was just passing by the islands and needing to get to his destination fast. And that just happens to be where our friends on the salvage ship are looking.'

The two of them looked at each other for a few seconds, before Andrew spoke.

'We need to get out there right away,' he said and lifted his eyebrows. 'I'll get Cathy to book two tickets and a place to stay as soon as possible. Then I'll call you. Probably later tonight. Let's go home and pack straight away. I'm not sure we will get anything more done here today. Alright with you?'

'It certainly is. I've never been to the Azores,' she smiled. 'But what do we do when we get there? We still don't know where to look for either the salvage ship or the wreck. All we know is that they are probably in the same place.'

'I'm not sure yet. We'll have to improvise, and see what we find,' said Andrew thinking that he sounded a lot more optimistic than he really felt. They had certainly made progress over the past few days, but the reality was that they had nothing to go on when they got to the Azores, except for the harbourmaster who might be able to tell them some more details about the salvage ship. They needed luck, and in Andrew's experience luck had an unpleasant tendency of staying absent when it was needed the most.

★ ★ ★

Prisoner #4264, or Kashim Khan as his name was, sat back in his seat. He was still sweating but knew that the worst part was now over. His false passport had worked perfectly through the two security checks, and his new appearance would have fooled even his own mother. With a short beard, heavy black spectacles and a few specially made and strategically placed pillows to make him appear obese, he now looked very different from a few days earlier when he had walked out through the hole in the prison wall. He had passed straight through the airport, and all the way to the departure lounge and onto the plane without any problems. Now sat in his business class seat, impatiently waiting for the plane to begin taxiing to the runway. A stewardess was already making her first round with cold drinks for the business class travellers. He asked for some orange juice with an ice cube. There was no need to start celebrating with alcohol yet. He would not feel safe until they were in the air. Next to him was what appeared to be a businessman. He looked to be American or European, and he was already busy typing something on his laptop computer. He hardly noticed the stewardess when she asked him what he would like to drink. After ordering a glass of water, he dove back down into his keyboard. That suited Sanjay just fine. The last thing he wanted right now was to have somebody next to him that enjoyed chatting with strangers.

The Airbus jerked slightly and then began rolling slowly backwards, pushed by a small but powerful towing vehicle. Having cleared its slot, the aircraft then began rolling along the taxiway, towards the end of one of the runways of the airport. There it held for a few minutes, which the stewardess used to collect empty glasses and flasks. The aircraft then rolled out onto the runway, and almost immediately the captain increased the throttle, pushing the aircraft forward in a powerful acceleration. Kashim Khan still felt tense as he was pushed back in his seat. He wasn't out yet. The Airbus continued to accelerate, causing the undercarriage to shake violently as it moved over the tarmac. Through the window, he could see the runway lights zooming past faster and faster until the nose of the aircraft pitched up, and then suddenly he was airborne. Instantly the shaking from the undercarriage disappeared, and a few seconds later Khan could hear the characteristic sound of it being retracted into the body of the aircraft. The plane rose steeply through the low clouds into the sky, and the higher it moved the more at ease Khan became. He had made it out. He had escaped from what would have been a lifetime of imprisonment. He knew that he was now indebted to the people that had made his escape possible. The fact that his debt was not talked about in terms of money and that the repayment hadn't been settled in any detail, didn't bother him too much right now. He was on his way out of a country where he would never again be able to walk as a free man, and that was reason enough for him to work off the debt for as long as it took. And moreover, he knew that he would enjoy his work and even get paid handsomely, so things were looking a lot brighter than they had just a few weeks ago.

When the Airbus reached cruising altitude, he unbuckled his seatbelt and leaned back in his seat. Putting on his headset, he closed his eyes and listened to the classical music that filled his ears. Flying had always made him feel free, but this was so very different from any trip he had ever made before. Now that freedom really meant something, he exhaled slowly and tried as best as he could to savour the moment. This was truly a new beginning in his life.

★ ★ ★

The salvage ship had finally passed through the Straits of Gibraltar that morning, and it was now heading deeper into the Mediterranean Sea. Onboard, Antonio and Ramon and the divers had thought it a bit strange that they couldn't disembark in Gibraltar and head back to Lisbon, but the contract they had signed had stated that they must remain aboard the ship until the cargo had been delivered safely to its destination. They hadn't been told what the destination would be, but a contract had been signed, and none of them wanted to back away from that.

It was now some eight hours since they passed through the Straits of Gibraltar, and it was getting dark. They were still going almost due east, but the seas had calmed considerably compared with the day before. Conditions were perfect, and as the freighter announced its arrival on the radio for their mid-ocean rendezvous, Hamza adjusted the course of the salvage ship, so that the two ships were on a near-collision course. It was a medium-sized freighter, ostensibly making its way from the Black Sea to Algeria, with its cargo hold full of coal. As its captain ordered engines to stop, it started drifting slowly forward in the twilight. The salvage ship moved to a parallel course and slowly started to move closer. Antonio entered the bridge where Hamza was guiding the salvage ship towards the freighter. He had a confused look on his face.

'What's going on?' he said as he walked to stand next to Hamza.

'Nothing. We're taking on supplies.'

'What supplies? We have plenty of supplies. And why don't we just go to port if we need anything?'

'Please, Mr. Pieza. I'm trying to concentrate,' said Hamza in an effort to make the man go away. 'Go back to your cabin. Everything is under control. It will only take half an hour,' he lied.

Antonio didn't like being ordered around, but he finally yielded and turned to walk back to his cabin. 'Alright. But make it quick,' he retorted and exited the bridge with a frown.

A few minutes later the salvage ship was right next to the freighter, and the two ships were now virtually stationary in the water. The arm of a large crane came out over the side of the freighter, and it began lowering a net containing a big black box. At the same time, Yusef came out onto the deck of the salvage ship, carrying a large plastic container, which he placed in the net. He then took the black box and walked to the railing of the salvage ship, where he started lowering it down along the side of the ship, using two steel wires. The net was hoisted aboard the freighter, as he lowered the black box down well below the water line. He then engaged the electronic switch, and the magnet in the box instantly caused the box to fix itself to the hull of the salvage ship with a metallic thump.

Hamza took out a pair of wire cutters and cut all the wiring around the radio and navigation aids. All of them went dead instantly, and he finished off by breaking out a fire axe and smashing all the control panels. A long rope ladder came over the side of the freighter, and immediately Yusef started climbing up. Neither of the two men said a word. On the railing of the freighter, appeared three men with sub-machine guns in case anything went wrong.

As Hamza began making his way up the ladder to where Yusef was waiting, Ramon suddenly appeared on the bridge of the salvage ship. Upon seeing the carnage that Hamza had left there, he ran to the side of the bridge facing the freighter and started yelling.

'Hey. What's going on here,' he shouted in a panicked voice.

He only just had time to finish his sentence, before one of the three men on the freighter opened fire, and a couple of bullets came through the windows of the bridge, shattering several of them.

'For Christ's sake. What the hell are you doing?' he yelled in a frantic voice as he dropped down onto the floor. At that moment Antonio came out onto the deck, and instantly bullets started hitting the deck and the ship's superstructure. It sounded almost like hail, except it was much louder. Antonio only made it about three meters away from the stairwell leading to the deck, when the first bullet hit him in the leg. He stumbled and fell face down on the hard steel deck, breaking his nose. He tried to stand up and move back towards the door, but as he stood, two more bullets hit him in the back, and he fell forward like a rag doll. After that, he didn't move.

Yusef was now safely over the railing of the freighter, and its captain immediately started pulling away from the salvage ship, which was now helplessly floating along on the sea with its controls wrecked. As the freighter cleared the salvage ship and began moving further away, the rest of the dive team made it up to the deck, alarmed by the noise and the screaming. Seeing Antonio in a pool of blood on the deck clearly stunned several of them, but one ran to the bow of the ship shouting something at the freighter. On the bridge, Ramon was frantically trying to fix the radio, but it was completely destroyed.

Yusef stood silently by the railing of the freighter and watched the doomed salvage ship slowly disappearing into the darkness. When he was sure that it was far enough away, he looked up towards the bridge of the freighter, where the captain was giving him the thumbs up. That meant that his radar indicated that there were still no other ships within at least ten kilometres. He pulled out a radio transmitter and switched it on. Looking at the salvage ship as it started to disappear in the darkness, he pressed the button and instantly there was a brief flash and then a column of water shot up vertically from the side of the salvage ship. Half a second later the sound of the muffled explosion reached the freighter. In spite of the distance of a couple of hundred meters, it was still powerful enough for him to feel it through his torso. An oil fire broke out on the ship, and it now became very visible. The screaming had stopped as most of the crew and the dive team had probably been killed, and he could already see the ship beginning to list heavily. Water was rushing in through the hole in the side, filling every compartment and leaving the former ship more akin to a large dead mass of metal that would surely sink to the bottom of the ocean. Then the bow disappeared below the waterline, and air started escaping from the ship's interior with a violent hissing sound. The more of the ship that went below the water, the quicker it all happened, and within seconds the ship had disappeared from sight. Left was just an uneasy patch of sea, where the remaining air from the ship bubbled to the surface. A small puddle of burning oil illuminated the water, but that vanished quickly, and then the sea was as calm as ever.

Yusef threw the radio transmitter over the railing and went inside the superstructure of the freighter. Everything was going as planned. In a day or so, he would reach his destination, and be celebrated as a hero. Arrowhead had informed him that the Alchemist had been set free from his captivity, and was now on his way to Arrowhead's location, which meant that there were now no obstacles for the plan to move ahead. With the Alchemist working for them now, they would be able to unlock the immense power that had first seen the light of day several thousand years ago, and that had been hidden on the ocean floor for the past half a century.

★ ★ ★

As it turned out, the trip to Pico went easier than they had expected, although it would end up taking almost twenty hours in total. Having got them to Lisbon, Catherine had managed to book two seats on a flight directly from Lisbon to the island of Pico. That meant that they didn't have to stop over on the main island of Sao Miguel first, saving them almost twelve hours including one night at a hotel. As they sat side by side on the plane to Pico, they went over the details of the information they had both retrieved, but nothing new came up. They would just have to pin their hopes on finding something new when they arrived. Fiona had spent a couple of hours already, reading one of the books that she had brought with her.

'What are you reading?' asked Andrew.

Fiona looked up as if yanked from a dream. 'Oh, this? It's just another book on the occult aspects of Nazi Germany. It's really quite amazing how deeply embedded in the workings of the Nazi party all these activities were.'

'How do you mean?'

'It's everywhere. Right from the beginning, with the establishment of esoteric brotherhoods such as the Thule Society. That society by the way seems to be the original and oldest one of them all. From that, to their affiliations with the socialist revolutionary parties, right up to the shaping of the SS and the Nazi party itself.'

'But that isn't really all that different from many other societies, even contemporary ones including our own. Many are based on religious writings, whose origins are difficult to assess with any degree of certainty. And in my opinion, there is no difference between religion and belief in the supernatural. It's all in the eye of the beholder. Christianity is no better or worse that Islam, Hinduism or Nordic Mythology. It's all just a matter of individuals craving a sense of belonging, and religions provide that for them.'

'So, you are not religious at all?'

'No. Unlike our friend Serbottendorf, who seemed to be a true believer' said Andrew and pointed at Fiona's books.

'Ok, well he certainly wasn't the only one at that time who was open to new ideas. The head of the SS, Heinrich Himmler was apparently also one of the founders of the Thule Society, and it seems that he took on the role of a high priest of sorts, and performed occult rituals in his private castle named Werwelsburg.'

'So, the man was delusional? Sounds like a Nazi to me.'

'Maybe. He does sound a bit unstable. Listen to this,' she said and began reading aloud. 'Werwelsburg functioned as Himmler's very own 'Camelot' of sorts, with high-ranking SS commanders cast as the Knights of the Round Table. Rooms were dedicated to figures of Nordic history and other mythology like the story of King Arthur, and he even had an exact copy made of the room in which the original round table was supposed to have been. Himmler modelled the entire SS on ancient orders of the Teutonic Knights, which he saw as representatives of the Aryan power that was to be resurrected by the Third Reich. The parallel between the knights and the SS order was very clear, and it didn't just limit itself to an occult methodology. Oaths and rituals, priesthoods, the swearing in of new members, and their unconditional submission to the Fuhrer, the Reich, and to God, in that order, was all a part of the SS. They even had their own catechisms. It went like this: *Why do we believe in Germany and the Fuhrer?* it asked. And the answer was: *Because we believe in God, we believe in Germany as he created it, and we believe in the Fuhrer Adolf Hitler who was sent to us by God.*'

'Wow. That definitely sounds like religion to me,' said Andrew.

'Quite,' said Fiona, lifting her eyebrows. 'They were all pretty dedicated from what I can see here, but Himmler himself certainly took the prize. His own room at Werwelsburg was dedicated to a certain King Heinrich I, founder of the first German Reich or empire. This was because Himmler believed himself to be the reincarnation of Heinrich.'

'Fool,' chuckled Andrew. 'Can you believe that those people actually ran a whole country for a decade and that they were initially elected by the people in a democratic process?'

'It was actually only Hitler who was elected,' Fiona pointed out. 'Himmler was appointed to office by Hitler. But yes, it is disturbing to think that the German people elected a dictator, thereby abolishing the system that ensured their own say in the way their society was to develop. No wonder many people became so scared that they actually fled the country altogether.'

'I would have as well,' said Andrew and shook his head.

'Me too, but I'm not sure that the German public was generally aware of just how pervasive the occult elements were in these relatively new political parties. Or maybe they didn't much care about that. Having lost the First World War, and been humiliated by the victors, and then having to pay war damages surely made its mark on the German people. They were eager to get back on the horse, so to speak, and start rebuilding not only their country but their self-esteem and national pride. All they needed was for someone to stand up and take it upon himself to carry the nation forward. Hitler provided just such a figure for them. And in the 1930's he actually delivered results, with German industry being revitalised and welfare increasing significantly for most of Germany's citizens. Given their recent history and the obvious improvements for the average German, I think most of them were more than willing to ignore what must at the time have seemed a minor eccentricity to them.'

'You're probably right. But looking back it just seems incredible that a whole people could be misled in such a dramatic manner.'

'I know. But I think the key here is that it all happened incrementally. People did notice the changes in their society of course, but it was mostly a slow process, during which most Germans experienced tangible improvements in their daily lives. But what they didn't see, of course, was what went on behind the scenes, or behind the thick walls of Werwelsburg. That would probably have scared most of them.'

'Definitely,' nodded Andrew.

'Himmler's spies and agents even infiltrated all kinds of religious and occult groups, and produced voluminous reports which they delivered to the Gestapo. Among those investigated were Jehovah's Witnesses, the Freemasons, the Rosicrucians and many astrological societies, which were all quite active back then. The Rosicrucians were particularly carefully scrutinised because they were daft enough to claim that they possessed certain universal secrets, which Himmler promptly concluded might be of value to the SS.

'What did Himmler hope to achieve with all of this voodoo nonsense?' asked Andrew.

'Well, it seems that one of his goals was to create a new spiritual focal point for the Third Reich, allowing its leaders to justify their actions, by referring to what was held up as ancient truths. To this end, Himmler set out to re-establish an ancient Aryan religion within Germany, as a basis for Nazi ideology. Himmler maintained that many ancient and sacred symbols of the Aryan religion had been stolen by other religions, such as Christianity, and that he and the SS had to recover them. One such symbol was the Holy Grail.'

Andrew looked at her incredulously. 'You mean, THE Holy Grail. The actual Holy Grail, also known as the Cup of Christ?'

'That's correct. The Cup of Christ, that ostensibly held the blood of Jesus after he had been crucified.'

'Now we are really beginning to enter the twilight zone,' said Andrew. 'So, the Nazis actually went looking for this thing?'

'They did. It's one of the most well-documented cases of the Nazi fascination with the occult. One of the leading academics recruited to the Nazi cause was Otto Rahn, who was an authority on the Holy Grail. He was brought into the SS to lead the search for it the world over. Himmler actually had a whole room set aside to house the Holy Grail, in the event that it was found. There was one expedition, which attracted particular attention. This happened before the war, and it was led by Otto Rahn himself. An *SS-Ahnenerbe* expeditionary team was sent to the Pyrenees Mountains to find the Grail.'

'SS what?'

'*SS-Ahnenerbe*. It was Himmler's archaeological and historical unit, also called the SS Ancestral Heritage Society, an affiliate of the Thule Society that was founded in 1935. It was led by Wolfram Sievers, who was later brought to trial in Nuremberg.'

'Ok. So, this Rahn character went to the Pyrenees?' Andrew was beginning to struggle with all the names involved.

'Yes,' said Fiona. 'According to folklore, the Holy Grail was believed to have been hidden by the Cathar Christian sect in Montsegur in France. Otto Rahn embarked on a mission to find it. They searched in many small churches and monasteries in France, and the whole thing stretched over many months.'

'So did they?'

'Did they what?'

'Find it, of course?'

'No. No reports have been uncovered to indicate that the Thule Society did find the Grail. But if they did, do you think it would be public knowledge?'

'Why wouldn't it be?'

'Because that might create religious tension, not just in our neck of the woods, but all over the world. There are hundreds of religious conflicts large and small the world over at any given time. Something like that could further ignite religious tensions.'

'I'm not convinced that would happen. But anyway, you are assuming that the people who might know of the existence and perhaps even the location of the grail are all capable of keeping a secret like this. That may be a bit optimistic, in my view.'

Fiona looked at Andrew with her dark curious eyes. 'You can be quite the cynic; did you know that?'

Andrew turned to look at her. Then he smiled. 'Maybe you are right. I just like to keep my feet on the ground, and not get too carried away.'

'Ok. So, if I were to suggest that the U-boat that left Bremerhaven in 1944 was carrying the crate Henke mentioned. And if I suggested that the crate contained something really important. Something like the Holy Grail, for example. Then you'd probably just laugh at me, wouldn't you?'

'That's not entirely unimaginable,' smiled Andrew and looked at her for a few moments. 'Do you really think that that was what the U-boat was carrying?'

'I don't know. It could also have been some other relic from another expedition. It is hard to say what it might have been. But think about the effort that was put into retrieving, storing and protecting it, and then finally to bring it out of Germany before the anticipated allied invasion and occupation. On the basis of that, it wouldn't be illogical to assume that it was of great significance, either to the German people or to the German war machine.'

Andrew nodded. 'Whatever it was, it was at least perceived to be of great importance to someone.'

With that, they both sat back in their chairs. Andrew wondered what Strickland would have said if he had been listening to the conversation he had just had with Fiona. Andrew was still very doubtful that there was any substance to any of these stories, but he had decided to go along with it and to let Fiona work as she thought it best. Unlike him, she was good at thinking in untraditional ways, and he didn't want to stand in the way of that.

SEVEN

Landing at Pico airport in the rain was not a pleasant experience. Andrew and Fiona had to disembark the twin-engine turboprop aircraft and run across the tarmac to the airport terminal. It rains quite a lot in the Azores, but for some reason, there was no protection against rain for their luggage, so when it entered the arrivals hall on the small conveyor belt, everything was completely drenched. Fiona was furious, as were several other passengers, but Andrew couldn't help chuckling when looking at them. He had been soaked through more times than he could remember, and most of those times, he had been hundreds of kilometres from the nearest hotel.

'Seems you have a bit of a temper, eh?' he smiled innocently.

'I'm Irish, remember? Don't push me,' she snarled.

Andrew was amused, but just nodded and kept quiet for a few minutes as they exited the building and hailed a taxi. Rooms had been booked for them at the Pico Hotel & Apartamentos close to the centre of Madalena. It was a long building by the side of the road to Madalena. The main building was a large white round structure, that housed the reception hall and lounge. It was one of the best places to stay on the island, and it had a nice big restaurant and a swimming pool outside. Looking south, guests could see the volcano stretching up into the air, and it seemed as if the hotel was right at the base of it. But that was the case almost regardless of where one was on the island. Even the locals regularly peered up at the peak, whether they were walking along the streets, driving their cars or working on the harbour. The volcano was a part of their identity, and it was always with them no matter where they went on the island.

After checking in at the hotel, Andrew and Fiona agreed to go for a quick swim in the pool, and then head for their rooms for a couple of hours of sleep. They were both tired after the long journey and needed the rest. At half-past three in the afternoon, they met again in the reception. The weather had improved, and the sun was now peeking through the disappearing clouds.

That was one of the peculiarities about the Azores islands in general and Pico in particular. Because the islands were volcanic, they almost all had a peak or a ridge running across them. There was always a light breeze carrying warm humid air over the islands, and so the air was constantly being pushed up along one side of the island, and down again on the other, creating clouds at the top. That meant that there was almost always one side of the island that was bathed in sunshine, while the other was covered with light clouds.

Winds often changed direction several times a day, so it was usually impossible to say where the sunshine going to be, much to the frustration of tourists as well as the local tourist office.

This afternoon was unusually hot, even for this time of year, and Fiona had taken the opportunity to change into a light blue summer dress. She was wearing small round sunglasses, and her hair was up. As she stood there smiling at Andrew coming up from the long corridor leading to the rooms, she looked to him like someone he might like to get romantically involved with.

That wasn't a new thought, but this was the first time it really annoyed him that he couldn't do anything about it. They had to keep this absolutely professional.

'You look nice,' she commented, looking at his holiday attire, which consisted of light beige cotton trousers, a white short-sleeved shirt, and walking boots.

'Thanks. So do you,' he said as casually as he could while trying to avoid sounding too impressed. 'Looks like the weather decided to be kind to us for the rest of the day. Shall we walk to the town?'

'Sure. Let's do that.'

Twenty minutes later they had reached the centre of Madalena. It had a square with everything a small community needed. A church, a supermarket, a post office, a souvenir shop, a bookshop and a couple of cafés and bars. Outside the wall surrounding the church sat a group of elderly men on a couple of benches. They looked as if they sat there all day and every day, commenting on whatever there might be to comment on, and telling stories of the time when Pico was a whaling station and its industry was thriving. Now, all that was left was a whaling museum a couple of kilometres east of town. The new business was tourism, as evidenced by the buses, loading and off-loading people coming from and going to the smaller island of Faial which was clearly visible just a few kilometres away.

On the other side of the square outside the bars, were the young men and women who had got off work or school. They now sat around small tables and laughed and occasionally shouted good-natured insults at each other. It all seemed very idyllic.

Looking like a pair of tourists, Andrew and Fiona went across the square and proceeded to the harbour area, where they quickly spotted the modern ticket office building that also housed the harbourmaster's offices.

'Let's go see if he is in today,' said Andrew.

The harbourmaster's office looked a lot nicer from the outside than from the inside. The walls were plastered with all kinds of pictures of ships and pieces of coastline, apparently all here from Pico. His desk looked as if it had been stolen from a severely under-funded school, and on the dirty carpet were stacks of old magazines about boats and sailing. This man was a sailor and not a sleepy public servant. The smell in the office was overpowering, and Andrew couldn't help wondering whether that was by design, in order to keep anyone out that didn't absolutely need to see him. The air was thick with tobacco smoke, reminding Andrew of his own father's study, and he couldn't help smiling as he remembered his father always saying that he didn't trust air he couldn't see.

'Can I help you,' asked a voice from beyond the smoke clouds.

Fiona closed the door behind them, and they took a few steps towards the harbourmaster who was sitting at his desk, comfortably leaning back so that he appeared to be almost lying down. He was a scruffy looking character with an unruly beard and thinning black hair. He was wearing a dirty striped shirt and a pair of dark brown trousers. In his mouth was a big pipe, which Andrew suspected never left his mouth, even in his sleep.

'Hello. My name is Andrew Sterling, and this is my assistant Fiona Keane,' he said and winked at Fiona. 'Are you the harbourmaster here in Madalena?'

'I am,' he responded in mediocre English. 'What can I do for you?' he continued in a voice that left none of the two visitors in any doubt, that he would much prefer not to have to do anything. And ideally, he would like to see them leave his office as soon as possible.

'I'd like to inquire about a boat that was here in this harbour a few days ago, Mr?'

'Sousa. Luis Sousa,' he said and blew a new cloud of smoke into the air.

'Right, Mr. Sousa. It was a salvage ship, painted blue with a white superstructure and a crane at the front. Do you remember that ship?'

'Of course, I remember,' said Luis. 'I'm the harbourmaster. That is my job!'

'Alright,' said Andrew politely. 'When did it arrive and when did it leave?'

Luis Sousa sat motionless in his chair and looked at Andrew. Then he shifted his gaze to Fiona, whom he evidently found very attractive, and then back to Andrew again. 'Who are you?' he asked suspiciously.

'I'm sorry Mr. Sousa. We are from London, and we are investigating a criminal case that may be quite serious. We have reason to believe that the salvage ship that was here may be connected to our case.'

Sousa hesitated. He was obviously unimpressed. 'Do you have identification?' he said and looked up at them with narrow suspicious eyes.

'Ms. Keane doesn't since she is just my assistant in this investigation, but you may have a look at mine,' said Andrew, and handed the harbourmaster his ID.

Sousa looked at the small plastic card with a picture of Andrew Sterling and the name of the SAS unit he worked for.

'You may write down my name and check it later if you'd like,' said Andrew trying to accommodate the man.

'No. it's fine,' he finally said and handed back the ID.

Then he dove into one of his drawers, and produced a leather-bound book, which he opened and slowly started paging through. 'This is where I log all ships that enter my harbour,' he said. 'And I remember the salvage ship very well. It has been a long time since one of those came here, you see.' After a few seconds, he stopped and leaned forward slightly. 'It came in nine days ago, and left again seven days ago.'

'Did you speak to the captain?' asked Fiona.

Sousa looked up from his book and smiled slyly to Fiona, revealing an uneven and poorly maintained set of teeth. It was probably the tobacco along with too much rum, she thought.

'I don't think so. I spoke to a man who said his name was Paul, but I think he was lying,' said Sousa.

'Why would he do that?' asked Andrew.

'How should I know? I just haven't ever seen anyone looking like that who was named Paul, that's all. He looked like somebody from the Middle East. Heavy accent.'

'Can you describe him in more detail?'

'Big. A little too much food and drink. Black beard. Curly hair. I didn't like him.'

'Why not?'

'It didn't seem like anything he said was true. I've been in this business all my life, and I can tell when a man is lying, and this man was lying.'

'Did he tell you where they were going?'

Sousa shrugged. 'He said they were going to look for the wreck of a small aeroplane that crashed a few years ago. He said it was his brother who flew the plane. But he was lying about that too.'

'How do you know?'

'Because my wife's brother knew the pilot of the plane that went down. He was from Piedade on the other side of the island,' said Sousa and pointed behind him into the dark wooden wall, 'and he was very thin and had blond hair. The man I spoke to could certainly not have been his brother. Of that, I am sure.'

Andrew and Fiona looked at each other. The harbourmaster might be a bit of a difficult person to deal with, but he was definitely right about the man's story sounding very dubious indeed.

'And when they left, did they say precisely where they were going?'

'No. But my cousin works as a guide taking tourists up to the peak almost every day, and he said that he had seen the ship anchored south-east of the mountain for a couple of days.'

'Really?' said Andrew in astonishment. 'So, it just lay there in the same position for several days?'

'That's what he said. And if he is right, then I know for sure that they were lying, because the aircraft that crashed in the sea went down north of the island just a few kilometres from the airport. Not on the other side of the island, ten kilometres away.'

'Mr. Sousa,' said Fiona and gave the harbourmaster her most endearing smile. 'Do you think it might be possible for us to have a talk with your cousin? It really would help us immensely,' she said and tilted her head slightly to one side.

Luis Sousa looked at her face for a few seconds and then smiled reluctantly. She had clearly won him over by now. 'Let me write down his telephone number,' he said and scribbled a number on a piece of paper, which he then handed to her. Fiona reached for it but as she grabbed it, he kept holding on to it and smiled cunningly.

'Maybe you would like to join me for dinner tonight?'

Andrew had trouble keeping a straight face, as he stood back and enjoyed the show. She had suddenly got more than she had bargained for.

'Uhm. What? No thanks, Mr. Sousa,' Fiona gabbled, taken aback by his advance. 'We're both very busy tonight. And tomorrow night,' she added. 'I don't think that will be possible, but thanks anyway,' she said and stood up, her eyes begging Andrew for them to leave soon.

'Well, Mr. Sousa,' said Andrew and gave him his hand. 'Thank you very much for your help. I'll go and call your cousin right away.'

'My pleasure,' he said and smiled at Fiona.

'Yes. Good day, Sir,' she said and hurried out of the office.

The clean ocean air was a big relief, after having spent just fifteen minutes in Mr. Sousa's office. As they walked away from the office and back towards the square, Andrew chuckled to himself.

'That's not funny,' she said feigning anger, but then burst into laughter herself.

'Don't do that again,' said Andrew, 'or I might not get you back to London with me.'

'Don't be an oaf,' she sneered through her smile. 'I can take care of myself, thank you very much Mr. SAS man.'

Andrew decided not to retort. There would be plenty of time for him to tease her with this later. As soon as they got back to the hotel, Andrew called the number he had been given.

Diego Sousa sounded like he might be quite a bit younger than his cousin Luis, and he spoke good English, which was probably necessary for being a tour guide. Andrew relayed what he had discussed with Luis, and Diego then agreed to take Andrew to the top of the volcano early the next day, so that he could point out to him the spot where the salvage ship had been anchored.

Andrew and Fiona spent the evening in the hotel's restaurant. There weren't too many guests now, so they enjoyed a pleasant evening with good food and wine. Andrew went to bed early, because he wanted to be well-rested for tomorrow's climb. He had been told that it would take between two and three hours, and that it would be quite steep in some places.

Diego had agreed to pick him up at six-thirty. That would enable them to avoid the sun for a few hours, but more importantly, it would increase the chances of avoiding the clouds during the descent, since they usually formed around noon, when the sun warmed up the ground and the winds started picking up.

The sun was due to come up over Madalena just after eight in the morning, but it was already lighting up the top of the volcano. Andrew was now sitting in Diego Sousa's truck, which was making its way up the road towards where the trail for the peak began. Diego was a man of about twenty-five years of age, with short dark hair and an easy smile. During the summer months, he took tourists to the top of the peak almost every day, so by now he was physically very fit. He had asked Andrew to wear warm clothes since it would be chilly at first. But as the sun came up, they could expect the temperature to shoot up. Seeing Andrew in his hiking boots, his trekking trousers and his camouflage jungle hat, he had smiled and asked if this was something Andrew had done before. Andrew had answered evasively with a story about a couple of walks in the Scottish Highlands that summer.

They started out from the trailhead at 1235 meters above sea level. That left them having to climb more than a kilometre straight up into the air, which seemed a daunting task, even to Andrew. He might be in good shape, but it had been some weeks since he had really pushed himself.

Looking towards the west, Andrew could see the town of Madalena with its white houses, the harbour with its characteristic two big rocks jutting up from the water just beyond the harbour entrance. A couple of kilometres beyond that was the smaller round island of Faial, which was covered in low wispy clouds. Except for Madalena, this side of Pico was almost completely enveloped in the shadow of the volcano, denying the inhabitants its warm morning rays.

Andrew yanked out his Garmin GPS system and marked the trailhead. He didn't doubt the abilities of his guide, but just in case, he liked to know that he would be able to find his way back. They started walking, and Andrew was quick to appreciate that Diego wasn't the talkative type. They walked quickly, and it didn't take more than ten minutes for Andrew's heart to start pounding, not least because the air was noticeably thinner here than at sea level. The trail started out as somewhat moist and soft, with various types of vegetation growing on the red-brown soil. But after half an hour they were walking on dark grey rock, which only supported tiny colonies of green and yellow moss.

He looked up at the peak towering above them and felt the familiar sense of awe that he always felt when walking in the mountains. But this was different. He had always been used to having other mountains around him when he was trekking, but here there was nothing on the horizon but the light blue ocean. It also had the effect of clearly letting him see how they increased their altitude as they walked, since the only good point of reference was Faial, and it was obvious how they began to see more and more of the island because they were increasingly looking down on it. As the sun came up, the cone-shaped shadow of the volcano crept closer and closer to its base, bathing ever more of the west side of the island in the sun. As it did, it became apparent that many smaller craters dotted the island. Some were small – the size of buildings. Others were the size of a football pitch.

As they neared the top, clouds started forming ever so slowly in small patches around the island and out to sea, and soon the town of Madalena was partially obscured from view. The last stage was also the steepest and most difficult. The entire top of the volcano was covered by very loose glass-like pieces of rock, from the most recent eruptions. As the lava was flung into the air, it cooled and often became completely hard before landing on the side of the volcano. This was what they were walking on, and it was extremely treacherous. On several occasions, Andrew had to quickly shift his weight from one foot to the other, in order not to lose his balance and cartwheel down the side of the mountain. When they reached the crater rim, a desolate grey and black moonscape revealed itself to them. The base of the crater was twenty meters below the crater rim, and in a few places, there was steam slowly rising from small fissures in the crater bed. The air had a slightly sulphurous smell, but not so much as to become too unpleasant. On the opposite side of the crater rim, was the smaller fifty-meter high cone where the latest minor eruption had occurred. They walked over to it and climbed up. Sitting on the peak at an altitude of two and a half kilometres, provided an excellent view, not only of Pico and Faial, but also of several of the other islands that made up the Azores. Towards the east stretched the majority of the island, and they could see almost every detail of it. They could even see the town of Piedade some thirty kilometres away. White clouds ran all along the north coast, but the interior of the island was in plain view. It was dotted with craters all along the ridge towards the east. This was typical for volcanic islands in the middle of oceans, including the Hawaiian Islands where Andrew had once gone on holiday.

Lava from inside the Earth would sometimes find a weak spot in the Earth's crust, and then force its way through under enormous pressure, creating an eruption on the surface, and even creating a whole new island if powerful enough. Then the eruption would die down as the pressure below the crust diminished. But during all of this, the tectonic plates of the crust would slowly move, thus carrying the most recently generated volcano away from the point where the lava had flowed out. The next eruption would therefore happen next to the former, and over many thousands of years, it would have the effect of generating a ridge of extinct volcanoes side by side, with the most recently active ones still smouldering.

The interior of Pico was therefore covered with smaller volcanoes, and they in turn were all covered with vegetation. The warm and humid climate, along with soil that was heavy in nitrates, created the ideal conditions for all sorts of plants to grow. Some of the extinct craters even had small lakes inside them.

'Beautiful, isn't it?' asked Diego with an enthusiastic smile on his face. He had been up here more times than he could remember, but the view always took his breath away.

'Yes. It really is a remarkable view,' said Andrew and pulled out his binoculars from the small bag he had been carrying on his back. He also powered up his GPS. It indicated 2.553 meters above sea level. They had taken just over two hours to get to the top, which was quite fast. They hadn't tried to rush things, but they both found that letting their bodies decide the optimal speed made for the safest way to travel. Andrew had learned from experience that intentionally trying to slow down, would often result in a loss of concentration, and then the risk of an accident grew much larger.

Andrew looked at Diego. 'So, when and where did you see the salvage ship anchored?'

Diego pointed towards the southeast. 'See how that part of the island sort of sticks out into the sea? That's where the town of Lajes Do Pico lies.'

Andrew pointed his binoculars towards the small fishing town.

Diego continued, 'And just beyond those huge rocks there, several kilometres out to sea, was where the ship was until just a few days ago.'

Andrew sat looking through the binoculars for a few seconds before speaking. 'Why did you notice the ship?'

'Because it was there,' he shrugged. 'We usually never have ships anchored off the coast here. They always go to one of the harbours. It was sitting there in the same spot for several days, and then one day it was just gone. I have never seen that happen before.'

'Do you think you could plot its position on a map if I gave you one?' asked Andrew looking again at the young man.

'I could. I have been here many times, and I made sure to note that it appeared to be directly above that large cliff sticking out, so I think I can tell you very precisely where it was anchored.'

'That is excellent,' smiled Andrew and took out two cans of Coke and a couple of chocolate bars.

They would need the sugar for the trip down. Descending was usually tougher on the body than ascending, because it required the use of muscles that the average person hardly ever used.

That turned out to be true for Andrew and Diego as well. They were both out of breath, tired and sweaty when they finally made it back down to the trailhead some three hours later. The whole trip had taken around seven and a half hours, including the stop at the peak, so Diego needed to rest his legs for ten minutes before getting into the car for the drive back to Madalena.

They had arranged to meet with Fiona outside the post office, but she had grown tired of waiting for them and had sat down by a table with a cup of coffee in one of the cafés. There she was reading a copy of the Herald Tribune, which was the only English language newspaper she could find. When she saw the two men park outside the post office, she paid the waiter and walked over to them.

'Diego. This is my partner, Fiona Keane. Fiona, this is Diego Sousa.'

'Hello Mr. Sousa,' she said and then quickly turned to Andrew, who enjoyed being considered a safe haven by her. 'Did you get up there?'

'Yes. It was a bit of a tough trek, but we made it. The view was fantastic. You must do it yourself someday.'

'Perhaps. And the ship?'

'Well, obviously it wasn't there anymore, but Diego promised me to plot its approximate position on a map.'

'And then what? We need to get out there, right?'

'Exactly. I actually thought about renting a boat, but maybe it won't be so easy finding one that is big enough,' he said and turned to Diego.

'What do you say, Diego. Can we rent a boat here?'

'That's not easy. Most tourists want to be taken to places. They don't like to sail the boats themselves.'

'What about that ship over there,' said Fiona and pointed to a boat that was bobbing calmly by the pier. At about fifteen meters long and 5 meters wide, the dark red fibreglass hull looked like it could accommodate several passengers for a long time. The back portion of the ship was covered with a hard white plastic canopy, under which the whale watching tourists would probably sit during the trip. It was powered by an internal engine, and it looked like it could sail quite fast if it had to.

'That is a whale-watching boat,' said Diego. 'You can't just rent that for several days, you know'

'I think that would probably depend on the price, don't you think Andy?' she said jovially.

He smiled and looked at Diego. 'Who owns that boat?'

'An American.' Replied Diego. 'Burke. I don't know his first name. Everybody here just calls him Burke. You can go and talk to him if you like.'

'Do you know where we can find him?' asked Fiona.

'Yes. He is right over there,' said Diego and pointed to a robust-looking man of about forty years of age, who was talking to some of the local fishermen.

He looked amicable with his thick black moustache and brown leathery skin. Spending every day of the summer in the sun, ferrying tourists out to see the whales that still lived here despite having been hunted almost to extinction, would do that to a man's face. He was wearing dark blue trousers, a green sweater and a red baseball cap, and he looked just like one of the locals.

'Thanks, Diego. We'll do that. I'll just go over and buy a map,' said Andrew and ran over to the bookshop, from where he returned a few minutes later with a map in Portuguese. 'Will this do?'

'Yes. That is Ok,' said Diego, and placed the map on the hood of the car. 'We started our walk here, and here is the peak, and over here is where the ship was,' he said and made a small 'X' on the map.

'X marks the spot, eh?' grinned Andrew.

'I'm pretty sure it was right there,' said Diego.

'Great. Thank you very much, Diego. How much do I owe you for that guided tour of the peak?'

'Let's just say 80 Euros,' he said and shrugged as if he wasn't too interested in the money.

'Alright. Here's 100. Thanks again.'

As they walked towards the American, Andrew looked briefly at Fiona. 'So how about Diego,' he said in a teasing voice. 'He seems to be a very nice lad, and he's much younger than Luis.'

Fiona didn't answer but glared at him briefly. He was pushing it now, he knew that. But he just couldn't help himself.

Just as they approached the American Diego had called Burke, the man turned and started to walk away from them.

'Excuse me, Mr. Burke?' said Andrew.

Immediately the American spun on his heels, to face the two people approaching him. 'Yeah?' His eyes were alert, and he looked good-natured.

'Are you Mr. Burke?' Fiona took over.

'That's right,' he responded in a southern drawl.

'Sorry guys. Didn't realise you wanted to talk to me.'

'That's alright, Mr. Burke. I'm Fiona Keane and this is Andrew Sterling,' she said politely.

'Oh, come on, let's cut the fancy talk, why don't we. I'm Roger,' he said and stuck out his hardy fist.

'Roger. Very good to meet you,' continued Fiona. It was clear that she liked him already. 'Where are you from?'

'Texas,' he said, pronouncing it *Tex's.*

'We've just talked to the harbourmaster's cousin about going out to sea for a few days, and he thought that maybe you could help us.'

'For a few days? What for, if ya don't mind my askin,' he said touching the tip of his red baseball cap.

'Well, Mr. Burke. Roger. We need to go and look for a wreck, and since we are not sure of the exact location, it might take a while to find it.'

'A wreck you say? What kind of wreck is it?'

'We'll get to that. Is it possible?'

'Possible? Of course, it's possible. This here boat was constructed by the Canadian Coast Guard in Wedgeport, Nova Scotia. It's got a big engine, powerful sonar, a heated cabin area, plus a galley and a washroom facility, so the ship can do it just fine. The only issue as far as I'm concerned is the pay. I usually take ten or twenty people out for a couple of hours, and they pay a fixed fee. You'd obviously have to pay a lot more than a simple fee, since I'd have to be gone for a while, without making any money from the whale watchin' business.'

'I'm sure we can accommodate you in that respect. It is a matter of national security for the British government,' said Andrew in a slightly lower voice. Not that he really expected someone to be eavesdropping. It was just an old habit.

'Now wait a li'll old minute there,' said Burke. 'What are you guys up to? I ain't gonna get involved in no covert operations or anything like that. Pretty sure that'd be bad for ma' health!'

'Roger,' said Fiona endearingly. 'I can assure you that this is not dangerous for you or your ship. All we need is for you to sail us to a certain spot and drop your anchor. Then we'll take care of the rest:'

'Excuse me Miss,' he said slightly offended. 'It ain't because I'm scared of nothin'. I was in the US navy for neigh on twenty years, and there ain't nothin' out there that scares me any. I just wanna be able to do my job and sail my boat the next day. Y'all will have to pay me big time for this.'

'We will,' said Andrew. 'Trust me. Money will not be a problem as long as we get to where we need to go.'

And with that Burke began to look more at ease. 'So, you just want me to sail you two to a spot and then back again a couple of days later, is that it?'

'Yes. We might even get it all over with in just one day.'

Burke considered the proposition while he looked from one to the other. Then his face lit up in a broad smile, exposing a row of strong white teeth. 'What the hell,' he grinned. 'I'll do it. When are we goin'?'

'When *can* we go?' asked Fiona. 'We'd like to leave as soon as possible.'

'How about tomorrow morning?'

'Don't you have whale watchers to take out to sea?'

'Nope. There's no booking in advance. People just show up on the pier with a few bucks, and we're off. If I'd like to take the day off, I just take the day off. That's the way I run ma'business.'

'Alright then,' smiled Andrew. 'How about eight o'clock tomorrow morning?'

Burke nodded. 'That'll do just fine. I'm gonna need a little time to get ready today anyway, so that's alright by me. Do y'all have diving equipment? If not, you can use mine. I have a couple of outfits on the boat. How deep will you need to go?'

Andrew pulled out the map and pointed to the little X that Diego had put on it. 'This is where we need to go. From this map, it looks like no more than a hundred meters.'

'Yeah. I think you're right, Son. It ain't too deep. A couple of regular dry suits should do just fine. You can use mine if you want?'

'That would be excellent. Is there anything we need to bring?'

'Just bring clothes and what you need to drink. I have plenty of food on the boat. So, what exactly is it you guys are looking for?' asked Burke and lit a cigarette.

'I'll tell you tomorrow after we leave the harbour,' said Andrew.

Burke looked at him for a few seconds and then chuckled while shaking his head. 'Sure sounds all cloak-and-dagger like. But alright. I'll wait.'

'Great,' beamed Fiona. 'We'll see you tomorrow at eight.'

★ ★ ★

Mullah Haq was sitting in the small room next to his bedroom. As a religious leader, he was responsible for guiding his fellow Muslims in the interpretation of the Koran. But he was more than that. He was one of only a few people who, due to the good grace of Allah, had been granted an opportunity to do his God's work.

Sitting in his room in the middle of prayer, the door in his apartment suddenly opened. His apartment consisted of four small rooms. On the other side of the front door in the corridor were two very large and very well-armed men, guarding him and his staff. In his small office just next to the front door, his accountants were working to coordinate the flows of finances that were needed to support the effort. In the corridor, a man was insisting on entering the apartment. He was not just any man. In fact, he was one of the most important men currently doing Mullah Haq's bidding, but he still needed to convince the guards that it really was important enough to interrupt the Mullah in the middle of prayer.

He was finally allowed inside and didn't stop to greet the two accountants who were sitting in the office. He made his way swiftly through the living room and into the bedroom where he slowed down and then walked cautiously towards the doorway to the small room in the back of the apartment. He stopped in the doorway, knowing that his master had heard him enter and that he would have to wait for permission to speak. The bearded grey-haired man sitting on the floor lifted his hand and beckoned the younger man to enter. He then rose and turned to hear what message could have been so important that he needed to be interrupted.

'What is it?' said the bearded man.

'They have it, Master. They have the Fist of God.'

As he said the words, the messenger could hardly contain his joy, and upon seeing this, Mullah Haq smiled calmly and placed his hand on the young man's shoulder.

'Do not seem so surprised, my son. It is the will of Allah that we should find it.'

EIGHT

The next day, Andrew and Fiona met with Burke on the pier at eight in the morning, as agreed the day before. The previous night after returning to the hotel, they had discussed how to go about the dive. Fiona had only ever taken introductory diving lessons, and was reluctant to go down that deep. Andrew had a Dive Master diploma from the SAS, and had descended countless times to about a hundred meters, so they decided that he should go down alone, even though it would be risky. They considered calling Strickland and asking for additional support, but they decided against it. It would simply take too much time to find someone and send him out here.

It was getting light very quickly now, and the sun was peaking over the side of the volcano, making its dark silhouette look even more imposing. Burke was loading a couple of crates onto the boat, and when he noticed Andrew and Fiona approaching, he stood up and saluted like a sailor, with a big grin on his face.

'Mornin y'all,' he called. 'You guys ready?'

Andrew waved back and turned to look at Fiona. 'He's certainly in a good mood.'

'Yes, well. We are also paying him very nicely,' she said and lifted her eyebrows. 'But I must admit, I do like him. He seems very honest and genuine.'

'I think you are right,' said Andrew. 'I hope we can find that wreck. Otherwise, we will really be stuck.'

When they reached the boat, Burke came out under the canopy from the wheelhouse.

'You can put your stuff in there,' he said and pointed through the wheelhouse to a small door that led to the living quarters. 'There's plenty of room in there for the two of you.'

'Thanks, Roger,' said Andrew. 'Is she ready to go?'

'Ready as she'll ever be,' he smiled confidently, revealing a certain amount of pride in his ship.

'How long will it take to get there, do you think?'

'Well, it's almost on the other side of the island, so it'll probably take a couple of hours. You guys can sit in the back and fish if ya like. There's plenty of tuna out here. You just throw out the bait and let it trail after the boat. And believe me - you'll know when they bite,' he grinned.

'Sounds like fun,' said Fiona enthusiastically. She had never tried deep-sea fishing before, and the prospect of two whole hours on a boat with nothing to do was not enticing.

Casting off the moorings, the boat sailed slowly out of the harbour, before heading south-east along the coastline. They had an excellent view of the volcano, and Andrew was even able to see where he had trekked up its side the day before. They tried catching some fish for the next hour or so, but it didn't amount to anything, much to Fiona's disappointment. Andrew took the opportunity to walk forward to the wheelhouse and tell Burke what they were looking for, without revealing why. He was surprisingly unexcited by what Andrew told him. It seemed he had heard many a strange tale from imaginative tourists before. Maybe he was just interested in the money.

After just under two hours, Burke eased back on the engine and came back out to the other two. 'I think this is close to where you need to go. At least it's right where that spot on your map is. I'm going to start looking with the sonar. You guys wanna watch?'

'Sure,' said Fiona and headed for the wheelhouse, happy to have something interrupt her boredom.

For the next half an hour they searched the seafloor without result, but then something big appeared on the sonar screen. It was about ninety meters below them, and more than fifty meters long.

'I think we've got her,' said Burke.

'I think you're right. I'll go and get ready,' said Andrew and disappeared down into the living quarters. A few seconds later he was back with some diving equipment. Then he walked down to the rear of the ship and started donning his dry suit.

'It's too deep to drop anchor,' said Burke to Fiona.

'Is that a problem?'

'No. Not really,' said Burke and turned the boat into the light breeze. 'I've marked the spot with the onboard GPS, so if we drift too far away from it, we can easily get back. I just need to keep an eye on it.'

Andrew was now almost done. As the very last thing, he put on the helmet that allowed him to breathe more freely than in a wet suit, as well as communicate with the boat. Fiona came back to help him make sure that he had everything he needed, and that his diving suit was secure. He had with him a camera with a strong flashlight attached to it, an extra flashlight in case the camera broke, a big diving knife attached to his right leg, and a harpoon. The camera was attached to a long cord that fed it power and ensured that Fiona and Burke topside could see what was going on below them.

When they had assured each other that everything was ready, Andrew climbed up on the railing and jumped in. He stayed on the surface for a few seconds, checking his breathing apparatus. It worked perfectly.

'Radio working?' he asked.

'Radio workin just fine,' said Burke and waived to him from inside the wheelhouse.

'Ok. I'm starting my descent,' he said and disappeared beneath the shallow waves.

The sea was a dark green, and the boat rolled ever so gently in the long calm waves of the Atlantic Ocean. Looking at the spot where Andrew had disappeared, Fiona couldn't help feeling a little uneasy about him going into the deep by himself. The only comfort was that Burke was in the wheelhouse, and also the fact that she could see the island of Pico not too far away. That was calming her nerves a bit. It would have been easier if she had been able to go with him. It was never pleasant to be the one having to look on at somebody else doing something dangerous. It was always much better to be the one doing the dangerous thing.

She walked into the wheelhouse, where Burke was watching the sonar and the screen transmitting the image from Andrew's camera. At the moment there was nothing to see, except a sea that was getting darker and darker as Andrew sank towards the bottom.

'You alright, Son?' asked Burke in an amiable voice.

'I'm good,' replied Andrew in a calm voice. 'I'm beginning to feel the pressure now, but I'm fine.'

'What's your depth?'

'Forty-two. It's getting quite dark already.'

'Yeah. We can see that. Just keep going.'

They could hear his breathing all the way down, and the sound remained calm and even. A few minutes later Andrew's voice came back over the loudspeaker.

'I've reached the bottom. It's quite soft and there is a thick layer of silt that is reaching my ankles. I'm starting to walk.'

On the screen, Fiona and Burke could see the image from Andrew's camera as he moved slowly over the grey ocean floor. Sometimes when he stopped for a few seconds to orientate himself, he would inadvertently kick up some silt, that would then float around in the water, obscuring their view until he moved on again. There were no discernible features around him, but he moved slowly in what he thought was the right direction.

'Still nothing. How close should I be?' he asked.

'About twenty meters,' answered Burke, 'but the current might have taken you a bit further away. Just keep on it.'

At that moment something to his right caught Andrew's eye. It was a dark shadow of about five meters in length that seemed to move in parallel to him. He stopped and watched for a few seconds.'

'Are you seeing this as well?' he asked.

'What?' said Fiona.

'That dark thing over there. It moved,' he said, his breath starting to quicken.

Burke looked at Fiona and shook his head.

'No,' said Fiona 'We didn't see anything.'

Andrew hesitated for a few seconds, but then began moving forward again. Almost instantly the shadow reappeared and began moving towards him.

'Look! Do you see it now?' said Andrew in a tense voice.

'Yeah. We see it,' said Fiona anxiously. 'Andrew, be careful.'

Andrew had stopped walking and just stood there as the shadow moved towards him, seemingly faster as it approached. The shadow was now just a few meters away and kept coming directly towards him. He pointed his spare flashlight at it and switched it on. At that moment it became clear that it was a large octopus looking for food. It had been attracted by the light in Andrew's camera and was now unable to resist it, much the same way a moth is attracted to a light bulb.

'Jesus. It's coming right at me,' he shouted.

He just had time to switch on the second flashlight before it reached him.

'Andrew, watch out. It's going to hit you,' Fiona shouted. Immediately thereafter the octopus barged clumsily into Andrew who fell over and landed in the silt with his arms and legs flailing, and the flashlight spinning in the water. He struggled to get to his feet, only to feel a tentacle wrap around his left leg. In a flash, he had his knife in his right hand and slashed violently at the tentacle. The knife cut deep into the tentacle, almost severing it. He then brought up his harpoon, but the octopus had vanished in the murky water, which was now filled with silt. Visibility was down to under a meter, and Andrew could feel a claustrophobic sensation creeping in on him.

He knew that the octopus was still very close and probably able to see his flashlight, but he was unable to see it. He decided that the only option was to start moving again and get away from the cloud of silt. He leaned forward and began walking as fast as he could while looking from side to side to see if the octopus was anywhere near him. After about five meters he turned around and started walking backwards so as to be able to see if it was coming towards him again. Another five meters and then he stopped to catch his breath.

'Andy,' Burke called out.

'What?' Andrew responded in the middle of a cough.

'You alright, Son?' asked Burke tensely.

'Yes. I think so. I think I managed to scare him off with my knife. But I'll just stand here for a while to make sure, if that's alright with you two?'

'Absolutely. Take it easy, now.'

Fiona was almost as out of breath from hyperventilating, as Andrew was from the strain of trying to move quickly through the water. Her eyes were fixed on the small screen in the wheelhouse, following the camera's every move as Andrew turned from side to side to see if the octopus was still there. After a few minutes, Andrew's voice came back over the speaker.

'I think it has had enough,' he said relieved, and looked down at the compass on his arm. He didn't think that an octopus would have been particularly dangerous to him, but it would probably be able to do serious damage to his suit, and that was not something he would like to have happen to him at this depth. 'I'm moving on now,' he said and started walking again.

After another few minutes, the wreck of the submarine suddenly loomed in front of him. It seemed positively huge as he walked closer to it. It was several stories high, and with the visibility at no more than twenty meters he could just about see half of it at any given time.

'Is that it?' asked Fiona.

'Yes. I've found it. I'm going in for a closer look.'

His panting was constant, as the ghostly shape towered above him, making him feel very small.

'I'm approaching the hull. It is in a remarkably good condition, by the looks of things.'

He walked to within five meters of the U-boat, and then stopped just under the tower. He turned a few times to let the light shine on different parts of the hull. It was clearly heavily corroded, but the U-boat was still structurally sound and not about to fall to pieces.

Then he turned right to walk along the hull towards the bow. Onboard the boat, Fiona and Burke could hear his heavy breathing through the speaker in the communications module, as he moved forward along the hull, twice having to walk around big pieces of twisted metal that seemed to have come from the U-boat itself. It wasn't until he reached the deck gun, that he realised the U-boat had no bow at all.

'Look at this. The whole bow is completely blown away. At least now we know why it went down.'

'Looks pretty horrific to me,' said Fiona. 'Can you see anything inside?'

Andrew began walking around the gaping hole. 'No. It's all a tangled mess. Christ, they must all have died almost instantly,' he said as he shone his light inside the unrecognisable wreck. 'I don't think anyone could have entered here either. It's too dangerous. And there are no signs of anything having been touched recently. I'm going to go down along the other side.'

'Watch the cable,' said Burke. You don't want it to get tangled up down there.'

'Right, Will do.'

He walked down along the hull of the U-boat and reached the tower again. It was leaning in his direction now, and he shone his light onto it.

'U-303. Are you guys recording all of this?'

'Every second,' said Burke.

Andrew proceeded past the tower and soon discovered what appeared to be a large black circular spot on the hull just half a meter above the seabed.

'Wait a minute', said Andrew a bit out of breath. 'What's this? Hang on. I'll have to move in closer to see.'

It wasn't until he was less than ten meters away, that he realised that it was not a dark spot, but rather a big hole that had been cut right through the hull of the U-boat.

Fiona looked at Burke, clearly uneasy with Andrew being down there by himself. For a few seconds, there was so much static on the line that the image flickered and went away, only to return in short flashes on the screen. They couldn't hear what Andrew was saying now. After a few seconds, he was back.

'You guys still there?' he asked in a perplexed voice.

'Yes, Andy. We're still here. We had a small problem with the signal but it seems to be fine now.'

'Oh. Good,' he replied, clearly relieved. 'I thought that I had lost you for a moment.'

'What are you seeing,' asked Fiona.

'Well, I think I can safely say that our friends have been down here. It looks as if they've cut a hole directly through the hull of the submarine. Do you see it?' he asked and held steady for a few seconds to let them see.

'Yeah, Andy.' Said Burke. 'We see it. It's big ain't it?'

'Yes, it is. It's more than big enough for me to pass through. Looks like it has been made very recently. See how the edges reflect the light from my flashlight? Some sort of high-temperature cutting tool, I'd guess.'

'Pardon me for asking,' said Burke. 'But what friends are you talking about now?'

'Well, Roger. They're not really our friends, to be honest. They came here looking for something, and we need to know what it was.'

'But let's talk about that when you get back up, okay?' interrupted Fiona and looked at Burke, who duly nodded and held up his hands to indicate that he didn't want to get in the way of what they were trying to accomplish.

A little bit out of breath from the action, Andrew was still panting slightly. The anticipation of what was to come also played its part.

'I'm going to go through, alright?'

A hundred meters above Andrew, Fiona and Burke exchanged anxious looks. This was suddenly very real. After all, he was about to enter a submarine that had been lying there for half a century, recently visited by people they knew almost nothing about. In addition, it happened to be the tomb of some fifty people who suffered a horrible death.

'Are you sure it is a good idea to enter by yourself?' asked Fiona nervously.

'I don't think it is dangerous. If there's something in there that I don't like, I'll just come straight back out again. Ok?'

'Ok,' said Burke. 'Be careful now as you move through the hole, Son. Those edges can be sharp as razors.'

'Right. I'll look out,' said Andrew as he moved slowly towards the hole, trying not to stir up too much of the sediment. Circular and approximately one and a half meters in diameter, the neatly cut hole offered plenty of space for him to move through. He put his right foot on the lower edge of the hole and hesitated for a second, but then proceeded through the opening. Halfway through, he could place his other foot on the inner hull, but then he had to kneel down. The hole had been made so that it led almost directly to one of the narrow corridors that ran the full length of the interior of the U-boat, but not quite. Andrew had to enter feet first through the gap to the corridor, but first, he had to fasten his flashlight to his belt.

A few seconds later he stood inside the corridor, which was pitch black, except for the light his helmet-mounted flashlight could produce. The walls were covered in a thin layer of corrosion, and small fish darted between his legs from time to time. They must have made their way through narrow passages from the front of the ship. It probably hadn't taken them long to settle here from the time the U-boat hit the bottom some fifty years ago.

Along the ceiling of the corridor ran several pipes and cables that had not been visibly affected by the seawater. Andrew assumed that the water in here had been very still for most of the time since the sinking of the U-boat. He estimated that he was at least twenty meters from where the bow had once been. Above him under the ceiling, a small pocket of air was developing, as the air he exhaled rose from his mask. Its shiny surface made it look like quicksilver as it moved along the corridor.

It felt eerie standing there, knowing that people had once lived and worked in this space. Orders had been given through the small loudspeaker box above his head. People had walked back and forth talking and making jokes, discussing whatever was on their minds, and thinking about their loved ones back in Germany. And that was when it really hit Andrew. This place was a giant tomb, and he was bound to find some of the dead sailors, or rather, what was left of them.

'Can you see anything, up there?' he asked with some trepidation.

'We see a corridor,' said Burke. 'You know where you are?'

'Yes, I think so. I spent last night looking at blueprints for several types of German U-boats, and I believe this is a Type VII from the end of the war. Anyway, the basic design is more or less the same for them all, so I should be on the upper deck somewhere near the caboose.' As he spoke, he shone his light up and down the corridor looking for anything that might provide him with an exact location.

Burke looked at Fiona, anxiety apparent in his eyes. With his right hand, he covered the microphone that sat on a small arm on the communications console. 'You guys owe me a serious God damn explanation once this is over, ya hear?'

'You will get one,' nodded Fiona. 'Don't worry.'

'How much air do you have left, Andy?' she asked calmly as Burke removed his hand from the microphone.

Andrew looked at his diving clock. 'Uhm. The gauge says thirty-five minutes, so including the reserve, I'd say about forty minutes.'

'Alright,' said Burke. 'You'd better start movin, Son. It'll take you at least fifteen minutes to get back up,' he warned.

Burke had never lost a passenger while he was at the helm of any ship, and he wasn't about to have one drown now. For a few seconds, he lifted his head and looked outside his boat, to see if there were any other ships in the vicinity. None were present. Although there was no reason for it, he felt as if they were doing something that they were not supposed to do. Maybe it was this whole secrecy business that threw him off, but he didn't feel quite as much in control as he usually did when he was out to sea. The ocean was his element, his friend, but now he also felt connected to the guy down below, and that was a place he had never endeavoured to explore. He wasn't exactly on home turf at this moment. He leaned over to one side and checked the GPS. They had drifted just fifteen meters since Andrew descended. They could easily compensate for that when he eventually began to ascend.

'I'm going to move further back now,' said Andrew and started moving slowly through the water in the narrow corridor. Because the water was confined to a small space, and because of his big bulky dry suit, it was harder to move forward in the corridor. He had to displace a lot of water, and that water could only go around him, so he was acting as a cork in a bottle. It was slow going, but eventually he reached the caboose.

'I'm in the caboose now. You guys hungry?' His attempt at a joke failed miserably. 'Ok. I'm proceeding to the cargo hold further back.'

'What about the captain's cabin?' asked Fiona.

'I'll take a look on the way back.'

Andrew had to go down a steep flight of stairs and started to worry slightly about his communications cable. If it got cut or caught in something, he would be on his own. But then he realised, that he was in fact all alone now. If something happened, there was nothing Fiona or Burke could actually do to help. It would simply take too long for Burke to get down to him.

On the boat, Burke was thinking exactly the same thing.

'Where are you going?' asked Fiona as Burke suddenly left the wheelhouse.

A few seconds later he returned with another dry suit. 'I'm going to put this on in case something happens.'

Safely down the stairs, Andrew turned the corner leading to the cargo hold. It was evident that someone else had moved the same way not too long ago. The sediment on the floor was disturbed, and in several places, he could actually see footprints from a suit similar to his own. He had just begun to wonder why he hadn't seen any bodies anywhere, when he suddenly stepped on something fragile that crunched under his weight. When he looked down it was a human ankle. It was attached to a whole body, or rather the pitiful remains of one. It lay face down in a room with only its feet sticking out into the corridor.

'Oh, bugger,' exclaimed Andrew.

'What is it?'

'Nothing. I've just made a ghost very unhappy,' he said, trying to sound jolly. He wondered if there might be a law about desecrating underwater tombs.

'Alright, you two. I believe I'm coming up on the cargo hold now,' he said as he approached a large steel door. He could tell from the scrape marks in the silt, that it had been swung open recently. As he approached the steel door, he noticed that its lock had been cut out of the door entirely. Apparently, someone had decided not to waste time trying to open it in a civilised manner. That was probably a good idea. The lock would have corroded so badly, that it would have been impossible to enter by any other means.

Fiona and Burke held their breath as they watched the helmet-mounted camera seemingly floating slowly towards the entrance to the cargo hold. For a few seconds, the camera tilted downwards and they could see Andrews's hand grabbing the second flashlight and pointing it forward. When he looked up again, he was standing in the doorway looking in.

'Alright,' said Andrew. 'The cargo hold is approximately three by four meters, and it's stretching from the corridor to what must have been the inner hull on the opposite side of the U-boat.'

Fiona strained their eyes to make out some recognisable features, but without any luck.

'What do you see, Andy?' she asked.

Andrew took a few steps inside the cargo hold and shone the light methodically around the interior. In the back corner of the room was a heap of unrecognisable debris. He walked towards it while shining his lights around the room. When he reached the corner, he knelt down and grabbed onto one of the pieces. It was a metal cap, that had once sat on the corner of a crate.'

'I think this used to be a wooden crate or something,' he said. 'But it's completely disintegrated now. Only the corner caps are left. It looks a bit messy, though. As if it was recently broken to bits.'

His hands searched through the crumbling debris, but he found nothing else there. Then he stood up and turned around.

'It's empty,' he finally muttered, sounding dejected. 'It is completely bloody empty. There's nothing here but two herrings and a baby squid. Whoever was here before us have cleaned it out completely. I think they smashed that crate to pieces and took what was inside.'

'Do you think that was the crate Henke spoke of?' asked Fiona and looked at Burke, who had given up trying to decipher their conversations.

'It could very well be,' said Andrew. 'Look, I'm going to go back up to the captain's cabin. There's obviously nothing left down here.'

He took a final look around the interior of the cargo hold, and then walked back out into the corridor and up the flight of stairs. On the way, he shone his light down along the corridor to what he thought must have been the engine room and wondered what the final thoughts of the people in there had been. He was careful not to step on the bones sticking out into the corridor once more.

Reaching the upper deck, he closed his eyes and visualised the blueprint he had studied the night before. The captain's cabin shouldn't be too far away. If there was one thing he had learned better than most people from his time in the army and in the SAS, it was to study and remember a map. In combat, you didn't have time to ask for directions or even to sit down and look at a map. He opened his eyes and proceeded briskly forward. Mindful of his air supply, he looked once more at his gauge. *Twenty-five minutes.* He was playing with fire, if such a thing was possible a hundred meters under the sea.

'Ok. This must be it. I think this is the captain's cabin,' said Andrew and stopped. He was standing in front of what appeared to be a closed wooden door. On closer inspection, it became clear that it was made of metal, but that it had once been laminated with thin sheets of wood, that was now slowly beginning to peel off.

'Is it locked?' asked Burke.

Andrew grabbed the handle and pushed, but the door didn't open. In fact, it didn't move at all. It was like grabbing and door handle mounted on a wall.

'Looks like the lock and the doorframe has corroded into one big piece of metal,' he Andrew.

'Andrew, you're running out of time,' said Burke. 'I think a bit of force might be called for here.'

Andrew stepped back a few steps. 'Alright. Here we go,' he said, and lifted his right leg up in front of him. Then he kicked the door right on the doorknob, and the whole thing disintegrated in front of him. He nearly lost his balance, and before he knew it, he was standing halfway inside the cabin.

'You alright?' asked Fiona. She couldn't see very much now that the water had become murky with debris and sediment being hurled around the cabin. With Andrew's flashlights shining brightly in the small compartment, it resembled driving in a snowstorm with the headlights on.

'Yes, I'm fine. Didn't realise that I was this strong,' he chuckled.

'Just don't get cocky now, ya hear?' said Burke. 'It's still dangerous down there.'

'Right,' said Andrew and started looking around. Virtually everything had decomposed, except for the metal in the bed, the sink, the chair, and what used to be a table. He walked towards the metal frame of the table and spotted a square indentation in the wall above it. He brushed aside the silt that had gathered on it, and immediately his heart started racing. 'Hey. Look at this. It's a safe.'

Fiona and Burke could just about make it out on the small screen in the wheelhouse, but both of them felt the thrill of what Andrew had found.

'Can you open it?' asked Fiona.

'I'm not going to try. It's probably airtight, so if water rushed in now, it might destroy whatever is inside.'

'Can you bring it back up?' asked Burke.

'I don't know,' said Andrew and moved in closer.

In the wheelhouse they could see his fingers moving along the edges of the safe, trying to discover a way to loosen it.

'It seems to be welded into the rest of the wall here, but if the water has done to this wall what it did to that door, then I might be able to get it out.'

'Just give it all you've got,' said Burke. 'I don't think you need to worry about the safe itself. That could probably withstand a minor explosion without receiving even a scratch.'

'Well,' said Andrew. 'It has worked once before.' He removed the remains of the table, and started kicking the wall below the safe. It was soft, but not as brittle as the door had been. After a few hard kicks, he had made a hole in the wall, but the safe was still well and truly stuck.

'I don't want to use up all my air on this,' said Andrew now out of breath, 'but I also wouldn't like to leave without this thing.'

'Just keep going, Andy,' said Fiona. 'You have about five minutes before you need to come up.'

Andrew continued to kick as forcefully as he could, but the water held on to his limbs, making it impossible to move his legs as quickly as he wanted to. After another minute, he had made a large hole in the wall below the safe, which was now just barely attached. A lot of debris was now floating in the water, and it was beginning to become difficult for Andrew to see more than just a meter ahead. But that was all he needed. He stepped forward, stuck both his arms inside the hole, and started feeling around. When he had found the back end of the safe, he repositioned his feet for better traction, gripped the safe firmly with both hands, and then exerted all his force. Every muscle in his body was strained to its limit in the pull, and when the safe suddenly came loose, it sent him flying backwards in the cabin across to the opposite wall, still holding on to the safe with both hands.

In the wheelhouse, the event looked more violent than it was, and Fiona instantly yelled at him. 'Andy. Are you ok?'

Andrew coughed a few times before answering. 'Yes, I'm fine thanks. Nice of you to ask,' he said as he slowly stumbled to his feet. 'I have the safe. Better get myself out of here before this place comes crumbling down on me.'

'Right,' said Burke. 'Better get a move on. We'll be waitin for ya.'

Andrew pulled out a bag made of a metal net that he had kept folded up in a sealed pocket in his suit. He put the shoebox-sized safe inside the net, closed the bag and attached it to his thick nylon belt. He then made his way through the murky water in the cabin and back out into the corridor. He wasn't lost, but even if he had been, he would have been able to follow the cable that ran all the way back to the ship. Within a minute he was at the hole where he had entered, and he leapt out and down onto the seabed. Then he made his way back along the hull of U-303 trying to pace himself in order not to use too much oxygen. Just then he received a warning in his earpiece, telling him that his oxygen supply was becoming critical.

'I think it's about time you hurried up,' said Burke.

'I know,' said Andrew. 'That alarm came a bit quicker than I had thought it would.'

'Ok,' said Burke calmly. 'Here's was you're going to do. You're going to surface right where you are, and we'll come and pick you up. No need to try to make it back to where you started out. Just dump your weights and come on up, alright?'

'Right,' said Andrew and immediately released the buckle that held his weight belt in place.

The belt weighed ten kilos and ensured that he achieved almost neutral buoyancy when wearing it, but still gave him enough weight to be able to walk underwater. As soon as it fell to the seabed, he started rising through the water.

'Belt released,' he announced. 'I'm coming up.'

He looked down and was treated to a bird's eye view of sorts of the whole wreck, except for what disappeared in the murky darkness. As he rose through the water, he directed his light towards the tower of the U-boat. The letters U-303 quickly faded from view, and after twenty seconds, he couldn't see the U-boat anymore. In fact, he couldn't see anything at all, except dark water all around him. If it hadn't been for the air bubbles that rose towards the surface, he would have lost his orientation in the uniform grey-blue darkness.

'My depth is now fifty meters,' he announced to the others. He was just beginning to sense light penetrating the water to where he was, when his ascent ended abruptly. It felt as if the cable was jerked violently downwards, but he quickly realised that he had simply stopped moving upwards. The cable must have got caught on something on the wreck as he started his ascent. *Fuck!*

He was suspended in the water, his positive buoyancy trying to bring him to the surface, but the cable was holding him firmly in place.

'What the hell,' he exclaimed.

Burke had started the engine of the ship, so he and Fiona didn't hear what he said at first. Fiona turned up the volume on the communications console and looked at the screen showing nothing but dark grey and blue.

'What was that, Andy?' she asked.

The communications cable was attached to a harness around Andrew's chest. The locking mechanism was directly behind his head, so that if there was ever a problem, a diver could be hoisted to the surface with his head first. Apparently, nobody had foreseen this particular event, because the positive buoyancy of Andrew's suit was causing his legs to rise, while his shoulders and chest was held in place. Within a few seconds, he was completely inverted in the water, trying to reach the locking mechanism on his back.

'Andy, are you Ok?' said a concerned Fiona.

'Not exactly,' gasped Andrew. 'My cable is stuck to something on the bottom. I can't get to the surface.'

Fiona looked up at Burke with wide terrified eyes. 'What are we going to do?'

Burke sprang over to the console. 'Can you reach the locking mechanism. It's right behind your head.'

Andrew snarled. 'I know. What do you think I'm trying to do!?'

His legs were flailing wildly and his body was spinning in the water as he desperately tried to free himself from the cable, but his own body prevented him from releasing the lock. The pull of his positive buoyancy simply kept the lock immovable. For a second, he considered using his arms to claw his way back down to where the cable was stuck, but the pull from his dry suit was too much, and he would not have the time to do it. His air supply was already so low, that he could distinctly feel the air getting thinner. He grabbed the cable and tugged violently in an attempt to pull it loose from whatever it was caught on. It was no use. Although it felt for a moment as though something snapped, he was still as stuck as a mouse in a trap.

Onboard the ship both Fiona and Burke had heard how the huffs and puffs had suddenly been replaced by utter silence.

'Andrew?' Fiona's voice revealed her terror. 'Andrew, can you hear us?' She looked at Burke. 'What happened?'

'Maybe the cable snapped,' he said in a hopeful but unconvinced voice. 'In that case, he is on his way to the surface right now.'

'And if it didn't?'

Burke suddenly flipped a switch and then leapt out of the wheelhouse. He had started to tow in the communications cable with the use of a small petrol engine under the canopy. He made it run as fast as it could, and quickly the cable rolled up onto a big spindle. After just a few seconds, the engine started straining as the cable became tighter and tighter, and then it was suddenly loose again.

Fiona stared at Burke. 'What was that?'

Burke didn't answer but continued to stand at the railing, looking at the cable coming back into the boat, as well as trying to see if Andrew might be coming up through the water. He knew that the speed with which he was pulling in the cable could cause diving sickness, also known as The Bends. But at this point, it was a risk he had to take. As far as he knew, Andrew was out of the air, and if they didn't bring him to the surface soon, he would surely die anyway.

Suddenly the end of the cable came flying over the railing, and what Burke had feared the most appeared to have happened. The spindle kept turning, flailing the end of the cable round and round until Burke killed the engine.

Fiona looked dumbfounded at Burke without a single word, but he could see tears from shock and grief beginning to form in her eyes. Burke kept looking over the side, scanning the waves for any sign of Andrew. Fiona's legs almost gave way under her. She leaned against one of the poles holding up the canopy, and slowly slid down onto the deck, where she sat motionless and ashen-faced.

Andrew knew that this was the worst moment to panic, so he let go of the lock, closed his eyes and relaxed for a few seconds, floating calmly in the water. Then he reached slowly up towards his leg and grabbed his diving knife. He gripped it firmly in his right hand and then grabbed the cable with his left. Then he started slashing at the cable, but it was slow going. The cable was reinforced with a sleeve made of flexible metal netting surrounding the communications cables, so he had to work his way through that, which wasn't an easy task hanging upside-down without being able to see what he was doing. At one point he felt the knife slip and cut into his left index finger, and that nearly caused the knife to slip out of his hands, which would almost certainly have meant his death. But he managed to hold on to it, and after a few seconds, he could feel that he was through the metal sleeve. He stuck the knife into the cable and pressed as hard as he could, and the knife went all the way through the cable. Using all his strength he then ripped the knife right through the cable, and immediately he started moving towards the surface again.

By then his air supply was virtually exhausted, and he was gasping for breath. He could see the surface approaching but didn't dare swim for fear of passing out from the lack of oxygen. He figured it would take a little more than a minute for him to reach the surface. As he rose through the water it seemed to him like an hour passed, and when he finally broke the surface, he instantly tore off his helmet and was greeted by the richest most invigorating mouthful of air he had ever experienced. Almost immediately, he could feel the oxygen being pumped around in his body again, and his senses coming back after having been dazed on the way up. He didn't have the strength to wave or shout, so he just lay there in the water with his eyes closed, feeling very lucky to be alive.

Burke spotted him almost as soon as he appeared some fifty meters away. He threw up his arm and pointed.

'There he is,' he shouted and ran into the wheelhouse and started to turn the ship to go and pick Andrew from the water.

Fiona leapt to her feet and looked out towards the spot Burke had pointed to. And sure enough, there was Andrew bobbing in the waves in his yellow dry suit. A few minutes later they passed close to him, and then hauled him aboard and helped him out of his suit. The safe was still attached to his belt. He produced an exhausted smile.

'I scared you there, didn't I?' he grinned and then started coughing.

'Don't you do that again, you bastard,' said Fiona and laughed reluctantly. 'Do you realise how frightened I was?'

'Yes. I must say I wasn't too happy about it myself.'

'What happened?' asked Burke.

'I don't know. I think the cable got stuck, so I had to cut it loose. That took me a while, and I think I accidentally sliced my finger as well,' he said and held forward his left hand. It was bleeding heavily and dripping onto the deck, but Andrew just calmly held it up high and looked at Burke. 'Do you have a first aid kit here? I think I might need a bandage.'

'Sure thing, Son,' said Burke and hurried below to the living quarters for some bandages and a bottle of vodka.

'Are you Ok?' asked Fiona. 'Apart from that thing,' she said and pointed to his bloody hand.

'I'm fine,' he said calmly. 'I've done this lots of times before,' he grinned.

Burke returned with the bandage, and ten minutes later they were all sitting in the living quarters, drinking hot tea and a glass of vodka. In front of them on the table was the safe. It was almost black due to decades of corrosion, and water still trickled from its sides. Its front was inset a couple of centimetres from the edges of the box, and on it was a small wheel, which with the proper combination would have opened the safe some fifty years ago. But now it was as good as welded shut by the corrosion.

'Do you reckon it has held the sea out for all those years?' said Burke to no one in particular.

Andrew tapped its top with his diving knife. It sounded hollow, but the steel plates were still hard and appeared undamaged by the seawater. 'I think that there has never been anything but air in there,' he said. 'But we need to wait until we get back to Madalena before we can open it.'

'What about the police?' asked Fiona.

The two men looked at each other.

'The police?' asked Andrew. 'What about them? We are not going to show them this, that I can tell you right now.'

'But isn't it Portuguese state property? I mean, it was recovered in their territorial waters.'

'That may be so, but couldn't you also argue that it is German property? After all, it was their U-boat. Or what about English property? We were probably the ones to sink her, so it might as well be considered war booty. And in addition, I'm not sure Colonel Strickland would appreciate us flying out here risking life and limb, and then handing over what we found to a bunch of coppers who probably don't care about it anyway.'

Fiona nodded. 'Right. I see your point. Let's just bring it back with us and open it ourselves. Now that we didn't find anything in the cargo hold, this is the best we have.'

Three hours later they were on their way back into the Harbour at Madalena. Andrew had taken the opportunity to explain to Burke in more detail precisely what was going on, but had subsequently asked him to keep it to himself for now. Burke had agreed, and it seemed to Andrew that he was a man he could trust.

After mooring the ship by the dock, they disembarked and shook hands. They were all content that they hadn't had to stay out for more than just that one day. The winds were picking up again, and clouds were gathering in the distance towards the west. It looked like a storm might be brewing, so they decided to go their separate ways for the day. Burke needed to ready the ship for another whale watching trip, and he also had to find a way to change the broken cable, which Andrew had already offered to pay for. Andrew and Fiona would go to a shop to buy some tools, and then head back to the hotel, and try to open the safe somehow.

The man had watched as the whale watching ship had entered the harbour at Madalena, and now he stood next to his car pretending to look at a tourist map. If the trio had been any closer, they might have noticed that the map he was holding was a map of the south of France. The man was tall and thin and had short blond hair. He was wearing dark trousers, a thick white sweater and a short black leather jacket to match his sunglasses. Even though he was standing just twenty meters away, he could not hear what they were saying, because of the noise from the ferry from Faial that was just in the process of offloading passengers.

He watched silently out of the corner of his eye, as they shook hands and said goodbye to each other. Then he got into a dark blue BMW with tinted windows and drove slowly after Andrew and Fiona as they left the harbour to find a shop that stocked an assortment of tools. As they got into a taxi and headed for their hotel, he followed at a distance. When they eventually stopped in front of the reception building and got out, he continued driving past without looking directly at them. He continued on for a few hundred meters and then pulled over by the side of the road, where he fetched his mobile phone from his inside pocket and speed-dialled a number in Austria.

NINE

The truck was a former military transport vehicle, and as it drove quickly along the hot desert road, plumes of dust whirled up behind it. The sun was now so low in the sky that the driver could see the shadow of the dust being cast ahead of him on the ground. Having the sun behind him made traversing the plateau much easier, as he was able to see more clearly where he was going. He and the other passengers were regularly lifted off their seats and jerked from side to side because of the poor condition of the road. It had actually stopped qualifying as a road after they passed through the last village on their way. That was over an hour ago, and since then they had seen no people or buildings or anything else indicating the presence of humans nearby. The landscape was dotted with small mountains and hills and the uniformity of its colours of beige, brown and yellow made it very difficult to assess distances.

There were two men seated in the front and two in the back of the truck, which was just as dirty and dusty on the inside as on the outside. The younger man sat in the passenger seat, looking at a map that had been handed to him just before they had departed from Al Raqqa. He was astonished by the change in the nature of the landscape as they had headed south through the countryside. As the place from which the Euphrates River sprang before making its way east through Syria and into Iraq, Al Raqqa was relatively fertile. Its suburbs were surrounded by fields and plantations, that generated exports mainly to countries in Europe. But just half an hour after leaving the city, they had reached the desert. It wasn't what most people thought of as a desert. It wasn't a sea of sand dunes, but rather a seemingly endless arid mountainous and above all dry landscape. It was infertile, and sandstorms were frequent, making it difficult even for the nomads to exist out here. The men had enough food to last them a couple of days should they get lost. Roads were often of a temporary nature in these parts, and a few times in the past, people had simply vanished in sandstorms that could rise up quite unpredictably from the desert plains in just a few minutes, enveloping anyone unfortunate enough to be travelling there. As a result, hardly anyone ever ventured into the desert without a very good reason, and these men had one.

The driver had his gaze fixed on the tracks in front of him, the two men in the front had not spoken since they left Al Raqqa. The road could be tricky, and getting lost or perhaps even damaging the cargo would be a serious problem, and they both knew that. The two men in the back did not know what they were carrying, and it was better that way. There simply wasn't any need for them to know, but perhaps more importantly, knowing might very well have made them nervous and unnecessarily clumsy.

The truck carrying the precious cargo was coming to the end of a four-hour-long journey. Following the rough tracks, the truck entered down into a long valley, where they spotted the steep cliff face to their left that was their destination. The cliff was about eighty meters tall, almost vertical and made of solid brown rock with a reddish hue that was amplified by the setting sun. A crevasse ran into the side of the cliff, and at its base, it expanded to an opening large enough to comfortably allow a truck or perhaps even a tank to enter. There was usually nothing outside the cave entrance to reveal its presence to prying eyes that they knew would be passing overhead from time to time.

The approaching truck had been observed by a guard from the top of one of the sides of the valley for more than ten minutes. That explained why there was a handful of guerrilla fighters dressed in light brown shabby clothes and armed with AK47s now waiting at the entrance to the crevasse.

As the truck approached and slowed down slightly, the driver flashed his headlights a few times and stuck his arm out of the window, waving. The soldiers then slung their weapons on their backs and stepped aside to let the truck roll into the crevasse where the Alchemist and his carefully assembled team would be arriving soon for the first phase of the project. They immediately followed the truck into the cave system, and within seconds the valley was deserted, only a little dust still drifting in the dry air revealing that anyone had been there a few moments earlier.

★ ★ ★

That evening Fiona and Andrew met in Andrew's room a couple of hours after dinner. Andrew had drawn the curtains of the windows facing towards the street, as the rooms were almost at street level. He had laid a towel out over a table and put the safe there along with an array of tools he thought they might need.

He was bending over, looking at the combination lock's wheel when Fiona suddenly entered the room. He snapped to attention and spun round to face her. 'Can't you knock?'

She looked at him and smiled. 'Can't you just lock your door? Are you ready?'

Andrew's shoulders dropped as he relaxed once again. 'Ready as can be. My main concern is making too much noise.'

She looked around his room. 'We could always put on some music or turn on the TV really loudly. But then people would probably just think we were shagging, and we wouldn't want that now would we,' she said with a teasing smile.

Completely caught out by her remark, Andrew did his best to laugh casually. The thought had crossed his mind several times in the past few days, but this was probably the worst possible time for him to get distracted by that. He cleared his throat and pointed to the safe on the table. 'I've thought about trying to drill out the combination lock. What do you think?'

She came over and stood next to him, and Andrew had to make an effort not to be distracted by her hair hanging down over her shoulder, as she leaned over the table in front of him.

'I'm not sure,' she said pensively. 'Don't you think the corrosion has welded the door to the rest of the box after all this time?'

'Yes. I did consider that. Maybe we should just go for brute force from the beginning, and start sawing through it.'

'That's probably the best way to go about it,' she replied and stood up again. 'But let's do that at one end, instead of cutting it in half. Less risk of damage to the content.'

With that, she picked up the safe, and shifted it slightly in her hands. 'Probably weighs about five kilos,' she said and then held it to one ear and shook it lightly. 'I can't hear anything moving, can you?'

Andrew took it and tilted it gently from one side to the other whilst listening. 'No, maybe it is empty.'

'Why would the captain of a U-boat have a private safe, and then not have kept anything in it?' asked Fiona.

'Maybe he emptied it before the U-boat went down.'

'If he did, why would he lock it before leaving his cabin?'

'Good point,' smiled Andrew and looked at her. 'I guess there's nothing else to do but to get cracking, so to speak.'

He picked up a small saw with a hardened steel blade and placed it near one end of the safe. 'Ready?'

'Go ahead,' she said, and sat down on a chair to watch as Andrew started sawing away at the steel box.

The outer layer of the safe was still hard, but softer than the day the safe was shipped from the factory. After half a centimetre, the saw met with the parts of the safe that had not been affected by the seawater in any way. It was hard as glass, and the saw began making a screeching noise. After thirty seconds, the noise had become so loud that they were both uncomfortable with it. Andrew looked up at Fiona.

'Now would be a good time for a little distraction,' he smiled, as small beads of sweat were beginning to form on his forehead.

Fiona walked over to the TV and switched it on. She quickly found a channel playing music videos, and turned up the volume to maximum. 'I feel like a teenager again,' she shouted through the noise and began laughing.

Andrew smiled, shook his head, and then resumed his work. The saw was about one-quarter of the way through, and it was obvious now that there was no water in the safe, so there probably never had been. Fiona stood next to Andrew and asked, 'Do you want me to take over?'

'No thanks,' said Andrew and continued. 'I think I'll be all the way through in a second.' He was looking intently down along the narrow slit that had formed from the top of one end of the safe, down to where the blade was slowly working its way through the steel sides.

After another minute, he stopped and slowly pulled the blade out from the slit. He had cut almost all the way through, and so he moved the safe to the edge of the table. Here he gripped the end of the steel box, and then simply broke off the end that had been almost completely severed.

'Anything?' asked Fiona.

Andrew stood up, turned the safe over and looked down into it. The inside of the box was a dark shade of brown. The safe might have been airtight, but condensation had caused a thin layer of rust to develop inside it. It had two small compartments separated by a metal shelf. In the top compartment was a small wooden box about the size of a cigar case, and a thick brown envelope. The wooden box had been jammed in on top of the envelope, which explained why Fiona hadn't heard anything when she shook the safe. In the bottom compartment was another smaller envelope, which Andrew reached for. He held it in his hands and turned it over a few times as if to try to gauge what was inside it.

'It is a letter addressed to a Kommandant Kaufmann. Might have been the captain's name.'

'Well, come on. Open it!' said Fiona impatiently. She was the historian and archaeologist of the two, and if it wasn't because it was Andrew who had invited her to join him on this trip, she would probably have grabbed the letter from his hand and ripped it open.

Andrew took out a large hunting knife from his suitcase, and carefully slit the envelope open. Inside was a single piece of paper folded once with the writing on the inside. He unfolded it and turned so that Fiona could see it as well.

'Do you speak German?' he asked and looked up and down the letter, which was in a remarkably good condition.

Fiona gently took the letter and put it down on the table next to the safe. Studying the files from the National Archive in Berlin a few years back, she had accumulated a good knowledge of the German language, and so she started reading the letter out loud.

'The letter is dated on October 2. 1944,' she said. 'It is addressed to a Kommandant Kaufmann.'

'Read it,' said Andrew curiously.

'Ok. To Kommandant Kaufmann,' she began.

These orders from the High Command of the Third Reich, are to be carried out by U-303 and her crew at all cost. You should now be at sea and therefore ready to have your orders revealed to you. U-303 has been chosen for an important mission for our Fatherland. As you were informed two days ago, a crate containing a very important cargo must be transported out of Germany immediately. The crate has now been placed in your cargo hold, where it will remain undisturbed until you reach your destination of Montevideo in Argentina. Upon reaching the harbour, you will be contacted by a unit of the SS, who are waiting for your arrival at this very moment. They will unload the crate, and transport it to its final destination.

The crate contains a set of four glass cylinders, in which are stored the last samples of a bacterium recently uncovered by the SS-Ahnenerbe. The pathogen has already been proven extremely deadly. It is vital that these microorganisms are contained inside the cylinders. If they are let loose inside

YOUR U-BOAT, YOU AND YOUR CREW WILL SUCCUMB TO IT WITHIN HOURS. THERE IS NO CURE.

YOU WILL DELIVER THE SAMPLES TO YOUR DESTINATION, FROM WHICH THEY WILL BE BROUGHT ON TO A MASS PRODUCTION PLANT, WHERE THE BACTERIA WILL BE WEAPONISED. THIS WILL ALMOST CERTAINLY WIN THE WAR FOR OUR FATHERLAND.

SINCE THIS IS A MATTER OF THE UTMOST IMPORTANCE FOR OUR COUNTRY, IT HAS BEEN DECIDED THAT YOU SHOULD BE INFORMED OF THE NATURE OF YOUR CARGO, SO THAT YOU MAY BETTER APPRECIATE HOW VITAL IT IS THAT IT REACHES ITS DESTINATION. UPON YOUR SUCCESSFUL COMPLETION OF THIS MISSION, YOU CAN EXPECT A POSITION OF HONOUR AND ENLIGHTENMENT IN THE BROTHERHOOD.

YOU MUST NOT FAIL. THE FUTURE OF THE REICH DEPENDS ON YOU. CREW EXPENDABLE.

Adolf Hitler

'Adolph Hitler?' exclaimed Andrew and grabbed the letter. The signature was smeared as if it had been written in a hurry, but there was no reason to believe that it was not genuine. 'Christ. Are you trying to tell me that almost seventy years ago, THE Adolf Hitler held this piece of paper in his hand?'

Fiona nodded slowly. 'That's how it appears. It has got to be real. Why else would it be lying in this box that has clearly not been opened since 1944?'

Fiona fell silent for a few seconds. 'You were in there, you know,' she finally said with a worried expression on her face.

'Where? The cargo hold?'

'Yes. Whoever was there before you, smashed the crate to get those glass cylinders out. What if they damaged one of them in the process? Then that stuff could have been floating in the water.'

'Look, Fiona. I don't think you need to worry about that.'

'Why not?'

'The crate might just have fallen in on itself after all that time in the water. They may very well have been able to just pick up the cylinders from the floor. And even if they did break one, I'm not too worried.'

'So, you think that those bacteria were dead? Then why would someone go down there now to get them?'

'I'm not saying that they were necessarily dead, or even that they didn't botch the whole thing and break a cylinder. But if bacteria were actually in the water and I came in to contact with them, then I would probably be dead by now. But since I'm not, I evidently didn't.'

'You sure?'

'Quite sure. But on the subject of whether the bacteria were dead, you're most likely right. I think that they are probably still very much alive.'

'After all those years?' said Fiona sceptically.

'Yes. A few years back, a group of scientists revived a colony of bacteria that had effectively been in hibernation for some 250 million years, just waiting for the right conditions to come along. They can be tough little buggers.'

'And these particular ones sound very nasty indeed,' said Fiona and picked up the letter again.

Still feeling stunned by having held a piece of paper with direct orders from Adolf Hitler, Andrew had almost forgotten the other items in the safe.

'Let's see what else we have here,' he said and reached into the top compartment of the safe. He carefully took out the wooden box, and the thick brown envelope.

'More letters perhaps?' he said.

'Maybe personal stuff. Open the box first.'

Andrew put down the brown envelope and turned the box over to have a look at it. It appeared handmade from a maroon type of wood that was very hard and cold to the touch. It had a shiny surface, and on its front was a small latch that held the lid down. Andrew gently pushed the latch from its hinge and opened the lid. The inside was covered with soft blue velvet, and in a neatly shaped indentation lay what at first appeared to be a medallion. It was made of a shiny metal with an engraved image, and it gleamed under the lights in the hotel room. A rectangular shape, it depicted a short stubby sword standing on its tip, with a couple of vines twisting around it. In the background was an unusually shaped swastika, with its ends curved around the centre, and what appeared to be rays of light coming out in all directions.

'What's this?' he said.

'Some kind of military medal? Like the Victoria Cross or something?'

'No. This is not military,' he said and picked it up.

'Wait a minute,' said Fiona suddenly. 'I've seen that before. It looks like the insignia that was on several of the documents I've read about the Thule Society. Yes, I'll bet a month's salary that this is that same insignia.'

'So, this captain Kaufmann was a member of the Thule Society?' asked Andrew and looked at Fiona suspiciously.

'He must have been. And look,' she said and picked up the letter again. 'There was a mention of a brotherhood here. What else could it be?'

Andrew nodded. 'You may be right. And if you are, then Captain Kaufmann was a member of the Thule Society along with Adolf himself. It probably wasn't a coincidence that they chose him for this mission. He was someone they could trust.'

'A true believer?'

'Yes. Something along those lines.'

★ ★ ★

While Andrew and Fiona were examining the safe in Andrew's hotel room, the tall man with the short blond hair and the black leather jacket was walking casually along the pier towards Roger Burke's boat. The sun had disappeared under the horizon a couple of hours earlier, and the dense cloud layer shut out any remaining light from the sky. There were a few lights scattered around the harbour area, but there were none where Burke's boat was moored. The man walked slowly towards the boat, trying to see if anyone was inside. There were no lights inside the boat either, and it looked completely deserted as it lay there bobbing in the water next to the pier.

Walking past the boat he glanced first into the wheelhouse and then through the small windows in the hull, where he could see the living quarters. There was no sign of anyone being present. He continued on and stopped fifty meters away at the end of the pier, lighting a cigarette and watching the harbour area. The only movement he could detect was a group of drunken teenagers, most likely tourists, that sat on top of a pair of garbage dumpsters where a narrow street led back to the town square. They were about one hundred meters from where he was, joking and making a lot of noise, which suited him just fine. Less attention on him.

After finishing his cigarette, he placed it between two fingers and shot it into the water below. Then he started walking back towards the boat. About three meters before he reached it, he started into a slow run and as he reached the boat he speeded up and made a running jump across the gap between the pier and the railing, and landed with both feet on the deck. His boots hit the front of the deck with a thumb. He knelt down and sat completely still for a few seconds, listening for any movement. If someone had been inside the boat, they would certainly have heard him by now. Having assured himself that all was quiet, he lifted his head and looked towards the youths on the dumpsters. A scuffle was breaking out among them, so no one had noticed anything.

Crouching, he moved slowly towards the wheelhouse and quickly slipped inside. He sat there for a few seconds to let his eyes get accustomed to the darkness. Then he rose and moved silently towards the communications console that had been transmitting those remarkable images earlier that day. He searched for the video recorder and quickly found it, and when he pressed the Eject button, a small disc appeared. He took it out and placed it on the console, then he turned his attention to the small door that led to the living quarters. It was a low double door, with a small padlock. He took out a pair of pliers from a bag and placed the beak around the lock. He was just about to squeeze hard on the handles when he heard voices outside on the pier. A young couple was walking slowly along the pier, talking softly to each other.

He waited until they had passed, and then squeezed the lock with all his strength. It crumpled silently, and he was now able to gently remove it from the door, which he then slowly opened. Down a few steps, he found a room with five beds and a table with seating for at least ten more. To his right was a tiny kitchen, and to his left an even smaller lavatory. He walked slowly forward, his eyes scanning for anything of interest. On the table was a map of the Azores. Next to that was another more detailed map of the island of Pico. A small 'X' had been drawn on the map. The man looked at it for a moment and then decided to take the map with him. He folded the map up and put it in the inside pocket of his jacket.

Just then, he heard someone jumping onto the boat. It shifted a little bit in the water as the person landed and started walking towards the wheelhouse. Suddenly feeling trapped, the man-made his way as quickly and as silently as he could towards the door and climbed up the steps to the wheelhouse, where he, still crouching, reached up and grabbed the disc with the recording.

Burke had the disadvantage of just having sat in a brightly lit bar, drinking a couple of beers. His eyes had not yet adjusted themselves to the darkness in the wheelhouse, and his left hand fumbled for the light switch on the wall next to the door. To Burke, the wheelhouse seemed pitch black, but the tall blond man could clearly recognise Burke's strong build as he stood there in a silhouette against the slightly brighter exterior. Burke finally found the switch and flicked it.

Knowing that it was now or never, the blond man launched himself directly at Burke's body and hit him with his shoulder in the abdomen. Burke, utterly unprepared for the attack, fell backwards gasping for air. The assailant dropped something that sounded like it was made of plastic, and then stumbled frantically to his feet.

'What the fuck!?' shouted Burke which seemingly scared the other man, who leapt clumsily onto the pier but fell again.

This gave the whale watching captain time to get back on his feet and jump after him. Burke, who had once been a line-backer on the Navy football team, threw himself vertically through the air and grabbed the man around his legs. The man fell over yet again, and the two of them rolled over a few times. The man kicked at Burke, attempting to free himself from his iron grip.

Unfortunately, at that moment the young man who had passed by the ship earlier with his girlfriend decided to play the hero. Hearing the commotion, he had turned and spotted the scuffle. He started running towards the two men who looked as if they had taken their bar brawl out into the streets. When he was just a few meters away, he started yelling something in French, which made Burke think that he now had more than one opponent. He turned his head to look at the new potential threat, and just then the blond man succeeded in planting his right boot squarely in Burke's face, breaking his nose and instantly causing him to let go of the man's legs.

Blood gushed out of Burke's nose as the man jumped to his feet, and started running away as fast as he could, with the cassette under his arm. The young man looked at Burke, clearly stunned and unable to decide whether to chase to other man or not. A few seconds later the burglar disappeared down a small street, and so the young man walked hesitantly towards Burke who was holding his nose with his right hand, blood running down his forearm.

'What are you looking at?' bellowed Burke. He had never considered himself an especially attractive man, but he had always been quite fond of his nose.

The young man walked backwards a couple of steps, hesitated and then turned to walk back to his girlfriend. Burke staggered to his feet and started walking back towards his boat, cursing and swearing at the coward who had inflicted this pain in his face. The stream of blood soon abated, but now he could feel swelling around his left eye as well. 'Fuckin' yellow chicken shit bastard,' he mumbled as he entered the wheelhouse.

Nothing was damaged or missing as far as he could see. Then he spotted the open doors to the living quarters. 'Arhg, Crap!' he exclaimed, diving into the first aid kit in search of some bandages to soak up the blood that was still trickling out.

He cautiously descended into the belly of his boat and switched on the lights. He went over every detail in the room looking for clues but found none. Then he remembered the sound of something made of plastic hitting the floor just when his attacker had barged into him. That could only mean one thing. He walked back up to the wheelhouse and looked down at the communications console.

'Shit,' he mumbled. 'Someone's definitely gonna be real unhappy about this.'

He got back out onto the deck and jumped back onto the pier. It was time to go to the hospital, which lay just a few hundred meters from the town square.

★ ★ ★

Back in the hotel room, Fiona picked up the thick brown envelope and opened it. Inside it was a stack of documents and a few black and white photographs. The black colour was seriously faded and looked as if it had been bleached, but it was still possible to make out a group of people huddled together on a lawn in front of a big white house. The group comprised young as well as old people all smiling, some of them raising their champagne glasses to salute the photographer.

'This must have been his family,' said Andrew. 'I wonder what happened to them after the war. They probably never knew that Kaufmann was leaving.'

'They definitely never heard from him again,' replied Fiona.

'His children must still be alive today. What if we could track them down?'

'What good would that do? I'm convinced that this chap never talked to anyone about his work, and if he really was a member of the Thule Society, I'm pretty sure that he would never discuss that with any outsiders either. Not even his wife.'

'Unless she was in there too,' said Andrew and smiled cunningly.

'Right,' said Fiona. 'We can't rule that out, let's just stick to what we think we know, shall we?'

She took out another picture. 'These people definitely weren't family,' she said and showed it to Andrew.

It was a photograph taken in what appeared to be a mountainous landscape. A circle had been drawn around one of the people standing at the back of a group. They were all wearing black SS uniforms, and in the background, a flag billowed in the wind. It was obvious that the photographer had waited until the right moment when the flag had been fully unfurled by a gust of wind so that he could see the whole thing. The flag was completely black, with a large white circle in the middle. Inside the circle was the same insignia that was lying in the wooden box next to Andrew.

'I think we have here the Thule Society out on a merry camping trip in the German alps,' he said. 'They sure look to be in good spirits. Maybe they've just been initiated or something.'

'No. I don't think so. Such things usually happen in dark candlelit dungeons under castles, during much chanting and reading aloud from old texts,' she said, trying to sound conspiratorial.

'Regardless of the occasion,' said Andrew, 'don't you think that these characters could be the people you told me about on the plane?'

'They might be,' replied Fiona.

'Let's see what else is in here,' said Andrew and emptied the content of the envelope onto the table next to the safe. A smaller envelope fell out. Fiona picked it up and swiftly opened it. 'Here's something interesting. It seems to be some sort of identification certificate.'

'Certifying his Aryan ancestry, no doubt?' Andrew chuckled.

'Well. You're actually not too far off. This document attests that Kaufmann was a so-called '*mitgleich das Thule Gesellschaft*'. A member of the Thule Society - Vienna district. Vienna?' she said and looked at Andrew sceptically. 'That's in Austria. Do you suppose he was Austrian by birth?'

'Could well be. Many Austrians joined the German army during the Second World War. After all, they are more or less one people. At least that's how many of them felt back in the 1930s.'

'Look here,' she said and pointed to the top corner of the document. 'There's even an address here at the top. That's a bit unusual for a secret society, isn't it?'

'Well, the Pentagon is a sort of secret society too, but even a rice farmer in Nepal could tell you where it is. What is the address?'

'Somewhere in Vienna. 15 Waldhoff Strasse.'

'We'll check out what is there when we get back. Probably a cheap hotel or a massage parlour.'

'The certificate is dated the 26th of May 1943. His membership number was 293.'

'An exclusive bunch, assuming he was one of the last members to be initiated.'

'Well. If you've found the mystical origins of your race, and untold powers await you, I guess you don't start running about town telling anyone and everyone,' said Fiona as her eyes scanned the document. 'His title or rank was that of Peon.'

'So, this chap was just a small fish, then.'

'Yes, but when called upon, this little fish did his duty, by the looks of things.'

'And he died in the process.'

'I guess so,' she said and sat down on the bed with the wooden box. 'So, when the Thule Society had got their hands on a nasty little bacterium and was in need of someone to transport it out of Germany, they called on Kaufmann. I bet he would never have been told of the cargo if it weren't because he just happened to be a U-bout commander. I doubt that all the members of the Thule Society knew everything about everything.'

'Probably not. Those appear to have been some very clandestine activities. Do you suppose that they actually did get their hands on such a deadly pathogen?'

'I don't think there's any reason to doubt it,' said Fiona pensively. 'So where does that leave us?'

'Well, you know what this means, don't you?' asked Andrew.

Fiona shifted her dark eyes from the shining insignia to Andrew. 'What it means?'

'Yes. It means that someone has just taken possession of a deadly pathogen, and you don't do that unless you are going to use it. And by that, I mean using it on other people.'

'Right,' mumbled Fiona. Ten minutes ago, she had only been excited about uncovering what was effectively the content of a fascinating time capsule. Now it began to sink in that this was serious. If the letter in the safe was genuine, and the content of the cylinders taken from the U-boat's cargo hold contained what the letter said they did, then something terrible was going to happen, sooner or later.

'We have to try to find them,' she said and looked intently at Andrew. 'We just have to. If this is something really deadly, we are the only people who know about it, except for the people who took it, and they are probably not going to warn anyone in advance.'

Andrew nodded pensively. 'You are right. This is no game. We also have to report back to Strickland as soon as possible.'

'Are you sure that is a good idea?'

Andrew looked up at her. 'What exactly do you mean?'

'Well, this could be a really big thing. How do we know who we can trust?'

Andrew looked incredulously at Fiona. 'Look. We can trust Strickland. He has saved my arse on several occasions, and I trust him completely. Let's not get all paranoid now, ok?'

'Ok,' Fiona nodded. 'I'm just saying, we have to be careful who we bring into this. And I definitely wouldn't like telling anyone before we are back in London.'

'You think we should bring all this with us?' asked Andrew and pointed to the items on the table.

'Sure. Just stuff it in a suitcase. No one will ask.'

Andrew thought about it for a second and then agreed. 'Fair enough. What do you say we try to get back tomorrow? I'll call Cathy first thing in the morning, and ask her to book some seats.'

'Great. I want to get back to the British Museum and search our international database. There's got to be more on this Thule Society, and I think I'll try to dig up something on Argentina as well.'

'Good idea. I'd like to talk this over with Colonel Strickland.'

'Ok. Let's get some sleep. My brain is exhausted,' she smiled.

They wrapped the safe in a towel and put it in Andrew's suitcase. He put the rest of the items in a side pocket of his hand luggage. He wanted the insignia and the documents where he could see them at all times. Including while he was on the plane.

★ ★ ★

They managed to get seats for the afternoon departure for Lisbon the next day, so Andrew and Fiona took the opportunity to go down to the harbour and say goodbye to Burke. He was standing in the bow of the boat with his back turned, so they didn't notice the bandage that covered most of his face until they were close enough for him to hear them. When he turned around, he startled both of them.

'What on Earth happened to you!?' asked Fiona concerned.

'No money for the bar bill?' attempted Andrew.

Burke jumped adroitly to the pier and strolled towards them with his hands in his pockets. 'Nah. Some asshole decided to rob my damn boat last night,' he said angrily.

'What? Who?' asked Fiona.

'Dunno,' said Burke and shook his head. 'Some blond guy. Tall and skinny. I tackled him right here where we're standing, but the bastard kicked me in the face and performed this little piece of surgery,' he said and pointed to his nose.

'Are you alright?'

'Yeah, sure. I'm fine. My nose is broken, but it'll be alright in a couple of weeks, they tell me. But the dude stole the recording.'

'Our recording?' asked Andrew.

'Yeah. The recording I made yesterday when you were down there playing 'Twenty Thousand Leagues Under the Sea', remember?'

'Oh, shit!' exclaimed Andrew. 'This could be a problem.'

'I didn't notice it at first, but after having recovered for a couple of minutes, I remembered the guy was carrying something when he ran, and that I had heard something hit the floor when he came at me. That must have been the disc. As far as I can tell, that thing was the only thing the guy decided to grab, so you almost get the feeling he knew what he was lookin for.'

Andrew looked at Burke, pondering how serious this might be.

'Did the console record both image and sound?'

'Yeah, of course,' answered Burke. 'You don't like people hearin what went on?'

'No,' said Andrew bitterly, cursing himself for not thinking about securing the recording immediately after they came into Madalena harbour. 'If they had just seen the images, the damage hadn't been that great, but I'm pretty sure that anyone seeing and listening to the recording, can sense that I was looking for something specific. And my little performance in the captain's cabin is a dead give-away.'

'Andrew, what if it's just a simple burglary?' asked Fiona. 'He'll never be able to use it for anything.'

'Fiona,' said a frustrated Andrew. 'A five-year-old child would be able to put two and two together here and see that we were looking for something very specific, and that there were others before us down there looking for the same thing. And what's even more, we've been looking into this damn thing for just over a week now, and I'm already faced with two burglaries. Do you really think that this third one is a coincidence?'

She looked at him calmly. She was a bit surprised at Andrew's outburst, which she thought was over the top. 'Look, Andrew,' she said sternly. 'I understand that this is stressful for you, just as it is for me, but there's no need to be rude. That's not very helpful to any of us.'

Knowing instantly that he had stepped over the line, Andrew was already chastising himself. 'Right,' he said bowing his head and holding up his hand as if to defend himself. 'I know. I apologise,' he sighed. 'That was uncalled for. I'm sorry.'

Burke intervened. 'Look kids,' he said calmly and put a hand of each of their shoulders. 'This here bickerin ain't gonna get you guys anywhere. And it sure's hell ain't something I wanna spend my day listening to, so if you're dead set on killing each other, could ya please go and do it someplace else?' he said, looking angry at first, until a disarming smiled appeared.

Both Andrew and Fiona looked up at the big man and felt immensely foolish. Without a word they just exchanged looks that conveyed their embarrassments, as well as their apologies.

'Right,' said Andrew. 'Where does this leave us?'

'Yes, let's try to think calmly about this,' said Fiona, eager to get on with things.

'I'm not sure,' replied Andrew. 'Except that someone knows we are here, and if they didn't already know what we were looking for, they are bound to know by now.'

'And that makes me very bloody uncomfortable, regardless of what they want,' said Fiona and looked nervously at Andrew. 'I thought we were the ones chasing them. Not the other way round?'

'We don't know for sure that they are the same people yet, do we?'

'No, but that would be obvious, wouldn't it? Somehow, they know that we are on to them, and now they are trying to prevent us from finding out what they are up to.'

Fiona looked from Andrew to Burke and back again, clearly not happy with the sudden turn of events.

'Well, I can't come up with anything more plausible than that,' said Andrew. 'I guess we will have to stay more vigilant from now on. Did you get a look at his face?' he asked and looked at Burke.

'No. The only thing that really left an impression on me was his right boot,' he grinned and pointed to his face. 'A size nine, I think.'

Fiona looked distinctly unconvinced that staying vigilant would be sufficient, but she couldn't think of anything more to say. There was nothing more they could accomplish here.

'You guys best be goin right about now if you're gonna catch that plane,' said Burke and looked at his wristwatch.

'You're right,' said Andrew. 'We had better be on our way. The plane leaves in just over one hour.' He looked at Burke and offered him his hand. 'Roger. I'm sorry we have to leave you looking like this,' he grinned, 'but we have to get back. I hope to see you again someday.'

'Likewise,' smiled Burke through the bandages.

'Take care,' said Fiona and gave him a cautious hug. 'And maybe it would be best if you just stick to whale watching in the future. I feel terrible about having placed you in this position.'

'Don't worry,' said Burke with a broad smile. 'I'll just send a nice big bill to Andrew's office. That'll take care of it.'

'Promise me that you won't talk to anyone about this, and that you'll give me a call if anything else out of the ordinary happens here, ok?' said Andrew.

'I will. You have my word,' said Burke and squeezed Andrew's hand.

★ ★ ★

Two hours later they were sitting on the plane with a drink and a couple of appetisers, heading for Lisbon. It would be another six hours before they were back at Heathrow, and an additional hour before they were all the way home, so they tried to make the best of it and relax as much as they could.

Andrew sighed and looked at Fiona. 'You know. In a way, I'm happy that the people who raided the U-boat were looking for something as down-to-earth as a bug, and not some supernatural weapon from ancient times.'

'Might be a really nasty bug, though,' said Fiona.

'Yes, that's how it sounds. I wish we could get a hold of a sample to study. I like knowing exactly what I am dealing with.'

'And I'd like to know where it came from.'

'It must have been something the Germans brought back from one of the expeditions. Otherwise, it wouldn't have been brought to the warehouse where Friedrich Henke worked.'

'Yes, but which expedition? And where to?'

'Good question. I think I'm going to fly over to Vienna and investigate the address that was mentioned in that certificate in Captain Kaufmann's safe.'

Fiona looked at him and shook her head. 'Christ, Andrew. Don't you ever get tired?'

'Yes. But I'm too curious to stay at home.'

'I honestly don't think you will find anything. It might just have been a private meeting place, and even if it wasn't, why would there be anything left now?'

'It's all we have right now. And there's no harm in trying.'

'Well. You'll have to do that by yourself. I'm going back to the Museum to dig some more.'

'That's ok. You were beginning to annoy me anyway,' lied Andrew and winked.

Fiona just laughed, leaned back in her seat and closed her eyes. 'Oh no, Mr. Sterling. You fancy me. I can tell.'

'Oh, can you now?' he asked unconvinced.

'Yup. I'm always right about these things,' she said confidently and smiled, still with her eyes closed. 'Good thing I don't find you totally repulsive.'

Unsure about how badly she was pulling his leg, Andrew just grunted and took out a newspaper and started reading. 'Oh shit,' he exclaimed causing a few of the other passengers to glance in his direction

'What is it?' asked Fiona and looked at him, puzzled.

'Chelsea lost this weekend.'

★ ★ ★

It was a quarter to eleven by the time their plane touched down at Heathrow airport. They were both tired, and they hardly spoke on their way through customs or as they sat in the shuttle speeding towards Paddington Station. To the other travellers, they probably looked like a young couple whose holiday had gone horribly wrong and ended in tears. As they said goodbye outside Paddington Station, Fiona took a step forward and quickly stole a hug before Andrew even had time to be surprised.

'I'm glad you decided to come back up to the surface after your little leisure dive,' she said and smiled sheepishly.

'Thanks. I appreciate that,' said Andrew, and then he took the opportunity to get even. 'You fancy me,' he chuckled. 'I'm never wrong about these things.'

Fiona wasn't in the mood for jokes. 'Shut up, Silly. That was really serious. You could easily have been killed.'

'I don't mean to sound like an old man, but I've been in situations more dangerous than that one,' he smiled.

'And I don't think I need to hear about them.'

'No. I guess not. Listen, I'll go to the office tomorrow and find out what's at that address we found in Kaufmann's papers. If it's sufficiently interesting, I'll try to get to Vienna sometime later in the day, and I'll probably be gone at least until the day after that. I suggest you go home and get some rest. Why don't you take the day off? You've earned it.'

'Thanks, but I think I'll scoot into the office tomorrow. Let's just talk when you get back, alright?'

'That's fine. Have a good evening.'

'You too, Andy.'

TEN

The next morning, Andrew woke up at half-past six, and took his time getting out of bed and making breakfast. Things had been quite hectic these past few days, and he needed to relax. Filled with tension and impatience, his body felt as if he had been drinking a couple of litres of coffee, so he knew he needed to slow down. Working while being stressed out was never a good idea. He had known a few people who had died that way. He didn't consider his own life to be in any immediate danger here in London, even if traffic was a killer.

As soon as he entered his office at around eight o'clock, he sat down at his PC and fired up a web browser. He wanted to find out what if any buildings there might be on 15 Waldhoff Strasse in Vienna. The easiest way to do that was not through the billion-pound intelligence systems that the British taxpayers had funded. Google won out every time.

Within a few minutes, Andrew had found an online Austrian phone guide. He entered the address and found that there were several streets by that name in Austria, so he chose the one in central Vienna. After a few seconds, he watched as the page loaded onto his screen.

'A monastery?' Andrew muttered to himself.

Number 15 Waldhoff Strasse appeared to be a monastery belonging to the Austrian Order of the Teutonic Knights. After a few seconds, Andrew remembered something Fiona had told him about the SS. They modelled their whole organisation of the Teutonic Knights. Was that a coincidence? Either way, it was certainly enough for Andrew to decide to fly to Vienna for a look. But he needed an excuse to make contact. He leaned back and stared at the ceiling of his office. At its centre was a large chandelier. It was gleaming with soft lights through hundreds of small pentagonal glass cylinders. It was old but very beautiful, and it must have cost someone a fortune to make.

That's it, he thought. *Money makes the world go around, doesn't it?*

On the right side of the screen was the telephone number for the building at 15 Waldhoff Strasse, which he promptly dialled. He could hear the faint clicks as the call was being routed through to the BT system that had been installed in the building, to an international relay station and then on to Austria and Vienna. The phone rang twice, before what sounded like a young man answered it.

'Ludvig Bauer hier.'

It suddenly occurred to Andrew that perhaps not everyone in the universe spoke English.

'Uhm. Hello? My name is William Taggart. Do you speak English?'

'Yes,' replied the young man with some hesitation.

'Good. I would like to enquire about the possibility of providing funds to some of the charities that the Order of the Teutonic Knights support. And also inquire about a possible membership?'

Andrew winced. He didn't have the faintest idea what he was doing, but it sounded about right.

'Well,' said Ludvig. 'We have a website where you can read about contributions. It is usually done by check or bank transfer. About the membership, I have to tell you that one cannot walk in from the street and acquire one. Other things have to be in order first.'

'Very well. But the thing is, I've just inherited a lot of money, and I would like to give some of it to Christian charities since the deceased woman was very religious. I have been looking at several religious orders, but I'm not sure if you are the right one. Would it be possible to come and visit you to discuss this?'

Once again, the young man hesitated. It was obvious that he wasn't the one making those kinds of decisions, but Andrew would like to speak to the one who was.

'How large of an amount were you considering, Mr. Taggart?' he finally asked.

'Oh,' replied Andrew in a casual tone. 'For now, I was thinking perhaps something in the region of a hundred thousand pounds.' Short pause. 'For several different charities, of course,' he added. He could almost hear young Ludvig Bauer's brain stop in its tracks.

'Mr. Taggart. I think it is probably better if you come to see our grandmaster, Herr Erich Strauss. He usually handles requests such as this. Would it be possible for you to come and see us this week?'

'Preferably tomorrow,' ordered Andrew.

'Oh. Could you just wait one moment, please?'

'Certainly,' said Andrew. He waited a couple of minutes, and then Ludvig Bauer returned sounding excited.

'Herr Taggart, the grandmaster would be delighted to see you tomorrow afternoon, if that suits you?'

'Excellent,' declared Andrew. 'Shall we say three o'clock at your offices?'

'Yes. Three is fine for us,' replied Ludvig.

'Marvellous. I'll see you then. Goodbye.'

'Thank you. Good day Herr Taggart. And may I say that we are all very much looking forward to seeing you.'

Andrew put down the phone. Perhaps he should have become a con artist instead of joining the army.

★ ★ ★

Former prisoner #4264 Kashim Khan held the water bottle between his hands in the passenger's seat of the jeep. He had become sick on the plane to Damascus, which was the first time that had ever happened to him. He suspected it might have been germs in the horrible food that had been served. How ironic that was. He had vomited a couple of times the previous night in his hotel in Damascus, and had hardly eaten anything today. Feeling extremely weak and irritable, he had lost his appetite completely. The only reason he had been drinking water, was because he knew that if he didn't, he would dehydrate within just a few hours.

Now he was sitting in a jeep that bounced along on the desert road, the driver seemingly disinterested in his condition. It was obvious that he wanted to get to their destination before dark. The locals' fear of the open desert at night seemed a little over the top to him. *Savages*, he thought.

How did these people ever accumulate the resources to put together an operation like this? Certainly not by using their brains. It was all due to the fact that they just happened to own land where there was an enormous amount of oil in the ground.

Most of those billionaires are probably illiterate, he thought to himself. But that really didn't matter now. What mattered, was that he had been granted funds to carry on with his research in a secure location, without the risk of being bothered by the government or those pesky international arms control agencies.

After too many hours with dusty air flying in the wind and sand sticking to his hair, they finally arrived at the valley. The jeep slowed down and was greeted by armed guards at the entrance to the cave. He didn't bother to look up at the guards but assumed that they knew who he was. After a few seconds, the jeep moved along and started making its way into the crevasse that continued some fifty metres, before it ended. The dusty crevasse had narrowed so that there was just room for one truck either going in or coming out. At that point, a large opening had been made directly into the brown rock. The jeep turned and entered a long tunnel that extended another 200 meters inside the mountain, and down approximately 25 meters.

The tunnel was lit up by a long row of white lights, which made it seem much longer than it really was. Halfway through the tunnel, there was a large area to the right that had been excavated or blasted into the rock, where various earthmoving and construction machines were parked. Next to them was a row of one-story buildings that looked like living quarters large enough for approximately 50 people. Outside the buildings, a group of around fifteen men were performing various chores but stopped to look at Khan as he passed by them.

Suddenly the tunnel opened up into a gigantic circular cave around 150 meters across and at least four stories high. It was the shape of a dome, with its highest point at its centre, and it had been blasted out of the mountain at a considerable cost, from what Khan had been told. Overhead, the ceiling was dotted with powerful lights that bathed the entire cave in soft light. At the far end of the cave was another set of one-story buildings, which Khan guessed were probably the home of his support staff. He had been told that they would number around twenty people.

Situated in the middle of the cave, was a large structure that must have seemed peculiar to anyone but Kashim Khan. His eyes lit up as he spotted it, coming through the tunnel opening. It was a large rectangular windowless building, with what appeared to be two corridors of some ten meters in length, jutting out at opposite ends of it. At the end of each corridor, there was a small shed with a door and no windows. The entire structure seemed to be constructed mostly of aluminium, and it had an exceptionally robust feel to it. The giant cave was completely silent, except for the distant humming of generators and air-conditioning equipment that fed new air into the cave, as well as providing a completely stable environment inside the main building.

Everything looked right to Sanjay. He jumped out of the jeep as soon as it parked alongside a couple of other vehicles including a large truck. Having almost forgotten how sick he had felt, he took a few steps towards the building and placed his hands on his hips.

What a beautiful sight, he thought.

In scale, this surpassed anything he had previously worked with, but what really excited him was that it was so apparent that the building was the centre of this giant operation. And he was in charge of that building and everything that was going to go on inside it. He felt like a million dollars, and that was probably even a low number.

'How is our Alchemist?' a voice boomed from behind him.

He turned to see a man in his thirties coming towards him, with his right hand stretched out to greet him, and the smile of a long-lost brother.

'I am Yusef,' said the man. 'I am responsible for making sure that everything here works to your satisfaction.'

Khan shook the man's hand and smiled vaguely. 'I am Kashim Khan. This is quite an impressive laboratory. And expensive they tell me.'

Yusef shrugged. 'It is worth it, I am sure. Did your trip go well?'

'Not really. I haven't eaten anything in twelve hours.'

'Come with me, my friend,' said Yusef and placed a hand on Khan's shoulder. 'We have plenty of food,' he said and pointed to what appeared to be a modern two-story office building next to the laboratory. 'I would also like to introduce you to the rest of the team, and of course show you your living quarters.'

Khan detested physical contact with other men, so he started walking towards the two-story office building to get some distance between himself and Yusef. 'Have all the stocks been replenished by now?' he asked.

'Yes. Everything is set up in accordance with the instructions sent to us.'

'How many canisters?'

'2,400 so far, but our network is expanding every day. It is easy for us to recruit new soldiers. There are plenty of young men willing to give themselves to the cause. I expect we will have many thousands in a few weeks.'

Khan nodded. He didn't personally understand their reasons, but he didn't really need to either. If that was what they wanted to do, he wasn't going to stand in their way. He was in it solely for the money, and that was as worthy a cause as any other he could think of.

'So, you will bring in more canisters if need be?'

'Yes, and the pens will be assembled in the room right here,' said Yusef as they entered the office building. To their right was a large room with a row of tables and several big boxes filled with cheap plastic pens.

'So simple, yet so effective,' smiled Yusef, seemingly completely unaffected by the nature of their endeavour. 'Let's go upstairs,' he said and motioned for Khan to go up the stairs to the second floor.

The second floor had a corridor running the length of the building, providing access to a number of offices. In the largest one, a group of people stood leaning over a table with a large flat computer screen showing the molecular structure of an enzyme, as far as Khan could tell. Upon seeing the two men in the doorway, they snapped to attention, which immediately made Khan feel at home. They might be savages, but they sure were trained well.

'This is your science team,' said Yusef and walked over to them. He put a hand on the shoulder of one who appeared to be the oldest person in the room, an Arab in his forties with a short black and greying beard. 'This will be your second in command, so to speak.'

The man stepped forward and politely held out his hand. 'My name is Ahmed Kamal Rashid,' he said, and performed a measured bow for his new boss. 'I have heard much about you.'

Feeling appropriately venerated, Khan shook Rashid's hand and smiled. 'Nice to meet you,' he said, actually meaning it this time. Rashid had the eyes of a bright and inquisitive scientist, and that was what Khan was looking for. Brilliant as he himself was, he still depended on having intelligent and hard-working people around him in order to achieve results.

'The team here has been assembled by me personally,' said Rashid and pointed to the other three men, who all bowed at the introduction and then came over to shake hands with their new boss. 'They have been handpicked from the best universities in this and a couple of neighbouring countries. You will find them most resourceful, I am sure,' smiled Rashid proudly. It was clear that to him, this was also a unique chance to work at the cutting edge of science with a team of highly trained specialists, and with an almost unlimited supply of funds.

Khan nodded and looked each one of them in the eye as he shook their hands. Each one of them impressed him with their bright eyes and their apparent enthusiasm. *Maybe they are not all savages*, he thought.

A couple of hours later he had been shown the rest of the facilities including his luxurious living quarters, and he had even had time for a short nap and some food. Feeling much better than when he arrived, he decided to go for a tour of the main laboratory. After all, this was where the action would be.

He exited the office building and walked over to the shed nearest to him and punched in the combination to unlock the heavy steel door. It swung open and he entered a white room with a familiar array of equipment. He took off his clothes, put them in a locker, and put on a one-piece full-body undergarment. He then donned his bright blue Level 4 protective suit and hooked it up to the air-canister on the side of the suit. It was completely airtight, and inside it, he could hear the faint hissing sound of the air supply. He ran through the security procedure a couple of times, and satisfied that everything was as it should be, he pushed a yellow panel and a door opened to the corridor.

It was brightly lit and looked like an ordinary corridor until he stepped inside it and the door closed behind him. Then a set of nozzles quickly generated a cloud of water and steam, which removed any large organic material on his suit. He then started walking slowly through the cloud and continued through a series of chemical cleaning procedures that ended with a fifteen-second halt at a designated point at the end of the corridor, where clean warm air-dried the exterior of his suit. Khan smiled inside the suit, pleased with the procedure. It all seemed very professional indeed.

As soon as the oversized blow dryer had stopped, the door in front of him opened, and he stepped into the laboratory. It was a large room with several separate rooms, all with their own individual air supply and decontamination systems. Each one was filled with advanced laboratory equipment, and Khan once again thought of the enormous resources that had been pumped into this project.

He walked over to one of the refrigerator-sized storage tanks and opened it. Inside were the small glass boxes that he had expected to see. He took one out and placed it carefully in a high-powered microscope. He adjusted the suit and leaned forward to look at the image that appeared on the computer screen next to him.

And there it was. The tiny organism, which gave off a bluish hue under the lights of the microscope, seemed so harmless. But it would soon bring untold devastation to its unsuspecting victims. He smiled and stood motionless for a minute, admiring its structure. So simple, yet so deadly.

'Wake up, little one,' he whispered. 'Daddy's here.'

★ ★ ★

William Taggart, AKA Andrew Sterling the charity benefactor extraordinaire, arrived in Vienna the next day carrying a briefcase and wearing an elegant grey suit and golden tie. He had spent the time on the plane reading up on the Order of the Teutonic Knights.

A medieval military order modelled on another order, the Hospitallers of St. John, first established itself in Acre in Palestine around 1190, after the third crusade. But it maintained many residences throughout Europe during the next many centuries. There, it took its place alongside the two other orders, the Templars and the Hospitallers. In 1291 however, the order was forced to leave Palestine, which had again fallen under the yoke of Islam.

But a new path had already opened up to their warlike and religious zeal, this time in Eastern Europe, against the pagans of Prussia. The Baltic, which had been difficult to access, had resisted the efforts of the Christian missionaries, many of whom had been killed trying to convert the locals. To avenge these Christians, a new crusade was launched, and the Teutonic Knights were offered the territory of Culm, with whatever they could wrest from the pagans, in return. The knight Hermann Balk, along with twenty-eight of his brother knights and a whole army of crusaders from Germany, began this struggle which lasted twenty-five years and was followed by German colonisation. From then on, the Order of the Teutonic Knights was associated with the Baltics and with Prussia.

In 1309 the fifteenth grandmaster, Siegfried Von Feuchtwangen, transferred his residence from Venice, where at that time the knights had their headquarters, to the Castle of Marienburg in northern Poland, which they made into a formidable fortress. When the Lithuanian Grand Duke finally embraced Christianity, the Teutonic Knights suddenly lost their *raison d'être.* From this point onwards, their history consists of incessant conflicts with the kings of Poland, which eventually lead to the ruining of their finances. After losing most of its possessions, the order settled in Vienna and there it has functioned as a hospital order ever since, also managing a number of parishes and schools. Their revenues now consist almost entirely of money raised through a variety of charity fundraisers.

Pleasant bunch of people, thought Andrew as he disembarked the aeroplane. But what does the Order of the Teutonic Knights have to do with the Thule Society? The fact that the order has held on to its headquarters in Vienna for so long indicates that the building was probably also theirs during the 1930s.

He walked out of the Arrivals Hall, and hailed a taxi, showing the driver a piece of paper with the address he needed to go to. The driver had to look it up on a map of the inner city, which wasn't surprising. He suspected that there probably weren't too many businessmen who needed to go to visit an ancient order of knights. It seemed a bit strange to Andrew as well, that someone would persist in keeping such an order alive. What would be the purpose? It was hardly because they wanted to resurrect the crusades, and go off to the Middle East and liberate the Holy Land.

Apart from the charity aspect, it was probably just a case of some people taking on an identity, which could give them the feeling of being more than simple believers. Maybe there was also a sense of history and grandeur, along with a feeling of being a part of something mysterious, secret and exclusive. *Humans like to feel special,* he thought.

In that sense, it wasn't that different from the Thule Society. There were probably a lot of people who didn't believe the supernatural nonsense that it preached, but were eager to join simply for the sense of belonging, and the sense of power and influence it could give them. At the end of the day, the Thule Society and its affiliates were political entities. They were working towards political aims and probably threw in the elements of the occult to add a bit of mystique. The exclusive nature was probably also an attraction to its members. Who didn't want to be part of a select few, initiated in the 'secrets of the order'?

It had all been done a thousand times before all over the world and all throughout history. More than anything else, it probably just demonstrated the extent to which individuals need to feel significant. This desire might very well be the root cause of many conflicts and even wars throughout history. In some sense, it could even be argued that the Second World War had started because of the desire of the German people to regain their sense of self, after the humiliating defeat in the First World War. A desire to once again feel strong and in control of its own destiny. And Hitler had identified that desire and had fed it, and astonishingly managed to blind a whole nation with powerful rhetoric and propaganda. Andrew was certain that the German people were no better or worse than any other people in the world. But through a long and complicated process, they had as a society slipped into a position that the people of other countries might also find themselves in, given a similar set of circumstances.

That was a frightening thought in itself, because if what had happened in Germany was a natural consequence of a set of very specific circumstances, then it was obvious that it would definitely happen again in some other place at some other time.

On that happy note, Andrew got out of the taxi and turned to face the building in front of him. There was no visible number on the building, but he had to assume that it was the correct one. It was a massive grey two-story block from some time in the eighteenth century. At one end it had a small tower with a golden spike adorned with a crucifix at its top. It looked more than anything like a chapel or a church, and facing the street was a large black double door.

Andrew walked up to it and knocked. He had to knock hard to make himself heard, since the heavy wooden door absorbed all the force of his fist. After a few seconds, he could hear a series of locks snapping, and then the door swung open revealing a short person, whose voice Andrew immediately recognised.

'Mr. William Taggart?' asked Ludvig Bauer. He was slightly chubby and wore round spectacles on his nose.

'That is correct,' said Andrew, finding himself strangely surprised that the man was wearing jeans and a white sweater and not a cloak of some sort that he thought would have been more befitting of a monk.

'Please come in,' the young man beckoned. 'I'll show you to the grandmaster,' he said, and led Andrew through a couple of impressive rooms filled with antique furniture and large paintings that hung on wood-panelled walls.

Every room had a beautiful chandelier, each one with a different shape. Everywhere they went, the wooden floors were so polished that he could almost see his own reflection in them. Bauer explained that most of the rooms were now used only as venues for charity fundraisers. They reached a flight of stairs and ascended to what appeared to be an office of some kind.

'Please wait here,' smiled Bauer.

Andrew nodded and waited, while the young man slipped through a wooden door with intricate carvings, into an adjoining room. A few seconds later he returned and motioned for Andrew to enter.

The grand master's office was as large as any Andrew had seen, and everywhere he looked, he saw what must have been a fortune's worth of antique furniture, paintings, small statues and above all books. The two walls that had no windows were covered with shelves that were packed with old books. Andrew wondered if they were all for show, but suspected that each one was related to the long history of the order.

A man in his late sixties was standing by one of the windows, holding a cup of tea in one hand and a newspaper in the other. As

Andrew entered the room, the man looked up from his newspaper and raised his eyebrows. At first, it looked to Andrew as if for some reason he was merely surprised at the appearance of the would-be benefactor, but then it seemed as if there was genuine consternation on the man's face. His hand started trembling slightly, and he almost dropped his newspaper on the floor.

Quickly, he put the newspaper on the desk, and nervously sipped his tea. The shock of the recognition was overwhelming. Grand Master Erich Strauss stood dumbfounded for a few seconds. Utterly bewildered by the stranger's appearance, and by the thought of what his intentions might be, the grandmaster finally regained his composure. He steadied his hand to stop it from trembling and spilling his tea, and then forced a smile. He then motioned for Andrew to come inside.

'Come in Mr. Taggart. I've been looking forward to seeing you.'

Andrew could have sworn that Strauss had looked shocked to see him, and he had not the faintest idea why that might be. As far as he could remember he had never laid eyes on the grandmaster or any other member of the Order of the Teutonic Knights. He tried to find an answer in the elderly man's face, but merely found eyes that darted across his own face, seemingly also trying to find answers.

Strauss was searching for and slowly finding his balance once again, and he now felt confident that he was hiding his thoughts. While keeping his face looking relaxed and amiable, his mind was racing. Could this man really be him? For a split second, it had seemed as if one of the Keepers had returned from the grave, but surely that was not possible, so there could only be one possible explanation. This had to be his son. He had the same dark eyes, the same chin, the same hair and even the same way of carrying himself. In his wildest dreams, Erich Strauss had never imagined that he would one day be standing face to face with the son of one of the Keepers.

Andrew searched the old man's face for clues but could find none. Now he was smiling and looking at Andrew with his gentle eyes, and Andrew started wondering whether he had imagined the whole thing. But he knew he hadn't. The grandmaster of this backward order had been visibly shaken at the sight of him, but there was not a single reason for it that Andrew could think of. He returned the smile, and shook the man's hand, noting his sweaty palm.

'Hello Mr. Strauss,' said Andrew and let go of the hand. 'It was very good of you to see me so soon.'

'My pleasure Mr. Taggart. Won't you please sit?' he said and moved over to a pair of dark red antique armchairs by one of the windows.

Two teacups had been placed there on a small round table, along with a silver teapot and some milk and sugar. As he sat down, Andrew noticed that what appeared to be an ancient map of the world had been painted on the top of the table. But it wasn't like any map he had seen before. It had Antarctica at its centre, and the other landmasses of the world placed around it in a circle. The map was inaccurate, with coastlines drawn in a slightly simplified manner, and the proportions of the continents clearly wrong. But it was a beautiful piece of craftsmanship, nonetheless.

'Did you have a good flight Mr. Taggart?' said a now entirely serene Erich Strauss.

'Yes, I did. Not a very long one, and the trip from the airport went very quickly indeed.'

'Oh, that's nice to hear,' smiled the old man and sipped his tea.

'Mr. Strauss. I'll come straight to the point if you don't mind,' said Andrew and opened his briefcase.

'Certainly,' said Strauss, his curious eyes peeking into Andrew's briefcase as it opened.

'As Mr. Bauer has no doubt relayed to you, I am in the process of distributing some of my inheritance to suitable Christian charities and organisations, and I'm considering giving part of it to your order.'

Andrew looked up at Strauss as he took out a sheet of paper from his briefcase, and the two men began discussing possible charities of the Teutonic Order that Mr. Taggart might see fit to support. They included several hospitals in Austria and a number of Christian Schools in Vienna.

While making an effort to sound sincere, Andrew pretended to be content with the options presented to him, and slowly started small talking about the order and its history. Strauss was visibly impressed by Mr. Taggart's knowledge of the order and soon began providing information of his own.

'You know, a church already stood on this site at the turn of the 12th and 13th centuries. As a result of two fires, only the spire of this church is left standing today. The present church was finished in 1395, and the House of the Teutonic Order was renovated in the baroque style between 1725 and 1735.'

Andrew looked engaged and listened intently to the old man, while attempting to jolt his memory into retrieving an image of Erich Strauss, but he could not for the life of him find any memory of ever having seen him anywhere. 'It's quite an impressive history you have, I must say. I imagine you must have very extensive records of that?'

'We certainly do,' said the grandmaster still wondering what was happening. Why was this man here, and what was he looking for? This could not be a coincidence. It just couldn't. He would have to contact the current Keeper in London as soon as possible.

'Hundreds of crates of records from all the provinces of the Order were sent to Vienna in the decades after it became the new seat of the grandmaster in 1809,' Strauss continued. 'In recent years, the documents have been catalogued in accordance with modern academic methodologies. The library contains some 10,000 volumes at present, and also holds some 1,000 old seals, treaties, inventories and catalogues.'

'And is this open to the public?' asked Andrew.

'No, but requests can be filed with me, and then I, along with the other council members, will decide whether to grant access. We usually just provide access to religious scholars.'

'Might I take a look inside?' asked Andrew innocently. 'I have always loved libraries.'

Strauss hesitated, but then decided that there could be no harm in allowing this man, whoever he was, to have a look around the library. After all, several hundred thousand pounds were at stake. 'Since you may prove to be one of our most important benefactors, I suppose a quick look around would be of no harm,' smiled the old man and rose. 'I'll have Ludvig give you a short tour. It's downstairs at the other end of the building. Please follow me.'

Andrew rose and followed the grandmaster out into the front office where Ludvig Bauer was waiting.

'Mr. Taggart would like to have a look at the library. A passion of his, is that correct Mr. Taggart?' asked Strauss and looked inquisitively at Andrew.

'Yes,' replied Andrew feigning embarrassment. 'I must have inherited that from my father. He loved books too.'

At the mention of the visitor's father, Strauss almost lost his composure again, but he managed to remain calm.

Does he know? thought Strauss. *Is he toying with me?* He looked again at Andrew's face. *It must be him.*

'Have a pleasant day, Mr. Taggart,' he said and offered the Englishman his hand. 'I hope you will decide to make a contribution to us. We would be most grateful,' he said and performed a small bow.

'Thank you for seeing me,' replied Andrew and shook the grand master's hand. 'I'll give it serious consideration.'

And with that, Ludvig Bauer led Andrew out of the front office, down the stairs to the ground floor and back through the splendidly decorated rooms. 'Right this way, Mr. Taggart,' said Bauer as they entered a passage leading to another flight of stairs. 'We are going to the basement.'

The stairs led an unusually long way down under the building, and at its base, it turned ninety degrees to the right for the final steps onto the basement floor. Andrew now found himself at the end of the stairs, in the corner of a large dimly lit rectangular room. The floor was made of big dark tiles of polished granite, and the parts of the walls that were visible were constructed from big solid blocks of grey rock, that appeared to have been hand chiselled from a quarry. All the walls were almost completely covered by bookshelves, except for the back wall, which featured a very large fireplace.

The ceiling appeared to be made of oak, with solid timber support columns spaced equidistantly throughout the room. The only light sources were eight wall-mounted artificial candles with small electric light bulbs, and it took Andrew a few seconds to adjust his eyes to the gloom. At the centre of the room ran a meter-high bookshelf, that continued almost all the way down to the other end of the room, where a couple of armchairs and a sofa were placed around a small table. On the table lay a number of books. Evidently, people sat there from time to time studying the writings of the collection.

'Quite dark in here, isn't it?' said Andrew.

'Yes,' shrugged Ludvig. 'I guess we have never really thought of it as a problem. It isn't a problem if you spend a whole day down here.'

'Do you do that often?'

'Sometimes we do. The history of the Order is rich and varied, and we often recount the exploits of the order for the students.'

Andrew walked slowly along the walls looking up at the many hundreds of old books. Some of them were obviously very old indeed, their backs frayed and worn, and most of them had thick layers of dust on top of them, indicating that they had not been touched for years.

With Ludvig following a few steps behind, Andrew strode along the bookshelves towards the back wall, his eyes now fixed on the fireplace. At first, he couldn't put his finger on it, but something wasn't quite right. Then he remembered that looking up at the building from the outside, there hadn't been a single chimney visible on the entire roof. Andrew stopped and looked down at the fireplace. On top of an iron grill lay several charred pieces of wood covered by a thin layer of dust, and below the grill there was not a single piece of charcoal. It was clear that the fireplace wasn't real, but that every effort had been made to make it appear that way. There was something very odd about this. Andrew wished that he could have had just a few minutes alone in the library.

Above the mantelpiece hung a large painting of what appeared to be one of the previous grandmasters of the order. Looking much like a nobleman with his feathered hat and his gold-embroidered jacket, he held in his hand a small gold chain, at the end of which dangled a golden cross. Below the painting was a shiny brass plaque with an inscription in German. The plaque seemed to be slightly worn at its centre.

'What does this say?' asked Andrew.

Bauer looked a bit uncomfortable. 'It translates roughly into something like. 'The Keepers Guard the Future,' he said, looking vaguely uncomfortable. 'It's just a silly old mantra of the order. It doesn't really mean anything anymore.'

'Really,' said Andrew, who had the distinct feeling that the young man was lying.

'Your founder?' asked Andrew as he looked at the painting.

'No. This is Albert of Brandenburg. He was one of the first German grandmasters at the beginning of the sixteenth century'

Andrew pointed to the charred wood on the grille. 'Must be nice to have a fireplace down here during the winter,' he said pretending to make small talk.

'Yes, it is. It has already become cold in Vienna, especially at night,' said Ludvig and stood next to Andrew, who turned and looked back towards the stairwell.

'What a marvellous collection,' he said admiringly.

'Yes. It is our most prized possession.'

'Well,' said Andrew and looked at his wristwatch. 'It's almost half-past four. I really should be going now. Thank you very much for the tour. I appreciate it.'

'My pleasure,' said Bauer and then he escorted Mr. Taggart back up the stairs and out to the front door. 'Nice of you to come all the way from London Mr Taggart. We hope to hear from you soon.'

'Thank you, Mr. Bauer.'

Andrew opened the front door and stepped out into the sun, which was now shining over the city of Vienna. As the door closed behind him, he looked up and down the street. It was a very quiet street with hardly any traffic. Just the occasional bicycle rolled past.

It seemed a completely different world out here. It was as if time stood still just beyond those doors behind him, and Andrew decided that he just couldn't go back to London. Not now, after having come all this way. He felt that something was waiting for him inside the building. Something just wasn't right about that place. He could feel it.

★ ★ ★

Bauer felt disturbed. There was something odd about Mr. Taggart, and what had happened to the grandmaster. He was so preoccupied that he forgot to press the panel on the wall to re-engage the locks on the front door.

As he was walking back up the stairs to his grandmaster, he wondered what had been the matter with him earlier. He had known him for quite a few years now and he had never seen the old man so shaken. Although he had hidden it well, it was obvious to Bauer that something was amiss. He knocked on the door to Strauss' office and entered. The grandmaster was sitting at his desk stirring his tea with a small silver spoon. He heard Bauer enter, but didn't move.

'Are you alright, Sir?'

'Please sit down, Ludvig,' he said, ignoring the question.

Bauer sat down in front of Strauss' desk.

'This man,' continued the grandmaster almost whispering. 'This man is not what he seems.'

'What do you mean?' said a perplexed Bauer.

'Exactly what I just said. I am sure of it. He is the son of a Keeper,' said Strauss and gave Bauer an ominous look.

Now thoroughly confused, Bauer didn't know what to say. 'How do you know?' he finally ventured.

'A mouth may lie, but the eyes do not,' said Strauss pensively while staring into his cup of tea. A few seconds later he awoke from his trance. 'We must contact the Keeper in London. Something is brewing and I need to know what it is.'

'Yes, Master, of course,' said Bauer, still clueless as to what was happening. 'What should I do?'

'Arrange for a meeting of the council members as soon as possible, and try to reach our man in London. I must speak with him. And fetch me the Book of Keepers right away.'

'Yes, Sir,' said Bauer and retreated, leaving the grandmaster alone with his thoughts.

★ ★ ★

It took Andrew a few seconds to realise what had just happened. Something out of place. Something that didn't fit. Then he realised what it was. The door behind him had been unlocked for him on the way in, but there had been no sound of the door locking again after he had left. This could be his chance. He glanced left, then right, to ensure that no cars or pedestrians were in the street. Then he turned around and gripped the door handle. Ever so carefully, he opened the door and peeked inside. There was no one there, so he slipped in and closed the door carefully behind him while listening for approaching footsteps. All was quiet. He proceeded through the hall and slipped silently into the passage that led to the stairwell from where he and Ludvig had emerged just a few minutes earlier. Here he stopped for a few seconds and listened. Still no sound. He walked quickly down the stairs to the library and made his way to the fireplace, where he knelt down to look at the grille and the charred pieces of wood. It was definitely fake. Looking up inside the fireplace, he could see that it was entirely sealed off.

So much for keeping warm in the winter, he thought and rose.

At that moment he heard footsteps coming from the stairwell, so he quickly ducked down next to the low bookshelf that ran through the centre of the room. He crept in close to the side of the shelf that faced away from the stairwell, hoping he wouldn't get spotted. A few seconds later a figure appeared from the stairwell and started walking towards the fireplace on the opposite side of the bookshelf. Andrew held his breath to avoid making any noise. The only things moving were his eyes, which followed the figure on the other side through the little gaps between books on the bookshelf.

It was Bauer, and he had clearly not noticed Andrew hiding in the room. He was walking at a brisk pace, as if in a hurry. Upon reaching the fireplace he placed his hand on the brass plaque. Andrew heard a loud 'clink', as if a lock was being released. Peeking out from his hiding place he saw the back wall of the fireplace move slightly. Bauer stooped down and stepped across the grille in the fireplace, pushed the back wall to the side, and vanished through the dark hole. Just before the back wall slid shut, Andrew noticed a faint light coming on inside the room on the other side, but he was unable to make out what was in there, or how big it was.

Andrew sat dumbfounded for a few seconds behind the bookshelf, before breathing again. This was beginning to look very strange indeed. The order's address on the note found in Kaufmann's safe, the grandmaster visibly shaken by Andrew's arrival and now this Ludvig Bauer stepping into a fireplace and vanishing. The past few weeks had already been odd enough, but as the days passed, things just seemed to get more and more strange.

He waited for a couple of minutes, and then Bauer appeared as suddenly as he had vanished, stepping over the grille and exiting the fireplace as if it was something he did every day. He was holding a thick book under his arm, and walking quickly back towards the stairwell where he disappeared. Listening to the footsteps receding, Andrew remained immobile until all was quiet again. Then he resolutely walked over to the fireplace and pressed the brass plaque. Sure enough, the lock clicked, and the back wall of the fireplace shifted a couple of centimetres inwards. He stooped and took a long step across the grille, pushing with one hand at the back wall. It swung open smoothly on its hinges, and when he stood back up again, he found himself inside a completely dark room. There was a smell of old leather and dry wood.

He pushed the door shut behind him as he searched with his hands for a light switch, but he couldn't find any. Although he didn't smoke, he always kept a lighter in his pocket. Offering a light to someone was always a good way of striking up a conversation. It was an old habit from his days in the army, when most of his fellow soldiers smoked.

He lit the lighter, and the small flame shone brightly in what turned out to be a room similar to the library, but much smaller. There were many books and some scrolls on the shelves. Then Andrew spotted a small gas lamp sitting on a table that was placed along one of the walls. Once lit, it shone brightly and illuminated the whole room. There were probably around a hundred books and other documents in here, and Andrew started going over the titles of those on the shelf closest to him. They all appeared to be about the exploits of the knights, from as far back as the 14th century up until the present. It was an extensive collection sorted according to age, and the oldest of the books seemed like they might crumble if touched, so Andrew decided to stay away from those. On a separate shelf was a large collection of books on all kinds of occult societies and practices, which struck Andrew as particularly odd for a supposedly Christian charity organisation.

He walked over to the shelf that seemed to contain the most recent additions to the collection. They included books as well as other documents. He took out a couple at random, and upon finding that they all concerned the beginning of the twentieth century, he took down almost the entire content of that particular shelf and placed them in a heap on the table. He then sat down and started to examine them one by one. Some of them contained lists of names, possibly of members of the order through the twentieth century, and Andrew noted that a number of them seemed to be British or American names. Others appeared to be records of meetings between previous grandmasters and people referred to as Major this or Colonel that. He paged through it without much in the way of results since it was all handwritten and in German. He wondered why the Order of the Teutonic Knight had been involved with the military, but then remembered what Fiona had told him. During the Second World War, the SS had modelled itself on the Order. Perhaps the Order was more than just a role model for the SS.

He put the handwritten documents aside, and that was when he saw it. One of the books carried on its leather cover the same insignia that they had found in the wooden box in Kommandant Kaufmann's safe. Andrew placed the heavy book in front of him, and just sat there looking at it for a few seconds. The connection between this place and the submarine at the bottom of the ocean was undeniable.

He opened the book carefully, to discover that it was more akin to a diary than anything else. At the top of each page was a date. All entries were made between 1937 and 1943. After a few seconds, it dawned on him that he was looking at a chronicle of several of the expeditions undertaken by the *SS-Ahnenerbe* in the 1930s. Dazed by the potential significance of his find, he looked towards the door almost expecting someone to enter and catch him red-handed. His head was swimming. What had he gotten himself into, and what did all this mean?

He started gently leafing through the pages, finding ever more records of expeditions, and they all seemed to be described in great detail. He started reading, but it was slow going. Although these chronicles were typed on a typewriter, his German wasn't sufficient to extract much more than the most basic content from them. However, it left him curious enough to decide that he had to take the book with him. If there had been a connection between the order of the Teutonic Knights and the *SS-Ahnenerbe* at the time when U-303 had left Germany, he needed to know what it was.

He put the book aside and went through the rest of the books in the pile. Several of them appeared to be of a more scientific nature with maps of the world, old as well as new. The name 'Thule' appeared repeatedly along with words like 'Civilisation' and 'Race'. Andrew decided to grab those too. They might provide useful clues.

★ ★ ★

Erich Strauss was poring over the old book that Bauer had brought to him from the secret library. In it was described the initiation ceremony for new Keepers, as well as the complete list of all the men upon whom that immense responsibility had been bestowed since the late 1930s. Back then, during its heyday, the society could function openly, and it soon gathered enough momentum to become a political force, as well as a basis for a new world order.

The grandmasters before him had worked tirelessly to achieve that goal, and with the backing of the SS they had slowly but surely taken over the order of the Teutonic Knights. When the war had come to an abrupt end in 1945, the Order had served as a convenient cover for the society, and now more than sixty years later, Grand Master Erich Strauss felt that perhaps he would be the one to deliver the prize to the Aryan race.

But as much as recent developments showed promise, there was also new threats to their existence. It even seemed as if they would have to accept merely monitoring their enemies, at least for now, finally striking when the time was right and the prize was discovered. As it was now, he could do nothing but passively follow the events that were in one respect leading him towards their coveted prize, but then simultaneously dragging him and the society towards the abyss. It was an almost unbearable balancing act, over which he had no control. At least not at present, so he simply had to wait. This seemed to him the worst possible option, even though he knew it was the only one.

He looked down at the list that lay before him on the table. Keeping the secret among as few people as possible was always preferable. Strauss ran his finger down the list of the initiated in Britain and stopped at the third from the bottom.

'It must be you,' he whispered.

★ ★ ★

Andrew turned out the light of the oil lamp and navigated back to the door using his lighter. He pulled the door in the fake fireplace open, and stepped out onto the smooth granite floor in the library, pulling the door shut behind him. He then walked silently across the room to the stairs and peeked around the corner. There was no sign of anyone there, so he started walking carefully up the stairs. Upon reaching the top, he stopped for a few seconds to ensure that it was safe for him to move on, and then he quietly darted across the hall and slipped out of the front door to the street.

★ ★ ★

Later that evening, the grandmaster of the Teutonic Knights received an unannounced visitor, but he was let in anyway. He was tall with short blond hair, and a slight tan indicating that he had spent some time outside during the past few days.

ELEVEN

Fiona got out of her yellow Peugeot 206 XR that she had just parked in the street outside Phillip Eckleston's house in a quiet suburban neighbourhood in north London. She had bought the second-hand car the year before, and it was the best car she had ever owned. It didn't really make much sense to have a car in the centre of London, but seeing it in the window of the dealer, she just couldn't resist. She had only had one car before this one, and that was a run-down old Fiat, which she had read, had the poorest safety record among all the small cars available. Her yellow Peugeot suited her perfectly with its stylish design and its small size. It was the ideal car for London traffic, and she particularly liked the colour.

She had called Eckleston in advance and asked to see him again, and he had happily accepted. It seemed to her that the good doctor was keen on discussing his ideas with kindred spirits. Fiona felt sure that the old man seldom got the opportunity to pour from his vast reservoir of knowledge, simply because there weren't too many people willing to accept his ideas. The scientific community had effectively shut him out several years ago, and he now lived off his pension plus what little money he could make from writing articles for various magazines.

Despite his reputation, Fiona had read a few of his books and articles, just to make sure she always kept an open mind. Eckleston was an avid writer on the subjects of ancient civilisations and the possibility of artefacts preserved through the millennia. In her opinion, some of the articles were bordering on the absurd, but they certainly provoked thoughts that she would never have produced herself without such an alternative source of intellectual stimulus.

Phillip Eckleston's house was a typical suburban two-story Victorian red brick house, with a dark grey slate roof. The garden was orderly and well kept, and as she walked towards the front door, she noticed a satellite dish in the backyard. That wasn't unusual in itself, except that this wasn't just a dish for receiving TV signals. This was an expensive communications dish capable of sending as well as receiving signals. She hadn't noticed that the last time she was here just over a week ago. Maybe his car had blocked her view then.

She rang the bell, and a few moments later the elderly man opened the door with a smile. He was wearing tweed trousers, a white shirt with thin blue stripes and a dark blue bowtie with small white dots. On his feet, he had a pair of slippers, and he gave the appearance of being a typical English pensioner living a quiet life in suburban London. But that wasn't entirely true, and that became evident as they moved into his living room. There were piles of papers everywhere, as well as articles and books all related to his favourite area of research. On the walls hung a few paintings that were a terrible match for his beige furniture.

'Please sit down, Miss Keane,' he smiled.

Fiona sat down in the same chair she sat in last time she was there, and Eckleston came over to pour her a cup of tea.

'What can I do for you today?' he asked amicably.

'I would appreciate it if you could help me understand some of your theories about ancient civilisations, particularly that of the mystical Atlantis. I am trying to determine to what extent it could be connected to the legend of Thule, that appeared prominently in several occult Nazi societies during the 1930s.'

Eckleston nodded and sipped at his tea. 'May I ask why you are looking into this?' he asked.

'I'm working with the government on an investigation, and we have stumbled across several references to Thule. Looking into this I've found out that Thule was similar in concept to Atlantis, in that they were both supposedly ancient but technologically advanced civilisations that existed thousands of years ago. As you know, I've done a bit of research on Nazi esoteric activity along with some work on their expeditions. What I'm looking for now is more background material on ancient civilisations.'

Eckleston seemed unfazed by the mention of a government investigation, and Fiona reckoned that he had become numb to the dealings of 'the establishment'. In particular, the scientific establishment, which had ridiculed him on numerous occasions, and often dismissed dealing with him altogether. None of this seemed to bother him. It was quite evident that he was convinced that he was right, and they were wrong.

'Very well. Where would you like to begin?' he asked and settled into his soft beige armchair.

'Could you just give me an overview of what you consider to be the most plausible theory of an ancient civilisation that might subsequently have been lost.'

'I certainly can,' said Eckleston. 'As you know the Greek philosopher Plato is the most often referenced source when people speak about Atlantis. And it is with good reason, in my humble opinion, even though he also to some extent led researchers astray. But I'll get back to that. In one of his dialogues, Plato gives a very captivating and immensely detailed account of this lost continent. As with all other narratives of creation, it begins with a bit of poppycock about the Greek gods spawning kings and peoples along with lands. One of these lands happens to be Atlantis. It is a great island nation beyond the Pillars of Hercules, which today we call Gibraltar, indicating that it was indeed situated in the Atlantic Ocean somewhere. Plato reports it to be greater in extent than Libya and Asia together, which is best translated as North Africa and the Middle East. There have obviously been many theories about the exact location of this lost continent, including Greek islands, Greenland, the Azores and even the Florida Keys. But I am convinced that what is mostly now a popular myth, was in fact very real some 12,000 years ago, and that there indeed was a highly advanced civilisation in what we now call Antarctica.'

'Yes. I believe you indicated as much last time I was here,' said Fiona politely.

'Oh, yes. Of course.'

'When exactly was this supposed to have happened?' asked Fiona.

'Well,' said Eckleston and adjusted his butterfly.

Plato asserts that the creation of Atlantis occurred some 9,000 years ago. But as I said, I personally believe it to be a couple of thousand years before that.'

'Based on what?'

'Just wait,' he said, holding up his index finger admonishingly. 'Let me get back to that. I'll just get the original text first,' he said, and then rose and walked over to a pile of documents, from where he pulled out a sheet of paper.

'This is a translation of the original wording of Plato's dialogue,' he continued as he sat back down in his armchair. 'These are direct quotes as near as the translation permits.'

'The whole island was said to be mountainous near the sea surrounding it, but the interior surrounding the main city was relatively flat and fertile. The interior plain itself was fashioned by nature, and by the labours of many generations of kings, through long ages. The defining feature of the entire kingdom was the many concentric canals that all connected to a giant circular canal surrounding the main city. The depth, width, and length of this canal were incredible. It was excavated to the depth of a hundred feet, and its breadth was a stadium everywhere.'

'That is about 50 meters,' said Eckleston and carried on.

'Further inland, likewise, straight canals of a hundred feet in width were cut through the plain, and led off into a huge canal leading to the sea. These canals were at intervals of a hundred stadia, and along them the Atlanteans brought down wood from the mountains to the city and transported grain and fruits to the city. In the centre of the city was the royal palace. The entire city was protected by a gigantic circular wall. The city was densely populated, and the canals and the harbour were full of vessels and merchants.'

Eckleston looked up for a reaction. 'Fantastic, isn't it?' he said.

Fiona was intrigued but no nearer understanding what it all meant. 'So, what do you make of all this?' she asked cautiously.

Eckleston appeared surprised that she hadn't caught on yet. 'Don't you see? This is a precise description of the layout of their city, similar to the Roman city-states. And it was clear that they were a sea-faring people with the great harbour mentioned many times in the texts, and the notion of the many vessels and merchants shows us that they had extensive contact with other parts of the world. This was more than ten thousand years ago,' he announced jubilantly.

Fiona looked at him, trying to follow and trying hard not to look as if she was lost. 'So how do you know that this continent was what we now call Antarctica?'

Eckleston jumped out of his chair, and fetched a file from his bookshelf, along with a big atlas. 'Look at this,' he said and spread out a copy of what appeared to be an old map.

'This is the Piri Reis map,' said Eckleston and laid it out in front of Fiona. 'It is an actual map from 1513 that you can get a copy of if you like, and it is one of the cornerstones of Charles Hapgood's theory. History tells us that Antarctica wasn't even discovered until 1818. But 305 years earlier, in 1513, a well-known Ottoman Admiral named Piri Reis drew this map of the South Atlantic, featuring the western coast of Africa, the eastern coast of much of North and South America, plus a rugged coastline at the bottom of the map.'

The map was a light brown colour, rectangular in shape and it fitted neatly on a standard page of A4. It was clear that it was a depiction of the continents, but it was quite inaccurate, particularly in terms of the relative sizes of the continents.

'It was discovered in 1929,' continued Eckleston, 'in the library of the old Imperial Palace in Constantinople, or Istanbul, in Turkey. In a series of notes written in his own hand on the map itself, the Admiral says that he was not responsible for the original surveying and cartography. Instead, his role was merely that of a compiler and copyist, and that the map was derived from a large number of source maps, which have now apparently been lost. It is possible that he himself found those in the Imperial Library at Constantinople, where he enjoyed privileged access.'

The middle of the map was evidently an ocean, with small ships drawn in as ornaments. In the top right corner was a fairly accurate depiction of the Iberian Peninsula, followed a bit further south by Gibraltar and the West African coast, which swung into what is now the Gold Coast. Here the coastline abruptly disappeared, indicating that beyond this point, the coast had not been explored at the time of the making of the map.

In the top left corner was a small oblong land feature, that with a bit of imagination could be said to look like present-day Florida. Below it followed a plethora of islands large and small, but one dominated, and that was without question what is today Cuba. Woefully out of proportion with the other landmasses, it was nevertheless possible to make out the Yucatan Peninsula, much of Central America and what appeared to be a highly accurate depiction of what is today the coastline of Brazil and Argentina. This coastline was very detailed and continued all the way down to the bottom of the map.

At the bottom of the page was another stretch of coastline, but Fiona couldn't make out what it might be.

'What's this?' asked Fiona and pointed.

'That, my dear, is Antarctica without the ice,' announced Eckleston proudly.

'I don't understand,' said Fiona confused. 'Without ice?'

'Don't worry,' he said. 'Most people didn't understand let alone pay much attention to it for a very long time, until Professor Hapgood took it upon himself to investigate. He was fortunate in the sense that at the time he threw himself into this endeavour, the US Airforce, more precisely the 8th Reconnaissance Squadron under SAC Command, had just completed a new type of mapping using a new radar technique. It entailed flying over the entire continent of Antarctica while bouncing radar waves off its surface. Some of the waves would penetrate the ice, and the returning radar energy enabled the Americans to produce an exact map of the landmasses below the ice. Comparing the Piri Reis map with the new and precise maps produced by the US Air Force, Hapgood was so intrigued that he immediately asked the Airforce to have a look for themselves. And this is how they responded on the 6th of July 1960,' said Eckleston and pulled out another sheet of paper.

'SUBJECT: ADMIRAL PIRI REIS WORLD MAP.'

'TO: PROFESSOR CHARLES HAPGOOD, KEENE COLLEGE, KEENE, NEW HAMPSHIRE.'

'DEAR PROFESSOR HAPGOOD. YOUR REQUEST FOR EVALUATION OF THE 1513 PIRI REIS WORLD MAP HAS BEEN REVIEWED. THE CLAIM THAT THE LOWER PART OF THE MAP PORTRAYS THE PRINCESS MARTHA COAST OF QUEEN MAUDE'S LAND, ANTARCTICA, AND THE PALMER PENINSULA, IS FOUND TO BE REASONABLE. WE FIND THIS IS THE MOST LOGICAL, AND IN ALL PROBABILITY, THE CORRECT INTERPRETATION OF THE MAP. THE GEOGRAPHICAL AND TOPOLOGICAL DETAIL IN THE SOUTHERN PART OF THE MAP ALSO AGREES VERY REMARKABLY WITH THE RESULTS OF THE SEISMIC PROFILE MADE ACROSS THE TOP OF THE ICE CAP BY THE SWEDISH-BRITISH ANTARCTIC EXPEDITION OF 1949. THIS APPEARS TO INDICATE, THAT THE COASTLINE HAD BEEN MAPPED BEFORE IT WAS COVERED BY THE ICE CAP. THE ICE CAP IN THIS REGION IS NOW ABOUT A MILE THICK.

WE HAVE NOT BEEN ABLE TO ASCERTAIN HOW THIS MAP CAN BE RECONCILED WITH THE SUPPOSED STATE OF GEOGRAPHICAL KNOWLEDGE ABOUT THAT PART OF THE SOUTHERN HEMISPHERE IN 1513.'

'The letter is signed, Harold Z. Ohlmeyer, Lt. Colonel, USAF, Commander,' concluded Eckleston and handed Fiona the letter.

'And look for yourself, first at the atlas here,' said Eckleston and showed her a detailed map of the entire Antarctica, 'and then at the Piri Reis map over here.'

Fiona had to concede that the two were remarkably similar. In fact, so similar that she was prepared to write off the deviations to the fact that the Piri Reis map was hand-drawn and produced using comparatively primitive navigation and positioning equipment.

It was unmistakably Queen Maude's Land to the right, and the oblong peninsula that jutted out on the left side of the map was surely the Palmer Peninsula extending north towards South America. All the islands in between, along with the coastline connecting the two features, showed her beyond any doubt that this was in fact a map of Antarctica, as it would appear if the ice could be melted away.

'But how could that be, if almost the entire continent was covered by kilometres of snow and ice?' asked Fiona perplexed.

'There is only one answer,' Eckleston smiled knowingly. 'The map was not made by Piri Reis. It was merely compiled by him from a range of other much older maps. He even intimated as much himself. As I told you, Antarctica wasn't discovered in modern times until 1818, and people didn't set foot there until 1821, and by then it had already been completely enveloped in ice for thousands of years, including the time when Piri Reis made the map. But it is evident from Reis' map, that the knowledge of the coastline existed in 1513. And the clearly distinguishable features of the Antarctica coastline could only have been made while the continent was free of ice. And according to the Earth Crust Displacement Theory, when was this?' he asked rhetorically.

Fiona was amazed by how well the puzzle pieces fitted together. '12,000 years ago,' she whispered.

Eckleston had completed his oratory, and it had achieved the desired effect. His eyes were shining, and his face beamed with delight as he watched Fiona absorb the implications of what he had said.

'The cartography is indisputable. Seafarers had knowledge of the Antarctic coastline as it was when there was no ice, some 12,000 years ago. And there is more,' he said and pulled out another map. 'This is called the Oronteus Finaeus Map,' he said and handed her a map made of two sections. One, of the Arctic seen from the North Pole, and the other of the Antarctic, seen from the South Pole. In terms of the quality of the map it was not much different from the Piri Reis map, but the depiction of the South Pole showed the landmasses as they now appear under the ice.

'In the Reference Room of the Library of Congress in Washington DC, this ancient map of non-glacial Antarctica was discovered by Professor Hapgood, who had teamed up with Dr. Richard Strachan of MIT. They jointly studied the map and concluded that it must have been copied and compiled from several earlier source maps because it shows non-glacial conditions in coastal regions of Antarctica that closely matched the seismic survey maps of subglacial land surfaces. Their conclusion was as follows.'

'THE PROPOSITION THAT ANTARCTICA WAS VISITED AND PERHAPS SETTLED BY MEN WHEN IT WAS LARGELY IF NOT ENTIRELY NON-GLACIAL, SEEMS VALID. IT GOES WITHOUT SAYING THAT THIS IMPLIES A VERY GREAT ANTIQUITY (AND) TAKES THE CIVILISATION OF THE ORIGINAL MAP MAKERS BACK TO A TIME CONTEMPORARY WITH THE END OF THE LAST ICE AGE IN THE NORTHERN HEMISPHERE.'

'Impressive, eh?' said Eckleston. 'Now, I said that Plato had also to some extent led us astray, and here is why,' he continued and again took out the Finaeus map. 'In recording the first known reference to Atlantis, Plato described its location as being in the 'true ocean'. Most people are used to seeing maps of the earth that employ the Mercator projection, where the surface of the planet is peeled off the spherical Earth, and flattened to fit a square piece of paper. This results in significant stretching near the edges of the map, thereby making landmasses and oceans to the far north and the far south appear much larger than they really are. The Mercator projection also led people to believe that this 'true ocean' was the Atlantic Ocean, since it is vast and has appeared at the centre of our maps for centuries, and it lies directly beyond the Pillars of Hercules. But when viewing the Earth from the South Pole, it becomes clear that the Earth has but one true ocean,' he said and pointed to the map. 'That ocean is the sum of the Atlantic, the Pacific and the Indian Ocean, and the continent placed at its centre is Antarctica. Today this ocean is even called the World Ocean by oceanographers.'

'Compelling,' said Fiona.

'And now that you have seen the maps, let me read to you the three sentences in Plato's Dialogue that describe where the island continent was supposed to have been located, relative to what we today call Europe and Africa.'

'IN THOSE ANCIENT DAYS, THAT OCEAN COULD BE NAVIGATED, AS THERE WAS AN ISLAND OUTSIDE THE CHANNEL, WHICH YOUR COUNTRYMEN TELL ME YOU CALL THE PILLARS OF HERCULES. THIS ISLAND WAS LARGER THAN LIBYA AND ASIA TOGETHER, AND FROM IT, SEAFARERS IN THOSE TIMES COULD MAKE THEIR WAY TO THE OTHERS, AND THENCE TO THE WHOLE OPPOSITE CONTINENT, WHICH IS ENCIRCLED BY THE TRUE OUTER OCEAN. THE WATERS WITHIN THE CHANNEL, ARE MANIFESTLY A BASIN WITH A NARROW ENTRANCE. WHAT LIES BEYOND IT IS THE REAL OCEAN, AND IT IS LAND ENCLOSING THAT OCEAN WHICH SHOULD RIGHTLY BE CALLED A CONTINENT.'

'This describes perfectly its size, and the fact that the island lay beyond the Straits of Gibraltar, which is a narrow channel, in the True Ocean. In addition, it describes that it was possible for the island's seafarers to sail to the 'opposite continent', which is the rest of the world as seen from Antarctica.'

Eckleston put down the quote and sat back. 'There is no doubt in my mind that Antarctica was the place of the lost civilisation.'

Fiona was flabbergasted by it all and sat for a few moments shifting her gaze from the Atlas to the Piri Reiss map, to the letter from the US Airforce.

'So, what happened to it? The continent, I mean.' she finally mumbled, looking up at Eckleston.

'Well, it is supposed to have sunk into the sea as a punishment from the gods, but I believe there to be a perfectly logical and scientifically very plausible explanation to its demise.'

'The Earth Crust Displacement Theory of Charles Hapgood?' said Fiona.

'Exactly right,' said Eckleston and pointed his index finger at her. 'It provides a simple logical solution that even fits perfectly with the time this catastrophe is supposed to have occurred. Huge amounts of geological evidence have proven beyond any doubt, that the Earth underwent sudden and dramatic temperature changes some 12,000 years ago, at exactly the time this civilisation perished. That point in time coincides with a period where huge amounts of ice had built up around what was then the poles. The Earth Crust Displacement Theory takes care of the rest. The violent shift in the Earth's crust simply tore the whole civilisation apart. There would have been volcanoes and tidal waves and earthquakes, and this would surely have destroyed everything. And the reason there isn't even a hint anywhere of other civilisations perishing in this disaster is because there simply were none. No other civilisation had advanced to anywhere near the level of that found in Antarctica. And note also that coincidentally, virtually every religion on the face of this planet to some extent takes its origin in a cataclysmic natural disaster. Earthquakes, floods and volcanic eruptions.

'Yes,' said Fiona. 'That is true. I remember reading about that so-called coincidence.'

Eckleston continued his monologue. 'Assuming that Hapgood's theory holds, as a result of the violent crust displacement, the forest-covered hills of the continent, would suddenly be situated in present-day Antarctica, where regeneration of the vegetation was impossible. The same would have been true for the existence of the ancient civilisation. The people who survived the cataclysm would have had no chance of surviving in arctic conditions, which must have gripped the land within weeks or even days of the displacement happening. It all makes sense. Add to all of this the fact that the Piri Reis map proves beyond any doubt that an ancient knowledge of the coastlines of this continent was present 12,000 years ago. That is to me more than sufficient evidence to prove that Antarctica is indeed the site of the lost civilisation.'

Fiona scratched her head, feeling herself wanting to believe the story, but having great difficulty overcoming a tendency to cling to more traditional scientific dogma. Perhaps she wasn't as open-minded as she liked to think.

'But don't you think it's a little odd that there are no traces of it anywhere?' she finally asked.

Eckleston smiled overbearingly. 'My dear girl. That is what is so beautiful about this. It didn't just vanish, and there are thousands of remnants all over the world.'

Fiona now looked puzzled. 'What do you mean?'

'Well. This was a highly advanced civilisation, much more so than other peoples on the planet, and through their navigation of the world's oceans and their extensive trading activities, they spread parts of that technology to various places on other continents. There are hundreds of examples of the exact same construction techniques being applied independently thousands of years ago in South America, South East Asia and in Egypt. Note for example that the Pyramids of Giza are aligned to star constellations as they appeared in the sky in the Age of Leo, which was around 10500 BC. But the pyramids are supposedly from 2500 BC. Don't you find that odd? There was plenty of time for the technology of the lost civilisation to spread out across the world. Recently, huge underwater structures have been uncovered in the ocean off southern Japan, that can only have been man-made.'

'Under the water?' asked Fiona sceptically.

'Yes. They are now, but 12,000 years ago they were above the water, as the sea level has risen at least 100 meters since then. These structures were the result of this dissemination of technology that happened in the heyday of the lost civilisation.'

'So, if there were any remains of an ancient civilisation in Antarctica, there is a good chance that they are under the water now?'

'Yes, unfortunately. There are actually very similar finds off the coast of Florida, but the evidence is inconclusive at this point.'

Fiona was a little overwhelmed by all the information she had received, but she had to admit that it made sense in a weird sort of way. She was still trying to overcome the internal barrier erected within her over the years by traditional science and by the accepted schools of thought on geology and anthropology.

'But you don't believe that anything is left in Antarctica today?' she asked.

'No. Definitely not. I think everything has been destroyed. It appears to me like the plain that is mentioned in Plato's dialog, upon which the main city-state of the civilisation was situated, might have been the result of thousands of years of sediment being washed down from the mountains of Antarctica. Settling in a valley, this layer of sediment would have provided excellent and rich soil for trees and human crops. But it would also have been a death trap for the city.'

'How so?'

'When the first violent earthquakes came, I think that the entire layer of sediment built up over millennia might have been shaken loose, so to speak, and simply slipped into the ocean, completely wiping out the city in an enormous landslide and burying it in the process. Hence the persistent legend that the lost civilisation sank into the sea. This phenomenon has been witnessed in many places around the world, most notably in the Norwegian town of Rissa back in the 1970s when an entire village slid into a fjord within the space of twenty minutes. Nothing was left of it. I believe the same basic principle applies here, only on a much bigger and more brutal scale. Add to that volcanoes and tidal waves, and it isn't very hard to understand why such an event was recounted by many different peoples across the globe as a cataclysm, probably caused by the anger of the gods. Legend has it that the ancient civilisation, and let's just call it Atlantis for now, sank beneath the waves, but logically it is highly unlikely that such a vast mountainous continent would just disappear. It is much more probable that instead of vanishing in the ocean, it ended up being covered by ice after the catastrophic events that destroyed it and most likely killed most of its inhabitants.'

'The city-state being washed into the sea?'

'Exactly.'

'So was Thule and Atlantis really the same thing?' asked Fiona and put down the copy of the Piri Reis map.

Eckleston smiled and looked at her as if she had just spoken the mantra of a long-lost religion. 'Yes,' he said, and continued in a solemn voice. 'I firmly believe that they were. I think that the Thule Society may have been very close to finding some artefacts from, or remnants of, the lost civilisation in other locations around the world, but I'm not entirely convinced that they actually succeeded. Principally, because I believe that their initial theories were a bit out of this world to be quite honest.'

'How do you mean?'

'Well, let me give you an example. Some of the most, shall we say 'open-minded' members of the Thule Society, believed that the Earth was like a hollow ball, with entry corridors in certain places, particularly near the poles.'

Fiona almost laughed out loud as she heard that, but she managed to compose herself, hoping that Eckleston didn't notice.

'Now, obviously that whole idea is preposterous, but this was a time of what you might call a very rapid scientific awakening of society as a whole, and not just in Germany. Similar ideas sprang from other places in the world including America and Britain. But this flood of alternative thinking within science resulted in some quite remarkable, and at times some remarkably silly, ideas. Richard Walter Darré, an Argentinean who was educated in England, proposed that anything of significance in life was to some extent linked with race. Darré believed that all great civilisations in the history of mankind had been founded by men with so-called Nordic blood in their veins, and he claimed that they had all fallen, because they hadn't managed to maintain racial purity. Coincidentally, this accords well with the legend that the people of Atlantis were initially pure in heart and spirit, since they were the children of the gods. But as they intermingled with the lesser races of the planet, they became vain and unruly, engaging in all manner of loathsome behaviour, until finally the gods lost their patience and destroyed them in a cataclysm.'

'It certainly does sound familiar,' said Fiona.

'Darré proposed that in order to prevent the corruption of modern German Society, all international and humanitarian organisations should be suppressed.'

'Well, it seems that you are right,' Fiona interjected. 'These ideas certainly do sound a little farfetched, I must admit.'

'They do indeed,' replied Eckleston. 'The theory of an Earth riddled with underground structures, has a strong racial element, in that it pre-supposes that these structures were inhabited by a form of super-beings, and this was exactly what the Nazis needed. As I have already told you, they were in search of something that could assert the proposition that the Germans were a master race that was destined for world domination.'

'Just as their supposed forefathers from Thule or Atlantis had been,' said Fiona.

'Exactly. Now, the main Nazi architect behind the plan for the extermination and replacement of Christianity and other religions was ironically a Jew, Alfred Rosenberg. Similarly to Darré, he claimed that all civilisations were the work of Nordic men and that they all originated from a common lost civilisation. This idea was then re-packaged and served to the German public as Aryan Theosophy, with claims that the Aryan race had dominated the world in ancient times. He went on to preach that this master race had spread out across the world in their Swan- and Dragon ships to found all the ancient civilisations that we know of today. Of course, this new religion invoked colourful images of a bold and kind-hearted people, that unselfishly spread its wisdom to the less endowed. In other words, it was just what a new religion needed.'

Eckleston shifted slowly in his armchair and raised his index finger. 'As I tell you these things about the occultism within the Nazi party, and the SS in particular, please keep in mind that every word of this is based on historical and verifiable facts. I am not making any of this up. You can go and check for yourself. Just so that you don't shoot the messenger, and have me dragged off to an asylum somewhere,' he said and smiled.

'Don't worry,' chuckled Fiona. 'I won't hold you responsible the day an army of Nazis emerge from their polar caves to flood the Earth. That reminds me. How does this tie into the expeditions that were mounted? You mentioned something about a fifth expedition the last time we spoke?'

'Oh, yes. The Nazi interest in sending out missions to far off places seems to originate from the legend of Agharti. It is an ancient Asian story of a great civilisation that once blossomed in the Gobi Desert, in present-day China, which fled underground to two subterranean cities called Schambhala and Agharti. It was hoped that if they could find the remains of these underground cities, they would be able to uncover clues to the lost civilisation of Thule, from where the Aryan race supposedly sprang. Himmler, through the SS-Ahnenerbe, sent out an expedition to Tibet to locate the entrance to these lost cities.'

'But you said that there were several expeditions.'

'Yes. I believe that they also sent people to Egypt, as well as Central and South America.'

'And the fifth expedition?'

'Well, this is purely speculation on my part, but it is conceivable that they dispatched an expedition to Antarctica to look for similar underground cities.'

'But you don't believe that they found anything?'

'Underground structures? No. If there ever was an Atlantis or Thule, it was surely destroyed in the cataclysm. Of that I am certain,' said Eckleston firmly.

'Does it really matter?' asked Fiona. 'Whether it is called Atlantis or Thule, I mean?'

'What?' said Eckleston, and jerked out of his brief moment of reflection. 'Oh. No, I suppose it doesn't really, does it?' he said dismissively. 'After all, what's in a name, eh?'

Fiona rose from her chair and looked at her wristwatch. 'Mr. Eckleston, I think I had better get going now. It's getting late in the day, and I would like to pop by the office.'

'Certainly,' smiled Eckleston and walked her to the front door which he opened for her. 'Please let me know if I can be of any further assistance in the future, won't you?'

'Thanks a bunch, Mr. Eckleston. It's much appreciated,' she smiled and walked out to her car.

As Fiona's car had disappeared from view, the telephone on the coffee table in Eckleston's living room rang. He picked it up and sat down on the sofa next to the small table.

'Eckleston,' he said, preparing to either entertain an enthusiastic journalist or to fend off another unrestrained critic.

'Good afternoon, Mr. Eckleston,' said an even and calm voice from thousands of kilometres away. 'This is Erich Strauss. We may have a problem.'

TWELVE

Ahmed Kamal Rashid donned his Level 4 biohazard suit and wiped a piece of cloth across the transparent plastic visor to remove specks of dust. He threw the cloth in the bin and punched the panel that opened the door to the decontamination corridor connecting the small shed with the main laboratory building. Walking calmly through the corridor he went through successive clouds of water and vaporised decontamination chemicals, that sprayed out of the many sets of nozzles that were affixed to the inside of the corridor. Each vapour cloud was different, but they all helped to ensure that the main lab remained completely sterile at all times. More importantly, they also ensured that the pathogens would never make it out of the lab by accident.

He had never worked in such an advanced scientific compound as this, and upon arriving at the huge cave some days ago after a long drive through the desolate desert, he had been dumbfounded by the sight that had greeted him. The dome inside the mountain was the largest underground structure he had ever seen, but he was even more impressed when Yusef had shown him the laboratory facilities.

Working previously at the University of Damascus, he had been one of the most influential scientists on campus, but that had not been able to change the fact that he was always lacking funds for his research. A common problem for scientists around the world, particularly within fields of study such as physics where huge equipment was often needed. In Damascus, this was also a persistent and frustrating problem at the Biology Faculty. Countless times he had been pursuing a research project and had commenced planning for the final stages of the programme, only to be frustrated by the lack of money to carry them out, as well as by the seemingly endless bureaucracy of the government.

Added to that was the fact that certain areas within his field of research were off-limits, in the sense that they conflicted with the story of creation recounted by the Koran, and as such was simply omitted from the University's research programme. This had never directly influenced his own work, but former colleagues of his had seen their research programmes terminated because they took their origin in Darwinian evolutionary theories, which made them unacceptable to the government. Being involved with microbiology had presented similar problems from time to time, but he had soon learned that this area of research was so complicated and demanded such a vast knowledge for anyone to be able to discuss it, that government bureaucrats simply gave up trying. That left him with the opportunity to tell them whatever he liked, which he promptly did without any moral qualms. In that way, he had avoided interference in his work based solely on religious issues, which for him was an absolute minimum requirement for performing serious and ambitious scientific research.

But that had never removed the money problems that dogged him and his colleagues, several of whom he now had working beside him under this great dome. His position at the university had provided him with the opportunity to carefully and discretely recruit young bright minds for this the greatest of research projects. And not just any bright students with top grades, but in particular those who had developed a clear sense of religious and political purpose for themselves.

There were plenty of the latter in Syria, but a combination of the two virtues, which is what he considered them to be, was not very prevalent. He had been extremely careful in his choices, but every single one of his young colleagues had accepted his proposition without much in the way of hesitation. The opportunity to break new scientific ground while at the same time pursuing a noble cause, was attractive enough for all of them to agree to living and working for an extended period in a cave in the desert. Exactly how long that period might end up being he didn't know himself, and he doubted that even the Alchemist knew.

★ ★ ★

A couple of hours earlier at Sheldrake Place in London, Andrew had arrived in his office to find a message from Colonel Strickland waiting on his desk.

'Have you seen the message?' asked Catherine. She had stuck her head into Andrew's office to ensure that Strickland's request was fulfilled. 'He asked me to ensure that you got it as soon as you came in,' she smiled.

'Right,' he said. 'I've got it. Thanks Cathy.'

Andrew quickly ran through his mail from the day before and checked his inbox on his PC. There was nothing there that required his immediate attention, so he got up a few minutes later and made his way to Colonel Strickland's office.

'Andy. Nice of you to stop by,' said the colonel, ever the courteous gentleman.

He was of the old school in more ways than one. Having been too young to fight in the Second World War, he had still been old enough to see his country very close to being run over by the enemy. This had given him a deep sense that freedom wasn't to be taken for granted. It was not always going to be there unless you made sure that you could hold on to it, and do it by force if need be. His reputation for professionalism was impeccable, and having been a member of the SBS for more than twenty years, seeing action in a number of conflicts, several of which far removed from the public eye, he had eventually joined the SAS. Performing his duties in a textbook manner as a squad leader, he had been promoted a number of times, eventually being appointed to head the division in the SAS which was responsible for identifying and combatting biochemical threats to the United Kingdom.

Gordon Strickland was always dressed in his uniform, although the house dress code was very relaxed, and would have allowed him to wear a suit or even just a shirt with no tie. But Strickland held on to what he considered essential standards, reflecting his desire to do things by the book as much as possible. The notion of doing things by the book had become a trademark for him over the years. He had earned a reputation for being a decisive commander who would rarely make the wrong decision, and who always did things the proper way. But what had made him perfect for the job in the SBS and later the SAS had been his ability to improvise when the situation demanded it. On several occasions during combat, particularly in the midst of close-quarter fighting, he had analysed the situation in a flash and taken the initiative with offensive action that had turned the situation to his advantage, often securing vital enemy positions and allowing other more conventional ground forces to move in. Right now, he looked like someone's friendly uncle as he stood there in his office with his pipe in his mouth.

'Sir. You've asked to see me?'

'Yes, Andy. As you might have guessed I've been following your investigation with interest but also with some trepidation, I must say.'

The Colonel looked a little uneasy, which was unusual.

'What do you mean?' asked Andrew.

'I understand that you've been talking to a Doctor Phillip Eckleston, is that correct?'

'Yes. Or rather, Fiona has,' said Andrew puzzled.

'I've had MI5 run a check on him, and what they came up with was somewhat ambiguous.'

'How is that?'

'Well, it seems the good doctor is an outcast in the scientific community due to some rather extraordinary theories of his. I must admit that I don't fully understand them, and quite frankly I haven't made an effort to do so.'

'But that's not all, I gather?'

'No. Apparently he affiliated briefly with a society called the Order of the Second Sanctuary when he was a young man at Cambridge.'

Andrew immediately got a bad feeling about Eckleston. He'd had his fair share of esoteric societies over the past few weeks. 'What do we know of this society?' he asked.

'Very little I'm afraid. In fact, we're not even able to determine whether it still exists or not. From what we can gather from a number of old student gazettes still kept at Cambridge, they worked for a united world, with all peoples conforming to a common culture, in order to prevent war and conflict.'

'That all sounds very harmless,' said Andrew.

'Granted,' responded Strickland. 'But since we cannot determine with any degree of certainty what their agenda was, how they aimed to achieve it, and indeed if they are still active, we are a little bit in the dark here, I'm afraid.'

'Are there no lists of previous members anywhere?'

'No. Apparently, it was quite an exclusive bunch of young lads.'

'But why so worried about a group of pacifists?' asked Andrew.

'Firstly, we can't actually be certain that they aimed to achieve their goals by peaceful means, and secondly when your investigation comes up with elements that smack of the occult, I think it is reasonable to be vigilant, even if it took place in the distant past. Especially given what we have uncovered recently.'

'I'm sure you're right,' conceded Andrew. 'I appreciate you telling me this. As it happens, Fiona is supposed to have talked to him only yesterday, so she might have something more about this for us. In fact, I believe she's waiting in my office as we speak.'

Strickland perked up and tapped Andrew on the shoulder in a fatherly fashion. 'Well, go on then, young man. Can't keep a young lady waiting, can you?'

'No. I suspect I can't. Not this one anyway. Is that all, Sir?'

'Yes. Good day to you, Andy.'

'Sir.'

★ ★ ★

Upon reaching the entrance to the main laboratory, Rashid waited patiently for the giant blow dryers to remove all the moisture from his suit, before pressing the access panel and walking inside through the sliding doors to the main laboratory. The Alchemist was standing motionless at the far end of the room, stooping over a high-powered microscope. He didn't react to the sound of the doors sliding open and shut, but seemed to be completely immersed in his work.

Rashid walked in the slow and controlled manner that by now had become a habit when working in the lab. Not just because sudden moves could destroy sensitive equipment or even ruin scientific experiments, but also because of the obvious risk of harming himself. If his suit tore open, he could potentially be exposed to the bacteria they were nurturing. It was highly unlikely that the pathogen should escape from its containers or from the extensive and extremely costly array of processing and testing equipment that was lined up within the labs. But that was no excuse to be careless.

They were still in the early phases of testing and characterising the original samples. They only had a very limited number to work with, so every single experiment that was carried out to determine the nature and characteristics of the bacterium was discussed extensively within the group before any work was commenced.

It had been a pleasure for Rashid to watch his young proteges blossom under his leadership. They worked tirelessly, and they constantly came up with new ideas and approaches, and they had even impressed Khan, whom Rashid suspected had initially been very sceptical about the abilities of the youngsters. In fact, much of the progress made so far was in no small part due to their efforts, but at this moment they were resting in their quarters in the office building.

Rashid walked over to an extremely precise spectroscopic tool, primarily used for the separation of molecular matter according to its mass. It was one of the most expensive pieces of laboratory equipment in the building. It had just finished an analysis of an organic crystalline residue that Rashid had inserted a few hours earlier. He sat down on the chair by the spectrometer and looked at the results. They would have to be analysed further by the team at a later time, but the preliminary results seemed encouraging. The microscopic organisms they were working with had the most astonishing properties he had ever seen or heard of. Rashid had developed a fascination with pathogens many years ago, but now he had finally got the opportunity to work on a project that had no constraints whatsoever.

Bacteria basically fall into one of two groups. Archaebacteria which are ancient forms thought to have evolved separately from other bacteria, and Eubacteria which have evolved as an integrated part of the rest of the bacteriological ecosystem. They are found in the bodies of all living organisms and on all parts of the planet, including the tallest peaks, the deepest and coldest ocean trenches, arctic environments, even highly acidic hot springs, and they have even been detected in the stratosphere. The only form of life on Earth for more than 3 billion years, these single-celled organisms essentially ruled the planet for a period that makes the perceived rule of Homo Sapiens look like a short ad break in an all-night movie marathon. For most of Earth's history, they were the real rulers of the planet, and in many ways, they could still be argued to be just that.

They were first observed by Antony van Leeuwenhoek in the 17th century, and have proven themselves remarkably adaptable to very diverse and often extremely harsh environmental conditions. Under unfavourable conditions, some bacteria form highly resistant spores with thick coverings within which the living material remains dormant in altered form until conditions improve. Others are able to repair their own DNA, making them resistant to even high doses of radioactivity.

Generally speaking, the genetic material within bacteria is organised in a continuous circular strand of DNA. This strand of DNA is located in an area called the nucleoid, but there is no membrane surrounding a defined nucleus within the cell, as is the case for cells in plants and animals. Similar to other living things, bacterium reproduction happens mainly by cell division, yielding identical daughter cells. In theory, these processes should produce identical cells, but the rapid rate of mutation possible in bacteria makes them very adaptable indeed.

This particular type of bacterium was entirely unlike anything Rashid had seen before, and their best guess was that this strain had been around since at least 200 million years ago. Since then, it had mutated many times over, making it ever more resistant to the hostile environment surrounding it. It was of the Anaerobic kind, which meant that it was unable to grow in the presence of free oxygen. Instead, it only developed in an environment where it was able to obtain oxygen from other compounds surrounding it.

This gave it useful characteristics as far as the science team was concerned since oxygen in a compound state basically functioned like a trigger. When it came into contact with oxygen contained within other compounds, and if at the same time it was subjected to an environment that offered a temperature of more than 30 degrees Celsius, it would develop and do so unfathomably quickly, as they had recently learned. The fact that it only awoke at a certain temperature also meant that, contrary to Saprobes that live off dead organic matter, this bacterium was only able to exist in its active form on and inside living warm-blooded creatures.

The real potency of the pathogen was that when it was exposed to oxygen in a gaseous form, it would secrete a bluish crystalline material that would create a protective casing around it, probably preparing it for hibernation if that should prove necessary. This crystallisation would happen in the phytoplasma of the infected cells, causing them to entirely crystallise virtually instantaneously, setting off a chain reaction through the tissue. They had performed several experiments on mice the day before, and it had been a shocking sight.

The experiments had been carried out in completely airtight Plexiglas containers, which had subsequently been incinerated. This was necessary because, as they had also discovered yesterday, as the animals succumb to its invasion, the bacterium in its crystalline form would become airborne, due to something akin to vitrification of the living tissue.

The bacterium had also proven very mobile, giving it the ability to move very quickly through its host's bloodstream and the lymphocytic conduits all over the body. Directly attacking the tissue immediately upon contact, the pathogen was autotrophic, meaning it manufactured its own food by way of chemosynthesis, which is similar to photosynthesis but requires no light. Self-supporting and without the need for light to live and propagate, it quickly invaded virtually every cell in the host, where it lived a short but violent life, before returning to its crystalline state, and then once more waiting for its chance to be resurrected.

As Rashid watched the result of the mass spectrometer, Khan came over with another sample from 'the Farm' as they now called the incubation chambers that had slowly started to produce controlled mutations of the pathogen.

'Run the analysis on this one as well,' he said through his headset and handed Rashid a tiny glass container.

'It's a modified form of crystal secreted from the strain that killed one of the mice yesterday. It appears to be somewhat more powerful than any of the previous ones.'

Rashid carefully took the container with both gloves, opened the spectrometer, and placed the sample inside. This was probably one of the most hazardous operations during the whole process. There simply wasn't a conveyor belt or anything else that could transport the samples from incubation chambers to the spectrometer after they had been extracted, so they had to perform that task manually. Being a scientist, Rashid knew that it would eventually go wrong as the number of times it was performed went towards infinity. So, from that perspective his most important task was to prevent that number from getting too high, which in turn meant making swift progress with the research programme, reaching an acceptable result, and to do it sooner rather than later.

'I'm going to go for a couple of hours sleep,' said Khan and walked behind Rashid towards the exit. 'How are the boys doing?'

'They are resting for now. But they will be back later today. You just can't keep them away, you know,' he said proudly.

'I have noticed,' replied Khan. 'They have shown themselves to be good scientists,' he concluded, making his way to the exit and entering the long decontamination corridor for another chemical disinfection procedure.

Rashid had already learned that those words amounted to a huge compliment coming from the lips of Kashim Khan. He seldom made himself heard when things were going according to plan, but would sometimes blow up in a fit of rage, if he felt that someone had been sloppy or unprofessional. A perfectionist, he simply didn't accept anything less than the utmost from every team member. And while that took its toll on some of them from time to time, they had to concede that Khan had been able to bring out the best in all of them, and the sum of their efforts had been nothing short of superb.

★ ★ ★

When Andrew arrived back at his office, Fiona was sitting in the front office chatting to Catherine. They were talking about holiday destinations and seemed very much to be enjoying themselves.

'Am I interrupting anything?' asked Andrew and stopped in the doorway to the front office.

Catherine looked up and smiled. 'No, not at all. Fiona here was just telling me about the Azores, and how you refused to let her come with you to the top of the volcano,' she said with a teasing smile.

'Really?' smiled Andrew. 'I think that was very much her own choice. She was busy catching young men on the harbour most of the time, as I recall.'

'Right,' interrupted Fiona. 'That story is getting old already. Let's get to down business.' She then rose and marched into Andrew's office without seeming to care whether he followed or not.

'Better do what the lady tells you,' giggled Catherine.

'So,' said Andrew as he entered the office and closed the double mahogany doors behind him. 'What did you come up with?'

Fiona began telling him about her experience at Eckleston's house, and all the while Andrew, kept in mind what Colonel Strickland had just told him. Despite the seemingly outrageous stories Fiona conveyed, there was no hint of a secret society.

Having been told about Strickland's reservations regarding Eckleston, Fiona could not think of anything that might have implied something odd. Except for when they had discussed whether an ancient civilisation called Atlantis or Thule might have been found by the Nazis. At that moment Eckleston had appeared fidgety. But whether that was significant or not, she couldn't say.

'After the meeting with Eckleston, I spent some more time researching the *SS-Ahnenerbe*. The amount of information on these people is surprisingly scarce, but I guess it's easier to think of the entire SS as a ragtag gathering of violent hoodlums and to disregard that some of them were actually very bright and scientifically minded, although perhaps a bit eccentric.'

'That's probably putting it mildly,' said Andrew and raised his eyebrows.

'Anyway,' continued Fiona. 'I discovered that the chief administrator of the *SS-Ahnenerbe*, Dr. Wolfram Sievers, had been heavily involved in medical experiments that were carried out on Jews in concentration camps, all to prove racial differences and the superiority of the Aryan race. After Germany's defeat in 1945, Sievers was brought before a war crimes tribunal, found guilty and sentenced to death. He was executed on June 2, 1948.'

'So?' asked Andrew.

'So, doesn't it strike you as a bit strange that one of the leaders of a supposedly archaeological and anthropological research division was involved with medical experiments on human subjects?'

'It does,' said Andrew pensively. 'What do you suppose they were experimenting with?

'Well, the only reason for Wolfgang Sievers to be involved in medical experiments, must have been that the experiments carried out had some relation to the *SS-Ahnenerbe* expeditions. This leads me to believe that the concentration camp prisoners were subjected to something brought back from one or more of the expeditions.'

'You could be right,' nodded Andrew. 'There's really no other obvious way of explaining it. The bacterium transported aboard the U-boat might have been one of them?'

'I think that is very likely,' said Fiona. 'And there is one other thing that caught my attention when I looked into this a bit further: Apparently, these events aren't necessarily a thing of the very distant past. As it says here in this book:'

'SCHOLARS INVOLVED IN AHNENERBE RESEARCH, CLAIMED THAT THEIR SOLE INTEREST WAS THE DEVELOPMENT OF THEIR SPECIFIC FIELD OF STUDY. BUT EVIDENCE SHOWS THEY KNEW OF, AND WERE COMPLICIT IN, THE NAZI CRIMES AGAINST HUMANITY. THEY WERE SS OFFICERS IN UNIFORM, AND THEY PARTICIPATED IN CLOSE DISCUSSIONS WITHIN THE COUNCIL OF AHNENERBE, WHILST SCIENTISTS WHO WOULD NOT GO ALONG WITH THE NAZIS WERE OSTRACISED. WHEN THE ARCHAEOLOGICAL ACTIVITIES OF THE SS DIED WITH HITLER, HIMMLER AND SIEVERS, THE SS-AHNENERBE TOO MELTED AWAY. MANY OF ITS TOP ARCHAEOLOGISTS HOWEVER, RETURNED UNPUNISHED TO UNIVERSITY LIFE AFTER THE WAR, ONLY TO RE-EMERGE AS LEADING ACADEMICS IN POST-WAR GERMANY.'

'So, what you're saying is, the SS-Ahnenerbe officially melted away, but it didn't necessarily disappear?'

'Correct. Many of its members were never even put on trial, and it even seems that some of them simply continued their careers in archaeology after the war.'

Thinking of the events of the day before, Andrew sat back in his chair for a few seconds while contemplating this new information. 'I suppose it is possible that one or more of them kept the Thule Society alive all the way up until now.'

'Do you think so?'

'I think it is possible,' said Andrew and then went on to recount the story of his visit to Vienna, which seemed at least as strange to Fiona, as her story had seemed to him.

'So, where's the book?' asked Fiona curiously.

'It's right here,' said Andrew and pulled it up from one of his drawers. 'Look at the insignia on the cover. Recognise it?'

'Of course. It's the insignia of the Thule Society, the same as the one we found in Kaufmann's safe.'

Andrew nodded and gave the book to Fiona. As she held it in her hand, she didn't quite know what to say.

'Damn. This is amazing,' she said. 'Have you looked at it yet?'

'Just briefly, but I don't understand German well enough to read it. I thought you might be able to.'

'Definitely,' she said and walked over to a sofa with a coffee table in front of it.

She placed the book carefully on the coffee table and opened it onto the first page. For about ten minutes she paged slowly through the book, scanning the pages superficially. Andrew remained quiet and let her focus. She eventually returned to the first page and looked up at Andrew.

'Well, these are definitely *SS-Ahnenerbe* records. Look down here,' she said and pointed to one of a number of names listed on the bottom half of the page. 'Rudolf Von Serbottendorf, and here Heinrich Himmler. This looks like a complete chronicle of four expeditions. The first one to Inca ruins on the Yucatan Peninsula in Mexico and Belize, the second to Tibet, the third to a couple of sites in Peru. And have a guess where the two last expeditions went,' she said and looked at Andrew who had sat down next to her on the sofa.

'That would have to be Antarctica?' he asked.

'Correct. So, Eckleston was right after all. The Nazis actually did send out a fifth expedition. Was this book the only one like it in the room?' asked Fiona.

'I think so. It didn't feel as if I had time to hang about for too long, so I searched through the shelves quite quickly. I don't think that there were any more books like this one, but I can't be sure.'

Fiona leaned back in the sofa and scratched her head.

'Why would these people have such a book there? How could the Order of the Teutonic Knights be connected to the Thule Society?'

'I've asked myself that question many times since I came back,' replied Andrew. 'And the only answer I can come up with is that they are in fact one and the same.'

'That could well be it. I must say, that I very much doubt that the Order of Teutonic Knights would hide a book with the Thule Society insignia on the cover, containing an original chronicle of

SS-Ahnenerbe expeditions, just because they want to preserve history for the benefit of all mankind.'

'Me neither,' nodded Andrew.

'But,' continued Fiona. 'The Thule Society is supposed to have crumbled with the collapse of the SS. The convictions of Himmler, Hess, Sievers and all the others at the Nuremberg trials should have pulled the rug from under its feet, so to speak.'

'I know,' said Andrew. 'But what if it didn't? What if they somehow infiltrated the Order of Teutonic Knights, which itself wasn't exactly foreign to the idea of Germanic dominance, and then simply used it to go underground after the war? It might even willingly have let itself become infiltrated. You have to admit that a supposedly humanitarian organisation would have been the perfect hiding place.'

'Yes, but it just seems strange that they would be able to stay hidden for that long. And why would they want to do that?'

'Well, one obvious explanation could be that they may be protecting some type of secret. I guess it isn't entirely inconceivable that some of these occultism buffs might actually believe in some of the superstitious nonsense about mystical artefacts and magic powers,' said Andrew. 'And it does seem as if there are some pretty strange people out there with some pretty damn strange ideas about the world.'

'Possibly,' said Fiona drumming her fingers on the table. 'Or perhaps, if we are indeed dealing with the Thule Society, it is simply still pursuing the same goals as they did almost a century ago.'

'So, you are saying that they may still be an active organisation, even though they are out of sight?'

'You can't rule it out.'

'All I know is that I had a very creepy feeling when I was down in that room. It sure didn't feel benign to me.'

'Right,' said Fiona as she flicked back and forth through the pages a couple of times. 'Look, Andrew. This is very extensive, so I'll need a day or two to go through all of it. Maybe some of the answers lie in here somewhere. Can we meet again the day after tomorrow? Then I'll go home and go through this in a more methodical way.'

Andrew thought about it for a few seconds. 'I'm afraid I'm going to have to ask you to work on the book inside this building. Since we are not yet sure what it contains, and since the way I acquired it was technically theft, I wouldn't like for it to leave here just yet.'

Fiona nodded. 'Fair enough. Do you think I can use the projector room again?'

'Certainly. I'll arrange for it. It'll be ready for you tomorrow.'

★ ★ ★

That evening Kurt Moltke checked out of the London hotel where he had spent a single night. He walked out to get into his car, which was parked in the underground parking lot. As he opened the driver's side door, he looked at his wristwatch. He did not want to arrive late tonight. He turned the key, and the car's engine immediately sprang to life. Backing out of the parking bay, he switched on the radio, but finding nothing but vacuous pop music, he pushed PLAY on the CD player. The car filled with Wagner, as he pulled out into the street and switched on the headlights. A slight drizzle gave the impression of a haze drifting down through the two cones of light that swept over the streets. After a few minutes, he was on his way north. He kept to the right side of the road since he would have to get off it soon.

His destination was not very far from the hotel, but so far, he had been there only once during the eight years he had been a full member. Driving carefully, he pulled off the main road and drove for ten minutes until he turned right to enter a quiet residential area.

He immediately recognised the house, even though they all looked very similar in this neighbourhood. There were no other houses in the area that had a big satellite dish in the backyard. Most people here would probably never dream of tarnishing their own gardens with a monstrosity like that, but the owner of this particular house had a reputation for not caring about such issues, much to the frustration of his neighbours.

There were lights in all the windows of the house, and as Kurt Moltke parked his car outside it in the street, he noted that he appeared to be the first one to arrive that evening. He got out of his car and walked casually up the footpath to the front door where he rang the bell. A few seconds later, through the frosted glass in the door, he could see a figure approaching. He recognised him immediately, from his stature and from the way he shuffled along as he walked. The man opened the door and beckoned Moltke inside.

'Good evening, Kurt,' he said as he closed the door.

Through the frosted glass, the two figures could be seen moving through the hallway and into the living room, where Moltke sat down in a chair. He had been asked to arrive well ahead of the others so that he would have time to tell Eckleston about what he had witnessed on the Azores.

'How much do you think they know?' asked Moltke.

'Difficult to say,' said Eckleston and scratched his chin, while his brain was spinning. 'It is a bit annoying that I didn't receive that telephone call from Strauss before I had the meeting with Miss Keane. I'm certain that I didn't reveal any information to her that might lead her to conclusions about us, but it would have been nice to know then what you have told me now.'

'Yes. They might be on to us. At least there is no doubt that they have a number of the pieces of the puzzle.'

'You are probably correct. But remember, Kurt. We want them to look. We just don't want them to find all that there is to find. It's a most difficult balance to strike.'

Kurt nodded. He was uncomfortable with the thought that someone, as yet not identified properly, might be working to reveal the precious secret they guarded. But he knew that he would lay down his life to protect it if it should ever come to that.

The two men talked for another half hour until the doorbell rang again. Another figure was let inside and then brought to the living room to sit down on the sofa. Ten minutes later yet another person arrived at the house, and the group of four was now just one person short.

The two latest arrivals were both supporters of the cause but had not yet been fully initiated. They were just two of many sympathisers spread out over the whole country, but they had been called tonight because they might possess information that could be valuable for the society. They had been handpicked because they each had special access to information that the society needed. Mostly, they merely functioned as passive messengers for the Keeper. During wartime, they would probably have been executed for spying and treason, but these were peaceful times, at least on the surface of things. However, their loose affiliation with the group, and the fact that they might not be able to continue supplying information indefinitely, meant that they would never have revealed to them the extent of the society's work, or the significance of its secrets. In the end, they all had their own reasons for letting themselves be used in this way. Each informer didn't demand to know all there was to know. They knew their place within the society, and in addition, they all knew that disloyalty would mean the end of their involvement altogether.

They all accepted that there might be secrets that only the Keepers and the grandmaster knew of. In time, some of the servants might be made aware of small additional pieces of insight, but as always there were degrees of truth, and ultimately everything was on a need-to-know basis. Every army needed its foot soldiers, sergeants, majors and generals, and most of them didn't need to know anything, except that they were fighting a just cause. Some also needed to know how to fight, and only a select few needed to know why.

Only the grandmaster and the four Keepers had been fully initiated, and they each carried a heavy weight on their shoulders. Knowledge was power, but it was also a burden. If revealed, the secret those five people guarded might well change the course of human history. Such power and responsibility took its toll, and required a strong mind and a healthy spirit. But above all, it required conviction, and Eckleston had plenty of that.

He rose from his armchair and looked out of the window. The rain was getting worse and the street seemed deserted. Then a car appeared at the far end of the street and rolled slowly to a stop outside Eckleston's house. It would be the last visitor to arrive that evening. After a few seconds, a woman got out and ran to the front door to escape the rain. Instead of ringing the bell, Pauline Edwards knocked on the door, wanting to make sure that she was heard. She had no intention of staying out in the rain for any longer than she had to.

Kurt had just gone to the kitchen for a cup of tea when Eckleston got up and let her in.

'Good evening, Pauline,' said Eckleston politely and extended his hand.

'Good evening,' she said and shook it.

Then she greeted the other people in the room. They were all familiar faces, even though they did not see each other very often. Almost all communication between them was conducted by encrypted e-mails. Even the national intelligence services were not able to crack the codes on a simple e-mail, once it had been encrypted with 256-bit encryption programmes that could be downloaded for free from the internet.

'And hello to you too, Mr. H.,' smiled the librarian knowingly, as Kurt emerged from the kitchen.

Kurt smiled and shook her hand. Every time he saw her, it seemed to him that she made an effort to look less attractive than she really was.

As Eckleston led the group through the hall and towards the stairs to the cellar, Pauline and Kurt exchanged looks. The two of them had a natural bond since both of their grandfathers had fought and died in the Second World War. The major difference was that whereas Kurt's grandfather had been German, Pauline's grandfather had been a British citizen, sympathetic to the idea of a new world order based on segregation of races. She would never have called Kurt 'Mr. H.' in public, but she knew that he wouldn't mind in this group. Kurt's grandmother had apparently had a fling with a Nazi officer. She had become pregnant, but out of fear of being ostracised, she had shied away from telling anyone, including the child's father. A few years later the officer could be seen on television and in newsreels, sitting in the courtroom in Nuremberg.

The woman had raised the boy by herself in a broken Germany, relying on friends and family to help her out in times of need, all the while keeping her secret. She had eventually told Kurt's father, who by then had become a father himself. Kurt had been an only child and had grown up believing that his grandfather had died in the war. It had been a shock for him to realise that his grandfather was Rudolph Hess, and that the old man was sitting in a prison in Berlin, convicted of war crimes and crimes against humanity, which were concepts the young boy had difficulty understanding.

Even now, it seemed unreal that his grandfather, who had died by his own hand in 1987, had been sitting in a cell for all those years. As Kurt had become an adult, he had turned against his father for abandoning his own father, and Kurt was reaching a point when he was preparing to apply for a visitation in Berlin, when he received the news of his grandfather's death. That experience had made him feel robbed, not only of his past but of his dignity. With his grandmother now dead as well, he had become a man with no identity, save for a family and a father who had never had the courage to face the truth and deal with it.

This had led him to begin a quest for his own identity, and what better place to start than to uncover all he could about Rudolph Hess, whom he slowly began to regard as a wronged idealist. A man who had sought greatness for his country and for his people, but who had also, in the final stages of the war, attempted to stop the destruction, not just of Germany but of other countries as well. He had risked his life in pursuit of peace during a dangerous but heroic flight in a small single-engine aircraft to Scotland, only to be ridiculed by the world as a madman and a simpleton.

Slowly, the anger had built up inside Kurt, and while taking it out on his spineless father had lessened the burden for a while, it eventually became apparent to him that the only way he could bring purpose to his own life, would be to right this wrong that had been committed against his family.

For months he had pondered what to do, while bitterness and the sense of futility mounted within him. History had been written, and in this world that meant it was written by the victors. Although he admired the energy and stamina displayed by so-called revisionist historians, he had come to believe that it was a lost cause. The only true way of bringing honour to himself and his grandfather was to fulfil the dream of re-establishing the Aryan civilisation. Out of the lack of direction and the feeling of bitterness and fury, came a sense of purpose. It was only now, looking back, that he realised that his own story of anger, followed by a new sense of purpose, was very similar to that of another young man. That man had been Adolf Hitler. He too had experienced anger and frustration at the way politicians had squandered the opportunity for German greatness. They had lost the First World War, and then shamefully betrayed the nation, and this had provided Hitler with his opportunity.

As a somewhat strange yet fulfilling testament to the memory of his grandfather, Hess had decided to take flying lessons and to acquire a license in the name of Kurt Hess. It might seem odd to others, but to him, it was a way of manifesting his pride in his family's history, and perhaps in a childish way to reconnect with what had been taken away from him.

Kurt Hess, as he now came to think of himself, began searching for ways to learn about his grandfather's work, and he had spent years trying to connect with like-minded people. He had finally struck gold, and his first meeting with Erich Strauss had been an unforgettable experience and a turning point in his life. He had come home after their meeting, and he knew right away that everything would be different from then on. Finally, he had found a way of channelling all his frustrated energy into something worth fighting for.

Strauss had quickly become a mentor for him, and unlike the pathetic young and unruly communists that marched down the streets yelling their toothless slogans, he had soon learned that staying hidden was much more effective in achieving goals, than making noise and burning tires.

Now twenty-eight years of age, he had found peace in the cause, as well as a sense of belonging. The small group of people around him had in a strange way become family, or at least kindred spirits.

They all shared the same dreams and the same goals, and while they were few, their determination was unmatched. There were groups such as this all over Europe, and they all felt strongly that if they could destabilise the world order as it was today, they would be able to free Germany from its chains and let the nation and its people rise to reveal its full potential.

What they needed was proof for all to see, that Aryans had indeed been the dominant race on the planet long before the so-called civilisations of today were created in the recent past. Proof that their destiny was one of greatness. The most important task for the secret society had been to preserve the knowledge that had been gathered, particularly by the *SS-Ahnenerbe* so many years ago. But to achieve their goals they needed to find what his grandfather and the SS had been searching for. They realised that they didn't have anywhere near the same resources, so the agreed-upon strategy was to identify and perhaps even encourage others to travel the same road, without necessarily pursuing the same goal.

Alerted by one of many sources within the German police, they had learned of the break-in at the National Archives. They themselves possessed copies of all of the documents in Vienna, but the fact that someone had stolen them from the National Archive in Berlin, indicated that others might be looking for the same thing as them. But they were perplexed as to who it might be. The only one to have shown himself on the scene so far, was this Mr. Taggart, whom they had learned was really someone else. That in itself had seemed suspect, but discovering that he was employed by the British government had come as a nasty surprise.

The group descended into the cellar, which was a single large room under the house. It was decorated sparsely but in good taste. There was a warm light coming from several antique lamps in the ceiling, the floor was covered with a number of Persian rugs, there were a couple of chesterfield sofas and armchairs arranged around two coffee tables, and on three of the walls hung giant oil paintings in elaborately carved and gilded wooden frames. The only thing that was missing in order for it to look like the study in a large countryside manor, was a fireplace and windows. The fact that there were no windows gave the room a slightly eerie feel, but then it wasn't designed to make people feel relaxed. On the fourth wall hung a big burgundy velvet banner, with the Thule Society's insignia embroidered in gold at its centre.

'Right. Welcome to all of you,' said Eckleston as they sat down in the armchairs and sofas around a small table at the centre of the room. He was no longer the jovial and slightly eccentric scientist that Fiona had met. His face was grim looking, and his voice was stern.

'As you have no doubt guessed, a somewhat precarious situation has arisen, and our grandmaster has deemed it necessary for us to discuss it amongst ourselves in order to determine its urgency. I have spoken with the grandmaster, and he has called a meeting of the Council of Keepers, which will be held very shortly in Vienna.'

He shifted in his chair. 'There are two points that we need to go over. Firstly, I want to verify that we have still not been able to uncover who stole the documents from the Office of National Records, is that correct?' he asked and looked at the informant whose day job was in the London Metropolitan Police.

'That is correct,' nodded the man embarrassed. 'No one has a clue so far. I'm sorry.'

'Alright,' said Eckleston in a voice that clearly betrayed his displeasure at the answer. 'It's not your fault that the police are incompetent. Keep working at it.'

'I will do what I can,' said the man.

'Secondly,' continued Eckleston. 'I had a discussion with Kurt earlier tonight, and he indicated that the headquarters of our society may have been compromised by agents of the British government. I can't tell you how we know this, but suffice it to say that we have good reason to believe that it has happened. At this point, we have also yet to discover what led them to us, but we must do so without attracting undue attention. Therefore, we must all be extra vigilant in the time ahead. Don't take any chances in anything you do. We can't afford any mistakes. We are investigating a certain person at this time. Although he may work under different aliases, we think his real name is Andrew Sterling. We have reason to believe that he may indirectly have a connection to our Society, but we are still uncertain. For this reason, we need to plant listening devices in his house, and that is why I have called you here tonight,' he said and pointed to one of the men, a commercial security systems engineer. 'I will provide you with details later.'

The man nodded silently.

'Apparently,' Eckleston went on, 'He has been aided by a woman who has been to see me recently. She is a colleague of yours,' he said and looked at Pauline.

'So, what do I do?' asked Pauline.

'You keep a close eye on her and see if you can plant a bug in her phone. Also, try to gain access to her e-mail accounts.'

'Got it,' said Pauline.

'And finally,' said Eckleston, looking at the last man in the group. 'You will attempt to hack into Sterling's computer at work. We have already determined where he works, and it should be easy to at least get connected to the building's mainframe. Do what you can,' he ordered.

Pauline cleared her throat. 'Mr Eckleston, may I ask? Do you think we have Fiona on board, so to speak? Did she take the bait?'

'I believe so,' replied Eckleston pensively. 'It is a delicate balancing act just now. Not too much information, and not too little. We need to keep her moving forward, but without allowing her to acquire the full picture.'

Pauline nodded. 'Let's hope for the best.'

THIRTEEN

Fiona spent all of the next day reading methodically through the chronicle from the secret room in the house in Vienna. Her German turned out to be considerably less rusty than she had feared, so after a few hours she had made good progress.

Sometimes she would get momentarily thrown off course by a word or a phrase that was particular to the time the document was written, but eventually she would decipher its meaning. Some of the texts were in the form of diaries, other parts seemed to be notes made after the return of the expeditions. Still others appeared to be no more than fragments of original diaries that had been placed in the book between other pages.

Amazingly the expeditions that had been documented in this book, went to all the places that Eckleston had talked about. On the second page of the book was a list of them.

AUGUST 1936 - OCTOBER 1936. UXMAL, YUCATAN PENINSULA.
DECEMBER 1936 – FEBRUARY 1937. CUSCO, PERU.
JUNE 1937 – SEPTEMBER 1937. YAMZHO YUMCO, TIBET.
DECEMBER 1938 – MAY 1938. QUEEN MAUDE'S LAND, ANTARCTICA.
APRIL 1939 – AUGUST 1939. VESTFJELLA, QUEEN MAUDE'S LAND, ANTARCTICA.

Carefully, Fiona started reading the chronicle of the first expedition, taking extensive notes and being as systematic as she could, particularly when she felt like skipping right to the end for a conclusion, as she might impatiently have done with any other book.

The first expedition concerned Mayan ruins in Uxmal on the Yucatan Peninsula, but it also included a trip to Belize where a number of ruins and statues from the Olmec culture had emerged deep in the jungle. The expedition had been severely hampered by illness, as their protection against the malaria-carrying mosquitoes had been inadequate.

They had spent days charting and photographing their finds, as well as determining the orientation of the ruins relative to the stars, and they found that when constructed, the buildings had been aligned with images in the night sky, as they looked 10,500 years ago. And those same images of constellations were still visible on the ruins themselves. That didn't mean that the current ruins were the remains of buildings 10,500 years old. In fact, they estimated them to be around 3,000 years old, but rather, that the original buildings on that site had been constructed at that earlier time.

Judging from the number of exclamation marks written in the margin, the expedition leader, Thomas Beck, was over the moon with excitement at having found what he considered to be proof of an ancient civilisation. There were even references to the honour he might receive upon returning to Berlin. After having completed the work in Uxmal, it appeared that Beck was anxious to get back home to report his success, so the expedition was apparently wrapped up sooner than some of his colleagues would have liked. Fiona deduced this from annoyed remarks in Beck's diary, about some of his colleagues wanting to stay and continue the work. But as far as Beck was concerned it wasn't an archaeological expedition in the traditional sense, where every stone needed to be turned.

He was acutely aware of the political motives behind the financing of the expedition, so in his mind they had already completed the mission successfully. They had even brought back some sculptures and other artefact that would allow them to demonstrate a connection to ancient Germanic works of art.

Fiona rose and walked out into the hall to get herself something to drink. She had been absorbed in the book for several hours already, and she began to doubt whether she would get it all done on that day. When she came back, she sat down again and tried to sum up the results and conclusions from the first mission she had read about so far. In addition to the records of where the expeditions went and what they encountered in terms of buildings and ruins, there were always accounts of extensive interviews with locals. These interviews revolved around local legends of creation and destruction, and they were astonishingly detailed, just as Eckleston had told her.

Apart from the tales of floods, earthquakes, and volcanoes, there were tales of tall gods arriving on big ships, and sometimes even coming down from the sky. And in all of those legends, there were elements of an ancient civilisation perishing in a great cataclysm, under the wrath of the gods.

On several occasions during their travels to and from the archaeological sites, the *SS-Ahnenerbe* had uncovered stories about a medallion made of four irregular and uniquely shaped triangles, that together would form a square about the size of a human hand with a pentagonal hole in the centre. The medallion was supposed to be made of a shiny metal unlike any other. According to the local legends of several of the places the *SS-Ahnenerbe* visited, the triangles would combine to produce a medallion that would lead whoever held it, to a great civilisation far away beyond the seas.

The German researchers initially believed that the four triangles might represent the four dimensions, i.e., the three physical dimensions that we can move around in, and also time. Subsequently, however, they agreed that the four triangular pieces represented the four elements, and that the central crystal represented the human at the centre of those. They took that to signify superior Aryan beings conquering all the forces of nature, and thereby achieving world domination.

This is really powerful stuff, thought Fiona. This was just what the SS needed. Apparent proof of an advanced and superior ancient civilisation, in control of the elements, and navigating the Earth's oceans, making contact with its lesser peoples.

On the subsequent expedition to Cusco in Peru, the chief of the entire *Ahnenerbe* programme Rudolph Von Serbottendorf had taken over the role of expedition leader, with Thomas Beck as his assistant. This would probably not have pleased Beck, but there were no signs of any dissent in Von Serbottendorf's notes. Even though all the members of the expeditions were part of the *Ahnenerbe* programme, they always wore civilian clothes, so as not to attract undue attention.

Upon arriving in Lima by aeroplane, they drove by truck to Cusco, which even today is a popular starting point for tourists wanting to see the Inca ruins in the mountains. In 1936 the area was virtually untouched, and mass tourism had not been invented yet. The only foreign visitors that ventured into the mountains were civilian scholars and scientists, so that was a perfect way for the expedition to travel. They spent several weeks traversing high mountain passes and deep lush valleys, and they uncovered several ancient ruins that had not previously been identified.

Fiona turned the page carefully and then continued reading Von Serbottendorf's diary entries.

FEBRUARY 22ND 1937

WE HAVE FOUND IT. IT IS A WONDEROUS OCCASION WHEN ONE CAN TRAVEL FROM ONE END OF THE EARTH TO THE OTHER, JUST AS OUR FOREFATHERS DID, TO DISCOVER SOMETHING THAT HASN'T SEEN THE LIGHT OF DAY FOR THOUSANDS OF YEARS. THIS MORNING WE WERE ABOUT TO BREAK CAMP, WHEN ONE OF THE SCOUTS CAME BACK AND TOLD US THAT HE HAD SPOTTED A LARGE RUIN NO MORE THAN A FEW HUNDRED METERS AWAY. UPON OUR ARRIVAL, WE IMMEDIATELY REALISED THAT IS WAS PART OF A LARGER COMPLEX OF BUILDINGS THAT EXTENDED FOR SEVERAL HUNDREDS OF METERS INTO THE THICK JUNGLE. THE AREA WAS ENTIRELY OVERGROWN BY VEGETATION, BUT WE SOON MANAGED TO IDENTIFY THE MAIN STRUCTURE, AND AS IF

DRAWN TO IT BY SOME MYSTICAL FORCE, I LEFT THE OTHERS BEHIND AND ENTERED THE HEART OF THE IMMENSE PYRAMID STRUCTURE. THERE I FOUND SOMETHING AKIN TO AN ALTAR IN THE MIDDLE OF A SMALL CHAMBER, UPON WHICH LAY A SHINING TRIANGULAR OBJECT. IT WAS A MOST EXTRAORDINARY SIGHT, SINCE EVERYTHING IN THE CHAMBER HAD DECAYED AND CRUMBLED, BUT THE OBJECT SEEMED AS IF IT HAD BEEN MADE ON THAT SAME DAY. AS I SHONE MY LIGHT ON IT, IT REFLECTED IT IN ALL DIRECTIONS, AND I REALISED THAT IT WAS MADE FROM SOME FORM OF METAL, BUT ONE THAT I HAD NEVER SEEN BEFORE. AS I PICKED IT UP, I WAS AMAZED AT ITS WEIGHT. ALTHOUGH THE SIZE OF AN EGG, IT SEEMED TO WEIGH NO MORE THAN THE FEATHER OF A GOOSE. I TOOK THE OBJECT WITH ME, AND IT HAS NOT LEFT MY SIGHT SINCE. WE HAVE SPENT ALL DAY SEARCHING THE COMPLEX, BUT WE HAVE FOUND NOTHING MORE. IT WAS AS IF THE OBJECT HAD JUST BEEN SITTING THERE WAITING FOR US TO FIND IT. I AM IN AWE AND CANNOT WAIT TO RETURN TO BERLIN TO ANALYSE IT.

The account continued with the discovery of several additional sites, but none as significant as the one the scout had found.

Rudolph Von Serbottendorf eventually brought the triangle home to Germany, and Fiona also discovered that it was indeed one of the items brought to the warehouse outside Berlin, which Friedrich Henke had told Andrew about. There were many other items mentioned in the book that revealed a large number of artefacts having been taken from the complex and brought to Berlin.

The following pages in the book described a set of tests performed on the triangle subsequent to its arrival in Germany, but none of them were able to determine what its purpose was or even what metallic material it had been made from. It was unfathomable dense and hard, yet extremely light.

The expedition to Lake Yamzho Yumco in Tibet was unusual, in that it appeared that Himmler had asked for them to seek out remains of an ancient civilisation, and if possible, make contact with its descendants. It was clear from Von Serbottendorf's diary that he thought Himmler was chasing pies in the sky. He didn't express it in so many words, but it became evident that there were quite different views on what one could realistically hope to find on an expedition such as that.

Himmler's orders to Von Serbottendorf apparently did not have much of an effect on the archaeologist. His goal was not to make contact with mystical beings, but to use science to uncover irrefutable evidence of an ancient superior race. If that meant working for someone like Himmler, then so be it. The archaeological prize of all time would be ascribed to him in any event, and it wouldn't change the impact such a discovery would have on the German spirit and indeed on the future of humanity.

Arriving at Lake Yamzho Yumco, the expedition began gathering village elders from near and far, asking them to reveal the ancient legends of their land. It turned out that there were substantial differences and inconsistencies between the accounts, but not enough to obscure the fact that they all believed in the same basic legend. Thousands of years ago, they had been sought out by tall fair-haired men, who had possessed knowledge that to them seemed divine. As a token of friendship, they had delivered them a shiny metal object, that they were then instructed to keep in a safe place, until such time as they were ready to travel the Earth themselves, and make contact with other peoples in other lands.

The visitors had been peaceful, and the towns and villages around Lake Yamzho Yumco had had many dealings with them over several hundred years. But then one day, they had simply vanished. Legend held that their island in a faraway sea had sunk beneath the waves, but they never received any evidence themselves of why the tall visitors disappeared so suddenly. According to the elders in the tribes, their forefathers had built a temple inside a cavern deep in the mountains, where the triangle had been safeguarded. Unfortunately, war had then ravaged the country for many years, and the temple had eventually been forgotten, lost to time and the inexorable growth of the thick jungle vegetation.

Using the information gathered from the people they interviewed, the Nazis had eventually found the temple after several months of searching.

AUGUST 23RD 1937

THE TEAM IS JUBILANT. WE HAVE FINALLY FOUND THE TEMPLE. IT WAS OVERGROWN AND PARTLY BURIED IN A LANDSLIDE, AND IT SEEMED TO HAVE REMAINED UNDISTURBED FOR AN EXTREMELY LONG TIME. WE REMOVED SEVERAL TONS OF ROCK, TO UNCOVER AN INTERIOR THAT WAS COVERED IN DUST AND DIRT. BUT AFTER DIGGING FOR HOURS AT THE BACK OF THE TEMPLE RUINS, WE FOUND A TRIANGLE SIMILAR TO WHAT I FOUND IN TIAHUANACO. IT IS A TRULY EXCEPTIONAL DISCOVERY, AND PROOF OF THE LINK BETWEEN THE TWO CIVILISATIONS. I FEEL NOW MORE THAN EVER, THAT OUR ASSERTIONS ARE CORRECT, AND THAT IT WILL ONLY BE A QUESTION OF TIME BEFORE THE TRUE COURSE OF HISTORY IS REVEALED TO US.

The rest of the account took up no more than one-and-a-half pages, and was just a simple narrative of their journey home. Some of the final notes indicated the beginnings of a theory about the triangles. Realising that the two pieces he had found were similar, he speculated that they might constitute a key to the gates of Thule. Upon returning to Berlin, it became evident that the pieces might somehow fit together, but it was as if he lacked a mechanism to hold the two pieces together. There were extensive ornamentations on one side of each triangle, and when placed next to each other, the ornamental patterns overlapped seamlessly and perfectly. Apart from his speculation on the purpose of the triangles, there was no mention of any other experiments carried out on any of the artefacts, subsequent to Von Serbottendorf's return to Berlin.

The chronicle then went straight to an account of an expedition to the Antarctic region in the winter and spring of 1938. The expedition had been planned so that there would be the least amount of ice in the Antarctic region, which meant that they would have to sail from Germany during the early winter, to reach the warmest summer months in the southern hemisphere. There were extensive notes about the planned route and the supplies that were needed for the expedition. They would have to bring all of their supplies, since they could not count on being able to re-supply on any of the South Sandwich Islands, the southernmost of which is incidentally called the Southern Thule Island.

Fiona turned the page and then found herself looking at a copy of the Piri Reis map, similar to the one that Eckleston had shown her. It seemed that the Germans had also used that map, which fitted nicely with the fact that it was supposedly rediscovered in 1929.

Might it actually have been German scientists that discovered it? Might they have discovered additional maps?

She got her answer immediately. Next to the Piri Reis map was a copy of another slightly smaller map that seemed to have been hand sketched.

From what she could gather from the notes below it, it was a copy of an ancient Egyptian map, made in 1665 by a German Jesuit priest named Athanasius Kircher.

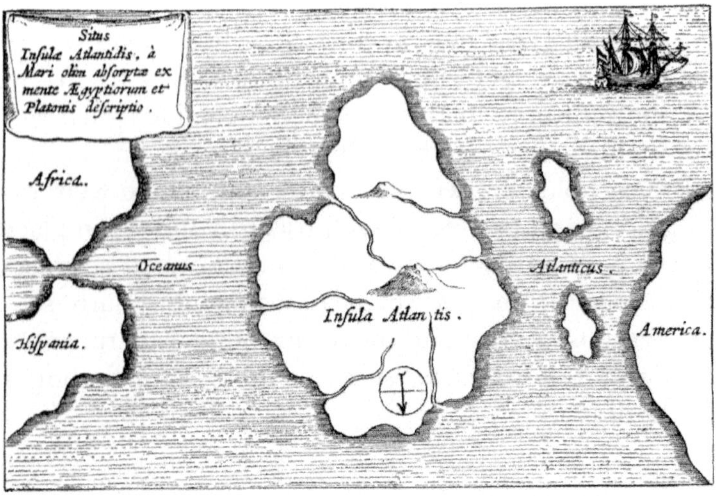

Fiona studied the map for a few seconds, and then read the translation of the Latin text in the top left corner.

'LOCATION OF THE ISLAND OF ATLANTIS - SWALLOWED BY THE SEA - FROM EGYPTIAN MINDS/MEMORIES, AND THE DESCRIPTION OF PLATO'.

The map showed the whole of the Antarctic continent lying at the centre of a great ocean, with South America on one side and Africa and Europe on the other. The map was upside-down relative to how modern maps are drawn, but it was unmistakably a map of sub-glacial Antarctica, and thus necessarily drawn before the continent was enveloped in ice.

On the next page was another copy of the map, but this time turned upside down and annotated with names of continents and islands. Stunned, Fiona stared at the map in disbelief. This map was more than 350 years old, created centuries before the 'discovery' of Antarctica.

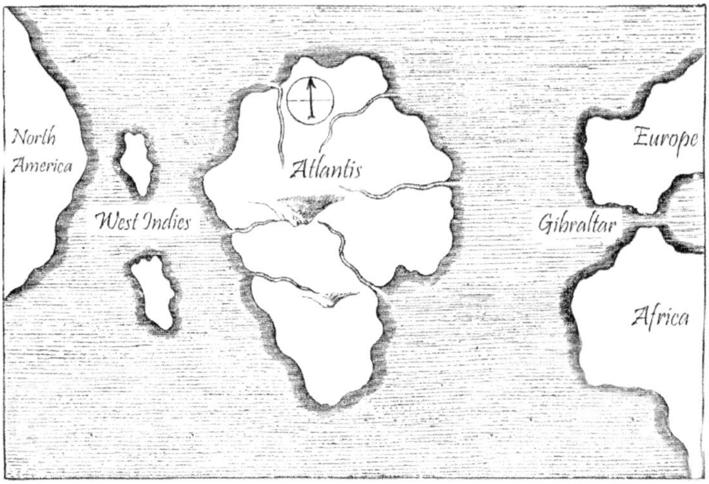

There was no doubt in her mind any longer. The legends had to be true. Between the Piri Reis map and the Kircher map, it was clear that Antarctica must have been mapped when it was free of ice, and humans had clearly travelled there thousands of years earlier than conventional wisdom held. The exact location of the lost continent was clearly wrong, as it was situated too far north on Kircher's map, but the fact that it was there at all, 'beyond the Pillars of Hercules' now had her convinced that there was a lot more to this than fanciful legends.

Much of the following was from Von Serbottendorf's diary, where he described setting out to sea from Cape Town towards Antarctica, after having had all his equipment and his entire team transported over several legs from Germany to South Africa. A ship capable of navigating the ice-filled Antarctic waters had been waiting for them in Cape Town, and within a couple of days, they were heading for Queen Maude's Land.

It was a long and arduous journey, which quickly became evident from Von Serbottendorf's diary. He was an impatient man and found himself struggling to pass the time on board the ship.

February 16th - 1938

Having left Berlin more than a month ago, we have finally entered the Southern Ocean. Far away over the horizon to the north, the African continent is slowly, much too slowly, slipping away, and to our west is the Southern Thule Island now close enough to spot with binoculars. We still have many days of sailing ahead of us. I am convinced that Thule is waiting for us. The ruins and artefacts uncovered in the most remote corners of the Earth, and the ancient maps of the continent's coastline are irrefutable evidence. As we sail ever closer to Antarctica, I sense that we are close to fulfilling our destiny.

The following pages were merely one-line notes, revealing the frustration and boredom that Von Serbottendorf and several other team members experienced during the long journey. But then came a long section, indicating that something had changed.

March 2nd - 1938
We have arrived, and I am exhilarated. After seemingly endless days on the open sea, our lookout spotted land this morning at first light. In the far distance there now stretches an immense white wall of ice from one side of the horizon to the other. It is dotted with black specks of huge rock formations, and our lookout can make out a couple of tall mountains further inland. This gives me hope that the coast will enable us to make landfall there. I suspect that we shall only have a few weeks here, before the ice may close off access again. Hopefully we can send out a landing party in a small boat either tomorrow or the next day. I yearn to be a part of that group of men, but I know that I must stay here on the ship for now.

The next entry read:

March 6th - 1938
Due to bad weather, we have been unable to attempt a landing until today. The men are rowing ashore as I write this. I hope they bring back good news. I am as excited as I am anxious. Could this be the day?

Then followed a few pages that recounted how the landing party returned with reports of a suitable place to establish a camp. He also described the efforts to bring their equipment and supplies to shore, and the difficulty in setting up a base in these weather conditions. Even though it was summer in the southern hemisphere, and the weather was comparatively mild, it was still very cold and it wasn't until three days later, that they had finally managed to establish themselves in a suitable location, thus allowing them to commence the search.

The next few pages recounted a number of small excursions further inland, as well as a two-day expedition up and down the jagged coast in search of traces of an ancient port. For a couple of weeks, they found nothing at all, even though they had brought sleighs and dogs, which enabled them to traverse tens of kilometres of terrain each day. Von Serbottendorf's notes became shorter and less enthusiastic as the days went on, until one day he wrote:

MARCH 17TH - 1938

A MONUMENTAL DAY. TWO DAYS AGO, I UNCOVERED WHAT WE BELIEVE TO BE THE ENTRANCE TO AN UNDERGROUND CAVE. IT WAS SPOTTED BY ONE OF OUR SCOUTS AND IS SITUATED MANY KILOMETRES INLAND TO THE SOUTHWEST OF THE CAMP. THE ENTRANCE IS QUITE NARROW BUT VERY VISIBLE AS IT SITS ON THE SHEER FACE OF A STEEP MOUNTAINSIDE. WE INITIALLY THOUGHT THAT IT WAS ANOTHER OF WHAT WE HAVE FOUND TO BE NATURALLY OCCURRING CAVES AND GROTTOES IN THESE MOUNTAINS, BUT ON CLOSER INSPECTION, IT WAS CLEAR THAT IT WAS MAN-MADE. WE DISCOVERED IT ONLY A FEW HOURS BEFORE IT BECAME DARK, SO WE DID NOT HAVE MUCH TIME TO INVESTIGATE, BUT I TOOK THE OPPORTUNITY TO WALK APPROXIMATELY FIFTY METERS INSIDE IT, AND WHAT MET ME WAS ASTONISHING. THE CAVE QUICKLY NARROWED TO A CORRIDOR THAT TURNED NINETY DEGREES SEVERAL TIMES TO THE RIGHT AND TO THE LEFT, EFFECTIVELY INSULATING THE INTERIOR FROM WHATEVER WEATHER MIGHT BE RAGING OUTSIDE.

I ONLY HAD A SMALL GAS LAMP, SO WHEN THE CAVERN EXPANDED INTO A LARGER AREA, I WAS NOT ABLE TO SEE MUCH, BUT IT IS CLEAR THAT WE HAVE UNCOVERED A LARGE STRUCTURE MADE BY HUMAN BEINGS. I HAD TO RETREAT SINCE THE OIL IN MY LAMP WAS RUNNING LOW, BUT I AM SPEECHLESS AT WHAT I DISCOVERED.

WE MADE IT BACK TO THE CAMP LATE TODAY, JUST AS DARKNESS CLOSED IN ON THESE COLD AND HOSTILE LANDS, BUT AS SOON AS POSSIBLE TOMORROW, I WILL TAKE A GROUP WITH ME TO EXPLORE THIS MOST ASTONISHING OF FINDS.

Fiona was amazed at the tale that unfolded on the pages in front of her. If this wasn't all some elaborate hoax, she was in the middle of discovering how history had been made many decades ago. Turning the page, she was puzzled by the date of the next entry, made more than two weeks later.

APRIL 3RD - 1938

IT IS WITH GREAT SADNESS THAT I MUST WRITE THAT RUDOLPH VON SERBOTTENDORF IS DEAD. AS OF TODAY I, THOMAS BECK, HAVE TAKEN COMMAND OF THIS EXPEDITION. AFTER LEAVING TO EXPLORE THE CAVERN ALONG WITH FIVE OTHERS, VON SERBOTTENDORF WAS NOT HEARD FROM AGAIN. WE WAITED FOR SEVERAL DAYS, BUT HE DID NOT RETURN. WE FINALLY DECIDED TO MOUNT ANOTHER MISSION TO LOOK FOR THEM, SO WE ENTERED THE CAVE, AND THERE, THE MOST HORRIBLE SIGHT MET US.

WE FOUND VON SERBOTTENDORF LYING ON HIS BACK, HIS FACE GLEAMING WITH A BLUEISH HUE IN THE LIGHT FROM OUR OIL LAMPS. IT WAS CLEAR THAT HE HAD DIED A HORRIBLY PAINFUL DEATH. THIS BECAME EVIDENT AS I MOVED CLOSER, COVERING MY FACE TO SHIELD MYSELF FROM THE EXPECTED STENCH. ONLY LATER DID I REALISE THAT THE EXTREME COLD WOULD PREVENT HIS DEAD BODY FROM DECAYING. HIS MOUTH WAS OPEN IN WHAT SEEMED LIKE A LAST CRY OF AGONY, AND THE INSIDE OF IT WAS POSITIVELY COVERED IN TINY BLUE CRYSTALS THAT SEEMED TO HAVE ACTUALLY GROWN FROM HIS OWN FLESH. NEXT TO HIM LAY HANS FINK, WHO HAD ALSO PERISHED IN A SIMILAR FASHION. HOWEVER, THERE WAS NO TRACE OF THE THREE REMAINING TEAM MEMBERS.

WE ARE ABANDONING OUR MISSION AND RETURNING TO BERLIN AS SOON AS POSSIBLE. WE ARE NOT EQUIPPED TO DEAL WITH WHATEVER IS LURKING IN THESE CAVES. WE WILL BE ENTERING THE CAVERN ONE FINAL TIME TOMORROW TO RETRIEVE SOME OF OUR EQUIPMENT AS WELL AS THE BODIES OF VON SERBOTTENDORF AND FINK. THEN WE WILL MAKE OUR WAY BACK TO GERMANY. WE ARE DEALING WITH SOMETHING WHICH WE CANNOT COMPREHEND. I ADMIT THAT I AM SCARED TO DEATH. WHATEVER THIS THING IS, IT IS SO GHASTLY THAT I FEAR FOR THE LIVES OF THE ENTIRE CREW.

Fiona leaned back, astounded by what she had just read. It seemed like a nightmare, and she could easily imagine what the remaining team members must have felt. She looked at her wristwatch. It was now five-thirty in the afternoon, and she was getting tired. Instead of stubbornly continuing, she decided to call it a day and walked to Andrew's office to tell him what she had learned. Andrew however, had left for the day and Catherine was gathering her things and getting ready to go home as well. So, after saying goodnight to Catherine, Fiona returned to the projector room to put on her coat. Then she also left for home.

★ ★ ★

At the same time as Fiona was leaving Sheldrake Place, a man was leaving her apartment. Wearing black clothes and a cap, he brought nothing out from the apartment that he hadn't brought in fifteen minutes earlier. Picking her lock had been easy, and finding the phones in the living room and in the bedroom and installing the listening devices had been child's play. People didn't realise how easy it was to break into a house or an apartment. They thought that if they got themselves a nice big lock, then everything would be just fine. What they didn't realise was that as long as there had been locks, there had been tools to pick locks with. And recently, that equipment had become available to everyone at the click of a mouse button. For just a few pounds, anyone could acquire tools that would enable them to defeat virtually any mechanical lock within seconds.

Earlier that evening he had paid a visit to a mansion just north of the city centre. He had cut the power to the security system and then calmly entered the house to plant bugs in the phones both upstairs and downstairs. The bugs were always on, which meant that they would pick up any sound in the room whether it was part of a telephone conversation or not. On his way out he had re-engaged the security system, and then left with no discernible sign of him ever being there.

★ ★ ★

Abdullah Soliman was originally of Egyptian descent but had moved to Syria at the age of 22. Having grown up on the outskirts of Cairo as the son of a plumber, he had, as the first in his family, gained admission to the Technical University of Cairo. In fact, he was one of only a few young people in his neighbourhood to have done so. Aware of his privilege, he had studied hard, and he had made a big effort to make his parents proud. But after only a few months of studying, he had soon become unhappy with what he regarded as sloppy education. The professors seemed to be more concerned with their positions in the university hierarchy than with undertaking research and making scientific progress. In addition, as he grew older and had begun to discover his faith as something more than just a way of conducting his everyday life, he had become increasingly angered by what he saw as western cultural imperialism aimed at the destruction of Islam.

Soliman had moved to Damascus two years earlier to join the renowned Professor Rashid, who was in need of young scientists with technical expertise that could be applied to constructing tailor-made biological research equipment. In spite of his frustration with the Technical University of Cairo, Soliman had achieved just such a level of expertise, and having applied for the position at Professor Rashid's side he had been thrilled to learn of his acceptance at Damascus University. But his admittance to the university and the inclusion into Rashid's research programme had turned out to be much more impactful than a mere working experience.

To Soliman's surprise, Professor Rashid had arranged group discussions for himself and his students, where scientific as well as political topics were debated, sometimes ferociously. During these debates, Soliman had managed to surprise himself a few times, especially when discussing the position of the Arab world in a global context. Whenever they debated the relationship between the western world led by the United States and the few Muslim states that had decided to stand up to the west, he started to feel a barely controllable anger and resentment welling up inside him. Rashid had encouraged him and the other students to express their views, and not to be shy about sharing them. He told them that the basis of scientific progress was the unrestrained discussion of ideas, and had encouraged them to become independent thinkers. Soliman had become just that, not just in terms of science but in terms of politics as well, and Rashid had taken the young man under his wing.

Because of his vigour and tenacity, he had gained a special place in Rashid's heart as well as in his team, and Soliman remembered clearly the evening where he had been invited to the home of the professor for a discussion of how to construct a laboratory environment that would allow for the safe isolation of a new highly active enzyme they had been working on. Soliman, who was beginning his fifth year at the university and was now working on his PhD, had thought of it as another group discussion, but upon arriving at Rashid's house, none of the other students were there. Instead, there was an elderly man with a long grey beard who was dressed in the traditional clothes of the Syrian upper-class, but his facial features were more like those of an Egyptian. When the man spoke to greet Soliman, he had been proven right. He wasn't told his name, but Rashid had told him that the man belonged to a political organisation that worked for the unification of all the Arab nations, and the expulsion of western culture from the Middle East.

Immediately, Soliman's heart had started pounding. Maybe here was a man who could help him fulfil his desire to fight for the Arab world and for Allah. He looked at Professor Rashid for guidance, and with one look and a smile, the professor had conveyed that this was indeed what Soliman had been searching for.

The bearded man was proposing a new scientific research programme, that would be carried out away from the university, and he said that he and Rashid had been discussing this for many months. He said that it was a very large programme and that it was already being prepared somewhere in the Syrian desert. Then he had looked Soliman straight in the eye with his calm dark brown eyes and asked him if he would be willing to take the step and become a servant of the Arabs and of Allah.

Soliman had felt as if he had been granted a chance that was beyond anything he could have hoped for. He had never thought that such organisations existed, but upon learning that perhaps his people wouldn't forever be trampled underfoot by the westerners, his heart had filled with hope and joy, and he had accepted without hesitation.

Rashid had once again judged correctly and had supplied the programme with another extremely talented and motivated asset. In time, these assets would help propel the effort forward, and he knew that he could expect complete loyalty, even to the point of death and thereby martyrdom.

Having just turned 28, Soliman was now a happy man. He had no wife or family, but that didn't bother him too much. He was fulfilled by the opportunity to serve God, and he had more or less accepted the thought that there was a chance that he might not live to see the final victory. As he donned his bio-suit and entered the laboratory, he didn't know how near death would turn out to be.

Upon joining the huge effort that was underway deep within the mountain, he had soon learned that its aim was not just to expel America and her allies from the Middle East. That had been attempted by way of negotiation for decades, but America had repeatedly invaded Arab nations, and continued to support Israel one-sidedly with no regard or respect for the interests of the Arab people who had been evicted from their lands to make room for the Jews long ago. America's arrogance was intolerable, and it had been decided that nothing short of the destruction of that nation, along with several of its allies was now the only solution. This was the only way to drive home the point that the Arab peoples wanted to govern themselves.

Soliman sat down at 'The Farm' and began collecting newly grown samples from the rows of heated glass containers that had been filled with horse blood and gelatine, to provide the optimal growth environment. This was the standard approach to growing colonies of bacteria, but they had needed to design a completely new system whereby the bacteria could grow in a vacuum, in order to prevent them from being exposed to gaseous oxygen, which would make them snap violently into hibernation mode, and generate their blueish crystal casing.

In the beginning phases of the project, they just had the raw original samples to work with, but as soon as they had determined their growth pattern as well as its potency, they had started to experiment with mutations of the bacterium. They had now assisted the bacterium in evolving into a much more powerful variant than the original, and they had begun producing it in larger volumes. Soliman transferred the latest ten samples to the specially designed aluminium containers that were about one centimetre long and three millimetres wide, and then put them in the small airlock that he had helped design. The small compartment was filled with air from the laboratory, and he could now reach in and grab the tiny containers. He put them on a plastic tray and made his way across the room to the transfer system, which was designed to enable the team to safely transport materials from inside the laboratory to the outside. He placed the tray in a compartment in what looked like an ATM and pressed a button. The compartment was then retracted into the machine and a chemical cleaning process began.

When he emerged in his own clothes outside the laboratory fifteen minutes later, after having moved through the decontamination corridor, he proceeded to where the transfer system was mounted on the outside of the laboratory wall. He pressed a button and the tray was extended from the machine standing on a small platform. He grabbed it and made his way across the cement floor of the cave to a storage depot in the far corner. On his way over there, he had to stop to let a small electric vehicle pass. It was one of the locals transporting a new supply of decontamination chemicals to the laboratory.

He didn't seem to be aware of what they were working on, because even though he saw Soliman carrying the plastic tray, he didn't slow down to let him pass. In fact, he sped up and swerved in an arc around him. There had been no actual danger of a mishap, but Soliman still decided to have a word with Rashid about it. They could not afford to have an accident occur. It could set the programme back several months, or even terminate it permanently.

The sample depot had been cut roughly five meters into the rockface, and at three meters in width and two meters in height, it presented ample room for the number of containers they needed to produce. It was kept at a constant temperature of twelve degrees Celsius, and was sealed off from the rest of the underground compound by a solid steel door with a small window at its centre. He entered the correct combination on the access panel, and the doors swung open. There were already several hundred containers arranged on a set of metal racks inside the storage depot, and Soliman couldn't escape an ominous feeling creeping up on him as he walked closer with his latest batch of bacteria. He tried not to think about the nozzles in the ceiling that would be able to fill the room with several nasty chemical compounds, principally acids, and that would be able to eat away anything organic that was in the room if necessary. He let the door remain open since he figured he'd be out of there a few seconds later.

Soliman would never know, but a cap on one of the cylindrical aluminium containers had not been fastened properly, and as he lifted the plastic tray and took it out to place it in the rack along with the others, the accident happened. As he pressed on the front of the cylinder it would not immediately slide into the rack as the others had done, so he pushed a little harder causing the thin aluminium foil to rupture. He immediately felt through his fingers how the container gave way, and thinking initially that it had merely slipped into place, he realised that it was now open and that the pathogen had most likely been released into the air. He froze, paralysed by fear.

He instinctively held his breath, even though he knew that it would make no difference now. Fear was fighting reason, and as he turned his head slowly towards the door, he realised that the cold air inside the storage depot would flow out into the cave, being replaced by warm air from out there. That would take the airborne pathogen outside and kill everyone within minutes. He took a deep breath and then yelled at the top of his voice for someone to close the door.

Only seconds later he started feeling the first effects of the pathogen entering his lungs. There was a slight tingling sensation, which soon grew to a painful sensation of tiny needles inside his lungs. He felt the pain spread quickly to the rest of his body as his pounding heart helped his blood carry bacteria around his entire body fast. He knew that he was doomed, so when a worker appeared in the doorway looking bewildered, he held up his hands to signal to him to stay away and close the door.

Soliman's throat was tightening painfully, and he could no longer speak. His entire body trembled for a few seconds, and then his legs gave way beneath him. The bacteria were now reproducing at a staggering speed, and they were already entering virtually every cell in his body. As they spread throughout his body, and started to crystalise, they broke down the cell membranes causing Soliman to start coughing up blood, which flew out of his mouth and splattered onto the floor, where it quickly transformed into the blueish crystalline material that he had seen numerous times in the mice. Now on his hands and knees and petrified by fear, he watched motionless for a few seconds as the crystals grew out of his blood on the floor in front of him, at a terrifying speed.

Then his entire body suddenly went into violent toxic shock. This caused uncontrollable vomiting, which was his body's last desperate attempt to rid itself of the pathogen.

Luckily for Soliman, he was as good as dead by then. His body triggered the only response it had left – unconsciousness, and thus he was spared the final agonising molecular disassembly that was now happening throughout his entire body. As the bacteria spread ever faster in a run-away chain reaction, they continued to break down cell walls, and as the microscopic crystals within the bacteria came into contact with the phytoplasma of the cell which didn't contain sufficient amounts of compound oxygen, the bacteria almost instantly secreted the bluish crystal in a protective coating, which in turn crystallised the entire cell.

The effect was horrible to watch. It had only been a few seconds since the worker arrived to see Soliman collapse on the floor, but as the shocked man walked hesitantly towards him, he could see Soliman's skin turning blue. But it wasn't the kind of blue he had seen in people found dead in the snowy mountains where he had grown up. This shimmered in the lights and it seemed to spread across Soliman's body at a truly shocking speed. It almost seemed as if it came from the inside, working its way rapidly out through the skin.

Completely dumbfounded by the scene playing out in front of him, the worker didn't say a word as he knelt down beside the young scientist, whom he knew only by name.

At that moment Rashid arrived at the storage depot, alerted by the shouting. Even before he had reached the storage unit, he had decided what to do. Immediately upon reaching the door, he hit the emergency close button next to the access panel, and the door slammed shut in an instant.

The worker had just grabbed Soliman's hand to see if he could feel a pulse, but the body had already turned strangely rigid. When the door slammed shut behind him, he was so startled that he jolted backwards, still holding Soliman's hand. Instantly, Soliman's hand separated from the rest of his body as the worker fell backwards, terrified at holding another man's severed hand in his. He instinctively threw the hand on the floor and it crumbled like brittle glass in the smashed windscreen of a car. The tiny crystals shot into the air like a fine dust and began drifting through the room.

Soliman was now a rigid crystal statue lying on the floor of the storage building, staring with dead blue eyes at the ceiling, and with a severed hand lying crumbled a few meters away. There was no blood coming from his wrist where his hand had been attached. His entire body had turned into a dead crystalline mass, with every cell perforated by billions of bacteria that had almost instantly turned into crystals as they spread. Their hibernation was merely a self-preservation mechanism, with no awareness of the impact this had on other living organisms in the vicinity. But the effect on their surroundings was devastating.

The worker leapt to his feet and ran for the steel door. Rashid could hear the thump as he hit the inside of it, and a few seconds later he could see the man's desperate face in the small window. His panicked eyes looked as if they were about to pop out of his head, and his mouth moved rapidly, shouting muffled cries for help.

The man continued hammering on the door with his bloodied fists, now completely enveloped by panic and the inevitability of his own death. He had seen what had happened to Soliman the young scientist within the space of a minute, and despite his ferocious attack on the door he probably knew that he was doomed.

Rashid stood calmly outside and watched the man slowly lose his strength as well as his control over his own body. After twenty seconds his eyes became unfocused and his hands were now flailing randomly across the bloodied window. A few seconds later he collapsed just inside the room, but an infinite distance from safety. Rashid had watched the man without compassion. He had been concerned with trying to determine whether he himself had been infected. If that was the case, the whole programme would fail, and that made the deaths here today seem insignificant.

Other workers and a couple of scientists including both Kashim Khan and Mohammed Yusef had arrived, but Rashid shouted to them to keep back and stay inside the living quarters. It might not help them much if he was indeed infected, but it seemed like the right thing to do. After a couple of minutes of standing still and trying to sense every part of his body, he concluded that none of the pathogen had escaped from the storage depot. Rashid slowly knelt down onto the cement floor and thanked Allah. Not because he was still alive, but because the weapon had been saved and the programme would be able to go on. The pathogen had presented an opportunity of unparalleled scale, and to lose control of it now would have been a catastrophe, irrespective of his own death.

'Seal it!' he shouted at some of the workers, and after a few seconds of disorganised bewilderment, they ran off to fetch the equipment that had been brought to the cave for an incident such as this. A few minutes later they returned and began covering the entire front of the storage depot with a thick sticky yellow polyurethane foam that hardened almost immediately upon contact with the air. Soon it covered the entire steel door and the surrounding rockface with a thick layer as hard as concrete, and then the workers began preparing for the construction of a concrete wall.

After having taken a shower and consumed a couple of cups of coffee, Rashid walked to the central control room of the facility. From here it was possible to control everything from lights to security cameras to support systems for the laboratory and the living quarters, as well as humidity and temperature in individual areas of the vast compound. The control system was also designed to deal with the type of situation that had arisen a few hours earlier. Rashid thought briefly about the loss of that remarkable man Abdullah Soliman, and he was truly saddened by the loss. But he found consolation in the knowledge that Soliman was now with Allah, where he would receive his reward for his sacrifice.

Rashid then accessed the control system for the storage facilities and punched in the correct code for the destruction of depot #2. He hit 'ENTER' and without anyone in the cave being able to hear it, the depot behind the newly constructed wall was drenched in an extremely potent acid that was squirting from the nozzles in its ceiling. The acid ate its way through everything in the room, including the outer layers of the reinforced walls, the steel door, the storage racks and through the aluminium containers which held the bacterium samples.

A lethal haze spread throughout the depot, as all of its content decomposed and turned into basic chemicals and gasses. Within half an hour the reactive potency of the acid was spent, and on the floor of the room was only a thick slurry comprised of liquid remnants of all the matter, organic as well as inorganic, that had been in the room thirty minutes earlier. That also included the bodies of Mohammed Soliman and the unfortunate worker who had tried to help him. There was now no trace of them, and they would never be heard from again.

FOURTEEN

Returning to the office the next day, Fiona found herself eager to get to work. She had been very tired when she had left the night before, but her curiosity had almost kept her in. Now she was ready for another day and another chapter in the extraordinary tale of the SS-Ahnenerbe expeditions. She had expected to read more about the retrieval of Rudolph Von Serbottendorf from the cave. But when she turned the page, she found only a short entry, presumably made by research staff in Berlin, indicating that all the members of the expedition, including Thomas Beck, were presumed to have perished.

She thought that was very odd, but the mystery was explained in the next section of the book, where she learned that another expedition was eventually dispatched after nothing was heard from Von Serbottendorf. It was evidently planned as a rescue mission, and its leader had been Jürgen Reitziger, one of Von Serbottendorf's closest aides. It had taken the SS more than six months to put together the mission, and the first documents written by Reitziger bore the mark of an impatient and frustrated man, much in the same way that Von Serbottendorf had felt frustrated on his way from Cape Town to Antarctica.

But the mission had finally got underway, and following the same route as the previous missions, it took them more than a month to reach the Antarctic continent. Because of the delay in arranging the expedition, it arrived during the early winter. They knew almost exactly where Von Serbottendorf had been headed on his way out, so they were able to determine his approximate landing point on the coast. But because of heavy ice, they had to make the last leg by sleighs, and this added to the time and effort required. Within a couple of days of reaching the shore, they found the remains of Von Serbottendorf's camp.

Most of it had been destroyed by the violent Antarctic weather, but several of the camp shelters had been partially dug into the ground and further reinforced by stone walls, so two living quarters and what appeared to be some sort of communal space was virtually intact. At temperatures some thirty degrees Celsius below freezing, the improvised rooms were as if frozen in time. Rudolph Von Serbottendorf's diary, which had later been taken over by Thomas Beck, was found on a table in one of the living quarters, along with various other notes concerning the progress of the expedition.

Fiona turned over the cover of the book to look at the insignia of the Thule Society. This was clearly a compilation made after all the expeditions had been completed. Apparently, someone with all the accounts and documents must have sat down in the following years to reconstruct the entire course of events.

Jürgen Reitziger had chronicled his own expedition, and noted what an eerie sensation it had been to uncover an empty camp with no trace of any of the team members from the previous expedition, except a diary similar to the one he wrote his own account in. Reitziger decided that the only thing they could do now was to find the cave entrance mentioned by Von Serbottendorf and Beck. Apparently, he succeeded.

JULY 18TH 1939

WE HAVE FOUND THE CAVERN AND ARE PLANNING TO GO INSIDE TOMORROW. IT IS IN PLAIN SIGHT FROM THE VALLEY, SO IT IS REALLY NO WONDER VON SERBOTTENDORF AND BECK FOUND IT. ITS NARROW ENTRANCE AT THE BACK OF THE CAVE IS EXACTLY AS DESCRIBED BY VON SERBOTTENDORF, WITH THREE 90-DEGREE TURNS

ALTERNATING LEFT AND RIGHT, THUS OFFERING ALMOST TOTAL PROTECTION FROM THE ELEMENTS, EXCEPT FOR THIS DREADFUL COLD.

The next day Reitziger's team evidently entered the caves for the second time in an effort to retrieve the bodies of their countrymen, as well as to explore the caves.

JULY 19TH 1939

WE HAVE RECOVERED THE BODIES. THOMAS BECK WAS RIGHT. IT IS A TRULY HORRIFIC SIGHT, AND WE ALL HAVE A FEELING THAT SOMETHING OMINOUS IS AWAITING US HERE. THERE IS NO TRACE OF LIFE ANYWHERE INSIDE THE CAVE, BUT IT IS CLEAR THAT VON SERBOTTENDORF AND FINK DIED NOT AT THEIR OWN HAND, AND NOT FROM ANY WEAPON. WE HAVE ENCASED THEM BOTH INSIDE BLOCKS OF ICE, TO ENSURE THEIR PRESERVATION IN THE STATE WE FOUND THEM. WE WILL BRING THEM BACK TO GERMANY FOR STUDY AND A DIGNIFIED FUNERAL. THERE IS NO TRACE OF BECK HIMSELF OR ANYONE ELSE FROM THE TEAM. THE SHIP, ALL OF HER CREW AND THE REST OF THE SCIENCE TEAM IS GONE. THEY MAY HAVE BEEN EATEN BY WILD ANIMALS, ALTHOUGH I AM UNSURE IF ANYTHING EVEN LIVES HERE. WE SEARCHED THE BACK OF THE CAVE, AND IT IS CLEAR TO US THAT THE MARKINGS ON THE SURFACES OF THE CAVE'S INTERIOR ARE MANMADE. AS WE PUSHED FURTHER INTO THE CAVE, WE ENTERED A WIDE IMMACULATELY CARVED CIRCULAR CORRIDOR EXTENDING SOME TEN METERS INSIDE THE BLACK ROCK, AFTER WHICH IT PROMPTLY STOPPED. IT SEEMS THAT A HUGE CAVE-IN HAD TAKEN PLACE, BECAUSE THE CORRIDOR WAS ENTIRELY BLOCKED BY SEVERAL TONS OF HUGE BOULDERS. WE WERE ALL IN AWE AT THE WALL SURFACES OF THE CORRIDOR, WHICH WERE AS SMOOTH AS POLISHED MARBLE. I HAVE NEVER SEEN SUCH CRAFTSMANSHIP, AND TO THINK THAT IT

WAS CARVED THROUGH SOME OF THE HARDEST ROCK ON THE EARTH IS ASTONISHING INDEED. UNFORTUNATELY, WE HAVE BROUGHT NO EQUIPMENT CAPABLE OF PENETRATING THE ROCK OR THE CAVE-IN, SO WE HAVE HAD TO RETREAT TO THE CAMPS. I HAVE SPOKEN WITH THE OTHER MEMBERS OF THE SCIENCE TEAM, AND WE ALL AGREE THAT THERE IS NOTHING MORE WE CAN DO HERE. WE WILL TAKE DOWN OUR CAMP AND PACK UP TOMORROW TO RETURN TO GERMANY. I ONLY HOPE THAT I MAY BE GRANTED ANOTHER OPPORTUNITY TO COME BACK. I FEEL THAT SOMETHING MAGNIFICENT IS WAITING FOR US WITHIN THIS MOUNTAIN.

The following pages described the trip over the ice back to the ship, which was precariously close to being locked in the ice. Reitziger speculated that Von Serbottendorf's expedition might have suffered the same fate. He considered it likely that some of the team had escaped from the camp alive, only to have their ship crushed by the ice. In that case, it might be sitting at the bottom of the ocean not far from the camp. Alternatively, it might be that the ship had escaped the ice, but that the crew had perished from the mysterious illness, after which the ship would have succumbed to the elements during one of the frequent and violent storms in the South Atlantic.

And with that, the diaries of the *SS-Ahnenerbe* expeditions ended. Fiona couldn't help but feel sorry for the men who had perished in such a horrific way. At the same time, she was fascinated by the notion that something so deadly could have laid dormant for so long, only to suddenly unleash its deadly potential on unsuspecting visitors.

What followed was an account of how the bodies were brought back to the Berlin storage facility, and how initial tests were carried out. Jürgen Reitziger may have thought about bringing them home for an honourable burial, but the first experiment, which was conducted in a sealed refrigerator room, entailed drilling a small hole through the ice and directly into the skull of Hans Fink. A sample of his brain was then extracted and put under a microscope. Inside the tiny blood vessels, they discovered minute amounts of the bluish crystal that had covered their bodies, when found by Reitziger. Various tests were carried out, and the pathogen was quickly recovered and isolated.

Initially, the highly capable team of scientists in Berlin left the bodies undisturbed, except for two more drilling attempts to verify that the two men, and most likely the rest of the crew, had died from the same thing. They then started to grow the bacteria in containers, and shortly thereafter had their first proof of its potency. One of the lab assistants accidentally inhaled some of the microscopic crystals containing bacteria, and had died a terrible death that evidently shocked the science team. Undaunted, however, they pressed on with the experiments, and after having discovered that the pathogen was capable of remaining active even when in an airborne state, there were no further accidents.

All of the experiments were conducted in specially designed labs in a heavily guarded storage room at the purpose-built facility outside of Berlin. Although turning out to be an arduous process, they were able to gradually refine the pathogen, making it significantly more deadly than the original samples found in Antarctica, shortening the incubation period from six to two hours. Eventually, the head of the *SS-Ahnenerbe*, Wolfram Sievers, shipped off several samples to a concentration camp, where he then supervised the most gruesome experiments on living human subjects, in order to study the lethality of the bacteria, as well as the hibernation mechanism.

He discovered that in the right conditions the pathogen would invade the entire body in under an hour, spreading to virtually every cell, causing them to crystallise in a rapid chain reaction, essentially causing the host to vitrify, and thereby killing it in a horrific fashion. Additionally, they verified that on several occasions the process would happen in a way that would allow crystal-encased microscopic bacteria to become airborne, thereby potentially infecting new victims.

Fiona wondered why she had never once in her life heard of any evidence of such tests carried out in the concentration camps. All she had ever heard about was how they gassed people by the hundreds of thousands. Perhaps the SS was able to erase any trace of the experiments before the Americans and the Russians had arrived to liberate the camps.

She had always been taught that the Nazis and in particular the SS were simply a bunch of sadists who enjoyed torturing and killing people. But now that she thought about it, it seemed extremely odd that the tens of thousands of people who were members of the SS, should suddenly run wild in an uncontrolled sadist extravaganza. Particularly when considering that all of them had been civilians before joining the army. Most had been youngsters perhaps sixteen or seventeen years of age. To just assume that they were all psychopaths was simply not credible.

There had to be something more, and if there was one thing in the history of mankind that could make otherwise ordinary people do extraordinarily cruel things, it was religion or the perceived threat of being trampled underfoot by an enemy. In other words, in order for these people to be able to do what they did to millions of political opponents, Jews and other ethnic minorities, they had to be motivated to believe that they were working for a greater good. They had to be convinced that it was for the benefit of their nation, and that their actions were justifiable.

The pathogen research programme wasn't just killing for the sake of killing. It was a barbaric yet systematic scientific programme, designed to refine the bacteria found in Antarctica into a material suitable for weapons of war. And all in the name of the ultimate goal of world domination, and a Reich that was to last a thousand years.

Fiona paused for a few minutes, sitting back in her chair holding her coffee cup with both hands, and staring at the wall. The accounts were hard to believe, but she didn't doubt their authenticity for one second. Everything she had learned up until this point fitted neatly in a larger puzzle. There were still important pieces missing, but they were making progress, and she knew that she just needed to keep pushing forward.

When it became apparent even for the most optimistic members of the SS-Ahnenerbe that the war would be lost, Himmler went to see Adolph Hitler, to petition for a transfer of the research facility to a place outside of Germany. At that point, it had only been a few months earlier that the entire research and production programme for the V1 and V2 rockets had been moved from Peenemünde deeper into the heart of Germany, in order to protect it from further allied aerial bombardments. The facilities at Peenemünde had been raided at great costs in time and money to the Nazis, but enough of the scientists, equipment and production facilities had survived, and were promptly transferred to sites in the south of the country. Himmler requested that the same should be done for the biological warfare research efforts. Hitler seemed to be reluctant, but when Himmler, seconded by Sievers, raised the risk of an accidental pathogen outbreak inside Germany, the Fuhrer had apparently yielded, and a plan was quickly drawn up.

The entire programme was to be moved to Argentina, where mass production would be able to commence within a few months. Hitler and his military staff had accepted that the United States would be able to continue sending an almost limitless number of troops and military equipment across the Atlantic Ocean. And despite the heroic efforts of the German U-boat crews, the only truly effective means of stopping that from continuing was to inflict serious harm on the Americans on their own soil.

An invasion was obviously completely out of the question, but an attack by a potent biological agent might stun president Roosevelt into withdrawing his troops, or at least halt the transfer of any additional resources for a while. That would enable Germany to regroup, concentrate its efforts, and beat the Russians and then the Allied forces in the West. After that, the entire European continent, as well as the British Isles would be under Nazi control, and in a fight between a united Europe and the United States, Hitler was convinced that his military machine would prevail. After that, it would be a question of time before world domination was achieved.

After a few months, and upon learning that the mass production facility in Argentina had been completed, Hitler had ordered all bio-facilities on German soil torn down, all scientific research documents erased from the records, and the remaining samples of the pathogen incinerated. The Russian army and the allied forces were moving ever closer, and even he was getting nervous that some of the research might fall into enemy hands before long. He then granted the submarine U-303 permission to embark on its journey from Bremerhaven to Montevideo in Argentina.

Wow, thought Fiona. *So that's what happened. If there really were samples of this stuff on the U-boat, no wonder someone was eager to get to it.*

She filled up her cup with more coffee, hardly taking her eyes off the texts in front of her, and forgetting the milk and sugar. Then she resumed reading.

Upon learning of the apparent failure of the U-boat to reach its destination, Hitler, in one of his fits of rage, denounced Himmler's programmes as being nothing but empty promises. He then ordered the destruction of all the facilities in Argentina, as well as the death of several of the leading scientists, who he accused of plotting against him. Fiona suspected that another reason might be that he didn't want the allies to get their hands on the German scientists. Hitler knew as well as anyone, that they could probably be convinced to change sides if presented with the right set of incentives.

A single sheet of paper at the back of the book indicated that Himmler then took the remaining records of the experiments to an undisclosed safe location, ostensibly in Vienna. What followed were a series of notes and pieces of text, that documented an elaborate system for keeping the triangular pieces of medallion safe and out of reach of the non-initiated. However, there were no references to where the triangles might be now.

Fiona had to stand up to stretch her legs now. She had been stooped over the texts for hours, and her back was aching. She paced the room for a few minutes, letting what she had learned fall into place in her head, along with all the other information she had poured in there over the past weeks. She could feel herself becoming more and more tense as the days went by, and the mystery unfolded. She felt excitement and impatience enveloping her, but also a sense of responsibility now that the true nature of this mystery had been revealed to her. These past few weeks might be interesting from a purely archaeological and historical point of view, but if her worst fears were to come true, it could also prove to be truly calamitous for the world. This was especially true now she knew that someone had probably recovered samples of the pathogen from U-303, just days before she and Andrew got to it.

★ ★ ★

Erich Strauss had remained in his office the whole day, and had decided not to go home before the meeting. His house was around twenty kilometres outside of Vienna in an exclusive area near a river, and driving there and back would take too long. He had asked Ludvig Bauer to leave at five in the afternoon, since there would be no further need for his services, and also because Strauss didn't want any uninitiated in the building when the Keepers arrived.

He had called the meeting only yesterday because of the unsettling visitor he had received a couple of days earlier. That had been reason enough for him to want to see the Keepers, but now there was something even more pressing to discuss. Upon entering the secret room in the library, to his utter horror, he had discovered that somebody, almost certainly the visitor, had entered the room and taken a book and a number of other documents. And it wasn't just a few random texts either. The culprit had stolen the documents that chronicled the efforts of the first members of the Thule Society, as they attempted to reach the goal they all shared, even now, so many years later.

The grandmaster and the four Keepers had all read and studied the documents, as had all their predecessors, so the information contained within them was by no means lost. The real issue was much worse than that. The theft had proven beyond any doubt that someone was pursuing, not only the goal they themselves were seeking to reach, but also pursuing them as a society, which was even more disconcerting.

Tonight, he would have to deliver the news to the Keepers and although he held the title of grandmaster, and as such in principle had absolute power and the final say in everything that happened in the society, he knew that they would not be pleased. He had not dared to communicate anything to anyone, save for the one telephone call to Eckleston, which had been brief and without specific details. He didn't dare send letters or even e-mails to anyone, for fear of being monitored.

Many times, he had arranged for others to be investigated and followed. As the protector of the Thule Society and its artefacts, there were times when he needed to determine whether someone presented a threat or not. The vast majority of the time there had been no reason to worry, and he had not thought twice about the fact that he had essentially meddled in other people's lives. But this evening he was having trouble getting used to the idea that perhaps it was now him that might be watched. And even more unpleasant was the fact that he wasn't sure who might be watching.

One by one the four men arrived. They were all elderly gentlemen, dressed smartly in suits, and looking more than anything like board members of a bank, on their way to attend a business meeting.

They arrived within five minutes of each other, and Strauss personally let them inside the hall. There were heartfelt greetings and handshakes between the men, most of whom had known each other for years. The most recent member of the group was Doctor Phillip Eckleston, who had left London for Vienna with a distinct feeling that his grandmaster had been right in fearing for the safety of their society, and possibly also their own lives. After one of the first British Keepers had been killed in a road accident, the title had been passed on to a headmaster of a boarding school, who had died from cancer only seven years later. With that, the honour and responsibility had been given to Phillip Eckleston, who had thus taken over the peculiar responsibility of being a Keeper who didn't actually possess a triangle. Two of the other three Keepers had the responsibility of guarding one triangle each, until the day all four were under the control of the Thule Society. The first Keeper was a retired German Airforce commander, the second was a leading member of the Austrian Parliament for the National Freedom Party, and the third, who didn't possess a triangle either, was the head of the French Rotary Society. As the fourth Keeper, Eckleston had, as he ought to, thrown himself at the task of uncovering the triangle that he rightly felt he ought to be responsible for.

So far, however, his efforts had not borne fruit, which was why he had conceived of the idea of luring someone else to start the search, not for the triangles, but for Thule. He didn't necessarily think that somebody else could do a better job than him, but he just couldn't rule out that someone might be able to uncover clues to where the fourth triangle might be. And as soon as that happened, he knew that the society would move heaven and earth to retrieve it, letting no man or woman stand in its way. This would allow them to bring the four pieces together, producing the medallion that would take them to the land of the ancients. The land of Thule. And as a bonus, they might even be able to find the means to achieve the goal of destroying the Jews and the Arabs. The bacterium which had so nearly won the Second World War for Germany, Hitler, the SS and the Thule Society, would be capable of that. The realisation of an ancient prophecy had been so close and yet had turned out to be so far away. For more than fifty years they had searched for the triangles, always taking immense care not to reveal their existence to anyone. Now, their goal seemed to be closer than ever, but at the same time, they were more vulnerable than ever before.

Strauss led the four people through his own office to a large and elegantly decorated meeting room that was only used for very special occasions. Not even the biggest benefactors of the Order of the Teutonic Knights would ever see this room. They were as ignorant of that, as they were of the fact that the Order they had donated large sums of money to, in good faith, represented something altogether more sinister than was portrayed to the world.

As the men sat down, the grandmaster straightened his tie and took on a sombre demeanour.

'Firstly,' Strauss started out. 'I must inform you of a meeting I had a few days ago, with a man from London calling himself Robert Taggart. I've already had a short discussion with Mr. Eckleston about this,' he continued while motioning to the chair in which Eckleston was sitting. 'And I think that we agree, at least in principle, about what is the best way to deal with this situation.'

The three other Keepers began to look slightly uneasy, sensing that something was not right. One shifted in his chair, while another straightened his tie and placed his glass of water on the table. They could all see that the grandmaster was about to deliver some bad news. Eckleston was the only one who had been informed, and so he had spent many hours planning for the best way of handling the situation that had arisen.

'This Mr. Taggart is not who he claims to be. He is not a charity benefactor in search of a good cause. His name is Andrew Sterling.'

Upon hearing that name, all four Keepers, except for Phillip Eckleston, froze and stared at the grandmaster.

'His is Andrew Sterling, son of Charles Sterling, the former Keeper who was killed in a car crash along with his wife a number of years ago.'

Strauss paused for a few seconds to let the men at the table absorb what he had said. As they did so, their reactions went from consternation to bewilderment to dismay.

'Do you mean to tell us,' said the Airforce commander in as stern a voice as he dared, 'that the son of a former Keeper has tricked you into letting him enter into this building and steal valuable documents from us?'

The commander knew that he was pushing the limit of how he could reasonably speak to the grandmaster, but none of the men had any doubt that this was a most serious issue.

'That is correct,' replied Strauss unfazed. 'We had no indication that he was not who he claimed to be, until he stood right there in my office,' he said and pointed to beyond the closed double doors. 'By then it became clear to me that something was very wrong about him, but it wasn't until he had left that I could put my finger on it.'

Instead of pointing out that it might have been wiser to ask him to leave as soon as the grandmaster had become suspicious, the Airforce commander yielded. He had never had an abundance of respect for the intellect of this grandmaster, but the position was not one that a person came into by accident. It was not a popularity contest, but a case of one of the Keepers being voted into that position upon the death of the grandmaster. Unfortunately, he had been selected as a Keeper, just after Strauss had taken up the title of grandmaster, so there was nothing he could do about it. Now, his worst fears had come true. The man had proven inadequate for the task, and the consequences could be catastrophic.

'As you are all aware,' continued the grandmaster, 'We still hold just two of the four pieces of the medallion. This has been the case ever since the end of the war, and I am not blaming any of you for that,' he said, to appease the head of the French Rotary Society, who tended to become defensive about that particular subject matter. 'My point is, that the situation now is fundamentally different from what it was before.'

The others all nodded without saying a word. There was clearly agreement around the table that something needed to be done swiftly, but as had been the case during most of their meetings, Eckleston proved himself to be the most energetic and resourceful in the group.

'If I may,' said Eckleston, and the grandmaster motioned for him to proceed. 'Previously we could set our own pace, calmly and quietly biding our time while waiting for the opportunity to strike if we thought that a credible source possessed valuable information. With an investigation against us apparently underway, and the theft of one of the most crucial texts for this society, we must go on the offensive. We must now be much more aggressive in the pursuit of our goals,' he said and tapped his knuckles on the polished wooden table as he spoke to emphasise his point. 'The time for being passive is over. We must be as active and aggressive as we can. Our history, and indeed our future is too important.'

'So, what do you suggest we do?' asked the Austrian Member of Parliament. He was as dedicated as any around the table, but it had never been in his nature to be aggressive. Previously working as a banker with the task of taking good care of the investment needs of wealthy clients, he had learned that most good things came to those who lived quietly and didn't attract too much attention to themselves.

'Simple,' replied Eckleston. 'We change the rules of the game. The hunter becomes the hunted, so to speak. We remain calm and vigilant as ever, but we also put all our efforts into identifying and monitoring the people who are investigating us. I have spoken with one of them, a woman by the name of Fiona Keane, and if my assertion is correct, she and her companions are looking for the exact same thing that we are, except they may very well have access to sources that we do not. If we keep a low profile, monitor their every move and never let them out of our sights, I am convinced that they will eventually lead us straight to our prize.'

'And then?' asked the head of the retired German Airforce commander.

'Then we do what we must, to ensure that we acquire all the pieces of the medallion,' said Eckleston resolutely.

'But isn't this risky?' asked the French Rotary Society.

'Yes,' interjected the grandmaster calmly. 'But not doing anything might be even more dangerous. I am very aware that aggressiveness is not traditionally a virtue of this society, at least not when it comes to the search itself, but given the circumstances with which we are confronted, we simply cannot afford to merely sit back and hope for the best.'

As he spoke, the grand master's voice slowly increased in pitch, revealing the anxiousness he felt at this moment. The fact that someone had been able to trick him and managed to steal one of their most important texts, had severely shaken his belief in his own abilities.

'Gentlemen,' he said, placing the palms of his hands on the table and leaning back in his chair. 'There are people out there who are looking at us, and they are apparently making a determined effort to find what we have been searching for through all these years. We cannot risk having them find the remaining pieces. If that were to happen, all the work that has been done by all of our predecessors, all the danger that they have put themselves and the society in over the years, would have been wasted. And I assume that we are all aware of the fact, that it would then be possible to point to each and every one of us and say that we did not perform our duty when it really mattered. It would be a disgrace, and we would have proven ourselves unworthy of the responsibility which has been placed on us.'

After a few seconds of silence, Erich Strauss outlined the plan, which was to be set in motion immediately after the meeting had ended. He then let Eckleston take over the meeting for discussion of the finer details.

The grandmaster sat back and watched as Eckleston spoke, thinking to himself that Eckleston would make an excellent grandmaster someday, and that he would certainly point to him as his successor when the time came.

Some 45 minutes later, the three elderly men emerged almost simultaneously from the front door of the building and began making their way to their homes. It had become dark, except for the faint glow on the horizon where the sun had set an hour and a half earlier.

Agent Nick Frost sat motionless in his car, which was parked under a chestnut tree in a square some 50 meters from the building. He had been following Eckleston from the hotel and would be following him back there now. He hadn't been informed in any detail about what was going on, except that this man Phillip Eckleston, about whom he knew next to nothing, was to be followed so that people back at MI5 headquarters could know whom he had gone to see. The job was easy but boring, and it actually demanded quite an effort to stay alert for several hours when absolutely nothing happened.

He made sure to take clear pictures of all the four men exiting from the building. Then he started the engine of the car, and calmly followed Eckleston's car. Ten minutes later, Eckleston's car pulled into the car park of the hotel he was staying at, and the elderly man got out and entered the foyer. Frost's day was over as far as work was concerned, so now he was going out for a pint of Austrian beer. But just the one, since he needed to be in place early the next morning to trail Eckleston in case he had additional business in Vienna.

FIFTEEN

The next day Fiona went straight to Andrew's office to tell him about what she had learned. She had brought the book and the other documents, and had outlined the chronicle for him as best she could without going into too much trivial detail. She told him of the first two expeditions to the Yucatan Peninsula and to Tibet, of Von Serbottendorf, Beck, Fink and Reitziger, and of the bacterium that had attacked and possibly killed all the members of the first expedition to Antarctica. She relayed the experiments undertaken once the samples had been brought back to Germany, and the attempt to move production to Argentina in a last desperate attempt to turn the war around.

Andrew sat back in his chair for a few moments, feeling slightly bamboozled by it all. He frankly thought that most of it sounded like something out of a movie, and he still had trouble with a few of the details.

'Why did the first team succumb to the pathogen, and not the second?' he asked.

'Well, it appears that the original bacterium was lying dormant deep within the cave where Von Serbottendorf somehow contracted it. He may have contracted it from rummaging around in the cave and thereby stirring up some of it into the air. Anyway, he almost made it out, but collapsed along with his assistant Hans

Fink close to the exit passage. Whether Fink contracted it from Von Serbottendorf is unclear, but apparently, the two men died almost simultaneously. When the rescue team arrived, the bodies had been covered in frost and ice, and the leader of the second expedition Jürgen Reitziger was by then aware of the danger. They protected themselves with air filters which probably didn't help much, but the fact that the two bodies were encased in ice meant that they were effectively sealed off completely.'

'But why didn't the bodies fall apart like in the experiments carried out later?'

'I think it was because they had become completely rigid from the sub-zero *rigor mortis*, but perhaps more importantly, the bacteria may not even have had the opportunity to spread throughout the entire body. One could imagine that it only made it to the internal organs and the major blood vessels, before Von Serbottendorf and Fink collapsed and their hearts stopped beating. After that it would have been only a short time before their body temperature fell below 30 degrees Celsius, effectively forcing the bacterium to stop its onslaught and go into hibernation.'

'Makes sense,' said Andrew. 'That would also explain why the bodies looked relatively undamaged when Friedrich Henke sneaked in to the refrigerator room and peeked inside the water tanks.'

'You're probably right. Anyway,' continued Fiona. 'Reitziger wisely decided to place the two corpses in tanks filled with ice-cold water, which then quickly encased them in giant ice cubes. These were then transported home to the storage facility outside Berlin. So, it seems likely that the bacteria never had a chance to either get airborne and into anyone's lungs, or exposed to temperatures above 30 degrees Celsius.'

Andrew nodded pensively. 'Let's assume that what I found in Vienna was proof that the Thule Society is alive and well in Vienna. If that is the case, then why didn't they return to Antarctica again? Why haven't they attempted a new expedition? If they knew where the cave was, they could have just gone back to retrieve some more samples, couldn't they? They should have been able to mount several new expeditions since the war, and probably without anyone ever finding out about it.'

'Well, we actually don't know for a fact that they haven't, but since there are no clear descriptions of the route taken or the landing point on the Antarctic coastline, it would seem pretty hopeless to travel down there. But the first expedition by Von Serbottendorf back in 1937 appears to have relied solely on ancient maps, such as that of Piri Reiss and Kircher. The funny thing is, that none of the chronicles of either expedition actually specifically mention where the cave was, except that it was somewhere in Queen Maude's Land. Now, I'm sure that the SS had the coordinates somewhere, but they may have been destroyed, or perhaps the Thule Society actually still has them somewhere else.'

'But didn't you say that for his expedition, Reitziger had followed the course taken by Von Serbottendorf and Beck?'

'That is what he himself wrote, but there is no mention of what that course actually was.'

Andrew scratched the back of his head. 'Either the Thule Society has the coordinates, or they were destroyed during the end of the war, or someone else could have them?'

'Right, said Fiona. 'We don't know, so we can't rule anything out at this point.'

Andrew grimaced, trying to make it all make sense inside his head. 'Ok, let's just back up for a second. How did the Nazis end up travelling to the various locations they ended up visiting?' he asked.

'Well,' said Fiona, 'It appears that there had initially been no direct connection between the choices of destinations, other than the belief that they would find remnants of ancient civilisations, that might then lead to clues about the original Aryan civilisation. I wouldn't call it random, but they apparently just started combing ancient sites around the world, believing that an original ancient civilisation would have left some trace somewhere. And having seen the evidence presented to me by Eckleston in the form of maps, having read about the similarities in legends among ancient civilisations that supposedly evolved separately, and having seen all this material from the expeditions, I'm actually beginning to believe that the Nazis were on to something.'

Andrew glanced at Fiona with a perplexed look on his face. 'Let me see if I understand you correctly. You now actually believe that there really was an ancient civilisation named Thule?' he asked perplexed.

'Look,' said Fiona. 'I frankly don't give a hoot what people call it, but you have to admit that there is a hell of a lot of evidence pointing in that direction, right?'

'Well, yes,' admitted Andrew grudgingly.

'Good. Now, I've come up with an idea,' said Fiona, and got up from her chair and started pacing the floor. 'The accounts of Rudolph Von Serbottendorf and Thomas Beck clearly indicate a connection between the ancient civilisations. At least their legends are often the same, and they all mention what they call superior beings that visited them in ancient times. Do you agree?'

'Yes, but what about the triangles? Why do you suppose these advanced beings would hand these out in different parts of the world, and where are they now?'

'Just wait a moment,' she said and raised her hand to ward off his impatient questions. 'My own interpretation is that the original ancient civilisation, which I'm beginning to believe really existed, sent out their own expeditions to the rest of the world to seek out other peoples. But upon finding, probably to their disappointment, I would imagine, that none of them were nearly as highly developed as themselves, they established the occasional contact with them, checking up on them from time to time, so to speak. Only on rare occasions was there any direct contact or technology transfer. Judging from various anthropological sources, these contacts happened several hundreds of years apart, and some civilisations recount just one such contact.'

'But,' said Fiona, raising her index finger. 'And this is the important bit. They did leave the more primitive civilisations with a tool that would enable them to find them, once they had reached a certain level of technological development. A sort of flag for having achieved a higher state of civilisation.'

'But why would they do it in such an elaborate and frankly convoluted way?' asked Andrew confused.

'Well, remember that the triangle was supposed to be able to guide them to the original civilisation?'

'Yes. So?'

'I believe that the general idea of the inhabitants of the ancient civilisation was the following: By delivering a piece of some type of navigation equipment to each of the less developed peoples they had discovered, they would ensure that those peoples would only be able to find their way to Antarctica if they worked together, combining the pieces to some sort of device that could guide them.'

'Sounds a bit like a Bible story to me,' said Andrew sceptically.

'I know it sounds just a bit farfetched, but I'm trying to put together a logical theory, Ok?'

'Ok. So, what you are saying is that only a peaceful and united people would be able to find the continent of the ancients? The idea being that they wanted to make contact with other civilisations, while avoiding getting run over by barbarian hoards?'

'Exactly,' said Fiona. 'At least that's one theory. Whether it holds, I don't know. And whether the whole idea of a peaceful and united people working to find their common ancestors was even realistic in the first place, that's equally difficult to say. Looking back through the history of exploration, it isn't exactly self-evident that this could work, but there's no reason to assume that 12,000 years ago the inhabitants of Antarctica would think or reason the way we do today. I would even go as far as to say that it is unlikely.'

'Alright,' said Andrew impatiently. 'Getting back to where the pieces of the medallion, the triangles, are now. I'm sure you've developed a theory on that as well,' he said and smiled wryly.

'Let me start out by saying that I have discovered that the head of the SS, Heinrich Himmler, decided to set up a system, at least until all the pieces of the medallion had been found, by which four of the most trusted members of the Thule Society would have bestowed upon them the responsibility of so-called 'Keepers'. Himmler, being the grandmaster, would hold the Ruby, and the four Keepers would guard the four pieces of the medallion when and if they were found. The Keepers were Himmler himself, Wolfram Sievers, Rudolph Von Serbottendorf and Thomas Beck, in other words, everyone who was anyone in the *SS-Ahnenerbe*.'

'Ok. Go on,' said Andrew.

'Well, the material that I have now spent hours reading, clearly states that one was found near Cusco in Peru, and another in Yamzho Yumco in Tibet. And I found a reference to a third triangle, which amazingly had been lying virtually forgotten in a museum in Paris for years until the German occupation of France. It was initially uncovered when, in an attempt to kick out the British, Napoleon invaded Egypt in 1798. He wasn't much of an archaeologist, to say the least, but he did feel fascinated by the ancient Egyptians and their monuments, as demonstrated by the huge obelisk which has been standing in the centre of Paris ever since he stole it and dragged it back with him. He is even supposed to have spent a night alone in the king's chamber inside the Pyramid of King Cheops outside Cairo.'

'But you're saying that this obelisk wasn't the only thing he brought back?'

'Lord, no,' laughed Fiona. 'He looted hundreds of archaeological sites, and even graves for what we would today consider priceless artefacts, but to him, they were merely shiny tokens of his most recent conquest. Some of them are very spectacular and still reside in Paris museums and private collections all over France, so it is no wonder that a small metal triangle didn't catch anyone's attention, particularly when nobody could figure out what it was.'

'So how did the SS get hold of it?'

'Simple. Remember that Himmler was a buff for all sorts of esoteric paraphernalia and ancient relics. So, when the Nazis occupied France, they systematically collected and impounded anything that might be connected to the occult. And since they had already been looking for artefacts from the ancient world for years, I would guess that several of those stored in Paris fit the bill very nicely. Also, remember that the *SS-Ahnenerbe* had already uncovered two triangles, so having the third triangle from Egypt eventually end up in the hands of the *Ahnenerbe* was virtually inevitable.'

'So, the triangle first stolen by Napoleon in Egypt and then by Himmler in Paris ended up being the third one in the *Ahnenerbe*'s possession?'

'Correct. That is what I understand after reading through this material,' she said and tapped the leather cover of the book.

'What about the fourth triangle then? Weren't the less developed people of ancient times supposed to have all four of them, to find Atlantis or Thule or whatever its name was at the time?'

'Yes. And I think I've figured out where it might be,' beamed Fiona.

'Oh, really?' replied Andrew sceptically. 'Where? And how?'

'It's quite simple really. When reading Thomas Beck's account from the Uxmal expedition it becomes abundantly clear, that at that point he wasn't particularly interested in the broader archaeological aspects of the excavations at Uxmal. All he wanted to do was to determine that it had indeed been built far earlier than was previously assumed. And having proven just that, as well as positively establishing the use of building techniques similar to those of the ancient Egyptians, he returned to Germany with a few prizes in the form of pottery and sculptures and even some spectacular gold jewellery.'

'What are you suggesting?'

'I'm not just suggesting. I'm convinced that Beck did a lousy job and never completed the excavations properly. Even his own staff was apparently upset that he pulled the expedition out and back to Germany as quickly after their arrival as he did.'

'But why didn't they go back to look again?'

'I'm sure that Beck did what he could to convince everyone that he had completed the task in the Yucatan Peninsula, and by the time they had found three of the triangles and needed the fourth, Beck was a corpse inside a big ice cube. Evidently, it never occurred to anyone to return to Uxmal, because there are no records of any further expeditions.'

'So, you think that there is still one more out there?'

'Exactly,' nodded Fiona. 'That is exactly what I think. Based on Beck's account, I believe that there is still a piece of the triangle hidden somewhere in those ruins on the Yucatan Peninsula, most likely in Uxmal.'

'So, let me guess. You want us to go there and look?'

'Yes. If we find the triangle it might help us find the lost civilisation, and that might lead us towards a way to find and deal with the pathogen.'

'If it's still there.'

'Yes. If it's still there.'

'But where exactly would we start looking? How would we know where it might be?'

'Well, Beck's account of his journey to the Yucatan Peninsula is actually very detailed. We should have no trouble finding the ruins he mentioned if we can hire an experienced guide from that area.'

'But what good would that do? Don't you think that they might all be excavated by now? It's unlikely that they should be discovered by a group of supposedly civilian German scientists back in 1937, and then be forgotten all over again.'

'I know,' nodded Fiona. 'But if they have indeed been excavated, we might still learn something we can use. And in any case, it's all we have right now, isn't it?'

Andrew shrugged. 'Yes, I guess you're right,' he said and poured himself another cup of tea.

'And moreover, it's been a while since I've had the opportunity to get my hands dirty at an archaeological site like that,' she said and smiled enthusiastically.

'Would you like some?' said Andrew and pointed at her with his silver teapot.

'Yes please,' she said and lifted her cup. 'I don't know about you, but I'd definitely like to get underway as soon as possible.'

'Well, I must say that I tend to agree with you. It is going to look a bit funny with me flying around the world like this, but as you just said, it's all we have at this stage.'

'Great,' exclaimed Fiona. 'Let's not waste any time then. Let's start planning this thing.'

'Fiona,' said Andrew. 'If what you've read is all true and the U-boat actually attempted to carry samples of this pathogen out of Germany, then you can be sure that this was what the people who entered the submarine before we did, were looking for.'

'I'm sure that's the case,' said Fiona.

'And that means that right now some lunatic is holding that stuff in his hands, and I'm pretty sure that he didn't go down there to get it just for the fun of it. In other words, someone is planning to use it on someone else, and they are probably working on it right now.'

'So, we have to try to find them!' said Fiona emphatically. 'If we don't, they might let the bloody thing loose somewhere, or perhaps it could escape by accident. In any event, it would be a disaster. We simply have to do something.'

'But how? We don't even know who those people are?'

'Well, it has to be those people you paid a visit to in Vienna, right? Who else could it be?'

'If it is them, how do you explain that some of the stuff from the burglary in London and Berlin was found in an apartment in Germany that was owned by a man affiliated with Middle Eastern terrorist networks?'

'Right,' said Fiona pensively. 'Some things just don't add up here. But in any case, if we can retrieve all the triangles, we should be able to find the location where the bacterium was first discovered by Von Serbottendorf. And that might enable someone to develop some type of cure or perhaps an antibiotic that might avert a disaster.'

'Yes,' said Andrew. 'That's probably the best way to do it.'

'We need to get ourselves to Mexico as soon as possible,' repeated Fiona.

'Guess so,' said Andrew. 'And if those people in Vienna have the other three triangles, then I'm afraid we'll have to break a few more laws to get them. Do you have any idea how that medallion is supposed to work?'

'No. Not a single clue. There was nothing in the texts I read, and Eckleston didn't give any details, but then he might very well be lying through his teeth just to confuse us. We'll have to try and figure it out later. Right now, I just don't know.'

'By the way, Fiona,' said Andrew, and gave her a serious look. 'There's something else I need to tell you.'

'What?' she said, already not liking the tone of his voice. He sounded as if he was about to tell her that he had run over her dog.

'I had a chat with Colonel Strickland yesterday, and he said that upon running a routine check on your friend Doctor Eckleston, it has been uncovered that he used to be a member of a rather shadowy group during his years at university.'

'University? That must have been ages ago.'

'It is quite a few decades back, but from what we can determine about that group's political aims, they could be interpreted to be quite similar to those of the Thule Society.'

'So?' asked Fiona visibly relieved. 'What's the big deal about that? Lots of people experiment with political organisations as students.'

'I know. But this one wasn't entirely political from what we could tell. Apparently, it was working towards a new world order based on racial ancestry. At least, that's what our people are guessing at this juncture. Sounds familiar, doesn't it?'

'Christ,' whispered Fiona. 'That is actually unsettling. I rather liked the old geezer. He seemed pretty eccentric, that's for certain, but otherwise completely harmless.'

'Well, I've spoken with Strickland again today, and in the light of what we are investigating, the MI5 has had a tail on him since they discovered his past affiliations. Yesterday he went to the airport and flew to Vienna, and guess where he went?'

Fiona didn't answer. There was no need to. She just stared dumbfounded at Andrew.

'I'm beginning to lean towards the conclusion that The Order of the Teutonic Knights are in fact the Thule Society, and that Eckleston is involved with them.'

'But why?' said Fiona. 'What could be his motive for getting involved with them? Do you suppose he believes in all that stuff about an Aryan race and world domination?'

'Well, I don't think he believes any of the nonsense about magical powers and underground structures near the poles. But you yourself have given a pretty good picture of the man. He is a scientist with, shall we say, an extraordinarily open mind, who is apparently convinced that the Aryan race and its origin are equivalent to the lost civilisation and the lost continent. He probably believes that Aryans once ruled the planet, and that they are destined to do so again. In any case, the fact that Eckleston has met with a group of people who might represent a Thule Society which seems alive and well even today, is a concern to me.'

'But why do you suppose Eckleston was so willing to provide information to me then?'

'First of all, to control the information that is out there. By making himself the most outrageous proponent of these and other ludicrous theories, he ensures that he is always one step ahead of anyone trying to investigate these matters. In a weird sort of way, he controls the narrative when it comes to these specific topics. Secondly, he is a believer in these theories, and he wants to draw us out to see what we want.'

'Well, I did notice how he went on and on about the Earth Crust Displacement theory but appeared to be mocking the Nazi expeditions and the beliefs that lay behind them. That might just have been a smokescreen, to draw my attention away from what he believes to be the truth. Perhaps you are right. Perhaps he really does believe that there once existed an Aryan super race and a superior civilisation.'

'But then that would also entail that he lied when he told you that the Nazis never found anything in Antarctica. From my talk with Friedrich Henke and from the material you have examined, we know for a fact that they brought something back from those expeditions'

'I suppose so,' said Fiona with a troubled look on her face. 'I guess we have to start being a lot more careful about who we talk to and about what, eh?'

'Exactly. Which reminds me,' said Andrew. 'I'll have to go and tell Strickland about this. His suspicions about Eckleston seemed to be justified after all.'

'Do you suppose he'll want to involve more people in this? I mean, it seems to grow bigger for every new turn we take.'

'That may be a good idea. I'll discuss that with him too. And I'll have Cathy arrange flights to the nearest international airport to the Uxmal ruins as soon as possible, but from then on, I'm expecting you to take over. You're the archaeologist, so I'm going to let you handle everything, ok?'

'Absolutely,' smiled Fiona cheerfully. 'You'll be in safe hands.'

★ ★ ★

Somewhere in the Syrian Desert, Kashim Khan and Ahmed Kamal Rashid were preparing for the arrival of the man they simply called 'The Russian'. His name was Sergei Ivanov, and over the past year, he had been instrumental in planning and equipping the laboratory that now stood finished some fifty meters underground deep inside a mountain. Both Khan and Rashid liked the man. He was jovial and had a good sense of humour, which was sometimes needed in this business. He was also completely unscrupulous and obsessed with money, the latter of which was a product of his many years in the Soviet scientific world.

Russia had always produced excellent scientists, but they had also been extremely underfunded, and the ability to exploit their scientific results had never come even close to matching the prowess of the scientists. Ivanov was now a 'freelance scientist', as he liked to call it. What this meant was that he provided his expert services to the highest bidder, just like people did in the west for all those years when he had been living off a salary no different from that of a coal miner in the Ural Mountains. That state of affairs had insulted and frustrated him to such an extent, that he had contacted a South Korean industrial chemicals company, that he knew had several large government contracts for compound chemicals for the South Korean weapons testing programme.

Through his limited number of contacts in the western scientific community, he had been able to set up a meeting with the company, and at that meeting, he had offered his services for anything they might like to do, no questions asked. Initially taken aback by his direct and somewhat brusque style, the timid human resource personnel that had received him, had eventually decided to go up the long chain of command with the Russian scientist's offer. Two months later Ivanov was contracted to work in the company's research department, where he had grown even more with every task presented to him.

At the time, he had not been aware that certain people were watching him, but one day he had been contacted by a man who had asked him to join him over dinner, to discuss a 'business opportunity', as he had put it. The offer had involved moving to the Middle East and working for an organisation about which he could not be told the details, except that it was working towards a 'curtailment of western influence in the region'.

Ivanov wasn't so stupid that he couldn't figure out exactly what that meant, but he had agreed to continue the talks nonetheless. Primarily because of the expectation of big money, but also because he felt that the West and the United States, in particular, had taken on an outsize role in the world. This had been especially evident in the way Russia's international influence had been suppressed after the fall of the Soviet Union. In addition, he also firmly believed that there were several just causes worth fighting for in the Middle East, including the expulsion of the Jews from what he thought was originally Arab land.

The man Ivanov had met for dinner, was clearly a professional who knew what he was talking about, and he had suggested several areas where Ivanov might be capable of contributing to various programmes that this organisation was sponsoring. They had eventually talked quite openly about chemical and biological weapons, and Ivanov had immediately sensed that, given the right impression, the man might be prepared to pay very handsomely for Ivanov's services. So, to make a point, Sergei Ivanov had retrieved from the most distant recesses of his memory, a story that he had once been told at the Science Academy in Moscow many years ago.

It was a story of a Russian army platoon that had taken part in overrunning Germany at the end of the Second World War. The platoon, which was part of one of the Russian armies penetrating the German defences, was making its way into southern Germany. In fact, this platoon was the southernmost of them all, much to their frustration, because they knew that they would be missing out on the fall of Berlin and the final defeat of the enemy.

The platoon leader had taken his men through a provincial town near Munich, and had been engaged in running battles from house to house and sometimes from room to room in the ruins of buildings in the town. They had reached what appeared to be a chemicals factory on the outskirts of town, where German soldiers were still fighting like madmen to keep the enemy at bay. In most parts of Germany, the soldiers were hoping to be captured by British or American troops instead of Russian troops, since they knew full well what the German army had done to the civilian population in Russia during its advance earlier in the war. The Russian army often showed no mercy, and simply killed off as many German soldiers as they could. At first, the platoon leader had thought that the German soldiers were scared to death of being captured alive by the Russian troops, but eventually, he had realised that the reason was something else entirely.

The German soldiers turned out to be an elite SS unit, and they fought the way they did because they defended an extremely important production facility. The plant was in the process of being dismantled, but apparently the rapid advance of the Russian mechanised armies had surprised the SS. Having shelled the remnants of the plant and killed most of the soldiers, the platoon leader had discovered a large office complex in addition to what appeared to be a research laboratory of some kind. There didn't appear to be anything left of the experiments themselves. However, there was still an extensive record of the activities of the scientists that had worked on the plant, and who had apparently fled as the Russian army approached. The platoon leader had then decided to secure the records and arranged for all the documents to be shipped off to Moscow for examination.

The war had barely ended before the Cold War was beginning, and at the time Stalin was in the process of developing nuclear as well as chemical and biological weapons of mass destruction, so the documents were received with enthusiasm by the scientists in

Moscow. They had contained detailed accounts of tests, as well as some spectacular if horrific accidents with a bacterium whose origin was unknown. The Russian scientists had read about the powerful effects and the pathogen, and had started evaluating its possible uses for weapons production, but there remained one small problem. There had been no trace of the bacterium itself, and there were no references to where any remnants of it might be found. So, after a short period of excitement, the scientists had gradually forgotten about the pathogen, and the documents detailing its nature and potency had ended up stored somewhere in the endless corridors of the academy's library.

The outcome of the meeting was positive for Ivanov to say the least. He had absolutely no idea of just how much money was actually sloshing around among certain people in this world. He had deliberately set the price for his cooperation at what to him seemed an outrageously high level, far in excess of his current salary at the time. But without hesitation the mysterious organisation had agreed to his demands, making him wonder how much more he could have asked for, and from that day on he had worked for the New Dawn, making millions of dollars in the process. He now had a house in Monaco and New York as well as his native city of Moscow.

He could never get tired of taking a ride around the former Soviet capital in one of his expensive cars, looking at the places he grew up, and looking at some of the people and neighbourhoods he remembered from back then. They were still there, looking exactly the way they did when he was young, but now he was sitting in his big car with the most expensive music system, a state-of-the-art security system and automatically regulated heating in all the seats.

Upon hearing that his new employer was endeavouring to find and recover possible remnants of the Nazi pathogen, Ivanov had thought them completely insane, but he had of course offered his assistance in any way possible. He had been tasked with retrieving copies of the original documents that were stored in the dusty file cabinets of the Academy of Science in Moscow. That had presented no serious problem, since the Academy, as was the case with most institutions in Russia, only functioned after an appropriate amount of lubrication in the form of hard currency. Within a few days of making contact with former colleagues at the Academy, he had been able to hand over to his employer, copies of every document that was recovered from the Nazi plant in southern Germany all those years ago.

Now, the 'nouveau riche' Russian was on his way out into the Syrian Desert in a corporate helicopter that was only a small step down from the executive jets that the heads of the world's largest corporation used. He had been instrumental in deciding that as a rule, personnel were to travel to the desert facility by car only, in order not to arouse any unnecessary attention. He was aware that his travelling by helicopter signalled that somehow, he was more important than anyone else, but this was partly the point. There were another couple of good reasons for him to travel this way. Firstly, he needed to attend to a rather urgent matter at the site. He had been informed of the accident the day before and had insisted that he came out there to see for himself. Khan had maintained that there was nothing to see now and that he would be wasting his time, but Ivanov insisted.

He knew that Khan didn't like visitors in general, but that was partly the result of the man being such a control freak. The Pakistani positively hated not being in charge, and to have some Russian scientist come out to inspect what Khan considered his personal laboratory, seemed like something of an affront to him. But knowing full well the way the system worked, he had yielded and arranged for Ivanov to be received by a couple of guards in a jeep, some two kilometres from the valley in which the facility was situated.

The second reason that he didn't see a problem in travelling by helicopter was the fact that it was several hours after sunset. There was a low dense cloud cover, which made the desert pitch black since there were no buildings or roads anywhere. This was not a problem for the pilot, as he was wearing state of the art night vision goggles, purchased through a middleman from the manufacturer in the United States. They offered the pilot a clear view of the desert in shades of green and enabled him to fly very close to the ground.

The helicopter raced over the undulating dunes, the pilot hugging the ground as he had been trained to do in the military. Ivanov wasn't entirely happy about this way of flying, because it meant that from time to time, he would become almost weightless as the helicopter cleared the top of a ridge and then dropped down into the valley beyond. Other times he would be pressed harder into his seat, and he had trouble understanding why that was necessary. He was as keen as anyone on maintaining the security and secrecy of the operation, but the fact was, that the Syrian air force and its radar equipment was so poor and had such a limited coverage, that the risk of being detected out here in the middle of nowhere was remote. But rules were rules.

The helicopter had taken off from a civilian airport just under an hour ago, flying through the normal air corridors surrounding the airport, after which it had dropped down low and changed course to head for the desert. At that point, the pilot had switched off all external lights, so the only light the helicopter emitted was a faint glow from the Multi-Function Displays or MFDs that the pilot used for showing a wide range of instrumentation and navigation data. The glow was not bright enough to be seen from the ground, and the helicopter appeared like a shadow moving quickly across the sky.

For anyone on the ground who happened to be in the helicopter's flight path, it would have been an eerie experience indeed. The helicopter was almost completely silent. It had been fitted with a special set of rotor blades that eliminated virtually all of the buffeting sound that could be heard from standard rotor blades. In addition, its engines were some of the quietest ever made, and their exhausts were covered by a muffler system that choked off most of the characteristic whining sound that jet engines usually produce.

It raced through the darkness across the rugged landscape at close to 250 kilometres per hour, effectively passing overhead only seconds after it could be heard, and then it would be gone before anyone but a trained ear could have determined what it was. As it came within two kilometres of the landing site the pilot signalled to Ivanov that he should get ready. Ivanov grabbed his briefcase from the floor of the helicopter and moved out to the side of its broad passenger seats in the back. Several hundred meters out, the pilot spotted the two guards and the jeep, which he had been told would be waiting for them. The men could neither see nor hear the helicopter until it was about one hundred meters away.

The pilot pulled back gently on the control stick which increased the pitch of the helicopter. At the same time, he pulled back on the throttle thereby reducing the lift of the rotor blades, causing the helicopter to move horizontally through the air while gradually bleeding off airspeed. When it was less than fifty metres from the two waiting guards who were covering their faces to avoid getting sand in their eyes, it came to a stop and hovered for a few seconds a couple of meters above the ground. Then the pilot switched on the landing lights, extended the retractable landing gear and set down on the rocky desert floor. The two guards, who had been standing in the dark, waiting for the helicopter to arrive for half an hour, were blinded by the bright lights. They were shone directly at them, causing them to turn away as the wheels touched the ground. The pilot didn't reduce the throttle further after the landing, as he would be taking off a few seconds later so as not to remain in the area for longer than necessary.

Ivanov jumped out of the side door and slammed it shut behind him. Then he ran crouched towards the jeep, and as soon as he had greeted the two guards he turned around and signalled for the helicopter to take off again. The pilot pushed the throttle forward, and as the helicopter quickly rose into the air, he pushed the right rudder with his foot causing the helicopter to rotate 180 degrees in just a couple of seconds. The pilot then increased the throttle and pitched down hard, causing the helicopter to point down steeply at the ground while accelerating rapidly away from the three men.

Within seconds they could neither see nor hear any trace of it, and Ivanov turned to the two guards. 'How far?' he asked.

'Fifteen minutes,' replied one of them, as he made for the jeep's driver's seat. 'We have to drive slowly with the light off,' he continued, sounding slightly annoyed.

'Yes. I know,' said Ivanov. 'I made that rule.'

That put a stop to any further conversations during the drive to the cave, which suited Ivanov just fine. He was here to see Kashim Khan and that professor he had hired. The programme had rapidly become a major operation after the launch earlier the same year. Nobody had seriously expected them to establish the laboratory and acquire qualified staff in such a short amount of time, but it had happened, and in no small measure due to Ivanov's efforts. He had been provided with a large purse, and that had enabled him to hire some of the best people in the business in record time.

Only once had he met the people who funded the whole operation, and he had soon learned that the organisation was only transparent in a downward direction. That meant that he had complete and absolute information about every single one of his subordinates, but he had virtually no information about how many and who were above him. It could be one layer or it could be five, or it could be an organisation without the hierarchical structure of western political and business entities. He had no idea, and he also didn't have a clue whether the organisation had other and perhaps similar projects scattered throughout the world, but in his own mind that seemed probable and even likely. These people were serious, and they had the funds to back it up.

By now he had earned more than enough money to retire comfortably if he wanted to, but he had signed a contract that guaranteed his commitment to the programme for at least two more years. And even though the contract had been a two-page text written on a blank piece of paper and signed in a hotel lobby in Geneva, he didn't doubt for an instant that his employers would become more than a little upset should he suddenly abandon his responsibilities, and run for the mansion in the hills. He was in it for the long haul, and that suited him just fine. Having been a neglected and overlooked resource in giant science programmes of the Soviet Union and then of the Russian Federation, he relished the opportunity to be the head of his own programme. He didn't much care about the purpose of it, but simply reasoned that if he hadn't taken the job, then someone else would have, so he might as well be the one to get rich.

★ ★ ★

At number 10 Downing Street, the Minister of Defence was arriving in a dark blue Jaguar to see the Prime Minister. He was driven swiftly through the gates at the back entrance, and try as they might, the journalists and photographers who were always on standby outside the Prime Minister's residence, couldn't see through the black-tinted bulletproof windows. As soon as the limousine had come to a stop away from the public, the Minister of Defence exited the car while still speaking on his phone. Under his arm was a stack of papers, and behind him followed his personal aide carrying even more documents. The minister was a busy man and hopeless at keeping appointments, so without his assistant, he would have been virtually disabled.

The door was opened by a police officer and they were rushed inside. After a few minutes, the Prime Minister was ready to see him. They had been friends since Cambridge, and had jointly held the government together on several occasions, by way of their personal influence on members of Parliament. The Prime Minister was a charismatic man, who always came across well in the mass media, and who had an uncanny ability to hold a baby in his arms whenever a photographer was nearby.

On the face of it, everything looked perfect for the Prime Minister. He had a perfect marriage with a beautiful and agreeable wife ten years his junior, and an impeccable political reputation and career. He also had a team of spin doctors, who were some of the best in the world at what they did. They had managed to present a very likeable image of the Prime Minister to the country, prior to his campaign for office. In fact, they had been so proficient at managing the media, that they had succeeded in turning a brilliant but at times unfocused and hot-tempered man into a political icon everyone seemed to trust. And for all the idealism suggesting that politics was about clear positions based on a coherent ideology, when push came to shove, it was just as much about simply being pragmatic. Excessive adherence to ideology often complicated the process of compromise that is needed in a parliamentary democracy. The Prime Minister had found a seemingly perfect balance between the two, depending on whether there was an election to be dealt with, or a government to be managed.

However, the Prime Minister could not have done it without his intellectual sounding board, the Minister of Defence. The two of them had effectively taken over power within the party, and then gone on to win the election. It was the combination of the Prime Minister's ability to appeal directly to the voters, and the Minister of Defence's brilliant strategic mind that had secured the victory.

This meant that, although more powerful than some people liked, the government was highly focused and firm in its political agenda, and even its staunchest opponents had to admit that it had achieved significant results in several areas that were of particular concern to the public. The opinion polls were ample proof of that, and The Duet as they were popularly known, was now stronger than ever.

The economy was growing steadily in tandem with the international economic environment, unemployment numbers were low and stable, Britain was proving itself a worthy and strong partner to the United States in foreign policy, the problems in Northern Ireland were a thing of the past, and the Prime Minister's wife was expecting her second child. Everything was going swimmingly.

That was why the Minister of Defence was reluctant to bother the Prime Minister with what he had initially thought was a trivial issue. He didn't exactly like looking paranoid, but on the other hand, it was his job to ensure that no threat to Britain was ever allowed to develop beyond being a mere threat. To that aim, he had at his disposal one of the best and most experienced foreign intelligence agencies in the world, as well as some of the best elite troops in service anywhere, and it was the former which had brought this issue to his attention.

A few days earlier they had intercepted a radio transmission that had originated from a point approximately in the middle of the Mediterranean Ocean, and then bounced off a satellite and been relayed to somewhere in the Syrian Desert. The exact location was impossible to determine since the so-called footprint of the satellite's signal comprised a very wide area. But they had been able to decrypt it, since it originated from a standard Iridium satellite telephone, whose encryption system both the British and American governments had a backdoor to. That effectively meant that there were no conversations carried out over satellite telephones that the intelligence agencies could not track, decrypt and listen in on.

At least that was the idea, but on this particular occasion, the signal had only been intercepted by the Americans, since it was their listening station next to their airbase on the Island of Terceira, that had identified it.

They had subsequently found that similar communications had been picked up from listening stations in the Middle-Eastern. The advanced voice recognition software at CIA headquarters in Langley, Virginia, had then been set to work analysing the data. Their computers were among the most powerful in the world, and they could process vast amounts of both digital and analogue data, but they could still only process a fraction of all the communications that were transmitted through the fibre optic networks and copper phone lines around the world. Therefore, the programmers at Langley had developed a unique search algorithm which they had dubbed The Puppy, since it worked on the same principle as the nose on a dog out for a stroll, having its nose subjected to millions of sensory inputs. If something passing by turned out to be of interest, it would stroll closer for another sniff, and if it proved more interesting, the dog would stroll even closer and so on and so forth, until the dog would be standing next to whatever was emitting the smell.

That principle was applied in the software, in that it would simultaneously take small fractions of perhaps a few seconds of audio, from millions of ongoing telephone calls, and then analyse those more or less instantaneously. Every call would then be assigned a score by the algorithm, in accordance with the degree to which that particular call matched with any of the thousands of stored voice profiles. The higher the score, the greater the likelihood of the programme taking another look a few seconds later, when it would analyse another bit of sound which would then be assigned a score. The scores would then be successively compounded, so that if the call was of great interest, the algorithm would dig more and more aggressively into that conversation, and possibly eventually end up recording the whole thing for a human analyst to listen to in its entirety. All of this happened in real time.

In this instance, the CIA's algorithm had indicated the possibility that several of the calls had been made by a well-known terrorist, who had previously been arrested in the United States on drug smuggling charges, as well as on one charge of attempting to smuggle scientific equipment out of the United States. The man had recently been released after serving three and a half years in federal prison in Florida. His voice match had prompted the algorithm to have one of the human analysts listen to all the bits and pieces of the transmissions that had been intercepted and recorded. The analyst and the algorithm had together concluded that in all likelihood the voice was that of Mohammed Yusef. He wasn't currently wanted for anything specific, and even though the fractions of his cryptic conversations only provided very few clues to what was going on, the analyst concluded that the call warranted further investigation.

The initial information and results had been passed on to MI5 in London, where a junior officer had just finished a report on the threat of chemical terrorist attacks on the United Kingdom. In his report he had noted several observed attempts to obtain equipment and trained scientists for such programmes, and that there had been two attempts at freeing jailed scientists from prisons in third world countries. One of these had succeeded, and two others had ended in significant bloodshed. The freed scientist had been an expert in biological and not chemical weapons, but the threat remained the same in principle. The officer received the report from the CIA, and began searching the records for previous attempts at chemical or biological terrorist attacks in Britain as well as in other places.

He had then come across a file, which contained some original documents from the Second World War, as well as a report produced immediately after the war ended. And as if that wasn't unusual enough, some of the documents that the report referred to were classified, and restricted to people much more senior than him.

He had gone to his section chief, whose clearance allowed for him to read those particular documents. The section chief, who sat on a government anti-terrorist advisory committee with Colonel Strickland, was by now familiar with the investigation currently undertaken by Andrew Sterling. The junior officer made his case, and after having presented the possible links between the American communications intercept, the man who had been detained in the United States and the recent attempts at freeing jailed scientists, the section chief asked the junior officer to pause his investigation for now. But he promised that he would return to him with an answer as soon as possible.

Now just days later, the Minister of Defence had held a meeting with the section chief of MI5 and with Colonel Strickland of the SAS, and it had turned out that they had all learned a great deal from each other. The various pieces of information that they each possessed were worrying by themselves, but the sum of them was certainly enough to bother the Prime Minister with.

Both the MI5 section chief and Colonel Strickland were instructed to keep quiet about the Prime Minister's involvement until further notice. That also meant that Strickland couldn't inform Sterling about anything other than the fact that the CIA had traced a possible terrorist, and that they would be working with MI5 to investigate further.

SIXTEEN

Sitting in his comfortable first-class seat, it occurred to Andrew that he had spent a lot of time in aircrafts lately. Although the check-in and security procedures could be a bit stressful at times, it was a very comfortable way to travel once one got under way. Having just reached its cruising altitude of ten kilometres, the Airbus 300 was crossing the Atlantic Ocean at over 900 kilometres an hour, and would be landing in Mexico City just after half-past six in the afternoon local time. Fiona was reading a magazine, while Andrew was relaxing with a glass of orange juice and some classical music that flowed out of the head-set he was wearing. The headset was connected by a wire to the right armrest on his chair, and he reached down for the small switch on the wire, and flipped it to ON. The switch engaged an anti-noise system that mixed the audio signal from the music with artificial cabin noise sound waves that had been inverted, so as to cancel out the naturally occurring cabin noise from within the aircraft. The result was almost complete silence, and since the artificial inverted noise signals were only targeted at cabin noise, it didn't affect his ability to hear what people were saying to him.

'Funny how my fear of flying has almost disappeared now,' said Fiona.

'You've suffered from that?'

'No, not always. It took me at least a year from the attacks on the World Trade Centre and the Pentagon in 2001 until I was able to sit in a plane again.'

'Really? So, you didn't go on holiday for a while, I guess'

'Oh, I did go on holiday, but that was in the Scottish Mountains.'

'You are aware that the risk of getting killed in an aircraft is minuscule compared to risk of dying in a car crash, right?'

'Yes. I know that. But the idea of falling out of the sky for several minutes before you hit the ground, is a lot more terrifying than the notion of being in a car accident.'

'Most aircraft accidents actually happen on the runway, during take-off or landing. It is extremely rare for an aeroplane to just drop out of the sky.'

'Yes, maybe. It's irrational I guess, but that how I've felt for a long time. I'm just about getting used to it again now.'

'Do you remember where you were that day in September 2001, when those two planes slammed into the World Trade Centre in New York?'

'Yes. That is something I don't think I'll ever forget. I was at work. I heard the murmurs among my colleagues slowly rising from quiet chatting to loud eruptions. When I went to the meeting room to see what was going on, my colleagues were all watching the TV. The first of the two towers had just collapsed, and people were more or less in shock. I remember not being able to grasp what had happened, and it took me several seconds to realise that a tower had collapsed, even though the giant clouds of dust and smoke told their story very clearly. I just couldn't process it.'

'I know. It was genuinely shocking to watch.'

'Where were you?' asked Fiona.

'I was actually sitting at home speaking on the phone, with a broker of mine.'

'With a what?'

'A stock broker. I like to manage my own assets, so I regularly speak with brokers about what stocks to hold and what stocks to stay away from. So, anyway. We were speaking on the phone and suddenly she broke me off and told me that a plane had just slammed into the World Trade Centre in New York. I immediately assumed that it was a small civilian aircraft, but then I switched on the TV, and I could see the massive gaping hole in the side of the building. I remember realising that the hole was at least ten stories high, so it had to have been a commercial aircraft. But we still thought that it was an accident. As we spoke, the second plane hit the other tower, and then we broke off our conversation. I turned up the volume on my TV, and a few minutes later the anchor said that the Pentagon was on fire, and that was when I started to get really worried. It was almost a claustrophobic sensation that was creeping in on me, but it didn't take me more than a few minutes to put two and two together and figure out that it had probably been Osama Bin Laden's work.'

'You thought of that by then already?'

'Yes. I was convinced of that pretty quickly. I just couldn't see who else it would be. If it had been another nation attacking the United States in that way, I am convinced that the president would have ordered a measured nuclear strike.'

'Really? Do you really think that would have happened?'

'I'm pretty sure of it. Such an attack was equivalent to a declaration of war on the United States, and given the savagery of the attack on those civilians, I'm convinced that the president would have thought it justifiable to use any means necessary, including nuclear weapons to punish whatever country was behind it.'

'I guess in that sense you must actually think that it was fortunate that you were right about Osama Bin Laden?'

'Yes. In a way, I guess you could say I was.'

'Do you know what I thought was the most frightening part of that whole thing?' asked Fiona.

'What?'

'It was, that even several weeks after the collapse of the World Trade Centre, nobody asked why it had happened. Everybody was focused on the effects of the attack, and not on the cause of it.'

'Isn't that natural? I mean, several thousand people had lost their lives. Wasn't that the main issue?'

'Of course it was, but it wasn't a natural disaster. It had clearly been carried out intentionally by other people, and I remember being so impatient to find out what the hell they might have been thinking. And when somebody finally did start to ask those questions, there seemed to be only one universally accepted answer, and that was that they were simply evil. They are evil and we are good, end of story. It was all completely black and white, without any nuance at all. And what was even worse, was that the public immediately accepted that as being a sufficient explanation. And it was repeated so many times that in the end, nobody questioned its validity. Not until the bombing of the Taliban in Afghanistan had begun, did a few journalists and commentators begin to dig into the real underlying reasons for the attacks. Insane and horrible as they were, it is a fact that they did happen, and that the people who carried them out were absolutely convinced that they were serving a just cause. Regardless of whether you believe that their cause is just, and even regardless of whether you believe that any cause can justify such an act, one has to accept that this is what happened.'

'Well, you are right about that. Writing it off as the work of a group of madmen isn't going to make the problem go away, even if they were mad.'

'Correct,' continued Fiona. 'And it certainly isn't going to stop similar acts of terrorism from occurring in the future. It also doesn't change the fact that these people had somehow come to be convinced that it was a just cause. Some people might dismiss their logic as being crazy, but in the end, who has the right to say what is sane and what is insane? The logic of achieving political and religious goals through acts of violence is as old as the human race, and not limited to any place or time, if I may remind you. The terrorists weren't crazy, but they certainly functioned on an entirely different premise and set of values from that of most people in the West. I'm pretty sure that nobody in their right mind would argue that these people were born that way. And valid cause or not, something made them into what they were. That is a fact.'

'Well, their deaths are certainly ample proof of their existence,' interjected Andrew.

'The point is: It has always been true that it serves a nation to have a well-defined enemy, and so the Pentagon and the CIA will at all times provide one for the American people to focus on. First, it was the USSR, then it was Vietnam, then Iraq and then Afghanistan, not to mention the likes of Castro or even Manuel Noriega. We demonise the current enemy just as they demonise us, so we can obtain the public's support for bombing the crap out of their tents in the desert. But then we simply forget about them. And that is probably the worst of all, and it is in large part exactly what they react against. By making enemies in the minds of our people, we quite literally create real flesh and blood enemies somewhere.'

'But you have to agree that something needed to be done, right?'

'Oh, absolutely. But going in and rooting out Al Qaeda and the Taliban network could never be enough. If something more wasn't done, I think that it would be inevitable that such actions, justified as they might have been, could be creating even more problems than they solved.'

'So, what you are saying is that the West is acting arrogantly towards third world countries?'

'To some extent they are. The basic problem is that the rest of the world simply doesn't matter to America. Only to the extent that it is forced upon them, as it was, in no small measure in September of 2001. And the depressingly obvious result was that the terrorists got what they wanted. They got the attention, and they got a renewed focus on the many conflicts in the Middle East. Not just on the Israeli-Palestinian conflict, but also the corrupt and undemocratic governments in countries like Saudi Arabia and Kuwait, which by the way the Western world supports to the tune of billions of dollars in aid each year, much of which is in the form of military hardware.'

'But are you saying that the United States got what it deserved?'

'No. Of course, it's not as simple as that, but I think that it is fair to say that it is not a great surprise that it eventually happened. There is clear cause and effect here. Frustration had been building up for years and years, but it only came to be expressed because one of the more militant sympathisers happened to be a billionaire.'

'I'm not sure that I agree with everything you've just said,' said Andrew. 'But I will grant you that the focus of the West tends to be somewhat arrogant and self-centred. I guess that could frustrate and anger people who live in poor countries, especially if their governments are corrupt but still propped up by the West.'

'Thank you,' smiled Fiona. 'It's not that often that someone actually agrees with me on this.'

'But you have to understand that I'm coming at this from a slightly different angle, having served in Afghanistan.'

'Of course I do,' she said. 'Like I always say. There are just about as many universes as there are people. It's all entirely subjective, and every person has his or her own unique set of values and yardsticks, whether we realise it or not.'

'True,' nodded Andrew. 'When you think about it, it's actually really amazing that we haven't killed each other off yet.'

'What? Mankind?' asked Fiona.

'Yes. Think about it. Thousands of years ago the worst thing a person could do to someone else was to find a big stick, hit the other guy over the head and kill him. But then that would be that. Along came bows and arrows, which enabled one person to kill several people. Then came rifles and guns and grenades, and by then, one person could kill hundreds of people, and as those weapons were developed, their killing power increased into the thousands. Now we have nuclear, chemical and biological weapons, and in principle, it is possible for just one person to eliminate hundreds of thousands, maybe even millions of people.'

'You think that can happen?'

'I know for a fact that it can happen, and I'm sad to say that I'm convinced that it will happen within our lifetime. Maybe not tomorrow or next year or for the next five years. But I'd be surprised if it didn't happen within fifty years.'

'Really? You are that pessimistic?'

'I don't think that I am being pessimistic. I am just extrapolating what has happened in the past. I really do believe that it is realistic to expect such a thing to happen. The destructive power of the individual has, pardon the expression, exploded over the past fifty years and I see no reason why that should stop. If anything, it will continue, and that can only mean that someday somewhere, we will have an unfathomable disaster on our hands.'

Fiona looked uneasy and shifted in her seat. 'You really know how to cheer people up don't you.'

'Sorry,' said Andrew and smiled. 'It's just that I've thought about this a lot.'

'Yes. I know. Is that why you are in the line of business that you are in?'

'No. Not exactly. That was more or less by chance, I guess. But once you've thought this through, it's never a problem to find the motivation to keep going.'

'I understand,' said Fiona and nodded. 'It certainly does put into perspective the stuff I read in that book. If something like that was to get out in a major city, the human race would be in serious trouble, don't you think?'

'If it's as powerful as it appears to be, then you might be right,' said Andrew and brought his seat back up, since the stewardess was approaching with a trolley carrying more drinks and snacks.

'You're not going to get drunk now, are you?' smiled Fiona accusingly.

'No. Don't worry,' grinned Andrew. 'I'm still on duty, so I think I'll stick to orange juice and then maybe a glass of wine for dinner later on.'

'Good. Remember what we discussed,' she smiled.

'Right,' he said and raised his hands in surrender. 'You're the boss on this trip.'

★ ★ ★

The jeep carrying Ivanov and the two guards rolled into the tunnel and appeared thirty seconds later under the hundreds of lights affixed to the ceiling of the giant dome. As the vehicle came to a halt, one of the guards jumped out and opened the door for Ivanov, who then stepped onto the concrete covered floor. He was greeted and led to a meeting room by Mohammed Yusef who was visibly nervous. Ivanov's visit had only been announced by Arrowhead a few hours earlier, but they all knew what it was about.

Arrowhead, the founding organisation in control of this and many other programmes, was responsible for ensuring that the enormous amounts of money that had been laid out, didn't go to waste. It was in many respects considered an investment like any other, with a certain amount of fixed and variable costs, and a certain level of expected return, except that the return was in this case difficult to quantify. After all, how does one quantify justice?

Kashim Khan and Ahmed Kamal Rashid were already sitting at the table in the meeting room when Ivanov entered. They rose and came over to greet him, and then the four men sat down with Ivanov presiding over the meeting from one end of the table.

'Gentlemen,' he calmly. 'Arrowhead has been informed of the accident that occurred here a few days ago, and quite frankly we have been unsure of where the problem lies.'

Khan sat immovable, but Rashid was clearly uncomfortable.

'So,' continued Ivanov. 'We would like for you to explain to us exactly what happened and why you think it will never happen again. Is that possible?' he said and looked straight at Khan.

'Certainly,' said Khan, who was apparently not at all intimidated by the Russian. 'The accident was caused by a worker who had not been trained correctly. In other words, human error was to blame.'

Yusef knew what that meant. Since he had been responsible for staffing and training in the facility, he was ultimately responsible for what had happened. At least according to what Khan was saying.

'But wasn't one of the deceased handpicked by you?' asked Ivanov and looked at Rashid who had begun to sweat.

'Well,' he said nervously. 'Yes. But he was a highly skilled employee, and he had never made an error anywhere in his work. This didn't have anything to do with a lack of training or sloppiness. As far as I could determine, it was caused by a fault in the equipment used.'

Khan turned his head slowly to look at Rashid, who didn't dare to return his gaze. Khan was responsible for the construction of the laboratory and all of the equipment in it, so if equipment failure was deemed to be the cause of the incident, then ultimately he could be held responsible.

The meeting was going exactly as Ivanov had anticipated. The truth was that he was annoyed by what had happened, but he also knew as well as any other scientist that accidents do happen, and that they tend to happen at the worst possible time. But now that it had happened, he was pleased that it had happened this early in the process, that it had been contained, and that the event had caused the plant to change its safety procedures. The aim of the meeting was not to determine which one of the three men should be dragged out into the desert and shot. This was an amusing although cynical experiment, designed to see how the group would function under pressure.

Because of the clandestine nature of the entire operation, it hadn't exactly been possible to hire a staffing agency to assemble the team, so they had needed to do it blind, hoping that the group would be able to function. One way to ensure this had been the extraordinarily large sums of money that had been offered to the leading figures in the venture, but there had been no way to predict how the group would react to direct pressure and danger.

Ivanov did his best to sound and look like he might be the danger, and it began to have its effect, because now even Khan was beginning to seem nervous. His hands were shaking ever so slightly and his voice trembled almost imperceptibly.

'Two people died, is that correct?' asked Ivanov.

'Yes,' said Khan, seemingly unaffected by the memory of their deaths. 'One scientist and one worker.'

'Are they replaceable?'

Khan looked to Rashid for an answer.

'Well,' said Rashid and shifted nervously. 'The worker is not a significant loss, but the scientist was one of my best and most dedicated students. I don't think that we can replace him very easily.'

'But it is not going to affect our time schedule, is it?' asked Ivanov suspiciously and looked at Khan.

'No,' responded the Pakistani resolutely. 'We can proceed without any major delay.'

'But wasn't the entire stock of the pathogen destroyed in the storage depot?' asked Ivanov.

'Well, yes. But what has taken the most time so far was to cultivate and develop new strains. The production process itself is not too difficult, and since we can now produce at scale, it should not take more than a week to produce the amount that was lost.'

'And you are sure of this?' asked Ivanov.

'Absolutely,' lied Khan. He was getting tired of the arrogant Russian and wanted the meeting to be over so that he could get back to work.

'Ok,' said Ivanov, and smiled at the other men. 'I have complete confidence in you all, and I am sure that this will not end up presenting a major problem for us. Just as long as you understand, that a similar event would be most undesirable for all of us.'

The three men knew exactly what that meant, and so they nodded enthusiastically, except for Khan who merely looked coldly at Ivanov, trying to gauge what he was really thinking.

As far as Ivanov was concerned, the group hadn't exactly passed the test with honours, but at least the meeting hadn't descended into infighting either. In spite of their egos and different cultural backgrounds, they seemed to be able to work together even under stress, so he felt confident that the programme would eventually be completed. It might take a little bit longer than initially planned, but they would get it done. He was sure of that now. Despite the accident and the setback, he felt content as he was driven off to the improvised landing site where the helicopter would come and pick him up again. He had no desire to stay the night in the cave. Firstly, he knew that he wasn't exactly welcome, and secondly, he didn't think that the scientists would get anything done if they felt that he was looking over their shoulder all the time.

Just over four hours after he had jumped out of the helicopter, the characteristic sound of the rotor blades could again be heard over the landing site. He would be back in his hotel a few hours after that, and then he would be able to bring good news to his own bosses.

★ ★ ★

'Yes, what?' said Pete Ryan as he grabbed the telephone, trying to sound as annoyed as he could. He had been much too busy for his own liking the whole morning, and the last thing he needed right now was for someone to call him up and ask him to look into something. Ringing telephones were almost never a good sign, so he wasn't in the best of moods.

'This is General Ingram,' said a voice. 'Do you have a moment, Pete?'

Ryan leaned back in his chair and forced himself to calm down a little. 'Yes, General. Sorry about my outburst. Right now?'

'Yeah. My office.'

'Sure thing. I'll be right there.'

Ryan hung up and rose from his chair to walk the distance to General Ingram's office. Being called in by the boss was never a favourite event to have happen to the employees at this newly established CIA counter-terrorist unit. General Ingram was known to be harsh with people if they weren't pulling their weight. But Ryan felt relaxed since he and General John Ingram had known each other for a number of years, and each respected the other. They were both men with strong characters, but Ryan would never even think about disrespecting the chain of command.

Pete Ryan was of Irish descent, with his great grandfather having emigrated to the United States from Dublin in Ireland to seek his fortune in the new land beyond the Atlantic Ocean. Having come from next to nothing back in Ireland, the Ryans had established themselves firmly in the new world as a large influential clan. Many of them were working in important positions within both politics and business, primarily in Boston and New York.

With his father being the mayor of Boston, Pete had grown up with politics as a part of everyday life, and for many years he had given serious thought to entering into local politics himself. But during his time in college, he had developed an interest in international geopolitics and had written his thesis on the conflicts in the Middle East. He had eventually accepted an offer from a well-renowned think tank based in New York, from where he had subsequently been headhunted for a position at the CIA. There, he had become an analyst with the anti-terrorist division, and two months ago he had been appointed operational head of a new department with the sole purpose of focusing on nuclear, chemical and biological terrorist threats from the Middle East, state-sponsored as well as privately funded.

Ryan reached Ingram's office and knocked on the open door.

'Pete! Come on in. How are you doing?'

'Pretty good. A bit busy,' he said trying not to sound too frustrated.

'I know,' said Ingram. 'Close the door and sit down. I want to talk to you about the messages that were intercepted by our people at the Terceira airbase.'

'Right,' nodded Pete, and began to retrieve that information from the memory banks inside his head.

'The British MI6 have come back to us on that issue. It seems they have an ongoing investigation into this matter, but they haven't been able to identify any persons involved.'

'So, there's no further progress for now?'

'Not exactly, but apparently they have found a pile of information dating back decades, on something pretty nasty that might be related to all of this.'

'What do you mean?' asked Ryan. He knew that General Ingram wouldn't call him into his office and ask him to close the door if it wasn't important.

'The CIA has been contacted by the MI6 directly on behalf of the British Minister of Defence,' began Ingram and went on to inform Ryan that he now had orders to leave whatever he was working on, and focus all of his attention on something entirely different.

★ ★ ★

Andrew looked at his wristwatch. It would be another three hours until they landed outside Mexico City, so it had to be around seven in the morning in London. Andrew pulled out the wired-in telephone from his armrest and dialled Colonel Strickland's number. He knew that the colonel always came in early. The signal was bounced off a satellite and a split second later the telephone in Strickland's office rang.

'Strickland here,' said the colonel.

'Sir. This is Sterling.'

'Andy. How are you?'

'I'm fine, Sir. I'm on my way to Mexico along with Miss Fiona Keane.'

'Good. You'll keep me in the loop on your progress, won't you?'

'Will do, Sir.'

'What's your first objective?'

'We'll spend the night in Mexico City and then fly on to Mérida on the Yucatan Peninsula. Fiona is convinced that one of the pieces of the medallion is still there. I think it's a long shot, but it is all we have right now.'

'Got your hands full, I would imagine?' chuckled the colonel.

'Well. She definitely knows her stuff, that's for sure,' said Andrew and turned to look at Fiona who stopped reading as her name was mentioned. 'But I've asked her to take over, so I don't get in the way,' he smiled disarmingly.

'Andy. On an entirely different issue, I'm afraid we've had a security breach here at Sheldrake Place.'

'What?' exclaimed Andrew. 'How?'

'Well not in a physical sense. We haven't had an intruder as such, but last night there was an attempt to hack into our central computer system.'

'So, what happened?'

'Not much apparently. That is to say, the intruder managed to gain access and establish a presence in our systems, but since it was detected right away, the intruder was led through to a virtual honey-pot network.'

'A what?'

'Yes, I know it sounds strange, and I admit that I don't fully understand it myself, but I've been told that parallel to the actual computer network that is in use every day, our cyber security department has simulated a second dummy network. This network contains no useful information at all, but it looks very real when looking at it from the outside. Any intruder can be led safely into this simulated network, where his behaviour within it can then be monitored. This enabled our security teams to determine what he was looking for, simply by watching his behaviour within the network.'

'What was he after?'

'Well, that was the unpleasant surprise. The intruder went straight for personnel files, or rather the false personnel files which of course contains no classified information, and pulled out your file, Andy.'

'Mine?' exclaimed Andrew. 'Christ Almighty. Well, do you have any idea who it was?'

'No, unfortunately, the system was unable to track the intruder outside this building, but right now we are working on trying to establish where the hacking attempt originated from. They tell me that it's unlikely that they will find anything since it apparently isn't that difficult to mask this sort of activity and make it impossible for the target to identify the attacker. My best people here tell me it is virtually impossible to find someone who doesn't want to be found.'

'So, what do we do about it?'

'Well, we've spoken to the cyber security teams at MI5, who have extensive experience with these types of intrusions, and they are going to come over later today for a meeting. They may be able to turn something up.'

'But the intruder didn't actually get his hands on anything, is that correct?'

'Yes. He got hold of a bunch of files that seem to contain information about you, but in reality, they contain a mixture of false and misleading information, so it'll probably confuse rather than inform whoever is reading it.'

'But it is still a fact that someone was trying to poke his nose into my personal files,' said Andrew angrily. 'Who the hell could it be?'

'As I've said, we don't know yet, but isn't it bound to be some of the people you are investigating? Let's say that you've got them scared, after your little visit to Vienna.'

'Possibly, but they are taking a huge risk in doing this. So far, they haven't done anything illegal as far as we can tell, but now they have attempted to break into a classified computer system owned by the British government. They could be put in jail for years.'

'I know, but I guess that tells us that we must be on to something. They must really be hiding something fairly significant for them to be so nervous of us.'

'Yes, I suppose you are right. That means we are heading in the right direction, I guess.'

'Exactly. And this leads me to the second thing I wanted to speak to you about. An agent of the MI5 was sent to monitor Phillip Eckleston when he went to Vienna less than two days ago. And it seems that the good Doctor met up with at least three other people at the headquarters of the Order of the Teutonic Knights.'

'Well, that's a surprise,' said Andrew feigning shock. 'Yes. I know. But the agent managed to get some really excellent snapshots of the other three, and we've identified all of them.'

'Really? That was quick.'

'Yes. We had a little help from the intelligence agencies of other European countries.'

'So, who were they?'

'Well, the first was a German Stuka-ace during the Second World War, the second is the head of the French Rotary Society, and the third, hold on to your hat, is a very prominent member of the Austrian Parliament. He has been known to express some pretty harsh views on immigration, but in reality, he has no real influence in the parliament. We don't know too much about the two others, because they are not very public figures. The Frenchman is mostly a figurehead for French Rotary, and it seems that he is pretty far removed from any of its real activities.'

'What a motley crew,' said Andrew. 'What do you suppose they have in common?'

'Well, isn't it obvious? They are obviously members of the order, and probably quite senior ones too. The agent suspects that the head of the order, Erich Strauss, whom you know quite well, was there also, so it would appear that something rather important needed to be discussed.'

'Right. Looks as if I've stepped in a hornet's nest.'

'Indeed. You seem to have rattled them quite badly with that little number you did on them.'

'But if they were the ones who tried to retrieve information about me from the computer servers at Sheldrake Place, how the bloody hell did they know my real name or where I work?'

'Hard to say. As I said, we are still working on it, so perhaps we'll have something when you get back.'

'Alright. I hope so. I really don't appreciate people knowing things about me that I haven't told them myself.'

'I understand. We'll do what we can. I should also let you know that we've talked to the Americans.'

'Really? Do they know anything about this?'

'No, not as such. But they contacted us because they had intercepted some communications that they believe might stem from a Middle Eastern terrorist organisation, or at least from people connected to one such organisation. They say some of it happened on the Azores islands just a few days before you arrived out there. It might lead to something, but in any event, I'll keep you informed, Ok?'

'Alright. Let's speak again in a couple of days. I'll call Cathy and leave her the number for the hotels we'll be staying at.'

'Excellent. Good luck, Andy. Speak to you soon.'

'Thanks. Goodbye.'

Andrew put the phone back into place inside the armrest and then told Fiona of the attempted intrusion into the SAS computer system, which instantly made her worry about her own computer at work. Not that she ever stored anything of any importance there, but thinking about someone else going through her messages made her feel very uncomfortable.

★ ★ ★

'Anything yet?' asked Eckleston.

'No,' said the voice on the other end of the line. 'I planted the bugs a couple of days ago, but she has hardly been home. She spent several days at Sheldrake Place, so they must have brought the books there.'

'Is there any way we can get to them while they are there?'

'No. Absolutely not. They have a security system that is completely impossible to penetrate, and if we were to try, we'd probably end up dead. It's just not possible.'

'Alright. Any luck with the computer system?'

'Yes, I think so. We managed to pull out some files on this Andrew Sterling character, and it is true that he works in that building, but he seemed to be listed as an accountant.'

'That's just a smokescreen,' said Eckleston dismissively. 'I know who he is and what he is, and he's certainly not an accountant. You've been fooled.'

The man didn't say anything for a few seconds but then ventured to defend himself. 'I think anyone would have been fooled. If those weren't the right files, then the whole system must be fake. It was as comprehensive as anything I've seen, so either the content of the files is correct, or the whole system is a sham.'

'Well, then the system is a sham,' said Eckleston raising his voice in annoyance. 'Sterling is a trained killer and a member of an elite SAS unit. He's a decorated war hero, for Christ's sake.'

Eckleston took a deep breath and calmed himself. 'Alright,' he said. 'Keep trying with their computer systems. We might find some interesting information yet. Goodbye.'

'Yes, Sir. Goodbye,' said the voice.

Eckleston had just been informed that Kurt Moltke, A.K.A Kurt Hess was on his way to Mexico to trail the two explorers. He had even been able to book a seat on the same plane, so it ought to be possible to stay on them. Eckleston couldn't help but feel a small amount of admiration for young Fiona Keane's tenacity, and he did have a small hope that she might be able to lead him and the Thule Society to what they were searching for.

He had himself gone to several of the archaeological sites on the Yucatan Peninsula that Thomas Beck had visited many years before, but he had always returned empty-handed, and in doubt as to whether he had been searching in the right place. Eventually, he had given up and decided to turn his attention to other locations, such as the Far East, but so far without much luck. This time might be different, but he had to put his trust in Hess to monitor their every move. Hess had been successful on the Azores, so why not in Mexico as well.

SEVENTEEN

Coming in to land at Mexico City International Airport wasn't much different from any other landing anywhere else in the world. The Airbus A300 banked to the left and began its final approach to the runway in a northerly direction. The sun, which was now low on the horizon and getting ready to dive below it, shone its orange light in through the tiny windows of the aeroplane and made it difficult for Fiona to see out. She held up her hand to block the sun, and looked down on the city racing past below her. She could feel as well as see the aeroplane coming closer and closer to the ground, as the pilot alternately increased and decreased the throttle of the engines, to get the landing speed just right.

Situated in the southern highlands at approximately 2,200 meters above sea level, Mexico City is believed to have been founded in 1325. Long before Christopher Columbus set off towards America, Mexico Valley was already an important trading centre. Different peoples have occupied the central area of the Mexican Plateau for at least 20,000 years, and the people that originally came there settled on the shores of its fertile lakes. One of those peoples were called the Mexicas, and when they arrived in the area, they built an island roughly one square mile in size, in one of these lakes. It is said that their leader had had a vision of an eagle holding a snake in its beak, and that he had promised his god that he would build a city for him where he saw such an eagle. That happened to be right on the lake. They built canals, some of which still exist today, in order to make trading easier. By the beginning of the 16th century, the city had turned into the capital of a huge military empire stretching from present-day Texas to Honduras. The city now stretches for as long as the eye can see and its population has long ago passed twenty million people.

On its final approach, the Airbus flew over what appeared to be slum. Most of the roofs on the small houses were made of big corrugated metal sheets, and the conditions down there looked dirty and poor from where she sat. But it stretched for several kilometres, until it suddenly changed into green well-kept grass, with the odd cement road here and there. They had passed over the airport perimeter, and the ground was now approaching fast. Twenty meters from the ground the runway suddenly appeared below her, and the aeroplane levelled off to touch down. The main landing gear touched the tarmac and a few seconds later the nose gear made contact with the runway as well. Immediately thereafter the pilot engaged the reverse thrusters and the Airbus braked rapidly, forcing the passengers to hold on to their seats. This runway was one of the shortest at the airport, so the pilot had to brake hard to avoid running through the fence at the other end.

Customs and luggage retrieval went smoothly, and half an hour later Andrew and Fiona were standing outside the airport waiting for a taxi. That didn't take long, since the taxi drivers could spot a foreigner a mile away, and had a tendency to dismantle the meter and stuff it in the glove compartment. That way they could charge just about whatever they wanted.

Twelve dollars and half an hour later they arrived at their hotel. They had picked one not too far from the airport since they needed to get up early the next day and catch a flight to Mérida in the north of the Yucatan Peninsula. From there, they would have to plan things on their own. Catherine had booked the airline tickets, but she didn't think it made sense to try to rent a car from London without knowing what the options were, and Andrew agreed.

He and Fiona went for dinner in the hotel's own restaurant, as none of them felt particularly adventurous after the long flight. Fiona ordered Paella, and Andrew got himself for a big grilled steak with potatoes and salad.

'How can you eat that?' asked Fiona after the waiter had left.

'What do you mean? Steak and potatoes?'

'Yes. You come all the way to a different country, and then you order the closest thing to home. Come on. Why don't you try something native?'

'This *is* native,' protested Andrew with a grin. 'Potatoes came from over here, you know. We didn't have those in Europe until they were brought over from the new world in the fifteenth century.'

'Alright. Sorry,' laughed Fiona. 'I just thought you might like to try some of the local cuisine that's all.'

'Do you think they serve the actual native food somewhere? You know, the things the natives ate before the Spanish arrived.'

Fiona shrugged. 'I don't know, but I'd like to try some.'

'What *did* they eat back then?' asked Andrew. 'If anyone should know, it should probably be you, right?'

'Look Mr. Sterling,' smiled Fiona. 'Just because I have a PhD in archaeology, doesn't mean that I know all there is to know about every single place and time in history. An anthropologist would probably know this better than me, anyway.'

'Yes,' said Andrew and motioned to the half-empty restaurant. 'But I don't see any here, do you?'

'Leave it, Andy,' she said, shaking her head and chuckling. 'I don't know. Ok? Go and look it up somewhere yourself.'

'Alright,' resigned Andrew. 'Then tell me this. I noticed that you were reading some books about Mexican history on the way over here. Exactly how old are the ruins we are going to examine?'

'Well, Uxmal is believed to be at least a couple of thousand years old in its present form, but that doesn't mean that the area wasn't inhabited long before that. People have been living here for at least twenty thousand years, so I'm pretty sure that some of the sites have been inhabited for much longer. In fact, it is likely that the ruins that exist today were built on the remnants of earlier structures, that may date back many thousands of years, just as is the case in many of the Egyptian archaeological sites. At the moment, the generally accepted theory is that Uxmal was built at least three times. Mostly because the name Uxmal actually means 'thrice built', in Mayan, reflecting the city's many phases of development, but there is still some disagreement among scholars as to when the previous two compounds were originally built. There might even have been more than two previous cities, but it's very difficult to say with any degree of certainty at this point. And as of yet, no one suggested digging up the whole thing, just to see how deep it all goes. But if there are previous buildings and temples there, then it is most likely that they lie somewhere beneath those that can be seen today.'

'So, was it a major city, or just sort of a regional town?'

'Oh no. It was one of the largest Mayan cities ever constructed. Considered to be one of the most splendid archaeological sites in the Pre-Hispanic era on the American continent, for thousands of years Uxmal was an important economic and political power in ancient Mesoamerica. But it is believed that its most important period was during the so-called Classic Period, which stretched from approximately 200 AD to 900 AD. This was when most of the structures that can be seen today were either completed or renovated. It is considered to be one of the great showpieces of Mayan architecture, and it is famous for its intricate artwork. Some call it 'The Athens of Mexico'. During its heyday, besides its scholarly activities, the town witnessed important intellectual and technological advances, especially in the field of construction.'

'So how much is left today?' asked Andrew.

'Well, quite a lot actually, but not all of it is in good shape. Although it was one of the most important Mayan cities in the area, most of the site is effectively just ruins. However, there are three main buildings that are reasonably intact, all of them arranged around a central plaza with a ball court. But I'll show you when we get there.'

'Wait,' said Andrew. 'What was that about a ball court? Did they play some sort of game there?'

'Well, that depends on how you look at it. The game's Spanish name was *Juego de Pelota*, and was played between two long walls with a big ring attached to one of them, roughly two and a half meters above the ground. The objective for the players was for them to hit a ball with their hips, to make it pass through the ring to score a point.'

'Sounds difficult. Was it some sort of big contest for the whole city?'

'Possibly, but the true aim of it was as a religious ceremony.'

'How? What did the winner get?'

'Death,' said Fiona with a strained smile.

'What? Death? What kind of prize is that?'

'Well, apparently it was a great honour to win the game and be sacrificed to the gods. I know it sounds gruesome, but that's how it happened according to texts that have been uncovered. And it is even written on some of the stone tablets that are there today.'

'Christ,' exclaimed Andrew. 'Talk about an alternative incentive scheme.'

'I know,' said Fiona. 'Not exactly the best thing to get you out of bed in the morning, eh? Speaking of which. When does the flight leave for Mérida tomorrow?'

'Eight fifty-five. So, I guess we'll probably have to get up around six o'clock. Shall we meet here in the restaurant at seven tomorrow morning?'

'Yes. Let's do that.'

They finished their meals without much more talk since they were both tired from the long flight. Andrew paid the waiter with one of the credit cards supplied to him by his employer, and then they went to their separate rooms.

The next morning, they met as agreed in the restaurant where they had their breakfast, and a couple of hours later they were checking in for the flight to Mérida. The weather had deteriorated, with rain falling from dark grey clouds and the wind had picked up. That delayed the entire schedule at the airport, and they had to wait almost an hour at the gate before being let onto the plane. They finally got underway and spent the next two and a half hours either reading or looking out the window at the landscape below.

They finally arrived at Mérida Airport, where they got off the plane and walked outside. The weather had improved a bit, but it was still very humid, and warm enough for them to wear only summer shirts and cotton trousers. They decided to rent a car in Mérida and drive to the town of Muna, which is around 75 kilometres south of Mérida but just a few kilometres from the Uxmal ruins. The car was a white model CJ5 Jeep with four-wheel drive and a set of huge black tires that appeared more appropriate for a moon buggy. The tires were about half a meter in width and protruded out about twenty centimetres from the side of the jeep. Each tire also had a powerful suspension system, and the entire car was elevated almost a meter from the ground, so driver and passenger had to step up into the vehicle rather than just into it. Its four headlights were each as big a human head and would be able to illuminate a huge area in front of the jeep. Behind the headlights was a big shiny grille made of galvanised steel, that made the jeep appear as if it had a permanent grin on its face. A powerful 250hp engine and two sets of gears for road and off-road driving would enable the jeep to traverse almost any landscape effortlessly. Fiona thought that renting such a monster was perhaps overdoing it slightly, but Andrew insisted that they rent a vehicle that could take them anywhere and back again.

Leaving Mérida behind, they drove through the countryside, which was covered with shrubs and big rocks protruding up through the soil. There were also patches of dense forest here and there. To Fiona, it was difficult to imagine how this rocky land with only underground rivers and what appeared to be poor soil, could have supported the hundreds of Mayan cities and towns that had laid scattered throughout the Yucatan Peninsula.

All of the towns and cities had been joined together by so-called 'scabés', or paved roads made of stones, similar to those constructed by the Romans throughout Europe during the heyday of the Roman Empire. But the Mayans, in spite of the poor soil, the absence of animals for ploughing the fields or moving timber or stone, and without any metal tools, had established one of the greatest civilisations the world has ever known.

Although eventually conquered by the Spanish conquistadors, this proud people was never fully defeated. Their original native tongue remains a living language in much of this part of Mexico, many of their homes are of the same type of oval plastered huts, and their religion is still a strange mixture of Christianity and ancient Mayan beliefs. As they passed fields and villages, it occurred to Fiona that farming, even today, was carried out in almost the same manner as it had been 2,000 years ago when the Mayan temple priests established the dates for seeding and harvesting.

The road continued south, passing through several small towns where they could see the wares in the shops from the road. Beautifully embroidered blouses and dresses hung from the shop doors, and signs for ice cream and cold sodas were displayed everywhere.

As they slowed down to pass through one of the towns, they decided to stop at a small store and buy some water. As Andrew parked the jeep and got out, another car pulled over to the side of the road, and a man who seemed strangely familiar to Andrew got out and walked quickly into a grocery store. He couldn't quite place him, but Andrew was sure that he had seen him before. After a few minutes, Fiona returned with a couple of litres of water and some fruit, and soon they were on the road again.

After reaching the town of Muna, a mid-sized regional town some 75 kilometres south of Mérida, they drove around in the city's central area, looking for a place to stay. Eventually, they found a two-star hotel, which appeared to be one of the best available there. The rooms were small but comfortable, and very cosy and clean. It was now around the middle of the afternoon, and the weather had improved significantly since they arrived in Mexico the day before. The skies were clearing and the air was less humid now, so they decided to go for a walk in the town, before eating dinner at a restaurant adjacent to the hotel.

The next day they packed some food and clean clothes and set off. They drove further south, and shortly after leaving Muna, the countryside became more hilly but also less rocky. Having been flat almost all the way from Mérida, the land began to rise sharply up the Puuc Hills. Here, there were many areas that seemed to have fertile fields, and this fertility had in no small part helped the city of Uxmal to thrive as a flourishing business, cultural and ceremonial centre on the peninsula. The road twisted up steep inclines, and occasionally heavily loaded bicycles appeared around a bend on their way downhill. The riders would adeptly hop off and pull their bicycles to the side of the road, which was quite narrow. After a few kilometres, they caught the sign for Uxmal and turned off the main road and headed along a smaller road towards the site.

Andrew parked the car off to the side of the road as they arrived at the compound. There were already a few tourist buses parked in the parking lot, and Andrew began to have serious doubts about whether they would be able to discover anything here that hadn't already been uncovered by someone else. He had to put his trust in Fiona, who seemed convinced that something was out there, just waiting to be found.

Entering through the gates to the compound, they both stopped and looked in astonishment at what lay before them. The main pyramid, called *La Pirámide Adivino* or Magician's Pyramid, loomed in front of them, and it was a breathtaking sight. At 38 meters in height, the elongated pyramid, with its characteristic rounded corners unique to this particular site, was truly majestic. With its nine levels, the pyramid is the dominant structure of Uxmal, decorated with ornate carvings of masks, birds and flowers, and Andrew and Fiona both stopped for a few seconds to take it all in.

'Amazing, isn't it?' said Fiona.

'I'll say. You haven't seen it before?'

'No. This is my first time here,' she replied, as she started walking slowly towards the centre of the compound.

'Look over there,' said Andrew and pointed. 'Is that the ball court you told me about?'

'Yes, it is. It says in this book that it is 34 meters in length and 10 meters wide. That's pretty large for a stone structure erected for a game.'

'Yes. But as you said, it must really have been serious business to them, and quite a spectacle with the rest of the mob looking on as they played.'

'Have a look at that building over there,' said Fiona and pointed to their left. 'This is the *El Palacio del Gobernador.* A 98-meter-long Governor's Palace. It is a masterpiece of latticework and mosaics.'

The long building stood out dramatically among its neighbouring structures. Built on three terraces, and decorated with patterns of 20,000 individually cut stones it was an amazing example of stone mosaic work, and one of the most magnificent buildings erected anywhere by the Mayans. Across from the long building and opposite from the centre of the plaza, lay the *Cuadrángula de las Monjas*, or The Nun's Quadrangle, which is one of the architectural complexes most representative of the Puuc style, which is found throughout the ruins. Considered to be the architectural jewel of Uxmal and one of the Mayan world's greatest treasures, the whole complex is characterised by ornate stone mosaics and geometric designs in finely sculptured limestone. Elaborate decorations of stone latticework, masks, coiling snakes and phallic figures cover every square centimetre of structures.

'This is really spectacular,' said Andrew, clearly impressed. 'I would love to be able to travel back in time and see this place in its pristine condition, with priests and soldiers and farmers going about their daily business in this square. It must have been a very peaceful life.'

'In a way it was,' said Fiona. 'The Mayans lived in perfect harmony with nature and their religion. They believed that humans, when they die, went from level to level in the afterlife. So, there was no rush to achieve everything as soon as possible in the way modern people do. But having said that, they frequently engaged in wars with other regional powers, so it wasn't all rosy all the time.'

'Well, particularly after the Spanish arrived,' said Andrew pensively. 'Think about the shock that must have been.'

'Yes. That's an interesting point. To them, the East was sacred and they believed that from there, white men with beards would one day come to them as gods.'

'Really? That was part of their belief system?'

'Yes. Amazing, isn't it? You can safely say that that turned out to be their undoing, because when the Conquistadors came from the East, the Mayans believed the gods had arrived, and so they did not resist at first.'

'Well, they certainly should have, shouldn't they?'

'In retrospect, yes. After the invaders had enslaved them and relieved them of their wealth, their civilisation died a violent death. And thereafter, all of their splendid cities were erased by the encroaching jungles, and only in the late 19th and early 20th centuries were a number of these towns such as Uxmal re-discovered by European and American archaeologists.'

'And that would include our friend Thomas Beck, I would imagine?'

'Exactly,' said Fiona. 'Unfortunately, some of the first people here were more akin to grave robbers than real archaeologists, so several of the sites were damaged and some even partially destroyed in the digging process. A real shame.'

'What do you say we walk up to the top of the Magician's Pyramid?' asked Andrew. 'I'd like to see it all from up high.'

'Sure. Let's go,' she said and the two of them walked across the central plaza towards the pyramid. It was oblong, almost oval in its shape and both its base and its top was rectangular. There were no sharp corners as on the pyramids of Egypt, but rather the corners were rounded off smoothly. A long series of steps led up one side of the pyramid at an angle of around sixty degrees, making for a rather steep climb. At the summit were a series of small temples, one of them with a giant mask of the water god Chaac with his mouth open against the backdrop of the majestic Puuc Hills.

When they reached the top, they sat down and looked out over the compound.

'You know they say that this pyramid was built by a Magician in one day?' said Fiona.

'Really?' replied Andrew. 'He must have had one hell of a construction team.'

'Yes,' chuckled Fiona. 'I have trouble getting a plumber to come and have a look at my pipes when they leak. It can take weeks for those lads to arrive.'

'Yes, I know. And even if it's an emergency, you'll be lucky to have them come by for the first twenty-four hours.'

'I don't believe in luck,' said Fiona pensively.

'I didn't mean it literally,' said Andrew.

'I know, but still. I don't believe that there is such a thing as luck.'

'Oh really?' asked Andrew sceptically. 'How about those people who win the lottery more than once?'

'Pure chance,' she dismissed.

'Do you mean to tell me that you have never thought of somebody as lucky, even when everything always seems to go their way? These people do exist you know. I've known a few of them in my time in the army.'

'Of course I have, but I am convinced that the whole concept of luck is an illusion.'

'Ok, look. Take this example. It's a true story. During the Falklands war, a British army sergeant was separated from his platoon in thick fog in the mountains, and as he found out later, he ended up walking right through enemy lines with machinegun nests on both sides. Incredibly he wasn't spotted even though he was only meters from the Argentineans, and he was then able to go in and capture an enemy ammo truck driving along a road. He killed three Argentinean soldiers in a firefight and then attempted to bring the truck back to a temporary British camp as soon as the fog lifted. The truck, however, broke down halfway there so he had to abandon it. And from a ridge no more than three hundred meters, away he watched the truck get blown to bits by a Rockeye bomb dropped by British Sea Harrier, who just happened to be in the area looking for so-called 'targets of opportunity'. Had the truck not broken down, he would have been reduced to minced meat. Now, wouldn't you call that particular sergeant just a little bit lucky?'

'Those are all just random events'

'What do you mean?'

'Well, let's take your other example and suppose that a man wins the lottery twice in a row. That is the product of two random events, because they are specifically designed to be just that, random. Logically it then follows that winning twice can be seen as one random event comprised of two random events. And yes, that is extremely unlikely, but by no means impossible.'

'So, you actually think that everything that happens can be reduced to probabilities?'

'In a way, yes. If you really wanted to, you could put probabilities on just about anything you like. Let's take your example of a man who seems besieged by luck. In everything he does, things always seem to go his way.'

'Yes,' said Andrew. 'I know a couple of those too.'

'Alright. Now, I can understand why primitive societies would think of this as luck, or even divine intervention of some sort, and that somehow this person was special. But try to think of it this way,' said Fiona and pulled out her pocket calculator.

'You never stop do you?' chuckled Andrew.

Fiona held up her hand to silence him. 'Shut up and listen, you unruly student,' she said and smiled. 'For simplicity, assume that every time the man is faced with a choice, he can choose between two options, each with some likelihood of occurring. In reality, those likelihoods or probabilities will almost always be different from each other. For example, if he decides to go and watch a football match, the likelihood that his team wins is perhaps fifty percent. At least on average. If he goes for a job interview, the chances of him getting the job may be perhaps twenty percent. If he decides to go for a drive in his car, there is probably a 99.9% chance that his car will start, as well as a similar chance of him making it safely to his destination without having an accident.'

'What's your point?' asked Andrew impatiently.

'My point is that on average it is not unreasonable to assume that when faced with all these random events that each have two outcomes, there is on average a fifty-fifty chance of things turning out the way he wants them to. Does that seem reasonable to you?'

'Yes, I suppose so, but that still leaves you to explain the lucky bastard who won the lottery twice, found the woman of his dreams at the age of eighteen, got his dream house and his dream car, and whose football team always wins the championship.'

'I guess he's not a Chelsea fan then?' teased Fiona. 'Ok,' she said and snapped back into scientist mode. 'Let's finally assume that on average that this man is faced with one significant choice or random event every day. It can turn out for or against him, and on average there is a 50 percent probability of each. Like flipping a coin. That means that…' said Fiona and punched away at her calculator. 'Over the span of a whole month, the chance of him betting on heads and getting heads every day is 1 in 1.074 billion.'

Andrew was baffled. 'Yes? So?'

'Well, that sounds like a vanishingly small number, but with 7.5 billion people on this planet, the odds are that there are around 7 people currently walking the face of the Earth, for whom every single significant event during a given month, that would ordinarily be considered random, turns out exactly in his or her favour. Even I will say that you could be forgiven for thinking that such things had to be caused by an extreme amount of luck. But statistically, it is really not at all unlikely for this to occur.'

Fiona was really getting into the swing of things now. 'Here's another example. Imagine if every person on Earth walked into a casino and placed a bet on a number at a roulette wheel. A roulette wheel has 37 numbers on it, so the chance of the ball landing on the number you picked is 1 in 37, or 2.7%. Doesn't sound so bad, right? Having the ball land on your number 5 times in a row, is a 1 in 69 million chance! That's an extremely low probability, and yet if everyone on Earth were to place their bet on a number five times in a row, there would end up being five people who managed to win every time. Most people would look at those five people, and assume that they were somehow endowed with special abilities. But it is just statistics.'

'Lucky bastards,' grinned Andrew, feigning frustration.

Fiona shook her head and laughed. 'You just don't get it, do you?'

'No,' said Andrew proudly. 'Not really. So, what are the lottery numbers for this week?' he grinned.

'You're hopeless,' chuckled Fiona dismissively.

'Probably,' smiled Andrew and looked at her endearingly. 'But as much as I think you are a nice person and as much as I like spending time with you, there's just no getting around the fact that you are a nerd.'

'Why is it that men always get uncomfortable when women have more than half a brain? I'm bloody sick of it.'

'Look, I'm sorry,' attempted Andrew, slightly taken aback by her fierce reaction. 'I meant it as a joke.'

She shook her head. 'Yes, you probably did, but that's because you don't stop to think before you express your sexist and stereotypical views. If I had been a man, you would have given this much more credence, but because I'm a woman it's perfectly alright to make jokes about it. You know, it's men like you who make it difficult for women like me to get anywhere in science.'

Andrew was caught completely off guard by her sudden outburst. He was about to offer yet another apology but then decided to let her calm down by herself and wait it out. And it didn't take more than a minute for her to have cooled off.

'Sorry if I blew my top there for a bit,' she said. 'I have a slight temper, as you may have noticed.'

Andrew nodded and smiled at her. 'I have noticed. But then so do I. You just haven't seen it yet.'

'I still meant everything I just said,' she declared.

'Having an X and a Y chromosome does tend to make it tougher than having 2 X's. At least if you want to be heard in the science community. I guess now I know what it must be like for Eckleston. On second thought, it's probably much worse for him. He really does come across as a bit of a nut.'

'I think you are right. His ideas are out of this world, to say the least, whereas you are just burdened with a sharp mind.'

'Thanks. I know,' she smiled. 'When the average man is so dumb, there's got to be somebody to counter that, right?' she winked and stood up.

Christ, thought Andrew and leaned back and closed his eyes, soaking up the sunshine. *She's bright, funny and strong-headed, and she doesn't hesitate to call me a sexist twerp when I deserve it. I like her more each minute.*

'Anyway,' she said. 'I want to get cracking. I have a few things I need to look at. Are you ready?'

'Sure. Shall we go down again?'

'Yep. Follow me.'

The two of them walked down the steps and proceeded to the centre of the central plaza.

'Do you have your GPS with you?' asked Fiona.

'Yes. Do you need it?'

'No, I need you to use it for me. Can you mark this spot?'

'Sure. Just right here?'

'Yes. Right here.'

Andrew flipped through to the page that enabled him to store the current coordinates. At his current location, there were more than enough navigation satellites available, so accuracy should be good.

'And then what?' he asked.

'Just follow me,' said Fiona and started walking towards the centre of the plaza that lay in the middle of the compound.

Andrew was walking along next to her, whilst looking down at the GPS tracker. He flicked through the different screens to get to the one that displayed the number of satellites that it was currently receiving a signal from, as well as the overall signal strength. The landscape was relatively flat, so the device was currently tracking six satellites from which to triangulate its own position.

Accuracy would normally be well below 10 meters, but one satellite orbiting approximately 300 kilometres above the Earth's surface, was apparently in the process of moving below the horizon, so the signal came and went making the accuracy gauge jump back and forth between nine and four metres. As they walked along, a small trail was plotted on the screen, indicating exactly where they had been. Normally this was a feature that came in handy in thick fog or at night when visibility was poor since it would allow the carrier to retrace their steps if need be. But Fiona apparently had a different purpose for it right now. Having reached the centre of the square, she stopped and turned towards Andrew.

'Where is North?' she said.

Andrew flicked through to the compass screen. 'That way,' he answered and pointed between two of the major temples in the compound.

'And how many meters from here to the point you just marked?'

'Hang on,' he said adjusting the gauge. '114 metres. What are you looking for?'

'One second,' said Fiona and pulled out a book from the bag she had slung over her shoulder. 'Let me just have a look here.'

She put down the bag and flicked through the pages until she found the illustration she had been looking for.

'What's that?' asked Andrew and examined the picture. It seemed to be a map depicting a number of buildings similar to the ones they were standing among.

'That is a temple in Cambodia that was discovered just a few years back. It is believed to be from around 1200 BC and the researchers think that it was constructed by a relatively small society that lived isolated from other societies or tribes. At least that's how the theory goes.'

'So, what does it have to do with this place then?'

'Look here,' said Fiona and pointed to the centre of the map. 'Let's assume that this is a square or plaza similar to the one we are standing in right now. Now look at these symmetrical lines that seem to emanate from the centre, towards each of the individual temples and other buildings out here on the perimeter of the compound.'

'Yes?' said Andrew, who wasn't really following. 'Then what?'

'Well, if the same principle of lines emanating from the centre of a plaza applies to this compound as well, then this point would be the centre of the plaza, and the lines should be emanating from this exact spot. Right?'

'Ok. And?'

'Mark this spot,' said Fiona and pointed to the GPS. 'No, wait. Give me the GPS instead. And hand me that map of yours.'

'This one?' said Andrew and pulled out a small map of the entire Uxmal compound, covering approximately eight square kilometres.'

'Yes,' said Fiona and took the map and the GPS tracker. 'Now show me how this GPS system works. Can it plot exactly where I'm walking?'

'Yes. Look here,' said Andrew and ran through the basic features of the gadget.

Ten minutes later, Andrew was sitting fifteen meters above the ground on one of the steps of the main pyramid, watching Fiona marching across the plaza towards a building a couple of hundred meters away. He wasn't sure exactly what she was doing, except that she wanted to do it by herself, which was fine by him. He had more or less ordered her to take charge of this excursion, and he couldn't very well go back on that now. She seemed to know what she was doing, and she walked briskly again and again from the centre of the plaza out towards several points on the perimeter of the compound.

Andrew sat back and took the opportunity to enjoy the sun and the light breeze that swept calmly over the compound. The air was remarkably fresh, and as far as the eye could see there was nothing but thick forest. Everywhere he looked, there was a green carpet of treetops that swayed gently in the wind.

What must have been about five kilometres towards the East, a solitary white pyramid protruded through the forest canopy, and when Andrew took out his binoculars and pointed them at the temple, he could just make out a couple of small black dots that seemed to be moving around on its top. Probably a couple of tourists having been transported out there by bus.

Thousands of people came to see these sites every year, and they were truly something to behold, but Andrew couldn't help but think that there might be much more hidden somewhere in the dense jungle. The temples and buildings were spread over a vast area all across the Yucatan Peninsula, and it seemed unlikely that all of it would had been discovered by now. The tourist attraction might even be partially to blame, since ironically when people came here and viewed the large compounds, they would simply assume that all of it had already been discovered. Why else would they be allowed to trample across the grounds? And with the planet having been mapped extensively by satellite imagery many times over, there didn't appear to be any reason to go and look anywhere else.

But Andrew knew that while the Earth's surface might have been mapped by satellites, that didn't mean that there had been people everywhere. And not everything could be identified or even noticed from orbit. On several occasions, he had been dropped along with a squad of men somewhere behind enemy lines in hostile territory, mostly on recognisance missions. More often than not, they had found their maps, supposedly the best and most accurate in the world, to be severely lacking in detail, which was what was needed on missions like that. To think that the entire Yucatan Peninsula had been mapped completely was an illusion. *Not even street maps are accurate*, thought Andrew and remembered the trouble the cab driver had experienced in finding their hotel in Mexico City, which was an ancient city by any standard.

After half an hour, Fiona began climbing up the wide stairs towards where Andrew was sitting. Huffing and puffing she slumped down next to him and lay back on the warm rock. She was sweating and fanning herself with a book.

'Great piece of equipment that GPS,' she exhaled.

'Yes,' said Andrew. 'It's very useful. So, what did you learn?'

Fiona waited a few seconds before answering. Her legs were tired from walking and climbing, and it occurred to her that she hadn't had enough to eat for breakfast. She sat up and took out a water bottle from which she had a big gulp.

'Well,' she said, still a bit out of breath. 'I learned that we are going to have to go for a long walk.'

'What do you mean?'

'See this chart here?' she said and laid out a piece of paper with a number of markings. 'This is the centre of the plaza. Right down there,' she said and pointed to the ground below. 'And all these are the buildings along the perimeter. I've drawn up a set of lines to emanate from the centre towards them, just as on the map of the compound in Cambodia.'

'And are they similar?' asked Andrew.

'Very much so, but that is not the most interesting part. What really caught my eye is that they seem to be constructed with almost exactly the same proportions.'

'How do you mean?'

'Well, the distances from the centre to the buildings on the perimeter are almost the same, which indicates that the sizes of the compounds are more or less identical. But if you compare the maps of the two compounds, what do you see?' she asked and laid out the two maps side by side.

'I see that the buildings are almost placed in the same pattern around the central plaza.'

'Yes, and the pattern of lines emanating from the centre is exactly the same. But there is more. Have a look at the scale,' said Fiona and pointed to the map of Uxmal.

'This map covers a much smaller area than that depicting the compound in Cambodia. And the compound in Cambodia has buildings that lie several kilometres from the central plaza.'

'So, what's your point?'

'My point is that this map of Uxmal doesn't cover the entire compound, but only the buildings that are immediately adjacent to the plaza. In other words, there has to be much more here.'

'But where?'

'Look,' said Fiona and pointed to one of the lines on the map connecting the centre of the plaza with a temple. 'I've drawn the pattern of lines that run through the compound in Cambodia, onto the map of Uxmal. These lines here all connect the perimeter with the central plaza, but apparently, this particular line goes nowhere. It just sticks out into nowhere. On the map of the compound in Cambodia that particular line leads to a temple.'

'Maybe there just isn't anything here.'

'Unlikely. Why should the two compounds be so similar in every other respect, but not this one,' she said and tapped the line that did not connect to any structure.

'So, what are you suggesting?'

'I think the temple must be further away.'

'How much further?' said Andrew and held the two maps closer together.

'Judging from the distances on the map of the compound in Cambodia, I'd say at least one and a half kilometres from the central plaza.'

'In which direction?'

'Well, if your GPS is reading correctly, then north is in that direction, so the temple would have to be that way,' said Fiona and pointed towards the southeast. 'But I can calculate the direction precisely.'

'There's nothing but forest and swamp out there according to the maps,' said Andrew and gazed out over the lush forest canopy towards the Southeast.

'Thanks. I know that,' said Fiona. 'But I'm convinced that something is there. We just have to look for it.'

'Well. It's not going to be today. We'll have to go back to Mérida first and buy some equipment. It may look harmless from up here, but moving one and a half kilometres through the thick undergrowth of this jungle is no picnic. What's the weather going to be like tomorrow, do you know?'

'I think it's going to be more or less the same as today, but at this time of year it can change rather quickly.'

'Alright. Is there anything more you want to do here?'

'Yes. I want to lay down here and relax for a minute. We just need to be back in Muna before dark, so there's plenty of time.'

Andrew was already planning for tomorrow's trip, and wanted to go and buy their equipment as soon as possible, but he could do with some rest as well, so he laid down next to her and closed his eyes. 'Alright then. But just for a few minutes. We have to get back before the shops close. Otherwise, we'll waste too much time tomorrow. Fair enough?'

'Sure thing. Whatever you say,' smiled Fiona.

★ ★ ★

Pete Ryan's plane landed at Heathrow Airport just after eight in the evening. He had been ordered to London on very short notice, and at this point, he wasn't even sure why, but General Ingram had told him that he would be informed upon his arrival. Looking like the average American tourist, he filed out of the aircraft along with the other passengers and made his way to pick up his luggage from the conveyor belt in the Arrivals hall. He liked to travel light, and so he only had a small wheeled suitcase, which he dragged behind him through customs.

To his left, a young couple was protesting at having the entire contents of their backpacks emptied out onto a table by a customs inspector. Either they had just been unlucky and been pulled out of the crowd at random, or perhaps they had behaved suspiciously in some way. The customs inspectors were well trained, and looking at literally hundreds of thousands of people each year passing before their eye, enabled them to spot the slightest hint of nervousness or exaggerated attempts at looking calm.

Ryan had heard of several of his countrymen, who had been tempted by greed, and accepted carrying drugs into the United States, only to be caught by customs. As far as he could remember, that usually entailed a hefty fine and possibly even jail, and he guessed that the same would be the case here in Britain. What the two youngsters probably did not realise, was that they had been lucky not to get caught on their way out of Thailand or Burma or wherever they came from. He had read about drug mules sitting in Thai jails along with murderers and rapists for several years in appalling conditions. Often the government of Thailand had ignored pleas by the families of the smugglers to let them come home and serve their sentence in a prison in their own country.

General Ingram had ordered him over here, but things had been arranged so that he would be a guest of the MI5, and would be stationed in a hotel close to the River Thames within walking distance of their fort-like headquarters right on the embankment of the river. He walked through the crowds in the Arrivals hall who were waiting for family or friends to arrive, and proceed down a flight of stairs and round a corner towards the airport train station. Having purchased a return ticket for the Heathrow Express at the ticket office, he took the elevator another two stories down to the platform. The trains ran every twenty minutes, and the trip to Paddington Station in the western part of central

London would take no more than twenty minutes. As the train arrived by the platform, he entered and sat down next to an elderly man simply because he assumed that that would enable him to sit back and relax for a few minutes.

As soon as the train started moving away from the platform and into the tunnel built under Heathrow Airport, the elderly man started fidgeting with his mobile phone. He attempted to dial a number, but because they were underground, he could not connect to the phone network. A few minutes later the train emerged from the tunnel and shot across the countryside towards London, and so the man was able to reach his wife on the phone.

The train came to a gentle halt at Paddington Station's Platform 6, and Ryan got out and walked briskly towards the exit where the cabs were parked. He liked the London cabs. Even though most of them had been replaced by newer models over the past few years, they had still maintained the old design, which was unique in the world as far as Ryan was aware. The only apparent change was the fact that they were not all black anymore. Some of them were a dark burgundy, but others were completely covered in brightly coloured advertisements.

Ryan got in line and waited his turn until he was directed to an available cab, which he then got in the back of. He told the driver where he needed to go, and then sat back and enjoyed the scenery, which was very different from what he was used to. The driver took a route through Hyde Park and past Westminster Abbey and the Houses of Parliament and then headed along the Strand on the north side of the river. After a few minutes, he turned left and then left again to park right outside the hotel. Ryan paid the driver, got out and entered the hotel's foyer where a concierge offered to take his luggage. He then walked to the reception and checked in, and ten minutes later he was in his comfortable room on the fifth floor, with a good view of the river.

He had been instructed by General Ingram to remain in the hotel for the first evening since he would be contacted there by Nick Frost of the MI5. He and the British spook would be working together for some time to come, and he was going to let him in on the details of the British investigation. Ryan was still in the dark about the nature of the operation that he was about to participate in. All he knew, was that it had something to do with the communications that had been intercepted a few days earlier, but apart from that, he had been told to remain patient and wait until he arrived in London to be briefed. That was a bit unusual since he was used to being in control of what went on around him, but it did make it clear to him that this was no trivial case. There had to be something important going on, and he was curious to know what it was.

EIGHTEEN

Fiona had never seen such a gorgeous sight in her life. As the first rays of the orange morning sun reached the top of the Magician's Pyramid, it lit up in a bright yellowish hue. It contrasted beautifully against the grey stone below that was still in shade, and the dark green forest in the background. At 38 meters, the pyramid protruded at least 25 meters above the tallest tree in its immediate vicinity, making for an awe-inspiring sight. The bright steps to the top of the pyramid were silhouetted against the rest of the pyramid as it lay there like a mountain in front of them. Both Fiona and Andrew had to stop for a moment to enjoy the view.

They had left Muna just after five o'clock in the morning, in order to reach the ruins before too many tourists arrived. The eight-kilometre drive had taken less than half an hour since there were hardly any other vehicles on the narrow roads. Now they were standing at the gates of the ruined compound, getting their equipment ready for what might turn out to be a long walk through the jungle towards the Southeast. On their backs were a couple of medium-sized rucksacks with food, water, extra clothes and a whole range of equipment as well as a couple of first aid kits. Andrew had bought them both new clothes suitable for the adventure ahead.

They were wearing light brown trekking trousers, hiking boots and long-sleeved shirts. Andrew had also purchased hats similar to those used by the SAS on jungle missions. He knew that they were going to have to move through thick undergrowth, and he wanted to protect his head as best he could. Fiona had left her hat hanging on a string around her neck for now.

'Look at that,' she said and pointed in awe at the pyramid as the sun's rays crept ever so slowly down its face. 'This structure might be less sophisticated than the cathedrals in Europe, but I'm still more impressed with this. Think of the manifestation of power this would have represented at the time.'

'Yes,' said Andrew. 'It's amazing that these things could be built out here and so long ago.'

'Yes, it is,' she said and lifted her rucksack from the ground that was still a bit moist from the dew that had settled during the night. 'Shall we get going?'

'Yep. Let's do it,' said Andrew and so they started walking across the central plaza towards the Magician's Pyramid.

The central plaza was still completely in the shade and the soil beneath their hiking boots gave off a pleasant smell. Upon reaching the pyramid, they turned left around The Nun's Quadrangle, and proceeded towards the edge of the forest that rose above them. It was a fairly abrupt change from the compound where almost every tree had been felled, to the thick undergrowth they now had to penetrate. Andrew had bought them both a machete, but those weren't necessary for the first fifty meters. It was clear that a few tourists had ventured in here, but the further away from the compound they went, the more impenetrable the jungle became.

A hundred meters into the thicket, Andrew pulled out his machete to cut down some branches that blocked their path, and they now constantly had to stop to evaluate the best way forward. After just ten minutes, Fiona looked back over her shoulder, but could now see no sign of the compound whatsoever. They might as well have been deep in the Brazilian rainforest for all she knew. There was nothing to suggest that anyone had ever walked where they were now, and any sign of a path like the ones that existed close to the compound was long gone by now. There were hardly any sounds, except for the leaves and small branches that snapped as they walked on top of them. A few birds were singing in the tall trees, and occasionally they could hear an animal scurrying away through the undergrowth.

As they walked along, Andrew's eyes scanned from left to right trying to spot any potential dangers. It was not a conscious act, but a result of both his training and actual combat experience in environments similar to this. It all seemed very peaceful, but he knew from bitter experience that this was precisely the time to be vigilant and careful. Danger came in all shapes and sizes, and even though this was far from being a secret mission in enemy territory, there were still threats to watch out for. A highly venomous snake had once bitten him while on a training exercise in the jungles of Burma, and that had happened as his squad had been on their way back from successfully destroying the mock target. They had become complacent by the successful destruction of their objective, and if it hadn't been for the antidote that had been handed to them prior to the mission, he would probably not have lived. Still dazed and feeling extremely nauseous and tired, and with the help of the other members of the team, he had managed to drag himself to the extraction zone for the helicopter pick-up almost two days later. That had been a lesson for him, but then it was better to learn during training than during combat.

Above their heads the thick green canopy almost covered them completely, and only when they came upon a tree that had toppled over could they see the blue sky. High above them, what appeared to be an eagle circled the area, gliding calmly along on the light breeze that swept over the jungle canopy. The terrain was much less flat than it had been closer to the central Uxmal compound. It was now undulating up and down, making it much more difficult to move forward, since they could easily slip on the dense layers of leaves and rotting branches. There were small natural ponds that they had to walk around, which made for an even longer trip than they had initially thought.

After almost an hour of strenuous walking, climbing, chopping and crawling, Andrew pulled out his GPS again and stopped for a few seconds to let it connect to a sufficient number of satellites to receive an exact coordinate. He had continuously monitored their progress, ensuring that they remained on course towards the point on the map, indicated by Fiona with a black dot.

'420 meters from the Uxmal compound,' he said and grinned.

'That's all?' said Fiona incredulous. 'It feels like miles.'

'Yes. It's slow going. How are you doing so far?'

'I'm Ok,' said Fiona and wiped the sweat from her face. 'I'm really glad we didn't wait until later in the day. That would definitely have killed me off.'

'I think it's actually going to remain relatively cool down here under the canopy,' said Andrew and pointed to the treetops with the GPS. 'Do you want to take a break?'

'No. Let's keep going for a while. How far is it?'

Andrew glanced at the GPS and winced. 'At least a kilometre yet to go. Be careful where you place your feet, Ok? If one of us trips and breaks an ankle out here, it's going to take a long time to get back to the roads.'

'Right,' said Fiona grinned, and then saluted him the way a soldier would salute his superior officer. 'Will do, Sir.'

★ ★ ★

Erich Strauss had made up his mind. What he had proposed, or rather, what he wanted to have carried out, went against the practice of the Thule Society as it had conducted itself for more than half a century. But there was no other way. Of that, he had become convinced.

The two triangles in the possession of the society were no longer to be kept privately by the Keepers. He had decided that in the present situation, it could not be ruled out that the British government might resort to the use of force. The investigation of the Order of the Teutonic Knights, and thereby of the Thule Society, that was clearly under way, might potentially endanger the entire future of their endeavour.

In his estimation, Sterling and that woman Fiona Keane would have no reason to suspect that the Thule Society was still active, at least not based on the documents Sterling had stolen, but that was really beside the point at this stage. It was a fact that the security and secrecy of the society's headquarters had been compromised, and that several crucial items had been stolen. And even if the thief didn't put two and two together and figure out that the Thule Society was alive and well, they might attempt to come back looking for more at some stage, and that was a risk he as grandmaster was unwilling to take. For a few seconds, he had actually considered involving the Austrian Police, since the society had at least a handful of sympathisers and affiliated members placed in important positions within the Austrian police force. However, on second thought, he had decided not to do it, at least for the time being. It would simply be too risky at this stage, and even though he might receive genuine help in investigating the reasons for the theft of the book and the other documents, it could all easily escalate into an international incident, embarrassing both the Austrian and the British governments, and that would surely lead to a much more comprehensive investigation of the order. In addition, the very last thing he needed right now was stories about the society being run in the newspapers.

For these reasons, they had decided on a more cautious approach to their own investigation. He had also decided that the only proper place for the safe keeping of the two triangles, were in the personal safe of the Austrian member of Parliament, in one of his banks. Short of war, absolutely nothing could make the bank open their safes to anyone but the owners. They would be able to remain there until the society had retrieved the remaining two pieces of the medallion.

He had announced his decision to the four Keepers, and not surprisingly, the retired German Airforce commander and the Austrian Member of Parliament had been the least enthusiastic. But none of them had protested, because at the end of the day they knew and accepted the fact that the grand master had at his disposal an extensive network of sympathisers and aides, spanning many countries and built up over the course of more than fifty years. These people were completely loyal and subservient to the wish of the grand master. No member had ever revolted openly against the society and lived, as far as anyone knew. The secrets of the society were so sacred and its mission so crucial, that no dissent was tolerated.

As Strauss sat in his chair behind his desk, reading summaries of various activities of the society around the world, he couldn't get his mind off the fact that their holiest of holy, the secret chamber in the library, had been entered and looted. He felt a deep sense of unease that the monumental efforts of the Thule Society before, during and after the Second World War were in real danger of being brought down by two nosy Brits.

When he thought about all the time, effort and money that had been spent on surveillance, bribery, intelligence gathering and analysis, and even a large number of actual expeditions to sites around the world in search of the two remaining triangles, it sent shivers down his spine. The prospect of being the one holding the title of grandmaster as the society was brought down, had initially filled him with dread. However, much of that had soon been turned into anger and then rage at those who would stand in the way of the society fulfilling its destiny. And that is exactly what Sterling and the girl were to him. They didn't realise that in their quest to uncover the truth about him and his organisation, they were in effect digging their own graves.

Soon the entire European continent would be flooded with militant Arabs, slowly eating their way into the heart of Europe. First, they would force the Jews to retreat from Israel towards the continent, and then they would take over the world bit by bit, with their radical religious ideas and cries of war against western civilisation.

Starting with Turkey, whose government made a big effort to make the country look western in order to gain membership in the European Union, but which in reality was a deeply Islamic state, they would proceed into the Balkans which held large Muslim populations. From there they would sweep up through Europe and even into Austria itself, possibly taking over the democratic institutions and break them down from within, replacing the elected parliament with a council of fundamentalists, exactly as had happened in Afghanistan a few years earlier. In central Asia, Muslim hoards would spill over from the border of Pakistan into

India and make their way towards their religious brethren in Indonesia, which held a mostly Muslim population of close to a billion people. Much of Africa was already largely Muslim as far as he could tell, and in the United States of America, Muslims were the fastest-growing segments of the population.

Strauss had seen all this happen in a dream or a vision as he liked to think of it, and he was now absolutely convinced that Europe would one day become the last bastion of western civilisation, and that the final showdown between civilisations would eventually happen there.

That prospect filled Strauss with disgust, and he felt more strongly than ever that without some hard evidence of the bygone magnificence and dominance of the Aryan race in ancient times, and of the fact that they were the ones who initially spread civilisation among the peoples of the world, the Aryan race might face permanent extermination.

He, along with thousands of others, either directly or indirectly affiliated with the Thule Society, would lay down their lives for the cause. What more valiant a service could he offer to his ancestors, than to sacrifice himself in the struggle to preserve the original Aryan heritage, ensuring that one day it might again shine over the world and put right all that had been lost since the fall of the Third Reich? He could think of none, and he firmly believed that the future of mankind lay in his hands. He was also convinced that if he didn't ensure the recovery of the two remaining pieces, which would then reveal the path to Thule and the immense powers that lay hidden within it, the Aryan race would be doomed. The re-discovery of Thule would prove their heritage, and the powers of the ancients would ensure their victory over the inferior races, and would once more place the Aryan race in control of the world.

★ ★ ★

The sun was now rising quickly in the east, and as rays of light found their way through the thick green canopy, the forest floor became dotted with small bright spots. The temperature had risen to around thirty degrees Celsius, and by now both Andrew and Fiona were sweating profusely. They didn't speak very much but spent most of their time watching carefully where they put their feet. Fiona pulled out her map and stopped for a few seconds to look at it. Unless the map was incomplete, they were now just over a kilometre away from the main Uxmal compound, and they were at least three kilometres from the nearest dirt road. Such a distance would take them many hours of walking through the thicket if it should become necessary to do so.

They had been underway for a couple of hours and were still at least 500 meters away from the spot that Fiona had indicated on the map. Andrew had programmed that point into his handheld GPS, and every few seconds he would glance down at the screen and check their position and course.

Having been invented by the American military, the GPS had gained widespread use in civilian shipping as well as aviation, but the military still held an advantage over the commercial equipment, since commercial products were blocked from using the full potential of the system. Whereas a navigation aid for a sailboat would indicate the position of the boat on the Earth's surface to within tens of meters, the military systems were able to determine a position to within just a few meters. This helped the so-called 'smart bombs', that were fitted with GPS equipment to autonomously and more accurately hit their targets.

They were still moving almost due southeast, but they constantly had to make their way around obstacles such as large tree trunks from toppled over trees, small ponds and swamps, and even huge rocks that seemed to have been placed on top of the ground by a giant hand. At one point, Andrew climbed on top of such a rock to try to scout further ahead, but strangely, the vegetation didn't seem any thinner five meters above ground, so visibility was still below thirty meters. Had he been on a mission with the SAS, Andrew would have been called the 'point man', as he was the one walking in front. As they were making their way through the jungle, he almost forgot that he wasn't on a mission right now. The sights, sounds and smells of the jungle automatically prompted his brain to switch into soldier mode. His sensory system was as alert as ever, and he even started moving through the vegetation in the same slow but steady and silent fashion that he had done so many times before in similar types of terrain. Several times he caught himself reaching for his weapon to check that it was securely fastened, only to realise that he and Fiona were both unarmed, except for the hunting knife he had purchased the day before.

Fiona noticed the change in his behaviour but didn't comment on it. She didn't feel entirely comfortable with being this far out in the jungle and moving further and further away from the civilised world, but with Andrew walking ahead of her, she felt reassured by his obvious self-confidence and proficiency at traversing this difficult terrain. She was also getting increasingly excited about what they might find when they arrived at their destination, even though so far, there was no indication that any human had ever been where they were.

Upon reaching a small natural clearing, most likely created by a group of trees falling over during a hurricane, they decided to stop and rest for a while. Ideally, they should have stopped for rests of ten minutes every half hour, but since they didn't know what lay ahead of them and how long it might take to get to their destination, they had proceeded without a sufficient number of breaks. That began to make itself felt now, at least in Fiona's legs, which were getting sore already.

'You alright, Fiona?' asked Andrew.

'Yeah,' said Fiona and grimaced as she leaned on a tree and stretched her legs. 'I just need a few minutes. How far to go?'

'Somewhere in the region of 650 meters. Let's sit down here for a while and rest.'

'I'm a bit hungry too,' said Fiona as she came over and plonked herself next to Andrew on a piece of rock protruding from the moss-covered ground at the centre of the clearing.

'Me too,' said Andrew and opened his rucksack. 'We need to eat and drink something even if we were not hungry or thirsty. Our bodies are losing several litres of water every hour in this heat, so we need to replenish at the same rate.'

'No problem there,' said Fiona and bit into a half-melted candy bar. 'I'm not going to let myself starve out here,' she grinned and winked at Andrew.

'No. I see that,' he smiled. 'I suggest you take your boots off for a few minutes as well. Letting blood circulation return to normal for a couple of minutes can save you from some pretty nasty pains later on.'

The two explorers rested for another fifteen minutes before putting on their rucksacks again and heading back into the undergrowth towards the southeast. They had spent around twenty minutes resting in the clearing to cool off and have a drink and a snack, but now after just a few minutes of walking through the thicket, they were once again sweating heavily. Andrew chopped away at the branches and other vegetation that seemed hell-bent on blocking them every step of the way, and they often had to crouch down to walk under thick branches or to avoid spikey plants and bushes.

Slowly and laboriously, they made progress through the jungle, and after another hour of walking and chopping, they suddenly reached a big mound of earth. It appeared to be about the size of a tennis court, and it rose quite abruptly from the jungle floor to a height of some five meters, but it was still possible to walk up along its sides to its flattened top. Initially, Andrew was about to go around it, but then looked at his GPS to find that they should be within fifty meters of the spot Fiona had marked on the map.

They ascended to the top and stood there silently for a few seconds as they turned around and looked at the mound and its surroundings. There was hardly any vegetation on it except for moss and a few patches of tall grass, and standing on its top they were able to look straight into the tops of some of the trees surrounding it.

'What a strange hill,' said Fiona excitedly. 'Is this the spot?'

'Yep. This is it,' replied Andrew and tapped on the GPS with his finger. 'North 020'35.992 and West 089'16.412. Unless there's some other unusual feature close to this spot, I think we are standing right where you've indicated on the map. And I guess that begs the question: What exactly are we standing on?'

Fiona walked around slowly on the top of the mound, which was almost entirely flat and about four meters from one side to the other.

'Well, this isn't exactly what I had expected,' said Fiona and scratched her head.

'What do you mean?' asked Andrew, and gulped down some of his water.

'I don't know. I guess I had expected to find a temple or something, but this looks like just another heap of dirt.'

'Maybe its placement has some significance,' suggested Andrew and looked at a map of the Yucatan Peninsula, and put his index finger approximately where they were standing.

'Maybe,' said Fiona and started walking towards him. 'It just seems a little odd that my hunch about another part of the Uxmal ruin was right, but then to find…'

Suddenly the ground beneath her left foot gave way, and her leg seemed to instantly disappear beneath her, as she fell down on her other knee, resting on both hands.

'Andrew! Help!' she yelled in shock and tried to get up again.

Andrew immediately dropped his water bottle, ran over to her and pulled her forcefully out from the hole. She got her leg out and fell forward onto the ground with a thump.

'Are you alright?' he asked as she kicked frantically to get away from the hole that was now visible in the mound's moss-covered surface.

She jumped to her feet, as if wanting to get ready to defend herself, and then backed away from the hole.

'Uh, Yeah. I guess so,' she said and bent over to examine her leg, which was now covered in dirt and green plant juices.

'You're not bleeding or anything?' Andrew asked and knelt down beside her to look at a tear in her trousers.

'No, I don't think so. What the hell was that?'

'Maybe a burrow made by an animal,' said Andrew and rose.

'No way,' said Fiona dismissively, and stepped back cautiously towards the hole and looked down. 'It was way too deep for that, and… Hey, look at this!' she exclaimed and knelt down next to the hole. 'These rocks have been shaped to fit with each other. This is not natural.'

Andrew walked over and knelt down next to Fiona. She was already busy tearing up the thick layer of green and yellow moss and throwing it aside. Andrew helped her and within a few seconds, they were looking at something that had to have been made by humans.

Under the moss were large square slabs of about half a meter across, made from what appeared to be some form of grey and black volcanic rock, which had then been fitted together with amazing precision, into an almost completely flat surface. The joins between each of the slabs were so narrow that Andrew couldn't get the blade of his knife into any of them. The hole that Fiona had fallen into was in fact one of those slabs, that must have cracked and had then crumbled under her feet. At the centre of each of the other slabs now being revealed from under the moss, was chiselled the same image. It was a face or mask, similar to those found on Mayan temples all over the Yucatan Peninsula. Some of the images had eroded somewhat over time, but it was evident what they were supposed to show.

'What the bloody hell have we found here?' asked Andrew stunned.

'Look!' said Fiona excitedly, and pointed to a slab with what was the best-preserved image. 'It's the same mask that was on the Magician's Pyramid,' she beamed and looked at Andrew. 'This means that this really is part of the Uxmal compound. Just as I predicted!'

'Very clever, Miss,' said Andrew.

'And it proves that the Cambodian compound and Uxmal are indeed similar,' said Fiona.

'Right,' said Andrew and nodded. 'But just what exactly are we sitting on here?'

'No idea,' admitted Fiona and held up her hands. 'But we are going to find out, that's for sure.'

'How?'

'We dig, of course,' she said and pointed at the hole.

'Dig?'

'Yes, what else would you do?'

'Well,' he said and shrugged. 'I suppose you're right. After all, you're the archaeologist. Let's get to work.'

They put down their rucksacks near the edge of the mound's top and pulled out the folding aluminium spades that Andrew had bought. They were not the best tools for the job, but the two of them managed to clear an area of about two by three meters on the flattened top of the mound. The moss, grass and loose soil was dumped in a couple of heaps off to the sides, and after half an hour of gruelling work as the sun climbed towards its zenith, they were looking at an impressive surface made from uniform slabs of dark grey stone with the same mask image chiselled into all them. In some places the layer of dirt and moss had been as much as thirty centimetres thick, leading Fiona to wonder how many years' worth of falling leaves and branches from the surrounding trees and bushes, it had taken to cover the structure by such a dense layer of soil.

They eventually cleared the area around the broken slab, and Andrew was now walking around the edge of it, stomping his feet to see if any of the other surrounding slabs were fragile or loose. They all seemed to sit firmly in place, and so he stepped across the hole, knelt down on one knee and stuck his spade into the hole while resting it on one of its edges. Attempting to use the spade as a lever, he put his weight down on the spade's handle, but the slab didn't budge at all.

'What are you doing?' asked Fiona as she came over, wiping the sweat from her forehead.

'I'm trying to pry this thing open, but it won't move,' huffed Andrew as he pulled out the spade.

'Here,' said Fiona. 'Let me have a look.'

She knelt down next to the hole with her flashlight, stuck it through the hole and switched it on.

'Can you see anything?' asked Andrew.

'It looks like,' said Fiona who was now attempting to stick her head as far into the hole as she could in order better to be able to see. 'It's a large room. I can see the floor but it's at least four meters below us, and stone columns on the floor support the whole ceiling we are standing on. I can't make out what it is, but there seems to be a large round boulder immediately below us at the centre of the room.'

She sat back up on the edge of the hole and looked at Andrew, her eyes gleaming with excitement. 'Andrew, we need to get in there. This is an amazing find.'

'Yes, I know,' he replied reluctantly. 'But maybe there's another way in there, somewhere nearer ground level.'

'I'll go look,' said Fiona and walked down to the base of the mound, while Andrew brought out his own flashlight and shone it into the hole.

Fiona walked briskly around the circumference of the entire mound, searching the surface of its sides and occasionally walking up a few meters to get a closer look at a feature that might have been a concealed entrance, but having walked all the way around it, she came back up shaking her head.

'There's nothing there,' she said. 'Nothing that I can see, anyway. I think this hole is our best option.'

'Alright. Wait here for a minute. I'll go and find us something else to use as a lever. Otherwise, we'll never get those slabs removed.'

Andrew grabbed his machete, walked down the side of the mound and proceeded into the jungle looking for a suitable branch. After a few minutes, he found a young slender tree roughly five meters tall and decided that it would do the job. He began chopping with the machete at the base of the tree. It would have been a lot easier with a saw, but he had not imagined they would need one.

He began sweating heavily again but continued undaunted, and after ten minutes he was able to topple the trunk over just by pushing it. Its top tore down through the thick undergrowth, and it took him another fifteen minutes to chop off the top three meters of it and clear the remaining log of branches. He then dragged the log through the undergrowth and up the side of the mound to the top where Fiona was sitting, paging through a book.

'Find anything?' she said and looked up just as Andrew dragged the log onto the top of the mound.

'Yes. I think this'll do,' he said and dropped the log.

'Jesus,' she said surprised. 'Do you really think we need such a big one to lift the slabs?'

'Yes. It's not that they are very heavy, but they are so neatly laid, that they bind each other in place.'

'I just hope the whole thing doesn't cave in under our feet,' said Fiona as she put away the book and rose.

'I don't think it will. A little help?'

Fiona walked over next to Andrew, and together they inserted the first half meter of the log into the hole, and then slowly applied more and more weight to the other end. As the log had been cut from a newly felled tree, it was still flexible and as they increased the weight on its end, it slowly began bending into an arch.

'Do you think it'll hold?' asked Fiona and grimaced.

'Let's see,' said Andrew as he leaned over and put his entire weight squarely onto the log, which translated into several times more lifting power at the other end of it.

The slab finally freed itself from the grip of the surrounding slabs, and gradually came loose. The more it came loose the faster it went, and suddenly the slab popped out of its position and flipped over on its face, leaving a hole that was now more than big enough for a person to climb through. They pulled out the log and let it drop down next to the hole.

'Wait,' said Andrew. 'We might still need the log. Place it across the hole.'

Fiona did as he asked and then Andrew produced a long rope from his rucksack, knelt down and then tied one end of it to the log. He then let the rest of the rope drop down into the hole.

'Would you like to go first?' he said and smiled at Fiona.

'No thanks,' she replied. 'I think I'll just let you test whether that rope is strong enough. You're heavier than me.'

'Alright,' said Andrew and sat on the edge of the hole, with his legs halfway into it. 'Here goes.'

He slid off the edge, and lowered himself through the hole, still holding on to the pole that now lay across it, and when his body was almost entirely hidden from view, he shifted his hands to hold on to the rope instead. Making sure he had a firm grip, he slowly began lowering himself down into the room. The first thing that met him was the smell of cold, stale humid air. He wondered for how many years this air had been trapped in there. His eyes had not yet been accustomed to the relative darkness, so he couldn't see very much, except for the huge round boulder below him. It looked almost like a great ball lying there in the middle of the room, but as he got closer, he could see that patterns had been chiselled into its top. He was now hanging about three meters below the hole above him when his feet made contact with the boulder. It was made from the same grey and black volcanic rock as the slabs in the ceiling. Still holding on to the rope, he lowered himself down along what seemed to be a flattened side of the boulder to the floor below.

'Are you alright down there?' shouted Fiona.

Andrew gave her a thumbs-up and looked up at the hole high above him. It seemed like a white sun in a black night sky, and the rays of sun fell almost vertically down on the round boulder.

'I'm fine,' he shouted. 'I'll just have a look around.'

He walked a few steps away from the boulder and then turned to find that the boulder wasn't just a big round piece of rock. It was a giant head apparently chiselled out of a solid piece of volcanic rock. It was round as a ball except for its square jaw, and it seemed to be wearing a helmet of sorts, with several patterns and what appeared to be glyphs. Its lips were full, its nose flat and wide, and the ears were small and lay flat against the skull.

'Damn,' he muttered to himself.

'What's that?' shouted Fiona.

'Nothing,' he shouted back. 'It's just that this boulder is a face or a head or something. It's chiselled out of one solid piece of rock by the looks of it.'

'Who does it look like?'

Andrew peered up at her, incredulously. 'What the bloody hell is that supposed to mean?'

'Is it an Indian face or not? Does it have Indian features?'

'Well, maybe. I don't know. Hard to tell, isn't it?'

'No! Try!'

'Alright. I guess he looks most of all like a black man,' shouted Andrew and wondered whether that had been politically correct.

'Get your butt up from there. I want to go down and have a look. This could really be something significant.'

'Alright. Hold your horses there for a second, Miss Keane. I'll just go and see what else is in here, ok?'

'Alright,' said Fiona disappointedly. 'But please hurry!'

She was very anxious to get down there and see for herself. This was what she lived for. Reading a book about archaeological expeditions was interesting, but this was exciting beyond anything she had ever experienced herself. She had been lucky enough to participate in a number of expeditions to Egypt, the Far East and India, but never on her own. She had always been the assistant of some professor that would mostly regard her as a pretty servant.

It suddenly struck her that what she and Andrew were in the process of doing might be said to be grave robbery or desecration. She didn't know for a fact that this was a grave, but what was definitely a fact was that any finds such as this one ought to be reported to the local authorities without delay, and they would then contact the proper government agency in Mexico City. But Mexico City and the proper government agency was almost a thousand kilometres away, and she was right here looking down at what was surely a significant historical find. There was not a chance that she was backing out now.

Andrew took out his flashlight and shone it around the room. It was about five by seven meters, and he figured that it was at least five meters to the ceiling. Thick evenly spaced stone columns rose from the floor to the ceiling at intervals of around two meters, and Andrew couldn't help but be impressed by the fact that they were able to hold the ceiling in place. Obviously, the builders of this place had been extremely skilful and had employed sophisticated construction techniques, especially for their time. The floor was made from large stone slabs similar to the ones in the ceiling, but it was covered with a thin layer of dirt and dust, probably accumulated over hundreds or perhaps even thousands of years.

He walked around the giant head while shining his flashlight onto the walls of the room. They were all covered with images, some carved or chiselled into the stone, others painted onto surfaces that had once been polished smooth. Now there wasn't much of the paint left, and it was difficult to tell whether they were even the same colours as when the images had been painted. They appeared to depict religious ceremonies, with priests standing around an altar upon which lay a person about to be sacrificed. One of the priests held a knife high in the air, while the person about to be delivered to the gods was held in place by four big men each holding on to a leg or an arm.

Another wall depicted what appeared to be the layout of a town, only it seemed to cover a very large area. Andrew couldn't make out the details, but it seemed to be a fairly accurate map of the coastal region facing the present-day Mexican Gulf towards the north. The third wall was badly eroded and several of the stones in the wall had fallen out and now lay on the floor of the room. Despite this, Andrew was able to make out that it had once been a smooth surface with neatly interlocking stones. It didn't look too stable though, so Andrew decided not to step over next to it.

The fourth wall had a hole in the centre, and only as Andrew walked closer to it, did it dawn on him that this was the door into the room. It was directly in front of the face of the giant head, and appeared to have once been a short corridor to the outside, but now it had caved in, and it even seemed as if huge amounts of soil had been thrown into it from the outside. As if the room had been intentionally sealed off at some point and then forgotten.

Andrew walked back to the stone head and looked up towards the bright hole in the ceiling. 'Fiona, I'm coming up.'

There was no answer.

'Fiona, are you there?' shouted Andrew, suddenly becoming anxious without knowing exactly why.

Then Fiona's head appeared in the opening. 'I'm here. Sorry, I was just reading something. I think I may already have figured out what this is. Approximately, at least.'

'Alright. Wait a minute. I'll come up and join you. Then you can come down afterwards and have a look for yourself.'

A few minutes later Andrew had slumped down next to Fiona, panting after the climb up the rope.

'There's an exit down there, but it has been blocked. The only way in and out is through this hole.'

'Well, if you don't mind, I'll just pull the rope up and tie a few knots,' said Fiona. 'Otherwise, I'll never make it back up here.'

'Be my guest,' said Andrew and wondered why he hadn't thought of that himself. 'So, what is it you think you have figured out from up here?' he asked.

'I think that what you were looking at down there was a head made by the Olmecs.'

'The what?'

'The Olmec culture. It is believed to be the mother of both the Aztec and Mayan cultures.'

'So, this structure is even older than Uxmal?'

'Yes, almost certainly. At least the head is. Similar stone heads have been found in many places across central and eastern Mexico, as well as in Guatemala and Belize.'

'Look here,' she said and showed him a book with a picture taken near an archaeological site in central Mexico called San Lorenzo. 'Is this it?' she asked and tapped her finger on the picture.

'Yep. That's close enough. It has the same eyes, lips, and face as the guy down there,' he said and pointed into the hole. 'Olmec, eh?'

'Yes. There is believed to have been three major Olmec centres spanning most of present-day Mexico from east to west.

'And when was this?' asked Andrew.

'It is estimated that the oldest Olmec cities date back to at least 1800 BC, so that's just under 4000 years ago,' said Fiona and started tying big evenly spaced knots on the rope. 'There is really no hard archaeological evidence before that, but it has been speculated that the precursor cultures were in this area as early as 8000 years ago.'

'Wow. That's impressive,' said Andrew.

'Yes, it is. But if like me you believe that the Mayan culture, which definitely succeeded the Olmecs, is older than most researchers believe it to be, then the Olmec culture must have been even older than that.'

'Is there a basis for believing that?'

'I definitely think so,' said Fiona confidently. 'I think both cultures may well be perhaps as much as eight or even ten thousand years old.'

'That would fit nicely with the theory of Eckleston and the Thule Society about an ancient civilisation?'

'Quite possibly,' said Fiona and nodded. 'Right now, we are closest to the easternmost of the three major power centres in the Olmec culture. We don't know what its original name was, but it is called *La Venta* in Spanish, and it is near the rich inlets of the coast, and probably provided crops such as cacao and rubber, and even salt from the sea. San Lorenzo, at the centre of the Olmec domain, controlled the vast flood plain of the *Coatzacoalcos* basin in central Mexico as well as river trade routes. The third one is called *Laguna de los Cerros* in the West, and is positioned near important sources of basalt, which is a stone needed to construct buildings and monuments.'

'Sounds like a pretty big operation. How long did this culture last?'

'Well, it's difficult to say when it came to an end since the Olmec culture was gradually replaced by the Aztecs and the Mayans, but most estimates say around 400 BC. So, it seems that it persisted for several thousand years. It is hypothesised that marriage alliances between Olmec centres helped maintain its power for such a long period.'

'So, were they the first people to settle here?'

'Yes. At least they were the first advanced civilisation to inhabit this region. There has been considerable controversy about where the Olmecs originally came from, and some have hypothesised that they had actually migrated from elsewhere. Recent excavations at La Venta and San Lorenzo, and subsequent radiocarbon dating revealed that La Venta and San Lorenzo were originally inhabited by people from the Gulf coast. They were corn farmers who supplemented their diet with fishing and hunting, and the first evidence of their existence was uncovered in 1862 when a colossal stone head was discovered in the state of *Veracruz* along the Gulf Coast of Mexico. In the years after that, artefacts turned up at sites in Mexico and other parts of Central America. The colossal heads, of which you have just seen one, are actually portraits of individual Olmec rulers, and the large symbol displayed on the 'helmet' of each of these colossal heads is a unique motif for that particular ruler.'

'So that was their way of honouring their kings, just like we do now with paintings and statues.'

'Exactly. The heads glorified the rulers while they were alive, and commemorated them as revered ancestors after their death. But they also built other things that were later carried through to the Aztec and Mayan cultures, such as the ball court we saw in Uxmal.'

'They played that game too?'

'Yes. Several rubber balls have been discovered near San Lorenzo, and that confirms that the game was also played by the Olmec. Archaeologists working at La Venta twenty years ago discovered what they hypothesised were the remains of a ball court there.'

'What is this?' said Andrew and pointed to a map with what appeared to be trails across Central America.

'Those are trade routes,' said Fiona. 'Geologists have concluded that the basalt used to make most of the monuments at San Lorenzo and La Venta came from the area of the Tuxtlas Mountains far to the south of here, and in 1960 an Olmec basalt quarry site and monument workshop was discovered less than ten kilometres from a major Olmec centre.'

'Ten kilometres? That can be a long way if you have to drag blocks of stone like the one down there,' said Andrew and motioned towards the hole.

'Yes. But in a similar way to the ancient Egyptians, the Olmec and later the Aztecs and Mayans had advanced systems for transporting large blocks of stone and rock. One of the head sculptures found at La Venta was cut from a stone quarried more than 80 kilometres from where the head was discovered. So, they must have had quite exceptional means of transportation. Particularly considering the terrain here.'

'Evidently, yes. The one down there is approximately three meters high and two and a half meters wide, so we are talking about upwards of ten tons of solid rock.'

'I know,' nodded Fiona. 'It is pretty amazing. Remember that wood and rock were the only materials available to them for construction, and so they developed expertise in handling those over thousands of years. Some of the most beautiful stone structures, apart from the heads, were altars on which they performed sacrificial ceremonies involving living humans, and sometimes infants. The altars were actually the thrones of Olmec rulers, and they had intricate carvings on the front of the throne, showing the ruler sitting in a niche that symbolises a cave entrance to the supernatural powers of the underworld. That scene communicated to the people their ruler's association with cosmological power.'

'Well,' said Andrew. 'There's a huge illustration of one of the ceremonies on one of the walls down there.'

'Really?' said Fiona excitedly. 'Right, I really need to get down there now. I'll tell you more later.'

She then threw the rope with the newly tied series of knots down through the hole and started climbing down towards the head. As she did so, Andrew watched her progress closely, making sure that she didn't fall or trip on the smooth surface of the stone head. Holding on to the rope, Fiona slid down the side of the head and walked around it until she reached its face.

'Holy shit!' she exclaimed when she saw it. 'I've never seen one so well preserved,' she laughed. 'This is amazing!'

She placed her hands on the cool rock and found herself caressing the features of the face. The eyes were big and wide, unlike the small and narrow eyes of the locals. The lips were full and protruded slightly from the face, and the wide flat nose seemed more akin to those found among people in Africa. She couldn't help but think that what she was looking at was not an image of a local king, even though he had lived several thousand years ago. The facial features of the head were so different from those of the local people, that she had to believe that it depicted someone else, possibly a visitor having appeared thousands of years ago. But who, and from where?

She knew that other heads had been found with similar features, and there had been intense speculation that the Olmecs had originally come from Africa. But it was also generally accepted that many original populations of countries like Cambodia and the Philippines have similar characteristics, and those might have been brought along when the first humans entered the Americas from Asia. The real question was when this had happened, and whether there had been other visitors from other places.

Fiona turned to walk along the walls and stopped in front of the image of a sacrificial ceremony. She had seen similar images in other parts of Central America, but this one had been extraordinarily well preserved. She walked past the crumbled wall to the caved-in corridor. Atop the opening was a small stone figurine, displaying the characteristic Olmec motif of a human face with a jaguar mouth, sometimes called a 'were-jaguar', as in 'werewolf'. Some scholars believe that elements of the Olmec religion included shape shifting by shamans, who were very powerful and were placed at the very heart of Olmec society. Several stone carvings of shamans or medicine men had been found, and in one in particular the shaman was riding a serpent snake, while holding in his hands a small bag, believed to hold plants and possibly fungi, to help him reach an alternate state of mind, in order to gain access to the spiritual realm.

Fiona continued on to the wall with an illustration she could not immediately identify. She tried to recall similar images from the books she had read, but nothing fitted with what she was looking at. Only then did she realise that it wasn't an illustration as such, but rather a map. As far as she knew, neither the Olmecs, Mayans or the Aztecs had ever drawn any maps, at least not any that had been recovered. But this was clearly a map of present-day Campeche Bay to the southwest of their location. She moved closer, shining her flashlight over the wall, but then walked back to the stone head and looked up towards the hole.

'Andrew,' she shouted. 'Can you throw me your flashlight? I need more light.'

'Sure,' he replied and dropped his flashlight down to where she was standing.

She caught it and then switched it on while walking back to the map wall. She placed one of the flashlights on a small rock on the ground, so that it shone its light upward over the entire wall. The other she held in her hand, as she approached the map. The map itself was approximately three meters in height and appeared to be very detailed. She could immediately identify several of the ruins that she already knew about, including the ruins at Uxmal, but also those of Tikal, which was another famous ruin complex in Guatemala several hundred kilometres away. Whoever had painted this, seemed to have an astonishingly detailed knowledge of the region. Not only did all the proportions seem to be correct, but the placement of the ruins and cities and rivers and mountains relative to each other across the Yucatan Peninsula seemed very accurate, from what she could remember. Even the mound within which she was standing was indicated on the map by a small triangle with a circle around it, a small distance southeast of Uxmal.

As she ran her fingers over the map, she noticed that a marker near the coast directly north of the city complex of La Venta was marked on the map. It was a small but noticeable square with a line drawn below it, but she didn't remember ever having seen or heard about a site in that location. The marker was right on the coastline, at a distance of what she estimated was perhaps ten or fifteen kilometres north of La Venta. All the other sites that she knew of were exactly where she would have expected to find them, but this little square caught her eye as well as her imagination. Was it an undiscovered mound similar to this one?

She stepped back a few meters to assure herself that she hadn't missed anything else, but after scanning the entire map, she concluded that the only anomaly compared with modern maps, was the marker on the coast. She reached into their rucksack and pulled out a camera. She stepped back another few steps towards the centre of the room, making sure to stand directly in front of the map so that the proportions of the picture would not get distorted. The map was bound to be at least a little bit off, so she couldn't afford to introduce any more errors if she was ever going to find whatever was at that marker.

After making a few rounds in the room taking snapshots of practically everything she saw, she walked back to the centre and climbed up onto the stone head. She had to place her right foot in the left eye of the chiselled face, which made her feel strangely uneasy and made her think about the curses that had come down on Egyptian explorers of the graves of kings. She quickly leapt to the top of the head and then began climbing towards the bright opening above her.

Sweating and panting, Fiona appeared on the surface of the mound. She had to squint as her eyes struggled to accustom themselves to the bright sunlight again. As she held on to the pole placed across the hole, Andrew came over, taking her hand and pulling her up and out of the hole.

'You got a couple of photos, did you?'

'Yes. Did you notice the map on one of the walls?' she said as she brushed the dirt from her clothes.

'Yes. It was Mexico, wasn't it?'

'Well, you could say that. What it actually showed was the Olmec Empire as it looked in the heyday of their civilisation. But that wasn't the most interesting bit. What struck me was that everything was so accurate. It is almost as if they had an aeroplane or some other way of seeing everything from up high. How else could they have drawn such a detailed and accurate map?'

'Planes?' said Andrew sceptically.

Knowing that it was a lost cause, Fiona didn't push it any further. She knew that when it came to alternative theories, Andrew was a sceptic, to put it mildly. But she had decided not to rule anything out just because it went against conventional wisdom.

'Well, regardless of how they managed to draw the map,' she said, 'there was one thing that seemed peculiar about it.'

'What, apart from the fact that it was on a wall in a room inside a mound deep in the jungle?' grinned Andrew.

'Yes,' smiled Fiona overbearingly. 'Apart from all those things, I noticed that every significant landmark was on it, except for one.'

'Where was that?'

'North of the site of La Venta that I told you about. I'm thinking perhaps it hasn't yet been discovered.'

'Do you think we can find it?' asked Andrew and began packing up their equipment.

'I'm not sure. But I've taken a few pictures of the map, and I'm hoping to be able to figure out approximately where this site might be.'

'What do you think we ought to do about this opening?' said Andrew and pointed to the gaping hole they had made in the ceiling of the structure.

'We should probably cover it up. I'm not sure the interior can handle being exposed to the elements. The map certainly can't. I think we need to try to leave it as we found it, as best we can. Once this is all over, we can contact the authorities.'

'Alright,' said Andrew. 'But first I need something to eat.'

'I can't wait to get back to the hotel tonight for a shower,' said Fiona and sat down with her water bottle.

'It's 4:30 now,' said Andrew looking at his wristwatch. 'We are not going back today.'

'We are not?' asked Fiona surprised. 'Why not?'

'Covering this thing up is going to take at least an hour, and then we have to walk back to Uxmal through the jungle. That'll take at least another two hours, possibly more since we are more tired than on the way out here. By then it'll be dark under the jungle canopy, and if there's one thing you don't want to do, it's to move about in the jungle at night.'

'Why not? Can't we just use our flashlights?'

'We could, but that might provoke a predator into attacking us, or we might step on something we couldn't spot in the dark, like a snake or something, and then we could be in real trouble. Most of the animals that live here only come out at night, including pumas, so we don't want to get in their way. And just the fact that we would have to move through the thicket in the dark will add several hours to the time it would take during the day.'

'Christ,' said Fiona unsettled. 'You are sure about this, aren't you?'

'Yep. It will be much safer to head back tomorrow.'

'Alright then. I guess we have to unpack the tent, then.'

'Yes. But let's cover this up first.'

'You did mark it on that GPS of yours, didn't you?'

'Yes. Don't worry,' said Andrew and flipped the loose stone slab over and pushed it back into place. 'We'll be able to find our way back here, if that's what you were worried about.'

'Good,' smiled Fiona cunningly. 'I want to be able to come back here on a real expedition before too long, and do some real work on this site.'

'That shouldn't be a problem,' said Andrew, as he started covering the stone surface with the soil they had removed just a few hours earlier. 'I don't think anyone is going to trip over this place.'

'I certainly hope not,' said Fiona and joined him.

When they were done levelling the soil over the top of the mound, they walked around on top of the loose soil for a few minutes to make it settle into place. They had covered the hole with Andrew's raincoat and then buried it under a thicker layer of dirt and covered that with leaves. Fiona had been concerned that a drastic change in humidity, possibly brought on by heavy rain, might speed up the erosion of the room's interior, some of which was already quite brittle and frail, in particular the map that was painted in the wall.

After the job was complete, the sun was beginning to approach the horizon, and so the trees surrounding the clearing were casting ever longer shadows across the mound. It was now just after six o'clock in the evening and the temperature was dropping rapidly. As a test, Andrew ran his hand through some of the thick tall grass on the side of the clearing that had entered into shade first that afternoon. As expected, it was already becoming moist from the condensation of water from the humid air, and he decided that they'd better set up camp right away. During the night the temperature would probably dip below ten degrees Celsius, and he wanted to get the tent set up before it got too damp.

All their equipment was of excellent quality, and in addition to weighing very little, it hardly took up any space in their rucksacks since it could be packed very tightly into specially made bags and containers. Their tent was a basic two-person temperate climate tent, not designed to withstand the forces of nature, but then that was the idea. They were unlikely to be facing any severe weather, so weight and size had been the primary concern when Andrew bought it. They hadn't bothered with mats, since it was easy to construct some from grass and leaves from the jungle.

The tent was erected on top of the mound, and around the perimeter of the flattened top, and next to it, they quickly built a small fire to cook some food on. They made a small indentation in the soil and placed stones around the edge of it to absorb and store the radiated heat from the fire. Finding dry bark and wood to get the fire going was easy, and within half an hour the flames were licking the larger pieces of wood that they had been placed onto it.

When they had finished the camp and eaten their meal, which consisted of boiled rice, chicken soup, some fruit and a chocolate bar, the sun had disappeared below the horizon and darkness had quickly closed in on them. As they sat there in the orange light from the fire, they could hear the creatures of the night start to move around and call out to each other in the surrounding jungle. Andrew set up a long piece of string connected to an aluminium casserole, which hung precariously on a stick above a rock. If an animal touched the string, the casserole would fall onto the rock and make sufficient noise for them to wake up. Andrew hadn't been particularly worried by the prospect of wild animals attacking them while inside the tent, and the noise from the casserole was more likely to scare any animal away than to do anything else. But Fiona insisted that they make some type of warning system. Andrew didn't think it was of much use, particularly when considering that most of the animals that would be lurking around in the night had excellent night vision, and would probably spot the string right away. But the improvised alarm system was duly set up, and the casserole put in place on the stick.

Fiona sat for a moment, pondering when she might be able to come back here and claim the discovery properly.

'It's amazing how these people just wouldn't lay down and die,' she said.

'How do you mean?' asked Andrew, and took a sip from his coffee cup.

'Well, even in the face of the overwhelming power of the Europeans, their culture was never really trampled underfoot, in the same way it has happened in other places around the world where colonial powers made their mark. Just take such a thing as their religion. On the flight over here, I read that they are basically orthodox Christians like the conquistadors were, but there are still significant remnants of their old belief systems embedded into their religion and the way it is practised. I just think that's amazing.'

'I guess it's the old saying that you can kill a man, but you can't kill an idea. Same thing with democracy really. Once established it's damn difficult to tear down. If people have tasted democracy once, there's just no going back. Just look at Russia or China.'

'Are you religious?' asked Fiona and looked at Andrew inquisitively.

'No. Not at all. You?'

'I don't know. I guess I like the thought that someone is looking out for me. It's sort of comforting.'

'Yes, and that is actually exactly my problem with the whole thing,' said Andrew.

'How so?'

'Well, I probably have a bit of an unusual view on religion, I wish people would wake up and realise that there is just us here on this tiny blue planet. We are here by ourselves, at least on this planet, and we can't blame anyone but ourselves for what goes wrong, or for what goes right. We are responsible for what happens here, more than any other creatures on the face of the Earth. And we are ultimately responsible for ourselves and for each other, and in times of crisis, there is no God that will come down from the clouds to save us. It is up to us to take that responsibility into our own hands, and do what is right for us and for this planet.'

'But that leaves us all alone, doesn't it?'

'Yes. That's exactly right. And that's what I believe we really are. Us humans, I mean.'

'But don't you ever feel like asking God for help?'

'Yes, I did when I was a child. I guess it is always tempting to ask for help when things are really tough. But if you need help, you should be asking a human being, because there is no God. I often wonder what might happen someday if we make contact with another intelligent civilisation out there in space,' he said and looked up at the clear night sky and the gleaming river of stars that ran across it. 'I don't believe that we humans will be able to truly make progress for ourselves and for our world, until we have our own existence put into perspective.'

'Put in perspective, how? By aliens,' asked Fiona and smiled sceptically.

'Well, just think about it for a second. If an extraterrestrial presence made itself known in some way, perhaps through those ultra-long wave radio transmissions that can penetrate the universe at extreme distances, everything would change instantly. If that were to happen, I'll bet that we would very quickly stop hitting each other on the head with our little clubs, and start wondering if it might be our turn to be wiped out by something much bigger than ourselves. I'm convinced that in a situation like that, the human race would truly become as one, and that we would leave our differences aside. At least for a time. And depending on the timing of such first contact, it just might save us from ourselves. In a manner, I might add, that no religion has ever been able to do. I know I sound like a hippie, but this actually makes sense to me.'

'But would you be able to shun religion in a life-or-death situation, where people, as you probably know from experience, have a tendency to suddenly find God?'

'I've tried it. I've been tempted at times, but I have found that if I remained active, in the sense of making decisions and staying in control of my own life, even in a very literal sense, I have always come out on top. If I had resigned myself to a passive state, and assumed that God was in control, I would almost certainly have got myself killed.'

'Well, I am a bit out of my depth here,' smile Fiona and trembled slightly from the cold. 'I can't say that I've ever been in a life-or-death situation, so I can't really say anything qualified about this. But I suppose in a sense you are right. Anyway, I am pretty tired after today, so what do you say we go to sleep?'

'Sound's good,' said Andrew and finished his coffee. He then put some more wood onto the fire and scooped the glowing embers up around them so that it could sustain itself for the rest of the night. The two of them then crawled into the tent and slipped into their sleeping bags. Fiona had never slept out in the open before, and the sounds of animals all around her near and far made her uncomfortable. She didn't like the thought of animals moving around in the jungle just outside their tent. Without asking, she soon tucked herself in close to Andrew's body with her back towards his chest, and he offered an arm as her pillow and held her tight with the other.

As they lay there together like two spoons placed neatly one behind the other, Fiona felt safer than she had done in a long time. Andrew in turn realised how important it was for him to have someone to feel protective of, and how good it felt to be there for someone else. For most of his life, he'd had only himself to worry about and take care of, but perhaps he could get used to this.

Andrew's slow steady breathing had a calming effect on Fiona, and she soon slipped off into a deep sleep. After a few minutes she stirred as though about to awaken again, but she just gripped Andrew's hand tightly and then fell asleep again. Upon feeling her body relaxing and her limp hand lying softly in his palm, Andrew tucked the sleeping bag tightly around her body to prevent her from getting cold, and after a few minutes, he fell asleep as well.

NINETEEN

When the big white jeep with the oversized wheels finally returned to the hotel and Sterling and Keane stepped out, Kurt Hess breathed a heavy sigh of relief. He had feared that he had lost them completely. When they drove off the previous morning, he had not had enough of a warning from the concierge, even though the lazy little bastard had been paid handsomely to call him at the first sign of them leaving. His phone had rung just as they had made their way to the parking lot in front of the hotel, and by the time he had scrambled out of bed, put on some clothes and rushed out to his car, they had been long gone. He could have choked the little Mexican shit right there and then, but he had forced himself to calmly get in his car and drive towards Uxmal.

Having followed them out there the day before, he couldn't think of anywhere else for them to go, even if there were literally hundreds of big and small sites within a day's drive on the peninsula. He had sped after them, but by the time he made it to the ruins, he had to park the car well away from the parking lot so as not to make his arrival known in case they were actually there. He was afraid that Andrew might have recognised him from when he had stopped along with them in the small town on the way to from Mérida to Muna, or even worse, from Madalena on the Azores. That would have spelt trouble and would have left him with no alternative but to abort and travel back to Germany. The grand master would have been furious.

Now, as he watched the big soft tires screech to a halt in the dusty gravel, and the two of them get out of the jeep and walk towards the front door of the hotel, his spirits lifted and he felt hugely relieved. As far as he could see, their clothes seemed dirty from moving through the jungle, and if they had come straight back from the ruins of Uxmal, they must have been under way for many hours through the jungle. As far as he could tell, they weren't carrying anything except for their rucksacks, but they still just might have found something out there.

He had considered staging a theft from their rooms to look for anything they might have brought back but then decided to wait for a better opportunity. If he broke into both rooms, they would know that it wasn't just a burglar, and that would surely make them aware that someone was monitoring them. In addition, he didn't want to ruin any further plans they might have for additional excursions. Instead, he had walked past their rooms and, passing their doors, he had placed tiny plastic boxes in the top right corners on the two doors.

The boxes, which were the size of a small matchbox but much thinner, were the same dark brown colour as the doors themselves, and wouldn't be noticed in the dimly lit corridor unless someone was actually looking for them. One side of the box had an adhesive material placed around the edges, which made it stick very tightly to the door. At the centre of the box was a small sensor that worked on the same principle as a hydrophone. Instead of picking up sound waves, it sensed and amplified the tiny vibrations in the wooden door as people in the room spoke. The vibrations were then converted into a digital signal that was sent to a receiver in Hess' room where it was recorded.

★ ★ ★

Fiona returned to her room after having been out to buy a very detailed map of Central Mexico. Andrew was waiting for her, sitting in an armchair reading one of Fiona's books about the Olmecs.

'Have a look,' she said. 'As far as I can see, the closest town from the marker we discovered, is at least thirty kilometres away. There is a main road running between Coatzacoalcos by the sea in the West and Villahermosa further inland in the East, but there are hardly any settlements on the coast along that stretch. The area mainly consists of swamps and wet lands, but the coast itself is very rocky and difficult to traverse, so if we want to get out there, we'll need to go by boat.'

'Or by helicopter,' said Andrew and stooped over the map on the table. 'That is probably the most flexible solution. We can't be sure how close to the coast the site may be, but with a helicopter, we can search a large area quite quickly.'

'Great,' said Fiona. 'I want to get down there as soon as we can. I suggest we leave right now.'

'Now? We don't even know how to get there.'

'Leave that to me. I'll go down to the local travel agent and ask about flights. There are plenty of local and regional flights out of Mérida Airport.'

'Alright. How long will you be?'

'Half an hour,' said Fiona and shrugged.

'Ok. See you later.'

While Fiona was away, Andrew took the opportunity to call London and inform Colonel Strickland of their progress. The colonel told him that he was in the process of setting up a joint US-UK task force to handle the investigation. He also told him that significant progress had been made and that some important new information had come to light, but he declined to tell Andrew about it. He wanted to wait until he and Fiona got back to London. This was unusual of Strickland, but Andrew decided to leave it alone, and wait until they could meet again.

After Fiona returned to the room, they began packing her things.

'We are leaving now, I assume?' asked Andrew, as she ripped out her clothes from the closets and drawers and began stuffing them into her suitcase.

'Yes. Start packing,' she said, panting from her jog back from the travel agent. 'We have a flight in two hours and twenty-five minutes from Mérida. They told me that there is an air charter service in Coatzacoalcos, so we might be able to charter a helicopter there. It's called Mayan Air Ventures, would you believe.'

Andrew looked at his wristwatch. 'But it's at least an hour's drive to Mérida from here,' he exclaimed.

'I know,' said Fiona and spun round to face him. 'So, get packing! It was the only flight today. Alternatively, we could drive down there, but it would take us six or seven hours. Come on!'

'Alright,' said Andrew and left for his room where he packed all his belongings in less than five minutes.'

He was used to travelling light, and he hadn't even bothered to unpack all his things. Within ten minutes he was at the reception handing over his credit card and arranging for a taxi to meet them at the car rental shop in Mérida, so that they could get to the airport as quickly as possible. Fiona joined him a few minutes later dragging her suitcase behind her, visibly surprised that Andrew was already there.

'Ready to leave?' smiled Andrew calmly.

'Yes. Have you paid?' asked Fiona impatiently.

'Yes. I have.'

'Ok. Let's go, let's go,' she said and started out the door to the parking lot.

Andrew placed their luggage in the back of the jeep, climbed up and started the engine. He then backed out into the road, put the car into first gear, and then they were off to Mérida. Andrew didn't know what the speed limit was, or if there even was one, but he fed the engine plenty of fuel, making the jeep virtually fly across the uneven road. Despite its high centre of gravity, the jeep handled very well even in tight corners. As Fiona held on to the door to steady herself, she kept looking at her watch.

Less than fifty minutes later, they pulled into the parking lot at the car rental shop in Mérida. As arranged, a taxi was waiting for them, and they were able to leave for the airport just a few minutes later. In the end, they arrived in plenty of time, and since the check-in and security procedures took only ten minutes, they were able to walk calmly to the gate to board the plane.

★ ★ ★

Timothy Jenkins was going through the results from the latest analysis based on transactions from British banks via First National Bank to accounts in Russia. He was employed in the UK's Terrorist Finance Tracking Program, and was currently trying to extract some sort of pattern from the fund flow data in front of him.

He had begun his career many years ago in this unusual line of work, as a controller in the fraud department of Barclays Bank in London. Living in Essex, he would take the train to work each morning, and then sit down at his desk to try to catch people who attempted to engage in credit card fraud against the bank. It was a laborious process, and mostly involved going over endless lengths of printouts from accounts that had attracted the suspicion of one of the bank employees in one of the branches. It was hopelessly slow, and gradually Timothy had on his own initiative begun using computers to match and search for suspicious transactions.

At first, it had involved simply checking the validity and history of individual accounts, to see if one account tended to either transfer money to or receive money from accounts that only existed for a short period of time. That wasn't necessarily a sign that something illegal was going on, but it had actually caught a few of the most amateurish attempts at money laundering for the Russian Mafia, which ran an extensive network of prostitution in the Greater London area.

It was still an arduous process, not least because even quite powerful computers took a long time to analyse all the transactions that needed to be examined. In fact, Timothy's efforts only covered a small part of the total amount of accounts investigated, but his approach had proved its potential.

Gradually, Jenkins had improved his techniques, and when he had eventually been assigned a programmer, whose work Timothy could manage as he saw fit, things had really begun to move quickly. Within a month, they had devised a search algorithm that was able to trace individual money flows through several accounts using a highly sophisticated system, that simply attempted to net out all the amounts transferred from one set of accounts to another. It was impossible to account for every single pound or dollar, since there was a large number of accounts in other banks that he didn't have access to. That was a significant amount of 'unknowns', but it had still enabled him to identify a number of people who tried to commit fraud or launder money in a multitude of ways.

One day, he had been called into his section head's office and been told that he was to be asked to leave for another job. At first, he had been shocked, since he thought that everything was going so well, but then he had learned that MI5 had expressed an interest in him, and that they thought he might fit perfectly into a new team that was in the process of being set up. Exactly how they had obtained information about him to make such a conclusion he didn't know, but then of course, they were an intelligence agency. He suspected that his rather posh boss at Barclay's had probably gone to university with one of the head spooks at MI5.

After his first meeting at MI5 headquarters, he had become convinced that what was being offered to him was too interesting to turn down. He would become the head of a team of four, whose task it would be to develop and implement new types of techniques to trace and identify money transfers between suspected terrorist groups around the world, using whatever means he thought necessary. He would be given absolute freedom to buy equipment and develop new techniques as he saw fit, and in addition, he would be responsible for establishing a working relationship with their US counterpart.

His fellow workers at Barclays were told that he was leaving for an analyst position at a brokerage house, and apparently nobody at the office thought that such a thing was unlikely, so they had all accepted the cover story. Within a week he was sitting in a comfortable office with a nice view of the Thames, and had started to interview people for the three other positions. He knew exactly what he needed in terms of the qualifications and competencies he wanted to bring to the team. Three weeks later the team had been fully staffed, and they had immediately set to work.

The starting point of their enterprise was basically an improvement of the model he had devised at Barclays, except they were now able to gain access to almost every account in any bank in the United States, Europe, most of Asia and many other countries around the globe. This enabled them to significantly shrink the amount of 'unknowns' the algorithm had had to work with, making it much easier to identify, track and characterise almost any flow of money, even if it went through several banks and shell companies. The project was now up and running, and additional computing capacity was constantly being brought online to aid in the endless amount of number crunching that needed to be done.

Two weeks earlier he had been given just one account number from a person about whom he knew basically nothing, except that he had been arrested in Dortmund in Germany on drug smuggling charges. Within hours, they had produced a list of significant amounts of money transferred to and from other affiliated accounts in other banks, and one of those had gone through an account in Switzerland, where it had facilitated the purchase of a salvage ship from a salvage company in Rotterdam that was going out of business. Most people seemed to believe that Swiss accounts were completely secret and sealed from any intrusion, but with the threat of international terrorism rising, and new legislation being enacted to combat it, no bank wanted to stand in the way of any investigation, for fear of being accused of colluding with terrorists.

This effectively meant that Jenkins had access to any account in any bank anywhere in Switzerland. This had proved valuable on several occasions since even the criminals apparently still believed that a money-laundering enterprise and a numbered account in Switzerland would be enough to cover their tracks. But that wasn't the case anymore, and after the purchase of the salvage ship had been flagged inside MI5, he had been instructed to focus on that particular money trail, and on any others connected to it.

Now, just over a week after setting to work on that particular project, he had uncovered what appeared to be a significant set of interrelated money transactions or Green Links as they called them. By going back through the history of the account of the man arrested in Germany, he had discovered that fairly large sums of money had been deposited there from a range of sources, whose endpoints were difficult to identify. But the team had been able to determine that those sources had also transferred money to several other individuals all over the world in a number of countries. One of those other individuals had immediately been flagged by a monitoring system within the algorithm, that interfaced with the CIA's database containing the identities of people who in some form or another were considered potential threats to the United States of America.

The man's real name was Sergei Ivanov, but he had a number of aliases and an even larger number of bank accounts. The CIA had long believed that he might be involved with one or more terrorist organisations, but they hadn't been able to prove anything. He had been, and still was a brilliant scientist, but his lavish international lifestyle seemed difficult to reconcile with his previous salary levels.

Jenkins felt that he might have discovered the source of Ivanov's funds, or at least come closer to doing so. The fact that the accounts from which money was transferred to him, had also transferred money to the man in the jail cell in Dortmund, made for an even stronger case. Jenkins started writing up a report, detailing the Green Links from the Russian to the chap in Germany, to the salvage ship and ultimately to the elusive original source. This might prove useful to the higher-ups.

★ ★ ★

Less than two hours later the twin-engine turbo-prop plane touched down at the small airport outside Coatzacoalcos in central Mexico, right on the coast facing Campeche Bay. Fiona had used the time on the plane to try to pinpoint the exact location on her newly purchased map, where they might be able to find the site indicated by the marker in the map room at Uxmal. There was a ten or fifteen kilometre stretch of swamp and wilderness between the ruin complex of La Venta to the east of Coatzacoalcos, and the rocky coastline to the north of it. It should have been straightforward since on the photograph she had taken of the map on the wall, the square lay directly north of La Venta, but it seemed to be too far away, judging by the modern maps. If the ancient map was correct, then whatever it was would be either right on the coastline or actually some way out to sea. This seemed odd to her, although she knew that the Mayans had built coastal forts, most famously at Tulum.

The Tulum site had showed archaeologists that the Mayans were a seafaring culture, but the actual layout of the fort had also demonstrated that they were very proficient in astronomy and celestial navigation. From writings found at the site, it was known that they also practised maritime trade and possibly even weather forecasting from this fort. Some researchers even believe that the fort was used as a lighthouse for very large seagoing canoes, indicating extensive naval activities in the region at that time.

Tulum was believed to have risen to prominence around 1200 AD, which was much later than the original Olmec civilisation, but there was no reason why the Olmecs shouldn't also have been seafarers and built similar forts on the coastline. Tulum was inhabited right up until the Conquistadors arrived, and so it was probably one of the first places where the Mayans encountered the invaders from across the sea.

Fiona discussed this with Andrew, and they concluded that they just had to go out there and see for themselves. The map might be somewhat inaccurate even though Fiona had been unable to discover any other errors, so they would have to fly over the area for a closer look. As they exited the airport, they were swamped by a hoard of young boys holding signs with the names of hotels and resorts. Fiona declined politely since she had already arranged for a place to stay. It was an old Spanish mansion near the harbour, where they shared a two-bedroom apartment on the second floor with a porch and a view of the harbour area. There were quite a lot of tourists walking along the streets and on the promenade below them, but as they had learned in Uxmal, once one got just a little bit away from the tourist centres, there was often not a soul in sight. Fiona felt sure that this would be the case where they were going as well, simply because it was so far away from any roads, and because the rocky terrain was so challenging to traverse.

While she sat down with a drink on the porch overlooking the harbour, Andrew called the air charter company Mayan Air Ventures, and asked about the possibility of chartering a helicopter for the next day, but it turned out that Mayan Air Ventures didn't have any helicopters, and apparently didn't know if there even were any in the area at all. But they did have something else that Andrew thought they could use. He arranged to meet with the owner the next morning.

'Any luck?' asked Fiona as Andrew emerged on the porch holding a glass of cool white wine.

'They don't have helicopters, so I've arranged for us to charter a small plane instead. They'll have it ready for us tomorrow morning at nine.'

'A plane? But how are we going to land anywhere?'

'The plane has pontoons instead of wheels. Apparently, the air charter service is right next to a canal that used to transport goods further inland, but now they use it as their landing strip.'

'That should be interesting,' lied Fiona and tried to imagine what the plane might look like. She had gotten herself used to flying large passenger planes again, but she had never liked small planes. They seemed so flimsy and frail to her, and she found herself hoping that the winds would be mild the next day so they would not get thrown about in the sky.

The two of them spent the evening exploring the narrow streets of the city of Coatzacoalcos, taking in the sights and sounds of the old part of town. There were still many houses there from the seventeenth and eighteenth centuries. They had dinner at a local restaurant that exclusively served fish and other sea creatures landed on the harbour only meters away. After an excellent dinner and a bottle of local wine, they walked back to the hotel.

★ ★ ★

Leaving for the bank, Ludvig Bauer felt the responsibility weighing heavily on him. Along with the parliamentarian, he would place the two triangles in a safe deposit box in one of the oldest and most renowned banks in all of Austria. Something like this had never been done before, and as far as he knew, two pieces of the medallion had not been this close to each other for more than sixty years.

For the Thule Society it had been a strict policy to keep them apart since before the Second World War when they had first been discovered. For its own safety, the society had until now insisted on the triangles being kept apart until the day when they had all been uncovered. Then they would be brought together and finally, the medallion would be able to show them the way to Thule.

Bauer walked as casually as he could along the street towards the bank where he had arranged to meet with a senior manager. Being the messenger of a Member of Parliament had its advantages. He could not have known that he was being followed, as he and every other known affiliate of the Thule Society had been for several days now. He felt a slight tingling in his right hand as he carried the ordinary-looking briefcase along with him. He might be imagining things, but he could have sworn that there was some strange energy emanating from the two triangles as they lay there close to each other inside the briefcase.

When he reached the entrance to the bank, the senior manager was already waiting for him, and after shaking hands and exchanging the usual pleasantries, they proceeded down into the vault that was located deep under the building in the basement. Bauer had brought the key that had been given to him by the honourable member of parliament, and after the manager had left him alone for the agreed-upon five minutes, he placed the briefcase on top of a polished steel table and entered the combination into the lock.

The lock flipped open, and he lifted the top of the briefcase to reveal two small wooden boxes. He stood motionless for a few seconds and then decided to have a look. He might never get the chance again. In fact, no one might ever get to see them again, unless the two remaining triangles could be located and acquired. Simultaneously he lifted the lids off the two wooden boxes, and there they lay. Gleaming and sparkling in the light from the many spotlights in the ceiling of the vault, the two triangles were truly a magnificent sight to behold. He looked from one to the other to see how they might fit together, and for an instant, he was tempted to pick them up and see if he could assemble them, but he fought off the urge to do so and placed the lids back on the wooden boxes. He then took out his key and placed it in the keyhole, turned it once and then opened safety deposit box #263.

★ ★ ★

The next morning Kurt Hess left for Mayan Air Ventures in his rented car and soon found the company just off the main road to Villahermosa. During the previous evening, he had dyed his hair black, and he hoped that this and a set of dark sunglasses would make him sufficiently difficult to recognise. He hadn't had time to put on a proper disguise, so he needed a bit of luck to be able to pull this off. The stakes were high, but he couldn't afford to lose track of them again. The charter service lay in what could best be described as an industrial area, and as he drove his car across the small bridge over the canal that was used as a landing strip, he could see some people walking in and out of the main hangar, where a couple of single-engine aircraft were parked.

He parked his car next to a group of other cars behind the hangar building and got out. Walking towards the hangar, he spotted what appeared to be a pilot walking back from a Cessna single-engine aeroplane that floated calmly on its pontoons in the canal about two hundred meters away. As the pilot came closer, Kurt raised his hand and waved.

'Hey there,' he said, trying to put on an American accent.

'Good morning,' said the pilot with a genuine mid-western accent.

'Just came back, did you?' asked Hess.

'No, but I'm leaving in about half an hour,' he said as they walked towards the hangar building. 'A couple of tourists want to see the coastline.'

'You probably get those a lot,' said Hess, while his eyes were discretely scanning the area around him to see if anyone else was in sight. He couldn't spot anyone else.

'No, not really,' responded the pilot. 'Most people want to fly over the ruins of La Venta or the city, but these two want to see the coastline. I guess it takes all sorts.'

'How many tourists do you fly out with each day?' asked Hess and put his right hand in his pocket.

'Depends,' said the pilot. 'Sometimes none. Sometimes four sets of people.'

'Is there a lot of paperwork that goes along with that?'

'No, not really. They just show up, pay with cash, and then we take them wherever they want to go. Are you thinking of flying somewhere?'

'I might be,' shrugged Hess casually. 'Perhaps just a quick tour round La Venta. But I guess you're all set to take someone else now, right?'

'Yep. I'm basically just waiting for the two of them to arrive. Just gotta sign my name in the logbook, and then I'll go and wait in the plane until they get here. You would be amazed at the quality of music systems they put in them these days,' grinned the pilot, and then he entered the hangar office building, which seemed to be empty of other people.

'Alright,' said Hess. 'Have a nice flight.'

After the pilot had entered the building, Hess produced a small steel wire from his right pocket and held it in his right hand behind his back. As the pilot re-emerged and started walking back towards the plane, he swiftly moved up behind him, and in a flash, he had put the steel wire around the pilot's neck and tightened it as hard as he could.

Immediately the wire cut into the man's neck and windpipe, and his attempts at screaming were reduced to disturbing hissing and gurgling noises. As Hess quickly pulled the pilot backwards towards the hangar and out of view of passing cars, the man started flailing his arms as he desperately tried to turn around to reach for Hess, but it was all to no avail. He fell backwards, and instantly Hess was on top of him tightening the wire even more, and as blood appeared where it was cutting through the pilot's skin, the wire completely shut off his ability to breathe. A few seconds later, his desperate bulging eyes just stared into empty space, and his arms flopped down next to his dead body.

Hess waited another ten seconds before loosening the wire, and as he looked up to see if he had been spotted, he quickly dragged the body towards a small maintenance shed. Once inside, he stripped him of his Mayan Air Ventures pilot's uniform, and put it on himself. He found a large plastic bag on the floor of the shed and stuffed the dead pilot into it. He stuck his head outside to check if anyone was out there, and then dragged the body swiftly towards a garbage container and dumped it in there. He then jogged back over to the point where he had initially attacked his victim. The whole procedure had taken less than five minutes, and nobody in the hangar had apparently noticed anything.

He began walking calmly towards the small aeroplane that waited a couple of hundred meters away. It was an all-metal, single-engine Cessna Skyhawk SP aircraft with a high-wing monoplane and room for four people: Two crew and two passengers, plus luggage. It was about nine metres long and eleven metres from wingtip to wingtip, and with its slightly modified Textron Lycoming engine delivering around 215 horsepower, it was capable of a cruising speed of 240 kilometres per hour, and in its current configuration with a set of pontoons attached to the undercarriage, it was able to take off on less than four hundred meters of water. It was in a white livery with a blue ribbon running from front to back, on which was written Mayan Air Ventures in big yellow letters.

With a confident smile, Hess strode over to the aircraft, crossed the jetty, got inside and switched on the engine and the music system.

At that moment, a taxi arrived and crossed the bridge to the hangar area. It parked next to the office building with the big sign above it, and two people got out. Seeing that it was a man and a woman, Hess' heart began to race. This was it. After a few minutes inside the building, they reappeared and started walking towards him. He adjusted his sunglasses and took a deep breath and then exhaled slowly. He had to stay cool.

Upon reaching the aircraft, Andrew and Fiona greeted the pilot with a wave, and he waved back at them. They opened the passenger door and climbed up into the aircraft.

'Hello there,' said Andrew and reached out to shake the pilot's hand. 'My name is William Taggart, and this here is my wife, Louise.'

Fiona smiled politely and sat back in the seat behind the pilot.

Hess had made sure to read the nametag on his uniform. 'My name is John. I'll be your pilot for today.'

'Excellent,' said Andrew and made himself comfortable. 'Let's get underway. I'll explain where we are going after we've taken off.'

'Alright,' said Hess and pulled on the small rope that had tied the plane to the jetty. The knot loosened, and then he gently pushed the throttle forward. The engine noise increased, and the plane began moving forward faster and faster along the canal. Soon the pontoons were just skimming across the surface of the water. At just over a hundred kilometres per hour, Hess pulled back slightly on the stick, and slowly and gracefully the aircraft lifted itself from the water and started accelerating as it climbed slowly into the air.

When they had reached a speed of 150 kilometres per hour, Hess retracted the flaps, banked the aircraft left and turned towards the east along the coast. The weather was excellent for flying. It was a clear blue sky with a few wispy clouds high above them, and winds were very weak and steady. As Coatzacoalcos disappeared behind them and to the right, they began looking out across the landscape passing beneath them. Close to the town, there were a couple of roads leading out to a few beaches to the east. Those quickly turned into narrow dirt roads winding their way through the terrain, and after just fifteen minutes of flying, there was no sign of buildings or people anywhere.

After twenty minutes they were about ten kilometres from Coatzacoalcos, and Andrew instructed the pilot to slow down. He wanted to fly no higher than a hundred meters above the ground and to try to follow the coastline as precisely as he could. In a straight line the coastline that they wanted to examine was a stretch of approximately five kilometres directly north of La Venta, but because of the many lagoons and inlets, the flight was somewhat longer than that. The water was an amazing azure colour and as clear as glass, and in several places, the waves pounded tall black rocks that towered above the water.

On and immediately behind the rocks that faced the sea, there was a lush green thicket of trees and bushes, sometimes no taller than a few meters and sometimes as tall as ten meters. Andrew and Fiona sat next to the windows on either side of the aircraft, scouting for any sign of a ruin of a coastal fort or some other structure, but they spotted none. The rocky coastline looked treacherous and extremely difficult to access on foot, and there probably hadn't been anyone in the area for years.

They eventually passed over the spot that Fiona had thought would be the most likely place to find something. It was a beautiful lagoon about a couple of hundred meters wide behind a coral reef, and it looked to have been the perfect natural port. But at the far end of the lagoon on the rocks above the breaking waves, there was no sign of anything made by humans. Just more rocks and bushes.

They flew on for a few more kilometres, but by then they were so far from the area of interest, that Fiona told the pilot to turn around and go back for another pass. As they came back over the lagoon again, Fiona strained her eyes to spot anything that might have been man-made, but there was nothing there except for large black volcanic rocks towering three meters above the water. Fiona was just about to sit back in her seat when something caught her eye. In the water directly below the sheer rocks, was a dark patch that at first looked like a shadow. But it was much too dark for that, and without taking her eyes off it she patted Andrew on the shoulder and then pointed to the spot below the water about a hundred meters away.

'Look!' she said quickly. 'Look down there.'

'What is it?' asked Andrew.

'Look at the shadow down there. It's got to be an underwater cave of some sort.'

Andrew strained his eyes to see, but by then the aeroplane had passed the lagoon, and the place where the water met the rocks was now out of sight.

'Turn back,' said Fiona to Hess, who was by now feeling quite relaxed, both with the handling of the aircraft and with posing as a pilot of a charter plane.

He turned the plane around again and came in slow for a third pass directly over the rocks.

'Do you see it now?' asked Fiona and looked at Andrew.

'Yes. I see it,' he said. 'Do you think it is a cave?'

'It has to be,' she responded. 'Let's set her down here in the lagoon. She leaned forward to make sure the pilot could hear what she said. 'Set her down in this lagoon. We need to take a look at the rocks below.'

Hess gave her a thumbs up and then sent the plane swooping down over the lagoon while pulling back on the throttle and lowering the flaps. The engine was brought back to idle and as the aeroplane glided gracefully towards the water, its airspeed dropped quickly and a minute later the pontoons cut through the tops of the waves in the lagoon. Because a reef was protecting the lagoon from the surf in Campeche Bay, there were only small shallow waves inside the lagoon, and as the plane set down on the water, it reduced its speed smoothly, and it ended up drifting slowly forward due to its momentum.

'I suppose you have a dinghy on board?' Andrew asked the pilot.

'Uhm...,' Hess hesitated and looked over his shoulder into the back of the aircraft, and at that moment Andrew felt he recognised the man from somewhere, but he couldn't put his finger on it.

'Try that compartment,' said Hess and pointed to a storage compartment behind the passenger seats. 'There might be one in there. I've never had to use one before.'

Andrew got up, crawled over his seat to the compartment and opened it. Inside was a range of equipment, including first aid kits, shovels, ropes, flashlight, emergency flares and even some military field rations that could probably sustain them for a few days if necessary. In the back of the compartment was an orange nylon sack shaped like a rolled-up sleeping bag.

'Here it is,' said Andrew and pulled it out. 'This'll do just fine.'

It was similar to some of the inflatable dinghies they had used in the SAS for covert beach landings deep in enemy territory, except that this dinghy was orange. It weighed about thirty kilos including the pressurised air canister, so he dragged it behind him over to the right passenger door which he opened. Stepping out onto the pontoon was a strange feeling. Aeroplanes were not really supposed to be bobbing along on the water, but this one did, and it seemed very unnatural to him.

Andrew knelt down and placed the orange sausage gently in the water, found the cord and then ripped the pin from the air canister. Immediately the dinghy began to fill up with compressed air, and soon it was floating nicely along the side of the aircraft's right pontoon.

'Get the oars, will you?' he said to Fiona.

Fiona handed him two small oars made from hard plastic, which wouldn't do much good if they had been drifting at sea, but for this purpose, they were more than adequate.

'Are you coming?' asked Andrew impatiently.

'Right,' said Fiona. 'I'll be right there.'

She decided to leave her bag in the plane and made her way out and down onto the pontoon. Andrew was already sitting in the dinghy, holding on to the pontoon with one hand to make sure it didn't drift away. There was hardly any wind, so the plane was in no danger of drifting towards the rocks more than a hundred meters away.

'Just wait here please,' Andrew shouted at the pilot.

'Ok,' Hess shouted back and waived to Andrew.

Fiona sat down, and a few minutes later, Andrew had taken them halfway to the sheer rock face that lay at the azure end of the lagoon. Some five meters below them on the bottom of the lagoon, they could see a bright carpet of white sand dotted with a few rocks here and there, and through the calm surface, they could clearly see fish and crabs near the bottom.

As they neared the rocks, the water became only a few meters deep, but that was not what Fiona was paying attention to. She had her gaze fixed at the dark hole in the rock face under the water. As they approached, it seemed to become much bigger, and Fiona's mind was racing to try to determine whether it was a natural cave, or made by human hands. A few metres from the rock face, Andrew stopped rowing and let the dinghy glide slowly towards it.

'Would you like to jump in, or shall I?' asked Andrew.

'Be my guest,' said Fiona and smiled.

Andrew stripped off his shirt and trousers and now sat in the dinghy with only his boxer shorts on.

'Don't get all embarrassed now,' he grinned and looked at Fiona.

'I won't,' she said indifferently. 'I've seen a naked man before.'

'Yes. I'm sure you have,' said Andrew and winked at her. Then he jumped headfirst into the water. When he reappeared, he swam back over to the dinghy and grabbed onto the side of it. 'I'll swim in and see how far back it goes, and then I'll come back, Ok? Just a quick recon mission.'

'Right,' nodded Fiona. 'I'll be waiting right here.'

'Ok. See you in a bit.'

And with that Andrew took a couple of deep breaths in quick succession, and then dove down towards the hole. Located almost at the sandy bottom of the lagoon, it was about three meters across, and from the surface, it appeared a lot darker than the surrounding rock. As Andrew came closer, he could see that it extended several metres into the rock face, but the most noticeable feature was its shape. The closer he got, the more it became clear to him that the opening in the rock face was completely square, and he immediately knew that it had to be manmade.

A few fish scurried away and out into the lagoon in astonishment at seeing the big creature swim into the opening, and as Andrew swam deeper into the hole, he could see that it extended about five meters horizontally into the rock face, and then seemed to turn upwards slightly. After a few more meters, he was running out of air and was just about to turn and swim back to the dinghy, when he spotted something odd. It was quite dark in the opening, but from the sandy bottom deep in the underwater corridor, there appeared to be a set of neatly made steps chiselled into the rock. At the top of the steps, he could see what appeared to be a pond of quicksilver floating along the ceiling up ahead, but he knew that it was in fact just an air pocket under the ceiling of the tunnel, and so he decided to swim up to it and take a breath of air.

His first thought was that there might have been divers in there before him and that their exhaled air had gathered in a pocket under the ceiling, but the air pocket was much too big for that. As he approached it, the light became dimmer and he had to move slowly upwards since he didn't want to bump his head on any rocks that might be just above the surface.

As his head broke through the surface and he exhaled, he was immediately struck by the sound it produced. He couldn't see anything in the dark but it was instantly clear to him that he was in a large room. The sound of his violent exhalation reverberated around him and his initial thought was that he had to be in a large cave of some sort. However, it was pitch black around him, and he couldn't see a thing. He shouted a few times to try to gauge the size of the space he was in. It was definitely big. The question was: Was it a natural cave, or was it made by someone? After a few seconds, he decided to swim back. This was a lot easier since all he had to do was follow the light from the white sandy bottom of the lagoon around fifteen meters away.

When he reappeared next to the dinghy and looked up at Fiona, he thought she looked upset. 'What the hell were you doing down there?' she asked angrily.

'What do you mean?' asked Andrew as he clung to the dinghy catching his breath.

'I mean, you were down there for almost five minutes. Are you crazy? How could you hold your breath for that long? I thought you had drowned!'

'Relax,' panted Andrew. 'I've found a cave.'

'What? Down there under the water?'

'No. This opening leads to a cave higher up inside those rocks,' he said and pointed to the rock face rising above them.

'Really? Well, in that case, I want to go down and have a look as well,' said Fiona determined.

'Fine, but we need a flashlight or something,' said Andrew as he clambered back up into the dinghy. 'There's hardly any light coming in from the lagoon, so it's pitch black in there. We'll have to row back to the plane first,' he continued and then grabbed the oars.

A few minutes later they reached the plane and floated alongside the pontoon again. Fiona climbed back up into the plane and into the back.

'We just need a flashlight,' she said to the pilot. 'My husband has found a cave, and he wants to go in there for a closer look.'

'Interesting,' said Hess, trying to sound as if he was just being polite.

Fiona grabbed a flashlight from the storage compartment and a transparent plastic bag, and then she climbed back down into the dinghy. A few minutes later the two of them were back next to the rock face. While Andrew had rowed the dinghy, Fiona had sealed the flashlight within the plastic bag, shielding it from the seawater. She put it down in the bottom of the dinghy and began to undress. Andrew pretended not to notice, but he couldn't stop his eyes from sweeping quickly across her body. When she had stripped down to only her red underwear, she grabbed the flashlight and looked up at Andrew. 'Are you ready,' she asked with a determined look on her face.

'Absolutely,' he said and nodded. 'Let's go.'

They both jumped over the side and let themselves float by the surface while hyperventilating in order to get as much air into their bloodstreams as possible. They exchanged looks to confirm that they were both ready, and then they dove down towards the bottom together. Fiona intentionally held back a little and let Andrew take the lead. He swam very determinedly down and into the opening, and within a minute he arrived in the cave with Fiona only a few seconds behind. He wiped the water from his eyes, slicked his hair back, and ever so slowly, his eyes began to get accustomed to the darkness.

At that moment Fiona emerged, and after a few seconds she switched on the flashlight. Several meters above them there was a rock ceiling with stalactites hanging down towards the surface of what appeared to be a small pond at one end of a large cave. The air was humid and stale, and it smelled slightly rotten. Only a few metres away Andrew spotted the steps.

'Over here,' he said and pointed towards it. 'There were some steps over this way. We can get up that way.'

They swam over and were able to walk up the steps from the water and into the centre of the cave. It initially looked a lot like most of the caves that are popular tourist attractions all over the world, but at the far end of it was a low tunnel that seemed to lead to another room beyond it. Fiona pointed the flashlight towards the small tunnel and tried to see what was on the other side, but the flashlight wasn't powerful enough.

'What do you suppose this is?' said Andrew.

'I don't know, but that tunnel sure isn't a naturally occurring thing,' she said and pointed ahead of them. 'Let's go through and see what's on the other side.'

'Be careful,' said Andrew. 'We have no idea what's in here.'

'Right,' said Fiona and began moving towards the tunnel.

The tunnel was only about a meter wide and less than one and a half meters tall, so they had to crouch down to move through it. Fiona went first with the flashlight pointed ahead of her, while Andrew followed, thinking that he would have liked to have some type of weapon with him, just in case. The tunnel was about five meters in length and on its sides were intricate patterns and motives chiselled into the rock. The imagery seemed similar to what Fiona had photographed inside the room in the mound near Uxmal.

As the tunnel ended, they were again able to stand up straight, but as Fiona's flashlight swept over the opposite wall just a few meters away, they were dumbfounded by the sight that met them. The whole of the opposite wall was one big map of much of the world, from what they could see. The Americas were depicted in astonishing detail but also the entire European and African coastlines were there, and at the bottom of the map was what was unmistakably the Antarctic. Fiona shone her light from one side of the map to the other, and slowly it began to sink in that this was probably as close to concrete evidence of an advanced ancient and global civilisation as they were likely to ever find.

'I am speechless,' said Fiona. 'This is fantastic.'

'That's probably an understatement,' said Andrew.

'What's that down there?' he said and pointed to what appeared to be a table of some sort at the base of the map.

'Perhaps it's some sort of altar or something,' replied Fiona.

'This place is spectacular and very well hidden. But why is the entrance underwater?'

'Well,' said Fiona. 'If this place is as old as I think it is, then the sea level would have been about a hundred meters lower back when it was originally constructed. So, the entrance would actually have been sitting in the side of a cliff facing the ocean. The coastline itself might have been several hundred meters away back then.'

'That certainly explains the steps that lead up here from the bottom of the lagoon.'

As they walked closer, it became clear that the table was actually part of the wall, and having been chiselled from the rock, it protruded out from the wall about a meter from the floor. Into the table was chiselled a small square basin about twenty centimetres deep, and lying inside it was a dark item about the size of a matchbox. But it wasn't square like a matchbox. It was a triangle. Fiona reached down and picked it up. It was surprisingly light and as Fiona turned it over in her hand, she rubbed the dirt off. It was some sort of metal, and the light from the flashlight reflected off it.

'Holy shit!' she exclaimed. 'I think this is it. This must be one of those triangles.'

Andrew stood next to her and leaned over to see. 'Look at those patterns here on its surface. Is it some kind of writing?'

'I don't know,' said Fiona. 'I've never seen anything like it. It could just be ornamental, but I actually doubt it.'

'Can I see it?' asked Andrew, and as Fiona gave it to him, she shone the flashlight over the map wall again.

'This is really amazing,' she said and looked at the area depicting the Antarctic region. There were no markings of any kind, and nothing pointing to any particular spot on the continent. In fact, there were no landmarks of any kind on the entire map. It showed the entire Atlantic Ocean and the continents that surround it, but no cities or ports were indicated.

'Look at these small features here,' said Andrew and pointed to one side of the triangle. 'The sides are shaped so that the other three pieces can lock into place.'

'Interesting how the basin was placed just under Antarctica,' said Fiona. 'You could take that as a sign that this thing actually would have led to the lost civilisation.'

'Didn't you say that all four triangles are needed for that?'

'Yes. But this place still seems to hint at the possibility that whoever built it, knew of another civilisation. In any event, it is clear that they had knowledge of the world that goes far beyond anything we have ever imagined before.'

'Not entirely,' said Kurt Hess with a smirk on his face. He had followed them into the cave and had silently slipped through the tunnel to the room holding the triangle.

Andrew and Fiona both spun around and looked at Hess in astonishment. The pilot was soaked, and he was holding a revolver in his hand and had switched on a flashlight as he began speaking.

'What you just worked out has been known to us for many years,' continued Hess. 'We just lacked the good fortune to find this place.'

'Who the hell are you?' sneered Andrew and looked at the pilot, his mind racing to think of a way to overpower him. 'And what do you want?'

'My name is Kurt Hess. You may have heard of my grandfather, Rudolph,' said the arrogant blond man, with poorly hidden pride. 'I have been sent here to retrieve this most significant artefact. So, what I want, is for you to hand me that triangle, and then I shall decide whether you deserve to die slowly or fast. Especially you Mr. Sterling. You've betrayed us, and you've betrayed your father.'

Andrew's eyes narrowed and locked onto Hess's face. *What!?*

'Oh,' said Fiona, sounding strangely calm, and sounding almost mocking. 'Hess. Wasn't he the loon who flew to Scotland late in the Second World War?'

Andrew was surprised by how cool Fiona appeared. It was as if she hadn't heard the man say that he was going to kill them. But Hess was clearly high on his perceived power over life and death, and blurting out his plans for the two of them was an obvious mistake. Fiona was already laying the groundwork for Andrew, by provoking the maniac, and it worked.

'Look,' said Hess angrily and pointed the gun at her face. 'Throw me the fucking triangle, or your brains will be dripping off that wall behind you.'

That seemed to scare Fiona sufficiently to make her hold up both of her hands and bow her head. 'Alright,' she said. 'I'll give it to you.'

She calmly lowered her hands again and then forcefully tossed the triangle up in the air towards the man in the pilot's uniform.

Unprepared for this sudden surrender of the artefact, Hess dropped the flashlight to catch the triangle. His eyes were completely fixed on it, and while it was still in the air, Andrew ripped the flashlight from Fiona's hand in a split second and hurled it at Hess' face.

Just as Hess caught the triangle, the flashlight struck him hard on the forehead causing it to break and turn off, and Hess staggered backwards a few steps while trying to keep his balance.

Still holding on to the triangle with one hand, he fired four shots randomly in the dark, hoping to hit them, but by then Andrew had crouched down and moved like a tiger in an arc to the side and around him.

Out of the corner of his eye, Hess saw movement and pointed his gun in that direction, but it was already too late. Andrew's fist slammed into his throat, and as he fell backwards with a choking sound, he dropped both the gun and the triangle onto the floor. The force of the blow had crushed his windpipe, and his desperate attempt to breathe only resulted in strange gurgling noises as blood began filling his throat. Andrew picked up the revolver and stood over him, as life slowly ebbed from his body.

'What the hell have you done?' shouted Fiona hysterically. 'Are you crazy? You've killed him!'

'I know,' said Andrew calmly. 'It was him or us. You know that, don't you?'

'Yes, but…' Fiona slumped down on the floor holding her head in her hands. 'I don't believe this. What is happening?'

'This chap was after the triangle and was prepared to kill us both to get it,' said Andrew. 'That's what's happening.'

Fiona looked up at Andrew who had knelt down to search the man. 'What are we going to do? Are we just going to leave him here?'

'I don't think it would be a good idea to bring him back to town, if that's what you are suggesting,' said Andrew matter of fact. 'My guess is that he was a lackey of the Thule Society, and it's probably best for us not to reveal that he has gone to meet his maker. Look, here's a hotel key ring, but it doesn't say which hotel.'

'I can't believe he was about to kill us for this little piece of metal,' said Fiona and shook her head. 'I don't know about you, but I'd really like to get out of here.'

'Are you sure there's nothing more for us to do?' asked Andrew.

Fiona thought it over silently for a few seconds. 'No,' she said and rose. 'This map is of no particular value right now. It's enough to know that it is here. We can always come back to it later if we need to.'

'I still think we should take some pictures,' insisted Andrew.

'Be my guest,' said Fiona, trembling from the burst of fear and excitement. 'You are welcome to go a get the camera. I'm not spending another minute in here.'

And with that, she picked up the flashlight and walked past the dead body of Kurt Hess into the tunnel leading to the cave on the other side. Andrew followed and decided to leave her be for a few minutes. Silently, they waded into the water and then dove to swim back out into the lagoon. The light in the clear azure water was overwhelming, and it was as pretty as any postcard down here. It was difficult to comprehend that the body of a dead man was lying just beyond the rock face towering over the dinghy. The setting was calm and peaceful, and as they rowed back towards the plane, a fishing boat, oblivious to the drama that had just unfolded, passed the lagoon a few hundred meters out to sea.

Fiona climbed up into the plane and handed Andrew the camera she had brought. Soon after, Andrew was rowing back towards the dark spot beneath the surface. He jumped into the water and emerged some ten minutes later with a wave to Fiona to indicate that he had gotten the pictures. Upon returning to the aeroplane, he climbed up next to Fiona and put his clothes on again.

'Any idea how to fly this thing?' asked Fiona.

'Well,' said Andrew. 'I've flown a few planes in my time, but it has been a while since I was last at the controls. I think we can manage though.'

'But what will we do when we get back to the landing strip? We can't just say that the pilot fell out of the aircraft.'

'No. We'll have to land away from the town, and then walk overland to the main road. And then I suggest we go back to our hotel and then get the hell out of here.'

'Sounds good to me,' nodded Fiona, who was still visibly shaken at having witnessed the killing of a human being.

'Alright,' said Andrew. 'Let's get this thing in the air.'

He pushed the button for engine start, and instantly the powerful engine sprang to life. Pushing the throttle forward a few notches, Andrew then stepped on the right rudder pedal causing the plane to move forward slowly while turning around to face the lagoon and the sea. He flipped the switch to extend the flaps, and then gradually pushed the throttle forward to maximum. The plane leapt forward through the water, and Andrew soon began pulling back slightly on the control stick to prevent the propeller from pulling the aeroplane onto the water and topple it over. They soon achieved take-off speed, and well before they reached the coral reefs that were shielding the lagoon from the sea, Andrew was able to pull back further on the stick and bring the plane into the air. As soon as the water let go of the pontoons, the airspeed climbed quickly and Andrew banked the plane gently to the left and headed along the coast towards Coatzacoalcos.

Visibly impressed with the way he had handled the aeroplane, Fiona took the opportunity to put on some dry clothes and then climbed into the back to place the rolled-up dinghy back in the storage compartment in the back of the plane. After just twenty minutes, they could see Coatzacoalcos in the distance, and Andrew dropped down closer to the water.

As Fiona looked out to the left at the cliffs and rock passing by, it felt like moving across the landscape by train, except this landscape was mostly water. As they reached a stretch of coastline with less rocks and tiny patches of sandy beaches, Andrew pulled back the throttle to idle and set the plane down. He steered towards a beach that looked to be around fifty meters long and maintained a speed of about twenty kilometres per hour. The pontoons hit the beach and the plane glided halfway up onto the sand. The waves still came up around the back end of the pontoons, but the plane was firmly planted in the white sand.

Andrew shut down the engine, and as they jumped out, both of them looked around for signs of anyone else that might be in the area, but they could see none. They quickly made their way up over the cliffs and headed inland, towards where they thought the main road was. Andrew had brought his GPS so they had a pretty good idea of how far it would be.

Half an hour later, they came across a small dirt road. It wasn't the main road that they had been looking for and it wasn't on the map, but it led towards Coatzacoalcos which was now less than two kilometres away. They walked briskly along the dirt road and soon reached the edge of town. Looking like a pair of tourists coming back from a hike in the rugged landscape, they wandered through the town towards their hotel, and as Andrew had suggested, they quickly packed and checked out. Fiona had the receptionist call the airport and inquire about flights to Mexico City, and it had turned out that there were plenty of seats available on the evening flight some four hours later. They then decided to also book flights back to Britain. It would mean a six-hour wait at the airport, but they both wanted to get going as soon as possible.

It turned out that the long wait gave them some much-needed rest. They were flying business class and took the opportunity to throw themselves into the soft furniture in the British Airways Business Lounge, where it was relatively quiet.

Fiona knew that bringing artefacts out of Mexico without authorisation was punishable by fines or even prison, so before they boarded the plane, she went into a souvenir shop and bought a heap of cheap copper jewellery that had been made to resemble original Mayan art. She also bought a small handbag for it all and put the triangle in there along with the jewellery. Apparently, that was enough to fool the man at the security checkpoint, because as he looked into the handbag, he just shook his head mumbling something unintelligible and let her pass.

Both of them slept for most of the flight to Heathrow, but Andrew also spent some time considering the possible implications of him having killed a man. Andrew wasn't sure whether to believe what the man had said about being Rudolph Hess' grandson, but he felt pretty sure that he was somehow affiliated with the Thule Society. And that meant that the Thule Society had found out who Andrew was, and that they weren't playing games now. This was deadly serious, and what made Andrew most uncomfortable was the fact that the now late Kurt Hess had mentioned his father, Charles. How did he even know of his father, who had been dead for over twenty years, and what had he meant by 'betrayal'?

TWENTY

Mohammed Yusef was sitting in his office, deep inside the mountain in the Syrian Desert, going over the lists of supplies that would be transported to them over the next week. Once each week a truck would bring them new supplies, both for their sustenance and for their work with the production of the pathogen.

From what he understood from Kashim Khan, work was now progressing more quickly than they had dared to hope only a few days earlier. Sergei Ivanov's visit had put things into perspective for them all, and they had realised that bickering amongst themselves would lead nowhere, and that what was required was a team effort. That same evening, they had all sat down together and discussed the meeting. Just the three of them, Khan, Rashid and himself. And each one of them, for their own reasons, had committed themselves to an all-out effort to meet the deadline and reach the goal they had set.

The team had also been a bit lucky, in the sense that one of Rashid's young apprentices had, in spite of the gruesome and spectacular death of one of his colleagues, displayed the focus and dedication to come up with a combined process for isolating and concentrating the pathogen. That had then cut close to a third off the previous production time, now actually placing them ahead of schedule. They had once more started to fill the little aluminium containers with small amounts of the bluish crystal bacteria, and as far as Yusef was informed, they were coming up on two thousand finished containers in total.

Even though he didn't need to look at it again, Yusef entered the password into the central computer system and pulled out the file that contained the list of all the foreign assets that would soon be employed in an attack that would shock the world and bring the West to its knees. The list was astonishingly long, but it revealed an impressive level of dedication to the cause. It also bore witness to the fact that victory would almost certainly be secured. With a coordinated effort such as this, Yusef could not even in his most pessimistic of moments, imagine what might go wrong now. The infidels would be crippled and made impotent, and like so many men before them, they would come to realise that they would reap what they had sowed.

★ ★ ★

Arriving back at his mansion at around eleven o'clock in the evening, Andrew was hungry as never before and suffering from jetlag. He immediately went upstairs and took a shower. Being back in London in familiar surroundings made the whole trip to the Yucatan Peninsula seem like a distant memory. But in his mind, he could still hear the sound and feel the sensation as his knuckles had struck Hess and crushed his windpipe. He had known instantly that it was a killing blow, but there really was no alternative. He had killed a number of people during his time with the SAS, but he had never taken any pleasure from it. In every instance, he felt he had been put in a position where there would be no other alternative. But as he took the shower he couldn't help feeling as if the water was somehow cleansing him of that deed. He knew that he wouldn't lose any sleep over it, but taking someone else's life was never something that he would get used to, and that was perhaps the way it should be.

He put on a kimono-like housecoat, which he had brought back from a trip to Japan some years back, and walked downstairs again, feeling clean and refreshed. Walking into the kitchen, he opened the refrigerator and got himself a glass of milk, some bread with cheese and an apple. He then proceeded down into the living room and switched on the TV. The room was large by anyone's standards. He had made an effort not to stuff his rooms full of furniture, to the extent that visiting friends would joke about him not being able to afford enough furniture for all the rooms. The walls were painted a light grey, and on them hung a series of hand-painted oriental images, which Andrew had bought. All the furniture was made of oak and kept in a simple and light design. Across from the low coffee table sat Andrew's SONY ultra-widescreen TV, which he promptly switched on to watch his favourite news channel, BBC World.

There was a story about the Prime Minister, Erwin Campbell, who had been subjected to an assassination attempt earlier that evening. Astounded by the news, Andrew sat down on his sofa and placed the glass of milk on the table in front of him.

The Prime Minister had been attending the opening of a new museum for modern art, when a man had leapt from the crowd and started firing at him with a handgun. The man had managed to get off three shots before being subdued by a number of security guards. The would-be assassin had been a poor shot, so the Prime Minister himself had escaped with just the shock, but one member of his security team had been severely wounded. Even though he had been wearing a bulletproof vest, which had stopped two of the rounds, the third one had hit him in the thigh and severed an artery. The man had been rushed to the hospital and was now reported to be in a stable condition, but had it not been for the quick response from the emergency services the man might well have died.

So far nothing was known about the assailant, except that his nationality was British and that the gun he had used was a 9mm Smith & Wesson, one of the most common handguns in circulation. The news presenter was already speculating that it might be an Islamic fundamentalist, but there was really no evidence pointing to that yet. Relieved that nobody had been killed, Andrew proceeded to eat his food, and after he finished, he leaned back and placed his feet on the coffee table in front of him.

The news continued to flow out of the presenter's mouth, and soon it all became an unintelligible stream of words, and within a few minutes Andrew had nodded off. He was abruptly woken up when the phone next to him rang. Dazed, he leapt up and grabbed it while squinting at the clock on the wall. It was ten minutes to five in the morning.

'Uhm. Yeah. Hello?' he mumbled.

'Andy. This is Strickland. We need you in as soon as possible.'

'What?' said Andrew and rubbed his eyes with his hand. 'What's going on? I just came back from Mexico a few hours ago.'

'I know, but this is important. The Prime Minister wants to see you.'

It took Andrew a few seconds to fully comprehend what Strickland had just said. 'What? The PM? Why?'

'We will get to that, Andy. But right now, you need to get up and get dressed. There will be a car waiting for you in about twenty minutes. It will take you straight to Number 10 Downing Street. Alright?'

'Uhm…Yes,' said Andrew hesitantly. 'I guess I don't really have a choice.'

'That is correct,' said Strickland. 'Sorry about this Andrew, but the Prime Minister has asked that we get underway as soon as possible, and that means right now.'

'Well, I can't argue with that,' said Andrew, who was now beginning to wake up. 'I'll get going right away. Will you be there as well?'

'I'm already here,' said the colonel. 'We are waiting. See you in a bit.'

And with that, they hung up and Andrew raced upstairs to throw some water in his face. Fortunately, he didn't need to shave since he had done that just after taking a shower only a few hours ago. He stopped in front of his closet and stared at his clothes. What does one wear when going to see the Prime Minister at five in the morning? He decided to put on a grey suit, white shirt and a blue tie, and fifteen minutes later he was exiting the mansion and making his way down to the street where a dark BMW limousine was parked with its lights on.

The chauffeur got out and held the door for Andrew who got in the back, and then he was whisked away towards Downing Street. There was hardly any traffic this early on a Sunday morning, and before long the car rolled through the gates of the back entrance to Number 10. Moments later, Andrew's door was opened by the driver and he got out now fully awake and alert. Strickland was there to meet him, and he was quickly led through a number of corridors to a front office where a secretary asked them to wait for a few seconds.

'Does this have anything to do with the shooting last night?' asked Andrew.

'No,' said Strickland. 'It's something else. Here we are,' he continued, as the door to the Prime Minister's office opened and the face of the Minister of Defence, William O'Toole appeared.

'Come in please,' said O'Toole and smiled. 'We might as well get underway. The others are already here.'

As Andrew entered the room, he saw a number of people sitting along one side of an oval table and the Prime Minister and an aide on the other. He hadn't seen any of the people in the room before except for Erwin Campbell, and that was only from TV. The others were men more or less the same age as himself, all in civilian clothes and all looking a bit uncomfortable. Apparently, they knew as little as he did about what was about to happen.

The Minister of Defence closed the doors behind them and then walked over to sit down next to the Prime Minister. He shuffled through a pile of papers and then nodded at the Prime Minister who cleared his throat and looked at each of the men sitting across from him.

'I'm sorry for having dragged you all out of bed like this,' said Campbell. 'But we have assembled you here this morning because of a rather urgent situation that has developed, of which several of you already have some knowledge. Peter, would you explain?' he said and looked at the Minister of Defence.

'Certainly, Prime Minister. Let me begin by stressing that this is regarded as a matter of national security, and that the Prime Minister and I are both putting an emphasis on resolving the issue as swiftly as possible.'

The Minister of Defence had still revealed nothing, but Andrew thought he knew what this was about. He had stuck his hand into a hornet's nest with that investigation into the Thule Society, and by the looks of it, things were now really beginning to snowball.

'I don't believe any of you have met before, so I'll just quickly run through a brief introduction. Out here on the right is Colonel Strickland of the SAS. He is the head of a relatively new anti-terrorist division working to contain nuclear, chemical and biological weapons threats. Next to him is Andrew Sterling also of the SAS. A distinguished and experienced soldier, he is currently engaged in an investigation pertaining to the issue we are here to discuss.'

O'Toole then pointed to the man who was sitting next to Andrew. 'This is Pete Ryan of the CIA's anti-terror unit, based in Langley Virginia in the United States. He is here to assist us in putting some of the pieces together, and possibly provide us with suggestions for steps to be taken in the future. And lastly out here on the left is Timothy Jenkins. He is the head of a small but very effective team at MI5, specialising in tracking and mapping money transfers between various organisations and people. They have tracked several suspicious transfers of large sums from accounts known to be either owned by or affiliated with Middle Eastern terrorist organisations. You are not quite done yet, as I understand it?' said the Minister of Defence and looked at Jenkins.

'That is correct, Minister,' replied Jenkins. 'We are still working to expand the network of people. But we could have a major breakthrough any day now.'

The Minister of Defence nodded approvingly, and then went on to lay out for them what had happened over the last several weeks, beginning with the initial investigation of the theft of documents from the Office of Historical Records at the Royal Navy.

As he recounted what each of the men had uncovered during the last weeks, it all fell into place for all of them. It turned out that Andrew knew most of the pieces in the puzzle, but he was surprised to hear that there were several other groups involved. As the Minister of Defence spoke about the possible existence of the Thule Society and a potential threat from a bacterium that might have been uncovered by them, it became clear to Andrew that they had been speaking to Fiona Keane before he came in. He wondered why she wasn't there, but concluded that it was probably because she wasn't officially on the payroll.

'You may wonder how this all got set in motion,' said the Minister of Defence. 'The answer is simple. The MI5 has a number of so-called SITMs within its information gathering and processing systems. The acronym stands for 'Sensitive Information Trigger Mechanism', and the basic principle is that some of the information that is gathered and stored by the MI5 over the years is earmarked, if you will. This means that if that particular piece of information is either read, or revisited in some way, a control officer is instantly alerted. And this is what has happened here. It all began very early on with the break-in at the Office of Historical Records. What was stolen there was loosely connected to highly classified information dating back to the end of the Second World War. Upon entering a concentration camp in central Germany, the British forces uncovered what appeared to be a compound designed to test biological weapons on the prisoners. They found highly advanced laboratory equipment and several documents about the tests, but no traces of any pathogen were ever found. That turned out to be rather fortunate, since the documents revealed that the Nazis had been working on a quite horrendous bacterium, that they were planning to use against the allied forces. As you have probably figured out, it is the same bacterium that Mr. Sterling has now uncovered the origins of. Our researchers have designated it B-CAP, or Blue-Crystalline Archaea Pathogen due to its appearance and probable origin and age.'

The Minister of defence then continued to reveal that, in addition, the British forces recovered several strange artefacts when raiding Heinrich Himmler's private castle of Werwelsburg. Among other things they included a triangle, that was later determined to be the private possession of Himmler himself as the head of the Thule Society. They also found documents with references to the Keeper system.

'All the evidence was brought back to Britain, but since no trace of either the bacterium or its origins were ever found, the case was simply filed in a top-secret archive, with an SITM attached. And that was then triggered a few weeks ago. Since then, the connection to the triangles was made from the material that Mr. Sterling obtained from Vienna.'

The Prime Minister shifted in his seat and looked at the men in front of him. 'We are quite frankly very concerned that either this Thule Society or some Middle Eastern terrorist organisation has obtained samples of the bacterium. For all we know, they could even be working together, although we do not know this for certain. As of now, it appears that only one group has actually obtained samples of the bacterium. In any case, it is imperative that we stop whatever it is they are planning to do with it. As has been made clear from what Mr. Sterling has uncovered, it seems that the bacterium originated somewhere on the Antarctic continent, so the best course of action might be to try to locate the original source.'

'I am sorry, Sir. Do you mean going to Antarctica?' asked Jenkins incredulously.

'Yes,' responded the Prime minister. 'As strange as it may sound, we think it will be easier to find this alleged lost civilisation, than to find the bacterium itself. This is simply because the bacterium might already have been mass-produced and dispersed all over the globe, making it effectively impossible to find everything and avert a potential disaster. It would be possible to grow more of it with just one tiny sample, so if it's already out there, we can never hope to find all of it. The only viable course of action is to find the original source and then develop a fast-working antibiotic specifically targeting this pathogen, or perhaps even a prophylactic. What do you think, Mr. Sterling? Do you believe that we should go to Antarctica and attempt to locate the source?'

Andrew was caught off guard by the direct question. 'Uhm...Well,' he said. 'That might just be the only thing we can do, really. Have we no idea where this Middle Eastern organisation might be?'

'No,' said the Minister of Defence. 'Mr. Ryan here has got some educated guesses and is working with other departments within the

CIA as well as the MI6 to try to determine a possible location, but at this point, we have nothing but intercepts of calls made by satellite phones.'

'Well,' said Andrew. 'In that case, I see no other option.'

'How do you propose we attempt to find this civilisation?' asked the Prime Minister.

'Uhm,' said Andrew and shifted self-consciously in his seat. 'It's got to do with these triangles.'

And then he went on to tell the group about the legends of the triangles, what was believed to be the purpose of them, and that he believed that the Thule Society might have the other two. He felt extremely silly sitting in No. 10 Downing Street and telling the Prime Minister of Great Britain these seemingly outlandish things, but Erwin Campbell as well as his Minister of Defence seemed unfazed by what he was saying.

'Well, Mr. Sterling,' said the Minister of Defence. 'It seems that we have no choice, really. I want you to look into how soon we can get underway with such a project, but of course, we'll need the two remaining triangles. As you might have guessed Colonel Strickland reported the progress of your investigation to MI6, and they have sent a man to Vienna to investigate further. I must say that I am not too thrilled about the fact that you stole those documents from the Order of the Teutonic Knights, or the Thule Society or whatever they call themselves, but considering the strength of our suspicion against them, we are willing to let that slide. Anyway, our agent in Vienna, who is a very capable man, was able to monitor the transport of items from the home of an Austrian Member of Parliament to a bank. We believe these may well be one or two of the remaining triangles, so he has been given the freedom to do whatever he can to retrieve them. And I have complete confidence in his ability to carry out this task.'

'Like a regular James Bond?' chuckled Pete Ryan.

'Well, yes.' said the Minister of Defence. 'We don't usually work like that but I suppose extreme danger calls for extreme measures. At any rate, we now need to locate the source of the bacterium.'

Ryan smiled disarmingly. 'Hey. It's no problem for us. As long as we get hold of what we want, we ain't too concerned with the way it's done. We are talking about national security here, right?'

'Yes,' responded O'Toole. 'That is how we see it as well. Can't make an omelette without breaking eggs.'

'Once assembled, have you any idea how this medallion might work?' asked the Prime Minister.

'No,' said Andrew. 'Not yet. But I hope to find out soon. I suspect Miss Fiona Keane might be able to figure it out. She's very bright.'

'Good,' said Campbell. 'It is important that we get to work on an antibiotic as soon as we can, but without the original bacterium it is as good as impossible, from what our experts tell me.'

'Am I authorised to dig into the personal accounts of this Sergei Ivanov anywhere I would like?' asked Timothy Jenkins.

'Mr. Jenkins,' said O'Toole. 'You are authorised to do whatever it takes to determine the location of that man, as well as any others that you suspect of being financially tied to him. If he really is the link between the terrorists and their benefactors, we need to get to him and choke off the money supply.'

'But that might involve poking my nose in the accounts of some very important people around the world, quite possibly politicians and heads of some of the world's largest companies. We should probably be prepared for some unpleasant repercussions if we are detected.'

'Mr. Jenkins,' said the Campbell. 'Just do whatever it takes, and leave the rest to us.'

Timothy Jenkins nodded. The Prime Minster then went on to inform them that they would continue working on their individual assignments, but that they were now all members of a task force established solely to handle this particular situation. Until further notice, they would all report directly to Colonel Strickland. He let them know that the purpose of the meeting was to make them aware of the wider context of their individual discoveries and to stress to them the importance of working closely together in the time to come. They then spent the next half hour coordinating their efforts, and after that, the group disbanded. Just as Andrew was about to leave the room, the Minister of Defence pulled him aside.

'Mr. Sterling I'll see to it that you get the piece of the medallion that is already in MI6 custody. You may do with it what you want, just make sure that we find that bacterium. If it were to be unleashed in a major city, it would create a disaster on a scale that we haven't seen before. I believe it has the potential to wipe humankind from the surface of this planet.'

'I understand, Minister. I've had that thought myself.'

'Good. Then we agree,' said O'Toole and placed a hand on Andrew's shoulder. 'There's one other thing that I need to discuss with you,' he said and took on a grim look on his face. 'I might as well put it to you straight. It has turned out that your father Charles was a member of the Thule Society.'

Andrew recoiled at those words and stared blankly into the eyes of the Minister of Defence. 'What?' he muttered.

'I know it must be difficult for you to comprehend,' said O'Toole. 'But I'm afraid that there is no doubt. For a period of several years, in fact, right up until his death in that terrible car accident, he was one of the Keepers of the society. After his death, he was replaced by another man who died soon after of natural causes, and after that Phillip Eckleston took over. He has been a Keeper ever since.'

Andrew felt his knees almost giving way under him, and had to steady himself against the wall. So that was what Hess had meant by betrayal. He must have been a member of the Thule Society himself. How else could he have known about his father?

'I don't believe this,' whispered Andrew stunned. 'My own father. Why?'

'We don't know,' said O'Toole sympathetically. 'As far as we have been able to ascertain, he never publicly expressed any views that might demonstrate his sympathy with the Nazis or with a belief in an Aryan master race. I guess we will never know.'

'I don't believe this,' repeated Andrew.

'This might not have been the best of times to tell you, but I felt that you might as well know. Perhaps it could help us in the investigation. Look, young man. Go home and try to relax.'

‘Right,’ said Andrew still dazed. ‘I think I’ll do that.’

‘Good. I realise that this is a stressful time, but I’d appreciate it if you’d just keep reporting your progress to Colonel Strickland. If any of you make significant progress, we’ll get together and coordinate our efforts again, Ok?’

‘Right,’ repeated Andrew, still in a daze. ‘Strickland.’

He then staggered outside and shook hands with the Minister of Defence and Colonel Strickland, and then he got into the BMW that was still waiting for him. He sat back in his seat and watched the streets pass by outside his window, not recognising anything and not knowing how long the trip took. When they arrived, he got out of the car and walked slowly up to the front door where he let himself in. The first rays of sunlight were coming in through his kitchen windows and he walked over to the refrigerator and took out a couple of eggs and some bacon to make himself a bit of breakfast. Not because he was hungry, but because he knew he’d probably need it.

After finishing it, he sat down by the kitchen table with his head in his hands, trying to make sense of it all. The father that he had loved, had been a member of the Thule Society. How could that be? And how come he had never noticed, or never even had an inkling that something like that was going on? And where was the evidence? Why had he never found anything to suggest that this might be true?

After a few minutes, Andrew rose and walked up the stairs to the first floor and then to the attic. He had only been up here a few times since the death of his parents, and as he walked up there and switched on the lights, he wondered why that was, but he couldn’t come up with an answer. Along the sides of the roof were crates and boxes with his parents’ belongings, at least those of them that hadn’t been inherited by other family members. Most of them were pieces of furniture that Andrew had put here. He was not a great fan of his parents’ taste in interiors, so he had bought his own furniture and gradually redecorated the whole house according to his own taste.

The boxes also contained things that his parents had bought for the house and then grown tired of. There were also a lot of items that his father had bought while living in South Africa, including paintings and books.

He started going through the boxes and crates systematically one by one, searching for anything that might reveal his father's involvement in the society. He spread the contents of the boxes out over the entire floor of the attic and worked non-stop for several hours, only interrupted for a few minutes by some old photos that his parents had taken before he was born. One of them showed his father along with a group of men, and suddenly the hairs stood up on the back of his neck. There, with his arm around his father's shoulders, was a young man who Andrew felt certain was Phillip Eckleston. It had to be him.

He looked exactly like the man in the picture on the back of one of Fiona's books. There was nothing to indicate where or when the photo had been taken, but it was clear that the two men had been friends. He could see it from the relaxed way in which they both smiled. Andrew stared at the photo for a few minutes and then tucked it in his shirt pocket.

Going through a box full of books, he discovered that several of them had to do with legends about lost civilisations and the traces they might have left behind. There were books about expeditions to almost any place imaginable on the surface of the planet, and most of them had apparently had their inception in one or more of a whole range of theories about ancient civilisations. There were also several books on geology and plate tectonics and at the back of one of the books Andrew found a loose piece of paper with a copy of the summary of Professor Hapgood's theory about Earth crust displacement. Even though it all pointed to his father holding many of the same views as Doctor Eckleston, it wasn't in itself enough to convince Andrew that his father had belonged to the Thule Society.

But then he lifted a thick book out of the box he was examining, and instantly felt that it was much too light to be an ordinary book. Its title was 'Megalithic Sites in Wales', but when he opened it, he was amazed to discover that it was in fact completely hollowed out. Inside was a rectangular compartment and in the compartment was a dark wooden box of a kind he had seen once before. It took a few seconds to register what he was actually looking at, but from its shape and size, he didn't even need to open it to know what was inside.

He lifted the box out of the rectangular compartment and dropped the book onto the floor. Sitting down right there and then, he slowly opened the box, almost hoping that he wouldn't find what he knew he was about to see. The shiny metal insignia of the Thule Society gleamed back up at him, and picking it up and turning it over in his hand he could see that it was identical to the one he had retrieved from U-303 in the Atlantic Ocean. He tried unsuccessfully to recall just the faintest of memories that might in hindsight reveal his father's hidden life, and then he placed the insignia back in the wooden box and put it aside.

He spent the next hour or so going through the remaining boxes, but found nothing that might give away further details. He wondered if his mother had known, and soon he got an almost claustrophobic feeling that maybe all his childhood memories were somehow fake. What if his mother had been involved too? What if they had both hidden it from him and everyone around them? Feeling himself becoming slightly paranoid, he packed all his parents' stuff back into the boxes and went downstairs, holding the small wooden box in his hand.

★ ★ ★

It was nearly noon and Nick Frost had been in his hotel room all morning perfecting his disguise. He had secretly taken a handful of pictures of Ludvig Bauer, and had taped them to his mirror. Using a standard kit issued to him before his departure, he was now turning himself into an almost exact copy of Bauer. It had been a long time since Frost had played a spy in this way. Mostly, a disguise was just in place to keep someone from recognising him at a later stage, but this time he needed to make sure that he was virtually identical in appearance to another man. As he placed the glasses on his nose and combed his newly dyed hair to one side, the job was complete. He was happy with the disguise and felt sure that only Bauer's own family would have been able to see that it wasn't really him.

Frost left the hotel and walked calmly down the street, holding a briefcase identical to the one Bauer had held in his hand on his way to the bank the day before. Arriving at the bank, he strode purposefully through the doors and walked over to the counter that dealt with special requests. He handed over his false identification papers and told the clerk that he wanted another secure box for some personal items. The clerk tapped a command into the computer system along with Bauer's account number, and within a split second the computer had found him an empty box. The clerk got out Bauer's file and opened it up. He then asked Frost to sign his name on the dotted line, and as he did so, Frost was provided with an opportunity to easily see what other boxes Bauer had access to. Boxes #263 and #174 were already Bauer's, and as he and the clerk walked down the stairs towards the vault, Frost repeated the numbers inside his head. Forgetting them now would just be unforgivably stupid.

Bauer's new box was #182, and as the clerk closed the door behind them and handed him the key to box #182, Frost pulled out what looked like a pepper spray. It contained a gas that worked almost like a tranquilliser gun, except it was much faster, and it left no mark on the victim. The small amount of gas burst into the clerk's mouth and nose, and as he staggered backwards in shock and bewilderment his legs began to give way under him, and soon he slid down onto the floor with his back against the wall and his eyes closed. A few seconds later he was motionless on the floor with his arms out to the sides but still visibly breathing. The gas was harmless but would put a man to sleep for at least half an hour, so Frost had plenty of time. He figured it would be at least fifteen minutes before anyone upstairs might wonder where the clerk had gone.

Frost placed his briefcase on the polished steel table and opened it. He pulled out two small plastic syringes, each with a different chemical in them. Ignoring box #182 he then walked over to box #263 and injected half of the content of the first syringe into the keyhole. Then he injected some of the second chemical into the hole, and immediately the two chemicals began reacting, creating a powerful acid that soon ate away at the small metal lock. The locks on the safety deposit boxes were there more for show than for anything else. The real protection from theft was the massive steel doors that one had to pass through to get into the vault, and the flimsy locks were eaten away by the acid within a couple of minutes. As the acid took hold it started sputtering out of the hole and onto the floor, but eventually, the reactive ability of the acid tapered off, and a small plume rose from what remained of the keyhole.

Extracting a large screwdriver from his briefcase, Frost quickly snapped the safe deposit box open and peered inside. Just as he had been told, there were two small wooden boxes inside it. He took them out and placed them in his briefcase. Looking at his watch, he discovered that he had only used seven minutes, so he decided to repeat the process with the second box, even though he knew that he had obtained what he had come for. A couple of minutes later, the second lock crumbled as he twisted the screwdriver through it and forced the box open. Inside, he found a flat unlocked metal box with a set of documents inside. He quickly flicked through them and decided to bring them with him, since he didn't have time to sit down and read them.

He put his tools back into the briefcase along with the documents and the wooden boxes and then left the vault. On his way out, he knelt down beside the clerk to feel his pulse. It was calm and regular so there was no danger of him suffering permanent damage. Frost walked confidently up the stairs and across the hall towards the exit, without arousing anyone's suspicion. All the other clerks were too busy with their own customers to notice that he was leaving the vault by himself. He walked calmly outside and then strode down the street towards his car, which was parked around the corner in an alley. A few hours later he was on a plane back to Heathrow Airport.

★ ★ ★

The next morning Andrew considered staying home for the day, but decided that it might be a bad idea to sit there by himself, so even though he needed more sleep, he got into his car and drove to work. He had arranged to meet with Fiona at eleven o'clock, and he didn't want to be late. Driving towards Sheldrake Place, he considered whether to tell Fiona about his father. On the one hand, he was embarrassed and uncomfortable with the fact that his father, unbeknownst to him, had been a part of an organisation that had essentially tried to kill both of them. But on the other hand, he felt that Fiona might be able to offer some constructive thoughts on the whole thing, and it was difficult to argue that this revelation didn't in some way impact their investigation.

When he reached Hyde Park his phone rang.

'This is Sterling.'

'Good morning, Andy. Strickland here. I thought I'd just tell you that yesterday, one of our boys from MI6 paid a visit to a certain bank in Vienna, and he was able to retrieve two of those triangles you've spoken about. At least, that's what they appear to be. You and Fiona will be able to have a look for yourself soon. I'm having them delivered to your office as we speak, along with the one that has been in our possession since 1945. They ought to be there when you arrive.'

'How do you mean 'paid a visit'?' asked Andrew.

'Well, I haven't been let in on the exact details, but it seems that Pete Ryan's assertion about a James Bond manoeuvre was quite accurate. Anyway, the important thing is that we've got them for you. I really hope that you two will be able to come up with something. Right now, you are the best hope we've got, and as you could tell from the meeting yesterday, the government is really quite concerned about this matter.'

'Well,' said Andrew. 'They have good reason to be. But don't worry, Gordon. We'll do what we can.'

'Excellent, Andy. Keep me up to speed, will you?'

'Certainly, Sir.'

When Andrew entered the front office, Catherine was standing next to her desk, chatting with two men wearing suits, but looking decidedly military from their demeanour. As soon as she saw

Andrew, Catherine started towards him with a flustered look on her face.

'Mr. Sterling, these men are here to deliver something to you. Isn't that correct?' she said, and turned to look at them.

'Yes,' said one of them, evidently the most senior of the two officers. 'Mr. Sterling, my name is Captain Lewellyn and this is Leftenant Harrison. We are currently working with the London Metropolitan Police, and we've been asked to deliver this to you on behalf of the Prime Minister,' he said and handed Andrew a briefcase. 'I've been told that you know what this is about.'

'Uhm…Yes,' said Andrew. 'Do I need to sign anywhere?'

'Yes, sir,' said Harrison and handed Andrew a pad with a single sheet of paper. 'Right there, Sir.'

Andrew didn't bother to read it. He quickly scribbled his name on the dotted line and then he handed the pad back to the leftenant. 'There you are.'

'Thank you, Mr. Sterling. Have a good day, Sir.'

And with that, the two men filed out of the front office, leaving Catherine staring at Andrew.

'The Prime Minister?' she said, looking astonished.

At that moment Fiona entered through the doorway.

'What?' she said and smiled cunningly. 'The Prime Minister? That wasn't him just down the corridor, was it?' she grinned.

'No,' smiled Andrew. 'That wasn't him, but I had a meeting with him and a few other people early yesterday. Fiona, would you like to step into my office? There's something I need to discuss with you. And Cathy would you be so kind as to fetch us some coffee?'

'Certainly,' smiled Catherine and left the front office for the tea room.

'What's going on?' asked Fiona after they had entered Andrew's office and he had closed the door.

'Well,' said Andrew. 'Considering the amount of time and effort it cost us to obtain just one of those bloody triangles, it's nothing short of amazing that we now have all of them.'

'What?' exclaimed Fiona. 'How?'

Andrew went on to tell her about the early morning meeting with The Prime Minister, the Minister of Defence and the international task force that had been set up, and that he had been asked to put together a mission to recover the bacterium, if possible. He also told her the story about how one of the triangles was recovered and brought back to Britain after the Second World War.

'So, we have all four of them?' she asked excitedly.

'We do,' said Andrew placing the briefcase on his desk and flipping the locks open. 'There ought to be three of them here,' he said and opened the lid.

In three of the four small compartments in the black Styrofoam interior of the briefcase, lay small wooden boxes. Andrew carefully lifted the lids off of all of them, and as Fiona walked over next to him to see for herself, he picked up one of the matchbox-sized triangles and held it in his hand.

'Amazing craftsmanship,' said Fiona admiring the intricate ornamental patterns on it. 'They must have been produced in moulds of some sort and then finished by hand.'

'Yes,' said Andrew and ran a finger along the side of it. 'Look at the finish on these small indentations here. They are clearly meant to lock together.'

'Well, come on. Try putting them together,' said Fiona impatiently.

Andrew picked up another triangle and placed the two of them next to each other in the palm of his hand. He turned them a few times to try to fit them together. At first, they didn't seem to fit, but when turning one of them slightly and pressing it against the other, there was a small 'click', and as the two metal pieces locked together to form one half of the medallion. A couple of small holes opened up on the edges that were still waiting to be connected to the other two pieces.

'Christ,' exclaimed Andrew. 'It's mechanical.'

He picked up another triangle and slid it into position, placing two small pins into the holes that had just been exposed. The third triangle effortlessly snapped into place and was now firmly fixed to the other two pieces. Turning the fourth triangle over in his hands a few times, Andrew then slipped it into the empty slot, and it instantly locked itself in place with the rest of the medallion. He now held in his hand what appeared like a solid piece of metal. The individual pieces were so finely crafted that it was almost impossible to see where they were joined. At its centre, was a small hole where, according to the legends, the ruby was supposed to sit.

'Do you think you'll be able to take it apart again?' asked Fiona.

'I'm not sure it's supposed to be taken apart once it has been assembled. In fact, I think those mechanisms locking the pieces together are specifically designed to ensure that once the pieces have found each other, so to speak, they would not lose each other again.'

'Makes sense, I guess,' she said.

'Feel the weight,' said Andrew and handed the medallion to Fiona.

'Amazing,' she smiled and looked at him. 'It's light as a feather. What do you suppose it's made of?'

'I have no idea. Perhaps we should try to get someone to find that out.'

'Does it matter? I mean, the important part is to get it to show us the way to the lost civilisation, and we don't even know how to do that yet.'

'Right,' nodded Andrew pensively. 'But how does it work?'

Fiona shifted it gently from one hand to the other. 'I have no clue,' she said. 'Perhaps it only works with the ruby that was mentioned in the legends. If that's the case, then it might not work at all now.'

Andrew shook his head. 'You know, this is getting a little too superstitious for me. Don't you think there might be a more down-to-earth approach to this? Something less fantastical?'

'Look, Andrew. After all we have seen and heard over the last few weeks, I'm willing to accept anything. If it works, I'll believe it.'

She then handed the medallion back to Andrew, who turned it over in his hand a few times and then placed it on the table.

'Fiona, there something else I think I need to tell you,' he said in a sombre voice.

'What's that?' said Fiona concerned.

'I've discovered that my father was involved in the Thule Society.'

'What?' exclaimed Fiona. 'How? And how do you know?'

'Well, the Minister of Defence told me yesterday, would you believe. He said that my father was a Keeper just like Eckleston for several years.'

'Are you sure this is correct?'

'Yes, I am. I found some things in the attic at home, including an insignia identical to the one we recovered from the U-boat. There's no doubt in my mind that he was part of it somehow. I just don't understand why.'

'Who knows. Strange things happen in life. There might be many reasons,' said Fiona. 'I guess Eckleston would have answers to those questions.'

'Yes, I suppose he would, but that will have to wait. We need to concentrate on finding the bacterium as soon as we can. And that requires us to figure out how this thing works,' he said and picked up the medallion again.

They spent the next few hours speculating about possible ways the medallion might work. Fiona suggested that the missing ruby might work as a lens, focusing light onto a map similar to the one on the wall of the cave north of La Venta. Andrew thought that if that was the case then it should have been the ruby and not a triangle sitting in that cave. There was of course the possibility that the ruby might be in a similar room somewhere, but they had no idea where that might be. Andrew called Strickland to check that no ruby had been found along with the triangle that had been recovered from Himmler's castle. The colonel confirmed that nothing like that had been brought back from Werwelsburg. Disappointed, they decided to let the issue rest for now.

They even considered leaving for Antarctica without the ruby or any idea of how to use it. After all, the *SS-Ahnenerbe* had navigated to Antarctica based on old maps by Piri Reiss and others. However, they soon gave up on that idea. Travelling to Antarctica on a whim like that seemed like a big gamble, and at this point, they needed to make sure that their time was spent efficiently.

They decided to give it some more time. Perhaps someone might suddenly come up with a bright idea as to the location of the ruby.

TWENTY-ONE

Erich Strauss slammed his fist down on the table as rage welled up inside him. It was no more than a few hours ago that he had heard that Hess hadn't returned to his hotel in Coatzacoalcos. It had all looked so promising when Hess had reported back to tell him that Sterling and the girl had come back from an excursion into the jungle and that they were planning to go somewhere very close to one of the most significant archaeological sites in Central America. But then it had apparently gone horribly wrong somehow.

Officially, Strauss was Hess' business associate, so he had been informed when the German had not come back to his hotel for three days. The police had entered his hotel room and found the telephone number for Strauss, and he had immediately known that something had gone wrong. When asked about the murder of a pilot working for a local air charter service, Strauss had denied knowing anything about it, even though Hess had informed him of his plans the evening before he had left the hotel to pose as a pilot with the company. And as if that wasn't bad enough, Bauer had just walked into his office and had told him that his safety deposit boxes at the bank had both been broken into and that the two triangles had been stolen.

Through the rage, Strauss still realised that he was ultimately to blame, not just because he was the grandmaster, but also because he had given the order for the two medallion pieces to be moved to the same location. Even though he was sitting down, his heart was pounding and his mind was racing to find a solution to this predicament. It was obvious that Sterling had to be behind it all, and the thought of having been robbed by the same man twice was almost too much to bear. He had to refrain from following his instincts that were telling him to simply kill the man. Sterling had to be working with someone other than this stupid little girl he was dragging around with him. Perhaps he had even involved other parts of the authorities, possibly the police and even Interpol.

Just minutes ago, Strauss had said goodbye to another of his young proteges, Wilhelm Müller, having asked him to go to London as soon as possible to aid in the surveillance of Andrew Sterling and Fiona Keane. Müller was instructed to contact Eckleston as soon as he arrived, and to take orders from him.

Strauss had confidence in him. Wilhelm Müller was as ambitious and dedicated as Kurt Hess, and it had not gone unnoticed by Strauss that Müller had felt very disappointed and angry as Hess had gradually gained an increasingly powerful position within the society. Now Müller would have his chance to prove what he was made of, and if Hess didn't come back, Müller would be the obvious choice to take over his position. That in itself ought to be motivation enough for him.

What Strauss hadn't told Müller, was that he had made the decision to leave his office and go home to his mansion outside of Vienna as soon as possible. There he would pack his things and then drive over the border to Italy. He knew that there were no serious checks at the border, and once inside Italy he had powerful friends and sympathisers within the new Italian government that would help him stay hidden until this thing blew over.

However, he also needed to contact the Keepers, and especially Eckleston, who was probably in even more danger. At that point he felt fortunate that his position as grand master was his for life. None of the Keepers, nor anyone else within the society, could change that. He knew that he was responsible for the failure in protecting the medallion pieces, but now that it had happened, he had to do everything he could to recover them. And if that meant sending Müller on a suicide mission, then so be it.

Little did he know that Phillip Eckleston had already been visited by the police earlier that morning, and politely asked to come down to the station for questioning. The police had asked him about Fiona Keane and whether he knew anything about her having been attacked while on holiday in Mexico. They were obviously grasping at straws, and whether the police might actually be able to charge him with anything was highly unlikely. But they clearly wanted to make sure that he understood that people were watching him now. After questioning, the police had driven him back to his home, but from that moment on there would always be someone watching him and ensuring that he didn't do anything foolish, like running off to another country.

★ ★ ★

On his way home from work, Andrew drove over the Thames to the British War Museum. He considered it one of the best museums in London, and they currently had an exhibition on about the recent conflict in Afghanistan, along with the usual exhibitions about the First and the Second World Wars. His favourite section, although small, was the one devoted to the publicised operations of the SAS. He didn't exactly relish the idea of his regiment's activities being displayed in a museum, but he did realise that it was an important part of its task. The public needed to know that they were there, and so did potential adversaries. And as impressed as most people were at seeing their capabilities and hearing about a few of their missions over the past thirty years or so, they probably didn't realise that what was on display here was only a tiny part of the operational history of the SAS. But it was good for the public's trust in the military to be able to see some of what they could do if called upon.

A group of young boys had gathered around one of the exhibits, and it was clear from them that they were very impressed and probably thought they wanted to be like that one day. Andrew thought of his own history and of how he had become a member of the SAS. His involvement with the SAS wasn't exactly an accident, but it also wasn't something that he had set out to achieve either, at least not initially. It had just turned out that way. Sometimes he wondered what else he might have done with his life.

He strolled through the rest of the exhibition and walked outside where it was becoming dark. The wind was picking up, and as he walked over to his car and got in, he noticed that there was a voice message on his phone. It was Fiona who had come up with another idea about the medallion. She suggested that it might be a radio transmitter of some sort. Andrew didn't know whether to take it seriously or not but decided to wait until the next day to see if she really meant it.

After returning home that evening, Andrew entered the kitchen to fetch something to eat. He wasn't much of a cook, so he quickly threw together some fried eggs, a couple of slices of bread and a piece of ham. He went into his living room and plonked himself on the sofa in front of his TV.

BBC World was showing a documentary about the Second World War, again. Although proud of his country's history, he sometimes felt that the British had a tendency to dwell on its past in general, and on the Second World War in particular. The war had certainly been a defining moment in the more recent history of Britain, but when he thought about how much had happened before and since then, he couldn't help but feel that it tended to get overexposed, relative to the rest of his country's history.

He switched to the Discovery Channel, where a former member of Monty Python's Flying Circus told the story of how explorers such as Cook and Magellan had used the stars to navigate the oceans hundreds of years ago. The sextant had been their primary way of determining their location for many hundreds of years, whereas the magnetic compass had served as the means of quickly determining a course to plot in order to get from one point to another. Compasses had served seafarers well for centuries, but they had one weakness that wasn't overcome until electronic navigation aides were introduced. Simple mechanical compasses are orientated towards the magnetic north pole, which is only approximately equivalent to the geographic north pole. Adding to the confusion was the fact that the magnetic north pole shifted gradually over time. For example, the narrator said, the current magnetic north pole was somewhere in Northern Canada several hundred kilometres from the geographic north pole. The end result of this confusion was that when sailing near the Earth's magnetic poles, the mechanical compasses of past explorers would increasingly point in a direction different that was from the geographic north pole. The same would occur close to the south pole. Today there was hardly a ship that wasn't equipped with some form of electronic navigation aid using either ground-based radio sources or GPS.

Andrew slowly put down his glass of white wine on the table and stared into the TV screen, his mind racing. He sat like that for a few seconds, and then looked up again focusing his eyes on the screen, but then grabbed the remote control and switched off the TV. He got up and walked upstairs to put on some more clothes. A few minutes later he came down into the hall again and walked straight out through the front door. He got into his car and sped off to Sheldrake Place, where he parked the car. A few minutes later he was heading into his office.

The office was dark and quiet except for the large aquarium, which was emitting a bluish glow and a low humming noise. He switched on all the lights, threw his coat over a chair and stopped next to the aquarium for a few seconds switching off the air pump and the lights. Then he removed the cover and placed it on the floor next to the tank. As the bubbles of air stopped coming out of the nozzle that lay behind a small stone, the water calmed and gradually stopped moving around in the tank. He turned and walked over to his personal safe, entered the combination on the keypad, opened the safe and pulled out the padded box in which the medallion now lay. He opened the box and took out the medallion, and without taking his eyes off it he walked slowly over to the aquarium where he stood for about a minute until the water in the aquarium had calmed completely. The fish were mostly hovering motionless near the bottom, probably wondering where the light and the air had gone and if it might come back anytime soon.

But Andrew wasn't interested in them. Instead, he reached for a lamp that was standing on the floor and turned it on to throw some more light onto the aquarium. With both hands, he then slowly lifted the medallion over the side and into the tank, where he gently set it down on the calm surface. Holding his breath, he let go of the medallion, and just as he had hoped it didn't sink to the bottom but merely bobbed slightly in the water and then settled calmly on the surface. Andrew placed both hands on the edge of the tank staring at the medallion without moving for about a minute, but then a big smile started spreading across his face as the medallion ever so slowly began to rotate around its own axis.

Very very slowly, remaining in the exact spot where Andrew had set it down, the medallion rotated until it was aligned with the Earth's magnetic field. It overshot by a few millimetres, but then slowly realigned itself perfectly. Andrew turned to look out the window, picturing inside his head the street map showing Sheldrake Place and the building he was in. Then he returned his attention to the medallion, which was now virtually locked in a fixed position as it floated on the water in the aquarium. The pointy corner with the small square indentation was pointing directly towards the south. Andrew was certain that it had to be pointing at a particular location in Antarctica, and in the midst of his excitement at this revelation, he forgot what time it was and grabbed his mobile phone.

'Fiona Keane speaking,' mumbled Fiona, sounding very drowsy.

'It's a compass!' blurted Andrew. 'The medallion is a compass.'

'Uhm. What?' said Fiona as she tried desperately to kick her brain into gear. 'What is?'

'The medallion. I put it in the aquarium in my office, and it just aligned itself, with the corner with indentation pointing towards the south.'

'Aligned? How?'

'With the Earth's magnetic field, of course. Just like any other magnetic compass,' he chuckled.

'That's amazing,' said Fiona and wiped her eyes. She was now slowly regaining all of her senses and beginning to understand the implication of what Andrew was telling her.

'Yes.' Andrew was almost laughing now. 'Can you believe that? All that superstitious voodoo rubbish and the bloody thing turns out to be a simple compass. It is amazing. Can you believe it's that simple?'

'What do you mean? Do you think that it's pointing to the lost civilisation?'

'Absolutely,' he said, sounding convinced. 'If there is anything left of it, that is.'

'Right,' said Fiona. 'I guess that is the really big question. Except of course, the second expedition lead by Reitziger seemed to indicate that there was something unusual there, right?'

'Yes. So, if he was right, then I am willing to bet my house that this medallion is pointing directly towards that.'

'But what if it's just pointing south?'

'I don't think it is. I think it's probably offset to point directly at wherever the main city was.'

'And if it is in a different place from where it was 12,000 years ago?'

'Then we are in trouble. But we have to trust this for now. You have to come and see it. It's amazing.'

Fiona looked at her alarm clock. 'Now? Andrew, it's 1:30 am. I'll come by and have a look tomorrow, okay?'

'Oh. Alright,' said a slightly disappointed Andrew, who was suddenly feeling a bit like a little schoolboy who had been carried away by the whole thing. 'Can you come to my office tomorrow morning?'

'I'll be there at eight o'clock, Ok?'

'Ok, fair enough. See you then.'

★ ★ ★

Timothy Jenkins spent an hour getting the information he had gathered in order, and then he left in a taxi for Colonel Strickland's office. He didn't really care who he had to report to, as long as that person had a brain and understood that Jenkins was an information analyst and not some guy with a crystal ball. Strickland seemed like he got it, and he and Jenkins were quick to establish a good constructive working relationship where each respected the other. Walking into the colonel's office, he brought out his laptop and placed it on Strickland's desk.

'These,' he said, 'are the latest green links I've been able to identify. As you know, our friend Sergei Ivanov is the owner of a number of residences in major cities around the world including New York, Hong Kong and Monaco. Our people have been able to confirm that he is not in Hong Kong right now, and following a request put through by Pete Ryan, the CIA has returned to us and indicated that he is not in the apartment in New York now either. They say he has not been there for several months. There are a number of others, but none of them seem to have been in use for quite a while. However, it appears that he may well be in Monaco at the moment, at least judging from the way his credit cards are being used there.'

'Could it not be his wife or a mistress?' asked Strickland.

'It could, but it is unlikely. I may be judgmental, but I think it is more likely that he is the one visiting strip clubs.'

'Right,' said Strickland hesitantly.

'In fact,' continued Jenkins. 'He seems to be going to the same place almost every night when he stays in Monaco, and the nitwit doesn't even bother to pay with cash. Apparently, he's not concerned with trying to keep a low profile, so he must not think of himself as being involved in anything terribly criminal.'

'Well, he may not be,' said Strickland. 'Although, the connections you've made so far do seem compelling. I think I'll send out a man to have a little chat with him. Could you prepare a report containing the details about his house and what we know about his lady friends in Monaco?'

'Already done, Sir. I have emailed you a link to the report,' he said. 'Let me know it there's anything else you would like me to have a look at once you've read it.'

'Good work, Jenkins. I will do that.'

As soon as Jenkins had left the office, Strickland called Andrew to discuss the best approach to paying Ivanov a visit. Andrew started off by telling Strickland about his discovery the night before, and that he thought it likely that they might be able to find the origin of the bacterium.

They then discussed asking the authorities in Monaco to apprehend him and hand him over to the British but decided that getting the paperwork done for that sort of thing would take too long, and that time was the only thing they didn't have. They would have to go in and get him themselves. It would require a person who was trained in getting close to people unnoticed, and who wasn't afraid of applying a bit of pressure to get answers. Without much hesitation, Andrew suggested his friend and former comrade in arms Colin McGregor. Andrew had complete confidence in the Scotsman, and even though Strickland would have preferred Andrew to go, he knew that he and Fiona would be on their way to Antarctica before long. They agreed that McGregor should be sent to Monaco, where he would meet up with Nick Frost of MI6 for details of his mission. The British consulate would be providing a base for him, as well as a place to obtain any hardware he might need in order to complete the mission.

'There's one more thing I would like to discuss with you,' said Andrew. 'I am going to need a small team of people who are capable of handling and transporting dangerous bacteria. If we do find a sample of the original pathogen somewhere in Antarctica, then we are going to need somebody to go in and get it. And it would be preferable if they could bring it back here without killing anyone.'

'Of course, Andy. I'll see what I can do and then come back to you later today.'

'Thank you, Sir.'

★ ★ ★

Determined to give his surveillance team the slip, Eckleston decided to do what none of the team members could ever have imagined. He peered out of the window to see if they were there, and sure enough, there was a car parked just on the other side of the road in plain view. Inside it, two men were looking in his direction, and upon seeing Eckleston by the window one of them even waved and smiled at him.

Eckleston was enraged by the arrogance of these people. They clearly had no idea about what was going on, and what was actually at stake here. Sometimes he wondered if his people were worth saving, but he knew that in all societies there would be dimwits who would just never understand. Hopefully, he and his brethren would be able to get rid of them before too long.

Eckleston calmly started pouring petrol onto the floor of the living room and continued out through the hall and into the bedroom. He then walked down into the basement and poured out some petrol there as well, and then went back up into the kitchen. He turned off all the lights in the house causing the surveillance team to think that he had gone to bed. They would remain where they were of course, but they could now take turns napping in the front seats of the car. Wearing a coat and carrying a large bag containing his most personal items, Eckleston opened the kitchen door to the backyard and took out a Zippo lighter from his pocket. He then stepped approximately five meters away from the house, lit the lighter, and then threw it onto the kitchen floor. He didn't bother to turn and watch as the flames quickly spread throughout his house. Although he had stored all of his work online, he was still a bit sad to have to let all the books in the living room go up in flames. However, this was a small price to pay, and the books were replaceable, whereas he was not.

As he slipped away through the darkness, he thought about how he had felt the noose tightening around his neck over the last few days. He knew that he couldn't stay here much longer. The authorities were on to him and the society, and it would probably only be a matter of time before it all caved in. The only solution was to disappear from sight for a while. From now on, he would make sure that Sterling and Keane didn't manage to interfere with the Thule Society anymore, and if they did decide to leave for Thule, then he would find a way to be there with them.

He now had to assume that the two of them had possession of all four triangles and thereby of the medallion, and so he and the grandmaster had agreed that this was an opportunity they could not allow themselves to miss. Eckleston would meet up with Müller and the two of them would do whatever it took to reach Thule along with Sterling and Keane.

★ ★ ★

'What was it you wanted to see me about?' said Colonel Strickland.

'This,' said Pete Ryan and placed several documents on Strickland's desk. 'As you know, the United States government has placed export restrictions on materials and equipment that could be used for weapons research and manufacturing purposes. These restrictions obviously cover military hardware such as tanks, fighter jets and guns, but they also cover nuclear, biological and chemical materials and equipment. Believe it or not, but the Defence Department has a whole section in its headquarters that does nothing but characterise, catalogue and evaluate all products made in the United States for precisely this purpose. If a certain product is deemed to have offensive capabilities, there will be restrictions imposed on who the company can sell the product to. Naturally, it primarily pertains to actual weapons, but in principle, all products are subject to these restrictions.'

'So have you had a request from someone you don't want to sell to lately?'

'Yes. But not only that. We've actually allowed the company to sell some equipment to them.'

'But, isn't that against the law?' asked Strickland.

'Well. Strictly speaking, yes. But it has been decided by the President and the National Security Council that the export restrictions can be waved if the sale has the potential to further other interests of the United States.'

'So, what does that mean, exactly?' asked a perplexed Strickland.

'I know it sounds a little cryptic,' said Ryan. 'But what it simply means is that a company based in the US can initiate the sale of hardware to the bad guys if the CIA runs the operation in order to obtain information about foreign governments or organisations that are deemed to be hostile to the US.'

'Do you then actually track the goods?'

'That and many other things. We trace and investigate bank accounts. We map business relationships between US and non-US companies and citizens, and if necessary, we use the whole operation to put in place surveillance networks for groups or individuals that we might want to monitor.'

'Clever,' said Strickland raising his eyebrows. 'But also risky.'

'Yes, at first glance it is. But the reality is that we never actually let a company ship out anything that could be used offensively. Once or twice, we have shipped out what was supposedly nuclear material and equipment for processing it, but in fact, both were harmless imitations. These types of operations can be a very effective means of getting inside clandestine organisations, but it requires a lot of work since these usually surround themselves with a huge network of affiliates and fronts to cover their tracks.'

'But you have had some results?'

'Yes. Some months ago, a small laboratory equipment company based in California, received a request for some pretty advanced hardware. As I said, the company is relatively small. As far as I can recall, it is not even listed on the stock market, but it specialises in developing sophisticated biological incubators for the health care industry, specifically biotechnology companies. These incubators are designed to grow and develop colonies of bacteria in a highly controlled environment. It is the sort of thing the United States Army uses for its biological weapons programme.'

'I didn't think it had any?' said Strickland and looked at Ryan.

'A biological weapons programme?' said Ryan casually. 'Well, officially they don't, but they have to keep ahead of the competition, right? Anyway, the request originated from a small health care equipment trading company in Ankara, Turkey. Upon further investigation, we were able to determine that this company in Turkey is owned by a construction conglomerate based in Syria.

That company is owned by an outrageously rich family, and several of the family's senior members are involved in so-called charity work, where they finance hospitals and food programmes, but also fundamentalist schools or 'madrassas' in various countries, including Syria, Lebanon, Sudan, Saudi-Arabia and Pakistan. We've had a few unpleasant experiences with people educated in these schools, so as you can imagine, that was enough to get our attention.'

'I would expect so,' said Strickland concerned.

'From what we were able to discover, and also working with the Turkish intelligence services, the laboratory equipment was actually destined for the city of Al Raqqa in Syria, from where it was supposed to have been shipped to an unknown location.'

'Well,' said Strickland. 'That does sound a bit unpleasant. What can we do to pursue this further?'

'I'm going to have a talk with British intelligence, as well as the guys back at Langley. The trading company in Turkey disappeared without a trace soon after we started our investigation, and we haven't been able to track any of the people who worked there.'

'We'll need to try to investigate that further,' said Strickland. 'And if possible, establish some sort of surveillance inside Syria. Now, whether that means actually putting people on the ground, I'm not entirely sure, but I'd appreciate it if you would present all the options as soon as you have them.'

'Will do, Sir. I'll get right on it.'

'Excellent. Thank you, Ryan.'

★ ★ ★

Andrew met Fiona the next day in his office. They discussed Andrew's discovery the night before and he demonstrated for her how the medallion floated and aligned itself pointing south. She was as amazed as he had been and tried it several times herself.

'You know,' she said. 'I've got this theory about the missing ruby.'

'Really? And what's that?'

'Well, gems and crystals are known to possess electrical attributes, right? I think that the ruby may have magnetic features that might increase the medallion's accuracy. Let's say that the ruby can become electrically charged, then it might somehow be able to amplify the effect of the Earth's magnetic field on the medallion, thereby making the medallion more receptive to that field.'

Andrew shrugged. 'Could be,' he said and walked over to the phone that had begun ringing just then. 'But since we don't have the first clue as to where it could be, we might never know what it does, or if it's really necessary. Anyway, we've been ordered to get underway as soon as possible, so we don't have time to look for it.'

He then picked up the phone, and upon hearing the voice on the other end of the line, he sat down by his desk to take notes. It was Colonel Strickland, who called to inform him that an agreement had been reached between the Prime Minister and the President of the United States to put together a mission to attempt to recover the original source of the bacterium. Both men had agreed that there was a considerable danger that samples of the pathogen could have fallen into the hands of terrorists and that these terrorists might have been able to mass-produce it somewhere. Since the investigation originated in Europe, it was agreed that the British would handle the coordination of the mission, but that it would be dealt with as a joint effort in all other respects. The Minister of Defence had then personally called the head of the British Antarctic research Station Halley, Sir Charles Goodwin, to ask him to arrange for the accommodation of a mission to Antarctica within a few days. For security reasons, Goodwin had been instructed to say nothing to anyone else on the research station about the exact nature of the mission. Strickland went on to tell Andrew that, as they spoke, living quarters were being prepared for them on the research station, so that they would be able to get to work soon after their arrival.

Strickland also informed him that he had been assigned two people to bring with him to Antarctica. One of them was John Marx, who was an expert on biological weapons and was employed by the British Army's bio-weapons research programme. The other was Bill Rosenbaum of the Centers for Disease Control in Atlanta, Georgia, in the United States. Rosenbaum had worked on identification and neutralisation of viral and bacteriological agents for almost twenty years and had seen his share of action. He was one of the first scientists to have been sent to the Congo when the Ebola virus had first been discovered, and he was also called on to deal with several cases of Anthrax bacteria immediately after the terrorist attacks on the World Trade Centre in 2001. Both of them had been instructed to bring along one assistant, as well as bio-suits that would be able to withstand the extreme temperatures of the Antarctic region. Marx would be travelling with Sterling, Keane and the rest of the British contingent to the British South Atlantic Island of South Georgia. There they would wait for the American team to arrive, and together they would be flown to the research station in Antarctica.

'And one other thing, Andy,' said Strickland. 'It appears that our friend Doctor Phillip Eckleston has made a run for it. He set his house on fire yesterday, and by the time the surveillance team got out of their car and up to the house he had slipped away.'

'Are you sure he wasn't inside when it went up in smoke?'

'Yes. We've had people in there to check, and they found no bodies. We believe that he'll probably try to leave the country as soon as he can. Airports and ports have been asked to keep an eye out for him. I trust that the police and the Border Force will do what they can, but the truth is that there are so many ways of travelling in and out of Britain that if he really wants to escape, then he'll probably succeed.'

'Alright,' said Andrew. 'I'll let you know if I spot him walking down the street one day. But then I'd probably want a little word with him myself.'

'Yes,' said Strickland. 'I understand that you are probably a bit upset about your father. We've been unable to come up with anything that might give us a hint about his reasons for joining such a society.'

'Maybe it chose him,' said Andrew pensively.

'How do you mean?' asked Strickland perplexed.

'Never mind,' said Andrew after a few seconds, and then cleared his throat. 'I suspect you have most of our travel arrangement already in place?'

'Indeed we do. In fact, we would like for you to leave tomorrow afternoon.'

'That soon?' said Andrew. 'But doesn't something like this take weeks of planning?'

'It normally would, but there are really no serious logistical issues since most of the equipment and supplies you will need are already there on Halley. They have plenty of supplies and they will be able to replace whatever you use at a later stage. The only thing that is a bit tricky is the scientific equipment that Marx and Rosenbaum need to bring with them. But we are working on that, and it ought to be solved today. It is possible that Halley might have most of what they need, since there are a range of scientific programmes in progress there, several of them revolving around current and prehistoric bacteriological life of the continent. But I'll call you both later this evening to let you know the exact time of your departure.'

As promised, Strickland called Andrew just after eight o'clock that evening to let him know that a British Army Gulfstream jet would be leaving for South Georgia the next day at 3 pm. A C-130 Hercules transport aircraft carrying research equipment and material would be dispatched several hours before that, and should arrive on South Georgia only a couple of hours after the teams got there.

An hour later Andrew got a call from Number 10 Downing Street, and a few seconds later the Prime minister came on the line to wish him luck and again stress the importance of success. Only then did Andrew begin to feel the pressure mounting. He was used to getting very precise orders from people in uniforms to do things he had already done hundreds of times before, but this was different. The truth was, that they had no idea if they would even be able to find anything, and if they did, nobody would know exactly what to do. Marx and Rosenbaum were both experts within their respective fields, but they would need time to come up with a solution, and Andrew was concerned that the people around him were having unrealistic expectations as to the speed of eventual success. The Prime Minister assured him that he had complete faith in him and the rest of the team, and that he understood that they wouldn't be able to perform miracles.

★ ★ ★

The next day at one o'clock in the afternoon, Andrew and Fiona were picked up by a car, and taken to London City Airport, just east of Canary Wharf. John Marx, who looked a bit bewildered by it all, met them there and it became clear that he had only been given the bare minimum of detail about what their objective was. Marx was in his mid-thirties and had a narrow face with small but intelligent-looking eyes. On his nose was affixed a pair of square glasses and on his chin was a small black beard.

His assistant was a 26-year-old woman named Alice Bailey, who also worked for the army's biological weapons research programme. She seemed shy and didn't say much to anyone for the first few hours. Eventually, she started to relax, and it turned out that she was actually a very chatty and agreeable person.

As they taxied out to the runway, Andrew engaged in small talk with the two, and it wasn't until they had got airborne and were well underway, that he told them all the details of the mission that lay ahead of them. The four of them spent the next few hours getting aquatinted, and in between the planning of the trip, the naps, the food, and the jokes about the food, they ended up getting along quite well. The flight to South Georgia took a gruelling seventeen hours, and when they finally landed on the windswept landing strip near the town of Stromness on the north side of the small mountainous island, they staggered out of the aeroplane and walked towards the tiny terminal building. It was just below freezing but the strong wind caused the wind chill factor to make it feel like ten degrees below zero. Luckily there was no snow falling when they arrived, but the clouds above them looked as if they would be able to release mountains of it, given half a chance.

In a hangar a couple of hundred meters away on the other side of the runway, they could see the C-130 transport plane being refuelled. They would only have a few hours on the ground before they would have to press on. Less than an hour after their arrival, the American contingent arrived in what appeared to be an all-white civilian Learjet, but as the plane touched down and rolled up to the terminal building, they could see the letters 'CDC' painted in blue along the side of the plane. The Americans were equally groggy from their long flight, and after having exchanged handshakes and pleasantries, they were all driven into town to meet with the mayor. He had arranged for a bit of breakfast for them, which was much needed.

There were three Americans on the team, since Bill Rosenbaum had insisted on taking two people who had worked closely with him for several years. Rosenbaum was a very inquisitive character, and he asked lots of questions about the events that had led up to them flying to Antarctica. Eventually, though, Andrew had to tell him that he simply couldn't answer all his questions, since the investigation was ongoing and some of the information was still classified.

Breakfast came to an end, and a few hours later they were driven back to the airport, where they boarded the de Havilland Dash-7 that had arrived soon after they had left for Stromness. It was a high wing, four-engine turboprop aircraft, capable of carrying as many as fifty-four people in its passenger transport configuration. Now it was configured to carry supplies as well, reducing the number of seats considerably. Like all the other aircraft used by the British in Antarctica, the aircraft was painted in a bright red colour, which made it easy to spot against the snow and ice-covered landscape. It had a wingspan of 28 meters, a length of 25 meters and a maximum take-off weight of 21 tons, making it capable of carrying a significant amount of supplies back and forth between Halley and the airport at Stromness.

Only a few hours after it had arrived, the aircraft had been refuelled and was now taxiing back out to the runway with its two crew and seven passengers. Getting clearance from the control tower, the pilot increased the throttle and the plane soon shot out over the runway, with its passengers sitting by the windows looking out on the cold grey and blue sea that surrounded South Georgia. As the aircraft climbed, the sea disappeared below a thick cloud layer, and soon they could see nothing but the soft white carpet of clouds that stretched as far as the eye could see in all directions.

As they flew onwards towards the south, there was nothing to reveal that they were now moving closer to the south pole than most people would ever get. The view was like that of any other flight, except the de Haviland flew a lot lower than most commercial passenger aircraft. Inside the warm and comfortable aircraft, the seven of them were enjoying coffee and the occasional snack. Several of them were reading books and magazines, and from time to time one or two would nod off to sleep. The flight would take just under 5 hours, and when they were about halfway there, the pilot informed them that the weather at the landing strip was excellent and that they would be greeted by Halley's current chief, Sir Goodwin.

'Have any of you guys heard of him before?' asked Rosenbaum.

'I have,' said Marx and nodded. 'He's actually quite famous in Britain, but mainly for his research on the fossils he's uncovered in the Antarctic region. I spoke to him a few months ago when they discovered some million-year-old bacteria locked in the ice. There was talk of me going to see him, and he and I were making preparation, but then the funding was pulled. I guess the powers that be see things a bit differently now,' he smiled meekly.

'Where exactly is this research station Halley?' asked Fiona.

'It's situated on the Brunt Ice Shelf,' said Marx 'The current station is actually called Halley VI since it is the sixth station to be built there. The first was established in 1956, and named after the astronomer Edmond Halley, so we've been down there for quite a long time now. Over the years the station has contributed significantly to studies in meteorology, glaciology, seismology, and even radio astronomy. Many of these studies have continued uninterrupted since their initial inception in the fifties. Halley is actually the UK's most isolated research station and is located on an ice shelf just off the mainland of Antarctica. The station itself is some 12 kilometres from the edge of the ice and considerably further from what is called the 'hinge zone', where the floating ice shelf is joined to the continent. In winter there is darkness for 105 days, but at this time of year, there should be plenty of light.'

'How many people live there now?' asked Alice Bailey.

'Well, it has a maximum capacity of 65 people, and it gets close to that number during the summer, but during the winter there can be as little as 15, so on average I guess there are about 35.'

'It must be a nightmare to supply all those people.'

'Yes. Supplies are brought to Halley twice a year by ship, which take it as far as where the ice shelf meets the sea. It is then towed on sledges by snowmobiles to Halley, so it is really a major undertaking, especially in the summertime with that many people there.'

'I hope they have enough beds for us,' grinned Rosenbaum.

'Don't worry,' said Andrew and smiled. 'It has been arranged so that there is plenty of space for all of us.'

As they approached the landing strip on the Antarctic ice shelf, and the plane began to descend through the clouds, the turbulence buffeted the wings quite violently, making them bend unnaturally up and down.

Fiona didn't feel safe at all as that was going on, but soon thereafter the plane broke through the clouds and ahead of them appeared a magnificent sight. It was close to noon, and the weather was clearing. Stretching from East to West was a white landscape like no other they had seen before. They were just passing over the boundary between the South Atlantic and the ice sheets that stretched hundreds of kilometres out from the continent. Below them, the dark blue ocean was abruptly replaced by a seemingly endless white blanket. The aircraft continued to descend towards the ice and in the far distance to their left, they could see a few mountains sticking up from the otherwise flat terrain. That meant that they were close to the research station, and soon the pilot pulled back on the throttle and the airspeed started to gradually bleed off as they approached the station. The 'Fasten Seatbelt' sign came on and they all found their seats and buckled up for what was expected to be a rough landing. Prior to the arrival of aircraft, the people on Halley prepared the landing strip with large snowmobiles that would drive along the entire length of the runways levelling out its surface.

It appeared that they had done a good job because as the pilot levelled the aircraft out over the ice, extended the flaps to maximum drag and the speed gradually reduced, he was able to set the plane down very gently on the ice. As they slid along the landing strip on the aircraft's skis, there were a few violent bumps that made them jump in their seats, but on the whole, the landing was surprisingly smooth. As they taxied to the end of the runway, they could see the station about five hundred meters to the East. It didn't look like much, and Andrew had trouble imagining how that many people could live there for as long as they did.

As soon as the aircraft came to a stop and the pilot switched off the engines, a small vehicle drove up to it and a man jumped out, immediately attaching long hoses with special nozzles to them. The hoses would pump warm air in through the engines to stop them from freezing, which would make it impossible to get them to start again. While the passengers exited onto the gleaming white snow, another vehicle drove up to the back of the aircraft and a couple of men began unloading the supplies as well as the luggage.

Still wincing from the sunlight bouncing off the snow, Andrew was greeted by Sir Charles Goodwin who came over to him with a big smile on his face. He was a tall grey-haired man with a strong handshake and a booming voice.

'Mr. Sterling. I am Charles Goodwin. We've been expecting you. How was your trip?'

'Long,' sighed Andrew. 'But the scenery here is almost worth it,' he smiled and gazed out over the shimmering expanse that lay before him.

'Yes. We tend to get used to it here, but it is nice to stop and appreciate it once in a while. Your transport is over there,' he said and pointed to a snowmobile the size of a station wagon, with a passenger compartment akin to a bus on skis towed behind it.

Then Goodwin proceeded to greet all the other members of the newly arrived team, and soon they were on their way to the research station. The compound was the most unusual building

Andrew had ever seen. From a distance, it looked like an extremely long-legged caterpillar sitting on the ice. It comprised 8 sections, each about 15 meters long, and all of them joined together consecutively to form one long habitat. All of the sections were blue, except for one in the middle, which was red and much larger than the others. This was the central hub, containing recreational spaces and the communal restaurant. All the other sections contained living quarters as well as labs and research facilities. All of the individual sections were sitting on stilts several meters above the ice, and the stilts were themselves attached to skis, which allowed the station to be relocated once per year, in order to prevent it from gradually getting buried in the snow. The reason for these efforts was that previous habitats were built directly on the ice, and they were each abandoned within a few years, having been buried and subsequently crushed by the snow and ice.

Arriving at their living quarters they were pleasantly surprised to find them very spacious and comfortable. Each room had large oval windows made of thick triple-glazing, allowing the occupants to admire the scenery both day and night. The Antarctic storms could produce gusts of several hundred kilometres per hour, so almost any object bigger than a tennis ball could potentially become a deadly missile. Most of them spent the first hours of the afternoon sleeping and resting, while Andrew and Fiona had a private meeting with Sir Goodwin to explain to him what they planned to do. Goodwin was very cooperative and pledged to offer any equipment or expertise that they might need. He also assured them that he would not tell anyone else on the research station about the real purpose of their stay.

A few hours later, the C-130 Hercules arrived to offload the equipment that Marx, Rosenbaum and their teams would need. They soon set up a fully functioning laboratory in one of the sections of the station. That section was then slowly dragged about 500 metres away from the main station on a set of skis. Andrew was still concerned about whether the bio-suits might work properly in these extreme conditions but there was only one way of finding out.

While Fiona supervised the construction of a small sealed water container for the medallion made from Plexiglas, Andrew was driven to the landing strip where a smaller plane, a de Haviland Twin Otter, would take him and Goodwin out for a small tour of the surrounding area. The aircraft was a twin-engine turboprop aircraft with a wingspan of just under 20 meters. Originally designed to be a bush aircraft, it was famous for its rugged construction and Short Take-Off and Landing or STOL performance. The version operated by the British Antarctic Survey, was the wheel/ski-equipped aircraft, which has the capability to land on both snow and ice or a hard runway. It was normally used for carrying scientists out to field locations for short periods of time. Its engine almost seemed too large for it, as it positively leapt off the improvised airstrip and the pilot banked it over to the right, making a full circle of the research station as he increased his altitude. They then flew at an altitude of a couple of hundred meters towards the east. To their left was about ten kilometres of flat ice, which eventually met the dark South Atlantic Ocean. It was summertime in the Southern Hemisphere, so this would be as close as the sea would ever get to them. To their right in the far distance was a mountain range with huge dark peaks protruding from the white glacial base. After about an hour's flight and a couple of hundred kilometres, a large mountain loomed ahead of them in the distance.

'What's that?' asked Andrew and pointed to the mountain.

'It is called Vestfjella,' said Goodwin. 'It is actually part of a large mountain range that stretches about a hundred kilometres into the continent. We've been there several times to collect geological samples. Those are some of the oldest mountains on Earth, so their composition is quite interesting from a geological perspective. We've had several scientists from other countries come here to study plate tectonics. I don't suppose that many people know this, but during the Jurassic period, 180 million years ago, Antarctica formed the core of a super-continent called Pangea. When that eventually split up, Africa, South America, India, Australia and New Zealand drifted away from the Antarctic core, and the southern oceans were born. The challenge for us here is to understand how tectonic forces interacted to produce the sequence of events during break-up. Our research programme uses methods from many branches of geoscience, including geophysics and geochemistry, and we study satellite imagery in order to identify surface features, as well as flying aeromagnetic and aerogravity surveys to determine deep crust structures. By doing this, we can uncover unique information about the Antarctic continent, and how and why the super-continent dispersed. Based on the results, we then feed it into a computer model for the dispersal of the fragments of the original super-continent. That then provides us with the most up-to-date reconstructions and animations of the break-up of the continent and the birth of the southern oceans, and this, in turn, helps us better understand how tectonic forces work in general.'

'Sounds complicated,' said Andrew and looked down on the mountain. 'And expensive.'

'Yes,' smiled Goodwin. 'I suppose it is. I'll admit that I am not an expert on these areas of research. My speciality is fossilised plants and animals.'

'So, have you found anything interesting?' asked Andrew as the aircraft passed over the mountaintop and started a low turn to head back towards Halley.

'Well, the polar region is often portrayed as being populated by relatively few animals. Most people would probably know about penguins and seals, but our study of biodiversity has found rich and diverse marine life. One of the challenges for us here is to use this approach to study how Antarctic animal communities respond to systemic changes in temperature and radiation.'

'Can you give me an example of one of the projects?' asked Andrew.

'Sure. Several of our investigations into the relationship between ecosystem diversity and stability, focus on the terrestrial and freshwater realm. So, what we do is collect a representative sample of micro-organisms, including fungi, mites, and bacteria from various sites. These are then transferred to the laboratory where soil and freshwater communities of varying levels of complexity are established, within sealed microcosms.'

'Like an aquarium?'

'Yes. Except that these are completely sealed. These experimental communities are then subjected to systemic changes in both temperature and UV radiation in order to determine which communities are the most susceptible to environmental changes and which are the most resilient. By doing this, we can investigate the probable effect of environmental changes such as global warming or increased UV radiation from space.'

'Well, it sounds as if some of your people might be able to have a very interesting discussion with some of mine, if it wasn't because of all this secrecy. How often do you venture out?'

'Quite often, although we spend most of our time at Halley, analysing and studying the samples we bring back.'

'Don't you ever get lonely out here? I mean, it's not as if you can take a snowmobile and go home whenever you like.'

'I guess it can get a bit lonely here from time to time, but we also realise that this is a great privilege that not very many people get to experience. And just thinking about the amount of money that our government pours into this place can make any man feel humble.'

'It must be an unforgiving place to work,' said Andrew and looked out across the beautiful but harsh continent.

'It can be. We've had a few deaths here since the fifties I'm sad to say, but we try as best we can to live in harmony with nature, as opposed to trying to conquer it. On this continent, man is but a small ant that may be stepped on by the forces of nature if it behaves foolishly.'

'What a colourful analogy,' smiled Andrew. 'But I suppose you are right.'

Andrew knew a thing or two about how tough an opponent the weather could be. He had tried being beaten back, not by an enemy force but by the forces of nature, on more than one occasion. His own experience with arctic conditions was limited, having fought mostly in jungle and desert conditions. He and his team had brought excellent equipment with them to Antarctica, so he wasn't concerned that any of them might get hurt, as long as they took care of themselves and didn't tempt fate.

The skis mounted under the wheels of the landing gear skidded across the hard snow and ice, as the plane bled off speed and finally slid to a halt at the end of the runway.

As the two men made their way back from the landing strip, they walked past a series of vehicles in all shapes and sizes, all painted the same bright red as the aircraft.

'I had expected you to do most of your travelling by sleigh,' said Andrew.

'Well, we hardly ever use dogs for pulling sleighs anymore. We have several motorised units. The Snow Scooters here are probably the best known to the average person,' said Goodwin and pointed to a couple of red and black scooters that were neatly parked alongside a container. 'They are easy to ride with just a twist grip throttle and a brake, and their maintenance is similar to that of a motorbike. They have a fully automatic transmission and a skilled rider can move across the ice at upwards of 80 kilometres per hour.'

'Wow. I'd like to try one,' said Andrew. 'I think they will probably be the best vehicles for our purposes.'

'We also have a number of snowmobiles,' said Goodwin, and walked over to a somewhat larger tracked vehicle. 'They are mainly employed as personnel transports, as are these Tucker Snow-cats, which we use in and around the station. Propelled by four tracks and powered by a 170 horsepower diesel engine, they can go just about anywhere you want to go, and they are virtually impossible to break. They can tow sledges with up to 8 tonnes in weight.'

'Impressive. I guess these are the workhorses of this station?'

'Yes. You might say that, but the largest of the machines available here is the Caterpillar D4H bulldozer that's parked over there on the other side of that building. It is by far the most powerful vehicle here. It is fitted with internal pre-heating equipment that heats the engine to its operating temperature before starting. It can start even if the temperature of the engine block is as low as –30 degrees Celsius. They burn aviation fuel which remains fluid down to –60 degrees Celsius, but the engines lose about 10 percent of their power at that temperature.'

'These are quite the beasts,' said Andrew as they walked up the ladder to the machine shop where Fiona was working on the container for the medallion. 'I guess you weren't joking when you said this place costs a lot of money to run.'

'The fuel cost alone is huge,' said Goodwin, 'Frankly, we are just very happy that the politicians continue to see a purpose in us being here, and continue to fund us.'

They entered the machine shop, and inside it, Fiona and two other people from the station were stooped over a table on which sat a strange contraption. It was a square box made entirely from Plexiglas with an orange fluid inside. At its centre, the medallion was held in place by a thin pole going right through the centre of it, where the ruby was supposed to have been.

'What is this gadget?' asked Andrew and walked closer to the transparent cigar case sized box.

'It's a primitive compass made with the medallion.'

'But what is that fluid you've placed it in?' he said and attempted to peer inside.

'That's actually unused engine oil. It's nice a thick. It ensures that the medallion doesn't spin around erratically if the box is shaken or tilted for a few seconds. It makes the whole thing more stable and reliable, but it also means that it responds more slowly than if it was placed in water. However, since I'm not expecting our destination to move around, I thought that this was a good idea.'

'Pretty good thinking,' said Andrew impressed. 'What about that pin at the centre? That's for holding it in place I assume.'

'Yes. I have simply squeezed a small rubber ball into the hole and then stuck a thin piece of metal through it, attaching both ends to each side of the box. This way the medallion can only move laterally even if the box is tipped over. But again, this ads to the rigidity of the system which is both good and bad. I think it probably needs a couple of minutes to align itself perfectly now.'

'I would have never guessed that there was an engineer inside you just itching to come out,' grinned Andrew. 'This looks very good. But where is it pointing now?'

'Uhm. Well,' said Fiona apprehensively. 'Not south, that's for sure.'

'What?' said Andrew puzzled. 'Let me see.'

He walked over next to the box and pulled out a small magnetic compass. If the magnetic compass was reading right, the medallion was pointing towards the east. Andrew looked at Goodwin and showed him the compass.

'Is this correct?' he asked.

'Yes,' said Goodwin. 'East is definitely in that direction,' he said and pointed to one of the walls.

'Well, you should know,' said Andrew and scratched his head while grimacing. 'What lies in that direction apart from those mountains we just flew over?'

'Nothing,' said Goodwin. 'Vestfjella is the only thing between us and the sea. If you continue in that direction you'll end up in the Indian Ocean.'

'Which mountains?' asked Fiona, annoyed at having the men talk over her head.

'We just flew over a mountain range a few hours ago while you were in here playing engineer. The largest of them is called Vestfjella, and it is about 200 kilometres from here, and it just might be that the medallion is pointing to that mountain.'

'Well, I'd say that it is very likely,' said Fiona. 'From the journals of Jürgen Reitziger, it is quite clear that the cave is on the side of a mountain.'

'Who?' asked Goodwin.

'Jürgen Reitziger,' said Andrew. 'A chap that was here a number years ago. I can't reveal more than that at this stage, I'm afraid. Sorry about that.'

'That's quite alright,' said Goodwin. 'I understand that this is a sensitive matter. Why don't the two of you discuss this in private,' he said, and then led the two mechanics outside.

'Vestfjella is almost at the centre of the coastline of Queen Maude's Land,' said Fiona after the three had left. 'So, I think the odds are pretty good that this is where the medallion is pointing.'

'Agreed,' said Andrew. 'We'll go there tomorrow.'

'By plane?' asked Fiona.

'Yes, I think it would be good to have eyes in the sky, so some of us should definitely fly out there. But we will also need snow-scooters to get closer to the mountain range. We're not guaranteed to be able to land the plane that close to the mountain. Anyway, I think we should bring at least three snow-scooters out there, leaving this station perhaps three hours ahead of the plane.'

'I would definitely prefer to fly out there,' said Fiona. 'It's going to take forever by snow-scooter.'

'I know. I'll lead a team out to an agreed-upon position as soon as I can tomorrow, and then you can follow in the small transport plane, Ok?'

'Great,' said Fiona. 'Let's go and join the others. I think that we are being given a small welcome dinner tonight over in the main building.'

Andrew and Fiona left the machine shop and walked through the other sections to the main hub of the station. The rest of the team was already mingling with the permanent residents of the station, and there were people laughing and joking. The atmosphere did not reflect the underlying tension felt by the new arrivals. Their endeavour was potentially a very hazardous one, but they all knew that they couldn't decline without the loss of much more than their jobs. Each of them understood that a failure would potentially place millions of people in peril. Andrew told them to rest for the remainder of the day since most of them would be leaving early the next morning.

TWENTY-TWO

Arriving at his Monaco hotel, wearing an expensive pin-striped suit, a white shirt and a purple tie, Colin McGregor strode through the foyer and headed for the reception. Behind him followed a concierge with his two large suitcases and his hand luggage. McGregor had made an effort to look like a high roller that had come to town to gamble. The idea was to make him blend in with the rest of the crowd, and that seemed to have worked, because everywhere he looked there were men in fancy suits and women in designer dresses, and the whole place positively oozed money. The entire second floor was a casino with everything a compulsive gambler could ever dream of.

Fortunes were won and lost every single night, and it was not unusual to see winners celebrating loudly at one table and losers starring apathetically ahead of them at another. In the basement, there was a large bowling alley, where the guests could take a break from the real games. Most of the people that stayed here were rich kids out to gamble away the family fortune, but as in every other place where there was money, there were also the people who follow it. Loan sharks, prostitutes and con artists were all part of the scenery, but the vast majority of the guests were people who stayed in the hotel for a few nights before moving on.

The hotel was situated on one of the hillsides that surrounds the town of Monaco, with no more than a five-minute walk to the harbour and easy access to the promenade. McGregor had been booked into one of the most expensive rooms available, which suited him just fine. He had never stayed in a hotel like this, and he had promised Strickland to go down into the casino on the night of his arrival in order to be seen. Gambling had never appealed to him, but he would of course do as ordered. He was here for business, not pleasure, and his business could be a messy one, so it made good sense to play the part of a sophisticated high roller just passing through town.

As the panting concierge dragged his suitcases through the door to his room, McGregor walked over to the window to savour the view. Out across the ocean to his right, the sun had just set, and already the casinos, restaurants and nightclubs that littered the town were trying to attract customers with their neon signs. Just as the night before and every other night for as long as anyone could remember, the tourists came like moths to a flame, most of them entering town with a healthy bank account, and some leaving a small fortune poorer. McGregor handed the concierge a generous tip, after which he quickly left the room, thinking about the bracelet he would buy for his hard-to-please girlfriend.

At half-past five, McGregor re-emerged from the bathroom feeling refreshed and ready to put on a show. He switched on the TV and then calmly took his time to get dressed. He was good looking and had often been called 'pretty boy' by his mates in the army, and as he stood there in his black tuxedo looking every bit the heir to a fortune, he knew that he would be able to make an impression here.

His placid exterior belied the fact that he was one of the best and most capable people in the service at the moment. This was far from his usual *métier*, but his senior officer and good friend Captain Andrew Sterling had specifically asked for him to do this mission. The reason for this was that Sterling expected things to potentially take a violent turn at some stage, and he wanted someone who could handle himself. Another reason was that McGregor and Sterling had worked closely together for several years both out in the field, back in London, as well as on the training grounds at Hereford, and because of the sensitive nature of the whole affair, Sterling needed someone he knew well.

His father had been a banker and his mother a teacher, and Colin had grown up in a suburb of Edinburgh with two older brothers and a younger sister. His sister was still in school, training to become a veterinarian, and both of his older brothers had gone to university and gone into banking like their father. Partially because of that, Colin had decided to do something different, and had joined the army at seventeen and had never looked back. Soon after joining, he had demonstrated a natural instinct for field operations, and after a few years, he had been selected for evaluation as an SAS candidate. Due to his physical and mental strength, he had completed the evaluation programme with one of the best scores ever, and had then joined the service soon thereafter. Having taken part in several covert operations in Indonesia, Iraq, and Afghanistan alongside Sterling, he had been asked to transfer to an elite anti-terrorist unit under the command of his friend.

Working primarily as an investigative unit, they would also need the ability to strike without having to involve other parties in the operation. So, McGregor, along with several others that had all been handpicked from the ranks of the SBS and the SAS, had been put together to form the core of the team. They hadn't yet been in action, but disciplined as they were, they spent countless hours at Hereford and made regular trips to jungles and desert abroad to hone their skills, and keep themselves sharp. The only thing that might have revealed a hint of his true nature now, was his lean muscular body that was quite evident, even under the tuxedo.

He left his room and took the elevator to the casino on the second floor, where people were already sitting around the tables wishing for Lady Luck to come their way. The casino never slept, and there were always people either convinced that this would be their day, or determined to win back what they had already lost.

McGregor took the grand tour along all of the tables and made sure to make himself seen and heard. He genuinely enjoyed himself, but that was mostly because he was spending money that wasn't his, and because he found it amusing to watch how people would flock around him like vultures when he was on a winning streak. At one point, a young female gold digger was trying so hard to look enticing that McGregor could have sworn that she would have been arrested for prostitution back in London.

Undeterred, he pressed on, and although he had been ahead by over forty thousand dollars at one stage, he decided to stop after having lost most of it again. There was no need to be too flippant about losing. That might seem suspicious.

After a few hours, he got up from the table he had been sitting at and walked downstairs. As arranged, Nick Frost was waiting for him in the hotel lobby. The two men shook hands like old friends, even though they had never met, and then proceeded outside for a stroll in the small park that lay in front of the casino. It was still early, so there was nobody there to listen in on their conversation.

'Everything alright so far?' asked Frost.

'Yep,' said McGregor and grinned. 'I'm up 6,000 dollars. Are you all set?'

'Yes. This is his house,' he said and handed McGregor a photo. 'It's not far from here. You can almost see it on the other side of that ridge over there,' he said and pointed to the top of a hill with relatively few houses. 'That is where the superrich people live, and Ivanov owns a house up there.'

'So much for the theory that he is just a good card player, eh?'

'Yes. Those houses cost tens of millions of pounds, and he has several others that are even more expensive in other cities around the world.'

'And you've verified that the source is Middle Eastern?'

'Yes. MI6 has proof that the accounts that transfer money to Ivanov, have also financed the purchase of large quantities of weapons that were subsequently delivered to Hezbollah and other groups. These people are definitely not your average friendly neighbour.'

'When is he at home?'

'Mostly at night of course, but driving past the house a few times today, it seemed to me that he might be home right now.'

'So, should we make our move tonight?'

'Yes. The orders are to get to him as quickly as possible, so I think we should take the opportunity and get it done this evening.'

'Security?' asked McGregor.

'Three or four people. There is always at least one guard patrolling the grounds in front of the house, and we believe that there is one close to the main entrance of the house and possibly two inside the house at all times. This man seems to believe it necessary to protect himself.'

'Right,' said McGregor rubbing his chin. 'Weather's fine. The clouds will block out the moonlight, so all I need to worry about is the light from the house. When do you think is the best time?'

'Well, he is probably going to go out again tonight, so I'd say our best chance is to move just before he gets home. It's a one-way street, so I should be able to warn you when he is approaching.'

'Just after midnight, then?'

'Yes. I think that's fine. That should leave you plenty of time to get ready to receive him.'

'Good,' said McGregor calmly. 'I'll expect you at twelve then.'

'Great. I'll see you then.'

'Right. Must get back to it,' grinned McGregor. 'It's a tough job, but someone's got to do it.'

★ ★ ★

Less than three hundred kilometres east of Halley, at the German research station of Neumayer on Crown Princess Martha's Coast, Phillip Eckleston and Wilhelm Müller were preparing to gear up for their own mission. Privately, Eckleston had hypothesised that Thule might lie somewhere within the Vestfjella mountain that was only a couple of hundred kilometres away from the German research station, but without the medallion, it would have been like looking for a needle in a haystack to go there.

However, now that he had solid information that Sterling was going to the British research station Halley on the other side of

Vestfjella, he felt his theory had been proven correct, and he was now convinced that they were on the right track. Although things had become unpleasantly complicated lately, his basic approach of having someone else lead him and the society to Thule, had been proven right. As such, he felt vindicated for the troubles that had befallen the society over the last few weeks, and now more than ever, he was filled with energy and determination.

Chartering a private jet from a company in Vienna, he and Müller, along with a group of three others had left for Neumayer as soon as the bugs in Andrew's mansion had revealed his destination. It would cost them a considerable amount of money, but after consulting with the grandmaster, now in hiding in Italy, they could think of no better way of applying those resources. Furthermore, the Thule Society was extremely wealthy after having financed itself from the theft of property from hundreds of thousands of wealthy Jews that had been sent to the concentration camps in the late 1930s and early 1940s. Ever since then, the assets of the society had been managed by hundreds of professional asset management organisations around the world, who had no idea where the money had initially come from.

It was clear to Eckleston that Müller thoroughly enjoyed it all. Formerly a member of an elite Austrian Mountain division, he had received extensive training in operating in cold and harsh conditions such as these, and as an added bonus, his position within the division had provided him with a good platform for recruiting several others that were sympathetic to the cause. People always looked to him when things got difficult or dangerous, and he'd had no trouble convincing three of those people to join him and Eckleston for the trip to Neumayer. They had accepted without hesitation, even though they were told that it might become dangerous and that neither the German government nor the research station itself would be informed prior to their arrival. As far as they were concerned, the German and Austrian governments were traitors to their own people. After half a century of pacifism, they simply did not see the immense potential hidden within themselves. For that reason, the men considered it a legitimate act to use Neumayer as they saw fit, including taking it over completely if that should be deemed necessary.

They were now mounting their vehicles, and getting ready to leave for Vestfjella, which the German scientists had told them had been surveyed by a British research aircraft the day before. That meant that they had probably arrived just in the nick of time, but also that they needed to move out immediately without resting. As far as they were concerned, the British could already be on their way to Vestfjella, and Eckleston knew that this was an opportunity that would only present itself once in a lifetime, or perhaps only once in a thousand years.

Weapons were handed out and the former soldiers slung them over their shoulders, but Eckleston settled for a small handgun. He had never actually fired a weapon in his life, but he felt quite prepared to do so now. Leaving the small contingent of 18 German scientists bound and gagged, but safe in the main building of the research station, they mounted their snow-scooters and raced off across the ice shelf towards the tall mountains that loomed ahead of them 50 kilometres away.

★ ★ ★

On a quiet road on the hillside above Ivanov's property, a black van moved along with its headlight off. The Russian's mansion was placed at the centre of a large property that lay on a hillside overlooking central Monaco. The mansion was a white two-story house with beautiful gardens and a swimming pool, and running across the grounds between the tall pine trees were small footpaths that were used for taking walks. As the van approached the back of the property, it slowed down and its side door opened. A few seconds later a figure adroitly jumped out and rolled a few times before lying still in the bushes by the side of the road.

The van drove away as quietly as it had arrived, and soon McGregor was on his feet and moving crouched through the bushes and down the hill towards the fence that surrounded Ivanov's property. He was wearing all-black light body armour designed to produce minimal noise, as well as provide protection from small arms fire. His chest and back were covered with a Kevlar vest and into his suit were embedded smaller patches of Kevlar over the arms and legs. Knees, shoulders and elbows were padded with a strong but flexible composite textile woven from ultra-thin strands of carbon fibre. His face was painted black and he wore a dark woollen cap over his head. In his ear was a small headset that would let him communicate with Nick Frost, who would by now be parked close to the entrance to the one-way street on which Ivanov lived.

In his belt, McGregor had a silenced 9 mm Beretta Model 92SD pistol. A favourite of several special operations forces around the world, it was lightweight and very quiet. Attached to the other side of his belt was a heartbeat sensor, which could detect the heartbeats of living beings even through a wall. Having been developed for search and rescue operations, it was not yet widely used, but it was a very effective means of locating other people. He also brought with him a pair of small night vision binoculars, which he used several times as he approached the fence.

The house was around 150 meters away, and he could not spot any movement from where he was. Normally, the SAS would use helmet-mounted night vision goggles, but McGregor needed to stay quiet and hidden for as long as possible so he didn't want to be carrying too much equipment.

'I've reached the fence,' he whispered to Frost through the headset, and then he crawled up to it and pulled out a pair of wire cutters and quietly cut a hole just big enough for him to slip through. Once on the other side of the fence, he continued to crawl closer to the house, which seemed eerily quiet. There was no one to be seen anywhere, and looking through the binoculars revealed no movement either. He crept up close to a tree and rested. If his pulse became too high, he would not be able to move as deliberately and silently as he needed to, so he sat there in the shadow for a few seconds without moving a muscle, while watching the windows of the mansion. There were twelve windows facing his way, and the light was on in several of them. Having assured himself that there was no one in sight, he got up and ran crouched to within ten meters of the house where he laid down in the bushes next to the swimming pool.

As he lay there, he spotted a man sitting in the kitchen downstairs with his back towards the glass doors that lead to the swimming pool. He was a large man with short dark hair and a gun holster around his torso. He was watching a small television set and periodically stuck his hand into a bag of chips, which he then stuffed into his mouth. McGregor watched the man for a few seconds.

Amateur, he thought. *His back to the window and the TV overpowering his senses. I guess Ivanov is still out of the house.*

'By the house,' he whispered. 'One guard in the kitchen.'

He was just about to get up and move around the building towards the front of the house, when a man carrying a large shotgun came walking around the corner of the house no more than five meters from him. The man was wearing black trousers, a blue jacket and a baseball cap, and as he turned the corner, he exhaled a big cloud of cigarette smoke. He held a cigarette between his fingers next to the trigger, and as he came closer, McGregor could see that he was looking out over the grounds the way a guard should. But as he walked past McGregor, no more than a meter from his head, he didn't notice the figure that lay silently at his feet.

McGregor lay perfectly still without breathing until the man had passed and gone all the way around the swimming pool.

A second after he had disappeared around the corner on the other side of the house, McGregor slipped past the glass door and moved swiftly along the mansion towards where the man had just disappeared. He moved swiftly towards the corner of the house, but his feet hardly made any sound in the soft grass. A few meters before reaching the corner, and still moving smoothly forward, McGregor unholstered his 9 mm Beretta, and held it out in front of him at an angle so that it pointed at the ground a couple of meters ahead of him.

Turning the corner, he immediately spotted the guard walking away from him some ten meters away. The guard, hearing a noise and thinking that it was one of his comrades, turned and began to say something in French, when he saw the dark figure silently coming towards him like a crouched tiger. It took him a couple of seconds to process what he was seeing, and then he immediately scrambled to flip the safety on the shotgun. As he did so he dropped his cigarette, which bounced off the ground creating a small cloud of glowing orange embers.

McGregor's senses were now at peak performance, and as he watched the shotgun coming up to point at him, it seemed like it was happening in slow motion. While still crouched and moving forward, McGregor brought up his pistol in one smooth movement, at the end of which he fired off two shots in quick succession. The gun produced two quick 'pop' noises, and the bullets both hit the guard in the forehead. He had not had a chance to fire his shotgun, and he instantly slumped to the ground like a ragdoll.

McGregor continued moving forward silently, and only stopped when he was kneeling down beside the man. He was well and truly dead and McGregor decided to leave him in the shadows where he had fallen. Unless someone actually tripped over him, he was unlikely to get noticed. Moving quickly to the next corner of the mansion he peered around it towards the front of the house where a couple of cars were parked in the driveway. There was nobody else in sight, and he concluded that there had only been one guard outside, just as Frost has indicated.

'One guard down,' he whispered and holstered his pistol.

'Roger,' replied Frost quietly.

McGregor had planned to go in through the patio doors in the kitchen, but because the guard was sitting in there watching TV, he decided to try to find an alternative way in. The exterior wall of the house, where the dead body lay, was covered with a thick compact network of vines, so he decided to crawl up to one of the windows on the first floor. Slowly, he made his way upwards, placing his feet carefully on the strongest vines and trying not to break them. Upon reaching the window, he placed a small suction cup on the windowpane and then twisted the knob at the centre of the cup, thereby cutting out a circular piece of the glass without making any noise. The hole was big enough for him to stick his hand through and a few seconds later he had opened the window and climbed inside.

Standing in a dark room, he listened for voices or footsteps but could hear none. He opened the door quietly, still listening for any movement outside in the hallway. Hearing nothing but the TV downstairs, he walked quietly and purposefully through the upstairs with his heartbeat sensor on, to check for any other guards. He found none, and so he moved silently downstairs with his gun out. As he did so, he could hear the guard in the kitchen getting up, opening a can of beer, and changing the channel on the TV. Hearing him sit down and dig into his noisy bag of chips again, McGregor then moved through the rest of the ground floor checking for other guards. The only reading on the heartbeat sensor was from the man in the kitchen, so McGregor moved silently towards the kitchen door. Pausing outside for a few seconds, he waited until he could again hear the crackling sound of the man supplying himself with yet more chips, at which time he slipped into the room pointing his gun at the man's face. Stunned at what he was looking at, the guard stopped chewing, let go of the bag of chips, which fell to the kitchen floor, and then he slowly raised both of his hands above his head.

'Ivanov?' asked McGregor in a stern voice.

The guard shook his head, but McGregor was unsure whether the guard thought he had asked if he was Ivanov, or if Ivanov was in the house. He motioned for the guard to stand up and turn around, but at that moment McGregor heard the sound of a car pulling into the gravel driveway outside, and then a couple of car doors slamming shut.

For a split second, McGregor lost his focus, wondering why Frost hadn't warned him that someone was coming. His brief lapse of attention was taken advantage of by the guard, who spun around grabbing a large knife from the kitchen table. But as he hurled himself at McGregor with the knife raised above his head, he found that man in the black outfit still had the gun trained on him, and the next thing he felt were three punches in his chest. He fell forward and dropped to the floor dead, while McGregor stepped backwards a few steps.

'Idiot,' he snarled at the dead guard. Things were about to get complicated.

He hurried into the living room next to the hall and waited for someone to enter through the front door. He didn't have to wait more than a few seconds before the door was opened and a tall muscular man stepped inside with his gun drawn. Immediately behind him followed Ivanov, who McGregor recognised from the photos. Apparently, they were expecting a guard to greet them outside the house, and when that hadn't happened, they had become suspicious. The two men walked swiftly across the floor in the hall towards the kitchen while calling the names of the two missing guards. McGregor had been kneeling behind a sofa when they entered, and as they slipped out of sight he rose and moved silently after them.

The tall man spotted him out of the corner of his eye and tried to raise his gun while at the same time pushing Ivanov away to safety behind him. That became his undoing, as it provided McGregor with plenty of time to take aim and fire a single shot into his head. Blood sprayed from his skull as the bullets struck, and it hit Ivanov in the face.

He had never seen anyone die before, and as the guard slumped down at his feet, he tried to take aim at McGregor. But his hand was shaking so badly that the shot missed, and shattered a vase behind McGregor. Although now that he had the upper hand, McGregor didn't exactly like being shot at, so even before the pieces of the shattered vase had begun hitting the floor, he had taken aim and fired a single shot into Ivanov's right shoulder causing him to drop his gun. McGregor then advanced quickly, still with his gun trained at the Russian who had placed his left hand on the wound and was wincing in pain as he staggered backwards.

Five minutes later McGregor had tied Ivanov to the chair in the kitchen, on which the dead guard had been sitting only a few minutes earlier. The guard was lying in a pool of blood at his feet, and that had the desired effect. Ivanov was rambling on about how rich he was, how he was more than happy to pay off his debt immediately, and how he was prepared to pay ten times what his assailant had been offered. McGregor slapped him across the face and held an index finger up over his mouth. He hated it when people became hysterical.

'Shut up,' he hissed, without trying to hide his accent. 'Sergei Ivanov. Are there more than three guards?'

The Russian looked at him, terrified, and then shook his head.

'Good,' continued McGregor. 'I'm not here about repayment of any debt. I need some information from you, but I'll start by telling you that you are no good to me dead. I'm sure we can agree that it would be much easier for both of us if I don't have to hurt you again. But do not doubt that I will,' he said aggressively, and then kicked the dead guard in the gut for effect. He then grabbed Ivanov's wounded shoulder and pressed a thumb into the entry hole, causing the petrified man to scream in the agony.

'Alright!' he shouted. 'Alright. I'll tell you whatever it is you want to know.'

'Good,' said McGregor calmly. 'We'll begin with a certain organisation which I'm sure you are familiar with. It calls itself New Dawn. Isn't that correct, Sergei?'

The Russian tried to escape from it all by closing his eyes, but when he opened them again McGregor was still there. McGregor in turn, could see that this would not take long. Ivanov knew that he was finished, and although he might be both greedy and unscrupulous and a lot of other things, he was not stupid, and he knew when it was time to fold. So that's what he did, all the while wondering what might become of him and all his money now.

★ ★ ★

Three hours later at a quarter to five in the morning, the alarm clock in Andrew's room at Halley came to life with the most obnoxious and incessant chirping sound he had ever heard. He had been tired after the long journey, and had therefore fallen into a deep sleep.

He did however feel fully rested now, which was good because he had a feeling that today was going to require a lot of energy and stamina. He quickly put on some clothes and went outside, where the sky was clear and the wind had slowed to a light breeze. It was almost completely quiet, except for a generator humming away in its steel container somewhere.

He looked out over the vast icy expanse and gazed at the sunrise. The sun was coming up over the mountainous horizon but it was actually less than three hours since it had set. As it had slipped beneath the horizon and wandered the short distance to where it would rise again, it had never been further under the horizon than to enable it to light up the sky with a faint orange glow, so it had never really been dark while Andrew and the others had been sleeping.

Within half an hour, the rest of the station began to come to life, and soon they were all seated in the restaurant in the main building. Andrew laid out his plan, and there was general agreement to go ahead with it. Andrew, John Marx, and Bill Rosenbaum would each take a snow-scooter and leave for Vestfjella immediately after breakfast. Taking the small de Haviland Twin Otter, Fiona and Alice Bailey along with Charles Goodwin, would leave two and a half hours later for the same destination. Along with them in the plane, they would bring bio-suits in case they found the cave that Reitziger had been the last person to see. In that event, it was agreed that Rosenbaum would take over during the recovery phase.

During the first few hours they would all stay in radio contact in case some unforeseen obstacle should slow the scooters down, but if everything went smoothly, they would arrive at the base of the mountain at approximately the same time just before noon that day. That would leave them plenty of daylight for the search. Goodwin suggested that they mount a combined magneto/gravity-sensor array in the pod below the aircraft since it might be able to reveal features of interest below the ice or even inside the mountain.

Along with Marx and Rosenbaum, Andrew then rose from the table, gathered his equipment and started to get dressed for the journey. That turned out to be a rather long process because of the many layers of clothing that were needed. Moving across the ice at up to 80 kilometres per hour in temperatures well below zero could result in serious frostbites and permanent skin damage if they weren't properly protected. While the three of them suited up and packed their snow scooters, some of the permanent personnel on the station checked the fuel tanks on their vehicles to make sure they were full. The scooters were designed for travelling long distances in rugged icy terrain, but that didn't mean that they couldn't break down if they weren't looked after, so one of the mechanics checked the engines as well.

Having been given the go-ahead by the mechanic, the three men mounted their scooters. They were all wearing bright blue heavily insulated arctic suits, as well as close-fitting hoods and ski masks. Andrew gave a quick wave to the mechanic, and then they set off towards the east. The rest of the team watched them shrink to tiny black specks in the distance until they became hidden by the huge blocks of ice that intermittently jutted up from the surface of the colossal ice shelf. Fiona called Andrew over the radio to check that their communication system was online, and then she started getting ready for her flight along with the two others.

They loaded the crates with the bio-suits as well as equipment to detect any bacteria that might be found. The equipment was experimental, sporting an impressive array of organic sensors and designed from the outset by researchers at the CDC to be a portable pathogen analysis system. However, it had never been field-tested, which caused some concern on the part of both Rosenbaum and Marx. But right now, it was their best shot at finding and recovering the B-CAP pathogen.

In addition, they brought emergency equipment in case anything went wrong. Most of it was the standard equipment that station regulars would use for excursions out into the Antarctic glacial plains. They were specially designed pyramid tents, made to withstand extremely high winds and ice storms. In case they would have to spend the night in these tents, they also brought groundsheets and inflatable airbeds to insulate them from the cold ground. They also brought double sleeping bags, designed to withstand below-freezing temperatures, even though the tents would almost certainly keep the air temperature inside above zero.

'This sure looks like professional stuff,' said Fiona.

'Yes,' said Goodwin as he pushed a crate up into the back of the aircraft. 'The equipment here is tried and tested. We have field parties camping out for as long as one hundred days during the Antarctic summer, but the weather still dictates how much work can be accomplished. The worst that can happen to a team is a so-called whiteout, where complete cloud cover or fog at low altitude races across the ice shelf at incredible speeds, with nothing to slow it down.'

'I guess you can't get much work done during such weather?' asked Alice.

'Nothing at all,' responded Goodwin. 'Everything is just completely white, and crevasses and the horizon are both effectively invisible, so it is dangerous to be moving around outside. Most of the people that have died during expeditions here have ventured out into a whiteout and not returned. These whiteouts happen regularly and when they do our days are spent 'lying up' inside the tent as we call it.'

'Well, at least you still have radio communication to stay in touch with the station, right?' asked Fiona.

'Yes, we do. We even have radio locators that can help us find people should they not report back. There's one attached to every vehicle here, and the scientists all wear one at all times.'

'So, we'll be able to track the three snow-scooters on their way to Vestfjella?'

'Yes. Easily.'

After packing all of their equipment into the back of the aircraft, Fiona, Bailey and Goodwin sat down in the warm sun along with the aircraft's crew of two and enjoyed some hot coffee. It was well below zero, but between the lack of wind, the dry Antarctic air and the summer sun rising in the sky above them, they might as well have been lying on a beach in California. Having finished their coffee, they marched over to the aircraft that had already been pre-heated and climbed aboard. The engines sprang to life without hesitation, and soon the twin-engine aircraft was gliding along the icy landing strip on its skis. It then lifted itself into the air, slowly banked left to fly back over the research station, and then headed for Vestfjella and the rendezvous point.

★ ★ ★

After three and a half hours of racing across the Brunt Ice Shelf of Queen Maude's Land on Antarctica, Andrew and his two companions finally reached the base of Vestfjella, which now towered up overhead. They would have to go between Lyddan Island and the part of the continent called Coats Land to get out onto the Riiser-Larsen Ice Shelf that lay beyond it, adjacent to Vestfjella. Standing next to it, it seemed like a colossal bulge of rock rising up into the sky, but it actually consisted of many smaller peaks, and the mountain range stretched far inland and disappeared behind the white horizon. It was almost noon when they parked their snow scooters and quickly set up a couple of the red cone-shaped tents. There were no clouds and the light reflected from the snow was so overwhelming that they would not have been able to see without the heavily tinted ski masks. Overall, the weather was excellent but it could change so quickly that they wouldn't have time to put up the tents if a storm broke out, so setting those up was the first order of business.

With snow and ice squeaking and cracking under his double insulated mountaineering boots, Andrew walked over next to Marx, took out his binoculars and pulled back his hood to look at the mountain range that seemed to have cut straight up through the flat ice shelf less than a kilometre away.

'It almost looks as if the mountain has just popped out of the ice a few days ago,' he said. 'There seem to be no foothills like near a regular mountain.'

'That's right,' said Marx. 'It's because the ice shelf here is several hundred meters thick. All the smaller hills that surround Vestfjella mountain are covered by ice, so only the peak sticks up.'

'How tall is it?'

'I think it is around 1,600 meters above sea level, but I'm not sure.'

'I haven't seen a single animal while we've been out here,' said Rosenbaum as he came over to join the two others. 'I wonder where they are?'

'Probably hiding from us,' said Marx. 'It isn't like we are trying to stay quiet,' he said and pointed to the scooters.

'Let's get a bite to eat,' said Andrew and walked over to his scooter and took out a bag with food.

They had been provided with the same types of rations that the regulars on Halley VI used for field trips like this. Their supplies usually consisted of freeze-dried meat as well as several varieties of dried soups and vegetables, rice, tea, coffee, orange drinks, biscuits, chocolate milk and multi-vitamin pills. The dried food was made edible by adding water to it. Andrew got out a paraffin fuelled stove, which was used for cooking all the various types of foods. Even though it was an old design, it was still the most dependable and robust system available. A few minutes later they gulped down their food and let the hot drinks soothe their sore bodies. Racing across the ice for several hours was taxing, physically and mentally.

The trip had gone quicker than expected, and it was another thirty minutes before they heard the faint sound of the de Haviland Twin Otter from the west. A few minutes later they spotted the aircraft coming towards them. They waved as it flew overhead and continued towards the mountain where it circled a few times before coming in to land a few hundred meters away from them. The ice was remarkably smooth here, so the small aircraft was able to glide over the ice all the way to the temporary camp that Sterling, Marx and Rosenbaum had set up. It eventually came to a halt, and as the engine was switched off, the doors opened and Fiona and Charles Goodwin climbed out, followed a few seconds later by Alice Bailey.

'So, this is it?' asked Fiona having walked over to the three men, who were just finishing their meals.

'Yes,' said Andrew. 'Did you have a good flight?' he said and winced from the bright light as he looked up at her.

'Yes. It is amazing out here. So beautiful,' she said as she turned to look at the entire horizon. 'This mountain is quite a bit bigger than I had expected. How are we going to go about this?'

'We'll want to get underway in a few minutes, so if you would take out the medallion and place it here,' he said and padded a spot on the ice. 'Then we'll see what we can see.'

'Right,' said Fiona and walked back to the aircraft.

'We can't stay here too long,' said Goodwin. 'The plane doesn't have an engine-heater, so we can only leave the engine off for about twenty minutes.'

'No problem,' said Andrew and rose from his comfortable seat in the snow. 'We should be underway before that.'

'Hey,' said Fiona as she came walking back from the aircraft carrying the transparent Plexiglas box containing the medallion. 'I've got an idea. If we let the medallion align itself right here and then move it a few hundred meters over in that direction and let it align there as well,' she said and pointed past the mountain. 'Then we ought to be able to triangulate the spot it is pointing to.'

'Excellent idea,' said Andrew. 'Set it down and let's see if it works.'

Fiona put the box on a level patch of snow that Andrew had made for it, and then they stood back and watched anxiously. If it didn't work, they might as well have stayed at home. Without the medallion giving them at least a hint of where to go, it would be impossible to find anything. For the first ten seconds, nothing happened.

'Shit,' exclaimed Fiona. 'I don't believe this.'

'Let's just wait a little bit longer,' said Andrew. 'The kerosene has become cold so its viscosity has probably changed. That might make it more difficult for the medallion to move.'

'Do you think we should heat it up?'

'No, let's wait.'

But after a few more seconds even Andrew was becoming concerned, but then the medallion finally started to move ever so slowly to one side.

'Look! It's moving,' said Fiona enthusiastically.

'Well, I'll be damned,' said Rosenbaum.

The medallion continued to turn ever so slowly inside the oil for what seemed like an age, before finally settling in its new position pointing towards the left side of the mountain.

'Can we mark this direction?' asked Goodwin.

'Yes,' said Andrew and took out his GPS. 'I will do it now. It is pointing to 92 degrees. Alright, let's get it moved.'

Andrew and Fiona, who was carrying the box, mounted a snow scooter and drove carefully towards the northeast around the base of the mountain. About a kilometre away from the camp, Fiona tapped Andrew on the shoulder.

'Let's stop here,' she shouted.

Andrew let the scooter roll to a stop and killed the engine. They both dismounted and walked a few meters towards the mountain. There, Fiona cleared a small area of loose snow and placed the box onto the ice. And just as before the medallion took its time to start moving but eventually it adjusted its orientation and came to a stop pointing to 137 degrees.

'Hand me your map,' said Fiona and pointed to the map sitting in a pocket in Andrew's jacket. It was a detailed map of Coats Land and the Riiser-Larsen Ice Shelf, which he had used for navigating to Vestfjella. 'If I draw a line pointing 92 degrees from the camp and another line from this spot pointing 137 degrees, then the two intersect right here,' she said and put a small X on the map.

'X marks the spot?' said Andrew. 'I seem to have heard that before somewhere.'

'Yes. I think this is as accurate as we can get. If this is correct, we need to move to this small valley here on the other side of that peak,' she said and pointed to a small peak that lay behind several larger ones from where they stood.

'Alright. Let's get back to the others,' said Andrew and started to walk back towards the snow scooter.

As he did so, he suddenly thought he heard the faint sound of another snow scooter far away. He motioned for Fiona to be quiet, and then stopped dead in his tracks to listen, but he couldn't hear anything except the slight breeze in his ears.

'What is it?' asked Fiona.

'I thought I heard an engine somewhere,' said Andrew. 'I guess it was nothing.'

'It's probably coming from the camp.'

'Yes. I suppose you are right.'

They mounted the snow scooter, and fifteen minutes later they were back at the camp. While Andrew and Fiona had been away, the others had taken the opportunity to load the bio-suits onto the snow scooters.

Fiona, Goodwin and Bailey then climbed back aboard the aircraft and the pilot fired up the engine that sputtered at first but then began growling smoothly. A few minutes later, the aircraft was bumping along over the ice and then it lifted into the air and turned back towards the mountain range as it climbed rapidly. Andrew and the two scientists Marx and Rosenbaum accompanying him had mounted their snow scooters and were now on their way towards the X that Fiona had indicated on the map. They initially had to go around and to the right of the main massif, before they could turn up into a long shallow valley that ran for a couple of kilometres into the mountain range.

The valley became narrower and narrower, and after ten minutes of driving, the steep sides of it were no more than a couple of hundred meters away from them. The spot they were looking for seemed like it should be at the end of the valley, and Andrew could see the aircraft already circling the area. But as far as he could tell, there was nothing but rocks and snow where the valley ended and turned abruptly upwards into a steep cliff that continued to the ridge high above them.

Followed by Marx and Rosenbaum, Andrew slowed down as they approached the spot, and then parked his scooter near a big boulder that had evidently come tumbling down from the cliff recently. Walking away from the boulder and looking up towards the circling aeroplane, Andrew took out his radio and called up Fiona in the plane.

'This is supposed to be it,' he said as he followed the aircraft with his eyes. 'There's nothing here that we can see. Have you got anything?'

'Hold on for a second,' shouted Fiona above the noise from the engine. 'Goodwin is looking at the sensors right now.' She broke off but then came back on the radio a few seconds later. 'He's getting a strange reading from a position directly ahead of you, but he was not sure what it is. It could be some sort of void or cavity.'

Andrew looked across the snow-covered rocks to the cliff face, but was unable to see anything that looked even remotely like an entrance. The black rock of the cliff was very smooth and nothing on the snow below it suggested that any human being had ever walked there before. The radio crackled again as the de Haviland Twin Otter flew over their position one more time, and then Fiona's voice could again be heard over the engine noise in the background.

'There's definitely something there, Andrew. Can't you see anything?'

'Not a thing,' he announced.

'What if it is below the ice,' asked Marx who had come over next to Andrew.

'What about ice?' said Andrew into the microphone. 'Couldn't it be covered by the ice?'

'I guess it is possible,' said Fiona. 'If the snow cover is substantially thicker now than when the Nazis were here, then the entrance they used might be below the ice now.'

'Are you guys sure that thing is working correctly?'

'Yes,' insisted Fiona. 'There's definitely something there, perhaps a cave or something. Keep walking forward, Andrew. I'll tell you when you are directly above the spot where we are getting a strong reading.'

Andrew continued for about thirty meters, and then Fiona told him to stop and mark the position on his GPS. He looked around at the ground surrounding him but there was nothing but snow and ice to be seen.

'It's got to be below you,' said Fiona. 'There's a significant reading just where you are standing.'

'Alright,' said Andrew. 'This is going nowhere. I'm going to bring out some explosives and blast this ice cover away. Rosenbaum, you packed the dynamite, didn't you?'

'Yes,' said Rosenbaum. 'But I have never worked with explosives before.'

'Don't worry,' said Andrew. 'I know a thing or two about it.'

'Be careful, Andrew,' said Fiona over the radio. 'You might set off an avalanche of snow and rocks from above you.'

'I will be,' he replied, and then took out a couple of emergency flares, lit one of them and knelt down to hold it to the ice at his feet.

The flares were designed to burn for several minutes, and soon the immense heat melted through the compact ice. After the flare burned out, Andrew had melted a hole so deep that he could only just reach the bottom with his arm. He then set off the second flare and dropped it into the hole. Steam rose from the hole as the flare melted its way further down into the ice, and when it finally died, the flares had created a hole more than two meters deep, straight down into the ice.

By then Rosenbaum had brought over two sticks of dynamite to the hole and Andrew quickly wired them together and attached them to the radio-controlled detonator that had been inserted into one of them. He lowered the dynamite into the hole, and two minutes later the three men had ridden their snow scooters away to a safe distance, where they had dismounted and were now looking in the direction of the hole.

'Are you ready?' Andrew asked into his radio.

'We're ready,' responded Fiona. 'I hope you don't break anything.'

'We've got no time to dig,' said Andrew. 'Here we go!'

He pressed the button on the transmitter, and instantly a column of snow, ice and rock lifted from the end of the valley. A split second later the sound wave hit them, and they could feel it through their chests as it reached their vantage point some two hundred meters away. As a shower of rocks and ice began falling back down over the site of the explosion, the three men mounted their scooters and headed back. Where the small melted hole had been there was now a huge crater around five meters into the ice. There was still a bit of steam rising from the centre of the hole, but they could see a dark patch below the remarkably clear ice at the bottom.

'It looks as if we've blasted all the way to the rock bed,' said Rosenbaum.

'Or maybe not,' said Marx and started down into the crater carrying a shovel.

As he came closer, he could see that over to the side of the bottom of the crater there was a distinct dark patch, which seemed to be perhaps a meter from the surface of the crater wall. Marx started hacking away at the ice, but it was slow going. It seemed as if it had been packed so densely together that all the tiny air bubbles had been squeezed out, leaving only hard clear ice. Andrew and Rosenbaum joined him with their own shovels, but their tools weren't meant to be used in this way so it took some time before they finally reached a smooth piece of rock that jutted out through the side of the crater. In fact, it was so smooth that they quickly concluded that it must have been manmade. Andrew called Fiona to tell her of their find, and she had been close to jumping out of the aircraft just out of sheer excitement.

The three men continued to remove the ice from around the rock and soon realised that it was part of a structure that continued horizontally much deeper into the ice. They discussed whether to use another explosive charge, but decided to keep digging for a while yet. That turned out to be the right decision because suddenly Rosenbaum's shovel broke through the ice to a point along the rock that seemed to have an opening.

'Can you see what it is?' asked Fiona as the aeroplane continued to circle above them.'

'No, but we'll keep hacking away at it.'

After another ten minutes, they had revealed what appeared to be a doorway some two meters high and about one meter across. They were all sweating like pigs by then, and in the excitement, they seemed to have forgotten why they were there in the first place. Suddenly Marx stood up and looked at the other two.

'Uhm. Guys! Excuse me, but shouldn't we be wearing bio-suits?'

They all stopped what they were doing immediately, and looked at each other sheepishly.

'Fuck,' said Andrew. Without another word, they all walked out of the crater and up to the scooters where they donned their suits. As far as both Marx and Rosenbaum knew, protective suits like these had never been used in arctic conditions, but there was no alternative than to trust them and keep working. They had come too far to turn back now.

When the opening had been made big enough for a man to squeeze through, Andrew got out his flashlight end entered through the doorway into the space on the other side, followed closely by the two scientists. Before they entered, they had switched on their internal air supply so that the suits were now hermetically sealed from the outside and completely self-contained. In several positions on the exterior of the suits were sensors that would pick up any bacteria or toxins in the air.

'Perhaps you two should go first,' said Andrew over the communications link. 'You know what you are looking for. I'm just here for the scenery.'

'Right,' said Rosenbaum apprehensively. 'I guess I'm the one who should be taking the lead.'

He then walked past the two others and proceeded deeper into the space. Rosenbaum checked the telemetry that was embedded in his suit, and it told him that humidity was close to 90 percent and that the temperature was a few degrees above zero. That was about fifteen degrees above the temperature outside so something had to have kept the air relatively warm. Rosenbaum was not a geologist but he speculated that it was possible that the heat was simply transported up through the rock from the Earth's interior. He couldn't come up with anything more plausible than that.

With their three flashlights, they were able to light up what turned out to be a completely rectangular room. They were easily able to discern that it was approximately three meters wide and ten meters long, and at the far end was another doorway similar to the one they had just come through. Standing in the room, it became clear that the sides of the doorways actually sloped inwards slightly as they approached the stone beams at the top.

The beams themselves were decorated with intricate patterns chiselled into the rock. As Rosenbaum lead the group through the room, they let their flashlights sweep over the walls, which revealed strange markings and glyphs that seemed like a blend of ancient Mayan, Egyptian and Asian writings. There were facemasks, motifs and various illustrations that to Andrew looked like something he had seen at Uxmal not so long ago, and several of the glyphs were unmistakably Egyptian. The dark walls themselves were very humid and gleamed in the light from the flashlights, but as far as they could see, the markings or writings appeared to be completely unaffected by the passage of time, however long that might have been. Andrew felt tempted to walk closer in order to get a better look, but he didn't want to fall behind the other two.

As they approached the other end of the room, Rosenbaum spotted something on the floor just on the other side of the doorway. At first, he had trouble seeing what it was through the condensation that had gathered on the inside of his visor, but as he came closer, he realised that what he was looking at was the scull and ribcage of a man wearing a German army helmet.

TWENTY-THREE

Colin McGregor had been able to leave Monaco for London that same morning, having stayed in the country for less than 24 hours. After having finished his business with Ivanov, and recording everything the man had said, Frost had driven up to the mansion after which they had loaded Ivanov into the back of the van. The bodies of the three guards were dragged into the basement, but they had made no effort to clean up. After changing clothes, they had taken the Russian to a safe house where Frost would keep him locked up until the whole thing was over.

Ivanov was kindly encouraged to tell Frost about anything else that he might remember about New Dawn, and in the process given the impression that it might be looked upon with gratitude when his future was going to be decided. Then McGregor had made his way back to the hotel, and a few hours later he had checked out and left town.

Back in London, he had filed a detailed report with Colonel Strickland, who had then summoned the rest of the team in for a briefing. The colonel had been impressed with McGregor's work, and with the results that it had produced. Ivanov had spilt his guts to McGregor and provided lots of details about New Dawn, its organisation, many of the people involved, the financing, and its ultimate purpose. The last part had been particularly chilling. The programme to recover and mass-produce the bacterium had just been one of the organisation's many projects. There were several others of which Ivanov didn't have any details, but he was sure that they might be as big and costly as the one he had been hired for. He had never met or seen anyone from the very top of the organisation, but he seemed convinced that they were sponsored by private benefactors as well as state funds from several countries in the Middle East.

The program itself was shrouded in secrecy, and even high-ranking members of the organisation knew very little. Each person knew only enough to carry out their task and nothing more, but Ivanov had been in a position where he had needed to be informed about a lot of different things. From what he had learned, the mass-produced bacteria were to be spread in urban areas in the West and also in Israel, but he did not know exactly how or when that would happen. He did say, however, that he thought it might be in the not-too-distant future.

Importantly, Ivanov had provided the approximate location of the production facility, and immediately after receiving it, Strickland and McGregor had begun discussing options. Strickland would have liked to have Sterling along in those discussions, but he seemed to have left research station Halley only hours before the call came in. They agreed that a covert operation would be the only way forward, as it would otherwise be impossible to reach the facility without being noticed. They didn't even consider asking the Syrian government, since they felt sure that such a move would result in the people at the facility being warned and fleeing immediately.

Strickland discussed the issue with Prime Minister Erwin Campbell and Minister of Defence William O'Toole, and he was given a green light to plan the mission. The final go-ahead would then have to be issued by the Prime Minister once all the plans had been drawn up in detail.

Pete Ryan started investigating whether the CIA had any information on organisations known to operate near the location in Syria indicated by Ivanov. He also began gathering satellite imagery of the area to assist in the planning of the mission and filed for permission to draw on analytical resources in the United

States. Within hours he was granted several more people for the task, working out of the CIA headquarters at Langley.

McGregor hadn't had much sleep before having to leave for Hereford to take charge of his team. Six men, in addition to himself, had been chosen to take part in the operation and he was going to oversee and participate in their preparation until they could be deployed. They were all more or less his age or a bit younger, and all of them had been chosen based on their individual skill sets.

Some were excellent close combat soldiers, while others were experts at recognisance, capable of moving swiftly and silently through any terrain. McGregor had also been assigned one of the best snipers the SAS had ever had. All of them were trained killers, but contrary to popular belief, none of them were trigger happy cowboys aching to get into a firefight. What was called for in special operations units was a calm and organised team effort, so most of the members were experienced men in their thirties with distinguished careers behind them. Most importantly, however, was that they were all capable of remaining cool and level-headed even under extreme pressure, and capable of adapting and continuing to work as a unit if a mission fell apart.

As experts in close combat Paul Grant, Kyle Thompson and Joe Kendall had all participated in operations behind enemy lines in Afghanistan along with US special forces units. They also had experience in urban anti-terrorist operations. The team's recognisance expert, Sean Logan, was nicknamed 'Ghost' by his fellow team members, because of his uncanny ability to sneak up close to the enemy while remaining undetected. Robbie Dunn was the team's explosives specialist, capable of laying or fixing explosive charges to almost any structure with the purpose of destroying or penetrating it. The final member of the team was Jeremy Wilks who was their sniper. He usually ended up firing by far the smallest number of bullets, but his effort could easily end up deciding whether a mission was a success or a failure. Typically positioned at a forward vantage point, a sniper could either hold off approaching enemy forces or clear the way for an assault by the rest of the team.

Each of them had their individual set of weapons, although they were very similar. For most missions, they would all carry the silenced Heckler & Kock MP5SD as their primary weapon, except for Wilks who carried a sniper rifle as his main weapon. They all had handguns for close-in combat, ranging from the small silenced 9 mm Beretta 92SD to the powerful HK .45ACP.

All of the men had combat experience from different hotspots around the world, but on most of their missions, their primary objectives had been to remain hidden for as long as possible.

A team could be comprised of excellent individuals, but if they didn't work well as a group, they would most likely end up dead sooner rather than later. The team that McGregor would lead had worked as a unit for a little over year now, and they had come to know each other very well. They all had strong personalities, and they were all very different people, but the amount of time they had spent together in training and on exercises had provided them with mutual respect for one another, as well as deep insights into each individual's special skills. Working closely together, they were trained to move and fight as one combat entity, and every team member had his duties to fulfil to ensure the safety of the whole team and the success of whatever mission they had been sent to accomplish.

Although they would mostly work to avoid direct contact with an enemy, they were quite capable of defending themselves and also of applying offensive pressure if need be. For every hour they spent carrying out actual combat missions, they had spent hundreds of hours training and honing their skills, either here at Hereford or on exercises in remote places around the world.

McGregor had no idea exactly what they would be up against on the upcoming mission to Syria, so there was no point in trying to prepare for something specific. All he knew was that they would be sent on a desert mission, most likely at night, but as far as he knew there was still no satellite imagery available of the site. He wasn't even sure if they had pinpointed it yet, but hopefully, some additional information would be coming in before too long.

This afternoon he and his team would run through a set of standard exercises beginning with so-called fire and movement, which meant exactly that. Training with live ammunition, they would practice moving while firing at both moving and stationary targets. As they would do on a real mission, they split up into groups of two or three, that would then move through a set of mock buildings and rooms, clearing them of any threats that they encountered. As they moved through an area, either a building or an open area, they would stay close together covering each other both in front and behind.

McGregor, Grant and Dunn were standing in that order in front of a wooden door to a mock apartment complex. As his primary weapon for this exercise, McGregor had selected the smaller 9 mm Heckler & Kock MP5K-PDW, which, with its folding stock and lower weight, was ideal for moving around in a tight environment such as this. Dunn moved quickly up from the back and knelt down next to the door while pulling out a door breaching charge. It was a device made from six small explosive charges all connected by wires to a device at the centre containing either a timer or a radio receiver depending on the desired mode of detonation. The charges were arranged in a circular pattern about half a meter wide, and it used a special adhesive to make them stick to almost any surface. Dunn spent no more than ten seconds affixing the breaching charge and then re-took his position behind Grant, moving in close to the wall next to the door. The explosives were designed to exert as much force inward as possible, making it relatively safe to stand on the outside. The vast majority of the energy from the blast would be directed into the door, effectively shattering it. In a holster on his back, Dunn carried a Benelli 12-gauge tactical shotgun, that would be able to blow open a door if need be.

On McGregor's signal, Dunn detonated the charges and with a loud bang, the explosion ripped the door apart and blew it into the hallway on the other side of the door. Even before the debris from the fractured door had settled on the floor inside, the three men were up and moving.

With McGregor taking the lead they moved swiftly through the smoke-filled hallway leading to a main corridor inside the building complex. Covering each other, they moved forward with firearms at the ready and in a slightly crouched posture, which made it easier for them to fire while moving if necessary. In a pattern they had rehearsed hundreds of times, they moved at a fast and steady pace through to the first room on the right side of the corridor. Here, McGregor knelt down while taking out a Flashbang from his belt.

Able to create a loud bang and a bright flash, both designed to overpower the senses of people in the immediate vicinity, the small grenade-like explosive charge was an effective tool for disorienting potential threats. Its effect was to blind and stun people, and the pressure from the blast could even make people standing too near it feel nauseous and start vomiting. Because of its relatively soft plastic casing, the charge didn't eject any fragments that would be able to harm anyone. It was merely a weapon designed to pacify potential threats.

McGregor pulled the cord and threw it into the room. A second later it exploded, generating a bright white flash and making the walls reverberate with the sound of the explosion. Within two seconds of entering, all three men had discharged their weapons at a number of mock targets in the room. Their weapons were set to three-round bursts for maximum accuracy and effect. Moving swiftly through the doorway, McGregor as the point man immediately spotted the first target next to a window, and while moving sideways alongside the wall to make room for Grant and Dunn he brought up his sub-machine gun and placed all three bullets squarely at the centre of the mock target's face. Split seconds after that, he heard the other two firing at three other targets and then the 'Clear' calls, as all targets had been eliminated.

They moved quickly out of the room and then cleared the remaining two rooms of threats. Each room was furnished differently with different numbers of targets placed in new locations each time, in order to keep training exercises challenging. The whole thing took less than two minutes, and after having cleared the building, they exited through a back door and walked over to a control room some two hundred meters away, where they would spend the next hour watching and discussing a video playback of their efforts. No matter how many times they did these things there were always things that could be improved upon, and the recordings were an excellent way of uncovering weaknesses that they didn't see themselves during the assault. An hour later they would try a similar assault on a different building, and this time they would employ two teams, the other consisting of Thompson, Kendall and Logan.

The three of them were currently practising on a more traditional firing range, where they would go through a series of standard exercises. Bringing his weapon up, Logan fired several short controlled bursts at a stationary target, while he walked swiftly towards it in a crouched posture. This enabled him to keep his sights on the target even as he approached it. He repeated this as he passed by several targets, and having expended his last magazine for the submachine gun, he let it fall to his chest and then quickly pulled out his HK .45ACP and fired several rounds at his next target while he kept moving.

The sniper on the team, Jeremy Wilks was off practising by himself on a shooting range some distance from the main compound. As the others carried out their training programme, they would regularly hear the loud dry crack of a rifle being fired. The basic task of a sniper is to move undetected to a position relatively close to an enemy, and then be able to hit his target the first time every time. One of the most important skills is the ability to control breathing, as the sniper will usually be faced with having to hit targets that are many hundred metres away. Each sniper must find a breathing pattern that suits him, where he will take aim and then breathe in and out calmly a few times, eventually holding his breath while gently squeezing the trigger until the bullet is fired. The sniper must also take account of wind and temperature since both of those will affect the way the bullet behaves over different distances.

The weapon usually preferred by Wilks for urban operations was the PSG-1, firing a 7.62 NATO round, although lately, he had fired several hundred rounds with the 50 calibre Barret 82A1, that was capable of firing at targets out to as much as 1.5 kilometres away. With this weapon, a sniper would be able to take out almost any target even at that range, and the massive projectile would be able to slam right through an engine block of a car, rendering it utterly useless. The downside was that it was relatively heavy and cumbersome to carry around. It was over a metre and a half in length and weighed more than thirteen kilos.

At the end of the afternoon, the men met in the cafeteria in the main building, laughing and exchanging stories. They all knew that they were about to be sent out on a mission, but none of them spoke about it since it served no purpose. They wouldn't be told where they were going until immediately before departure, so there was no sense in speculating. Knowing this, McGregor was also aware that there was a limit to the amount of time a team could be put on standby. Being told to get ready to leave and then sitting in the barracks for days could be seriously demotivating to a soldier, and that would end up being dangerous for all of them. But McGregor was fairly confident that they would be given orders to leave before very long.

After the day's training, McGregor sat in the cafeteria with the other men drinking coffee. It was important to him that his team functioned well both on and off duty since they would be living together for several weeks at a time when on missions. This team was particularly well-integrated and homogeneous, and there wasn't a man in the room who would be nervous about putting his life in the hands of one of the other team members.

McGregor decided to go to his office and call colonel Strickland to ask if there was any progress in determining the location of the facility. Surprisingly, even given the information they had now retrieved from Sergei Ivanov, they had not been able to find the exact location of the production facility. He had been asked to point to a map of central Syria and the area around Al Raqqa, but it actually seemed as if he didn't know exactly where it was. He had always been transported to and from the facility by jeep or helicopter, and had apparently never learnt its precise location. Shown the map, he had only been able to point to a 10 square kilometre area, where he could say with a reasonable degree of certainty that it was situated. So now Pete Ryan had concentrated all the resources at his disposal on finding the site. He had even requested that a military spy satellite be directed to pass over the area indicated by Ivanov, in the hope that it might reveal something. The fact that the facility was buried under a mountain obviously meant that they wouldn't be able to spot it directly, and so they would have to use other ways of tracking it down. According to Ryan, it would be difficult, but Strickland had asked him to have his people work on it 24 hours a day until they found it.

★ ★ ★

Rosenbaum knelt down next to the skeleton in the doorway and shone his flashlight over the grey bones. As he got closer, he could see that it was lying in a rectangular room similar to the one they had just passed through, except that the doorway where the skeleton lay was at its centre, and at each of its ends were two more doorways similar to the first. Rosenbaum leaned in carefully, peering at the human remains through the visor of his bio-suit. He gently tapped the dead soldier's helmet with his flashlight and as he did so tiny strands of the dead man's hair fell out from under it. All of his flesh and muscles had rotted and withered away in the humid air. Had he been buried in the ice outside for this long, he would probably have been almost perfectly preserved, but in here his tissue had completely decomposed. The uniform, that had once been grey was now almost black, and it had virtually disintegrated and fallen off the skeleton in most places. There were, however, several flimsy pieces still draped over his ribcage and legs, and as the two others came up behind Rosenbaum, he carefully lifted a shred of the frail cloth from the corpse's shoulder.

'Christ,' said Andrew, looking sombre. 'It's a German soldier.'

'*Was* a German soldier,' said Rosenbaum. 'And look at the collar of his uniform. He was SS.'

'This guy must have been dead for over sixty years,' said Marx and looked at the soldier's empty eye sockets in disgust. 'What a place to die.'

'Well,' said Rosenbaum and carefully nudged the soldier's ribcage with his glove. 'Whatever it was that killed this man, I don't think it was the B-CAP pathogen, at least not if the accounts of the infection process that the British army recovered during World War Two are to be believed. There are no signs of the crystallisation process that is supposed to have occurred in those victims. Most likely this guy died of hunger, or maybe someone shot him. But I'm pretty sure it wasn't a bug.'

Andrew knelt beside Rosenbaum and took off the soldier's helmet. He placed it on the cold stone floor and carefully turned the skull from one side to the other.

'He definitely wasn't shot in the head,' said Andrew. 'And I can't see any sign that he took a bullet to the rest of his body. And look at the way he is lying there on his back with his legs stretched out, as if he just laid back and died. I'll go with starvation for now.'

'Does any of this look like anything you've seen described?' asked Marx and looked at Andrew.

'No. The entrance that was described in the chronicles was different from this one. Whatever this is, it isn't what the Germans found.'

'Do you mean to say that we are in the wrong place?' asked Rosenbaum and rose.

'Yes and no. This is definitely not the same place the Nazis found back in the thirties, but it *is* where the medallion was pointing.'

'Let's just continue,' said Marx. 'Watch your organic sensors. If they pick up any bacteria, they will let you know.'

The three men rose and decided to go left to the doorway at the end of the second rectangular room. The doorway itself was identical to the two they had already moved through, but this one led through a series of alternating 90 degree left and right turns until they exited into a giant dome-shaped room about thirty meters across. The first thing that alerted them to the size of the giant room was the acoustics, as the sound of their heavy boots reverberated through it. It was at least fifteen meters to the ceiling at the centre of the dome, and apart from an unrecognisable pattern of lines and markings chiselled into the smooth stone floor there was nothing in the room, and there was only the one doorway leading to it.

The curvature of the dome itself ended about two meters from the floor, the same height as the doorway, where it turned into a vertical wall that went all the way around the dome's interior in a smooth circular fashion. Every three meters or so, a small platform half a square meter jutted out from the vertical wall. The wall sections directly above the platforms were reflective, and it appeared that they might once have been used to place lamps on, in order to light up the whole room.

'What is this place?' said Marx as he led the group cautiously into the huge chamber.

'No idea,' said Rosenbaum. 'It looks almost like a chapel or something.'

Andrew shone his light up onto the dome above them and realised that there was a pattern of little specks of some sort. 'Look at this,' he said and pointed upwards, upon which the two others pointed their lights to the ceiling as well. The interior of the dome was completely black and the rock had been made so smooth that it reflected some of the light from their flashlights back at them. The whole surface of the entire dome was littered with sparkling dots of all sizes, spanning from a small coin to the hand of a grown man. On closer inspection, they turned out to be chiselled into the surface of the dome, and each one was covered on the inside with some sort of shiny metal, possibly gold or brass. There were thousands of them, and they stretched from the edge of the dome to its zenith in large patterns that at first looked as if they had been placed at random. Across from one side of the dome to the opposite, a band of about two meters in width stretched across the dome.

'Holy shit. Those are stars,' exclaimed Rosenbaum. 'This ceiling depicts all the stars in the sky. And the broad band of them running across the dome must be the Milky Way.'

'Christ,' said Andrew, looking up at the dome in awe. 'I think you are right.'

Stunned, the three men walked slowly further into the room leaning back as much as their bio-suits would allow them, looking up in amazement at the thousands of stars in this replica night sky. Reaching the centre of the room, they stood for a few minutes turning and watching this spectacular snapshot of the night sky as it had appeared long ago.

'Any of you two good at astronomy?' asked Rosenbaum.

'I know something about that,' said Marx. 'Why?'

'Because my father used to teach me how to find the North Star, and if I haven't completely forgotten, then that must be it right there,' he said as pointed to a particularly large star near the virtual horizon.

'Yes, I think you are right,' said Marx. 'That must be it.'

'Are you two sure about this?' said Andrew.

'Pretty sure,' said Marx. 'It looks like it is positioned in the constellation of Ursa Minor, right where it should be. Why?'

'Well, because the North Star shouldn't be visible from the South Pole at all.'

'He's right you know,' said Rosenbaum puzzled. 'That star is only supposed to be visible north of the equator.'

'Unless this place hasn't always been near the South Pole,' Andrew whispered to himself, as he gazed up at 'Polaris', as his father had always called it.

'You are talking way over my head here,' said Rosenbaum. 'What do you mean by that?'

'It's a long story,' said Andrew. 'I'll tell you about it some other time.'

'You know, someone should be able to date this place based on the stars as they are depicted here,' said Marx. 'The night sky changes over time as the stars and galaxies move relative to each other, so from the relative positions of these stars we'll probably be able to deduce the age of this place pretty accurately.'

'Provided that this depiction of the stars was accurate to start with,' said Rosenbaum.

'There's no reason to believe that it isn't,' replied Marx. 'The people who built this place knew what they were doing, that's for sure.'

'Yes, I agree,' said Andrew. 'If they could construct such a structure inside a mountain, then I think they'd be able to paint an accurate picture of the sky as well. The really big question is: Who were they?'

'Well, we sure can't answer that question right now,' said Rosenbaum. 'That's probably going to take a whole bunch of archaeologists. Let's move on to the other end of that corridor out there.'

They left the domed room as cautiously and calmly as they had entered, stealing a last look at the magnificent work of art high above their heads as they exited through the doorway. Andrew then led them back through the series of 90-degree turns past the dead soldier and down to the other end of the second rectangular room. The doorway there had crumbled a bit and there was a disturbingly large crack in the support beam above it.

'I hope this place doesn't cave in on us,' said Marx. 'I'd like to live to tell the tale of this place.'

'Me too,' said Andrew. 'Let's try to be careful and not touch anything, Ok?'

They proceeded through the doorway and encountered another of the strange twisting corridors. As far as Andrew could see, it was identical to the one they had just passed through at the other end of the corridor. After a few minutes, they came out into another narrower corridor of about 25 meters in length that ran straight ahead and seemed to end in a black void beyond another doorway. There were no features on the smooth walls.

'This is becoming claustrophobic', said Marx nervously and swallowed hard. 'I hope we get out of here.'

'Are you ok?' asked Andrew and placed a hand gently on his shoulder.

Marx looked down at the ground, took a deep breath and exhaled slowly. Then he nodded and looked at Andrew. 'Yeah,' he replied as if trying to convince himself. 'I'll be ok. Let's continue.'

With Rosenbaum in the lead, they walked briskly to the other end of the corridor. They passed through it and suddenly found themselves standing on a narrow ledge in a gigantic dark cavity that was at least five times as big as the dome containing the night sky. This massive room inside Vestfjella, seemed to be rectangular in shape, perhaps as much as 300 meters in length and at least 150 meters wide. From the floor to the ceiling was a distance of some 30 meters and the ledge the three men were standing on was approximately 25 meters above the floor. The floor itself was not really a floor but seemed to be perforated by several long fissures a few meters wide that ran parallel to the walls from one end of the vast room to the other.

Although powerful, their three flashlights had trouble illuminating even a small portion of the giant room. They merely produced narrow and sharply outlined cones of light as they shone through the mist that hung in the humid air. As they stood there gazing at the strange sight below them, they suddenly realised that what they were looking at was a small town. The floor below them was actually the flat tops of houses cut directly from the rock, and the fissures between them were narrow streets. There seemed to be several hundred dwellings down there, making the town big enough to house a huge number of people. But now it was quiet as the grave, and it might well have been this way for thousands of years.

'Incredible,' mumbled Marx and wiped his visor.

'Are you guys getting a reading?' asked Rosenbaum, looking at his suit's sensor array that apparently hadn't picked up any living organisms in the air.

'No,' said Marx, and pointed his light at the opposite wall across the giant cavity

'Me neither,' said Andrew. 'Let's get down there.'

Cut straight into one of the end walls of the giant room, the ledge they were standing on was no more than a meter wide. It led off to the right along the wall and soon turned into a series of steps that took them all the way down to the houses and streets below. Andrew walked at the front of the group on the way down and then proceeded along what appeared to be the main street, running from one end of the cavity to the other. But he took only a few steps before noticing a figure lying on the floor a few meters away. Calling it a figure was hardly accurate. It was a heap of badly crumbled bones almost reduced to a powder, but the outline of a human being was unmistakable.

As Marx and Rosenbaum followed him down the steps and came over to stand on either side of him, it became clear that the entire street was littered with hundreds of similar heaps of crumbled remains. Marx proceeded through the doorway into one of the houses that consisted of a single room about three by four meters in size. It had apparently been cut out of the rock, but all the surfaces were smooth as glass and at the far wall was a number of beds, several of them with heaps of dust and crumbled bones similar to those in the street outside.

'There are more of them in here,' he said as he came back out into the street, a pained look on his face. 'Some of them appear to have been children.'

'My God,' said Andrew. 'What happened here?'

Rosenbaum cautiously walked over to one of the heaps and knelt down next to it, picking up some of the dust and letting it run through his fingers. As he did so, he shone his light at the fine sparkly grains that fell like a tiny dusty waterfall back to the floor, and the light that was reflected back had a decidedly bluish hue to it.

'Well, I believe we've found our bug,' he said, as the sensor array on his bio-suit began chirping away quietly.

'There's definitely some type of bacterium in the air here.'

'Take a sample,' said Andrew. 'It must be in that dust.'

'Already on it,' said Rosenbaum as he pulled out a small cylindrical metal canister and unscrewed the lid. Tiny trails of vapour were rising from the rubberised surface of his bio-suit. The heat was building up inside their suits now, and as water suspended as mist in the cold air condensed on them, it soon evaporated from the heat inside their bio-suits.

'I wonder how many caves there are like this one,' said Marx and crossed over to the other side of the street where he looked inside another house. 'Several more of them in here. There must be thousands of human remains here.'

While Rosenbaum scooped up a spoonful of crumbled bones and decayed flesh now turned to dust, Andrew walked past him and continued cautiously down the central street past the houses that all seemed to be identical. Everywhere he looked, there were the unsettling piles of remains of people having succumbed to the devastating B-CAP pathogen that Rosenbaum was now collecting samples of.

Andrew considered their next course of action. He wanted to explore this cavity and find out if there were more of them inside this mountain, but he also knew that time was limited. Their orders were to recover the bacterium, as quickly as possible, so they had to turn back as soon as Rosenbaum was happy with his samples. He and Marx would need enough of it to run a preliminary analysis back at Halley, and if that turned out to be promising, then the samples had to be transported back to Britain, where a team of scientists would immediately launch themselves into developing an antibiotic, or a prophylactic that could potentially prevent infection altogether.

Andrew walked on, trying his best to avoid the hundreds of human remains that lay scattered in the street. It was a testament to the potential dangers of having the pathogen released in a densely populated area. Such an event would be able to develop into a cataclysm, destroying entire civilisations. He had never seen so many dead people before, and even though they were hardly recognisable as human beings anymore, it was an eerie feeling indeed to walk along inside this giant, cold and humid tomb.

Having walked halfway towards the other end wall that loomed above him, he reached a square structure about half a meter high sitting in the middle of the street. As he came closer, he could see that it appeared to be a well, with a vertical shaft running straight down at the centre. He leaned over the side and shone his light into it, but all he could see was a white mist that seemed to be slowly swirling around some ten meters below him. Movement meant that there was some sort of energy there and the only energy he could think of was heat, so perhaps the shaft led down to less cold sections of the rock. In that case, it would have to be quite deep, so he looked around for a loose stone. Not finding one, he was eventually able to kick one loose from the side of the small structure surrounding the shaft. He held it out into the centre of the hole and let it drop. As he followed it with his eyes, it fell through the mist, but try as he might, Andrew was unable to hear it reach anything below. Either his suit was muffling the impact sound, or the stone was still falling.

He then proceeded to the end of the street, where a set of steps similar to the ones they had descended at the other end of the cavity, rose up to yet another doorway. Andrew looked over his shoulder towards his companions at the other end of the street and then gazed back up at the doorway some 25 meters above him. He wanted to go up there and see what lay beyond it, but in the end, he decided to head back towards the others. He was not an archaeologist and he would just be wasting his time playing Indiana Jones in here, while Marx and Rosenbaum were working to complete their mission. Someone like Fiona was much better at this than he could ever be.

He started walking back towards his two companions, and as he reached the shaft where he had dropped the stone, he thought he spotted something in the doorway high above their heads. At first, he thought his eyes were playing tricks on him, but then he saw it again. A light flashed over the ceiling near the end of the long corridor just inside the doorway. Then it happened again and after a few seconds, he recognised the characteristic dance of light cones from flashlights as the people holding them walked along through the corridor. With his eyes fixed on the doorway high above on the end wall, he started to jog back towards Marx and Rosenbaum.

'We've got company,' he said as calmly as he could over the communications link.

'What?' said Rosenbaum and stood up. 'Where?'

By then Andrew was running back towards them, feeling increasingly nervous about the situation. There was no way Fiona and the others could have landed close enough for them to be able to walk up to the entrance this fast. And if it wasn't them, who else could be out here on this vast desolate continent? His question was soon answered as Phillip Eckleston flanked by four men carrying guns appeared on the ledge above him.

'Stop,' shouted Eckleston, as Müller pointed his gun at Andrew while the three others trained their weapons at Marx and Rosenbaum. 'Walk this way ever so slowly, please,' he said and then started to come down the steps towards the street. 'What a magnificent place, wouldn't you agree?'

Andrew didn't answer but focused on the weapons and tried to figure out if the men holding them knew what they were doing.

'I've been waiting to meet you Mr. Sterling,' continued Eckleston in an arrogant tone of voice. 'You have quite a reputation, but not an altogether enviable one. In case you haven't realised it, my name is Phillip Eckleston. I knew your father, by the way. Never really trusted the chap I must admit, but he did the job he was supposed to do.'

Andrew knew that Eckleston was trying to throw him off by poking at his emotions, but he kept calm and didn't let himself get angry. This was definitely not the time to lose his head.

'How about that lovely Miss Keane? Do you have her with you somewhere?' Eckleston sounded relaxed. Arrogant even. Clearly convinced that he was in total control of the situation.

'No,' said Andrew calmly. 'She couldn't come.'

'Oh, what a pity,' said Eckleston as he reached the bottom of the stairway and walked calmly towards Andrew and his two companions. 'She is really a nice girl. Shame she is so nosy. Walk over here to the others,' he said and pointed to Marx and Rosenbaum. 'Are those your only companions?'

'Yes,' said Andrew. There was no point in lying about that.

'Good. And by the way. Thanks for telling us exactly where you were. That explosion was impossible to overhear. A bit of a crude way to get in here I must say, but it worked of course.'

'How did you get here?' asked Andrew trying to keep his composure.

'That's not important. Search them for weapons,' ordered Eckleston and motioned for one of Müller's hired guns to approach them.

While Müller and two of his men fanned out a few meters, still pointing their guns at the three men in bio-suits, the third hired gun came over and frisked them, looking and feeling for concealed weapons either on the outside or inside of their suits. At that moment Andrew was happy that he hadn't brought a gun, since that would have meant that he would be forced to open up his sealed bio-suit. But he needed to try to draw Eckleston's attention somehow.

'What are you hoping to accomplish with this little adventure of yours, Eckleston?' sneered Andrew angrily, while trying to think of a way to turn the situation to his advantage.

'Accomplish?' laughed Eckleston mockingly. 'Isn't it obvious,' he continued and motioned to their surroundings. 'You and I are standing in the middle of what is without question the most significant archaeological find since the beginning of time. You are looking at the cradle of the first advanced civilisation in human history. This is proof of the magnificence of the Aryan race. This is what the Thule Society has been searching for since the beginning of the previous century. This, my dear fellow, justifies our goal of a world ruled by Aryans, and it will serve as a rallying cry to all descendants of the original Aryan race. We shall all stand together and rise up to take what is rightfully ours.'

'And what would that be?' asked Andrew unimpressed.

'This planet is ours!' shouted Eckleston. 'We developed it. We cultivated every civilisation that has ever existed. We are responsible for every technological advance the human race has ever produced, and you,' he said and looked Andrew in the eye, and then seemed to calm down a bit. 'You ought to be proud of that. They are your ancestors too, you know.'

Speaking loudly enough for Eckleston to be able to hear him, Rosenbaum leaned over to Andrew and said: 'This guy sure as hell is one beer short of a six-pack.'

'Shut up, you pathetic little fool,' shouted Eckleston. 'You just do not understand, do you? You don't realise what this means to the future of this planet and to the future of the human race. This is the most profound revelation in our history. Everything that people think they know about our place in this world needs to be re-written. And it shall be done by us, the descendants of the people of Thule. The rightful heirs to this world.'

'Eckleston,' interrupted Andrew sharply. 'Haven't you wondered why we are all dressed like this?'

Eckleston gazed at him, apparently without understanding the question and them looked from Marx to Rosenbaum and them back at Andrew.

'Look around you,' continued Andrew. 'How do you think all these people died?'

It wasn't until then that Eckleston seemed to realise that the little dark patches of dust that surrounded him were human remains. His face began to turn ashen, and as he took a few steps backwards, he grabbed Müller by the arm. 'Move back,' he said and pulled Müller with him. 'There might be a dangerous bacterium in here.'

Hearing the fear in Eckleston's voice, the soldier who had just searched the three men, and who was now standing less than two meters from Andrew facing him, turned his head to look over his shoulder at Eckleston.

'What?' he blurted out.

At that moment Andrew took a step forward towards one of the heaps of dust that lay between him and the soldier and kicked it up into the air. The resultant cloud of dust sprayed all over the soldier who staggered backwards while coughing and rubbing his eyes.

Several of the tiny crystals had already entered the man's lungs, and within seconds the pathogen came to life from its hibernating state and began to spread throughout his body as fast as the bloodstream could carry it. Having rubbed the dust from his eyes, the soldier winced and looked in astonishment at Andrew, who just stood there watching him.

The soldier coughed once and brought his hand up to his mouth. Andrew could see in his eyes that he was already beginning to feel something happening inside him. He brought his hand back out in front of his face, and when he saw the blood on his glove, his eyes became wide with panic. Suddenly he convulsed a couple of times and then lost his balance and dropped to his knees with a desperate look on his face. He fell forward towards Andrew, while he exhaled with a strange moaning sound as the pain spread throughout his entire body from every artery and every blood vessel. Landing flat on his face his head slammed into the cold damp floor, and in a last desperate attempt to stay alive his body managed a final breath of air. But as he exhaled, it became clear that he was already dead, and in the light from the flashlight of the shocked spectators, his skin took on a visibly sparkly blue tint, as the pathogen rapidly worked its way out from the blood vessels that had by now crystallised completely, and through the tissue to the skin.

The whole ordeal took less than twenty seconds, and during that time they had all stood dumbfounded at the horrific scene playing out in front of their eyes. Andrew was the first to regain his composure, and he knew that he needed to do something fairly drastic to get out of this situation alive.

For a split second, he considered diving into one of the doorways of one of the small houses, but that would have left Marx and Rosenbaum as cannon fodder. He sprinted the first few meters towards the dead soldier, and before Eckleston, Müller and the remaining two soldiers could react, he kicked the head of the dead man as hard as he could, as if it had been a football. Weighing several kilos, it hurt like hell despite the protection of his big mountaineering boots, but the head instantly severed from the body with a nauseating crack, like when breaking a biscuit in half. With every bit of fluid in his body having turned into tiny crystals, the soldier's entire body was now brittle, and as the head detached from the rest of his body, bouncing across the floor and leaving a trail of dust and blue crystals, it rolled right past Müller's feet.

Apparently, that was enough to make the former member of the elite Austrian Mountain division lose his composure, and Andrew exploited his hesitation. He sprinted towards him. Marx and Rosenbaum were quick to follow his lead, but as Andrew reached Müller, the Austrian seemed to recover from his state of shock. Andrew slammed into Müller's chest, knocking him over. Müller's gun went off as he landed on his back but it only had the effect of making the other two soldiers retreat while holding their gloves over their mouths and noses for fear of catching whatever it was their comrade had just died from. Now only concerned with their own survival, they hardly reacted as Marx and Rosenbaum sprinted past them and followed Andrew to the foot of the steps leading to the doorway 25 meters above them.

Shouting through a handkerchief that he had pulled out and placed over his mouth, Eckleston pointed to the three men running up the stairs as fast as their legs would carry them. 'Shoot them,' he screamed. 'They must not get away. Kill them!'

At first, the two soldiers merely looked up at the three escapees. Then Müller staggered to his feet and pulled his scarf over his mouth and nose. Then he aimed his gun at the three men running up the steps. This jolted the two other hired guns into action, and they opened fire as well. Eckleston was already making his way towards the base of the stairway and started up after Andrew and his companions, even as the bullets slammed into the rock no more than ten meters ahead of him. The three men now had a head start of around twenty seconds, and seeing that they were about to reach the doorway, Müller ceased firing and sprinted after Eckleston up the stairway while the two other soldiers continued to shoot.

Andrew and Rosenbaum made it all the way up to the top of the stairs and through the doorway, but just as Marx reached the top, he was hit by several bullets within a couple of seconds, fell forward and landed on his face right in front of the doorway. Andrew instantly recognised the thudding sound of bullets hitting flesh. He grabbed Rosenbaum by the arm, and the two of them immediately stopped and turned back towards Marx while trying to stay out of reach of the soldiers' bullets. Rosenbaum crouched down and grabbed Marx's bio-suit by the shoulder, and attempted to drag him along with him, but halfway through the doorway Andrew spotted the bloody bullet holes in Marx's bio-suit.

'No,' shouted Marx from inside the bio-suit. Then he coughed up pink blood which began trickling out of the left side of his mouth. He had been shot through the lungs. 'You have to leave me here. My bio-suit is penetrated. We can't run the of risk me carrying the bacterium out of here with me.'

'No way,' said Rosenbaum and knelt down next to Marx to pick him up. 'We are not leaving you here.'

But as he was about to lift Marx off the ground, Andrew placed a hand on his arm and looked him straight in the eye. 'He's right,' he said. 'We have to leave him here. If that thing is allowed to leave this place inside a living being, it will be uncontrollable. It's simply not an option.'

'Get out now,' coughed Marx and pushed Rosenbaum away from him. 'Run, damn it. Before it's too late.'

Reluctantly Rosenbaum got up, his eyes still fixed on the bleeding colleague at his feet. Andrew grabbed him by the arm and started to drag him towards the doorway. At that moment Müller and his men had reached the bottom of the stairway and began running up as fast as they could without risking falling off. That finally made Rosenbaum turn around, and he and Andrew hurried through the doorway and through the long corridor towards the exit. They bolted through the strange alternating turns and past the skeleton of the German soldier. As they did so, Rosenbaum shouted to Andrew through the communications system. 'We shouldn't have left him there, God damn it. He'll die.'

'He would have died anyway,' panted Andrew. 'His lungs were already filling with blood. Without a hospital, there's nothing we can do. He'd be gone in a couple of minutes.'

'If the pathogen hasn't finished him off already,' sneered Rosenbaum angrily.

Andrew decided not to respond but continued running towards the doorway leading to the crater. Behind them, he could hear the loud footsteps of Eckleston, Müller and the remaining two soldiers, but they had gotten a good head start, and thirty seconds later they bolted out through the final corridor and exited into the crater. They then sprinted up the side of the crater, and Andrew was about to follow Rosenbaum away from it, when he had an idea. He turned and ran over to Rosenbaum's scooter where he fetched a stick of dynamite with a fuse attached to it. While running back towards the crater he could hear the voices of Eckleston and his goons somewhere inside the underground structure. He ran past the crater and reached the steep cliff face where he lit the fuse and then hurled the stick of dynamite up towards a huge block of snow and ice sitting on an overhang some fifteen meters above the crater. The snow had accumulated there for a long time and Andrew aimed for the lower part of the overhang. The stick of dynamite flew in an arc above the overhang, and as it landed in the snow, Andrew turned and sprinted back past the crater.

Just then, Eckleston appeared at the bottom of the crater with Müller close behind him. A split second later the dynamite exploded, sending several tons of snow, ice and rock falling mercilessly down towards the crater. Andrew continued to run away as fast as he could, getting out of the way just in time. But it was too late for Eckleston, Müller and the two goons. Stunned, Eckleston looked up at the huge volume of blackened snow and ice that was hurtling in free fall towards him.

'No,' he screamed desperately as he cowered back inside the doorway. He screamed at Andrew: 'You don't know what you are do…' and with that, the sound of his voice disappeared as abruptly as when turning off a radio. The white and black mountain that had descended on the crater slammed down into it in a series of loud rumbling thuds, trapping the men inside. After only a few seconds, there was only the gentle sound of loose snow and small pieces of ice slithering down from the mound that now completely covered the crater. Eckleston, Müller and the two others were gone. Buried alive.

Andrew had thrown himself on the snow, covering his head for fear of being hit by chunks of rock or ice, and fifty meters away Rosenbaum was beginning to walk back towards him. At that moment the de Haviland Twin Otter appeared over the crest of the valley and flew directly over their heads. It swooped down towards them and passed no more than two hundred meters above the ground just as the earpiece in Andrew's suit crackled and Fiona's voice appeared.

'Are you two OK?' she shouted, sounding like she was panicking.

Rosenbaum gave a thumbs up.

'Yes. We are fine. But Marx didn't make it.'

'What? What happened?'

'Eckleston and his goons came in after us and started shooting. Where the hell were you? Why didn't you warn us?'

'There was no radio contact. A few minutes after you disappeared through the entrance, we saw them arrive and move down over the slopes. We tried to fly lower but they opened fire at us, so we had to leave. Can't we get Marx out?'

'No. I'm sure he is dead. If not from his wounds, then from the bacterium.'

'You found it?'

'Yes. It even took out one of Eckleston's goons for us. But I'm afraid that it has already found its way to Marx as well. Rosenbaum has got it in a small container. We need to bring it back to Halley as soon as we can.'

'Alright. We'll fly back to the camp and wait for you there.'

'Ok. I think it would be best if we left the snow scooters out here and all flew back to Halley on the plane. I'm not very keen to spend another three hours on that thing, and we need to get Rosenbaum back to the lab as soon as we can.'

'Agreed. We'll see you shortly.'

'Alright. But wait until we've washed ourselves down with the chemicals, Ok? The outside of our suits might still be contaminated, but the decontamination chemicals will take care of that.'

'Understood.'

A few seconds later the plane banked and headed away from them down the valley and out towards the camp on the ice shelf a few kilometres away.

TWENTY-FOUR

Pete Ryan had asked for another meeting with Colonel Strickland, to inform him of his latest results. He had spent hours analysing footage from cameras mounted on surveillance satellites that had passed over the Al Raqqa area in Syria over the past year. His aim was to spot new buildings or structures in the huge 50 square kilometre box southeast of Al Raqqa, that had been designated as most likely to contain the pathogen production facility. It was an enormous area and together with colleagues across the Atlantic, with whom he spoke several times a day, he had looked at every frame of film that had been stored in the CIA's image archive. Even using images with a resolution below ten centimetres, it was difficult to determine where it might be.

During the past year, which was when Ivanov had said the facility had been constructed, there had been a few new buildings erected in the area he was looking at. But for the most part, they were small sheds or houses and nothing like a guardhouse or something else that might reveal the presence of a high-tech laboratory facility. Ivanov had said that the facility was underground in a valley, but Ryan had still expected to find some type of building to reveal its position. He had been just about to call Langley and ask them to widen the search area when they had called him and said that they had found something interesting. In one of the frames that they had looked at they had spotted what appeared to be a helicopter. They had then digitally enhanced the image and determined that it was a corporate helicopter of which there were only two registered in Syria. One of those was registered in the city of Al Raqqa where it seemed to be coming from, judging from its heading.

Ryan had then called up a detailed map of the area they were focusing on, and then superimposed a narrow cone starting at the point where the helicopter had been spotted and designed to indicate its probable route after that. That had significantly reduced the search area, and after an hour he came across an image of a set of tracks leading down through a valley and out on the other side. That wasn't in itself particularly interesting, but what was very interesting, was that about a third of the way through the valley a less visible set of tracks had peeled off to the left and apparently gone straight into the mountainside.

A few hours later, following a request to the people at Langley who ran a database containing old satellite recognisance images of the entire planet, he had received a set of images of that exact spot. They had each been cut from films taken by different satellites that had passed overhead at different times during the day and night, and that turned out to be the key. On a couple of them, the images had been shot at a slight angle, letting him see the mountainside in the valley, and he had been thrilled to find that there in plain view, there was a large opening right into the rock just as Ivanov had described to McGregor. On one of the images, there was even a figure standing just outside the opening, and that was just as a truck was entering the valley a few hundred meters away.

Ryan was now sure that he had found what he was looking for. After having determined the exact latitude and longitude of the location, he alerted the team at Langley to direct another satellite over the area as soon as possible. He was told that it would take another eight hours before a satellite carrying a camera with sufficient resolution would pass overhead.

He then decided to go and see Strickland with the preliminary results, while he waited for new pictures to come in. Strickland decided to pass the information on to McGregor who was preparing his team at Hereford. Strickland had already been in contact with the United States Airforce, which had offered their assets on airbases in south-eastern Turkey to be used for the operation. A plan for the attack was then drawn up.

McGregor and his team were to fly to the airport at the city of Ganziantep in southern Turkey. From there they would be transported by road to a temporary forward airbase some 30 kilometres south of the town of Sanhurfa, which was less than 10 kilometres from the Syrian border. Once there, they would suit up for the mission and mount a Blackhawk helicopter that would transport them across the border into Syria and over the desert to the valley.

The mission would be carried out at night, so every team member would be wearing night-vision goggles. McGregor had asked for more details, but Strickland told him to be patient for a little while longer and prepare for a night mission within a day or two. It would take some time to set up the mission and take care of all the practical issues that were involved with transporting the team to Turkey and mounting a cross border mission. Firstly, the Turkish government, a fellow member of NATO, needed to be persuaded. Secondly, they needed to set up a coordinating task force consisting of Britons, Americans and Turks, from which they could be absolutely certain that nothing would be leaked about their endeavour. Finally, aircover in the form of fighters and drones needed to be allocated and readied.

That evening, McGregor and his team spent several hours practising night combat as well as moving stealthily over terrain with little or no cover, which was what they would be faced with down in the valley.

★ ★ ★

In an apartment with the curtains drawn in the city of Al Raqqa in central Syria, a man was sitting on a sofa smoking a cigarette and watching TV. It was a hot day and his air-conditioning had broken down again. Despite his access to ample funds, he had not been able to arrange for someone to come by and repair it. Now, he was considering buying a new one. His shirt was soaked in sweat, and on the table in front of him lay the remains of his last meal and the revolver that hardly ever left his side. Outside the window, a satellite dish was mounted on the wall, enabling him to watch close to a hundred TV stations, even the foreign ones like BBC and CNN, which he didn't pay much attention to. Their reporting was always heavily biased towards the policies of the west, if not outright propaganda and misinformation.

The phone rang a few times before it was picked up. 'Masood,' said the man in an annoyed voice.

'Hamza, this is Yusef.'

'Oh, it's you,' said Hamza embarrassed. 'I didn't expect your call so soon. How are you?'

'Could have been better. How are things in Al Raqqa?'

'They are fine. The trucks are being readied and will leave for the cave tomorrow morning.'

'Good. At least something's working.'

'Is something wrong?'

'It's the Russian. I can't reach him anywhere. He was supposed to be in Monaco, but he doesn't answer on any of his numbers. Has he indicated to you that he might be travelling?'

'No. But as you know, I hardly ever speak to him.'

'Yes, I know,' said Yusef, sounding irritated. 'This is so frustrating. Just now when we are on the verge of completing the program, he goes and disappears. I never trusted that man. He has been in it for the money the whole time. Just another infidel that can be made to do anything.'

'Have you tried contacting Arrowhead?'

'Yes. They have not heard from him since he returned from the visit with us.'

'Did they sound worried?'

'No, but when do they ever sound worried? I am concerned that something is wrong.'

'It could be that he is just away from his phone for a while. You know how he likes to go out and have fun with the western women.'

'Yes. He is a weak man, and that is what worries me. I don't trust him not to betray us, given the right amount of money. He has no morals.'

'Yusef. We have known each other for a long time now, and as your friend I will tell you that I think you are worrying too much. Everything has gone smoothly until now, except for the little mishap at the plant. But we have met our deadline, and just think of all the courageous soldiers who are waiting to hear from us. We can't let them down now, and we can't spend our time worrying about a drunken Russian when we have such a glorious task ahead of us.'

'I suppose you are right, Hamza. I shall see you tomorrow then.'

'Yes, Yusef. Allah is great.'

★ ★ ★

Rosenbaum was stooped silently over the microscope, while he watched the tiny bacteria encapsulated in blue crystal. They were placed inside a small glass container that was rotating around its vertical axis below the optics. He had managed to isolate several of the crystal-covered bacteria and had placed them in a number of Petri dishes like the one he was looking at now. All the crystals he had managed to isolate, seemed to have exactly the same size and shape, and inside their protective crystalised cocoon, the bacteria lay dormant waiting for the temperature and humidity to rise again.

Rosenbaum wondered for how long they could stay in hibernation like that, but after what they had found inside Vestfjella, it would appear to be several thousand years. He was sitting by himself in the laboratory, and he had wanted to be alone for the first few hours after coming back from the mountain. Leaving Marx to die inside the cavity was the worst thing he had ever had to do. He understood full well, that the risk of Marx unwittingly transporting the pathogen outside was too great, but running away from a dying man had still torn him up inside. Sterling had seemed strangely unaffected by it, but it wasn't difficult for Rosenbaum to work out why that was. What Sterling did inside that mountain was literally just his day job. If it hadn't been for Andrew's quick thinking, they would probably all have been lying dead in the snow at the end of the valley.

It was getting darker outside and the wind was picking up, but he was safe and warm inside the laboratory that had been set up the day before as a temporary workplace where preliminary tests could be run. They had come back from Vestfjella a few hours earlier, and after communicating with London they had agreed that a Royal Airforce Gulfstream would pick them up from South Georgia in approximately 35 hours and fly them and the B-CAP samples back to Britain. That left them at least 15 hours before they would have to start packing up for the trip north with Halley's de Haviland Dash-7, and Rosenbaum had decided to use every minute of it to try to learn something about the pathogen. He knew that other people were already working to mass-produce what was probably an ever more deadly and faster working version of it, so there was no time to waste.

Inside the hermetically sealed analysis chamber was a small amount of horse blood that had been watered down to decrease its viscosity. It was just enough to cover the bottom of the petri dish it was sitting in. Above it was a small mechanical arm that had a tiny sample of just a few of the B-CAP pathogens sitting on top of it. Rosenbaum engaged a pump that replaced the air in the small chamber with an inert gas, and after a few seconds, the chamber had been emptied of all oxygen molecules and replaced by argon. This should prevent the bacterium from triggering its crystallisation mechanism.

He then watched through the microscope as he turned up the heat in the analysis chamber to above 30 degrees Celsius, and a few seconds later the tiny crystals that had encapsulated the bacterium disintegrated, exposing the bacterium to the primitive growth matter that Rosenbaum had just injected. Within seconds of making contact with the horse blood, the bacteria began to stir and divide into more bacteria in an exponential process that soon filled the entire field of view of the microscope. Rosenbaum was about to reset the magnification when he discovered that he could actually now see the rapidly growing colony of bacteria with the naked eye. As he watched, it spread rapidly across the surface of the diluted horse blood, and within ten seconds it covered the entire interior of the petri dish.

Amazed, Rosenbaum decided to proceed with the real test that he had planned. If his hunch was correct, then one of the properties of the pathogen, namely its crystallisation, was somehow related to exposure to free oxygen, and he had decided to attempt to test that.

'Here goes nothing,' he whispered to himself, and reversed the flow of the air pump, thereby extracting the argon from the chamber, and replacing it again with oxygen.

Immediately, the horse blood, now completely saturated with the B-CAP pathogen, crystallised in a rapid and violent chain reaction starting from the centre of the container where the original bacteria had been, to quickly and completely cover the inside of the petri dish in blue crystals. While this was happening, Rosenbaum saw something else that he hadn't noticed before. As the crystallisation happened, the volume of the horse blood seemed to expand by about 20 percent, not dissimilar to the way water expands as it turns into ice. This revelation explained why people who were infected seemed to almost fall apart as the infection and crystallisation rapidly took hold throughout their bodies. The pathogen quite literally disintegrated every cell wall, every muscle fibre and every other physiological structure that held a human body together.

Stunned, Rosenbaum picked up the container and turned it over a few times in front of his eyes. The colony had infected every square millimetre of horse blood within seconds, penetrating every blood cell and then crystallising as soon as oxygen had been re-introduced. This was what he had witnessed happen to the man inside Vestfjella, and thinking about the effects it might have if released back in London sent a shiver down his spine. It was imperative that a prophylactic antibiotic was developed as quickly as possible, but it would take time that he wasn't sure they even had at this point. An antibiotic was not something that could be made to order within a few hours. It was usually a slow and painstaking process.

The principle of using organic compounds to treat infectious diseases seems to have been around since ancient times. Evidence has been uncovered of the use of certain cheese moles for the treatment of infections at that time. All antibiotics have the property of selective toxicity, which means that they are more toxic to an invading organism such as a bacterium than they are to a human host. Used to kill or treat the growth of infectious organisms, antibiotics are chemical compounds that were first discovered in 1880 by Louis Pasteur, who discovered that certain bacteria were able to kill the feared Anthrax bacilli. This opened the door for the development of a range of anti-infectious organisms to fight diseases.

Eager to start testing, Rosenbaum had spoken to Goodwin who had kindly provided a set of soil samples that had been brought from London. Although having been brought to Halley for the purpose of investigating and providing a natural growth medium for any bacteria found in the ice, no one could have anticipated that they would one day be employed to tackle a problem of this magnitude. There were literally thousands of tiny samples of soil from around the world, and the principle of their use was to subject the fungi living within them to a bacterium, and subsequently test them for antibacterial activities, in other words naturally generated antibiotics.

The method had originally been established by the pharmaceutical company Pfizer in the 1950s, which would become one of the largest drug manufacturers in the world. They began by asking airline pilots, missionaries, travelling salesmen, vacationers and soldiers to bring back soil samples from around the world. They then performed similar tests of bacteria to the ones now performed on Halley, and ended up having built up a library of more than 20,000 samples. Each sample was isolated and tested more or less in the same manner that Rosenbaum had tested the B-CAP pathogen.

The company subjected cultures of fungi from the soil samples to various pathogenic bacteria, to determine if the fungi were able to respond. If successful, a fungus would automatically generate inhibitors that would either slow or completely stop the bacterial growth. Successful tests demonstrating anti-bacterial responses would then lead to more sophisticated testing with animal test subjects, to determine if the antibiotic was harmful or perhaps even lethal to the animals. Most fungal antibiotics tested actually proved to be as lethal as the disease they were trying to stop, but there were also a number of successes, most notably Penicillin which had been discovered by accident much earlier in 1928.

Rosenbaum had no illusions about being able to produce an antibiotic in this simple laboratory. In fact, what he was doing represented one of the most basic forms of antibiotic research, but the results of the tests might still help give the team back in London a head start in determining what they were up against. Currently, more than 10,000 antibiotic substances have been identified, and approximately 300 new substances are characterised each year, so that would give them a vast pool of antibiotics to choose from in their attempt to produce an effective vaccine to prevent B-CAP infection. Their approach would probably be to develop a so-called Narrow-Spectrum Chemotherapeutic Antibiotic, that would be active only against a limited number of organisms. But that would only be part of the solution. Possible antibiotic resistance of the pathogen would most likely become a serious issue at some stage, but they would have to cross that bridge when they came to it.

Even back in the 1940s, scientists knew that the more an antibiotic is used, the quicker it loses its potency and effectiveness. The reason is that while most bacteria exposed to a particular antibiotic are killed, some of the strongest may survive and pass their special characteristics on to offspring, which will then be just as tough to kill. If the same antibiotic is used continually, the resistant pathogens will begin to proliferate, and adding to this danger is the fact that bacteria that have become resistant to one antibiotic, also seem to find it easier to build resistance to others. But all that would only be the beginning of their work. The effects of infection were so horrendous that Rosenbaum knew that the only viable solution would be widespread vaccination of the population, first in densely populated areas like major cities, and then across every single country on the planet.

As he sat by his desk, testing fungus after fungus, Rosenbaum saw ahead of him a massive effort to vaccinate people all over the planet, and he expected that it would have to be on the same scale as smallpox, with vaccinations at birth or soon thereafter. As the hours went by, he called London several times by satellite phone to inform them of his preliminary results, in an effort to give them the best possible preparation for the task that lay ahead of them. If successful, they would be able to completely remove the pathogen as a threat to the human race, and that would be enough motivation to keep him up all night and well into the morning when their flight would be leaving for South Georgia. If they failed, the entire modern world was at risk of crumbling.

★ ★ ★

Spending most of his time in the restaurant at Halley, Andrew tried not to think about the implications of what they had found inside the mountain. But as much as he was against the Thule Society reaching its goals, he had to admit that Eckleston had been right about that discovery changing the way humans would have to look at themselves in the future. He just hoped that it would serve to bind people closer together and not be exploited by extremist groups to widen the divides between them.

He chose to stay optimistic, but he also had to concede that power, whether it was military might or information, had always been used by one group of people against another, so perhaps things didn't look that bright after all.

Fiona had taken a long walk on the ice surrounding Halley, trying to console Marx's assistant Alice Bailey, who had been devastated by the death of her colleague and friend. They had agreed that a few drinks wouldn't hurt, and half a bottle of wine later Alice had gone to bed to try to get some rest. Fiona had then spent a couple of hours interrogating Andrew about every single detail of what he had seen inside Vestfjella. She had been more interested in the star dome than the small town, and had pointed out several similarities between the room on the coast north of La

Venta in Mexico, and what Andrew had seen in the domed room inside the mountain.

It was clear to her that the inhabitants of the city he had found, had been skilled seafarers and that they would have used their accurate depictions of the night sky to navigate the seas. But she also speculated that there might be at least one similar room with a depiction of the night sky from other positions on the planet. She also wondered whether the underground town they had discovered had been some sort of refuge after the earth crust displacement that she was now convinced had taken place.

Andrew began to feel frustrated that he hadn't had time to go up the stairway at the other end of the cavity, to see what was on the other side of the doorway. There might well have been more of the same or perhaps even something bigger and more spectacular. He would also have liked to have brought a camera, and he chastised himself for that particular oversight.

Fiona was convinced that what he had seen was in fact just a small part of what had once been a much larger complex, but also conceded that it was nothing like what Plato had written. According to his account, the city was supposed to be out in the open with easy access to the sea, but with the geological and environmental changes that had resulted from the violent earth crust displacement, it was perhaps not surprising if there wasn't anything outside the mountain now. She then speculated that the main city might have been hundreds of kilometres away on Parker Land that stretched north towards South America, and that what they had found was akin to a reception area. She believed that if the lesser peoples of the Earth should figure out how to get to their continent, the people of this ancient civilisation wouldn't want them to suddenly show up at the gate to their main city. It would be much safer and manageable to have them reach a different location further away, from where they would then be funnelled to the capital city. After having run out of questions, Fiona had gone to her living quarters to take a shower. Andrew was sure that there would be several more questions to come later on, but he wouldn't be going anywhere for quite a while. The wait for the plane to South Georgia seemed like it would last forever, so there would be plenty of time to talk about how they might one day return and investigate what they had found.

Andrew put on his coat, filled up his Styrofoam cup with freshly brewed coffee, and walked outside where the sun had descended for its short sideways trip below the horizon. He climbed down the ladder to the ground and walked across the ice towards the laboratory, listening to the pleasant sound of his mountaineering boots on the soft snow. The wind had picked up and there was a small amount of snow in the air. According to Goodwin, the weather could change in ten minutes, but it could also stay the same for weeks. He only hoped that they would be able to fly out of there as soon as possible and get the samples of the pathogen back to London.

★ ★ ★

The team had spent the whole of the previous day at Hereford doing target practice, as well as mock helicopter drops while wearing full combat gear. With McGregor in the lead, they would stand on a wooden platform some ten meters above the ground and then lower themselves along a rope from each side of the platform to simulate the exit from a Blackhawk helicopter. The trip down took only a couple of seconds, and as the first of them hit the ground they would immediately fan out to provide cover for the rest of the team.

In the evening, McGregor had been called in for a preliminary briefing and been told that they would be leaving early the next morning. Operating out of the forward airbase in southern Turkey, the helicopter ride to the facility would last as little as 25 minutes, depending on the weather. They would arrive at the drop zone around two kilometres from the valley where they expected the production facility to be. From there, the plan was to move on foot to the entrance of the facility using their night vision equipment and then move through the tunnel to the cave.

This was where the plan ended. Ivanov had supplied them with an approximate layout of the compound and the buildings inside it, including the laboratory, the office building and the living quarters. From that point on they would have to improvise, but that was something they excelled at. In fact, it was one of the most important qualities in a member of the SAS or any other special operations unit. Given that their missions were often to get very close to the enemy, any fighting that might break out would almost by definition become close combat and that was something that couldn't be planned. Therefore, in situations as fluid and dynamic as those, the team needed to be able to adapt and change tactics quickly, depending on the unfolding battle.

Now, mounting the Blackhawk helicopter roughly 30 kilometres southeast of Sanhurfa, at a temporary base that had been set up by the Turkish and British Armies, McGregor and his men were as ready to go as they would ever be. It had been less than 12 hours since they had left Hereford, and only an hour since the team members had been briefed. All of their equipment had been prepared and laid out for them prior to their arrival at the forward airbase, and having been flown out in a comfortable Gulfstream jet, the team members were well rested, calm and ready for whatever might face them.

It was getting dark now, and in the hours before sunset, the team members had checked and re-checked their equipment to make sure that everything was the way they wanted it. McGregor had been glancing out to the horizon, willing the sun to disappear behind the mountain range that lay far away to the west. They were all eager to get out there and prove themselves yet again, but as darkness fell and the time to leave approached, a quiet calm descended on them all, as each of them focused on the job ahead.

McGregor mounted the helicopter and moved over to the opposite side of the passenger cabin directly behind the pilot and the navigator who were sitting side by side at the front. He sat down next to the sliding door from which he would be exiting out into hostile territory in less than half an hour. Grant, Thompson and Kendall came in right after him and took their assigned seats next to him. Then followed Logan, Dunn and Wilks, who sat down on the seats opposite McGregor and the two others. They all strapped themselves tightly into the harnesses that were an integrated part of the seats. They would be flying low, or 'nap of the earth', as it was called by the pilots, in order to avoid being picked up either by a military radar or by airport radar systems, so it might get a little bumpy at times.

With the engines already running, the pilot disengaged the rotor lock and the blades slowly began to whirl around over their heads. Within a minute the Blackhawk lifted off from the ground, pitched down gently and then began moving forwards faster and faster as the helicopter rose into the sky and the pilot engaged the rudders to set it on its precise course. Their route would first take them away from the main road that ran from Sanhurfa to the border with Syria. Then they turned east for about ten kilometres over farmland and then into a mountain range that would allow them to slip unseen into Syria. The helicopter was flying at close to 300 kilometres per hour at an altitude of between 30 and 100 meters, and the pilot would regularly jink the helicopter to the side or pitch it up hard to pass safely between hills and over peaks.

As they got further into Syria it became overcast and it was now pitch black outside the comfortable passenger cabin. Even though the flight plan had aimed to avoid populated areas, the helicopter frequently had to climb over the tops of low mountains and then swoop down along their side through valleys where faint lights would sometimes reveal the houses of farmers and other people living in the area. Mostly the pilot and his navigator, both wearing night-vision goggles mounted on their helmets, saw only barren hills and desert, and as they passed through the mountain range near the border, the landscape levelled out somewhat and then turned into a nearly flat plain of sand and rock. That made the ride much more comfortable for the seven passengers and it also enabled the pilot to fly lower and faster.

Detection by the Syrian military would most likely start a very public and very embarrassing international diplomatic incident, and so that was simply not an option the Ministry of Defence in the UK, and the Department of Defence in the US, wanted to have to consider. Flying low and fast would minimise the risk of that happening, as it would keep them below the ground-based radar, and also mean that they had to spend less time in Syrian airspace.

A risk that remained and would be hard to avoid, was the look-down radar of the ageing Mig-25 fighter jets that the Syrian Airforce possessed. Although older than most of the military hardware currently flying in most air forces around the world, it was a very rugged and reliable jet, capable of easily shooting down a relatively slow-moving helicopter. For that reason, one of the AWACS aircraft participating in enforcing the No-Fly Zone over northern Iraq, had been directed to patrol interchangeably over north-western Iraq and south-eastern Turkey. With its huge airborne radar system contained inside a black dish that was mounted on top of the fuselage, it would make sure that no air threat came close enough to detect the lone helicopter now traversing the Syrian desert.

15 minutes into the flight, the helicopter raced from north to south across Lake Assad at a quarter of the speed of sound, with Al Raqqah off to their left in the distance. The pilot was skimming across the water at less than 10 meters altitude, and the vortex behind the helicopter left a long but faint trail of water spray hanging in the air behind it. Coming back in over land, the helicopter climbed another 10 meters, in anticipation of trees and small hills that would need to be avoided. Ahead in the distance, they could now see the mountain range where the valley containing the drop zone was located.

After 27 minutes of elapsed mission time, the red light in the ceiling of the passenger cabin came on, indicating that it was now roughly two minutes until they would reach the drop zone. The team checked their equipment one last time and then unbuckled their harnesses. About a minute after that, they felt the helicopter slowing down and then pitch up to rapidly bleed off speed. It then went into a hover some fifteen meters above the ground, and a few seconds later the two doors on either side of the passenger cabin slid open. There was an instant rush of air and engine noise into the cabin, but moments later they were on their way down the specially designed ropes that allowed them to slide to the ground quickly. They moved fast, but made sure they descended to the ground safely. Elite soldiers or not, a fall from fifteen meters onto a rock could still kill a man.

Kendall and Wilks were the last two down, and as soon as they had given McGregor their OK, the team leader signalled to the helicopter and it immediately turned 180 degrees on its axis, pitched down hard, and then accelerated quickly in almost horizontal flight as the pilot threw open the throttle in order to pick up speed fast, and get out of there. Within thirty seconds, the helicopter was gone from view, and lying flat on the ground the seven men used both their eyes and ears to scan their surroundings. After another couple of minutes without a word being exchanged between them, McGregor got up to rest on one knee while calling on every team member to verify that none of them had sustained injuries during the quick descent from the helicopter. Each year several men broke ankles or legs just performing practice drops at Hereford, so it was a real risk, but all of them had reached the rocky ground without incident.

McGregor then got out his handheld GPS system and waited a few seconds for it to track a sufficient number of satellites. Then he selected the pre-programmed position of the cave entrance at North 35.06579 and East 38.59080, and engaged the 'Go to' feature. Immediately, an arrow popped up on the small high-resolution screen pointing almost due west. They were in a perfect position some two and a half kilometres from the northern entrance to the valley. Signalling the others, he then rose and began walking at a measured pace towards the position indicated on his GPS, and the other six members of the team immediately fell into a V-shaped formation behind him. Not a word was said, and until they reached the valley they would not have to communicate unless something unforeseen happened.

A gentle breeze blew over the desert, with the occasional gust of wind sending a handful of sand into the air. The temperature had dropped rapidly from above twenty degrees during the day to now less than ten degrees. The cloud cover held some of the heat near the ground, but before morning the temperature might well end up close to freezing.

Now completely focused, and with their weapons at the ready, they walked swiftly across the desert towards the valley, while constantly scanning their surroundings for any unwelcome visitors.

Once in a while Wilks and Kendall, who walked furthest back in the formation, would turn 360 degrees as they walked, to check if something might be approaching from behind. But there was not a soul to be seen anywhere. In fact, there was no visible sign of anybody having been there for a long time, and as he scanned the landscape ahead of him through his night vision goggles, McGregor somehow found it hard to believe that there might be a terrorist base not far away.

Everything looked and felt peaceful, but he knew that was a false sense of security, and he had long ago learned to overcome it since it was without question one of his worst enemies. As soon as a soldier becomes complacent, he is a lot closer to death than if he had stayed alert and watchful. Too many times he had heard about soldiers becoming overconfident, arrogant or just forgetful and then died as a result. He was determined that this was not going to happen to him or any of his team members on this mission.

After half an hour, the GPS tracker indicated that it was now less than three hundred meters to the valley entrance where a waypoint had been placed into the navigation system. In shades of green through his night vision goggles, McGregor could see the valley entrance as the hills rose up on either side of it towards the southeast. As they came closer, they saw what the satellite images could not see, namely that the valley actually extended down into the ground as much as the small mountains surrounding it protruded up from the desert floor. That meant that the bottom of the valley was somewhat further down than the entrance, and that the valley was a lot more difficult to spot from afar than they would have expected.

Ever more careful as they moved closer, they reached the mouth of the valley where McGregor signalled for the others to stop. They then all lay down on the ground and switched their comms on. Each of them had an earpiece in their left ear, and a small lightweight microphone reaching down along the cheek to the mouth for easy communication between the team members. The signal was sent over a closed and encrypted wireless system, whose encryption algorithm was changed for each mission, to one of several million available, so they would always be able to trust that no one would be listening in on the orders being issued by the team leader.

As they did so, McGregor crept forward some twenty meters to the crest of the valley entrance where the dirt road turned down into it. Here he got out his night vision binoculars, flipped up his goggles and placed the binoculars in front of his eyes. It took a little bit of getting used to, after half an hour with the goggles, but he quickly found the place on the left side of the valley where the cliff became very steep and almost turned into a wall of rock some 30 meters high. At the base of it was a large black opening around 250 meters away from their position, just as Ryan had said there would be. From inside the opening, he could just make out a faint light of some sort, but it was barely enough to be seen with the naked eye.

'Hello there,' McGregor whispered to himself and smiled, as a lone guard came walking casually out of the cave entrance dangling an AK47 in his right hand.

He was wearing what appeared to be shabby clothes and sandals. He looked decidedly bored and pulled out a cigarette, which he promptly lit. As he leaned his head back and blew the first small cloud of smoke up into the cold evening air, another two guards emerged from the entrance. Now McGregor wasn't smiling anymore. One of the most difficult parts of the mission would be to get close to the entrance without begin detected, and for all he knew there could be ten guards in there that he couldn't see.

He turned and looked back over his shoulder, then waved for Wilks to join him. The sniper rose, and holding the heavy 50 calibre Barret 82A1 in both hands, he moved in a crouched position up next to McGregor where he lay down.

'The entrance is down there,' whispered Andrew. 'There are at least three guards. Move over to the opposite side of the valley, use your scope and report back how many you can see inside the opening. We'll hold our position here.'

'Roger,' said Wilks. Then he rose and began to jog as quietly as he could, first away from the valley's mouth, and then along the opposite side of the valley from where the cave entrance was.

It was several hundred meters to where Wilks needed to set up position, so McGregor took the opportunity to call up Logan, whose specialty was reconnaissance. He instructed him to crawl to the other side of the valley entrance and prepare to move closer on his orders. As Logan crept silently to his position some fifty meters away, McGregor took another look at the guards. They were smoking and talking, and once in a while they would even push each other amiably, and then distant laughter could be heard all the way across to McGregor's position.

Five minutes later Wilks called in from his position opposite the cave entrance and reported seeing two guards in addition to the three that McGregor had already spotted. Wilks also reported that just inside the entrance was a truck. This was the only vehicle he could see, and as far as he could tell, the tunnel went at an angle down into the base of the cliff.

McGregor ordered Logan to begin to crawl forward by the side of the dirt road itself, and then told Wilks to hold his position and await further orders. Then he called for Grant, Kendall, Thompson, and Dunn who had stayed behind until now, to move up next to him. He told them to fan out in a line with two on each side of him and three meters between them, and then the five men began to slowly make their way towards the cave entrance. As they crept along, one of the guards wandered back inside, and a few seconds later they heard a car door open, and then slam shut a moment later. Now, about 150 meters away, McGregor saw the guard re-appear, with what he guessed was a fresh packet of cigarettes, which he tossed to one of the other guards as he approached him. Having got this close, McGregor could now clearly see the light coming out of the cave entrance. It seemed to come from a simple light bulb mounted in the ceiling, and its bright light would mean that the guards' eyes never had a chance to adjust to the darkness outside. This in turn meant that their ability to spot anything was extremely limited. Even if the light bulb was switched off, it would take them several minutes before their eyes would get used to the darkness, and be able to see even an outline of the men that were silently creeping ever closer.

That gave McGregor an idea. He stopped and signalled for the others to do the same, and then he asked Logan if he could see how far it was from the first to the second light bulb inside the tunnel. Logan continued to creep forward on the dirt road for a few more seconds until he reached the tracks that led to the entrance. He now had a clear view all the way through the tunnel to the cave 100 meters into the mountain and reported back that it was approximately 10 meters between each light bulb. McGregor figured that would be sufficient, and ordered Logan to move close enough to be able to hit the first one. As he did so, McGregor, Grant, Kendall, Thompson, and Dunn moved to within 50 meters of the guards who had no inkling of what was about to happen.

Whispering a few sentences into his microphone, McGregor assigned each man a target, and after waiting a few seconds for all six to call in with an OK on having acquired their respective targets and having them in their sights, he gave the command for Logan to open fire. A second later his silenced Heckler & Kock MP5SD produced three short clicks in quick succession, and instantly the first light bulb in the tunnel splintered into a thousand pieces.

Hearing nothing but the shattering glass, the three guards outside turned around with no apparent sense of urgency and a second later McGregor whispered. 'Weapons free.'

Instantly the five silenced weapons clicked with three-round bursts, and virtually every bullet hit its intended target. At the same time, a dry crack was heard from the other side of the narrow valley as Wilks fired his sniper rifle at a target inside the tunnel entrance. Standing still outside the tunnel, the three guards were easy prey, and each of them got hit by at least ten bullets from the MP5s within the three seconds the firing lasted. Two of them slumped down on the ground as if they were robots that had just had their batteries removed, but the third guard saw the faint flashes from the muzzle that pointed towards him and attempted to bring up his weapon. He had already been hit in the chest and in one arm, and as he fell backwards, his finger squeezed the trigger causing his AK-47 to fire a short burst, but then they all fell silent.

'Wilks?' called McGregor.

'I got both,' reported Wilks calmly.

'Both?' said McGregor perplexed. He was sure that the sniper had only fired once. 'Say again, Wilks. You got both?'

'Yes, Sir. One of them stepped in front of the other.'

Wilks had fired a single round from his 0.50 Calibre rifle, which had taken the head clean off the first guard and then slammed right through the man behind him. Both had dropped to the ground dead before any of them knew what hit them.

McGregor and the four other team members leapt to their feet and began moving swiftly but cautiously towards the entrance to the cave. As they did so, they all heard Logan's voice in their earpiece. 'All clear,' he said. 'Nobody in the tunnel.'

As the four men reached the entrance to the tunnel, they switched off their night vision goggles, detached them from their helmets and put them in specially made bags on their belts.

'Logan. On me,' said McGregor, and a few seconds later they were six in the group now preparing to enter the tunnel to the production facility. They divided into two groups of three men, McGregor leading Thompson and Kendall, and Grant leading Logan and Dunn. They made their way quickly through the entrance and started down along the walls towards the cave. Their attention was directed firmly ahead of them, knowing that Wilks was watching the entrance from the outside and would warn them if anyone showed up unexpectedly. The sniper scanned the perimeter of the entrance, as well as the area further away at both ends of the small valley, but there was no one in sight anywhere.

As the two groups of soldiers moved swiftly and silently through the tunnel, there was an eerie quiet that made McGregor uneasy. He would have expected whoever was inside to hear the sound from the sniper rifle or the discharge of the guard's AK47, but they could neither see nor hear anyone. As he focused his eyes down towards the end of the tunnel, he could just make out the back of a truck parked close to a building of some sort further inside the cave.

As they moved closer, he was beginning to appreciate the sheer size of the complex, when suddenly two men bolted around the corner and into the tunnel less than 30 meters away. They immediately began firing their submachine guns, and as the first bullets whistled over their heads and ricocheted loudly off the tunnel's granite walls, three more men carrying weapons emerged and opened fire. Within a few seconds, sparks flew as the hail of bullets slammed into the rocks and bounced off the ground and the walls.

Upon seeing the first two men, McGregor had knelt down close to the wall with his MP5 up, and before the three others had appeared, he had fired several three-round bursts and hit the first man square in the chest. He immediately dropped to the ground, dead. Incredibly, none of the team members were hit by the hail of bullets that the guards had sent their way, and within a split-second Grant, Thompson and Kendall also opened fire and Dunn hurled a flashbang towards them, which landed right at their feet. A second later it exploded with a loud reverberating bang close to where the tunnel exited into the cave, which visibly stunned their opponents. The explosion gave McGregor and his team the upper hand, and as the remaining four guards staggered backwards while raising their weapons yet again, a hail of bullets came from McGregor and his team as they switched their weapons to automatic fire and let loose. The MP5 can empty a magazine with 30 bullets in about 2 seconds, so the team sent a torrent of lead at the remaining four men within just a few seconds.

Although the MP5 submachine gun has one of the weakest recoils among their available weaponry, such free firing made it much more difficult to hit the targets, and only about one in ten bullets found its mark. But with the number of shots fired, it still meant that their targets each got hit by multiple bullets in the chest and the head, making them spin, arms flailing, and falling to the ground like rag dolls. One of the guards was able to turn and begin to run back to the cave only to be cut down by three bullets that pounded into his back and made him stumble forward and land on his face without moving again.

As the firing stopped, Thompson, Kendall and McGregor took the opportunity to reload and switch magazines. None of them believed that it would be over already. McGregor knew that they were in a precarious position inside the tunnel, and gave the order to advance further towards the cave complex.

With their hearts pounding and their blood full of adrenaline, they reached the cave. McGregor and Grant both moved forward and looked around the corner inside the vast space that had been cut into the rock. The whole place was flooded with light from the hundreds of lights that were affixed to the inside of the dome high above them. To their right along the cave wall was a couple of two-story buildings, and in the centre was a strange-looking aluminium structure with no windows. At the far end of the aluminium structure next to what looked like a storage room set into the cave wall, were parked two trucks, of which McGregor had seen the rear of one from inside the tunnel.

A couple of men were frantically loading metal crates from the storage depot onto the trucks, but upon seeing the small team of black-clad men with guns, they pulled out pistols from holsters in their belts, and bolted away from the trucks whilst firing wildly towards the tunnel entrance. Grant immediately dropped one of them, who fell on his face with a thump on the concrete floor but the other managed to slip from view behind the aluminium structure. McGregor ordered Grant to take Logan and Dunn towards the two-story structures, and as they did so McGregor, Thompson and Kendall remained near the tunnel with their weapons at the ready in case there were more people eager to take a shot at them.

When they reached the main door to the living quarters, Grant grabbed the door handle, while the others prepared to open fire. The door was locked. Dunn then moved up to the door and quickly placed a breaching charge on it. He was just about to move back to detonate the charge, when the second man who had been loading the crates on board the truck, appeared around the corner of the aluminium structure some 50 meters away. Holding down the trigger on his AK47, he began spraying bullets in their direction. Before Logan was able to take aim and drop him, Dunn was hit in the shoulder and fell backwards with a loud grunt that sounded more like annoyance and frustration than actual physical pain. Logan's bullets hit the man in the centre of his chest and he fell backwards onto the ground, but Logan kept aiming in that direction while Grant knelt down next to Dunn to check his injury.

'You're alright,' said Grant. 'The Kevlar stopped the bullet, but you may have dislocated your shoulder. Stay here and cover us while we go in.'

'Fuck. Ok,' grimaced Dunn, and sat up leaning against the wall.

Just then, they heard voices shouting inside the building and a single shot rang out. Then Grant and Logan moved back behind Dunn, and an instant later the breaching charge went off splintering the door and sending thousands of fragments hurtling at several hundred kilometres per hour through the air inside the hallway.

A man who was kneeling on the floor inside the corridor with his AK47 pointed at the door, expecting it to be knocked down, got lifted off the floor and carried backwards a couple of meters through the corridor and then slammed into the back wall. As the smoke cleared a few seconds later, Grant leaned sideways to peek through the doorway, and on the floor at the opposite end of the corridor sat the lifeless body of a soldier, with most of his face torn off from the shrapnel that had once been a door.

At the sound of the explosion, McGregor, Thompson and Kendall started running and moved towards the laboratory at the centre of the cave. Having reached the small shed closest to them, they knelt down and trained their guns at the two windows in the office building. They would be providing covering fire as the three others entered the building.

With Dunn still sitting outside the building, Grant and Logan moved swiftly through the corridor and checked all the rooms downstairs, but there was no one there. They then cautiously proceeded up the stairs to the second floor and into the first office, and as they did so they heard the sound of feet running towards them out into the corridor. A few seconds later a man dressed in a white lab coat bolted through the door with a pistol, but before he could discharge it even once, both Grant and Logan had brought up their weapons and released a three-round burst each. The man dropped to the floor with a thud, and his gun slid across the floor. Logan moved over to him and kicked the gun away, while Grant exited into the corridor to ensure that there would be no more suicidal scientists coming their way. Then Logan came up behind Grant, and the two of them proceeded through the next three offices.

The first two were empty but in the third, a man in a similar white uniform sat slumped against the wall in a corner of the room. The wall behind and above him was smeared in blood and he was holding his stomach and bleeding badly. With their weapons trained at the man, Grant and Logan moved closer to him. As far as they could see, he had no weapons.

'Do you speak English?' asked Grant quickly.

'Yes,' said the man and grimaced. 'Don't shoot. I'm injured,' he continued in what sounded to Grant like an Indian accent.

Looking closer at his face, Grant could see that the man definitely wasn't an Arab, but more likely Indian or Pakistani.

'How many people are inside the laboratory?'

'No one. Production is finished,' he winced, as a stab of pain ran through his body.

'Have you done this yourself?' asked Grant pointing to his wound.

'No, you imbecile,' sneered Kashim Khan. 'It was that rabid Arab man you just shot. Is he dead?'

'Never mind,' said Grant. 'Show me your hands.'

'But I'm wounded,' protested the man.

'Shut up,' shouted Grant, and tied Khan's hands with a small plastic zip-tie he had pulled from his pocket. Then he spoke to McGregor through his microphone. 'We have a live one, Sir. I've tied him up. The building is secure.'

'Roger,' said McGregor. 'Get out here.'

Grant and Logan then left the protesting scientist and ran downstairs and out into the cave, where they took up position next to the office building where they could see most of the complex. Suddenly they heard the engine on one of the trucks parked on the other side of the laboratory start up, and at the same time, a man appeared from the building containing the living quarters around 100 metres away at the other end of the cave. His right hand was raised above his head and in his left hand, he held an Uzi submachine gun. Tied around his waist was a thick belt, and McGregor immediately recognised it as being explosives. As he sprinted forward, the Uzi sprayed bullets in all directions, many of them hitting the ground and the structures close to the two teams.

'Take cover,' yelled McGregor. 'He has a bomb.'

They all dove down behind cover while training their weapons at the man that was now zigzagging towards them while firing wildly and shouting continuously in Arabic. McGregor also threw himself on the ground and took aim at the man who had now reached the small shed attached to the main laboratory building.

As McGregor fired, so did several of the other team members. The result was that the man almost stopped from the force of the bullets slamming into his body, and as he fell forward, his legs were still attempting to run. Somehow, he was able to flip the switch in his hand, detonating the explosives.

The shock wave of the blast pulverised the small shed next to where he had fallen, and almost lifted the office building off the ground and shattered its windows. The corridor connecting the shed to the main laboratory building had been ripped open and folded back alongside the opposite side of the building like a can of sardines. Most of the lights in the ceiling were damaged, and about half of them went out instantly, but more disconcertingly, pieces of rock began dropping from the ceiling of the cave.

Outside in the valley, Wilks saw the flash from inside the tunnel and a second later there was a huge violent gush of air suddenly coming out of the tunnel entrance, blowing up a lot of dust. He immediately called McGregor over the comms system.

'McGregor! Are you guys ok?' he asked in an agitated voice. 'What the hell happened in there?'

At first, there was no answer, but after a couple of seconds McGregor came on the line, sounding a little confused and out of breath.

'We are alright. Just a few scratches. Wilks, there's a truck leaving the cave. It should be coming up through the tunnel right now. Stop it. Don't let it get away, do you understand?'

'Roger,' replied Wilks. 'They won't be going anywhere.'

Then he leaned his head in to touch the stub of his 0.50 Calibre Barret M82 sniper rifle, looked calmly through the sight, took two deep breaths and then settled in his firing position. Through his 10x sights he could see a dark shadow moving towards him up the tunnel that was now filled with dust and smoke, and suddenly it switched on its headlights. That would probably not make it any easier for the driver to see anything, but it gave Wilks a perfect opportunity to determine its approximate speed and as it approached the entrance to the tunnel his finger caressed the trigger, and he placed the crosshairs right on the bumper of the truck. It was an easy shot. The range was less than 300 meters, and the truck was coming straight towards him at about 50 kilometres per hour, heading for the dirt road that ran the length of the valley.

Meanwhile, inside the cave, the ceiling was crumbling and huge blocks of rock were beginning to fall around them with loud thuds. Several rocks had already hit the laboratory, punching straight through its ceiling. None of them knew if there might still be pathogens in there, so McGregor told Grant and Logan to run back into the office building to get the wounded scientist out and to take as many documents with them as they could carry. Then he ordered them all to leave the cave as quickly as possible. After pointing his gun at Khan's head and asking nicely, Grant had quickly recovered the scientist's two laptops. They would prove to contain virtually all they could ever want to know about the programme and the way it was being financed.

Keeping the crosshairs exactly on the Syrian number plate on the front bumper, Wilks squeezed the trigger when the truck was about halfway to the dirt road. A loud crack rang out through the night as the rifle recoiled violently and a bright flash exited from its muzzle. A split second later the 0.50 Calibre bullet went through the grille at the front of the truck as if it was a sheet of paper, and then it tore right through the engine block, including two combustion chambers. That caused the engine to seize up instantly, and the truck to screech violently to a halt in a cloud of dust, as the wheels stopped turning.

The two men in the front were thrown forward, and the one in the passenger seat continued through the windscreen that had shattered. He then rolled out over the front of the truck and landed on the ground, just as it came to a complete stop. The driver, who had managed to cling on to the wheel during its violent braking, swung the door of the cab open, bolted out and began running away with no apparent plan as to where to go. Wilks placed the crosshairs about half a meter in front of him and fired. The huge bullet tore right through the driver's chest, flinging him off to the side in a bloody mess.

Meanwhile, the guard in the passenger's seat had stumbled to his feet and seen the muzzle flash from the second shot. He knelt down and brought up his AK47, which he emptied in Wilks's direction. Having spent one magazine, he ripped it out and slammed a new one in place, and then continued to send a hail of bullets towards Wilks's position. The sniper could hear the bullets impact the sand and rocks around him and ricocheting off into the air, but he calmly took his time to reload and then placed the crosshairs right over the guard's head. He fired and a fraction of a second later, the bullet hit the guard squarely in the face and his head exploded in a red puff of blood and brains that splattered up over the front of the truck. It wasn't a pretty sight, but it did make him stop firing immediately, as his headless body slumped to the ground.

Wilks could hear the rumbling sound from inside the cave all the way across the valley to where he was. As he looked through his scope into the tunnel, he could see a number of figures that seemed to be making their way out through the dust and smoke. At that moment all the lights inside the cave went out and the entrance to the tunnel became a black hole on the side of the cliff.

Seconds later he got confirmation from McGregor that they were on their way out, so he switched on his Satcom system and called the forward airbase in Turkey to ask for immediate exfiltration. McGregor also asked for the Blackhawk to bring along a medic, as they had one seriously wounded prisoner. A couple of minutes after that, McGregor and the rest of his team exited from the tunnel entrance and hurried past the smoking truck. Two of them were carrying a third person and Wilks could clearly see that it wasn't one of their own.

'Wilks, you can come down and join the rest of us now,' said McGregor. 'Thompson and Kendall, check the truck. Dunn, set up explosives inside the tunnel. We need to seal off that cave completely.'

Dunn got his kit out and walked back inside the tunnel. His shoulder still hurt like hell, but it wasn't nearly enough to stop him from doing what he liked best. About fifteen meters in, he affixed several satchel charges to the walls of the tunnel and then activated the radio receiver that would set them off. He walked calmly outside and came over to McGregor.

'Done,' he said. 'I think we should move a little further away.'

'I know,' said McGregor. 'Thompson, what's on that truck?'

'I'm not sure, Sir. Thousands of small aluminium canisters. I didn't touch anything but it seems that none of them are damaged.'

'Good,' said McGregor. 'That will be the pathogen. They must have tried to escape with some of it. Take a couple with you. Someone might want to have a closer look at those.'

'For all we know they could already have shipped some out,' said Kendall.

'That is correct, but we can only deal with what we've got here. Can we push the truck back inside before we seal the cave?'

'No Sir,' said Wilks, who had just come back down the opposite side of the valley. 'Not a chance. The engine is just a dead chunk of metal now. The transmission and the wheels are completely locked.'

'Alright. We'll have to do it a bit differently, then. Logan and Wilks, you two carry our new friend here. Be careful with him. He might have a lot of useful information.'

McGregor walked over to the truck along with Thompson and marked the position on his handheld GPS. Then they moved out towards the end of the valley, heading for the exfiltration zone. Their Blackhawk had been on standby at the forward airbase and had already taken off, so it would arrive within half an hour. As they reached the end of the valley, they all took cover and then Dunn switched on the radio transmitter and flipped the switch causing the satchel charges to explode simultaneously inside the tunnel. There was a violent blast of fire, smoke and air from the cave entrance, followed by the distinct rumbling sound of tons upon tons of rock falling down in a massive cave-in inside the tunnel. The cave was now completely sealed off from the outside world, but what would have to be done with it now was not their concern. Someone else would have to take care of that.

McGregor called for the helicopter to come in closer to their position than was originally planned, but given their desire to get out of there quickly, and the fact that the wounded scientist might die without rapid medical attention, he felt that he had no alternative.

Twenty minutes later they heard the Blackhawk out in the distance, and McGregor cracked a green glowstick and waved it over his head. The helicopter moved smoothly to their position and they all climbed aboard. Within a few minutes, they were racing back across the Syrian desert towards the border with Turkey.

Less than an hour later, after the team had arrived safely at the airbase and Kashim Khan had been operated on and brought out of danger, a United States Navy cruiser on patrol in the Persian Gulf launched two Tomahawk cruise missiles, which lifted off the deck of the ship and then arched over and settled on their pre-programmed course that would take them north towards Iraq. The missiles flew at around 900 kilometres per hour and made their way towards their target at an altitude of less than 100 meters. They made their way all the way up to northern Iraq where they changed course and headed over the border into Syrian airspace.

Eight minutes later, some thirty seconds apart, they swooped down into the valley southeast of Al Raqqa and descended to 20 meters. As the first one passed right over the truck that was loaded with small metal canisters, it exploded in a huge fireball that enveloped the truck and everything around it. The high explosive charge was designed so that it directed all the force downward, causing the shock wave to slam the truck and its content towards the ground in an inferno of fire and heat reaching several thousands of degrees Celsius.

Thirty seconds later the second cruise missile reached the coordinates fed into it before launch and ejected several hundred bomblets that spread out over a large area surrounding the truck. None of them exploded but they dropped to the ground in their little parachutes and landed close to the truck at the entrance to the caved-in tunnel. There they would serve as a dense carpet of land mines, hopefully deterring anyone from entering the area before a plan to deal with the destroyed pathogen facility could be made over the next day or two.

TWENTY-FIVE

The entire contents of the two laptops found in the cave was sent securely via satellite to the servers at Sheldrake Place, where Pete Ryan had then downloaded it onto the hard drive of his own computer and had started sifting through every file. He had spent several hours just trying to get an overview of the huge amounts of information stored on them and had soon discovered that most of it was highly technical science-speak.

Sterling and the rest of the Antarctic team would be arriving within eight hours, and he had hoped to get Marx to help him with the analysis, but had been dumbfounded when told that the Brit had died during the expedition. Ryan had then spoken to Strickland, and the two of them had agreed to hand over the technical documents to the British Army's bio-weapons research programme who were keen to get a chance to review them as soon as possible. Ryan had then concentrated on the files that he did understand, and it turned out that they contained records of money transfers between accounts that were as yet unidentified, but the owners of which Timothy Jenkins was hoping to reveal before long. In addition to the extensive information about financial transactions and purchases of a wide range of scientific equipment that had subsequently been transported to Al Raqqa and on to the cave compound, he had uncovered encrypted messages between the people in the cave and an address in

Khartoum in Sudan. Strickland had arranged for the messages to be sent to GCHQ for possible decryption, but they had been told that, if decryption was even possible it might take a long time.

There were several hundred messages on one of the laptops, but only a handful had been left decrypted by whoever had used it, and it was difficult to conclude anything from the information found in them. Most interesting among those were a list of so-called foreign assets, that had turned out to be many individual lists of people under headlines of cities around the world. Among the cities were New York, Washington and San Francisco in the United States, virtually all capitals in Europe including the administrative centre of the European Union in Brussels, as well as Tokyo, Sydney and several Israeli cities. The lists containing the names were very long indeed, several of them containing as many as 150 names in just one city. Ryan had no idea what they might be, but he had the distinct feeling that something horrific had been planned. Information about a deadly airborne pathogen found along with lists of several thousand people in cities around the world could not be a good thing.

Two hours later he was sitting in colonel Strickland's office flanked by the man who had taken over Marx's responsibilities in the task force. George Halliday, who despite the untimely death of his colleague, had thrown himself at the task of analysing the first test results sent back from Rosenbaum, who was now enroute from Halley along with the rest of the team.

Halliday was a shy but very bright scientist who performed his best work when given time to sit in his office or his laboratory and ponder some problem that had come up. He would do so for hours, but would often single-handedly come up with a solution to a complex problem. His superiors, while regularly asking him to be more of a team player, had to admit that he was one of the very best scientists working for the programme. Now Halliday was sitting next to Ryan in Strickland's office, ready to present his first preliminary results.

'Well,' said Halliday and shifted in his chair. He didn't much like the attention being focused on him, and so he was a little nervous as he sat there in unfamiliar surroundings in the company of two relative strangers.

'What I have found so far, based on Mr. Rosenbaum's results as well as those of my team and I, is that the pathogen samples do indeed seem to be of a very aggressive nature. But it is not entirely inconceivable that we may be able to adapt one of our existing antibiotic substances to treating, or rather preventing infection.'

Colonel Strickland nodded approvingly.

'So,' he continued. 'The one that Rosenbaum and I are focusing on, based on the preliminary test results carried out by him on Halley, is an antibiotic that was originally developed to fight Anthrax. It is easily injected into humans without significant side effects, but in its current form, it is probably utterly useless against the B-CAP pathogen. I suspect it will require quite extensive work to come up with a derivative of this antibiotic that will work satisfactorily and that will be easy to mass-produce and distribute. As I say, I believe that there might be a good chance of success, but we'll have to wait for Rosenbaum's arrival with the samples before we can say anything more.'

'And the paper documents retrieved from the cave?'

'We are waiting for them to get sent to us. I'm told they should be here any minute now'

'Good,' said Strickland. 'Let's hope for the best. And if there is anything you need either from us or from the CDC, please do let me know immediately. I have it from the Prime Minister personally that we should spare no expense in this matter.'

'Thank you,' said Halliday. 'I shall keep that in mind.'

'Now, Mr. Ryan.' said Strickland and looked at the CIA agent sitting across from him on the other side of the table. 'What have you come up with so far?'

'Not that much, unfortunately. Much of the information stored on those two laptops is encrypted, but I found lists of hundreds of names of people, as well as the names of major cities all over the world, and I think that all these individuals may be living in those particular cities. What it means exactly is unclear, but I suspect that we may be dealing with a planned terrorist attack on much of the western world on an unparalleled scale. Based on the information supplied by McGregor's team, the pathogen had been stored in thousands of small containers. These were incinerated by the cruise missile, but if they were destined for the people listed in these files, I have to say that I think all of them were planning to release the pathogen in those cities. With that many people involved, it would have been impossible to stop such a coordinated attack, and the consequences would have been absolutely horrific. We are talking about hundreds of thousands, perhaps even millions of fatalities, within just the first few hours.'

Strickland was visibly shaken by what he had been told. 'Any news from GCHQ on the encrypted files?' he asked.

'No. Not yet.'

'And the location in Khartoum?'

'Nothing yet. The boys back at Langley are working hard for me right now on satellite imagery, trying to determine an exact location, and I should have it within a few hours.'

'Good stuff,' said Strickland. 'Let me know when you have something.'

★ ★ ★

In a room at an Army Hospital on the outskirts of Ankara in Turkey, protected by two guards posted there by the military police, McGregor, who was now dressed in a grey suit, a blue shirt and a black tie, was leaning over Kashim Khan's bed. The Pakistani was not looking very healthy, with his abdomen having taken a bullet and an infection having flared up. The military doctors had got it under control relatively quickly, and after hours of surgery, he was now in a stable condition, although he still had a high fever and seemed to have difficulty concentrating. McGregor had just spoken to Strickland ten minutes earlier and been informed of what had been found on the two laptops recovered from the cave. Now it was his turn to get some information.

'Mr. Khan,' said McGregor. 'Please listen to what I have to say.'

The Pakistani opened his eyes and looked at McGregor with an empty stare which lasted for a few seconds until he recognised the face of the man that had led the assault team in the attack on the production facility. Then his eyes narrowed and he swallowed a few times while waiting for the soldier to speak.

'I am a representative of the British government, and I need answers to some questions. Now, I am going to ask you nicely and I'm sure you'll find it in your best interest to comply. But let me tell you that the Pakistani government, does not know whether you are currently dead or alive, so that matter is still to be decided, if you understand what I am saying?'

The implications of the words took a few seconds to sink in, but Khan did not miss the point. He winced and then nodded to signal his willingness to co-operate. 'I'll tell you what you want to know,' he moaned.

'Good,' said McGregor. 'Clever chap. I'll be recording this, to make sure that there are no misunderstandings. Mr. Khan, we know who you are and what you were doing in that facility in Syria. We also have your Russian friend Sergei Ivanov, and he has kindly provided us with all the information we have requested of him. I suggest you do the same.'

Khan sighed and glanced up at the dialysis machine that had taken over his liver function after the bullet had pierced it. It was evident that his physical condition had taken a heavy toll on his mental strength, and it was soon to become clear that he was willing to co-operate unreservedly. He knew that the game was up and that his best chance was to play along with his captors. He nodded again.

'How much of the pathogen was produced?'

'About 3,000 canisters,' replied Khan as he stared at the wall.

'And each canister. How much did it contain?'

'About 50 grams.'

'How much is needed to kill a person?'

'Almost nothing,' replied Khan, as McGregor thought he spotted a tiny amount of pride in his voice. 'Less than one milligram.'

'So, each canister could kill thousands?'

'Theoretically, yes. If used correctly.'

'And what does that mean? We've found thousands of names on computers taken from the cave. Were they going to spread the pathogen?'

'Yes. They were sure that they would become martyrs. Stupid bastards.'

'What do you mean? Were they going to die themselves?'

Khan sighed again. 'It's very simple,' he said, speaking slowly so as not to upset his wounds that had just begun to heal. 'Each one of those men had been recruited by New Dawn. After the American war in Afghanistan, literally thousands of young men all over the world volunteered to become martyrs in the Jihad that was declared against the US.'

McGregor had heard this a hundred times before but resisted the urge to push Khan to speed things up. The Pakistani paused for a sip of water from a plastic cup.

'Several shipments were to be made to America and Europe and the canisters were to be distributed inside small innocent looking black plastic pens. Each pen contained one canister.'

'Pens? How was that meant to work? What were they going to do with them?' asked McGregor impatiently.

'Again,' sighed Khan. 'Everything was kept extremely simple, in order to ensure that the plan could actually be executed. Simultaneously on the 21st of December of this year at 4 PM UTC, in Europe, Israel, New York and other cities like San Francisco and Los Angeles, the jihadists were to seek out their pre-planned targets. They would then open the canisters, inhale some of the crystallised pathogen and spread the rest in the air around them.'

McGregor looked sceptically at Khan, who was explaining the horrific plan as calmly as if he had been recounting a morning walk in a park.

'Pre-planned targets? Like what?'

Khan shrugged. 'Well, that's pretty obvious, isn't it? Anywhere public with lots of people. Mainly shopping centres, but also tourist attractions, airports, public transportation, schools, churches.'

McGregor was stunned but didn't let it show. 'And being a good scientist, I suppose you have estimated the number of deaths?' McGregor sneered, although he tried not to.

'They figured 50 in the immediate vicinity and then a couple of hundred, maybe more, as the bodies decayed from the crystallisation process and the pathogen spread through the air.'

'So, in all those cities combined?'

'Maybe a million people, in the initial stages. But there would probably be many more later on.'

Incredulous, McGregor looked coldly at Khan who was evidently unaffected by the potential horrors of his work.

'What the hell were you trying to do?' asked McGregor, now unable to maintain his calm demeanour. 'Start a world war? Kill off humanity?'

Khan chuckled but then grimaced as the pain stabbed through his abdomen. 'You westerners don't realise this, but the hatred of the west is very profound in the Middle East, and many young men are raised to believe that martyrdom is something to strive for. So, they are not afraid. They are convinced that they will go to heaven, and that they will have a special place at the side of Allah.'

As Khan spoke, McGregor could sense that Khan seemed to share those feeling towards westerners.

'How many trucks?' he asked. 'Were there more than the two we saw?'

'No. Those were the only ones.'

McGregor suddenly grabbed the man's face in the iron vice of his powerful hand, and twisted his face towards himself.

'Don't you fucking lie to me,' he hissed menacingly.

Khan groaned in pain, his terrified eyes looking helplessly into McGregor's. He knew the soldier could snap his neck in a flash if he wanted to, and he was desperate to convince him that he was telling the truth. Khan had nothing left to gain from lying.

'It's true,' he yelped, looking pleadingly at McGregor. 'They were going to transport the canisters out that morning. Production had essentially finished already, and much quicker than we had dared to hope. It was the last stage of the operation.'

'And you? What did you get out of it?' said McGregor, letting go of Khan.

Khan looked at him with an innocent, almost childlike expression on his face. 'Money,' he said. 'What else? I don't agree with the policies of the United States in the Middle East. The war in Afghanistan was misguided and unjust and more akin to rape than anything else. But it's not something that I would dream of giving my life for. I was offered the opportunity to participate in this venture and I took it, along with the money of course. Let New Dawn wage war if they like. I'm not going to get involved with that. But if someone wants to offer me a huge amount of money, I am not going to say no. Would you?'

McGregor ignored the question. He looked Khan straight in the eye with a menacing look on his face, and then grabbed the plastic tube that was attached to the dialysis machine next to the bed.

'Who planned all this? What is New Dawn?'

Khan's eyes darted sideways to look at McGregor's hand, petrified with fear at what the crazy Scotsman might do. 'I hardly know anything about them,' he blurted. 'It was Yusef who took care of that. I never talked to any of them.'

'Yusef?'

'Yes. Mohammed Yusef. He was part of it, and so was a man called Hamza Masood. Yusef talked to the Russian, and he also talked to their headquarters sometimes. Arrowhead, he called it.'

'Arrowhead,' repeated McGregor. 'What do you know of it?'

'Almost nothing. It is in Sudan somewhere. Near Khartoum, I think. They have several training camps for their holy warriors there, but they also have their headquarters placed in the mountains somewhere. I don't know exactly where.'

'What do you know about them?'

'Not much, but I do know that they are not just a bunch of idealistic amateurs. I have heard phone conversations between Yusef and Arrowhead, and I am sure that they are extremely well organised and funded. I think they might be sponsored, not by individuals but by countries. I know for a fact that the Syrian government aided with logistics and equipment, and that some of the money we spent came from Saudi Arabia. Once Yusef boasted that he could buy anything we needed. All he had to do was make a phone call, and he turned out to be right. Everything we needed, we got.'

'Are you sure you don't remember anything else about them?' asked McGregor calmly and tightened his grip on the plastic tube.

'Yes,' said Khan, his eyes moving nervously from the tube to McGregor's eyes and back. 'I swear, that's all I know.'

McGregor released his grip on the tube and leaned back in his chair. Everything the Pakistani scientist had said had checked out with the information Ivanov had provided. There was nothing to suggest that Khan was lying, so McGregor decided to find out a bit more about the man.

'So, it was only ever about the money for you? What about the people who would die? Don't you care about that?'

'We are all part of nature,' he sighed and paused. 'Everything we humans do to this world, and to each other, is as natural as flowers that bloom in the spring, or the sun that comes up after another night. We are part of a whole, and so are the bacteria which we helped to develop in our laboratory. We are not above such an organism, and perhaps it serves us right to be reminded of that. To be reminded that we are not all-powerful.'

'You admire it don't you?' asked McGregor, with disdain in his voice.

'I admire what it can do,' responded Khan in a matter-of-fact fashion. 'I admire its power. I admire the fact that this tiny creature can sit there inside a mountain for hundreds of millions of years, biding its time, waiting for the right moment, and then it can completely wipe out thousands of supposedly highly advanced animals just by being what it is. Unlike humans, it possesses no evil intent but also no morals. It is unclouded by conscience or remorse. It just is. In a sense, it is more pure than we will ever be, and while it may be small, it could take back this planet from us if it were given the chance to do so.'

'Exactly,' interjected McGregor 'If it was released globally, this pathogen might wipe out mankind, and that would include yourself.'

'I think I would survive, and so would the human race. To me, we are much like bacteria ourselves, having sprung from the once dead surface of the planet and evolved through eons of time. The only difference is that we consist of more cells than they do, and we developed much later than it did. You might say that they rightfully own this planet, and that we are only temporary tenants. If we are worthy of survival, then we will survive even this. If not, the bacteria of this world will take over again.'

'You see nothing wrong with what you have done?'

'No,' shrugged Khan. 'Think of it as the plague, the Black Death. Events like that are a form of population control, much like we sometimes decide to almost wipe out certain types of animals, in the name of maintaining balance, as we would see it. Things like the Black Death reminds us humans that we are fragile and that we are not the supreme beings that we have lulled ourselves into believing we are. It might teach us to be humble and make us realise that we cannot control nature. We are a part of it and we can only survive by respecting it.'

Some of what the wounded scientist lying in the bed was saying seemed like the ramblings of a mad man, but some of it sounded disconcertingly sensible. McGregor decided to stop the recording and end the interrogation. He found himself feeling slightly uncomfortable with agreeing with what the scientist had just said, but all it really proved was that he was actually not crazy. He might have a different set of values, but he was apparently completely sane, unlike the thousands of people who had volunteered to die as martyrs, killing endless scores of innocent civilians. As McGregor rose, Khan lifted his hand and looked at him.

'What will happen to me,' said a now more humble Khan.

'You will stay here until your wounds have healed,' said McGregor. 'What happens after that is beyond my control. And frankly, I don't care.'

Then he left the room. On his way out, he told the two guards not to let anyone inside except for the nurse. They did not want Khan to die from secondary infections of the wound. They might still need him in the future, and death somehow seemed like it was too lenient a punishment.

★ ★ ★

Some seventeen hours later the Gulfstream touched down at London City Airport, and taxied calmly to a cordoned off area away from public eyes. Rosenbaum had made an effort to get as much rest on the flight as he could, since he knew what a monumental task lay ahead of him and his new British colleagues. He had also considered asking for additional personnel to be flown over from the CDC. There were a couple of people there that he knew might be able to contribute to the research process, but he'd have to talk to Colonel Strickland about that first.

As the doors opened and the team stepped out onto the tarmac, a car was waiting to take the samples of the pathogen to the laboratory that had been set up for that specific purpose. The location was part of Marx's research facility, so it was fitting that it should now be used in the attempt to find an antibiotic for the pathogen that had most likely ended up killing him. The samples had been brought there in a locked steel box that looked like a simple toolbox, but the people responsible for the transport handled it very carefully indeed. Rosenbaum bid farewell to Andrew and Fiona and then got in the car along with his two colleagues as well as Alice Bailey, who seemed to be slowly recovering from the shock of losing her colleague.

Andrew had spoken to Colonel Strickland several times during the flight, and the two of them had arranged the details of the mission that would be carried out within two days.

'Well,' said Fiona. 'I guess all we can do now is go home, right?'

'Yes. We've done our bit. Now it's up to the science team to get cracking and find a solution as soon as they can. They found the terrorist production facility, you know.'

'They did? Where?'

'I can't tell you that, but I'm pretty confident that they'll be out of business permanently. And the stash of pathogens that had been manufactured and intended to be disseminated around the world, has all been destroyed.'

'So, is that the end of it?'

'Not quite. There still a mopping-up operation to be carried out.'

'Did some of them get away?'

'They might have, and they might even have taken samples with them. This is what Defence Minister O'Toole meant when he said that it might be easier to find an antibiotic than to eradicate the pathogen. We might be chasing around after these samples for years, without ever getting them all. But if we could find an antibiotic that could work as a prophylactic, then we'd have nothing to worry about.'

'Well. At least not in this respect. I think sooner or later these people will think of something else to throw at us.'

'You are probably right. Unless we can remove them completely.'

'Is that what this mopping up mission is about?'

'Between you and me, yes. It is an attempt to eliminate the entire organisation that was behind this.'

'Is that the New Dawn organisation that we found references to?'

'Yes. They might very well be planning other similar attacks using other means, and we simply can't allow that to happen. Having a sophisticated judicial system designed to take care of criminals after they have committed their crimes simply isn't good enough in these kinds of situations. Waiting until after the fact is not an option we are willing to accept, so we need to strike them before they can strike us. And that is what we intend to do shortly.'

★ ★ ★

The telephone in the temporary office set up in the hanger building rang three times before it was picked up. The Turkish Airforce captain exchanged a few words with a dispatcher, first in Turkish and then in English. He then handed the telephone to

Colin McGregor, who had just asked his men to start packing up for the return trip to Hereford.

'Colin, this is Andrew. How are things?'

'Andy. Good to hear from you. We're alright. Dunn is moaning a bit about his shoulder, but you know him. He's always been a bit of a cry-baby. Where are you?'

'We are back in London. Have you been told that we recovered the original pathogen?'

'Yes,' replied McGregor, now in a more subdued tone of voice. 'I also heard that you had a problem down there.'

'Yes. Bloody awful thing, what happened to Marx,' said Andrew in a sombre voice. 'But we've been fortunate enough to get someone to take over. His name is George Halliday, and he is supposed to be brilliant, so at least now we can begin working on antibiotics.'

'Were you briefed on our mission into Syria?'

'Yes. Good job. Sorry about Dunn. Is he alright now?'

'Yes, he's fine. The vest stopped the bullet, but his shoulder took quite a bruising. He should be fit for fight within a day or two.'

'Good stuff,' said Andrew. 'Because you have two days to rest before you are shipping out again.'

'We are going back?'

'No. It's not Syria this time.'

'Let me guess. Khartoum?'

'Precisely. We've been asked to take care of it as soon as possible.'

'I have good news regarding that. We've had Frost talk to our friend Ivanov again, and with a remarkable effort from both the MI6 and the CIA both in the States and on the ground in Sudan, we've been able to determine the location of the headquarters of this organisation calling itself New Dawn.'

'How?'

'Well, GCHQ was able to extract much of the encrypted information from the computers you recovered. The encryption system was not very clever from what I understand, and from the content of those two computers, we were able to determine a location near Khartoum. Using images from the CIA's surveillance satellites, we were able to pinpoint the location of their headquarters. Some of the images are good enough for them to say that they believe that at least three known terrorists are there. How they've recognised them, I don't know, but we have to trust them on this.'

'Where is it, exactly?'

'Apparently it is some way away from Khartoum itself, so that makes things a lot easier for us.'

'So, someone needs to go in there and get them?'

'Yes. And that is your team. The option of a cruise missile strike has been considered, and we will probably send in a few of them. But since we only know the layout of the compound and not the exact location of the leadership, we have to send a platoon in there to make sure that they don't get away.'

'I'm guessing we're not taking any prisoners?'

'Correct,' said Andrew. 'The Minister of Defence and his American counterpart both agree on this point. Bringing these people out of Sudan would be a nightmare, so they are to be terminated.'

'So, what's the plan?'

'You will be flown out of Turkey to a US marine carrier group in the Red Sea. It will then sail close to the coast of Sudan and from there you will fly in at night in a helicopter for a dawn attack. The helicopter will not have time to fly back to the ship, so it will have to stay in the area until you finish your business.'

'Sounds a bit risky,' said McGregor.

'Yes. But logistically it is the only way we can do it.'

'Ok. When do we ship out?'

'Tomorrow morning. You'll have around fifteen hours onboard the aircraft carrier before you go in, so that should be sufficient to get some rest and go through the mission plan.'

'When do we receive that plan and a layout of the compound?'

'As soon as you arrive on the aircraft carrier. Strickland and I will produce a preliminary plan, which you and I will then discuss and alter if necessary once you are aboard.'

'Alright. I'll update the men.'

'Good. Any other questions?'
'No. We'll be ready.'

★ ★ ★

Later that evening Andrew was sitting on the sofa in his living room looking at the medallion, which he had placed on the table in front of him. The TV was on, but he had muted the sound. As the medallion lay there on the table gleaming in the light, he looked at the hole in its centre where the ruby was supposed to have been, wondering whether that might have made a difference.

Perhaps Fiona had been right that it might strengthen the magnetic properties of the medallion, but then maybe it was something else. It might have been that it would have resulted in the medallion pointing to somewhere else. He closed his eyes in an attempt to recall the layout of the magnificent domed room inside Vestfjella and the astonishing underground city that they had found. Perhaps Eckleston and his fellow fanatics were still alive in there. If they stayed close to the exit, then they might not become infected with the pathogen, but then they would surely die of starvation. There was not a chance of them digging themselves through that many tons of snow and rock, no matter how desperate they were.

Andrew considered the possibility of them somehow making their way across the giant room full of small dwellings to the opposite end, where the steps leading up might take them out somehow. The chance of that happening was slim, but if they did make it, they would probably also be able to make it back to Neumayer, where they had set out from.

Andrew decided that he was more than happy to leave that whole situation with Strickland. After all, Andrew and his men had killed a couple of German or Austrian citizens, so that might result in a bit of diplomatic jostling, but he was sure that it would not cause a public stir.

The next morning, he would have to get up very early indeed and leave for Sheldrake Place where he and Strickland would be able to follow the operation in Sudan. Every soldier would be fitted with helmet-mounted cameras and encrypted transmitters that would send images back to the helicopter, which would then relay them to the carrier. From there they would be bounced off a military satellite and back to a select few offices in Washington D.C. and London in real-time. In theory, this would enable them to communicate directly with the SAS team as the mission unfolded, and direct them as they went. That, however, would not have been a good idea. They could provide aerial reconnaissance information from drones overhead, and updates on possible threats nearby, but McGregor was more than capable of leading the team in and executing the mission, and he didn't need anyone looking over his shoulder.

★ ★ ★

The compound was roughly the shape and size of a football pitch, with its main building at one end, and several sheds, buildings and an obstacle course at the other, where the Mujahedin, the holy warriors, would be trained to fight the infidels in the name of Allah. Currently, there were as many as 30 fighters in the barracks next to the main building. Most of them were young men in their mid-twenties, eager to receive training and then to go off to battle wherever their Mullah might send them. In addition to military training, they also received schooling in the Koran at the camp, or rather the legal interpretations of it, known as the Sharia. These classes were designed to make it clear to the students that they were fighting for a just cause, and that death would result in martyrdom in the eyes of Allah.

It was early in the morning, and practically everyone was sleeping. The sun had not yet come up over the horizon but its golden glow could be seen on the horizon to the east.

Some three hundred meters away in a ditch, McGregor and his team were waiting. They had fanned out so that there were approximately five meters between them, except for Wilks who was lying prone about 50 meters to their left under a bush, which he was using as cover. He had put on light brown camouflaged clothes, and since he wasn't supposed to get any closer to the compound than this, he had decided only to wear the lowest level body armour.

Resting in his arms as he lay there was his silenced PSG-1 sniper rifle, with a scope powerful enough to let him read the brand name on a cigarette packet from two hundred meters away. Right now, he had set the scope so that he could see the entire compound without having to shift his rifle from one side to the other. It was dead calm, and all he could hear were the chirps of birds in the fields not far from them. The compound was situated in an area of low rolling hills, a couple of kilometres from a small village. The team had been inserted a few hours earlier about five kilometres away, and the whole trip in from the US marine carrier ship had been uneventful.

The terrain they had flown over during the 320-kilometre trip from the carrier group was sparsely populated, and the helicopter, which now sat silently in a narrow gorge nearby guarded by five marines, had set down without incident and was now awaiting the signal for it to come in and extract the SAS team. After moving out from the landing site, they had made their way silently across the terrain without seeing a soul anywhere. They were now in position for the final attack on the New Dawn headquarters, which both Khan and Ivanov had called Arrowhead.

The organisation might be well funded, but it evidently didn't spend its money on training facilities. If anything, that was a testament to the fact that assets, in the form of new recruits, were a plentiful and almost free resource, who didn't need huge amounts of training in order to carry out their tasks.

McGregor glanced at his GPS coordinates again. North 16.40440, East 34.25492. This compound was definitely the one. Most of it was surrounded by barbed wire fences, and at one end of it was an iron gate some 2 meters tall. The gate was made of massive metal bars, and just inside it, Wilks could clearly see two guards sitting on their stools on opposite sides of the road leading in, facing each other but apparently without speaking. He and the rest of the team had spent around half an hour observing the compound from afar, but the two guards were the only people currently visible. It didn't seem as if they received visitors very often, at least not this early in the day. Today would be different.

McGregor looked at his watch. Another minute or so before the cruise missiles would arrive. Wilks called in to say that he had acquired one of the targets at the gate, and a few seconds later McGregor gave permission to fire. There was a 'click' of the bolt in the rifle, a firm recoil into his right shoulder, and a split second later the bullet hit the first guard in the chest with a hard thud.

'First guard down,' said Wilks calmly and took aim at the other guard.

Shocked by the almost silent impact, but still not quite realising what had happened, the first guard attempted to stand up, but he just fell forward out of his chair and remained on the ground with his face buried in the dirt. The other guard only had time to jump up and look at his fallen comrade before he too was hit by a bullet. Wilks had aimed for the head but the projectile sliced through the guard's throat and sent him flailing to the ground, whilst trying desperately to scream. It only resulted in a pitiful gurgling sound, as the blood spewed from the wound. He managed to creep several meters towards the main building. Wilks fired again.

'Second guard down,' reported Wilks.

About thirty seconds later, they heard the distant whine of a jet engine, and looking east they spotted two small specks against the morning sky. They watched the specks grow bigger and bigger, and the sound became louder and louder, until the missiles were right over their heads, at which point they all took cover to shield themselves from the blasts. A few seconds later the Tomahawks reached their pre-programmed coordinates and detonated. One exploded over the main building, and the other over the barracks. The barracks were hit first but there was no more than ten seconds between the two blasts.

As the fireball enveloped the barracks building, and the blast ripped apart every piece of wood and concrete and sent it hurtling in all directions, the other missile found the main building and detonated directly above it. The main building contained the nerve centre of the whole organisation, including offices and computers as well as the living quarters of its leaders and their communications equipment. It was made entirely of wood, so the explosion completely blew it apart and flattened the structure so that only the concrete foundation was left as the smoke cleared a few seconds later.

Still, with smoking debris landing close to their position, the team loaded their weapons, moved swiftly out of the ditch and proceeded in tight formation towards the compound. As they came closer, Wilks spotted a man staggering out through the smouldering rubble that had been the barracks only a few seconds before. Although apparently confused and with tattered clothes hanging from his body, he was carrying a rifle of some sort, so without hesitation, Wilks fired a single shot at him. With the rest of the team on their way in, he wasn't about to take any chances. The bullet struck the man in the chest, and with a loud scream and his arms flailing, he dropped to the ground.

Mohammed Yusef had only spent a few nights there, but he was already beginning to get bored. Sudan was a primitive backwater compared with where he normally lived in Al Raqqa, and he missed the busy streets full of people walking about in the bazaars looking for a bargain to take home. He was lying in his bed reading a book when the massive explosion over the barracks building had sent him jumping out of his bed. The whole underground bunker complex shook violently and dust and bits of soil came down from the ceiling. Bewildered, he reached for his clothes as the rest of the men were screaming and shouting in Arabic, trying to figure out what had happened.

Yusef had figured it out already, but he was caught off guard as the second missile detonated right over their heads. The door from the main building to the first level of the office complex was blown down the steps and splintered as it slammed into the floor five meters below at the end of the stairs. The shock wave was powerful enough to fling the two guards that had been standing by the stairwell into the back wall and kill them instantly. Fire and heat also reached down into the first level of the complex and scorched two more guards as well as New Dawn's head of security.

In his private apartment, down in the back of the second level close to Mullah Haq's three-room underground apartment, Yusef's ears popped at the sudden increase in pressure from the explosion. A second later, he felt the gush of air out of the complex as the heat above them sucked out several cubic meters of air from the first level. The shouting intensified, and he could hear the sound of feet running outside in the corridor. The lights flashed a few times and then went out, leaving him in complete darkness, but a few seconds later they came back on. He put on a jacket, pulled out a drawer in his desk and grabbed his gun, which he loaded and stuck into the holster in his belt. Then he made his way out into the hall.

There was smoke and dust in the air, and to his left at the far end of the corridor, were a couple of the veteran Mujahedin from Chechnya and Afghanistan. They were hired guns, who were part of a team of elite guards protecting Mullah Haq who, aided by a handful of trusted advisors, effectively ran the New Dawn organisation himself.

Yusef looked at their faces, and he could see that they were nervous but ready to fight and die defending their leader. Each man in this compound was there because he had pledged his life to the cause, and there was no doubt that they would all fight to the last drop of blood as ordered by the Mullah. They were all Mujahedin, and considered themselves to be singled out by Allah to fight and die for this cause. Each of them had faced death on numerous occasions, but had fought on and won, and they had all prepared themselves for the fact that they might not live. In a battle of life and death, this was their greatest asset. The infidels were all afraid to die, which made them weak and cowardly, but a true Mujahedin was proud to become a martyr, and thus had no fear as he flung himself into battle. They were prepared for death and they knew that the glorious day had now arrived when they would go to join Allah.

Looking at their eyes, Yusef could feel that he did not himself possess the calm that these men were able to muster. As he walked up the stairs to the first level, where there was widespread carnage and people either lying motionless on the ground or creeping along the walls of the corridor whimpering, the unpleasant realisation began to sink in. He had always thought of himself as a warrior worthy of entering paradise, but now, as he faced his first real fight to the death, he could feel his mental strength ebbing away, and his heart cowering inside him. He felt fear, and he knew it and felt ashamed. He pulled out his gun and made his way towards the bottom of the stairway to the surface, where the shattered access door lay. He could see light coming down from the stairwell and was shocked to realise that the whole building on the surface had been blown away completely.

He walked over the shattered door and took two steps up before he realised that there was someone standing completely still at the top of the stairwell looking down on him. He winced a few times trying to clear his eyes from the dust that hung in the air and then realised that the man, who seemed immobile like a statue, was carrying a submachine gun. Yusef tried to bring up his pistol to point it at the man, but a split second later the muzzle of the man's gun flashed three times, and the MP5 produced an angry growl as three bullets hit him in the chest and the neck.

McGregor had opted for weapons without silencers because he had been informed that they might have to move through very tight passages, and the shorter the weapon the better. In addition, he knew that the sound of the rapid submachine gunfire would probably strike fear into the fighters in the compound. And so it should.

Yusef staggered backwards and fell onto his back, whilst still trying to fire a shot. Another three-round burst left McGregor's MP5 and slammed into his face knocking his shattered skull back onto the dirty floor. Seconds later McGregor, followed by Grant, Logan, and Dunn, moved quickly down the stairwell where they stopped for a few seconds, waiting to see if any threats might reveal themselves. Kendall and Thompson were still topside, ensuring that no one appeared without being noticed. They, in turn, were covered by Wilks who had moved about 50 meters closer to the complex.

McGregor made his way slowly down the corridor, covered by Grant, Logan and Dunn, while checking each room one by one searching for targets. Suddenly a man carrying an AK47 bolted from a room at the other end of the corridor and sprinted towards them firing wildly while yelling something in Arabic. A second later, all four of them opened fire, and instantly between ten and twenty bullets thudded into his body which seemed to stop him in mid-air, after which he flipped backwards and landed like a ragdoll on his back, next to a guard who had evidently died from the explosion of the cruise missile. His legs twitched a couple of times but after that, he moved no more.

They had barely started moving again when two more men came up the stairwell at the far end of the corridor. As soon as they saw the three black-clad figures in the smoky corridor, they threw themselves down on the ground and started firing. McGregor and his companion returned fire while moving through a doorway into a room that appeared to have been a small office of some sort. It was now in shambles, with the furniture having fallen over and stacks of paper strewn all over the place. Everything was covered in dust and dirt from the explosion.

As soon as they were all inside the room, Logan spun around and took out a hand grenade, which he pulled the pin on. He waited about a second and then leaned out of the room and hurled it down the corridor. As he did so, the two men opened fire once more. One of the bullets struck Logan in his right thigh. His leg buckled under him, and he fell down on his side out into the corridor.

Seeing the grenade hit the ground a few meters away and roll towards them, the two guards stopped firing and scrambled back towards the stairwell. McGregor grabbed Logan's left leg and yanked him back into the room.

One of the guards managed to get two steps down the stairwell while the other was still in the corridor when the grenade exploded. It had rolled almost all the way down to the end of the corridor, so the blast buried several pieces of shrapnel into the back of the guard in the stairwell and then threw him forward and into the air halfway down the steps. Here he landed head first and then cartwheeled to the corridor on the second level below. The other guard was virtually on top of the explosion when it occurred, and he was killed instantly by the razor-sharp pieces of shrapnel that has been flung out violently through the air at several hundred kilometres per hour.

McGregor knelt down next to Logan while Grant covered the corridor with his submachine gun to ensure that they wouldn't be surprised again. Logan grimaced in pain as his hands found their way down to the leg where the bullet had hit. Blood was already trickling out of the wound, soaking his trousers.

'Are you alright, mate?' asked McGregor while he ripped open a small hole in Logan's trouser.

'I'm not sure,' winced the wounded soldier. 'It felt pretty bad.'

McGregor wiped the blood away and then pulled a bandage from a side pocket in Logan's trousers. 'It looks as if it has passed right through the muscle without hitting the bone. You're lucky.'

McGregor quickly bandaged the leg, and almost stopped the bleeding. He then ordered Dunn to help Logan up to the surface. He would not be able to continue.

There were no other people on the first level and McGregor, followed by Grant, moved to the end of the corridor, where he peeked down the stairwell to the second floor. There was no one to see, so the two of them made their way down to the bottom of the stairs. Once again, McGregor peeked around the corner and he was instantly met by a hail of bullets that slammed into the wall right next to them, sending tiny pieces of concrete flying through the air.

The two guards outside Mullah Haq's luxury apartment had both opened fire with their AK 47s, and as McGregor jerked back his head to avoid being hit, he could hear first one and then the other changing their magazines. Across from the stairwell, about a meter closer to the guards was a room that appeared empty. McGregor signalled to Grant that he was going to try to reach it, and then he pulled out a flashbang. He pulled the pin and hurled it across the corridor and into the room. He and Grant then closed their eyes and held their hands over their ears. Two seconds later it went off, creating a deafening bang and a bright flash of light, as well as a cloud of smoke. As soon as it had gone off, he bolted across to the room where he threw himself on the ground and rolled over to stand up with his weapon at the ready. The guards had been so startled by the explosion that by the time they spotted McGregor throwing himself across the corridor and through a doorway, he was halfway there, and only one of them managed to fire at him without hitting anything except the floor.

McGregor heard a door open and quickly peeked out into the corridor. Behind the two guards, the door to the Mullah's apartment had been opened and two more men had appeared, also armed with AK47s. McGregor signalled to Grant to lay down cover fire. Grant immediately held his MP5 out into the corridor without exposing his head and blind-fired a series of short bursts down towards the door at the end of it. McGregor used the opportunity to throw a grenade down towards the men, who were taking cover from Grant's bullets.

They spotted the grenade instantly and were able to make it inside the apartment and slam the door shut. Seconds later the door was blown into the room as the grenade exploded, and immediately thereafter McGregor and Grant jumped out into the corridor and advanced close together towards the doorway, weapons up.

There was still smoke from the explosion hanging in the air, which made it difficult to see anything, and pieces from the ceiling were dropping to the floor. The two men kept moving swiftly forward at a steady controlled pace while training their MP5s at the doorway. Inside the room, one of the guards was lying on his front, a few meters away from the doorway. Apparently, he hadn't made it away from the blast and had been killed by shrapnel. Another one of the guards had thrown himself to the side and had thus been sitting on the floor right next to the door when the grenade went off. Suddenly he appeared around the corner near the floor and pointed his gun at the advancing SAS soldiers.

McGregor and Grant were no more than five meters away from him and they could see the wild look on his face. He was by no means calm but looked more as if he was throwing himself into the arms of death. Grant gave him what he wanted, and while on the move towards him, fired a three-round burst into his face. As the bullets struck, brains and blood squirted out of the back of the guard's skull. His head snapped back and flopped to the side, and then his body toppled over and hit the floor with a thump. Without hesitation, McGregor pulled out another flashbang and threw it inside the room. A couple of seconds after it went off, the two of them entered.

The apartment was comprised of just three rooms arranged in a line with doors connecting them. As the flashbang went off in the first room, the two remaining men had been stunned and had recoiled from the intense noise and the bright flash. They were now trying to recover to put up a fight. But it was already much too late, and none of them had a chance to fire their weapons before the MP5s cut them down. They were each struck by several bullets, and both men fell down onto the floor without ever managing to get a shot off. One of them appeared to be dressed in civilian clothes, but McGregor felt pretty sure that there were no civilians in the underground complex.

The room was apparently an office, and lavishly decorated with expensive furniture and paintings, and on the floor was a thick red carpet. McGregor and Grant continued moving through the office and into the next room, which was a living room. Their advance had speed, momentum and aggression, which were the essential ingredients in a successful assault, and the smartest thing for them to do was to press on and clear the whole apartment fast.

There was nobody in the living room, and the bedroom next to that was empty as well. Suddenly a single shot rang out from a small room next to the living room. McGregor, followed by Grant made his way through the bedroom to where the sound of the shot had come from. He kicked in the door and instantly saw a man kneeling down on the floor. He had a thick beard, and McGregor estimated him to be in his late fifties. He was dressed in a long white robe and seemed to be bending forward, with his forehead almost touching the ground. On the wall in front of him was a picture of a desert landscape and on the floor was a book.

It didn't take McGregor more than a few seconds to spot the blood trickling from his forehead onto the carpet, and the blood-spattered wall next to him. Mullah Haq had ended his own life, to avoid being captured.

‘No heaven for you,’ muttered McGregor.

* * *

Andrew parked his Jaguar outside the British Museum and walked across the street to the main entrance. He made his way up the stairs and to the left, and at the end of the corridor, he stopped and leaned into an office. He knocked on the door, and Fiona, who was sitting at her desk writing something on her computer, turned around and smiled at him.

‘Hello there,’ said Andrew.

‘Hi, Andy. How are you?’

‘I’m alright. Yourself?’

‘Great,’ she said and pointed to her screen. ‘I’m putting together an expedition for the spring. I’ve just spoken to my boss, and he is willing to discuss the possibility of me going back to the Yucatan Peninsula so that I can officially discover what I have already discovered once,’ she smiled.

‘Good,’ laughed Andrew, as he came up behind her and placed his hand on her shoulder. ‘How many times will you have to do that, I wonder.’

‘Did your meeting go well?’

‘Yes,’ shrugged Andrew. ‘The Prime Minister was obviously very grateful to all of us for our efforts, and it has earned us both a long vacation. So, I thought we might go to Tibet.’

‘Tibet? You are not going to tell me that you want even more adventure now, are you?’

‘No. I just always wanted to go there.’

‘Alright,’ she said teasingly. ‘I’d love to. If the international community can handle another crisis, then fine by me.’

‘If you are referring to the jobs in Syria and Sudan, then there’s no need to worry. Nothing will ever be made public about this, but I think it is fair to say that certain countries in the Middle East will be somewhat more cooperative with the international community in the future. At least for a while. The whole incident is obviously a great embarrassment to a few of those governments, so those countries probably feel the need to compensate somehow.'

'Diplomatic arm-twisting?'

'Something like that.'

'Did they ever find traces of the pathogen in Sudan?'

'No. There was not a hint of it anywhere, so with the UN-led clean-up work that's coming to an end in Syria, we should be relatively safe.'

'There might still be more out there,' said Fiona.

'Yes, but I've spoken to Rosenbaum today, and he says that he believes they are only weeks away from a breakthrough in the antibiotic research.'

'What about all those names of people they found.'

'That's a bit more disconcerting. It turns out that none of the people can be identified. There were several names on the lists that matched the names of people living in the cities mentioned, but none of them seem to have any connection to a terrorist network of any kind.'

'Then what does it mean?'

'We are not sure, but the names were probably all cover names, and we have no way of determining who they really are.'

'Are you saying they are all still out there?' asked Fiona appalled.

'Yes, I believe so. Not much we can do about it at this stage.'

'Christ. So, we have not seen the last attempted terror attack, I guess.'

'I'm afraid not. But at least we stopped this one in its tracks.'

'Let's hope we did,' said Fiona pensively. 'Anyway. Let's not talk about that right now. Have you arranged for a place?'

'Yes, of course,' smiled Andrew. Are you ready to go? You still like Chinese, don't you?'

'Yes,' she smiled. 'Just a second. I'll just finish this e-mail.'

After a few minutes, she turned off her computer and rose. As they walked out of her office, he ran his hand down her back, and she turned her head to smile at him. The end of the whole B-CAP business had made it possible for them to stop just being colleagues, and start being together the way they had both wanted to. They were still living separately and that was the way they both preferred it, for now at least.

'What happened to your colleague Pauline Hanson?' asked Andrew as they walked down the corridor towards the stairs.

'It was the strangest thing,' smiled Fiona knowingly. 'She disappeared. One day she just wasn't at her desk, and it seems that she had left her apartment without telling anyone where she went. She has completely vanished, without a trace. I wonder if she is even in the country anymore.'

'Well, just as long as she hasn't gone to Tibet,' smiled Andrew.

THE END

NOTE FROM THE AUTHOR.

Thank you very much for reading this book. I really hope you enjoyed it. If you did, I would be very grateful if you would give it a star rating on Amazon and perhaps even write a review.

I am always trying to improve my writing, and the best way to do that is to receive feedback from my readers. Reviews really do help me a lot. They are an excellent way for me to understand the reader's experience, and they will also help me to write better books in the future.

Thank you.

Lex Faulkner

Printed in Great Britain
by Amazon

25502824R00320